P9-DXL-335

BY PIERCE BROWN

Red Rising

Golden Son

Morning Star

MORNING
STAR

MORNING STAR

Pierce Brown

DEL REY

NEW YORK

Copyright © 2016 by Pierce Brown
Illustration copyright © 2016 by Joel Daniel Phillips

All rights reserved.

Published in the United States by Del Rey, an imprint of Random House, a division of Penguin Random House LLC, New York.

DEL REY and the HOUSE colophon are registered trademarks of Penguin Random House LLC.

ISBN: 978-0-345-53984-7

ebook ISBN: 978-0-345-53985-4

Printed in the United States of America on acid-free paper

randomhousebooks.com

2 4 6 8 9 7 5 3 1

First Edition

Book design by Caroline Cunningham

To sister, who taught me to listen

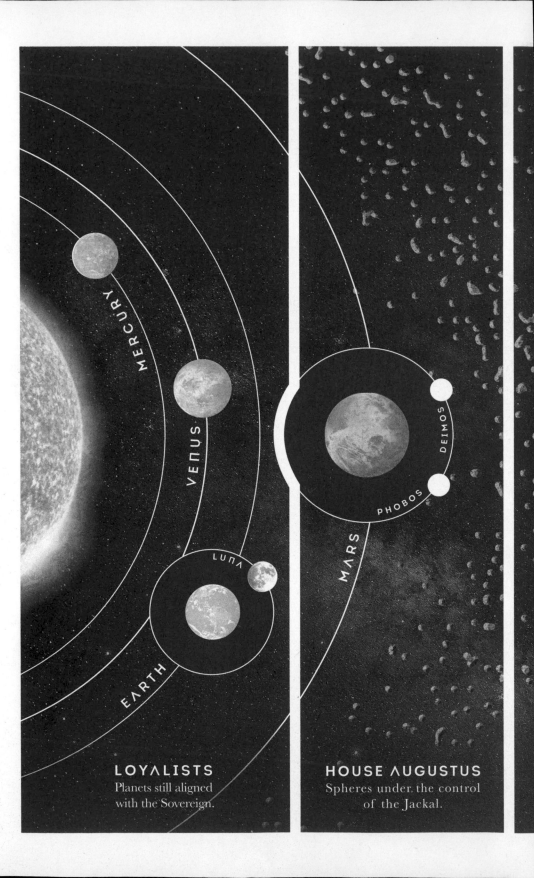

LOYALISTS
Planets still aligned
with the Sovereign.

HOUSE AUGUSTUS
Spheres under the control
of the Jackal.

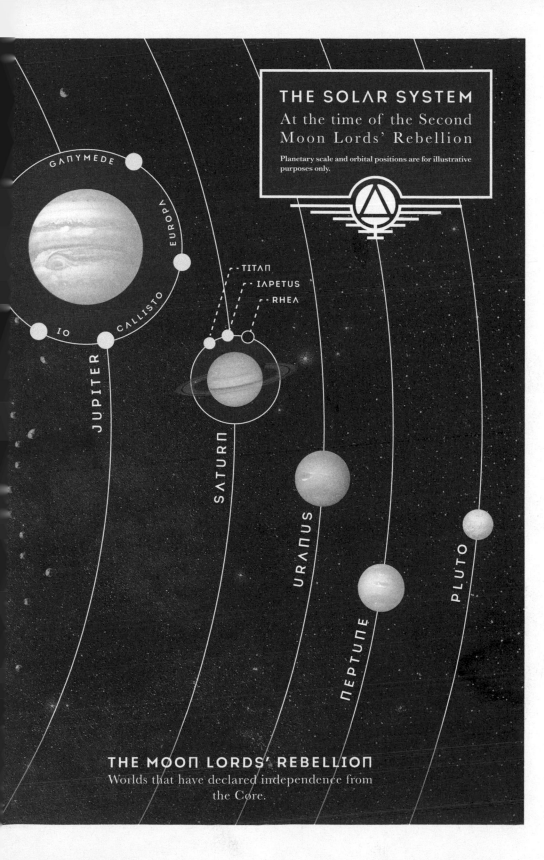

THE STORY SO FAR . . .

Red Rising

Darrow is a Red, a lowly miner slaving away below the surface of Mars. He toils to make the surface of his planet habitable for future generations, but he and his kind have been betrayed: the surface is livable and ruled by the unscrupulous Golds. When they hang his wife for voicing rebellious ideas, Darrow joins a revolutionary group known as the Sons of Ares. With the help of the Sons, Darrow is physically transformed into a Gold and sent to take the Society down from the inside.

He enters the Institute, a training school for the Gold elite that turns spoiled teenagers into the best warriors in Society. There Darrow learns the ways of warfare and how to navigate through the often treacherous—but sometimes genuine—friendships and complex political climate of the Golds. Only by changing the paradigm and relying on his new friends is Darrow able to best the Institute and all of its dangers.

Golden Son

From his victory at the Institute Darrow wins prestige and a position in the employ of the ArchGovernor of Mars, Nero au Augustus. However, he finds that it is difficult to live up to his own legend, as Darrow is unsuccessful at the Academy, where Golds train in ship-to-ship combat. Bested by a familial rival of his employer, Darrow's worth quickly declines in the eyes of the ArchGovernor, until that is, Darrow gives the power-hungry Gold what he wants: civil war.

Playing the Augustus clan against the Bellonas, Darrow throws

Society into disarray, sowing the seeds of chaos everywhere he goes. After amassing an impressive army and some dubious allies, Darrow leads a successful assault on Mars, ousting the Bellonas from control of the planet. But at the Triumph held to honor his military victory, betrayal once again rears its ugly head and all that he has worked for is undone. His friends and allies killed or missing, Darrow is captured and his secret identity is discovered; the fate of the rebellion balances on a razor's edge . . .

DRAMATIS PERSONAE

Golds

OCTAVIA AU LUNE   Reigning Sovereign of the Society

LYSANDER AU LUNE   Grandson of Octavia, heir to House Lune

ADRIUS AU AUGUSTUS/JACKAL   ArchGovernor of Mars, twin brother to
Virginia

VIRGINIA AU AUGUSTUS/MUSTANG   Twin sister to Adrius

MAGNUS AU GRIMMUS/THE ASH LORD   The Sovereign's Arch Imperator,
father to Aja

AJA AU GRIMMUS   The Protean Knight, chief bodyguard to the Sovereign

CASSIUS AU BELLONA   The Morning Knight, the Sovereign's bodyguard

ROQUE AU FABII   Imperator of the Sword Armada

ANTONIA AU SEVERUS-JULII   Half sister to Victra, daughter of Agrippina

VICTRA AU JULII   Half sister to Antonia, daughter of Agrippina

KAVAX AU TELEMANUS   Head of House Telemanus, father to Daxo

DAXO AU TELEMANUS   Heir and son of Kavax, brother to Pax

ROMULUS AU RAA   Head of House Raa, ArchGovernor of Io

LILATH AU FARAN   Companion of the Jackal, leader of the Boneriders

CYRIANA AU TANUS/THISTLE   A former Howler, now a lieutenant of the
Boneriders

VIXUS AU SARNA   Former House Mars, lieutenant of the Boneriders

Mid and LowColors

TRIGG TI NAKAMURA   Legionnaire, brother to Holiday, a Gray

HOLIDAY TI NAKAMURA   Legionnaire, sister to Trigg, a Gray

REGULUS AG SUN/QUICKSILVER   Richest man in the Society, a Silver

ALIA SNOWSPARROW   Queen of the Valkyrie, mother to Ragnar and Sefi, an Obsidian

SEFI THE QUIET   Warlord of the Valkyrie, daughter to Alia, sister to Ragnar

ORION XE AQUARII   Ship captain, a Blue

Sons of Ares

DARROW OF LYKOS/REAPER   Former lancer of House Augustus, a Red

SEVRO AU BARCA/GOBLIN   Howler, a Gold

RAGNAR VOLARUS   New Howler, an Obsidian

DANCER   Ares lieutenant, a Red

MICKEY   Carver, a Violet

I rise into darkness, away from the garden they watered with the blood of my friends. The Golden man who killed my wife lies dead beside me on the cold metal deck, life snuffed out by his own son's hand.

Autumn wind whips my hair. The ship rumbles beneath. In the distance, friction flames shred the night with brilliant orange. The Telemanuses descending from orbit to rescue me. Better that they do not. Better to let the darkness have me and allow the vultures to squabble over my paralyzed body.

My enemy's voices echo behind me. Towering demons with the faces of angels. The smallest of them bends. Stroking my head as he looks down at his dead father.

"This is always how the story would end," he says to me. "Not with your screams. Not with your rage. But with your silence."

Roque, my betrayer, sits in the corner. He was my friend. Heart too kind for his Color. Now he turns his head and I see his tears. But they are not for me. They are for what he has lost. For the ones I have taken from him.

"No Ares to save you. No Mustang to love you. You are alone, Darrow." The Jackal's eyes are distant and quiet. "Like me." He lifts up a black eyeless mask with a muzzle on it and straps it to my face. Darkening my sight. "This is how it ends."

To break me, he has slain those I love.

But there is hope in those still living. In Sevro. In Ragnar and Dancer. I think of all my people bound in darkness. Of all the Colors on all the worlds, shackled and chained so that Gold might rule, and I feel the rage burn across the dark hollow he has carved in my soul. I am not alone. I am not his victim.

So let him do his worst. I am the Reaper.

I know how to suffer.

I know the darkness.

This is *not* how it ends.

PART I

||||||||||||||||||||||||||||||||

THORNS

Per aspera ad astra

1

|||||||||||||||||||||||||||

ONLY THE DARK

Deep in darkness, far from warmth and sun and moons, I lie, quiet as the stone that surrounds me, imprisoning my hunched body in a dreadful womb. I cannot stand. Cannot stretch. I can only curl in a ball, a withered fossil of the man that was. Hands cuffed behind my back. Naked on cold rock.

All alone with the dark.

It seems months, years, millennia since my knees have unbent, since my spine has straightened from its crooked pose. The ache is madness. My joints fuse like rusted iron. How much time has passed since I saw my Golden friends bleeding out into the grass? Since I felt gentle Roque kiss my cheek as he broke my heart?

Time is no river.

Not here.

In this tomb, time is the stone. It is the darkness, permanent and unyielding, its only measure the twin pendulums of life—breath and the beating of my heart.

In. *Buh . . . bump. Buh . . . bump.*

Out. *Buh . . . bump. Buh . . . bump.*

In. *Buh . . . bump. Buh . . . bump.*

And forever it repeats. Until . . . Until when? Until I die of old age? Until I crush my skull against the stone? Until I gnaw out the tubes the Yellows threaded into my lower gut to force nutrients in and wastes out?

Or until you go mad?

"No." I grind my teeth.

Yessssss.

"It's only the dark." I breathe in. Calm myself. Touch the walls in my soothing pattern. Back, fingers, tailbone, heels, toes, knees, head. Repeat. A dozen times. A hundred. Why not be sure? Make it a thousand.

Yes. I'm alone.

I would have thought there to be worse fates than this, but now I know there are none. Man is no island. We need those who love us. We need those who hate us. We need others to tether us to life, to give us a reason to live, to feel. All I have is the darkness. Sometimes I scream. Sometimes I laugh during the night, during the day. Who knows now? I laugh to pass the time, to exhaust the calories the Jackal gives me and make my body shiver into sleep.

I weep too. I hum. I whistle.

I listen to voices above. Coming to me from the endless sea of darkness. And attending them is the maddening clatter of chains and bones, vibrating through my prison walls. All so close, yet a thousand kilometers away, as if a whole world existed just beyond the darkness and I cannot see it, cannot touch it, taste it, feel it, or pierce that veil to belong to the world once again. I am imprisoned in solitude.

I hear the voices now. The chains and bones trickling through my prison.

Are the voices mine?

I laugh at the idea.

I curse.

I plot. *Kill.*

Slaughter. Gouge. Rip. Burn.

I beg. I hallucinate. I bargain.

I whimper prayers to Eo, happy she was spared a fate like this.

She's not listening.

I sing childhood ballads and recite *Dying Earth, The Lamplighter,* the *Ramayana, The Odyssey* in Greek and Latin, then in the lost languages of Arabic, English, Chinese, and German, pulling from memories of dataDrops Matteo gave me when I was barely more than a boy. Seeking strength from the wayward Argive who only wished to find his way home.

You forget what he did.

Odysseus was a hero. He broke the walls of Troy with his wooden horse. Like I broke the Bellona armies in the Iron Rain over Mars.

And then . . .

"No," I snap. "Quiet."

. . . men entered Troy. Found mothers. Found children. Guess what they did?

"Shut up!"

You know what they did. Bone. Sweat. Flesh. Ash. Weeping. Blood. The darkness cackles with glee.

Reaper, Reaper, Reaper . . . All deeds that last are painted in blood.

Am I asleep? Am I awake? I've lost my way. Everything bleeding together, drowning me in visions and whispers and sounds. Again and again I jerk Eo's fragile little ankles. Break Julian's face. Hear Pax and Quinn and Tactus and Lorn and Victra sigh their last. So much pain. And for what? To fail my wife. To fail my people.

And fail Ares. Fail your friends.

How many are even left?

Sevro? Ragnar?

Mustang?

Mustang. What if she knows you're here . . . What if she doesn't care . . . And why would she? You who betrayed. You who lied. You who used her mind. Her body. Her blood. You showed her your true face and she ran. What if it was her? What if she betrayed you? Could you love her then?

"Shut up!" I scream at myself, at the darkness.

Don't think of her. Don't think of her.

Why ever not? You miss her.

A vision of her is spawned in the darkness like so many before it—a girl riding away from me across a field of green, twisting in her saddle and laughing for me to follow. Hair rippling as would summer hay fluttering from a farmer's wagon.

You crave her. You love her. The Golden girl. Forget that Red bitch.

"No." I slam my head against the wall. "It's only the dark," I whisper. Only the dark playing tricks on my mind. But still I try to forget Mustang, Eo. There is no world beyond this place. I cannot miss what does not exist.

Warm blood trickles down my forehead from old scabs, now freshly broken. It drips off my nose. I extend my tongue, probing the cold stone till I find the drops. Savor the salt, the Martian iron. Slowly. Slowly. Let the novelty of sensation last. Let the flavor linger and remind me I am a man. A Red of Lykos. A Helldiver.

No. You are not. You are nothing. Your wife abandoned you and stole your child. Your whore turned from you. You were not good enough. You were too proud. Too stupid. Too wicked. Now, you are forgotten.

Am I?

When last I saw the Golden girl, I was on my knees beside Ragnar in the tunnels of Lykos, asking Mustang to betray her own people and live for more. I knew that if she chose to join us, Eo's dream would blossom. A better world was at our fingertips. Instead, she left. Could she forget me? Has her love for me left her?

She only loved your mask.

"It's only the dark. Only the dark. Only the dark," I mumble faster and faster.

I should not be here.

I should be dead. After the death of Lorn, I was to be given to Octavia so her Carvers could dissect me to discover the secrets of how I became Gold. To see if there could be others like me. But the Jackal made a bargain. Kept me for his own. He tortured me in his Attica estate, asking about the Sons of Ares, about Lykos and my family.

Never telling me how he discovered my secret. I begged him to end my life.

In the end, he gave me stone.

"When all is lost, honor demands death," Roque once told me. "It is a noble end." But what would a rich poet know of death? The poor know death. Slaves know death. But even as I yearn for it, I fear it. Because the more I see of this cruel world, the less I believe it ends in some pleasant fiction.

The Vale is not real.

It's a lie told by mothers and fathers to give their starving children a reason for the horror. There is no reason. Eo is gone. She never watched me fight for her dream. She did not care what fate I made at the Institute or if I loved Mustang, because the day she died, she became nothing. There is nothing but this world. It is our beginning and our end. Our one chance at joy before the dark.

Yes. But you don't have to end. You can escape this place, the darkness whispers to me. *Say the words. Say them. You know the way.*

It is right. I do.

"All you must say is 'I am broken,' and this will all end," the Jackal said long ago, before he lowered me into this hell. "I will put you in a lovely estate for the rest of your days and send you warm, beautiful Pinks and food enough to make you fatter than the Ash Lord. But the words carry a price."

Worth it. Save yourself. No one else will.

"That price, dear Reaper, is your family."

The family he seized from Lykos with his lurchers and now keeps in his prison in the bowels of his Attica fortress. Never letting me see them. Never letting me tell them I love them, and that I'm sorry I was not strong enough to protect them.

"I will feed them to the prisoners of this fortress," he said. "These men and women you think should rule instead of Gold. Once you see the animal in man, you will know that I am right and you are wrong. Gold must rule."

Let them go, the darkness says. *The sacrifice is practical. It is wise.*

"No . . . I won't . . ."

Your mother would want you to live.

Not at that price.

What man could grasp a mother's love? Live. For her. For Eo.

Could she want that? Is the darkness right? After all, I'm important. Eo said so. Ares said so; he chose me. Me of all the Reds. I can break the chains. I can live for more. It's not selfish for me to escape this prison. In the grand scheme of things, it is selfless.

Yes. Selfless, really . . .

Mother would beg me to make this sacrifice. Kieran would understand. So would my sister. I can save our people. Eo's dream must be made real, no matter the cost. It's my responsibility to persevere. It is my right.

Say the words.

I slam my head into the stone and scream at the darkness to go away. It cannot trick me. It cannot break me.

Didn't you know? All men break.

Its high cackle mocks me, stretching forever.

And I know it is right. All men break. I did already under his torture. I told him that I was from Lykos. Where he could find my family. But there is a way out, to honor what I am. What Eo loved. To silence the voices.

"Roque, you were right," I whisper. "You were right." I just want to be home. To be gone from here. But I can't have that. All that's left, the only honorable path for me, is death. Before I betray even more of who I am.

Death is the way out.

Don't be a fool. Stop. Stop.

I lurch my head forward into the wall harder than before. Not to punish, but to kill. To end myself. If there is no pleasant end to this world, then nothingness will suffice. But if there is a Vale beyond this plane, I will find it. I'm coming, Eo. At last, I am on my way. "I love you."

No. No. No. No. No.

I crash my skull again into stone. Heat pours down my face. Sparks of pain dance in the black. The darkness wails at me, but I do not stop.

If this is the end, I will rage toward it.

But as I pull back my head to deliver one last great blow, existence groans. Rumbling like an earthquake. Not the darkness. Something beyond. Something in the stone itself, growing louder and deeper above me, till the darkness cracks and a blazing sword of light slashes down.

2

||||||||||||||||||||||||

PRISONER L17L6363

The ceiling parts. Light burns my eyes. I clamp them shut as the floor of my cell rises upward till, with a click, it stops and I rest, exposed, on a flat stone surface. I push out my legs and gasp, nearly fainting from the pain. Joints crack. Knotted tendons unspool. I fight to reopen my eyes against the raging light. Tears fill them. It is so bright I can only catch bleached flashes of the world around.

Fragments of alien voices surround me. "Adrius, what is this?"

". . . has he been in there this whole time?"

"The stench . . ."

I lie upon stone. It stretches around me to either side. Black, rippling with blue and purple, like the shell of a Creonian beetle. A floor? No. I see cups. Saucers. A cart of coffee. It's a table. That was my prison. Not some hideous abyss. Just a meter-wide, twelve-meter-long slab of marble with a hollow center. They've eaten inches above me every night. Their voices the distant whispers I heard in the darkness. The clatter of their silverware and plates my only company.

"Barbaric . . ."

I remember now. This is the table the Jackal sat at when I visited him after recovering from the wounds incurred during the Iron Rain.

Did he plan my imprisonment even then? I wore a hood when they put me in here. I thought I was in the bowels of his fortress. But no. Thirty centimeters of stone separated their suppers from my hell.

I look up from the coffee tray by my head. Someone stares at me. Several someones. Can't see them through the tears and blood in my eyes. I twist away, coiling inward like a blind mole unearthed for the very first time. Too overwhelmed and terrified to remember pride or hate. But I know he stares at me. The Jackal. A childish face in a slender body, with sandy hair parted on the side. He clears his throat.

"My honored guests. May I present prisoner L17L6363."

His face is both heaven and hell.

To see another man . . .

To know I am not alone . . .

But then to remember what he's done to me . . . it rips my soul out.

Other voices slither and boom, deafening in their loudness. And, even curled as I am, I feel something beyond their noise. Something natural and gentle and kind. Something the darkness convinced me I would never feel again. It drifts softly through an open window, kissing my skin.

A late autumn breeze cuts through the meaty, humid stink of my filth and makes me think that somewhere a child is sprinting through snow and trees, running his hands along bark and pine needles and getting sap in his hair. It's a memory I know I've never had, but feel like I should. That's the life I would have wanted. The child I could have had.

I weep. Less for me than for that boy who thinks he lives in a kind world, where Mother and Father are as large and strong as mountains. If only I could be so innocent again. If only I knew this moment was not a trick. But it is. The Jackal does not give except to take away. Soon the light will be a memory and darkness will return. I keep my eyes clenched tight, listening to the blood from my face drip on the stone, and wait for the twist.

"Goryhell, Augustus. Was this really necessary?" a feline killer purrs. Husky accent smothered in that indolent Luna lilt learned in the courts of the Palatine Hill, where all are less impressed by everything than anyone else. "He smells like death."

"Fermented sweat and dead skin under the magnetic shackles. See the yellowish crust on his forearms, Aja?" the Jackal notes. "Still, he's very much healthy and ready for your Carvers. All things considered."

"You know the man better than I," Aja says to someone else. "Make sure it is him. Not an imposter."

"You doubt my word?" the Jackal asks. "You wound me."

I flinch, feeling someone approach.

"Please. You'd need a heart for that, ArchGovernor. And you've many gifts, but that organ, I'm afraid, is dearly absent."

"You compliment me too much."

Spoons clatter against porcelain. Throats are cleared. I long to cover my ears. So much sound. So much information.

"You really can see the Red in him now." It's a cold, cultured female voice from northern Mars. More brusque than the Luna accent.

"Exactly, Antonia!" the Jackal replies. "I've been curious to see how he turned out. A member of the Aureate genus could never be so debased as this creature here before us. You know, he asked me for death before I put him in there. Started weeping about it. The irony is he could have killed himself whenever he chose. But he didn't, because some part of him relished that hole. You see, Reds long ago adapted to darkness. Like worms. No pride to their rusty race. He was at home down there. More than he ever was with us."

Now I remember hate.

I open my eyes to let them know I see them. Hear them. Yet as my eyes open, they are drawn not to my enemy, but to the winter vista that sprawls out the windows behind the Golds. There, six of the seven mountain peaks of Attica glitter in the morning light. Metal and glass buildings crest stone and snow, and yawn upward toward the blue sky. Bridges suture the peaks together. A light snow falls. It's a blurred mirage to my nearsighted cave eyes.

"Darrow?" I know the voice. I turn my head slightly to see one of his callused hands on the edge of the table. I flinch away, thinking it will strike me. It doesn't. But the hand's middle finger bears the golden eagle of Bellona. The family I destroyed. The other hand belongs to the arm I cut off on Luna when we last dueled, the one that was re-made by Zanzibar the Carver. Two wolfshead rings of House Mars encircle those fingers. One is mine. One his. Each worth the price of a young Gold's life. "Do you recognize me?" he asks.

I crane my head to look up at his face. Broken I may be, but Cassius au Bellona is undimmed by war or time. More beautiful by far than memory could ever allow, he pulses with life. Over two meters tall. Cloaked in the white and gold of the Morning Knight, his coiled hair lustrous as the trail of a falling star. He's clean-shaven, and his nose is slightly crooked from a recent break. When I meet his eyes, I do all I can to not fall into sobs. The way he looks at me is sad, nearly tender. What a shadow of myself I must be to earn pity from a man I've hurt so deeply.

"*Cassius,*" I murmur with no agenda except to say the name. To speak to another human. To be heard.

"And?" Aja au Grimmus asks from behind Cassius. The most violent of the Sovereign's Furies wears the same armor I saw her in when first we met in the Citadel spire on Luna, the night Mustang rescued me and Aja beat Quinn to death. It's scuffed. Battle-worn. Fear overwhelms my hate, and I look away from the dark-skinned woman yet again.

"He's alive after all," Cassius says quietly. He turns on the Jackal. "What did you do to him? The scars . . ."

"I should think it obvious," the Jackal says. "I have unmade the Reaper."

I finally look down at my body past my ratty beard to see what he means. I am a corpse. Skeletal and pallid. Ribs erupt from skin thinner than the film atop heated milk. Knees jut from spindly legs. Toenails have grown long and grasping. Scars from the Jackal's torture mottle my flesh. Muscle has withered. And tubes that kept me alive in the darkness erupt from my belly, black and stringy umbilical cords still anchoring me to the floor of my cell.

"How long was he in there?" Cassius asks.

"Three months of interrogation, then nine months of solitary."

"Nine . . ."

"As is fitting. War shouldn't make us abandon metaphor. We're not savages after all, eh, Bellona?"

"Cassius's sensibilities are offended, Adrius," Antonia says from her place near the Jackal. She's a poisoned apple of a woman. Shiny and bright and promising, but rotten and cancerous to the core. She killed my friend Lea at the Institute. Put a bullet in her own mother's head, and then two more into her sister Victra's spine. Now she's allied with the Jackal, a man who crucified her at the Institute. What a world. Behind Antonia stands dark-faced Thistle, once a Howler, now a member of the Jackal's Boneriders by the looks of the jackal skull pennant on her chest. She looks at the floor instead of at me. Her captain is bald-headed Lilath, who sits at the Jackal's right hand. His favorite personal killer ever since the Institute.

"Pardon me if I fail to see the purpose of torturing a fallen enemy," Cassius answers. "Especially if he's given all the information he has to give."

"The purpose?" The Jackal stares at him, eyes quiet, as he explains. "The purpose is punishment, my goodman. This . . . *thing* presumed he belonged among us. Like he was an equal, Cassius. A superior, even. He mocked us. Bedded my *sister*. He laughed at us and played us for fools before we found him out. He must know it was not by chance that he lost, but inevitability. Reds have always been cunning little creatures. And he, my friends, is the personification of what they wish to be, what they will be if we let them. So I let time and darkness remake him into what he really is. A *Homo flammeus,* to use the new classification system I proposed to the Board. Barely different from *Homo sapiens* on the evolutionary timeline. The rest was just a mask."

"You mean he made a fool of *you,*" Cassius parses, "when your father preferred a carved-up Red to his blood heir? That's what this is, *Jackal.* The petulant shame of a boy unloved and unwanted."

The Jackal twitches at that. Aja's equally displeased by her young companion's tone.

"Darrow took Julian's life," Antonia says. "Then slaughtered your family. Cassius, he sent killers to butcher the children of your blood as they hid on Olympus Mons. One would wonder what your mother would think of your pity."

Cassius ignores them, jerking his head toward the Pinks at the edge of the room. "Fetch the prisoner a blanket."

They do not move.

"Such manners. Even from you, Thistle?" She gives no answer. With a snort of contempt, Cassius strips off his white cloak and drapes it over my shivering body. For a moment, no one speaks, as struck by the act as I.

"Thank you," I croak. But he looks away from my hollow face. Pity is not forgiveness, nor is gratitude absolution.

Lilath snorts a laugh without looking up from her bowl of soft-boiled hummingbird eggs. She slurps at them like candy. "There *is* a point when honor becomes a flaw of character, Morning Knight." Sitting beside the Jackal, the bald woman peers up at Aja with eyes like those of the eels in Venus's cavern seas. Another egg goes down. "Old man Arcos learned the hard way."

Aja does not reply, her manners faultless. But a deathly silence lurks inside the woman, a silence I remember from the moments before she killed Quinn. Lorn taught her the blade. She will not like seeing his name mocked. Lilath greedily swallows another egg, sacrificing manners for insult.

There's animosity between these allies. As always with their kind. But this seems a stark new division between the old Golds and the Jackal's more modern breed.

"We're all friends here," the Jackal says playfully. "Mind your manners, Lilath. Lorn was an Iron Gold who simply chose the wrong side. So, Aja, I'm curious. Now that my lease on the Reaper is up, do you still plan to dissect him?"

"We do," Aja says. Shouldn't have thanked Cassius after all. His honor isn't true. It's just sanitary. "Zanzibar is curious to discover how he was made. He has his theories, but he's champing at the bit for the specimen. We were hoping to round up the Carver that did the deed, but we think he perished in a missile strike up in Kato, Alcidalia province."

"Or they want you to think that," Antonia says.

"You once had him here, didn't you?" Aja asks pointedly.

The Jackal nods. "Mickey's his name. Lost his license after he carved an unlicensed Aureate birth. Family tried sparing their child the Exposure. Anyway, he specialized in blackmarket aerial and aquatic pleasure mods afterward. Had a carveshop in Yorkton before the Sons recruited him for a special job. Darrow helped him escape my custody. If you want my opinion, he's still alive. My operatives place him in Tinos."

Aja and Cassius exchange a look.

"If you have a lead on Tinos, you need to share it with us now," Cassius says.

"I have nothing definitive yet. Tinos is well hidden. And we've yet to capture one of their ship captains . . . alive." The Jackal sips his coffee. "But irons are in the fire, and you'll be the first to know if anything comes of them. Though, I rather think my Boneriders would like the first crack at the Howlers. Wouldn't you, Lilath?"

I try not to stir at the mention of the name. But it's hard not to. They're alive. Some of them, at least. And they chose the Sons of Ares over Gold. . . .

"Yes, sir," Lilath says, studying me. "We'd relish a real hunt. Fighting the Red Legion and the other insurgents is a bore, even for Grays."

"The Sovereign needs us home anyway, Cassius," Aja says. Then, to the Jackal: "We'll be departing as soon as my Thirteenth has decamped from the Golan Basin. Likely by morning."

"You're taking your legions back to Luna?"

"Just the Thirteenth. The rest will remain under your supervision."

The Jackal is surprised. "My supervision?"

"On loan till this . . . *Rising* is fully snuffed out." She practically spits the word. A new one to my ears. "It's a token of the Sovereign's trust. You know she is pleased with your progress here."

"Despite your methods," Cassius adds, drawing an annoyed look from Aja.

"Well, if you're leaving in the morning you should, of course, dine with me this evening. I've been wanting to discuss certain . . . policies regarding the Rebels in the Rim." The Jackal is vague because I'm listening. Information's his weapon. Suggesting my friends betrayed me. Never saying which. Dropping hints and clues during my torture, before I was sent into the dark. A Gray telling him that his sister is waiting in his salon. His fingers smelling like frothed chai tea, his sister's favorite drink. Does she know I am here? Has she sat at this table? The Jackal is still prattling on. Hard to track the voices. So much to decipher. Too much.

". . . I'll have my men clean Darrow up for his travels and we can throw a feast of Trimalchian proportions after our discussion. I know the Voloxes and the Corialuses would be delighted to see you again. It's been too long since I had such august company as two Olympic Knights. You're in the field so often, skirting around provinces, hunting through the tunnels and seas and ghettos. How long has it been since you had a fine meal without worry of a night raid or suicide bombers?"

"A spell," Aja admits. "We took the Brothers Rath up on their hospitality when we passed through Thessalonica. They were eager to show their loyalty after their . . . behavior during the Lion's Rain. It was . . . unsettling."

The Jackal laughs. "I fear my dinner will be tame by comparison. It's been all politicians and soldiers of late. This gorydamn war has so impeded my social calendar, as you can imagine."

"Sure it's not your reputation for hospitality?" Cassius asks. "Or your diet?"

Aja sighs, trying to hide her amusement. "Manners, Bellona."

"Not to fear . . . the enmity between our houses is hard to forget, Cassius. But we must find common ground in times like these. For the sake of Gold." The Jackal smiles, though inside I know he's imagining sawing off both their heads with a dull knife. "Anyway, we all have our schoolyard stories. I'm hardly ashamed."

"There *was* one other matter we wished to discuss," Aja says.

It's Antonia's turn to sigh. "I told you there would be. What does our Sovereign require now?"

"It pertains to what Cassius mentioned earlier."

"My methods," the Jackal confirms.

"Yes."

"I thought the Sovereign was pleased with the pacification effort."

"She is, but . . ."

"She asked for order. I have provided. Helium-3 continues to flow, with only a three point two percent decrease in production. The Rising is struggling for air; soon Ares will be found and Tinos and all this will be behind us. Fabii is the one who is taking his—"

Aja interrupts. "It's the kill squads."

"Ah."

"And the liquidation protocols you've instituted in rebellious mines. She's worried that the severity of your methods against the lowReds will create a backlash comparable to earlier propaganda setbacks. There have been bombings on the Palatine Hill. Strikes in latfundias on Earth. Even protests at the gate of the Citadel itself. The spirit of rebellion is alive. But it is fractured. It must remain so."

"I doubt we'll be seeing many more protests after the Obsidians are sent in," Antonia says smugly.

"Still . . ."

"There is no danger of my tactics reaching the public eye. The Sons' abilities to propagate their message has been neutered," the Jackal says. "I control the message now, Aja. The people know this war is already lost. They'll never see a picture of the bodies. Never glimpse a liquidated mine. What they will continue to see is Red attacks on civilian targets. MidColor and highColor children dead in schools. The public is with us. . . ."

"And if they do see what you're doing?" Cassius asks.

The Jackal does not immediately reply. Instead, he signals a barely dressed Pink over from the couches in the adjacent sitting room. The girl, hardly older than Eo was, comes to his side and stares meekly at the ground. Her eyes are rose quartz, her hair a silvery lilac that hangs in braids down to her bare lower back. She was raised to pleasure these monsters, and I fear knowing what those soft eyes of hers have seen. My pain seems suddenly so tiny. The madness in my mind so quiet. The Jackal strokes the girl's face and, still looking at me, shoves his fingers into her mouth, prying her teeth apart. He moves the girl's head with his stump so I can see, then so Aja and Cassius might.

She has no tongue.

"I did this myself after we took her eight months ago. She attempted to assassinate one of my Boneriders at an Agea Pearl club. She hates me. Wants nothing more in this world than to see me rotting in the ground." Letting go of her face, he pops his sidearm out of his holster and thrusts it into the girl's hands. "Shoot me in the head, Calliope. For all the indignities I have heaped upon you and your kind. Go on. I took your tongue. You remember what I did to you in the library. It will happen again and again and again." He returns his hand to her face, squeezing her fragile jaw. "And again. *Pull the trigger, you little tart*. Pull it!" The Pink shakes in fear and throws the gun on the floor, falling to her knees to clutch his feet. He stands benevolent and loving above her, touching her head with his hand.

"There, there, Calliope. You did well. You did well." The Jackal turns to Aja. "For the public, honey is always better than vinegar. But for those who war with wrenches, with poison, with sabotage in the sewers and terror in the streets, and nibble at us like cockroaches in the night, fear is the only method." His eyes find mine. "Fear and extermination."

3

||||||||||||||||||||||

SNAKEBITE

Blood beads where buzzing metal pinches my scalp. Dirty blond hair puddles onto the concrete as the Gray finishes scalping me with an electric razor. His compatriots call him Danto. He rolls my head around to make sure he's got it all before clapping me hard on the top of it. "How 'bout a bath, *dominus*?" he asks. "Grimmus likes her prisoners to smell nice 'n civil, hear?" He taps the muzzle they strapped to my face after I tried to bite one of them. They moved me with an electric collar around my neck, arms bound still behind my back, a squad of twelve hardcore lurchers dragging me through the halls like a bag of trash.

Another Gray jerks me from my chair by my collar as Danto goes to pull a power hose from the wall. They're more than a head shorter than I am, but compact and rugged. The lives they live are hard—chasing Outriders in the belt, stalking Syndicate killers through the depths of Luna, hunting Sons of Ares in the mines . . .

I hate them touching me. All the sights and sounds they make. It's too much. Too gruff. Too hard. Everything they do hurts. Jerking me around. Slapping me casually. I try my best to keep the tears away, but I don't know how to compartmentalize it all.

The line of twelve soldiers crowds together, watching me as Danto aims the hose. They've got three Obsidian men with them. Most lurcher squads do. The water hits me like a horse kick in the chest. Tearing skin. I spin on the concrete floor, sliding across the room till I'm pinned in the corner. My skull slams against the wall. Stars swarm my sight. I swallow water. Choking, hunching to protect my face because my hands are still pinned behind my back.

When they've finished, I'm still gasping and coughing around the muzzle, trying to suck in air. They uncuff me and slip my arms and legs into a black prisoner's jumpsuit before binding me again. There's a hood too that they'll soon jerk over my head to rob me of what little humanity I have left. I'm thrown back into the chair. They click my restraints into the chair's receptacle so I'm locked down. Everything's redundant. Every move watched. They guard me like what I was, not what I am. I squint at them, vision bleary and nearsighted. Water drips from my eyelashes. I try to sniff, but my nose is clogged tight with congealed blood from nostril to nasal cavity. They broke it when they put the muzzle on.

We're in a processing room for the Board of Quality Control, which oversees the administrative functions of the prison beneath the Jackal's fortress. The building has the concrete box shape of every government facility. Poisonous lighting makes everyone here look like a walking corpse with pores the size of meteor craters. Aside from the Grays, the Obsidian, and a single Yellow doctor, there's a chair, an examination table, and a hose. But the fluid stains around the floor's metal drain and the nail scratches on the metal chair are the face and soul of this room. The ending of lives begins here.

Cassius would never come to this hole. Few Golds would ever need or want to unless they made the wrong enemies. It's the inside of the clock, where the gears whir and grind. How could anyone be brave in a place so inhuman as this?

"Crazy, ain't it?" Danto asks those behind him. He looks back at me. "All my life, never seen something so slaggin' odd."

"Carver musta put a hundred kilos on him," says another.

"More. Ever see him in his armor? He was a damned monster."

Danto flicks my muzzle with a tattooed finger. "Bet it hurt bein' born twice. Gotta respect that. Pain's the universal language. Ain't it, *Ruster*?" When I don't respond, he leans forward and stomps on my bare foot with his steel-heeled boot. The big toenail splits. Pain and blood rupture from the exposed nail bed. My head lolls sideways as I gasp. "Ain't it?" he asks again. Tears leak from my eyes, not from the pain, but from the casualness of his cruelty. It makes me feel so small. Why does it take so little for him to hurt me so much? It almost makes me miss the box.

"He's only a baboon in a suit," another says. "Leave off him. He don't know any better."

"Don't know any better?" Danto asks. "Bullshit. He liked the fit of master's clothes. Liked lording over us." Danto crouches so he's looking into my eyes. I try to look away, frightened he'll hurt me again, but he seizes my head and pulls open my eyelids with his thumbs so we're eye to eye. "Two of my sisters died in that Rain of yours, Ruster. Lost a lot of friends, ya hear?" He hits the side of my head with something metal. I see spots. Feel more blood leak from me. Behind him, their centurion checks his datapad. "You'd want the same for my kids, wouldn't you?" Danto searches my eyes for an answer. I have none he'd accept.

Like the rest, Danto's a veteran legionnaire, rough as a rusted sewer grate. Tech festoons his black combat gear, where scuffed purple dragons coil in faint filigree. Optic implants in the eyes for thermal vision and the reading of battlemaps. Under his skin he'll have more embedded tech to help him hunt Golds and Obsidians. The tattoo of an *XIII* clutched by a moving sea dragon stains all their necks, little heaps of ash at the base of the numeral. These are members of Legio XIII Dracones, the favored Praetorian legion of the Ash Lord and now his daughter, Aja. Civilians would just call them dragoons. Mustang hated the fanatics. It's a whole independent army of thirty thousand chosen by Aja to be the hand of the Sovereign away from Luna.

They hate me.

They hate lowColors with a marrow-deep racism even Golds can't match.

"Go for the ears, Danto, if you wanna make him yelp," one of the Grays suggests. The woman stands at the door, nutcracker jaw bobbing up and down as she gnaws on a gumbubble. Her ashen hair is shaved into a short Mohawk. Voice drawling in some Earthborn dialect. She leans against the metal beside a yawning male Gray with a delicate nose more like a Pink's than a soldier's. "You hit them with a cupped hand, you can pop the eardrum with the pressure."

"Thanks, Holi."

"Here to help."

Danto cups his hand. "Like this?" He hits my head.

"Little more curve to it."

The centurion snaps his fingers. "Danto. Grimmus wants him in one piece. Back up and let the doc take a look." I breathe a sigh of relief at the reprieve.

The fat Yellow doctor ambles forward to inspect me with beady ocher eyes. The pale lights above make the bald patch on his head shine like a pale, waxed apple. He runs his bioscope over my chest, watching the visual through little digital implants in his eyes. "Well, Doc?" the centurion asks.

"Remarkable," the Yellow whispers after a moment. "Bone density and organs are quite healthy despite the low-caloric diet. Muscles have atrophied, as we've observed in laboratory settings, but not as poorly as natural Aureate tissue."

"You're saying he's better than Gold?" the centurion asks.

"I did not say that," the doctor snaps.

"Relax. There's no cameras, Doc. This is a processing room. What's the verdict?"

"It can travel."

"It?" I manage in a low, unearthly growl from behind my muzzle.

The doctor recoils, surprised I can speak.

"And long-term sedation? Got three weeks to Luna at this orbit."

"That will be fine." The doctor gives me a frightened look. "But I would up the dose by ten milligrams per day, Captain, just to be safe. *It* has an abnormally strong circulatory system."

"Right." The captain nods to the female Gray. "You're up, Holi. Put him to bed. Then let's get the cart and roll out. You're square, Doc. Head back to your safe little espresso-and-silk world now. We'll take care of—"

Pop. The front half of the centurion's forehead comes off. Something metal hits the wall. I stare at the centurion, mind not processing why his face is gone. *Pop. Pop. Pop. Pop.* Like knuckle joints. Red mist geysers into the air from the heads of the nearest dragoons. Spraying my face. I duck my head away. Behind them, the nutcracker-jawed woman walks casually through their ranks, shooting them point-blank in the backs of their heads. The rest pull their rifles up, scrambling, unable to even utter curses before a second Gray double-taps five of them from his place at the door with an old-fashioned gunpowder slug shooter. Silencer on the barrel so it's cool and quiet. Obsidians are the first to hit the floor, leaking red.

"Clear," the woman says.

"Plus two," the man replies. He shoots the Yellow doctor as he crawls to the door trying to escape, then puts a boot on Danto's chest. The Gray stares up at him, bleeding from under the jaw.

"Trigg . . ."

"Ares sends his regards, motherfucker." The Gray shoots Danto just under the brim of his tactical helmet, between the eyes, and spins the slug shooter in his hand, blowing smoke from the end before sheathing it in a leg holster. "Clear."

My lips work against my muzzle, struggling to form a coherent thought. "Who . . . are you . . ." The Gray woman nudges a body out of her way.

"Name's Holiday ti Nakamura. That's Trigg, my baby brother." She raises a scar-notched eyebrow. Her wide face is blasted by freckles. Nose smashed flat. Eyes dark gray and narrow. "Question is, who are you?"

"Who am I?" I mumble.

"We came for the Reaper. But if that's you, I think we should get our money back." She winks suddenly. "I'm joking, sir."

"Holiday, cut it." Trigg pushes her aside protectively. "Can't you see he's shell-shocked?" Trigg approaches carefully, hands out, voice soothing. "You're prime, sir. We're here to rescue you." His words are thicker, less polished than Holiday's. I flinch as he takes another step. Search his hands for a weapon. He's going to hurt me. "Just gonna unlock you. That's all. You want that, yeah?"

It's a lie. A Jackal trick. He's got the *XIII* tattoo. These are Praetorians, not Sons. Liars. Killers.

"I won't unlock you if you don't want me to."

No. No, he killed the guards. He's here to help. He has to be here to help. I give Trigg a wary nod and he slips behind me. I don't trust him. I half expect a needle. A twist. But all I feel is release as my risk is rewarded. The cuffs unlock. My shoulder joints crack and, moaning, I pull my hands in front of my body for the first time in nine months. The pain causes them to shake. The nails have grown long and vile. But these hands are mine again. I charge to my feet to escape, and collapse to the floor.

"Whoa . . . whoa," Holiday says, hefting me back into the chair. "Easy there, hero. You've got mad muscle atrophy. Gonna need an oil change."

Trigg comes back around to stand in front of me, smiling lopsided, face open and boyish, not nearly as intimidating as his sister, despite the two gold teardrop tattoos that leak from his right eye. He has the look of a loyal hound. Gently he removes the muzzle from my face, then remembers something with a start. "I've got something for you, sir."

"Not now, Trigg." Holiday eyes the door. "Ain't got the seconds."

"He needs it," Trigg says under his breath, but waits till Holiday gives him a nod before he pulls a leather bundle from his tortoise pack. He extends it to me. "It's yours, sir. Take it." He senses my apprehension. "Hey, I didn't lie about unlocking you, did I?"

"No . . ."

I put my hands out and he sets the leather bundle in them. Fingers trembling, I pull back the string holding the bundle together and feel the power before I even see the deadly shimmer. My hands almost drop the bundle, as frightened of it as my eyes were of the light.

It is my razor. The one given to me by Mustang. The one I've lost twice now. Once to Karnus, then again at my Triumph to the Jackal. It is white and smooth as a child's first tooth. My hands slide over the cold metal and its salt-stained calf-leather grip. Touch wakening melancholy memories of strength long faded and warmth long forgotten. The smell of hazelnut drifts back to me, transporting me to Lorn's practice rooms, where he would teach me as his favorite granddaughter learned to bake in the adjacent kitchen.

The razor slithers through the air, so beautiful, so deceitful in its promise of power. The blade would tell me I'm a god, as it has told generations of men who came before me, but I now know the lie in that. The terrible price it's made men pay for pride.

It scares me to hold it again.

And it rasps like a pitviper's mating call as it forms into a curved slingBlade. It was blank and smooth when last I saw it, but it ripples now with images etched into the white metal. I tilt the blade so I can better see the form etched just above the hilt. I stare dumbly. Eo looks back at me. An image of her etched into the metal. The artist caught her not on the scaffold, not in the moment that will forever define her to others, but intimately, as the girl I loved. She's crouched, hair messy about her shoulders, picking a haemanthus from the ground, looking up, just about to smile. And above Eo is my father kissing my mother at the door of our home. And toward the tip of the blade, Leanna, Loran, and I chasing Kieran down a tunnel, wearing Octobernacht masks. It is my childhood.

Whoever made this art knows me.

"The Golds carve their deeds into their swords. The *grand, violent* shit they've done. But Ares thought you'd prefer to see the people you love," Holiday says quietly from behind Trigg. She glances back to the door.

"Ares is dead." I search their faces, seeing the deceit there. Seeing the wickedness in their eyes. "The Jackal sent you. It's a trick. A trap. To lead you to the Sons' base." My hand tightens around the razor's grip. "To use me. You're lying."

Holiday steps back from me, wary of the blade in my hand. But Trigg is ripped apart by the accusation. "Lying? To *you*? We'd die for you, sir. We'd have died for Persephone . . . Eo." He struggles to find the words, and I get a sense he's used to letting his sister do the talking. "There's an army waiting for you outside these walls—does that register? An army waiting for its . . . its *soul* to come back to it." He leans forward imploringly as Holiday looks back to the door. "We're from South Pacifica, the ass end of Earth. I thought I'd die there guarding grain silos. But I'm here. On Mars. And our only job is to get you home. . . ."

"I've met better liars than you," I sneer.

"Screw this." Holiday reaches for her datapad.

Trigg tries to stop her. "Ares said it was only for emergencies. If they hack the signal . . ."

"Look at him. This is an emergency." Holiday strips her datapad and tosses it to me. A call is going through to another device. Blinking blue on the display, waiting for the other side to answer. As I turn it in my hand, a hologram of a spiked sunburst helmet suddenly blossoms into the air, small as my clenched fist. Red eyes glow out balefully from the helmet.

"Fitchner?"

"*Guess again, shithead,*" the voice warbles.

It can't be.

"Sevro?" I almost whimper the word.

"*Oy, boyo, you look like you slithered out of a skeleton's rickety cooch.*"

"You're alive . . . ," I say as the holographic helmet slithers away to reveal my hatchet-faced friend. He smiles with those hacksaw teeth. Image flickering.

"*Ain't no Pixie in the worlds that can kill me.*" He cackles. "*Now it's time you come home, Reap. But I can't come to you. You gotta come to me. You register?*"

"How?" I wipe the tears from my eyes.

"*Trust my Sons. Can you do that?*"

I look at the brother and sister and nod. "The Jackal . . . he has my family."

"*That cannibalistic bitch ain't got shit. I got your family. Grabbed them from Lykos after you got snagged. Your mother's waiting to see you.*" I start crying again. The relief too much to bear.

"*But you gotta sack up, boyo. And you gotta move.*" He looks sideways at someone. "*Gimme back to Holiday.*" I do. "*Make it clean if you can. Escalate if you can't. Register?*"

"Register."

"*Break the chains.*"

"Break the chains," the Grays echo as his image flickers out.

"Look past our Color," Holiday says to me. She reaches a tattooed hand down. I stare at the Gray Sigils etched into her flesh, then look up to search her freckled, bluff face. One of her eyes is bionic, and does not blink like the other. Eo's words sound so different from her mouth. Yet I think it's the moment my soul comes back to me. Not my mind. I still feel the cracks in it. The slithering, doubting darkness. But my hope. I clutch her smaller hand desperately.

"Break the chains," I echo hoarsely. "You'll have to carry me." I look at my worthless legs. "Can't stand."

"That's why we brought you a little cocktail." Holiday pulls up a syringe.

"What is it?" I ask.

Trigg just laughs. "Your oil change. Seriously, friend, you really don't want to know." He grins. "Shit will animate a corpse."

"Give it to me," I say, holding out my wrist.

"It's gonna hurt," Trigg warns.

"He's a big boy." Holiday comes closer.

"Sir . . ." Trigg hands me one of his gloves. "Between your teeth."

A little less confident, I bite down on the salt-stained leather and nod to Holiday. She lunges past my wrist to jam the syringe straight into my heart. Metal punctures meat as the payload releases.

"Holy shit!" I try to scream, but it comes out as a gurgle. Fire cavorts through my veins, my heart a piston. I look down, expecting to see it galloping out of my bloodydamn chest. I feel every muscle. Every cell of my body exploding, pulsing with kinetic energy. I dry-heave. I fall, clawing at my chest. Panting. Spitting bile. Punching the floor. The Grays scramble back from my twisting body. I strike out at the chair, half ripping it from its bolted place in the floor. I let out a stream of curses that'd make Sevro blush. Then I tremble and look up at them. "What . . . was . . . *that*?"

Holiday tries not to laugh. "Mamma calls it snakebite. Only gonna last thirty minutes with your metabolism."

"Your mamma made that?"

Trigg shrugs. "We're from Earth."

4

||||||||||||||||||||||||

CELL 2187

They escort me like a prisoner through the halls. Hood on my head. Hands behind my back in unlocked manacles. Brother on my left, sister on my right, both supporting me. The snakebite lets me walk, but not well. My body, jacked with drugs as it is, still feels slack as wet clothes. I can barely feel my busted toe or feeble legs. My thin prisoner's shoes scrape the floor. My head swims, but there's a hyper speed to my brain now. It's focused mania. I chew my tongue to keep from whispering, and to remind myself that I am not in the darkness like before. My body is shuffling down a concrete hall. It is walking toward freedom. Toward my family, toward Sevro.

No one here will stop two dragoons of the Thirteenth, not when they have clearance and Aja herself is here. I doubt many in the Jackal's army know I'm even alive. They'll see my size, my ghostly pallor, and think I'm some unlucky Obsidian prisoner. Still, I feel the eyes. Paranoia creeping through me. *They know. They know you've left bodies behind. How long till they open that door? How long till we are discovered?* My brain races through the possible ends. How it could all go wrong. The drugs. It's just the drugs.

"Shouldn't we be going up?" I ask as we descend on a gravLift deeper into the heart of the mountain citadel's prison. "Or is there a lower hangar bay?"

"Good guess, sir," Trigg says, impressed. "We've got a ship waiting."

Holiday pops her gum. "Trigg, you've got some brown on your nose. Just . . . there."

"Oh, shut your hole. I'm not the one who blushed when he was naked."

"Sure about that, kiddo? Quiet." The gravLift slows and the siblings tense. Hear their hands click the safeties off their weapons. The doors open and someone joins us.

"*Dominus*," Holiday says smoothly to the new company, shoving me to the side to make room. The boots that enter are heavy enough for a Gold or Obsidian, but Grays would never call an Obsidian *dominus*, and an Obsidian would never smell like cloves and cinnamon.

"Sergeant." The voice scrapes through me. The man it belongs to once made necklaces of ears. Vixus. One of Titus's old band. He was part of the massacre at my Triumph. I shrink into the side of the grav-Lift as it descends again. Vixus will know me. He'll sniff me out. He's doing it now, looking our way. I can hear the rustle of his jacket collar. "Thirteenth legion?" Vixus asks after a moment. He must have noticed their neck tattoos. "You Aja's or her father's?"

"The Fury's, for this tour, *dominus*," Holiday replies coolly. "But we've served under the Ash Lord."

"Ah, then you were at the Battle of Deimos last year?"

"Yes, *dominus*. We were with Grimmus in the leechCraft vanguard sent to kill the Telemanuses before Fabii routed them and Arcos's ships. My brother here put a round in old Kavax's shoulder. Almost took him down before Augustus and Kavax's wife broke our assault team."

"My, my." Vixus makes a sound of approval. "That would have been a gorydamn prize and a half. You could have added another tear to your face, legionnaire. I've been hunting that Obsidian dog with the Seventh. Ash Lord's offered quite the price for his slave's return."

He snorts something up his nose. Sounds like one of the stim canisters Tactus was so fond of. "Who's this, then?"

He means me.

I hear my heart in my ears.

"A gift from Praetor Grimmus in exchange for . . . *the package* she's taking home," Holiday says. "If you understand me, sir."

"Package. Half a package, more like." He chuckles at his own joke. "Anyone I know?" His hand touches the edge of my hood. I cower away. "A Howler would warm the heart. Pebble? Weed? No, much too tall."

"An Obsidian," Trigg says quickly. "Wish it was a Howler."

"Ugh." Vixus jerks his hand back as though contaminated. "Wait." He has an idea. "We'll put him in the cell with the Julii bitch. Let 'em fight for supper. What do you think, Thirteen? Up for some fun?"

"Trigg, kill the camera," I say sharply from beneath my hood.

"What?" Vixus asks, turning.

Pop. A jamfield goes up.

I move, clumsy but fast. Snapping my hands out of the shackles, I pull free my hidden razor with one hand and rip off my hood with the other. I stab Vixus through the shoulder. Pin him to the wall and head-butt him in the face. But I'm not what I was, even with the drugs. My vision swims. I stumble. He doesn't, and before I can react, before I can even focus my vision, Vixus pulls his own razor.

Holiday shields me with her body, shoving me away. I fall to the ground. Trigg's even faster on the take; he jams his slug shooter straight up into Vixus's open mouth. The Gold freezes, staring down the metal length of the barrel, tongue against the cold muzzle. His razor pauses centimeters from Holiday's head.

"Shhhhhh," Trigg whispers. "Drop the razor." Vixus does.

"The hell are you thinking?" Holiday asks me angrily. She's breathing heavily and helps me back up. My head's still spinning. I apologize. It was stupid of me. I steady myself and look over at Vixus, who stares at me in horror. My legs tremble, and I have to hold myself up by one of the gravLift's railings. My heart rattles from the strain of the drug in my system. Stupid to try to fight. Stupid to use a jammer.

The Greens watching will piece it together. They'll send Grays to investigate the prep room. Find the bodies.

I try to paste my splintering thoughts together. Focus. "Is Victra alive?" I manage. Trigg pulls the gun out past the teeth so Vixus can answer. He doesn't. Not yet. "Do you know what he did to me?" I ask. After a stubborn moment, Vixus nods. "And . . ." I laugh. It stretches like a crack in ice, spreading, widening, about to shiver a thousand different ways, till I bite my tongue to cut it short. "And . . . and still you have the balls to make me ask you twice?"

"She's alive."

"Reaper . . . they'll be coming for us. They'll know it's jammed," Holiday says, looking at the tiny camera node in the elevator's ceiling. "We can't change the plan."

"Where is she?" I twist the razor. "Where is she?"

Vixus hisses in pain. "Level 23, cell 2187. It would be wise not to kill me. You might put me in her cell. Escape. I will tell you the proper path, Darrow." The muscles and veins under the skin of his neck slither and rise like snakes under sand. No body fat to him. "Two backstabbing Praetorians won't get you far. There's an army in this mountain. Legions in the city, in orbit. Thirty Peerless Scarred. Boneriders in southern Attica." He nods to the small jackal skull on the lapel of his uniform. "You remember them?"

"We don't need him," Trigg snaps, fingering his gun's trigger.

"Oh?" Vixus chuckles, confidence returning as he sees my weakness. "And what are *you* going to do against an Olympic Knight, tinpot? Oh, wait. There are two here, aren't there?"

Holiday just snorts. "Same thing you'd do, goldilocks. Run."

"Level 23," I tell Trigg.

Trigg punches the gravLift controls, diverting us from their escape route. He pulls up a map on his datapad and studies it briefly with Holiday. "Cell 2187 is . . . here. There will be a code. Cameras."

"Too far from evac." Holiday's mouth tightens. "If we go that way, we're cooked."

"Victra is my friend," I say. And I thought she was dead, but somehow she survived her sister's gunshots. "I won't leave her."

"There's not a choice," Holiday says.

"There's always a choice." The words sound feeble, even to me.

"Look at yourself, man. You're a husk!"

"Back off him, Holi," Trigg says.

"That Gold bitch isn't one of us! I won't die for her."

But Victra would have died for me. In the darkness, I thought of her. The childish joy in her eyes when I gave her the bottle of petrichor in the Jackal's study. "I didn't know. Darrow, I didn't know," was the last thing she said to me after Roque betrayed us. Death around, bullets in her back, and all she wanted was me to think well of her in the end.

"I won't leave my friend behind," I repeat dogmatically.

"I'll follow you," Trigg drawls. "Whatever you say, Reaper. I'm your man."

"Trigg," Holiday whispers. "Ares said—"

"Ares hasn't turned the tide." Trigg nods to me. "He can. We go where he goes."

"And if we miss our window?"

"Then we make a new one."

Holiday's eyes go glassy and she works her large jaw. I know that look. She doesn't see her brother as I do. He's no lurcher, no killer. To her he's the boy she grew with.

"All right. I'm in," she says reluctantly.

"What about the Peerless?" Trigg asks.

"He puts the code in and he lives," I say. "Shoot him if tries anything."

We exit the elevator at level 23. I wear my hood again, having Holiday guide me along as Vixus walks ahead as if escorting us to a cell, Trigg ready with his gun close behind. The halls are quiet. Our footsteps echo. I can't see past the hood.

"This is it," Vixus says when we reach the door.

"Put in the code, asshole," Holiday orders.

He does and the door hisses open. Noise roars out around us. Horrible static from hidden speakers. The cell is freezing, everything bleached white. The ceiling flaring with light so bright I can't even look directly at it. The cell's emaciated occupant lies in the corner, legs curled up in a fetal position, spine to me. Back painted with old burns and striped with lash marks from beatings. The mess of white-blond hair over her eyes is all that shields the woman from the blazing light. I wouldn't know who she was except for the two bullet scars at the top of her spine between the shoulder blades.

"Victra!" I shout over the noise. She can't hear me. "Victra!" I shout again, just as the noise dies, replaced over the speakers by the sound of a heartbeat. They're torturing her with sound, light. Sensation. The exact opposite of my own abuse. Able to hear me now, she whips her head my direction. Gold eyes peering ferally out from the tangle of hair. I don't even know if she recognizes me. The boldness with which Victra wore her nakedness before is gone. She covers herself, vulnerable. Terrified.

"Get her on her feet," Holiday says, pushing Vixus to his belly. "We gotta go."

"She's paralyzed. . . ." Trigg says. "Isn't she?"

"Shit. We'll carry her, then."`

Trigg moves quickly toward Victra. I slam a hand back into his chest, stopping him. Even like this, she could rip his arms from his body. Knowing the terror I felt when I was pulled from my hole, I move slowly toward her. My own fear retreating to the back of my mind, replaced by anger at what her own sister has done to her. At knowing this is my fault.

"Victra, it's me. It's Darrow." She makes no sign of having heard me. I crouch down beside her. "We're going to get you out of here. Can we lift—"

She lunges at me. Throwing herself forward with her arms. *"Take off your face,"* she screams, *"Take off your face."* She convulses as Holiday rushes forward and jams a thumper into the small of her back. The electricity isn't enough.

"Go down!" Holiday shouts. Victra hits her in the center of her duroplastic armor chestpiece, launching the Gray meters back into the wall. Trigg fires two tranquilizers into her thigh from his ambi-rifle, a multipurpose carbine. They put her down quick. But still she pants on the ground, watching me through a slitted eye till she falls unconscious.

"Holiday . . ." I begin.

"I'm Golden." Holiday grunts, lifting herself up. The chest piece has a fist-sized dent in the center. "Pixie can hit," Holiday says, admiring the dent. "This armor is supposed to handle rail rounds."

"Julii genetics," Trigg mutters. He hoists Victra up on his shoulders and follows Holiday back out into the hall as she snaps at me to hurry after them. We leave Vixus belly-down in the cell. Alive, as I promised.

"We'll find you," he says, sitting up as I go to shut the door. "You know we will. Tell little Sevro we're coming. One Barca down. One to go."

"What did you say?" I ask.

I step suddenly back into the cell and his eyes light with fear. The same fear Lea must have felt those many years ago when I hid in the dark while Antonia and Vixus tortured her to lure me out. He laughed as her blood soaked into the moss. And as my friends died in the garden. He would have me spare him now so he could kill again later. Evil feeds on mercy.

My razor slithers into a slingBlade.

"Please," he begs now, thin lips trembling so that I see the boy in him too as he realizes he made a mistake. Someone somewhere still loves him. Remembers him as a mischievous child or asleep in a crib. If only he had stayed that child. If only we all had. "Have a heart. Darrow, you're no murderer. You're no Titus."

The heartbeat sound of the room deepens. White light silhouetting him.

He wants pity.

My pity was lost in the darkness.

The heroes of Red songs have mercy, honor. They let men live, as I let the Jackal live, so they can remain untarnished by sin. Let the villain be the evil one. Let him wear black and try to stab me as I turn my back, so I can wheel about and kill him, giving satisfaction without guilt. But this is no song. This is war.

"Darrow . . ."

"I need you to send a message to the Jackal."

I slash open Vixus's throat. And as he slumps to the ground pulsing out his life, I know he is afraid because nothing waits for him on the other side. He gurgles. Whimpers before he dies. And I feel nothing.

Beyond the heartbeat of the room, alarm sirens begin to wail.

5

||||||||||||||||||||||||

PLAN C

"Shit," Holiday says. "I told you we didn't have time."

"We're fine," Trigg says.

We're together in the elevator. Victra on the floor. Trigg, helping her into his black rain gear to give her a semblance of decency. My knuckles are white. Vixus's blood trickles over the inscribed image of children playing in the tunnels. It drips over my parents and stains Eo's hair red before I wipe it from the blade with my prisoner jumpsuit. I forgot how easy it is to take a life.

"Live for yourself, die alone," Trigg says quietly. "You think with all those brains, they'd have sense enough not to be such assholes." He looks over at me, brushing hair from flinty eyes. "Sorry to be a prick, sir. Y'know, if he was a friend . . ."

"Friend?" I shake my head. "He had no friends."

I bend down to brush Victra's hair from her face. She sleeps peacefully against the wall. Cheeks carved out from hunger. Lips thin and sad. There's a dramatic beauty to her features even now. I wonder what they did to her. The poor woman, always so strong, so brash, but always to cover the kindness inside. I wonder if any is left.

"Are you prime?" Trigg asks. I don't respond. "Was she your girl?"

"No," I say. I touch the beard that's grown on my face. I hate how it scratches and stinks. I wish Danto had shaved it off as well. "I'm not prime."

I don't feel hope. I don't feel love.

Not as I look at what they did to Victra, to me.

It's the hate that rides.

Hate too for what I've become. I feel Trigg's eyes. Know he's disappointed. He wanted the Reaper. And I'm just a withered husk of a man. I run my fingers against my cage of ribs. So many slender little things. I promised these Grays too much. I promised everyone too much, especially Victra. She was true to me. What was I to her but another person who wanted to use her? Another person her mother trained her to be prepared against.

"You know what we need?" Trigg asks.

I look up at him intensely. "Justice?"

"A cold beer."

A laugh explodes out of my mouth. Too loud. Scaring me.

"Shit," Holiday murmurs, hands flying over the controls. "Shit. Shit. Shit . . ."

"What?" I ask.

We're stuck between the 24th and 25th. She punches buttons but suddenly the lift jerks upward. "They've overridden the controls. We're not going to make it to the hangar. They're redirecting us. . . ." She lets out a long breath as she looks up at me. "To the first level. Shit. Shit. Shit. They'll be waiting with lurchers, maybe Obsidians . . . maybe Golds." She pauses. "They know you're in here."

I fight back the despair that rushes up from my belly. I won't go back. Whatever happens. I'll kill Victra, kill myself before I let them take us.

Trigg is hunched over his sister. "Can you hack the system?"

"When the hell do you think I learned how to do that?"

"I wish Ephraim was here. He could."

"Well, I'm not Ephraim."

"What about climbing out?"

"If you want to be a skid mark."

"Guess that leaves one option. Eh?" He reaches into his pocket. "Plan C."

"I hate Plan C."

"Yeah, well. Time to embrace the suck, babydoll. Unpack the heathen.

"What's Plan C?" I ask quietly.

"Escalation." Trigg activates his comlink. Codes flash over his screen as he connects to a secure frequency. "Outrider to Wrathbone, do you register? Outrider to—"

"*Wrathbone registers,*" a ghostly voice echoes. "*Request clearance code Echo. Over.*"

Trigg references his datapad. "13439283. Over."

"*Code is green.*"

"We need secondary extraction in five. Got the princess plus one at stage two."

There's a pause on the other line, the relief in the voice palpable even through the static. "*Late notice.*"

"Murder ain't exactly punctual."

"*Be there in ten. Keep him alive.*" The link goes dead.

"Goddamn amateurs," Trigg mutters.

"Ten minutes," Holiday repeats.

"We've been in worse shit."

"When?" He doesn't answer her. "Should have just gone to the goddamn hangar."

"What can I do?" I ask, sensing their fear. "Can I help?"

"Don't die," Holiday says as she slides off her backpack. "Then this is all for shit."

"You gotta drag your friend," Trigg says as he starts picking tech off his body except his armor. He pulls two more antique weapons from his pack—two pistols to complement the high-powered gas ambi-rifle. He hands me a pistol. My hand shakes. I haven't held a gunpowder weapon since I was sixteen training with the Sons. They're vastly inefficient and heavy, and their recoil makes them wildly inaccurate.

Holiday pulls a large plastic box from her pack. Her fingers pause over the latches.

She opens the plastic box to reveal a metal cylinder with a spinning ball of mercury at its center. I stare at the device. If the Society caught her carrying it, she'd never see daylight again. Vastly illegal. I eye the gravLift's display on the wall. Ten levels to go. Holiday grips a remote control for the cylinder. Eight levels.

Will Cassius be waiting? Aja? The Jackal? No. They would be on their ship, preparing for dinner. The Jackal would be living his life. They won't know the alarm is for me. And even when they do, they'll be delayed. But there's enough to fear even without one of them coming. An Obsidian could rip these two apart with his bare hands. Trigg knows. He closes his eyes, touching his chest at four points to make a cross. A wedding band glints softly in the low light. Holiday minds the gesture, but doesn't do the same.

"This is our profession," she says quietly to me. "So swallow your pride. Stay behind us and let Trigg and I work."

Trigg cracks his neck and kisses his gloved left ring finger. "Stay close. Nut to butt, sir. Don't be shy."

Three levels to go.

Holiday readies a gas rifle in her right hand and chews intensely on her gum, left thumb on the remote control. One level to go. We're slowing. Watching the double doors. I loop Victra's legs in my armpits.

"Love you, kiddo," Holiday says.

"Love you too, babydoll," Trigg murmurs back, voice tight and mechanical now.

I feel more afraid than I did when I lay encased in a starShell in the chamber of a spitTube before my rain. Not just afraid for me, but for Victra, for these two siblings. I want them to live. I want to know about South Pacifica. I want to know what pranks they pulled on their mother. If they had a dog, a home in the city, the country . . .

The gravLift wheezes to a halt.

The door light flashes. And the thick metal doors that separate us from a platoon of the Jackal's elite hiss open. Two glowing stunGrenades zip in and clamp to the walls. *Beep. Beep.* And Holiday pushes the device's button. A deep implosion of sound ruptures the elevator's quiet as an invisible electromagnetic pulse ripples out from the spherical EMP at our feet. The grenades fizzle dead. Lights go black in the elevator, outside it. And all the Grays waiting beyond the door with their hi-tech pulse weapons, and all the Obsidians in their heavy armor with their electronic joints and helmets and air filtration units, are slapped in the face with the Middle Ages.

But Holiday and Trigg's antiques still work. They stalk forward out of the elevator into the stone hall, hunched over their weapons like evil gargoyles. It's slaughter. Two expert marksmen firing short bursts of archaic slugs at point-blank range into squads of defenseless Grays in wide halls. There is no cover to take. Flashes in the corridor. Gigantic sounds of high-powered rifles. Rattling my teeth. I freeze in the elevator till Holiday shouts at me, and I rush after Trigg, hauling Victra behind me.

Three Obsidians go down as Holiday lobs an antique grenade. *Whooomph*. A hole opens in the ceiling. Plaster rains. Dust. Chairs and Coppers fall through the hole from the room above, crashing down into the fray. I hyperventilate. A man's head kicks back. Body spins to the ground. A Gray flees for cover down a stone hall. Holiday shoots her in the spine. She sprawls like a child slipping on ice. Movement everywhere. An Obsidian charges from the side.

I fire the pistol, aim horrible. The bullets skitter off his armor. Two hundred kilograms of man raises an ionAxe, its battery dead, but edge still keen. He ululates his kind's throaty war chant and red mist geysers from his helmet. Bullet through the skull-helm's eye socket. His body pitches forward, slides. Nearly knocks me off my feet. Trigg's already moving to the next target, driving metal into men as patiently as a craftsman driving nails into wood. No passion there. No art. Just training and physics.

"Reaper, move your ass!" Holiday shouts. She jerks me down a hall away from the chaos as Trigg follows, hurling a sticky grenade onto the thigh of an unarmored Gold who dodges four of his rifle shots. *Whoomph*. Bone and meat to mist.

The siblings reload on the run and I just try not to faint or fall. "Right in fifty paces, then up the stairs!" Holiday snaps. "We've got seven minutes."

The halls are eerily quiet. No sirens. No lights. No whir of heated air through the vents. Just the clunk of our boots and distant shouts and the cracking of my joints and the rasping of lungs. We pass a window. Ships, black and dead, fall through the sky. Small fires burn where others have landed. Trams grind to a halt on magnetic rails. The only lights that still run are from the two most distant peaks. Reinforcements with tech will soon respond, but they won't know what caused this. Where to look. With camera systems and biometric scanners dead, Cassius and Aja won't be able to find us. That might save our lives.

We run up the stairs. A cramp eats into my right calf and hamstring. I grunt and almost fall. Holiday takes most of my weight. Her powerful neck pressing up against my armpit. Three Grays spot us from behind at the bottom of the long marble stairs. Shoving me aside, she takes two down with her rifle, but the third fires back. Bullets chewing into marble.

"They've got gas backups," Holiday barks. "Gotta move. Gotta move."

Two more rights, past several lowColors, who stare at me, mouths agape, through marble halls with towering ceilings and Greek statues, past galleries where the Jackal keeps his stolen artifacts and once showed me Hancock's declaration and the preserved head of the last ruler of the American Empire.

Muscles burning. Side splitting.

"Here!" Holiday finally cries.

We reach a service door in a side hall and push through into cold daylight. The wind swallows me. Icy teeth ripping through my jumpsuit as the four of us stumble out onto a metal walkway along the side of the Jackal's fortress. To our right, the stone of the mountain surrenders to the modern metal-and-glass edifice above. It's a thousand-meter drop to our left. Snow swirls around the mountain's face. Wind howls. We push forward along the walkway till it circles part of the fortress and links with a paved bridge that extends from the mountain to an abandoned landing platform like a skeletal arm holding out a concrete dinner plate covered in snow.

"Four minutes," Holiday hollers as she helps me struggle across the bridge toward the landing pad. At the end, she dumps me onto the ground. I set Victra down beside me. A hard skin of ice makes the concrete slick and smoky gray. Snowdrifts gather around the waist-high concrete wall that fences in the circular landing pad from the thousand-meter drop.

"Got eighty in the long mag, six in the relic," he calls to his sister. "Then I'm out."

"Got twelve," she says, tossing down a small canister. It pops and green smoke swirls into the air. "Gotta hold the bridge."

"I've got six mines."

"Plant them."

He sprints back down the bridge. At the end of it is a set of closed blast doors, much larger than the maintenance path we took from the side. Shivering and snowblind, I pull Victra close to me against that wall to escape the wind. Snowflakes gather atop the black rain gear she wears. Fluttering down like the ash that fell when Cassius, Sevro, and I burned Minerva's citadel and stole their cook. "We'll be fine," I tell her. "We'll make it." I peer over the short concrete wall to the city beneath. It's oddly peaceful. All her sounds, all her troubles silenced by the EMP. I watch a flake of snow larger than the rest drift on the wind and come to rest on my knuckle.

How did I get here? A boy of the mines now a shivering fallen war-lord staring down at a darkened city, hoping against everything that he can go home. I close my eyes, wishing I was with my friends, my family.

"Three minutes," Holiday says behind me. Her gloved hand touches my shoulder protectively as she looks to the sky for our enemies. "Three minutes and we're out of here. Just three minutes."

I wish I could believe her, but the snow has stopped falling.

6

||||||||||||||||||||||||

VICTIMS

I squint up past Holiday as an iridescent defensive shield ripples into place over the seven peaks of Attica, cutting us off from the clouds and the sky beyond. The shield generator must have been out of the EMP's blast range. No help will come to us from beyond it.

"Trigg! Get back here!" she shouts as he plants the last mine on the bridge.

A single gunshot shatters the winter morning. Echoing brittle and cold. More follow. *Crack. Crack. Crack.* Snow kicks around him. He sprints back as Holiday leans to cover for him, her rifle rocking her shoulder. Straining, I push myself up. My eyes ache as they try to focus in the sun's light. Concrete explodes in front of me. Shards rip into my face. I duck down, shivering in fear. The Jackal's men have found their backup weapons.

I peer out again. Through squinting lids, I see Trigg pinned down halfway to us, exchanging gunfire with a squad of Grays carrying gas-powered rifles. They pour out of the fortress's blast doors, now opened at the opposite end of the bridge. Two go down. Two more step near a proximity mine and disappear in a cloud of smoke as Trigg shoots it at their feet. Holiday picks another off just as Trigg staggers back into cover, hit with a round in the shoulder. He jams a stimshot into his thigh and pops back up. A bullet slaps into the concrete in front of me, kicks up into Holiday to impact her ribs just under the armpit of her body armor with a meaty thud.

She spins down. Bullets force me to crouch beside her. Concrete rains. She spits blood and there's a wet, phlegmy echoing to her breath.

"It's in my lung," she gasps as she fumbles with a stimshot from her leg pouch. Were the circuits of her armor not fried, meds would inject automatically. But she has to crack open the case and pull a dose manually. I help, pulling free one of the micro-syringes and injecting her in the neck. Her pupils dilate and her breath slows as the narcotic drifts through her blood. Beside me, Victra's eyes are closed.

The gunfire stops. Carefully, I peek out. The Jackal's Grays hide behind concrete walls and pylons across the bridge, some sixty meters away. Trigg reloads. The wind is the only sound. Something's wrong. I search the sky, fearing the quiet. A Gold is coming. I can feel it in the battle's pulse.

"Trigg!" I shout till my body shudders. "Run!"

Holiday sees the look on my face. She struggles up, wheezing in pain as Trigg abandons his cover, boots slipping on the ice-slicked bridge. He falls and gains his feet, scrambling toward us, terrified. Too late. Behind him, Aja au Grimmus rips out of the fortress's door, past the Grays, past the Obsidians who lurk in the shadows. She's in her black formal jacket. Her long legs reel Trigg in now. It's one of the saddest sights I've ever seen.

I fire my pistol. Holiday unloads her rifle. We hit nothing but air. Aja sidesteps, twists, and, when Trigg is ten paces from us, spears him through the torso with her razor. Metal glistens wetly from his sternum. Shock widens his eyes. His mouth makes a quiet gasp. And he screams as he's hauled into the air. Pried upward by Aja's razor like a twitching pond frog on the end of a makeshift spear.

"*Trigg . . .*" Holiday whispers.

I stumble forward, toward Aja, pulling my razor, but Holiday jerks me back behind the wall as bullets from the distant Grays rip into the concrete around us. Her blood melts the snow under her. "Don't be stupid," she snarls, dragging me to the ground with the last of her strength. "We can't help him."

"He's your brother!"

"He's not the mission. You are."

"Darrow!" Aja calls from the bridge. Holiday peers out where Aja stands with her brother, her face bloodless and quiet. The knight holds Trigg up on the end of her razor with one hand. Trigg wriggles on the blade. Sliding down it toward her grip. "My goodman, the time for hiding behind others is over. Come out."

"Don't," Holiday murmurs.

"Come out," Aja says. And she tosses Trigg off her blade over the side of the bridge. He falls two hundred meters before his body splits against a granite ledge below.

Holiday makes a sick choking sound. She brings up her empty rifle and pulls the trigger a dozen times in Aja's direction. Aja ducks before realizing Holiday's weapon is empty. I pull Holiday down as a sniper's bullet aimed at her chest slams into her gun, shattering it and kicking it from her grip, mangling a finger. We sit shivering, backs to concrete, Victra between us.

"I'm sorry," I manage. She doesn't hear me. Her hands shake worse than mine. No tears in her distant eyes. No color in her lined face.

"They'll come," she says after a hollow moment. Her eyes following the green smoke. "They have to." Blood leaks through her clothing and out the corner of her mouth before freezing halfway down her neck. She grips her boot knife and tries to rise, but her body is done. Breaths wet and thick, smelling like copper. "They'll come."

"What is the plan?" I ask her. Her eyes close. I shake her. "How will they come?"

She nods to the edge of the landing pad. "Listen."

"Darrow!" Cassius's voice calls over the wind. He's joined Aja. "Darrow of Lykos, come out!" His rich voice is unfit for this moment. Too regal and high and untouched by the sadness that swallows us. I wipe the tears from my eyes. "You must decide what you are in the end, Darrow. Will you come out like a man? Or must we dig you out like a rat from a cave?"

The anger tightens my chest, but I don't want to stand. Once I would have, when I wore the armor of Gold and thought I would tower over Eo's killer and reveal my true self as his cities burned and their Color fell. But that armor is gone. That mask of the Reaper gnawed away by doubt and darkness. I am just a boy, and I shiver and cower and hide from my enemy because I know the price of failure, and I am so very afraid.

But I will not let them take me. I will not be their victim, and I will not let Victra fall into their hands again.

"Slag this," I say. I grab Holiday's collar and Victra's hand and, eyes flashing with the strain, blinded by the sun on the snow, face numb, I drag them with all my strength from our hiding place across the landing pad to the far edge where the wind roars.

There's silence from my enemies.

The sight I must make—a tottering, withered form, dragging my friends, sunken eyes, face like that of a starving old demon, bearded and ridiculous—is pitiful. Twenty meters behind me, the two Olympic Knights stand imperious on the bridge where it meets the landing pad, flanked by more than fifty Grays and Obsidians who have come from the citadel doors behind him. Aja's silver razor drips blood. But it's not her weapon. It's Lorn's, the one she took from his corpse. My toes throb inside my wet slippers.

Their men seem so tiny against the face of the vast mountain fortress. Their metal guns so petty and simple. I look to the right, off the bridge. Kilometers away, a flight of soldiers rises from a distant mountain peak where the EMP did not reach. They bank toward us through a low cloud layer. A ripWing follows.

"Darrow," Cassius calls to me as he walks forward with Aja off the bridge onto the pad. "You cannot escape." He watches me, eyes unreadable. "The shield is up. Sky blocked. No ships can come from beyond to retrieve you." He looks to the green smoke swirling from the canister on the landing pad into the winter air. "Accept your fate."

The wind howls between us, carrying flakes of snow stripped from the mountain.

"Dissection?" I ask. "Is that what you think I deserve?"

"You're a terrorist. What rights you had, you've given up."

"Rights?" I snarl over Victra and Holiday. "To pull my wife's feet?

To watch my father die?" I try to spit, but it sticks to my lips. "What gives you the right to take them?"

"There's no debate here. You are a terrorist, and you must be brought to justice."

"Then why are you talking with me, you bloodydamn hypocrite?"

"Because honor still matters. *Honor is what echoes.*" His father's words. But they are as empty on his lips as they feel in my ears. This war has taken everything from him. I see in his eyes how broken he is. How terribly hard he is trying to be his father's son. If he could, he would choose to be back by the campfire we made in the highlands of the Institute. He would return to the days of glory when life was simple, when friends seemed true. But wishing for the past doesn't clean the blood from either of our hands.

I listen to the groaning wind from the valley. My heels reach the end of the landing pad. There's nothing but air behind me. Air and the shifting topography of a dark city on the valley floor two thousand meters below.

"He's going to jump," Aja says quietly to Cassius. "We need the body."

"Darrow . . . don't," Cassius says, but his eyes are telling me to jump, telling me to take this way out instead of surrendering, instead of going to Luna to be peeled apart. This is the noble way. He's putting his cape over me again.

I hate him for it.

"You think you're honorable?" I hiss. "You think you're good? Who is left that you love? Who do you fight for?" Anger creeps into my words. "You are *alone,* Cassius. But I am not. Not when I faced your brother in the Passage. Not when I hid among you. Not when I lay in darkness. Not even now." I grip Holiday's unconscious body as hard as I can, looping my fingers inside the straps of her body armor. Clutch Victra's hand. My heels scrape the concrete's edge. "Listen to the wind, Cassius. Listen to the bloodydamn wind."

The two knights tilt their heads. And still they do not understand the strange groaning sound that drifts up from the valley floor, because how would a son and daughter of Gold ever know the sound of a clawDrill gnawing through rock? How would they guess that my people would come not from the sky, but from the heart of our planet?

"Goodbye, Cassius," I say. "Expect me." And I push off the ledge with both legs, flinging myself backward into open air, dragging Holiday and Victra into thin air.

7

||||||||||||||||||||||||

BUMBLEBEES

We fall toward a molten eye in the center of the snow-covered city. There, among rows of manufacturing plants, buildings shiver and tip as the ground swells upward. Pipes crack and spin into the air. Steam hisses through ruptured asphalt. Gas explosions ripple out in a corona, threading lines of fire through streets that buckle and heave, as if Mars itself were stretching six stories high to give birth to some ancient leviathan. And then, when the ground and city can stretch no more, a clawDrill erupts out into the winter air—a titanic metal hand with molten fingers that steam and grasp and then vanish as the clawDrill sinks back into Mars, pulling half a city block with it.

We're falling too fast.

Jumped too soon. I lose my grip on Victra.

Ground rushing up to us.

Then the air cracks with a sonic boom.

Then another. And another, till a whole chorus resounds out from the darkness of the clawDrill-carved tunnel as it gives birth to a small army. Two, twenty, fifty armored shapes in gravBoots scream up out of the tunnel toward us. To my left, my right. Painted blood-red, pouring pulsefire skyward behind us. My hair stands on end and I smell ozone. Superheated munitions ripple blue from friction as they tear through air molecules. Miniguns mounted on shoulders vomit death.

Amidst the rising Sons of Ares, a crimson, armored man with the spiked helmet of his father zips forward and catches Victra seconds before she impacts on the roof of a skyscraper. The howling of wolves babbles from his helmet's speakers. It's Ares himself. My best friend in all the worlds has not forgotten me. He has come with his legion of empire breakers and terrorists and renegades: the Howlers. A dozen metal men and women with black wolfcloaks kicking in the wind fly behind him. The largest of them in pure white armor with blue hand-prints covering the chest and arms. His black cloak is stained with a red stripe down the middle. For a moment I think it's Pax come back from the dead for me. But when the man catches me and Holiday, I see the glyphs drawn in the blue paint of the handprints. Glyphs from the south pole of Mars. It is Ragnar Volarus, prince of the Valkyrie Spires. He tosses Holiday to another Howler and pushes me behind him so I can wrap my arms around his neck, digging my fingers into the rivets of his armor. Then he banks through the smoking valley city toward the tunnel, shouting to me: *"Hold fast, little brother."*

And he dives. Sevro to the left, clutching Victra, Howlers all around, their gravBoots screaming as we plummet into the darkness of the tunnel's mouth. The enemy pursues. The sounds are horrible. Screaming of wind. Rupture of rock as pulsefire rips into the walls behind us and weapons warble. My jaw rattles against Ragnar's metal shoulder. His gravBoots vibrate at full burn. Bolts from the armor dig into my ribs. The battery pack above his tailbone slams into my groin as we weave and dart through pitch black. I'm riding a metal shark deeper and deeper into the belly of an angry sea. My ears pop. Wind whistles. A pebble slams into my forehead. Blood streams down my face, stinging my eyes. The only light the glowing of boots and the flash of weapons.

The skin of my right shoulder flares with pain. Pulsefire from our pursuers misses me by inches. Still, my skin bubbles and smokes, lighting my jumpsuit's sleeve on fire. The wind kills the flames. But the pulsefire rips past again and boils into the Son's gravBoots just ahead of me, melting the man's legs into a single chunk of molten metal. He jerks in the air, slamming into the ceiling, where his body crumples. Helmet ripping off and spinning straight toward me.

Red light throbs through my eyelids. There's smoke in the air. Meaty. Stings the back of the throat. Fat tissue charred and crispy. Chest hot with pain. A swamp of screams and howls and cries for mother all around. And something else. The sound of bumblebees in my ears. Someone's above me. See them in the red light as I open my eyes. Screaming into my face. Pressing a mask to my mouth. A damp wolf-cloak dangles from a metal shoulder, tickling my neck. Other hands touch mine. The world vibrates, tilts.

"Starboard! Starboard!" someone screams in the distance, as if underwater.

We're on a ship. I'm surrounded by dying men. Burned, twisted husks of armor. Smaller men atop them, bent like vultures, saws glowing in their hands as they peel the armor away, trying to free those dying of their burns inside. But the armor's melted tight. A hand touches mine. A boy lying beside me. Eyes wide. Armor blackened. The skin of his cheeks is young and smooth beneath the soot and blood. His mouth not yet creased by smiles. His breaths come shorter, quicker. He mouths my name.

And he's gone.

8

||||||||||||||||||||||||

HOME

I'm alone, far away from the horror, standing weightless and clean on a road that smells of moss and earth. My feet touch the ground, but I cannot feel it underfoot. To either side stretches the grass of wind-beaten moors. The sky flashes with lightning. My hands are without Sigils and drift along the cobbled wall that meanders on ahead to either side. When did I start walking? Somewhere in the distance, wood smoke rises. I follow the road, but I feel I have no choice. A voice calls to me from beyond a hill.

> *Oh tomb, O marriage chamber, hollowed out*
> *house that will watch forever, where I go.*
> *To my own people, who are mostly there;*
> *Persephone has taken them to her.*
> *Last of them all, ill-fated past the rest,*
> *shall I descend, before my course is run.*
> *Still when I get there I may hope to find*
> *I come as a dear friend to my dear father*
> *To you, my mother, and my brother too.*

All three of you have known my hand in death
I wash your bodies . . .

It is my uncle's voice. Is this the Vale? Is this the road I walk before death? It can't be. In the Vale there is no pain, but my body aches. My legs sting. Still I hear his voice ahead of me, drawing me through the mist. The man who taught me to dance after my father died, who guarded me and sent me to Ares. Who died himself in a mineshaft and dwells now in the Vale.

I thought it would be Eo who greeted me. Or my father. Not Narol.

"Keep reading," another voice whispers. "Dr. Virany said he can hear us. He just has to find his way back." Even as I walk, I feel a bed under me. The air around cold and crisp in my lungs. The sheets soft and clean. The muscles in my legs twitch. Feels like little bees are stinging them. And with each sting, the dream world fades and I slide back into my body.

"Well, if we're gonna read to the squabber, might as well be something Red. Not this poncy Violet shit."

"Dancer said this was one of his favorites."

My eyes open. I'm in a bed. White sheets, IVs going into my arms. Under the sheets, I touch the ant-sized nodes that have been stuck to my legs to channel electrical current through my muscles to combat atrophy. The room's a cave. Scientific equipment, machines, and terraria litter it.

It was Uncle Narol I heard in the dream after all. But he's not in the Vale. He's alive. He sits at my bedside, squinting down at one of Mickey's old books. He's grizzled and wiry, even for a Red. Callused hands trying to be gentle with the frail paper pages. He's bald now, and deeply sunburned on his forearms and the back of his neck. Still looks like he was cobbled together out of cracked old leather. He'll be forty-one now. Looks older. More savage. A brooding danger to him, lent teeth by the railgun in his thigh holster. A slingBlade has been sewn onto his black military jacket above a Society logo that's been peeled off and inverted. Red at the top. Gold the foundation.

The man's been at war.

Beside him sits my mother. A bent, fragile woman since her stroke.

How many times did I imagine the Jackal standing over her, pliers in hand? She's been safe the whole time. Her crooked fingers weave needle and thread through tattered socks, patching the holes. They don't move like they used to. Age and infirmity have slowed her. Her broken body is not what she is on the inside. There she stands tall as any Gold, broad as any Obsidian.

Watching her sit there breathing quietly, intent on her task, I want to protect her more than anything else in the world. I want to heal her. Give her all she never had. I love her so much, I don't know what to say. What to do that can ever show her how much she means to me. "Mother . . ." I whisper.

They look up. Narol frozen in his chair. My mother setting a hand on his and rising slowly to my bedside. Her steps slow, wary. "Hello, child."

She stands above me, overwhelming me with the love in her eyes. My hand is almost larger than her head, but I gently touch her face as if to prove to myself she is real. I trace the crow's-feet from her eyes to the gray hair at her temples. As a boy, I did not like her as much as I liked father. She would hit me at times. She would weep alone and pretend nothing was wrong. And now all I want is to listen to her hum as she cooks. All I want are those still nights where we had peace and I was a child.

I want the time back.

"I'm sorry . . . ," I find myself saying. "I'm so sorry . . ."

She kisses my forehead and rocks her head against mine. She smells like rust and sweat and oil. Like home. She tells me I am her son. There is nothing to apologize for. I am safe. I am loved. The family is here. Kieran, Leanna, their children. Waiting to see me. I sob uncontrollably, sharing all the pain my solitude forced me to hoard. The tears a deeper language than my tongue can afford. I'm exhausted by the time she kisses me again on the head and pulls back. Narol comes to her side and puts a hand on my arm. "Narol . . ."

"Hello, you little bastard," he says roughly. "Still your father's son, eh?"

"I thought you were dead," I say.

"Nah. Death chewed on me a bit. Then spat my bloody ass back out. Said there was killing that needed doin' and some wild blood of mine that needed savin'." He grins down at me. That old scar on his lips joined by two new ones.

"We've been waiting for you to wake up," Mother says. "It's been two days since they brought you back in the shuttle."

I can still taste the smoke from burned flesh in the back of my throat.

"Where are we?" I ask.

"Tinos. The city of Ares."

"Tinos . . . ," I whisper. I sit up quickly. "Sevro . . . Ragnar . . ."

"They're alive," Narol grunts, pushing me back down. "Don't rip out your tubes and resFlesh. Took Dr. Virany hours to thread you up after that bloody mess of an escape. Boneriders were supposed to be in EMP radius. They weren't. They ripped us to pieces in the tunnels. Ragnar's the only reason you're living."

"You were there?"

"Who do you think lead the drillteam that punched up into Attica? It was Lykos blood, Lambda and Omicron."

"And what about Victra?"

"Easy, boy." He sets his hand on my chest to stop me from trying to get up again. "She's with the doc. Same for the Gray. They're alive. Getting patched."

"You need to check me, Narol. Tell the doctors to check me for radiation trackers. For implants. They might have let me go on purpose, to find Tinos. . . . I need to see Sevro."

"Oy! I said easy," Narol says sharply. "We checked you. Two implants were in you. But both fried in the EMP. You weren't tracked. And Ares ain't here. He's still out with the Howlers. Came back just to deliver the wounded and scarf down grub." There were almost a dozen wolfcloaks. So he's recruited. Thistle betrayed us, but Vixus mentioned Pebble and Clown. Wonder if Screwface is with them too.

"Ares is always on the move," mother says.

"Lots to do. Only one Ares," Narol replies defensively. "They're still out looking for survivors. They'll be back soon. By morning, luck holds." My mother shoots him a harsh look and he shuts up.

I lean back in the bed, overwhelmed by speaking to them. By seeing them. I can barely form sentences. So much to say. So much unfamiliar emotion running through me. All I end up doing is sitting there, breathing fast. My mother's love fills the room, but still I feel the darkness moving beyond this moment. Pressing in on this family I thought I lost and now fear I cannot protect. My enemies are too great. Too many. And I too weak. I shake my head, running my thumb over her knuckles.

"I thought I would never see you again."

"Yet here you are." Somehow she makes it sound cold. So like my mother to be the one with dry eyes when both the men can barely speak. I always wondered how I survived the Institute. It damn well wasn't because of my father. He was a gentle man. Mother is the spine in me. The iron. And I clutch her hand as if such a simple gesture could say all that.

A light knock comes at the door. Dancer pokes his head in. Devilishly handsome as ever, he's one of the only Reds alive who makes old age look good. I can hear his foot dragging slightly behind him in the hall. Both my mother and uncle nod to him in deference. Narol steps aside respectfully as he approaches my bedside, but my mother stays put. "This Helldiver's not done yet, it would seem." Dancer grips my hand. "But you gave us a hell of a scare."

"It's bloodydamn good to see you, Dancer."

"And you, boy. And you."

"Thank you. For taking care of them." I nod to my mother and uncle. "For helping Sevro . . ."

"It's what family is for," he says. "How are you?"

"My chest hurts. And everything else."

He laughs lightly. "It should. Virany says that crank the Nakamuras gave you almost killed you. You had a heart attack."

"Dancer, how did the Jackal know? Every day I've wondered. Picked it apart. The clues I left him. Did I give myself up?"

"It wasn't you," Dancer says. "It was Harmony."

"Harmony . . ." I whisper. "She wouldn't . . . she hates Gold." But even as I say it, I know how reckless her hate is. How vengeful she must have felt after I did not detonate the bomb she gave me to kill the Sovereign and the others on Luna.

"She thinks we've sold out the rebellion," Dancer says. "That we're compromising too much. She told the Jackal who you were."

"He knew when I was in his office. When I gave him the gift . . ."

He nods tiredly. "Your presence proved her claims. So the Jackal let us rescue her and the others. We brought her back to base, and an hour before his kill squads came, she disappeared."

"Fitchner is dead because of her. He gave her a purpose . . . I understand how she could betray me, but him? Ares?"

"She found out he was a Gold. Then she gave him up. Must have given the Jackal the base's coordinates." Ares was her hero. Her god. After her children died in the mines he gave her a reason to live, a reason to fight. And then she discovered he was the enemy, and she got him killed. It crushes me to think that's why he died.

Dancer surveys me quietly. It's clear I'm not what he expected. Mother and Narol watch him almost as carefully as they watch me, deducing the same.

"I know I'm not what I was," I say slowly.

"No, boy. You've been through hell. It's not that."

"Then what is it?"

He exchanges a look with my mother. "You're sure?"

"He needs to know. Tell him," she says. Narol nods too.

Dancer hesitates still. He looks for a chair. Narol rushes to pull one out for him and set it near the bed. Dancer nods his thanks and then leans over me, making a steeple of his fingers. "Darrow, you've gone too long with people hiding things from you. So I want to be very transparent from here forward. Until five days ago, we thought you were dead."

"I was close enough."

"No. No, I mean we stopped looking for you nine months ago."

My mother's hand tightens on mine.

"Three months after you were captured, the Golds executed you on the HC for treason. They dragged a boy identical to you out to the steps of the citadel in Agea and read off your crimes. Pretending you were still a Gold. We tried to free you. But it was a trap. We lost thousands of men." His eyes drift over my lips, my hair. "He had your eyes, your scars, your bloodydamn face. And we had to watch as the Jackal cut off your head and destroyed your obelisk on Mars Field."

I stare at them, not fully comprehending.

"We grieved for you, child," Mother says, voice thin. "The whole clan, city. I led the Fading Dirge myself and we buried your boots in the deeptunnels beyond Tinos."

Narol crosses his arms, trying to seal himself off from the memory. "He was just like you. Same walk. Same face. Thought I had watched you die again."

"It was likely a fleshMask or they Carved someone, or digital effects," Dancer explains. "Doesn't matter now. The Jackal killed you as an Aureate. Not as a Red. Would have been foolish for them to reveal your identity. Would have handed us a tool. So instead you died just another Gold who thought he could be king. A warning."

The Jackal promised he would hurt those I love. And now I see how deeply he has. My mother's façade has broken. All the grief she's kept inside thickens behind her eyes as she stares down at me. Guilt straining her face.

"I gave up on you," she says softly, voice cracking. "I gave up."

"It's not your fault," I say. "You couldn't have known."

"Sevro did," she says.

"He never stopped looking for you," Dancer explains. "I thought he was mad. He said you weren't dead. That he could feel it. That he would know. I even asked him to give up the helm to someone else. He was too reckless searching for you."

"But the bastard found you," Narol says.

"Aye," Dancer replies. "He did. I was wrong in it. I should have believed in you. Believed in him."

"How *did* you find me?"

"Theodora designed an operation."

"She's here?"

"Working for us in intelligence. Woman's got contacts. Some of her informants in a Pearl Club caught word that the Olympic Knights were taking a package from Attica back to Luna for the Sovereign. Sevro believed *you* were that package, and he put a huge portion of our reserve resources behind this attack, burned two of our deep assets . . ."

As he speaks, I watch my mother stare distantly at a crackling lightbulb in the ceiling. What is this like for her? For a mother to see her child broken by other men? To see the pain written in scars on his skin, spoken in silences, in far-off looks. How many mothers have prayed to see their sons, their daughters return from war only to realize the war has kept them, the world has poisoned them, and they'll never be the same?

For nine months, Mother has grieved for me. Now she's drowning in guilt for giving up and desperation in hearing the war swallow me again, knowing she's helpless to stop it. In the past years, I've trampled over so many to get what I think I want. If this is my last chance at life, I want to do it right. I need to.

". . . But now the real problem isn't materiel, it's manpower we need. . . ."

"Dancer . . . stop," I say.

"Stop?" He frowns in confusion, glancing at Narol. "What's wrong?"

"Nothing's wrong. But I'll talk with you in the morning about this."

"The morning? Darrow, the world is shifting under your feet. We've lost control over the other Red factions. The Sons will not last the year. I have to give you a debriefing. We need you back. . . ."

"Dancer, I am alive," I say, thinking of all the questions I want to ask, about the war, my friends, how I was undone, about Mustang. But that can wait. "Do you even know how lucky I am? To be able to see you all again in this world? I haven't seen my brother or my sister in years. So tomorrow I'll listen to your debriefing. Tomorrow the war can have me again. But tonight I belong to my family."

I hear the children before we reach the door. I feel a guest in someone else's dream. Unfit for the world of children. But I've little say in the matter as Mother pushes my wheelchair forward into a cramped dormitory cluttered with metal bunks, children, the smell of shampoo, and noise. Five of the children of my blood, fresh from the showers by the looks of their hair and the little sandals on the floor, are scrumming on one of the bunks, two taller nine-year-olds holding an alliance against two six-year-olds and a tiny little cherub of a girl who keeps head-butting the biggest boy in the leg. He hasn't yet noticed her. The sixth child in the room I remember from when I visited Mother in Lykos. The little girl who couldn't sleep. One of Kieran's. She watches the other children over her glossy book of fables from another bunk and is the first to notice me.

"Pa," she calls back, eyes wide. "Pa . . ."

Kieran bursts up from his game of dice with Leanna when he sees me. Leanna's slower behind him. "Darrow," he says, rushing to me and stopping just before my wheelchair. He's bearded now too. In his mid-twenties. No slump to his shoulders like there used to be. His eyes radiate a goodness that I used to think made him a little foolish, now it just seems wildly brave. Remembering himself, he waves his children forward. "Reagan, Iro, children. Come meet my little brother. Come meet your uncle."

The children line up awkwardly around him. A baby laughs from the back of the room and a young mother rises from her bunk where she was breastfeeding the child. "Eo?" I whisper. The woman's a vision of the past. Small, face the shape of a heart. Her hair a thick, tangled mess. The sort that frizzes on humid days, like Eo's did. But this is not Eo. Her eyes are smaller, her nose elfin. More delicacy here than fire. And this is a woman, not a girl like my wife was. Twenty years old now, by my count.

They all stare at me strangely.

Wondering if I am mad.

Except Dio, Eo's sister, whose face splits with a smile.

"I'm sorry, Dio," I say quickly. "You look . . . just like her."

She doesn't allow it to be awkward, hushing my apologies. Saying it's the kindest thing I could have said. "And who's that, then?" I ask of the baby she holds. The little girl's hair is absurd. Rust red and bound together by a hair tie so it sticks straight up on top of her head in a little antenna. She watches me excitedly with her dark red eyes.

"This little thing?" Dio asks, coming closer to my chair. "Oh, this is someone I've been wanting to introduce to you since Deanna told us you were alive." She looks lovingly to my brother. I feel a pang of jealousy. "This is our first. Would you like to hold her?"

"Hold her?" I say. "No . . . I'm . . ."

The girl's pudgy little hands reach for me, and Dio pushes the girl into my lap before I can recoil. The girl clings to my sweater, grunting as she turns and wriggles around till she's seated according to her liking on my leg. She claps her hands together and laughs. Completely unaware of what I am. Of why my hands are so scarred. Delighted by the size of them and the Gold Sigils, she grabs my thumb and tries to bite it with her gums.

Her world is alien to the horrors I know. All the child sees is love. Her skin is pale and soft against mine. She's made of clouds and I of stone. Her eyes large and bright like her mother's. Her demeanor and thin lips like Kieran's. Were this another life, she might have been my child with Eo. My wife would have laughed to think it would be my brother and her sister together in the end and not us. We were a little storm that couldn't last. But maybe Dio and Kieran will.

Long after the lights have dimmed throughout the complex to ease the burdens on the generators, I sit with my uncle and brother around the table in the back of the room, listening to Kieran tell me his new duties learning from Oranges how to service ripWings and shuttles. Dio went to bed long ago, but she left me the baby, who now sleeps in my arms, shifting here and there as her dreams take her wherever they may.

"It's really not that wretched here," Kieran is saying. "Better than the stacks below. We have food. Water showers. No more flushes! There's a lake above us, they say. Bloodydamn dazzling stuff, the showers. Children love it." He watches his children in the low light. Two to a bed, shifting quietly as they sleep. "What's hard is not knowing what'll be for them. Will they ever mine? Work in the webbery? I always thought they would. That I was passing something down, a mission, a craft. You hear?" I nod. "I guess I wanted my sons to be helldivers. Like you. Like Pa. But . . ." He shrugs.

"There's nothin' to that now that you got eyes," Uncle Narol says. "It's a hollow life when you know you're being stepped on."

"Aye," Kieran replies. "Die by thirty, so those folk can live to a hundred. It ain't bloodydamn right. I just want my children to have more than this, brother." He stares at me intensely and I remember how my mother asked me what comes after revolution. What world are we making? It was what Mustang asked. Something Eo never considered. "They have to have more than this. And I love Ares as much as anyone. I owe him my life. The lives of my children. But . . ." He shakes his head, wanting to say more but feeling the weight of Narol's eyes on him.

"Go on," I say.

"I don't know if he knows what comes next. That's why I'm glad you're back, little brother. I know you've got a plan. I know you can save us."

He says it with so much faith, so much trust.

"Of course I've a plan," I say, because I know it's what he needs to hear. But as my brother contentedly refills his mug, my uncle catches my eye and I know he sees through the lie and we both feel the darkness pressing in.

9

||||||||||||||||||||||||||

THE CITY OF ARES

I't's early morning as I sip coffee and eat a bowl of grain cereal my mother fetched me from the commissary. I'm not yet ready for crowds. Kieran and Leanna have already gone to work, so I sit with Dio and Mother as the children dress for school. It's a good sign. You know a people have given up when they stop teaching their children. I finish my coffee. Mother pours me more.

"You took an entire pot?" I ask.

"The chef insisted. Tried to give me two."

I sip from the cup. "It's almost like the real thing."

"It is the real thing," Dio says. "There's this pirate who sends us hijacked goods. Coffee's from Earth, I think. Jamaca, they said."

I don't correct her.

"Oy!" a voice screams in the hallways. My mother jumps at the sound. "Reaper! Reaper! Come out and play-e-ay!" There's a crash in the hall and the sound of stomping boots.

"Remember, Deanna told us to knock," says a thunderous voice.

"You are so annoying. Fine." A polite knock comes at the door. "Tidings! It's Uncle Sevro and the Moderately Friendly Giant."

My mother motions to one of my excited nieces. "Ella, do us kind." Ella darts forward to open the door for Sevro. He bursts through, scooping her up. She shrieks with joy. He's in his undersuit, a black sweat-wicking fabric that soldiers wear under pulse armor. Sweat rings stain the armpits. His eyes dance as he sees me, and he tosses Ella roughly onto a bed and charges toward me, arms outstretched. A weird laugh escapes his chest, hatchet face split with a jagged grin. His hair a dirty, sweat-soaked Mohawk.

"Sevro, careful!" my mother says.

"Reap!" He slams into me, spinning my chair sideways, clacking my teeth together, as he half lifts me out of the chair, stronger than he was, smelling of tobacco and engine fuel and sweat. He half laughs, half cries like an excited dog into my chest. "I knew you were alive. I bloodydamn knew it. Pixie bitches can't fool me." Pulling back, he looks down at me with a rickshaw grin. "You bloodydamn bastard."

"Language!" my mother snaps.

I wince. "My ribs."

"Oh, shit, sorry brotherman." He lets me sink back into the chair, and kneels so we're eye to eye. "I said it once. Now I'll say it twice. If there's two things in this world that can't be killed, it's the fungus under my sack and the Reaper of bloodydamn Mars. Haha!"

"Sevro!"

"Sorry, Deanna. Sorry."

I pull back from him. "Sevro. You smell . . . terrible."

"I haven't showered in five days," he brags, grabbing his groin. "It's a Sevro soup in here, boyo." He puts his hands on his hips. "You know, you look . . . erm . . ." He glances at my mother and tames his tongue. "Bloody terrible."

A shadow falls over the room as a man enters and blocks the overhead light near the door. The children cluster joyously around Ragnar so he can barely walk.

"Hello, Reaper," he says over their shouts.

I greet Ragnar with a smile. His face is as impassive as ever. Tattooed and pale, callused from the wind of his arctic home, like the hide of a rhinoceros. His white beard is braided into four strands, and the hair on his head shaved except for a tail of white that is braided with red ribbons. The children are asking him if he's brought them presents.

"Sevro." I lean forward. "Your eyes . . ."

He leans in close. "Do you like 'em?" Buried in that squinting, sharp-angled face, his eyes are no longer that dirty shade of Gold, but are now as red as Martian soil. He pulls back his lids so I can better see. They're not contacts. And the right is no longer bionic.

"Bloodydamn. Did you get Carved?"

"By the best in the business. Do you like 'em?"

"They're bloodydamn marvelous. Fit you like a glove."

He punches his hands together. "Glad you said that. Cuz they're yours."

I blanch. "What?"

"They're yours."

"My what?"

"Your eyes!"

"My eyes . . ."

"Did yon Friendly Giant drop you on your head in the rescue? Mickey had your eyes in a cryobox at his joint in Yorkton—creepy place, by the by—when we raided it for supplies to bring back to Tinos to help the Rising. I figured you weren't usin' 'em, so . . ." He shrugs awkwardly. "So I asked if he'd put 'em in. You know. Bring us closer together. Something to remember you by. That's not so weird, right?"

"I told him it was odd," Ragnar says. One of the girls is climbing his leg.

"Do you want the eyes back?" Sevro asks, suddenly worried. "I can give them back."

"No!" I say. "It's just I forgot how crazy you are."

"Oh." He laughs and slaps my shoulder. "Good. I thought it was something serious. So I'm prime keeping them?"

"Finders keepers," I say with a shrug.

"Deanna of Lykos, may we borrow your son for martial matters?" Ragnar asks my mother. "He has much to do. Many things to know."

"Only if you return him in one piece. And you take some coffee with you. And bring these socks to the laundry." My mother pushes a bag of freshly patched socks into Ragnar's arms.

"As you wish."

"What about the presents?" one of my nephews asks. "Didn't you bring any?"

"I've got a present for you . . ." Sevro says.

"Sevro, no!" Dio and my mother shout.

"What?" He pulls out a bag. "It's just candy this time."

". . . and that's when Ragnar tripped over Pebble and fell out the back of the transport," Sevro cackles. "Like a dumbass." He's eating a candy bar over my head as he pushes my wheelchair recklessly through the stone corridor. He sprints fast again and hops on the back to coast till we swerve into the wall. I wince in pain. "So Ragnar falls straight into the sea. Thing was at full chop, man. Waves the size of torch-ships. So I dive in too, thinking he needs my help, just in time for this huge . . . I dunno what the hell you'd call it. Some Carved beasty . . ."

"Demon," Ragnar says from behind. I hadn't noticed him following. **"It was a sea demon from the third level of Hel."**

"Sure." Sevro guides me around a corner, clipping the wall hard enough to make me bite my tongue, and sending a cluster of Sons pilots scattering. They stare after me as we trundle on. "This sea"—he looks back at Ragnar—"demon apparently thinks Ragnar is a tasty-looking morsel, so he gobbles him up almost as soon as he hits the water. So I see this, and I'm laughing my ass off with Screwface, as one would because it's bloodydamn hilarious, and you know how Screwface loves a good joke. But then the beasty dives. So I follow. And I'm chasing it, shooting my pulseFist at a bloodydamn sea"—he looks at Ragnar again—"*demon* as it swims to the bottom of the damn Thermic Sea. Pressure's building. My suit's wheezing. And I think I'm about to die, when suddenly Ragnar cuts his way out of the scaly bitch." He leans close. "But guess where he came out? Come on. Guess. Guess!"

"Sevro, did he come out the sea demon's rectum?" I ask.

Sevro squeals with laughter. "He did! Right out the ass. Shot like a turd—" My chair rolls to a stop. His voice cut short, followed by a thump and sliding sound. My wheelchair rolls forward again. I look back and see Ragnar pushing it innocently along. Sevro isn't in the hallway behind us. I frown, wondering where he went, till he bursts out of a side passage.

"You! Troll!" Sevro shouts. "I'm a terrorist warlord! Stop throwing me. You made me drop my candy!" Sevro looks at the floor of the hallway. "Wait. Where is it? Dammit, Ragnar. Where is my peanut bar? You know how many people I had to kill to get that. Six! Six!" Ragnar chews quietly above me, and though I'm probably mistaken, I think I see him smile.

"Ragnar, have you been brushing your teeth? They look splendid."

"**Thank you,**" he preens as much as a man eight feet tall can preen past a mouthful of peanut butter bar. "**The wizard removed my old ones. They pained me greatly. These are new. Are they not fine?**"

"Mickey, the wizard," I confirm.

"**Indeed. He also taught me to read before he left Tinos.**" Ragnar proves this by reading every single sign and warning we pass in the hall till we enter the hangar bay some ten minutes later. Sevro follows behind, still complaining about his lost candy. The hangar is cramped by Society standards, but is still nearly thirty meters high and sixty wide. It's been cut into the rock by laser drills. The floor is stone, blasted black from engines. Several dilapidated shuttles sit in berths beside three shining new ripWings. Reds directed by two Oranges service the ships and stare at me as we wheel past. I feel an outsider here.

A motley group of soldiers ambles away from a battered shuttle. Some are still in armor with their wolfcloaks hanging from their shoulders. Others are stripped down to their undersuits or go bare-chested.

"Boss!" Pebble cries from under Clown's arm. She's as plump as ever, and she grins at me, hauling Clown along to move faster. His puffy hair is matted with sweat, and he leans on the shorter girl. Both their faces are bright when they approach, as if I were exactly as they remembered. Pebble shoves Clown off her shoulder to give me a hug. Clown, for his part, gives a ludicrous bow.

"Howlers reporting for duty, Primus," he says. "Sorry about the kerfuffle."

"Shit got prickly," Pebble explains before I can speak.

"Exceedingly prickly. Something different about you, Reaper." Clown puts his hands on his hips. "You look . . . slender. Did you trim your hair? Don't tell me. It's the beard . . . terribly slimming."

"Kind of you to notice," I say. "And to stay, considering everything."

"What, you mean you lying to us for five years?"

"Yes, that," I say.

"Well . . ." Clown says, about to light into me. Pebble thumps his shoulder.

"Of course we'd stay, Reaper!" she says sweetly. "This our family . . ."

"But we have demands. . . ." Clown continues, wagging a finger. "If you desire our full services. But . . . for now, we must be off. I fear I have shrapnel in my ass. So I beg your leave. Come, Pebble. To the surgeons."

"Bye, boss!" Pebble says. "Glad you're not dead!"

"Squad dinner at eight!" Sevro calls after them. "Don't be late. Shrapnel in your ass is not an excuse, Clown."

"Yes, sir!"

Sevro turns to me with a grin. "Sods didn't even bat an eye when I told them you were a ruster. Came with me and Rags to fetch your family right off. Was wicked telling them what was what, though. This way."

As we pass the ship Pebble and Clown exited, I see up the ramp into its belly. Two young boys work inside, blasting the floors with hoses. The water runs brownish red down the ramp onto the hangar deck, flowing not into a drain, but down a narrow trough toward the edge of the hangar, where it disappears over the edge.

"Some dads leave ships or villas for their sons. Asshat Ares left me this wretched hive of angst and peasantry."

"*Bloodydamn,*" I whisper as I realize what exactly I'm looking at.

Beyond the hangar is an inverted forest of stalactites. It glitters in the artificial subterranean dawn. Not only from the water that dribbles along their slick gray surfaces, but from the lights of docks, barracks, and sensor arrays that give teeth to Ares's great bastion. Supply ships flit between the multiple docks.

"We're in a stalactite." I laugh in wonder. But then I look down at the horror beneath and the weight on my shoulders doubles. A hundred meters below our stalactite sprawls a refugee camp. Once it was an underground city carved into the stone of Mars. The streets are so deep between the buildings, they're more like miniature canyons. And the city spills over the floor of the colossal cave to the far walls kilometers away, where more honeycombed homes have been built. Streets switchback up the sandstone. But over that a new roofless city has spawned. One of refugees. Muddled skin and fabrics and hair all writhing like some weird, fleshy sea. They sleep on rooftops. In the streets. On the switchback stairs. I see makeshift metal symbols for Gamma, Omicron, Upsilon. All the twelve clans that they divide my people into.

I'm stunned by the sight. "How many are there?"

"Shit if I know. At least twenty mines. Lykos was small compared to some of the ones near the larger H-3 deposits."

"Four hundred sixty-five thousand. According to the logs," Ragnar says.

"Only half a million?" I whisper.

"Seems like a hell of a lot more, right?"

I nod. "Why are they here?"

"Had to give them shelter. Poor bastards all come from mines the Jackal has purged. Pumping achlys-9 into the vents if he even suspects a Sons presence. It's an invisible genocide."

A chill passes through me. "The Liquidation Protocol. Board of Quality Control's last measure for compromised mines. How do you keep this all a secret? Jammers?"

"Yeah. And we're more than two clicks underground. Pop altered the topographical maps in the Society's database. To the Golds, this is bedrock that was depleted of helium-3 more than three hundred years ago. Clever enough, for now."

"And how do you feed everyone?"

"We don't. I mean, we try, but there haven't been rats in Tinos for a month. People are sleeping toe to nose. We've started moving refugees into the stalactites. But disease is already ripping through the people. Don't have enough meds. And I can't risk my Sons getting sick. Without them. We don't have teeth. We're just a sick cow waiting to be slaughtered."

"And they rioted," Ragnar says.

"Rioted?"

"Yeah, almost forgot about that. Had to cut rations by half. They were already so small. Those ungrateful shitheads down there didn't like that much."

"Many lost their lives before I descended."

"The Shield of Tinos," Sevro says. "He's more popular than I am, that's for damn sure. They don't blame him for shit rations. But I'm more popular than Dancer, because I have a badass helmet and he's in charge of the nitty-gritty shit I can't do. People are so stupid. Man breaks his back for them and they think he's a dull-wit pennypincher. Least the Sons love him—and your uncle."

"It's like we've fallen back a thousand years," I say hopelessly.

"Pretty much, except for the generators. There's a river that runs underneath the stone. So there's water, sanitation, power, sometimes. And . . . there's lecherous shit too. Crime. Murders. Rapes. Theft. We have to keep the Gammas slags separate from everyone else. Some Omicrons hanged this little Gamma kid last week and carved the Gold Sigil into his chest, ripped the Red Sigils out of his arms. They said he was a loyalist, a goldy. He was fourteen."

I feel sick. **"We keep the lights bright. Even at night."**

"Yeah. Turn them off, it gets . . . otherworldy downstairs." Sevro looks tired as he stares down at the city. My friend knows how to fight, but this is another battle entirely.

I stare down at the city, unable to find the words I need to say. I feel like a prisoner who spent his whole life digging through the wall, only to break through and find he's dug into another cell. Except there will always be another cell. And another. And another. These people are not living. They're all just trying to postpone the end.

"This is not what Eo wanted," I say.

"Yeah . . . well." Sevro shrugs. "Dreaming's easy. War isn't." He chews on his lip thoughtfully. "You see Cassius at all?"

"Twice, at the end. Why?"

"Oh, nothing." He turns to me, eyes glittering. "It's just that he's the one who put Pops down."

10

||||||||||||||||||||||||

THE WAR

"Our Society is at war . . ." Dancer tells me in the Sons of Ares command room. The facility is domed, skinned in rock and illuminated by pale bluish lights above, and a corona of computer terminals that glow around a central holographic display. He stands to the side of the display drenched in the blue light of Mars's Thermic Sea. With us is Ragnar, several older Sons I don't recognize, and Theodora, who greeted me with the graceful kiss on the lips popular in Luna's highColor circles. Elegant even in black utility pants, she has an air of authority in the room. Like my Howlers, she was not invited by Augustus to the garden after the Triumph. Not important enough, thank Jove. Sevro sent Pebble to get her out of the Citadel as soon as it all went down. She's been with the Sons ever since, helping Dancer's propaganda and intelligence wings.

". . . Not just the Rising against Gold forces here and our other cells across the System. But *among* Gold itself. After they killed Arcos and Augustus, as well as their staunchest supporters at your Triumph, Roque and the Jackal made a coordinated play to seize the navy in orbit. They feared Virginia or the Telemanuses would rally the ships of the Golds murdered in the garden. Virginia did, not just with her father's own ships, but with those of Arcos, under the command of three of his daughters-in-law. It came to battle around Deimos. And Roque's fleet, even outnumbered, crushed Mustang's and sent them into flight."

"She's alive, then," I say, knowing they're wary of how I'd react to knowing the information.

"Yeah," Sevro says, watching me carefully, as do the rest. "Far as we know, she's alive." Ragnar seems about to say something, but Sevro cuts him off. "Dancer, show him Jupiter."

My eyes linger on Ragnar as Dancer waves his hand and the holographic display warps to show the great marbled gas giant of Jupiter. Surrounding it are the sixty-three smaller asteroidlike satellites and the four great moons of Jupiter—Europa, Io, Ganymede, and Calisto.

"The purge instituted by the Jackal and Sovereign was an impressive operation that spanned not just the thirty assassinations of the garden, but over three hundred other assassinations across the Solar System. Most carried out by Olympic Knights or Praetorians. It was proposed and designed by the Jackal to eliminate the Sovereign's key enemies on Mars, but also Luna and throughout the Society. It worked well, very well. But one grand mistake was made. In the garden, they killed Revus au Raa and his nine-year-old granddaughter."

"The ArchGovernor of Io," I say. "Sending a message to the Moon Lords?"

"Yes, but it backfired. A week after the Triumph, the children of the Moon Lords whom the Sovereign keeps on Luna as wards to ransom their parents' loyalty escaped. Two days after that, the heirs of Raa stole the entirety of *Classis Saturnus*. The whole Eighth fleet garrison in its dock at Calisto with the help of the Cordovans of Ganymede.

"The Raas declared Io's independence for the Moons of Jupiter, their new alliance with Virginia au Augustus and the heirs of Arcos, and their war on the Sovereign."

"A Second Moon Rebellion. Sixty years after the burning of Rhea," I say with a slow smile, thinking of Mustang at the head of an entire planetary system. Even if she left me, even if there's that hollowness in the pit of my stomach when I think of her, this is good news for us. We're not the Sovereign's sole enemy. "Did Uranus and Saturn join? Neptune surely did."

"All did."

"All? Then there's hope. . . ." I say.

"Yeah, you'd think. Right?" Sevro mutters.

Dancer explains. "The Moon Lords also made a mistake. They expected the Sovereign would find herself mired on Mars and would be plagued with lowColor insurrection in the Core. So they assumed she would not be able to send a fleet of sufficient size six hundred million kilometers to quash their rebellion for at least three years."

"And they were dead wrong," Sevro mutters. "The idiots. Got caught with their panties down."

"How long did it take for her to send a fleet?" I ask. "Six months?"

"Sixty-three days."

"That's impossible, the logistics on fuel alone . . ." My voice trails away as I remember the Ash Lord was on the way to reinforce House Bellona in orbit around Mars before we took the planet. He was weeks away then. He must have continued out to the Rim, following Mustang the entire way.

"You should know better than anyone the efficiency of the Society Navy. They're a war machine," Dancer says. "Logistics and systems of operation are perfect. The longer the Rim had to prepare, the harder it would have been for the Sovereign to wage a campaign. The Sovereign knew that. So the whole Sword Armada deployed straightaway to Jupiter orbit, and they've been there for nearly ten months."

"Roque did a nasty," Sevro says. "Snuck ahead of the main fleet and jacked that moonBreaker old Nero tried to steal last year."

"He stole a moonBreaker."

"Yeah. I know. He's named it the *Colossus* and chosen it as his flagship. The ponce. It's a nasty piece of hardware. Makes the *Pax* look tiny by comparison."

The holo above shows the Sovereign's fleet coming upon Jupiter, where the moonBreaker waits to welcome them. The days and weeks and months of war speed past.

"The scope of it . . . is manic," Sevro says. "Each fleet twice again as large as the coalition you summoned to pound the Bellona . . ." He says more, but I'm lost watching the months of war speed past, realizing how the worlds kept turning without me.

"Octavia wouldn't have used the Ash Lord," I say distantly. "If he even went past the asteroid belt, there would be no reconciliation. The Rim would never surrender. So who leads them? Aja?"

"Roque au Buttsucking Fabii," Sevro sneers.

"He leads the entire fleet?" I ask in surprise.

"I know, right? After the Siege of Mars and the Battle of Deimos, he's a bloodydamn godchild to the Core. Regular Iron Gold pulled from annals past. Never mind you snuck in under his nose. Or he was a joke at the Institute. He's good at three things. Whining, stabbing people in the back, and destroying fleets."

"They call him the Poet of Deimos," Ragnar says. **"He is undefeated in battle. Even against Mustang and her titans. He is very dangerous."**

"Fleet warfare is not her game," I say. Mustang can fight. But she's always been more a political creature. She binds people together. But raw tactics? That's Roque's province.

The warlord in me mourns having been kept away for so long. For having missed such a spectacle as that of the Second Moon Rebellion. Sixty-seven moons, most militarized, four with populations more than one hundred million. Fleet battles. Orbital bombardments. Asteroid hopping assault maneuvers with armies in mech suits. It would have been my playground. But the man in me knows if I hadn't been in the box, this room would be missing people.

I realize I'm internalizing too much. I force myself to communicate.

"We're running out of time. Aren't we?"

Dancer nods. "Last week, Roque took Calisto. Only Ganymede and Io hold strong. If the Moon Lords capitulate then that navy and the Legions with it return here to aid the Jackal against us. We will be the sole focus of the united military might of the Society, and they will eradicate us."

That was why Fitchner hated bombs. They bring the eyes, wake the giant.

"So what about Mars? What about our war? Hell, what is our war?"

"It's a bloodydamn mess is what it is," Sevro says. "It spilled over into open war about eight months ago. The Sons have stayed tight. Don't know where Orion is. Dead, we reckon. The *Pax* and your ships are gone. And now we've got paramilitary armies that aren't Sons-affiliated rising up in the north, massacring civilians and in turn getting wiped out by Legion airborne units. Then there's mass strikes and protests in dozens of cities. The prisons are overflowing with political prisoners, so they're relocating them to these makeshift camps where we know for a fact that they are pullin' mass executions."

Dancer pulls up some of the holos, so I see blurry images of what look like large prisons in the desert and forest. They zoom in on low-Colors disembarking transports at gunpoint and filing into the concrete structures. It switches to a view of rubble-strewn streets. Men with masks and Red armbands firing over the smoking remains of city trams. A Gold lands among them. The image cuts out.

"We been hitting them hard as we can," Sevro says. "Gotten some hardcore business done. Stole a dozen ships, two destroyers. Demolished the Thermic Command Center . . ."

"And now they're rebuilding it," Dancer says.

"Then we'll destroy it again," Sevro snaps.

"When we can't even hold a city?"

"These Reds are not warriors." Ragnar interrupts the two. "They can fly ships. Shoot guns. Lay bombs. Fight Grays. But when a Gold arrives, they melt away."

A deep silence follows his words. The Sons of Ares are guerilla fighters. Saboteurs. Spies. But in this war, Lorn's words haunt me. "How do sheep kill a lion? By drowning him in blood."

"Every civilian death on Mars is blamed on us," Theodora says eventually. "We kill two in a bombing of a munitions manufacturing plant, they say we killed a thousand. Every strike or demonstration, Society agents infiltrate the crowd masquerading as demonstrators to shoot at Gray officers or detonate suicide vests. Those images are dispersed to the media circus. And when the cameras are off, Grays break into homes and make sympathizers disappear. MidColors.

LowColor. Doesn't matter. They contain the dissent. In the north, like Sevro said, it's open rebellion."

"A faction called Red Legion is massacring every highColor they find," Dancer says darkly. "Old friend of ours has joined their leadership. Harmony."

"Fitting."

"She's poisoned them against us. They won't take our orders, and we've stopped sending them weapons. We're losing our moral high ground."

"The man with voice and violence controls the world," I murmur.

"Arcos?" Theodora asks. I nod. "If only he were here."

"I'm not sure he'd help us."

"Lamentably, it seems as if voice doesn't exist without violence," the Pink says. She folds a leg over the other. "The greatest weapon a rebellion has is its *spiritus*. The spirit of change. That little seed that finds a hope in the mind and flourishes and spreads. But the ability to plant that idea, and even the idea itself has been taken from us. The message stolen. We are voiceless."

When she speaks, the others listen. Not to humor her like Golds would, but as if her position was nearly equal to Dancer's.

"None of this makes any sense," I say. "What sparked open war? The Jackal didn't publicize killing Fitchner. He would have wanted it quiet as he purged the Sons. What was the catalyst? And also, you say we're voiceless. But Fitchner had a communication network that could broadcast to the mines, to anywhere. He pushed Eo's death to the masses. Made her the face of the Rising. Did the Jackal take it out?" I look around at their concerned faces. "What aren't you telling me?"

"You didn't tell him already?" Sevro asks. "The hell were you doing when I was gone, picking your asses?"

"Darrow wanted to be with his family," Dancer says sharply. He turns to me with a sigh. "Much of our digital network was destroyed during the Jackal's purges in the month after Ares was killed and you were captured. Sevro was able to warn us before the Jackal's men hit our base in Agea. We went to ground, saved materiel, but lost massive amounts of manpower. Thousands of Sons. Trained operators. The next three months we spent trying to find you. We hijacked a transport going to Luna, but you weren't on it. We searched the prisons. Issued bribes. But you'd disappeared, like you never existed. And then the Jackal executed you on the steps of the citadel in Agea."

"I know all this."

"Well, what you don't know is what Sevro did next."

I look to my friend. "What did you do?"

"What I had to." He takes control of the hologram and wipes Jupiter away, replacing it with me. Sixteen years old. Scrawny and pale and naked on a table as Mickey stands over me with his buzzsaw. A chill trickles down my spine. But it's not even my spine. Not really. It belongs to these people. To the revolution. I feel . . . used as I realize what he's done.

"You released it."

"Damn right," Sevro says nastily, and I feel all their eyes settling on me, now understanding why my blade is painted on the roofs of Tinos's refugees. They all know I was once a Red. They know one of their own conquered Mars in an Iron Rain.

I started the war.

"I released your Carving to every mine. To every holoSite. To every millimeter of this bloodydamn Society. The Golds thought they could kill you off. That they could beat you and make your death mean nothing. I'll be damned if I'd let that happen." He thumps his hand on a table. "Damned if I'd let you disappear facelessly into the machine like my mother. There's not a Red on Mars that doesn't know your name, Reap. Not a single person in the digital world who doesn't know that a Red rose to become a prince of the Golds, to conquer Mars. I made you a myth. And now that you're back from the dead, you're not just a martyr. You're the bloodydamn messiah the Reds have been waiting for their entire lives."

11

|||||||||||||||||||||||

MY PEOPLE

I sit with my legs dangling off the edge of the hangar, watching the city beneath teem with life. The clamor of a thousand hushed voices rises to me like a sea of leaves brushing together. The refugees know I'm alive. SlingBlades have been painted on walls. On roofs. The desperate silent cry of a lost people. For six years I've wanted to be back among them. But looking down, seeing their plight, remembering Kieran's words, I feel myself drowning in their hope.

They expect too much.

They don't understand that we can't win this war. Ares even knew we could never go toe-to-toe with Gold. So how am I supposed to lift them up? To show them the way?

I'm afraid, not just that I can't give them what they want. But that by releasing the truth, Sevro's burned the boat behind us. There's no going back for us.

So what does that mean for my family? For my friends and these people? I felt so overwhelmed by these questions, by Sevro's use of my Carving, that I stormed out without a word. It was petulant.

Behind me, Ragnar moves past my wheelchair and slides down next to me. Legs dangling off the edge like mine. His boots comically large. The breeze of a passing shuttle catches the ribbons in his beard. He says nothing, at ease with the silence. It makes me feel safe knowing he's here. Knowing he's with me. Like I thought I would feel near Sevro. But he's changed. Too much weight in that helm of Ares.

"When I was a boy, we always wanted to know who the bravest of us was," I say. "We'd sneak out of our homes at night and go down into the deeptunnels and stand with our backs to the darkness. You could hear the pitvipers if you were quiet. But you could never tell how close they were. Most boys would break and run after a minute, maybe five. I always stood the longest. Till Eo found out about our game." I shake my head. "Now I don't think I'd last a minute."

"Because you now know how much there is to lose."

Ragnar's black eyes hold the shadows of a vast history. Nearly forty, he's a man who was raised in a world of ice and magic, sold to the Gods to buy life for his people, and served as a slave longer than I've been alive. How much better does he understand life than I do?

"Do you still miss home? Your sister?" I ask.

"I do. I long for the early snow in the throes of summer, how it stuck to the fur of Sefi's boots as I carried her on my shoulders to see *Níðhǫggr* break through the spring ice."

Níðhǫggr was a dragon who lived under the world tree of the Old Norse societies and spent his days gnawing at the roots of Yggdrasil. Many Obsidian tribes believe he comes up from the deep waters of their sea to break the ice that blocks their harbors and open the veins of the pole for their spring raiding boats. In honor of him, they send the bodies of their criminals to the deep in a holiday called Ostara, the first day of true spring light.

"I sent friends to the Spires and the Ice to spread your word. To tell my people their gods are false. They are in bondage, and we will soon come to free them. They will know Eo's song."

Eo's song. It seems so fragile and silly now.

"I don't feel her anymore, Ragnar." I glance behind us to the Oranges and Reds who spare glances our direction as they work on the ripWings in the hangar. "I know they think I'm their link to her. But I lost her in the darkness. I used to think she was watching me. I used to talk to her. Now . . . she's a stranger." I hang my head. "So much of this is my fault, Ragnar. If I hadn't been so proud, I would have seen the signs. Fitchner would be alive. Lorn would be alive."

"**You think you know the strands of fate?**" He laughs at my arrogance. "**You do not know what would have happened if they lived.**"

"I know I can't be what these people need."

He frowns. "**And how would you know what they need when you are afraid of them? When you can't even look upon them?**" I don't know how to answer. He stands abruptly and extends a hand to me. "**Come with me.**"

The hospital was once a cafeteria. Rows of gurneys and makeshift beds now fill it along with coughs and solemn whispers as Red, Pink, and Yellow nurses in yellow scrubs move through the beds checking the patients. The back of the room is a burn ward, separated from the rest of the patients by plastic containment walls. A woman's screaming on the other side of the plastic, fighting a nurse as he tries to give her an injection. Two other nurses rush to subdue her.

I feel swallowed by the sterile sadness of the place. There's no gore. No blood dripping on the floor. But this is the aftermath of my escape from Attica. Even with a Carver as good as Mickey, they won't have the resources to mend these people. The wounded stare up at the stone ceiling wondering what life will be like now. That's what this feeling is in this room. Trauma. Not of flesh. But lives and dreams interrupted.

I'd retreat from the room, but Ragnar rolls me forward to the edge of a young man's bed. He watched me as I came in. His hair is short. His face plump and awkward with a prominent under bite.

"What's what?" I ask, my voice remembering the flavor of the mine.

He shrugs. "Just dancin' time away, hear?"

"I hear." I extend a hand. "Darrow . . . of Lykos."

"We know." His hands are so small he can't even wrap his fingers around mine. He chuckles at the ridiculousness of it. "Vanno of Karos."

"Night or day?"

"Dayshift, you pigger. I look like some saggy-faced night digger?"

"Well, you never know these days . . ."

"True enough. I'm Omicron. Third drillboy, second line."

"So that was your chaff I'd be dodging deep."

He grins. "Helldivers, always lookin' themselves in the eye." He makes a lewd motion with his hands. "Someone's gotta teach you to look up."

We laugh. "How much did it hurt?" he asks, nodding to me. At first I think he's asking about what the Jackal did. Then I realize he's referring to the Sigils on my hands. The ones I've tried to cover with my sweater. I unveil them now. "Manic shit, that." He flicks it with his finger.

I look around, suddenly aware that it's not just Vanno watching me. It's everyone. Even on the far side of the room in the burn unit Reds push themselves up in their beds to look at me. They can't see the fear inside. They see what they want. I glance at Ragnar, but he's busy speaking to an injured woman. Holiday. She nods to me. Grief still very much at home on her face for her lost brother. His pistol is on her bedside, his rifle leaning against the wall. The Sons recovered his body during the rescue so he could be buried.

"How much did it hurt?" I repeat. "Well, imagine falling into a clawDrill, Vanno. A centimeter at a time. First goes the skin. Then the flesh. Then bone. Easy stuff."

Vanno whistles and looks down at his missing legs with a tired, almost bored expression. "Didn't even feel this. My suit injected enough hydrophone to knock out one of them." He nods to Ragnar and draws air through his teeth. "And least I still got my prick."

"Ask him," a man beside him urges. "Vanno . . ."

"Shut up." Vanno sighs. "Boys have been wonderin'. Did you get to keep it?"

"Keep what?"

"*It.*" He looks at my groin. "Or did they . . . you know . . . make it proportionate?"

"You really want to know?"

"I mean . . . not for personal reasons. But I've got money riding on it."

"Well." I lean forward seriously. So do Vanno and his bedmates nearby. "If you really want to know, you should ask your mother."

Vanno stares at me intensely, then explodes into laughter. His bedmates laugh and spread the joke to the far edges of the room. And in that tiny moment, the mood shifts. The suffocating sterility cut through with amusement and crude jokes. Whispering suddenly seems ridiculous here. It fills me with energy to see the shifting tide and realize it's because of a single laugh. Instead of retreating from the eyes, from the room, I move away from Ragnar down the lines of cots to mingle more with the injured, to thank them, to ask where they're from and learn their names. And this is where I thank Jove that I've a good memory on me. Forget a man's name and he'll forgive you. Remember it, and he'll defend you forever.

Most call me sir or Reaper. And I want to correct them and tell them to call me Darrow, but I know the value of respect, of distance between men and leader. Because even though I'm laughing with them, even though they're helping heal what's been twisted inside me, they are not my friends. They are not my family. Not yet. Not until we have that luxury. For now, they are my soldiers. And they need me as much as I need them. I'm their Reaper. It took Ragnar to remind me. He favors me with an ungainly grin, so pleased to see me smiling and laughing with the soldiers. I've never been a man of joy or a man of war, or an island in a storm. Never an absolute like Lorn. That was what I pretended to be. I am and always have been a man who is made complete by those around him. I feel strength growing in myself. A strength I haven't felt in so long. It's not only that I'm loved. It's that they believe in me. Not the mask like my soldiers at the Institute. Not the false idol I built in the service of Augustus, but the man beneath. Lykos may be gone. Eo may be silent. Mustang a world away. And the Sons on the brink of extinction. But I feel my soul trickling back into me as I realize I am finally home.

|||||||||||

With Ragnar at my side I return to the command room where Sevro and Dancer are hunched over a blueprint. Theodora's in the corner exchanging correspondences. They turn as I enter, surprised to see the smile on my face and to see that I'm now standing. Not on my own, but with Ragnar's help. I left the chair in the hospital and had him guide me back to the command room I fled only an hour prior. I feel a new man. And I may not be what I was before the darkness, but perhaps I'm better for it. I have humility I didn't have before.

"I'm sorry for how I acted," I say to my friends. "This has been . . . overwhelming. I know you've done the best you can. Better than anyone could, given the circumstances. You've all kept hope alive. And you saved me. And you saved my family." I pause, making sure they know how much that means to me. "I know you didn't expect me to come back like this. I know you thought I'd come back with wrath and fire. But I'm not what I was. I'm just not," I say as Sevro tries to correct me. "I trust you. I trust your plans. I want to help in whatever way I can. But I can't help you like this." I hold up my thin arms. "So I need your help with three things."

"Always so dramatic," Sevro says. "What are your demands, Princess?"

"First I want to send an emissary to Mustang. I know you think she betrayed me, but I want her to know I'm alive. Maybe there's some chance it'll make a difference. That's she'll help us."

Sevro snorts. "We already gave her the opportunity once. She almost killed you and Rags."

"But she did not," Ragnar says. "It is worth the risk, if she will help us. I will go as emissary so she does not doubt our intentions."

"Like hell," Sevro says. "You're one of most wanted men in the System. Gold have shut down all unauthorized air traffic. And you won't last two minutes in a space port, even with a mask."

"We'll send one of my spies," Theodora says. "I have one in mind. She's good, and a hundred kilograms less conspicuous that you, Prince of the Spires. The girl's in a port city already."

"Evey?" Dancer asks.

"Just." Theodora looks my direction. "Evey's done her best to make amends for the sins of the past. Even ones that weren't hers. She's been very helpful. Dancer, I'll make the arrangements for travel and cover, if that's all right with you."

"It's all right," Sevro says quickly, though Theodora waits for Dancer to nod his agreement.

"Thank you," I say. "I also need you to bring Mickey back to Tinos."

"Why?" Dancer asks.

"I need him to make me into a weapon again."

Sevro cackles. "Now we're talking. Get some man-killing meat on your bones. No more of this anorexic scarecrow shit."

Dancer shakes his head. "Mickey's half a thousand clicks away in Varos, working on his little project. He's needed there. You need calories. Not a Carver. In the state you're in, it could be dangerous."

"Reap can handle it. We can get Mickey and his equipment here by Thursday," Sevro says. "Virany has been consulting with him anyway about your condition. He'll be tickled Pink to see you."

Dancer watches Sevro with strained patience. "And the last request?"

I grimace. "I have a feeling you're not gonna like this one."

12

||||||||||||||||||||||||

THE JULII

I find Victra in an isolated room with several Sons guarding the door. She lies with her feet sticking off the edge of a medical cot, watching a holo at the foot of her bed as Society news channels drone on about the valiant Legion attack on a terrorist force that destroyed a dam and flooded the lower Mystos River Valley. The flooding has forced two million Brown farmers out of their homes. Grays deliver aid packages from the backs of military trucks. Easily could have been Reds who blew up the dam. Or it could have been the Jackal. At this point, who knows?

Victra's white-gold hair is bound in a tight ponytail. Every limb, even the paralyzed legs, is cuffed to the bed. Not much trust here for her kind. She doesn't look up at me as the holo story kicks over to a profile on Roque au Fabii, the Poet of Deimos and the newest heart-throb of the gossip circuit. Searching through his past, conducting interviews with his Senator mother, his teachers before the Institute, showing him as boy on their country estate.

"Roque always found the natural world to be more beautiful than cities," his mother says for the camera. "It's the perfect order in nature that he so admired. How it formed effortlessly into a hierarchy. I think that's why he loved the Society so dearly, even then. . . ."

"That woman would look much better with a gun in her mouth," Victra mutters, muting the sound.

"She's probably said his name more in the last month than she did his entire childhood," I reply.

"Well, politicians never let a popular family member go to waste. What was it Roque once said about Augustus at a party? 'Oh, how the vultures flock to the mighty, to eat the carcasses left in their wake.'" Victra looks at me with her flashing, belligerent eyes. The madness I saw in them earlier has retreated but not vanished entirely. It lingers like mine. "Might as well have been talking about you."

"That's fair," I say.

"Are you leading this little pack of terrorists?"

"I had my chance to lead. I made a mess of it. Sevro is in charge."

"Sevro." She leans back. "Really?"

"Is that funny?"

"No. For some reason I'm not surprised at all, actually. Always had a bigger bite than bark. First time I saw him, he was kicking Tactus's ass."

I step closer. "I believe I owe you an explanation."

"Oh, hell. Can't we skip this part?" she asks. "It's boring."

"Skip it?"

She sighs heavily. "Apologies. Recrimination. All the trifling shit people muddle through because they're insecure. You don't owe me an explanation."

"How do you figure?"

"We all enter a certain social contract by living in this Society of ours. My people oppress your tiny kind. We live off the spoils of your labor. Pretending you don't exist. And you fight back. Usually very poorly. Personally, I think that's your right. It's not good or evil. But it's fair. I'd applaud a mouse that managed to kill an eagle, wouldn't you? Good for it.

"It's absurd and hypocritical for Golds to complain now simply because the Reds finally started fighting well." She laughs sharply at my surprise. "What, darling? Did you expect me to scream and rant and piss on about honor and betrayal like those walking wounds, Cassius and Roque?"

"A little," I say. "I would. . . ."

"That's because you're more emotional than I am. I'm a Julii. Cold runneth through my veins." She rolls her eyes when I try to correct her. "Don't ask me to be different because you need validation, please. It's beneath the both of us."

"You've never been as cold as you pretend to be," I say.

"I've existed long before you ever came into my life. What do you really know of me? I am my mother's daughter."

"You're more than that."

"If you say so."

There's no artifice to her. No coy manipulation. Mustang's all smirks and subtle plays. Victra's a wrecking ball. She softened before the Triumph. Let her guard down. But now it's back and it's as alienating as when I first met her. But the longer we speak, the more I see her hair is shot with gray, not just pale Gold. Her cheeks are hollow, her right hand, the one on the opposite side of the cot, clenching the sheets.

"I know why you lied to me, Darrow. And I can respect it. But what I don't understand is why you saved me in Attica. Was it pity? A tactic?"

"It's because you're my friend," I say.

"Oh, please."

"I would rather have died trying to get you out of that cell than let you rot in there. Trigg did die getting you out."

"Trigg?"

"One of the Grays who were behind me when we came into your cell. The other one is his sister."

"I didn't ask to be saved," she says bitterly, her way of washing her hands of Trigg's death. She looks away from me now. "You know Antonia thought we were lovers, you and I. She showed me your Carving. She taunted me. As if it would disgust me to see what you are. To see where you came from. To see how I had been lied to."

"And did it?"

She sneers. "Why would I care what you were? I care about what people do. I care about truth. If you had told me, I wouldn't have done a single thing differently. I would have protected you." I believe her. And I believe the pain in her eyes. "Why didn't you tell me?"

"Because I was afraid."

"But I wager you told Mustang?"

"Yes."

"Why her and not me? I at least deserve that."

"I don't know."

"It's because you're a liar. You said I wasn't wicked in the hall. But you think it deep down. You never trusted me."

"No," I say. "I didn't. That's my mistake. And my friends have paid for it with their lives. That . . . that guilt was my only company in the box he kept me in for the nine months." By the look in her eyes I know she didn't know what had been done to me. "But now I've been given a second chance at life, I don't want to waste it. I want to make amends with you. I owe you a life. I owe you justice. And I want you to join us."

"Join you?" she says with a laugh. "As a Son of Ares?"

"Yes."

"You're serious." She laughs at me. Another defense mechanism. "I'm not really into suicide, darling."

"The world you know is gone, Victra. Your sister has stolen it from you. Your mother and her friends have been wiped out. Your house is now your enemy. And you're an outcast from your own people. That is the problem with this Society. It eats its own. It pits us against one another. You have nowhere to go. . . ."

"Well, you really know how to make a girl feel special."

". . . I want to give you a family that will not stab you in the back. I want to give you a life with meaning. I know you're a good person, even if you laugh at me for saying it. But I believe in you. Yet . . . all that doesn't matter—what I believe, what I want. What matters is what you want."

She searches my eyes. "What I want?"

"If you want to leave here, you can. If you want to stay in this bed, you can. Say what you want and it's yours. I owe you that."

She thinks for a moment. "I don't care about your rebellion. I don't care about your dead wife. Or about finding a family or finding meaning. I want to be able to sleep without them jacking me full of chemicals, Darrow. I want to be able to dream again. I want to forget my mother's caved-in head and her vacant eyes and her twitching fingers. I want to forget Adrius laughing. And I want to repay Antonia and Adrius for their hospitality. I want to stand above them and that piece of shit, Roque, as they weep for the end as I gouge out their eyes and pour molten gold into the sockets so they scream and writhe and spread their urine upon the floor and beg forgiveness for ever thinking they could put Victra au Julii in a gorydamn cage." She smiles ferally. "I want revenge."

"Revenge is a hollow end," I say.

"And I'm a hollow girl now."

I know she's not. I know she's more than that. But I also know better than anyone that wounds aren't healed in a day. I'm barely stitched together myself, and I have my entire family here. "If that is what you want, that is what I owe you. In three days the Carver who made me into a Gold will be here. He will make us what we were. He'll mend your spine. Give you your legs back, if you want them."

She squints at me. "And you trust me, after what trust has cost you?"

I take the magnetic key given to me by the Sons outside and press it to the inside of her cuffs. One by one they unlatch from the bed, freeing her legs, her arms.

"You're dumber than you look," she says.

"You might not believe in our rebellion. But I saw Tactus change before his future was robbed from him. I've seen Ragnar forget his bonds and reach for what he wants in this world. I've seen Sevro become a man. I've seen myself change. I truly do believe we choose who we want to be in this life. It isn't preordained. You taught me loyalty, more than Mustang, more than Roque. And because of that, I believe in you, Victra. As much as I've ever believed in anyone." I hold out my hand. "Be my family and I will never forsake you. I will never lie to you. I will be your brother as long as you live."

Startled by the emotion in my voice, the cold woman stares up at me. Those defenses she erected forgotten now. In another life we might have been a pair. Might have had that fire I feel for Mustang, for Eo. But not in this life.

Victra does not soften. Does not crumble to tears. There's still rage inside her. Still raw hate and so much betrayal and frustration and loss coiled around her icy heart. But in this moment, she is free of it all. In this moment, she reaches solemnly up to grasp my hand. And I feel the hope flicker in me.

"Welcome to the Sons of Ares."

PART II

IIIIIIIIIIIIIIIIIIIIIIIIIIIIIIIIII

RAGE

"Shit escalates."

—Sevro au Barca

13

||||||||||||||||||||||||||

HOWLERS

"It's gorydamn infuriating being kept in the dark," Victra mutters as she helps me rack the weights on the bench press. The sound echoes through the stone gymnasium. It's bare bones in here. Metal weights. Rubber tires. Ropes. And months of my sweat.

"Don't they know who you are?" I say, sitting up.

"Oh, shut up. Didn't you found the Howlers? Don't you have any say over how they treat us?" She nudges me off the bench to take my spot, laying her spine on the padded surface and pushing her arms up to grip the barbell. I take a few weights off. But she glares at me and I put them back on as she fixes her grip.

"Technically, no," I say.

"Oh. But seriously: what's a girl got to do to get a wolfcloak?" Her powerful arms thrust the bar up off from its rack, moving it up and down as she talks. Nearly three hundred kilos. "I shot a Legate in the head two missions ago. A Legate! I've seen your Howlers. Aside from . . . Ragnar, they're tiny. They need . . . more heavies if they want to . . . take on Adrius's Boneriders or the Sovereign's . . . Praetorians." She grits her teeth as she finishes her last repetition, racking the bar without my help, and standing to point to herself in the mirror. Hers is a powerful, laconic form. Shoulders broad and swaying with a haughty walk. "I'm a perfect physical specimen, on and off my feet. Not using me is an indictment on Sevro's intelligence."

I roll my eyes. "It's probably your lack of self-confidence he's worried about."

She throws a towel at me. "You're as annoying as he is. Swear to Jove if he says one more thing about my 'nascent poverty' I'm going to cut his head off with a gorydamn spoon." I watch her for a moment, trying not to laugh. "What, you have something to say as well?"

"Not a thing, my goodlady," I say, holding up my hands. Her eyes linger on them instinctively. "Squats next?"

The ramshackle gymnasium has been our second home since Mickey Carved us. It was weeks of recovery in his ward as her nerves remembered how to walk and both of us tried to put on weight again under the supervision of Dr. Virany. A gaggle of Reds and a Green watch us from the corner of the gym. Even after two months, the novelty hasn't worn off seeing how much two chemically and genetically enhanced Peerless Scarred can lift.

Ragnar came in to embarrass us a couple weeks back. Brute didn't even say a word. Just started piling weights onto a barbell till no more would fit, power-cleaned it, and then gestured for us to do the same. Victra couldn't even get the weight off the ground. I got as far as my knees. Then we had to listen to the hundred idiots who flocked after him chant his name for an hour. Found out afterward Uncle Narol had been overseeing bets on how much more Ragnar could lift than I. Even my own uncle bet against me. But it's a good sign, even if the others don't think of it this way. Gold can't win everything.

It was with Mickey and Dr. Virany's help that Victra and I regained control of our bodies. But regaining our sense in the field has taken just as long. We started with baby steps. Our first mission out together was a supply run with Holiday and a dozen bodyguards, not for the supply run itself, but for me. We didn't do it with the Howlers. "Gotta work your way up to the A squad, Reap. Make sure you can keep up," Sevro said, patting my face. "And Julii has to prove herself." She slapped his hand when he tried petting her.

Ten supply runs, two sabotage missions, and three assassinations later Sevro was finally convinced that Holiday, Victra, and I were ready to run with the B squad: the Pitvipers, led by my own Uncle Narol—who has become a bit of a cult hero to the Reds here. Ragnar's a godlike creature. But my uncle is just a rough old man who drinks too much, smokes too much, and is uncommonly good at war. His Pitvipers are a motley collection of hardasses specializing in sabotage and thievery, about half are ex Helldivers, the rest are a spattering of other useful lowColors. We've completed three missions with them, destroying a barracks and several Legion communications installations, but I can't shake the feeling we're a snake eating our own tail. Every bombing is twisted by the Society media. Every pinprick of damage we do seems only to bring more Legions from Agea to the mines or the smaller cities of Mars.

I feel hunted.

Worse, I feel like a terrorist. I've only ever felt this way once before, and that was with a bomb on my chest walking into the gala on Luna.

Dancer and Theodora have been pressing Sevro to reach out to more allies. Trying to bridge the gap between the Sons and other factions. Reluctantly, Sevro agreed. So earlier this week, the Pitvipers and I were dispatched from the tunnels to the northern continent of Arabia Terra, where the Red Legion had carved themselves a stronghold in the port city of Ismenia. It was Dancer's hope I could bring them into the fold in a way Sevro hadn't been able to, maybe pull them away from Harmony's influence. But instead of finding allies, we found a mass grave. A gray, bombed-out city shelled from orbit. I can still see that pale bloated mass of bodies writhing on the coastline. Crabs skittering over the corpses, making meals of the dead, as a lone ribbon of smoke twirled and twirled up to the stars, the old soundless echo of war.

I'm haunted by the sight, but Victra seems to have moved past it as she plows through her workout. She's pushed it to that vast vault in the back of her mind where she compresses and locks away all the evil she's seen, all the pain she's felt. I wish I were more like her. I wish I felt less and was less afraid. But as I recall that ribbon of smoke, all I can think is that it presages something worse. As if the Universe is showing us a glimpse of the end we're rushing toward.

It's late night and the mirrors have fogged with condensation when we're done with our workout. We wash up in the showers, talking over the plastic dividers. "Take it as a sign of progress," I say. "At least she's speaking to you."

"No. Your mother hates me. She'll always hate me. Not a damn thing I can do about it."

"Well, you could try being more polite."

"I'm perfectly polite," Victra says in offense, turning off her shower and exiting the stall. Eyes closed against the water, I finish shampooing my hair, expecting her to say more. She doesn't, so I finish rinsing the shampoo out and exit the stall when I'm done. I feel something's amiss the moment before I see Victra naked on the floor, hands and legs hogtied behind her back. A hood over her head. Something moves behind me. I whirl around just in time to see a half dozen ghostCloaks slipping through the steam. Then someone inhumanly strong slams into me from behind, wrapping their arms around mine, pinning them to my sides. I feel their breath on my neck. Terror screams through me. The Jackal's found us. He's snuck in. How? "Golds!" I shout. "Golds!" I'm slick from the shower. The floor is slippery. I use it to my advantage, wriggling against my attacker's arms like an eel and lashing back with my head in his face. There's a grunt. I twist again, feet slip. I fall. Smacking my knee on the concrete floor. Scramble to my feet. Feel two attackers rushing me from the left. Cloaked. I duck under one, putting my shoulder into his knees. He catapults over my head and smashes through the plastic barriers that divide the shower behind me. I grab the other by the throat, blocking a punch, and throw him into the ceiling. Another slams into me from the side, prying at my leg with his hands to take my balance. I go with it, jumping in the air, twisting my body in a Kravat move that steals his center of gravity and puts us both on the ground, his head between my thighs. All I need do is twist and his neck breaks. But two more sets of hands are on me, thumping me in the face, more are on my legs. GhostCloaks rippling in the vapor. I'm screaming and thrashing and spitting, but there are too many, and they're nasty, punching the tendons behind my knees so I can't kick and the nerves in my shoulders so my arms feel heavy as lead. They shove a hood over my head and bind my hands behind my back. I lay there motionless, terrified, panting.

"Get them on their knees," an electronic voice growls. "On their bloodydamn knees." *Bloodydamn?* Ah, shit. As I realize who it is, I let them lift me up to my knees. Hood is removed. The lights are out. Several dozen candles have been set on the shower floor, throwing shadows about the room. Victra's to my left, eyes furious. Blood coming from her now-crooked nose. Holiday has appeared to my right. Fully clothed but similarly bound, she is carried in by two black-clad figures and forced down on her knees. A big grin splits her face.

Standing around us in the bathroom steam are ten demons with black-painted faces staring out from beneath the mouths of the wolf pelts that hang from their heads to their mid-thighs. Two lean against the wall, in pain from my rabid defense. Beneath the pelt of a bear, Ragnar towers beside Sevro. The Howlers have come for new recruits and they look bloody terrifying.

"Greetings, you ugly little bastards," Sevro growls, removing the voice synthesizer. He stalks forward through the shadows to stand before us. "It has come to my attention that you are abnormally devious, savage, and generally malicious creatures gifted in the arts of murder, mayhem, and chaos. If I am mistaken, do say so now."

"Sevro, you scared the shit out of us," Victra says. "The hell is your problem?"

"Do not profane this moment," Ragnar says menacingly.

Victra spits. "You broke my nose, you oaf!"

"Technically, I did," Sevro says. He jerks his head to a lean Howler with Red Sigils on his hands. "Sleepy helped."

"You little dwarf . . ."

"You were squirming, love," Pebble says from somewhere among the Howlers. I can't tell which she is. Voice resounding off the walls.

"And if you keep talking we'll just gag you and tickle you," Clown says sinisterly. "So . . . shhhh." Victra shakes her head but keeps her mouth shut. I'm trying not to laugh at the solemnity of the moment. Sevro continues, pacing back and forth before us.

"You have been watched, and now you are wanted. If you accept our invitation to join our brotherhood, you must take an oath to be always faithful to your brothers and sisters. To never lie, never betray those under the cloak. All your sins, all your scars, all your enemies now belong to us. Our burden to share. Your loves, your family will become your second loves, your second family. We are your first. If you cannot abide this, if you cannot conscience this bond, say so now and you may leave."

He waits. Not even Victra says a word.

"Good. Now, as per the rules set forth in our sacred text . . ." He holds up a little black book with dog-eared pages and a white howling wolfhead on the front. ". . . You must be purged of your former oaths and prove your worth before you can take our vows." He holds up his hands. "So let the Purge begin."

The Howlers pitch back their heads and howl like maniacs. What comes next is a blur of kaleidoscopic oddities. Music thumps from somewhere. We're kept on our knees. Hands tied. The Howlers rush forward. Bottles are brought to our lips and we chug as they chant around some weird looping melody that Sevro leads with bawdy aplomb. Ragnar roars with satisfaction when I finish the bottle they bring me. I almost puke then and there. The liquor burns, scouring my esophagus and belly. Victra's coughing behind me. Holiday just chugs on and the Howlers cheer as she finishes her bottle. We waver there as they surround Victra, chanting as she gasps and tries to finish the liquor. It splashes over her face. She coughs.

"Is that your best, daughter of the Sun?" Ragnar bellows. **"Drink!"**

Ragnar roars with delight when she finally finishes the swill, coughing and muttering curses. **"Bring forth the snakes and the cockroaches!"** he shouts.

They chant like priests as Pebble wobbles forward with a bucket. They push us together so we surround the bucket and in the wavering light can see the bottom of it wriggling with life. Thick, shiny cockroaches with hairy legs and wings crawl around a pitviper. I reel back, terrified and drunk as our binds are cut. Holiday's already reached inside and grabs the snake; she slams it on the floor till it dies.

Victra just stares at the Gray. "What the . . ."

"Finish the bucket or get the box," Sevro says.

"What does that even mean?"

"Finish the bucket or get the box! Finish the bucket or get the box!" they chant. Holiday takes a bite of the dead snake, tearing into it with her teeth.

"Yes!" Ragnar bellows. "She has the soul of a Howler. Yes!"

I'm so drunk I can barely see. I reach into the bucket, shivering as I feel the cockroaches crawl over my hand. I snatch one up and jam it into my mouth. It's still moving. I force my jaw to chew. I'm almost crying. Victra is gagging at the sight of me. I swallow it down and grab her hand and force it into the bucket. She makes a sudden lurching movement, and I'm too slow to realize what it means. Her vomit splashes onto my shoulder. At the smell of it, I can't hold my own in. Holiday chews on. Ragnar shouts her praises.

By the time we finish the bucket, we're a huddled pathetic mass of drunk, bug- and guts-covered filth. Sevro's saying something in front of us. Keeps swaying back and forth. Maybe that's me. Is he talking? Someone shakes my shoulder from behind. Was I asleep? "This is our sacred text," my little friend is saying. "You will study this sacred text. Soon you will know this sacred text inside and out. But today, you need know only Howler Rule One."

"Never bow," Ragnar says.

"Never bow," the rest echo and Clown steps forward with three wolfcloaks. Like the fur of the wolves at the Institute, these pelts modulate to their environment and take on a dark hue in the candlelit room. He holds one out for Victra. They free her bonds and she tries to stand, but can't. Pebble reaches to help her up, but Victra ignores the hand. Tries again and tilts down to a knee. Then Sevro kneels beside her and extends a hand. Looking at it through sweat-soaked hair, Victra snorts out a laugh as she realizes what this is about. She takes his hand, and only with his help can she walk steadily enough to take her cloak. Sevro takes it from Clown and drapes it around her bare shoulders. Their eyes meet and linger for a moment before they move to the side so Holiday can be helped up by Pebble to gain her cloak. Ragnar helps me, draping mine over my shoulders.

"Welcome, brother and sisters, to the Howlers."

Together, the Howlers pitch back their heads and let loose a mighty howl. I join them, and find to my surprise that Victra does as well.

Hurling her head back in the darkness without reservations. Then suddenly the lights flare on. The howls die as we look around in confusion. Dancer trudges into the showers with Uncle Narol.

"The bloodyhell is this?" Narol asks, eying the cockroaches and the remains of the snake and the bottles. The Howlers look at the ludicrousness of one another awkwardly.

"We're performing a secret occult ritual," Sevro says. "And you are interrupting, subordinate."

"Right," Narol says, nodding, a little disturbed. "Sorry, sir."

"One of our Pinks stole a datapad from a Bonerider in Agea," Dancer says to Sevro, not amused by the display. "We found out who he is."

"No shit?" Sevro says. "Was I right?"

"Who?" I ask, drunkenly. "Who are you talking about?"

"The Jackal's silent partner," Dancer says. "It's Quicksilver. You were right, Sevro. Our agents say he's at his corporate headquarters on Phobos, but he won't be for long. He's bound for Luna in two days. We won't be able to touch him there."

"So Operation Black Market is a go," Sevro says.

"It's a go," Dancer admits reluctantly.

Sevro pumps his fist in the air. "Hell, yeah. You heard the man, Howlers. Get scrubbed. Get sober. Get fed. We've got a Silver to kidnap and an economy to crash." He looks at me with a wild grin on his face. "It's gonna be a hell of a day. A hell of a day."

14

||||||||||||||||||||||||

THE VAMPIRE MOON

*P*hobos means fear. In myth, he was the offspring of Aphrodite and Ares, the child of love and war. It's a fitting name for the larger of Mars's moons.

Formed long before the age of man, when a meteorite struck father Mars and flung debris into orbit, the oblong moon floated like a cast-off corpse, dead and abandoned for a billion years. Now it is the Hive teeming with the parasitic life that pumps blood into the veins of the Gold empire. Swarms of tiny, fat-bodied cargo ships rise from Mars's surface to funnel into the two huge gray docks that encircle the moon. There, they transfer the bounty of Mars to the kilometer-long cosmos-Haulers that will bear the treasure along the great Julii-Agos trade routes to the Rim or, more likely, to the Core, where hungry Luna waits to be fed.

The barren rock of Phobos has been carved hollow by man and wreathed with metal. With a radius of only twelve kilometers at its widest, the moon is ringed by two huge dockyards, which run perpendicular to each other. They're dark metal with white glyphs and blinking red lights for docking ships. They slither with the movement of magnetic trams and cargo vessels. Beneath the dockyards, and at times rising around them in the form of spiked towers, is the Hive—a jigsaw city formed not by neoclassical Gold ideals, but by raw economics without the confines of gravity. Six centuries' worth of buildings perforate Phobos. It is the largest pincushion man has ever built. And the disparity of wealth between the inhabitants of the Needles, the tips of the buildings, and the Hollow inside the moon's rock, borders on hilarious.

"Looks larger when you're not on the bridge of a torchShip," Victra drawls from behind me. "Being disenfranchised is so damn tedious."

I feel her pain. The last time I saw Phobos was before the Lion's Rain. Then I had an armada at my back, Mustang and the Jackal at my side, and thousands of Peerless Scarred at my command. Enough firepower to make a planet tremble. Now I'm skulking in the shadows in a rickety cargo hauler so old it doesn't even have an artificial gravity generator, accompanied only by Victra, a crew of three Sons gas haulers, and a small team of Howlers in the cargo bay. And this time I'm taking orders, not giving them. My tongue plays over the suicide tooth they put in my back right molar after the Howler initiation. All the Howlers have them now. Better than being taken alive, Sevro said. I have to agree with him. Still. Feels strange.

In the aftermath of my escape, the Jackal initiated an immediate moratorium on all flights leaving Mars for orbit. He suspected the Sons would make a desperate bid to get me off planet. Fortunately, Sevro isn't a fool. If he had been, I'd likely be in the Jackal's hands. Ultimately, not even the ArchGovernor of Mars could ground all commerce for long, and so his moratorium was short-lived. But the shock waves it sent through the market were staggering. Billions of credits lost every minute the helium-3 did not flow. Sevro found it rather inspiring.

"How much of it does Quicksilver own?" I ask.

Victra pulls herself beside me in the null gravity. Her jagged hair floats around her head like a white crown. It's been bleached and her eyes have been blackened with contacts. Easier for Obsidians to move about the rougher ends of the Moon than it would be without the disguise, and being one of the largest Howlers, she hardly could pass for any other Color.

"Hard to guess," she says. "Silver ownership is a tricky thing, in the end. The man has so many dummy corporations and off-grid bank accounts I doubt even the Sovereign knows how large his portfolio is."

"Or who is in it. If the rumors of him owning Golds are true . . ."

"They are." Victra shrugs, which tips her backward. "He's got his fingers everywhere. One of the only men too rich to kill, according to Mother."

"Is he richer than she was? Than you are?"

"Were," she corrects, shakes her head. "He knew better than that." There's a pause. "But maybe."

My eyes seek the Silver winged-heel icon that is stamped on the greatest of Phobos's towers, a three-kilometer-long double helix of steel and glass tipped with a silver crescent. How many Gold eyes look on it with jealousy? How many more must he own or bribe to protect him from all the rest? Perhaps just one. Crucial to the Jackal's rise was his silent partner. A man who helped him secretly gain control of the media and telecommunications industries. For the longest time I thought that partner was Victra or her mother and he closed the loop in the garden. But it seems the Jackal's greatest ally is alive and prospering. For now.

"Thirty million people," I whisper. "Incredible."

I can feel her eyes on me. "You don't agree with Sevro's plan, do you?"

My thumb picks at a wad of pink gum stuck to the rusted bulkhead. Kidnapping Quicksilver will get us intel and access to vast weapons factories, but Sevro's play against the economy is more concerning. "Sevro kept the Sons alive. I didn't. So I'll follow his lead."

"Mhm." She eyes me skeptically. "I wonder when you started believing grit and vision were the same thing."

"*Oy, shitheads*"—Sevro squawks over the com unit in my ear—"*if you're done sightseeing or humping or whatever the hell you're doin', it's time to tuck in.*"

||||||||||||

Half an hour later, Victra and I huddle together with the Howlers in one of the helium-3 containers stacked in the back of our transport. We can feel the ship reverberate beyond the container as it links its magnetic coupling to the docks' ringed surface. Beyond the ship's hull, Oranges will be floating in mechanized suits, waiting to steer the weightless cargo containers onto magnetic trams that will in turn take them to the cosmosHaulers awaiting the journey to Jupiter. There they will resupply Roque's fleet in his war effort against Mustang and the Moon Lords.

But before the containers are transported, Copper and Gray inspectors will come to examine them. They'll be bribed by our Blues into counting forty-nine containers instead of fifty. Then an Orange bribed by our contact will lose the container we're in, a common practice for the smuggling of illegal drugs or untaxed goods. He'll deposit it in a lower-level berth for machine parts, whereupon our Sons contact will meet us and escort us to our safe house. At least, that's the plan. But for now we wait.

Eventually gravity returns, signaling we're in the hangar. Our container settles on the floor with a thud. We steady ourselves against helium-3 drums. Voices drift beyond the metal walls of the container. The hauler beeps as it decouples from us and returns out the pulse-Field to space. Then silence. I don't like it. My hand twists around the leather grip of my razor inside my jacket sleeve. I take a step forward toward the door. Victra follows. Sevro grabs my shoulder. "We wait for the contact."

"We don't even know the man," I say.

"Dancer vouched for him." He snaps his fingers at me to return to my place. "We wait."

I notice the others listening, so I nod and shut my mouth. It's ten minutes later that we hear a solitary pair of feet click against the deck outside. The lock thuds back on the container doors, and dim light seeps in as they part to reveal a clean-cut, goateed Red with a toothpick in his mouth. Half a head shorter than Sevro, he clicks his eyes over each of us in turn. One eyebrow climbing upward when he sees

Ragnar. The other follows when he looks down the muzzle of Sevro's scorcher. Somehow he doesn't step back. Man's got a spine in him.

"What can never die?" Sevro growls in his best Obsidian accent.

"The fungus under Ares's sack." The man smiles and glances over his shoulder. "Mind lowerin' the nasty? We gotta move, now. Borrowed this dock from the Syndicate. 'Cept they don't really know about it, so unless you wanna tangle with some professional uglies, we gotta box the jabber and waddle on." He claps his hands. "'Now' means now."

Our contact goes by the name of Rollo. Stringy and wry, with sparkling, bright eyes and an easy way with the women, even though he brings up his wife, the most beautiful woman who has apparently ever walked the surface of Mars, at least twice a minute. He also hasn't seen her in eight years. He's spent that time on the Hive as a welder on the space towers. Not technically a slave like the Reds in the mines, he and his are contract labor. Wage slaves who work fourteen-hour days, six days a week, suspended between the megalithic towers that puncture the Hive, welding metal and praying they never suffer a workplace injury. Get an injury, you can't earn. Can't earn, you don't eat.

"Mighty full of himself," I overhear Sevro saying under his breath to Victra in the middle of the pack as Rollo leads on.

"I rather like his goatee," Victra says.

"The Blues call this place the Hive," Rollo's saying as we head toward a graffiti-smeared tram in a derelict maintenance level. Smells like grease, rust, and old piss. Homeless vagrants festoon the floors of the shadowy metal halls. Twitching bundles of blankets and rags that Rollo sidesteps without looking, though his hand never leaves the worn plastic hilt of his scorcher. "Might be to them. They got schools, homes here. Little airhead communes, sects, to be technic, where they learn to fly and sync up with the computers. But let me learn you what this place really is: just a grinder. Men come in. Towers go up." He nods his head at the ground. "Meat goes out."

The only signs of life from the vagrants on the floor are little gouts of breath that plume up from their lumpy rags like steam from the cracks in a lava field. I shiver beneath my gray jacket and adjust the bag of gear over my shoulder. It's freezing on this level. Old insulation, probably. Pebble blows a cloud of steam through her nostrils as she pushes one of our gear carts, looking sadly left and right at the vagrants. Less empathetic, Victra guides the cart from the front, nudging a vagrant out of the way with her boot. The man hisses and looks up at her, and up, and up, till he sees all 2.1 meters of annoyed killer. He skitters to the side, breathing through his teeth. Neither Ragnar nor Rollo seems to notice the cold.

Sons of Ares wait for us on the run-down tram platform and inside the tram itself. Most are Red, but there's a good amount of Oranges and a Green and Blue in the mix. They cradle a motley collection of old scorchers and strafe the other hallways that lead to the platform with edgy eyes that can't help but jump our direction and wonder just who the hell we are. I'm thankful more than ever for the Obsidian contacts and prosthetics.

"Expecting trouble?" Sevro asks, eying the weapons in the Sons' hands.

"Grays been sweeping down here last couple months. Not hollow-ass tinpots from the local precinct, but knotty bastards. Legionnaires. Even some Thirteenth mixed in with Tenth and Fifth." He lowers his voice. "We had a nasty month, where they shred us up real bloody-damn bad. Took our headquarters in the Hollows, stuck Syndicate toughs on us too. Paid to hunt their own. Most of us had to go to ground, hiding in secondary safe houses. Main body of Sons have been helping the Red rebels on the station, obviously, but our special ops hasn't flexed muscle till today. We didn't wanna take chances. Ya know? Ares said you lot got important business. . . ."

"Ares is wise," Sevro says dismissively.

"And a drama queen," Victra adds.

At the door to the tram, Ragnar hesitates, eyes lingering on an antiterrorism poster pasted onto a concrete support column in the tram's waiting area. "See something, say something," it reads, showing a pale Red with evil crimson eyes and the stereotypical tattered dress of a miner skulking near a door that says "restricted access."

Can't see the rest. It's covered in rebel graffiti. But then I realize Ragnar's not looking at the poster, but at the man I didn't even notice
who's crumpled on the ground beneath it. His hood's up. Left leg is an
ancient mech replacement. A crusted brown bandage covers half his
face. There's a puff. The release of pressurized gas. And the man leans
back from us, shivering, and smiling with perfectly black teeth. A
plastic stim cartridge clatters to the floor. Tar dust.

"Why do you not help these people?" Ragnar asks.

"Help them with what?" Rollo asks. He sees the empathy on Ragnar's face and doesn't really know how to answer. "Brother, we barely
got enough for flesh and kin. No good sharing with that lot, ya
know?"

"But that one is Red. They are your family . . ."

Rollo frowns at the bare truth.

"Save the pity, Ragnar," Victra says. "That's Syndicate crank he's
puffing. Most of them would slit your throat for an afternoon high.
They're empty flesh."

"Empty what?" I say, turning back to her.

She's caught off guard by the sharpness of my tone, but she's loath
to back off. So she doubles down instinctively. "Empty flesh, darling,"
she repeats. "Part of being human is having dignity. They don't. They
carved it out themselves. That was their choice, not Golds'. Even if
it's easy to blame them for everything. So why should they deserve my
pity?"

"Because not everyone is you. Or had your birth."

She doesn't reply. Rollo clears his throat, skeptical now about our
disguises. "Lady's right about the slit-your-throat part. Most of 'em
were imported laborers. Like me. Not counting the wife, I've got plus
three in New Thebes that I send money back to, but I can't go home
till my contract's up. Got four years left. These slags have given up on
tryin' to get back."

"Four years?" Victra asks dubiously. "You said you were already
here eight."

"Gotta pay for my transit."

She stares at him quizzically.

"Company doesn't cover it. Shoulda read the fine print. Sure, it was my choice to come up here." He nods to the vagrants. "Was theirs too. But when the only other choice is starving." He shrugs as if we all know the answer. "These slags just got unlucky on the job. Lost legs. Arms. Company doesn't cover prosthetics, least not decent ones. . . ."

"What about Carvers?" I ask.

He scoffs. "And who the hell do you know that can afford flesh work?"

I didn't even think of the cost. Reminds me of how distant I am from so many of the people I claim to fight for. Here's a Red, one of my own more or less, and I don't even know what type of food is popular in his culture.

"What company do you work for?" Victra asks.

"Why, Julii Industries, of course."

I watch the metal jungle pass outside the dirty duroglass window as the tram pulls away from the station. Victra sits down next to me, a troubled look on her face. But I'm a world away from her, my friends. Lost in memory. I've been to the Hive before with ArchGovernor Augustus and Mustang. He brought the lancers to meet with Society economic ministers to discuss modernizing the moon's infrastructure. After the meetings she and I snuck away to the moon's famous aquarium. I'd rented it out at absurd cost and arranged a meal and wine to be served to us in front of the orca tank. Mustang always liked natural creatures more than Carved ones.

I've traded fifty-year-old wines and Pink valets for a grimmer world with rusting bones and rebel thugs. This is the real world. Not the dream the Golds live in. Today I feel the silent screams of a civilization that has been stepped on for hundreds of years.

Our path skirts around the edges of the Hollows, the center of the moon where the latticework of cage slum apartments festers without gravity. To go there would be to risk falling into the middle of the Syndicate street war against the Sons of Ares. And to go any higher into the midColor levels would be to risk Society marines and their security infrastructure of cameras and holoScanners.

Instead, we pass through the hinterlands of maintenance levels between the Hollows and the Needles, where Reds and Oranges keep the moon running. Our tram, driven by a Sons sympathizer, speeds through its stops. The faces of waiting workers blur together as we pass. A pastiche of eyes. But faces all gray. Not the color of metal, but the color of old ash in a campfire. Ash faces. Ash clothes. Ash lives.

But as the tunnel swallows our tram, color erupts around us. Graffiti and years of rage bleeding out from the ribbed and cracking walls of its once gray throat. Profanity in fifteen dialects. Golds ripped open in a dozen dark ways. And to the right of a crude sketch of a reaper's scythe decapitating Octavia au Lune is an image of Eo hanging from the gallows in digital paint, hair aflame, "Break the Chains" written diagonally. It's a single glowing flower among the weeds of hate. A knot forms in my throat.

Half an hour after we set out, our tram grinds to a halt outside a deserted lowColor industrial hub where thousands of workers should diverge from their early-morning commute from the Stacks to attend their functions. But now it's still as a cemetery. Trash litters the metal floors. HoloCans still flash with the Society's news programs. A cup sits on a table in a café, steam still rising off the top of the beverage. The Sons have cleared the way only a few minutes before. Shows the extent of their influence here.

When we leave, life will return to the place. But after we plant the bombs we've brought with us? After we destroy the manufacturing, won't all the men and women we intend to help be just as unemployed as those poor creatures in the tram station? If work is their reason for being, what happens when we take it away? I'd voice my concerns to Sevro, but he's a driven arrow. As dogmatic as I once was. And to question him aloud seems a betrayal of our friendship. He's always trusted me blindly. So am I the worse friend for having doubts in him?

We pass through several gravLifts into a garage for garbage disposal haulers, also owned by Julii Industries. I catch Victra wiping dirt off the family crest on one of the doors. The speared sun is worn and faded. The few dozen Red and Orange workers of the facility pretend not to notice our group as we file into one of the hauler bays. Inside, at the base of two huge haulers, we find a small army of Sons of Ares. More than six hundred.

They're not soldiers. Not like us. Most are men, but there's a scattering of women, mostly younger Reds and Oranges forced to migrate here for work to feed Mars-side families. Their weapons are shoddy. Some stand. Other are seated, turning from conversations to see our pack of Obsidian killers stalking across the metal deck, carrying bags of gear and pushing two mysterious carts. A small sadness grows in me. Whatever they do, wherever they go, their lives will be stained by this day. If it were my duty to address them, I'd warn them the burden they're taking on, the evil they'll be letting into their lives. I'd say it's nicer to hear about glorious victories in war than to witness them. Than to feel the weird unreality of lying in bed every morning knowing you've killed a man, knowing a friend is gone.

But I say nothing. My place now is beside Ragnar and Victra, behind Sevro as he spits out his gum and stalks forward, giving me a wink and an elbow in the side, to stand in front of the small army. His army. He's tiny for an Obsidian male, but still scarred and tattooed and terrifying to this company of small-handed garbage men and hunched tower welders. He tilts his head forward, eyes smoldering behind his black contacts. Wolf tattoos looking evil against his pale skin in the industrial light.

"Greetings, grease monkeys." His voice rumbles, low and predatory. "You might be wondering why Ares has sent a pack of hardcore nasties like us to this tin shithole." The Sons look to one another nervously. "We aren't here to cuddle. We aren't here to inspire you or give long-ass speeches like the bloodydamn Sovereign." He snaps his fingers. Pebble and Clown wheel the carts forward and unlatch the tops. The hinges squeal open to reveal mining explosives. "We're here to blow shit up." He throws open his arms and cackles. "Any questions?"

15

||||||||||||||||||||||||

THE HUNT

I float in the back of the trash collector with the Howlers. It's dark. The night vision of my optics shows the garbage that orbits us in shadowy green. Banana peels. Toy packaging. Coffee grounds. Victra makes a gagging sound over the com as toilet paper sticks to her face. Her mask is a demonHelm. Like mine, it's pupil black and shaped subtly like a screaming demon face. Fitchner managed to steal them from Luna's armories for the Sons more than a year back. With them, we can see most spectrums, amplify sound, track one another's coordinates, access maps, and communicate silently. My friends around me are in all black. We wear no mechanized armor, only thin scarabSkin over our bodies that will stop knives and occasional projectiles. We have no gravBoots or pulseArmor. Nothing that will slow us, cause noise, or trip sensors. We wear oxygen tanks with air enough for forty minutes. I finish adjusting Ragnar's harness and look to my datapad. The two Reds crewing the old trash collector are giving us a countdown. When it reaches one, Sevro says, *"Tuck your sacks and pop your cloaks."*

I activate my ghostCloak and the world warps, distorted by the cloak. It's like looking through refracted, dirty water, and I already feel the battery pack heating up against my tailbone. The cloak's good for short bursts. But it burns up small batteries like the ones we pack and needs time to cool and recharge. I grope for Sevro and Victra's hands, managing to grasp them in time. The rest partner up as well. I don't remember feeling so frightened before the Iron Rain. Was I braver then? Maybe just more naïve.

"Hold tight. We're in for some chop," Sevro says. *"Popping top in three . . . two . . ."* I tighten my grip on his hand. *". . . one."*

The collector's door retracts silently, bathing us in the amber light of a holoDisplay screen on a nearby skyscraper. There's a burst of air and my world spins as the trash collector ejects its load of garbage from the back of its hold. We're like seed chaff thrown into the city. Spinning with debris through a kaleidoscope world of towers and advertisements. Hundreds of ships funneling along avenues. All a flashing, liquid blur. We continue to spin head over heel to mask our signatures.

Over the com, I hear the grousing of a Blue traffic controller, annoyed at the spilled trash. Soon there's a company Copper on the line threatening to fire the incompetent drivers. But it's what I don't hear that makes me smile. The police channels drone on their usual slant, reporting a Syndicate airjacking in the Hive, a grisly murder in the ancient art museum near the Park Plaza, a datacenter robbery in the Banking Cluster. They haven't seen us amidst the debris.

We slow our spin gradually using small thrusters in our helmets. Bursts of air bring us to a steady drift. Silent in the vacuum. We're on target. Along with the rest of the trash, we're about to impact on the side of a steel tower. Has to be a clean landing. Victra curses as we drift closer, closer. My fingers tremble. Don't bounce. Don't bounce.

"Release," Sevro orders.

I pull my hands from his and Victra's, and the three of us impact jarringly against the steel. The trash around us bounds off the metal, cartwheeling backward at odd angles. Sevro and Victra stick, compliments of the magnets in their gloves, but a piece of debris impacting in front of me bounces off the steel and hits me in the thigh, altering my trajectory. Tipping me sideways, hands windmilling for a grip, which causes me to spin.

My feet hit first and I bounce backward toward space, cursing. "Sevro!" I shout.

"Victra. Get him."

A hand grabs my foot, jerking me to a halt. I look down and see a warped invisible form grasping my leg. Victra. Carefully, she pulls my weightless body back to the wall so I can clamp my own magnets onto the steel. Spots race across my vision. The city is all around us. It's dreadful in its silence, in its colors, in its inhuman metal landscape. It feels more like an ancient alien artifact than a place for humans.

"Slow it down." Victra's voice crackles in my helmet. *"Darrow. You're hyperventilating. Breathe with me. In. Out. In . . ."* I force my lungs to breathe in sync with her. The spots soon fade. I open my eyes, face inches from the steel.

"You shit your suit or something?" Sevro asks.

"I'm good," I say. "A little rusty."

"Ugh. Pun intended, I'm sure." Ragnar and the rest of the Howlers land thirty meters beneath us on the wall. Pebble waves up to me. *"Got three hundred meters to go. Let's climb, you pixies."*

Lights glow behind the glass of Quicksilver's double-helix towers. Connecting the double helixes are nearly two hundred levels of offices. I can make out shapes moving inside at computer terminals. I zoom in with my optics to watch the stock traders sitting in their offices, their assistants moving to and fro, analysts signaling furiously on holographic trading boards that communicate with the markets on Luna. Silvers, all. They remind me of industrious bees.

"Makes me miss the boys," Victra says. Takes me a moment to realize she's not talking about the Silvers. The last time she and I tried this tactic, Tactus and Roque were with us. We infiltrated Karnus's flagship from vacuum as he refueled at an asteroid base during the Academy's mock war. We cut through his hull with aims of kidnapping him to eliminate his team. But it was a trap and I narrowly escaped with the help of my friends, a broken arm my only reward for the gambit.

It takes us five minutes to climb from our landing place to the peak of the tower, where it becomes a large crescent. We don't go hand over hand, so climbing isn't the true term. The magnets in our gloves have fluctuating positive and negative currents that allow us to roll up the side of the tower like we have wheels in our palms. The toughest part of the ascent, or descent, or whatever you'd call it in the null grav, is the crescent slope at the extreme height or end of the tower. We have to cling to a narrow metal support beam that extends out among a ceiling of glass, much like the stem of a leaf. Beneath our bellies and through the glass lies Quicksilver's famous museum. And above us, just over the peak of Quicksilver's tower, hangs Mars.

My planet seems larger than space. Larger than anything ever could be. A world of billions of souls, of designer oceans, mountains, and more irrigable acres of dry land than Earth ever had. It's night on this side of the world. And you could never know that millions of kilometers of tunnels wind through the bones of the planet, that even as its surface glows with the lights of the Thousand Cities of Mars, there is a pulse unseen, a tide that is rising. But now it looks peaceful. War a distant, impossible thing. I wonder what a poet would say in this moment. What Roque would whisper into the air. Something about the calm before the storm. Or a heartbeat among the deep. But then there's a flash. It startles me. A spasm of light that flares white, then erodes into devilish neon as a mushroom grows in the planet's blackness.

"Do you see that?" I ask over the coms, blinking away the cigar burn the distant detonation made in my vision. Our coms crackle with curses as the others turn to see.

"*Shit,*" Sevro murmurs. "*New Thebes?*"

"No," Pebble answers. "*Farther north. That's the Aventine Peninsula. So it's probably Cyprion. Last intel said the Red Legion was moving toward the city.*"

Then comes another flash. And the seven of us hunker motionless on the crest of the building, watching as a second nuclear bomb detonates a thumb's distance away from the first.

"Bloodydamn. Is it us or them?" I ask. "Sevro!"

"*I don't know,*" Sevro says impatiently.

"*You don't know?*" Victra asks.

How could he not know? I want to shout. But I grasp the answer, because Dancer's words now haunt me. "Sevro's not running this war," he told me, weeks ago after another failed Howler mission. "He's just a man pouring gas on the fire." Maybe I didn't understand how far gone this war is, how far reaching the chaos has become.

Could I have been wrong to trust him so blindly? I watch his expressionless mask. The skin of his armor drinks in the colors of the city around, reflecting nothing. An abyss for light. He turns slowly from the explosion and begins to climb again. Already moving on.

"*HoloNews has it,*" Pebble says. "*Fast. They say Red Legion used nukes against Gold forces near Cyprion. Least that's the story.*"

"*Bloodydamn liars,*" Clown snaps. "*Another bait and switch.*"

"*Where would Red Legion get nukes?*" Victra asks. Harmony would use them if she had any. But I wager it was Gold using the bombs on Red Legion instead.

"*Doesn't mean shit to us now. Lock it up,*" Sevro says. "*Still got to do what we came to do. Get your asses in gear.*" Numbly, we obey. When we reach our entry zone on the crescent of the double helix tower, rehearsed routine takes over. I pull a small acid flask from the pack on Victra's back. Sevro releases a nanocam no larger than my fingernail into the air, where it hovers above the glass, scanning for life inside the museum. There is none—not a surprise at 03:00. He pulls out a pulseGenerator and waits for Pebble to finish her work on her datapad.

"*What's what, Pebble?*" he asks impatiently.

"*Codes worked. I'm in the system,*" she says. "*Just have to find the right zone. There it is. Laser grid is . . . down. Thermal cams are . . . frozen. Heartbeat sensors are . . . off. Congratulations, everyone. We're officially ghosts! So long as no one manually pulls an alarm.*"

Sevro activates the pulseGenerator and a faint iridescent bubble blooms around us, creating a seal, so that the vacuum of space doesn't invade the building with us. Would be a quick way to be discovered. I put a small suction cup on the center of the glass then open the acid container and apply the foam to the window in a two-meter-by-two-meter box around the suction cup. The acid bubbles as it eats through the glass, creating an opening. With a small rush of air from the building into our pulseField, the glass pane pops up where Victra grabs it to keep it from flying into space.

"*Rags first,*" Sevro says. It's a hundred meters to the museum floor below.

Ragnar clamps a rappelling winch to the edge of the glass and clips his harness to the magnetic wire. Pulling his razor out, he reactivates his ghostCloak and pushes through the hole. It's disturbing to the senses seeing his near-invisible form accelerate down to the floor, gripped by the skyhook's artificial gravity while I'm still floating. He looks a demon made of the heat that shimmers above the desert on a summer day.

"*Clear.*"

Sevro follows. "*Break an arm,*" Victra says, pushing me into the hole after him. I float forward, then feel myself gripped by gravity as I cross the boundary into the room. I slide down the wire, picking up speed. My stomach lurches at the sudden influx of weight, food sloshing around. I land hard on the ground, almost twisting my ankle as I pull up my silenced scorcher and search for contacts. The rest of the Howlers land behind me. We crouch back to back in the grand hall. The floor is gray marble. The length of the hall is impossible to gauge, because it curves according to the crescent, bowing upward and out of sight, playing with gravity and giving me a sense of vertigo. Metal relics tower around us. Old rockets from man's Pioneer Age. The coat of arms of the Luna Company marks the hull of a gray probe near Ragnar. It looks decidedly like Octavia au Lune's house crest.

"*So this is what it's like to feel fat,*" Sevro says with a grunt as he takes a small jump in the heavy gravity. "*Disgusting.*"

"*Quicksilver's from Earth,*" Victra says. "*Jacks it up even higher when he's negotiating with anyone from low-grav birthplaces.*"

It's three times what I'm used to on Mars, eight times what they prefer on Io or Europa, but in rebuilding my body, Mickey jacked the simulators up to twice Earth's gravity. It's an unpleasant sensation weighing nearly eight hundred pounds, but it works the muscles something horrible.

We strip our oxygen tanks and stow them in the engine rim of an old space shuttle painted with the flag of pre-empire America. So we're left with our small packs, scarabSkin, demonHelms, and weapons. Sevro pulls up Victra's crude maps of the tower's interior and asks Pebble if she's found Quicksilver yet.

"I can't. It's odd. The cameras are off in the top two levels. Same with biometric readers. Can't pinpoint him like we planned."

"Off?" I ask.

"Maybe he's having an orgy or wankin' off and doesn't want his Security to see." Sevro grunts with a shrug. *"Either way, he's hiding something, so that's where we're headed."*

I cue Sevro's personal line so the others can't hear us. *"We can't wander around looking for him. If we're caught in the halls without leverage—"*

"We won't wander." He cuts me off before addressing the Howlers. *"Cloaks on, ladies. Razors and silenced scorchers. PulseFists only if shit gets dirty."* He ripples transparent. *"Howlers, on me."*

We slink from the museum into a maze of otherworldly hallways, following Sevro's lead. Floors of black marble. Walls of glass. Ten-meter-high ceilings made from pulseFields, which look into aquariums where vibrant reefs of coral stretch like fungal tentacles. Reptilian mermaids one foot long with humanoid faces, gray skin, and skulls shaped like crowns swim through a kingdom of scalding blue and violent orange. Hateful little crow eyes glare down at us as they pass.

The walls are moodGlass and pulse with subtle alternating colors. Now heartbeats of magenta, soon rippling curtains of cobalt-silver. It's dreamlike. Amidst the maze are little alcoves. Miniature art galleries showcasing works of contemporary dot holographs and twenty-first century AD ostentaciousism instead of the reserved neoclassical Romanism so in vogue with Peerless Scarred. Recharging our battery packs to our ghostCloaks, we duck into a gallery where lurks a gaudy purple metallic dog shaped like a balloon animal.

Victra sighs. *"Goryhell. Man's got the taste of a tabloid socialite."*

Ragnar cocks his head at the dog. ***"What is it?"***

"Art," Victra says. *"Supposedly."*

The tone of condescension Victra strikes intrigues me, as does the building. It pulses with artifice. The art, the walls, the mermaids, all so on the nose of what the Peerless Scarred would expect of a newly moneyed Silver. Quicksilver must know Gold psychology intimately in order to have been allowed to grow so wealthy. So I wonder, is this extravagance all something far more clever? A mask so obvious and easy to accept that no one would ever think to look beneath it? Quicksilver, for all his reputation, has never been called stupid. So perhaps this tawdry dreamscape isn't for him. It's for his guests.

Which makes me think something here is amiss as we reach an unlit atrium with unpolished sandstone floors perforated by pink jasmine trees and slink across the floor in a V formation toward the set of double doors that leads to Quicksilver's bedroom suite. Cloaks deactivated so we can better see. Razors rigid and held out, metal drifting centimeters above the sandstone.

This isn't a home. It's a stage. Made to manipulate. Sinister in the cold calculation with which it was constructed. I don't like it. I key Sevro's frequency again. "Something's wrong here. Where are the servants? The guards?"

"Maybe he likes his privacy . . ."

"I think it's a trap."

"A trap? Your head or your gut talkin'?"

"My gut."

He's quiet for a breath, and I wonder if he's speaking to someone else on the other line. Maybe he's speaking to all of them. *"What's your rec?"*

"Pull back. Assess the situation to see. . . ."

"Pull back?" He snaps the question out. *"For all we know, they just dropped nukes on our people. We need this."* I try to interrupt, but he steamrolls me. *"Shit, I've run thirteen ops just to get intel on this Silvery asshole. We leave now, that's all slagged. They'll know we were here. We won't have this chance again. He's the key to getting the Jackal. You gotta trust me, Reap. Do you?"*

I bite back a curse and cut the signal short, not sure if I'm angry with him or with myself, or because I know the Jackal removed the spark that made me feel different. Every opinion I have feeble, and malleable to others. Because I know, deep down, beneath the intimidating scarabSkin, beneath the demon mask, is a callow little boy who cried because he was scared of being alone in the dark.

Purple light suddenly floods the room as a luxury vessel cruises past the wall of windows at our backs. We hastily line up to either side of the door to Quicksilver's suite, preparing to breach. I watch the vessel drift along through my black optics. Lights pulse on one of its decks as several hundred Pixies writhe to some Etrurian club beat that's all the rage on far-off Luna, as if a war didn't wage on the planet beneath this moon. As if we didn't move to rupture their way of life. They'll drink champagne from Earth in clothes made on Venus in ships fueled by Mars. And they'll laugh and consume and screw and face no consequences. So many little locusts. I feel Sevro's righteous wrath burn in me.

Suffering isn't real to them. War isn't real. It's just a three-letter word for other people that they see in the digital newsfeeds. Just a stream of uncomfortable images they skip past. A whole business of weapons and arms and ships and hierarchies they don't even notice, all to shield these fools from the true agony of what it means to be human. Soon they'll know.

And on their deathbeds, they'll remember tonight. Who they were with. What they were doing when that three-letter word gripped them and never let go. This pleasure cruise, this hideous decadence is the last gasp of the Golden Age.

And what a pathetic gasp it is.

"Of course I trust you," I say, tightening my grip on my razor. Ragnar's watching us, even though he can't hear our signal. Victra's waiting to breach the door.

The light fades, and the ship disappears into the cityscape. I'm surprised to realize I don't feel satisfaction in knowing what's about to happen. In knowing their age will fall. Neither does it bring joy to think of all the lights in all the cities across this empire of man dimming, or all the ships slowing, or all the brilliant Golds fading as their buildings rust and crumble. Would that I could hear Mustang's take on this plan. Before, I've missed her lips, her scent, but now I miss the comfort that comes knowing her mind is aligned with mine. When I was with her, I did not feel so alone. She'd probably chastise us for focusing on breaking rather than building.

Why do I feel this way now? I'm surrounded by friends, striking at

Gold as I have always wished. Yet something itches in the back of my brain. Like eyes watch me. Whatever Sevro says, something is wrong here. Not just in this building, but with his plan. Is this how I would have done it? How Fitchner would have done it? If it succeeds, what do we usher in after the dust has settled and the helium no longer flows? A dark age? Sevro is a force unto himself. His rage a thing to move mountains.

I was once like that. And look what that got me.

"Kill his guards. Stun the Pinks. Smash, grab, and go," Sevro is saying to his Howlers. My hand tightens on my blade. He gives the signal, and Ragnar and Victra slip through the doors. The rest of us follow into the dark.

16

|||||||||||||||||||||||||

PARAMOUR

The lights are off. It's tomb silent. The front room empty. An electric-green jellyfish floats in a tank on a table, casting weird shadows. We move through to the bedroom, smashing through the gold filigreed doors. I guard the door with Pebble, crouching on a knee, silenced railgun cradled in my hands, sheathing my razor on my arm. Behind us, a man sleeps in a four-poster bed. Ragnar grabs him by the foot and jerks him out. Clad in expensive sleepwear, he sprawls onto the floor. Waking midair and screaming silently into Ragnar's hand.

"*Shit. It's not him,*" Victra says behind me. "*It's a Pink.*" I glance back. Ragnar kneels over the Pink, blocking him from my view.

Sevro hits the bedpost, cracking it. "*It's three in the morning. Where the hell is he?*"

"*It is four p.m. market time on Luna,*" Victra says. "*Maybe he's in his office? Ask the slave.*"

"*Where is your master?*" Sevro's mask makes his voice warble like a steel cable struck by an iron rod. I keep my eyes trained on the living room until the Pink's whimper makes me look back. Sevro's got his knee in the man's groin. "*Pretty pajamas, boyo. Wanna see what they look like in red?*"

I flinch at the coldness in this voice. Knowing the tone all too well. Hearing it from the Jackal as he tortured me in Attica.

"Where is your master?" Sevro twists his knee. The Pink wails in pain, but still refuses to answer. The Howlers watch the torture in silence, bent, faceless stains in the dark room. There's no discussion. No moral question at play, I know they've done this before. I feel dirty in the realization, in hearing the Pink sobbing on the ground. This is more a part of war than trumpets or starships. Quiet, unremembered moments of cruelty.

"I don't know," he says. "I don't know."

The voice. I remember that voice from my past. I rush from my post at the door and join Sevro, pulling him off of the Pink. Because I know the man and his gentle features. His long, angular nose, rose-quartz eyes, and dark honey skin. He's as responsible for making me what I am as Mickey ever was. It's Matteo. Beautiful and fragile, now gasping on the ground, arm broken. Bleeding from his mouth, holding his groin where Sevro beat him.

"The hell's your damage?" Sevro snarls at me.

"I know him!" I say.

"What?"

Taking advantage of my distraction, and seeing nothing but the black demon visages of our helms, Matteo lunges for a datapad sitting on the bed stand. Sevro's faster. With a meaty thud the hardest bone density in the species of man meets the softest. Sevro's fist shatters Matteo's fragile jaw. He gags and falls convulsing to the floor, eyes rolling back into his head. I watch in a haze, the violence seeming unreal and yet so cold and primitive and easy. Just muscle and bone moving the way it shouldn't. I find myself reaching for Matteo, falling over his twitching body, shoving Sevro back.

"Don't touch him!" Matteo's been knocked unconscious, mercifully. I can't tell if he has spinal damage or brain trauma. I touch the gentle curls of his now-dusky hair. It has a blue sheen to it. His hand's clutched tight like a child's, a slender silver band on his ring finger. Where has he been this whole time? Why is he here? "I know him," I whisper.

Ragnar's bending beside him protectively, though there's nothing we can do here for Matteo. Clown tosses the datapad to Sevro. *"Panic switch."*

"What do you mean you know him?" Sevro asks.

"He's a Son of Ares," I say, in a daze. "Or he was. He was one of my teachers before the Institute. He taught me Aureate culture."

"Goryhell," Screwface mutters.

Victra toes his wrist where little flowers embellish his pink Sigils. *"He's a Rose of the Garden. Like Theodora."* She glances to Ragnar. *"He costs as much as you, Stained."*

"You're sure it's the same man?" Sevro asks me.

"Of course I'm bloodydamn sure. His name is Matteo."

"Then why is he here?" Ragnar asks.

"Doesn't look like a captive," Victra says. *"Those are expensive pajamas. He's probably a paramour. Quicksilver's not known for celibacy, after all."*

"He must have turned," Sevro says harshly.

"Or he was on an assignment for your father," I say.

"Then why didn't he contact us? He's defected. Means Quicksilver has infiltrated the Sons." Sevro spins to look at the door. *"Shit. He could know about Tinos. He could know about this bloodydamn raid."*

My mind races. Did Ares send Matteo here? Or did Matteo leave a sinking ship? Maybe Matteo told them about me before Harmony did. . . . It's a knife in the gut thinking that. I didn't know him long, but I cared for him. He was a kind person, and there's so few of those left. Now look what we've done to him.

"We should get the hell out of here," Clown is saying.

"Not without Quicksilver," Sevro replies.

"We don't know where Quicksilver is," I say. "There's more to this. We have to wait for Matteo to wake up. Someone have a stimshot?"

"Dose would kill him," Victra says. *"Pink circulatory system can't handle military crank."*

"We don't have time for talking," Sevro barks. *"Can't risk being pinned in here. We move now."* I try to speak, but he rolls on, looking to Clown who is using Matteo's datapad. *"Clown, waddya got?"*

"I've got a food request on the internal server's kitchen subsection.

Looks like someone has ordered a whole host of mutton and jam sandwiches and coffee to room C19."

"*Reaper, what do you think?*" Ragnar asks.

"It could be a trap," I say. "We need to adjust—"

Victra laughs scornfully, cutting me off. "*Even if it is a trap, look who we're packing. We'll punch through that shit.*"

"*Bloodydamn right, Julii.*" Sevro moves toward the door. "*Screwface. Bring the Pink and stow him. Fangs out. Ragnar, Victra in front. Blood's comin'.*"

One level down, we meet our first security team. Half a dozen lurchers stand in front of large glass door that ripples like the surface of a pond. They wear black suits instead of military armor. Implants in the shape of silver heels stick out from the skin behind their left ears. There's more patrolling this level, but no servants. Several Grays in similar suits took a coffee cart into the room a few minutes earlier. Strange that they wouldn't use Pinks or Browns for delivering coffee. Security is tight. So whoever is in Quicksilver's office must be important. Or at least very paranoid.

"*We're flowing quick,*" Sevro says, leaning back around the hallway corner where we wait thirty meters from the group of Grays. "*Neutralize those shitheads, then breach fastlike.*"

"*We don't know who is in there,*" Clown says

"*And there's only one way to find out,*" Sevro barks. "*Go.*"

Ragnar and Victra go first around the corner, ghostCloaks bending the light. The rest of us follow at a dead sprint. One of the Grays squints down the hall at us. The implanted thermal optics in his irises throb red as they activate and see the heat radiating from our battery packs. "GhostCloaks!" he shouts. Six sets of practiced hands flow to scorchers. Far too late. Ragnar and Victra tear into them. Ragnar swings his razor, cutting off one's arm and severing the jugular of another. Blood sprays over the glass walls. Victra fires her silenced scorcher. Magnetically hurled slugs slam into two heads. I slide forward between falling bodies. Stick my razor through a man's rib cage. Feeling the pop and give of his heart. I retract my blade into whip form to free it. Let it stiffen again back to my slingBlade before the man drops.

The Grays haven't managed to fire a single shot. But one has pressed a button on his datapad, and the deep throbbing sound of the tower's alarm echoes down the hall. The walls pulse red, signaling an emergency. Sevro cuts the last man down.

"*Breach the room. Now!*" he shouts.

Something's wrong. I feel it in my gut, but Victra and Sevro are propelling this forward. And Ragnar's kicking in the door. Ever a slave to momentum, I plunge in after him.

Quicksilver's conference room is less flamboyant than the rooms above. Its ceiling is ten meters high. Its walls are of digital glass that swirls subtly with silver smoke. Two rows of marble pillars run parallel on either side of a giant onyx conference table with a dead white tree rising from its center. At the far end of the room, a huge viewing window looks out at the industry of the Hive. Regulus ag Sun, hailed from Mercury to Pluto as Quicksilver, richest man under the sun, stands before the window, mauling a glass of red wine with a fleshy hand.

He's bald. Forehead wrinkled as a washboard. Pugilist lips. Hunched simian shoulders leading to butcher fingers that sprout from the sleeves of a high-collared Venusian turquoise robe embroidered with apple trees. He's in his sixties. Skin bronzed with a marrow-deep tan. A small goatee and mustache accent his face in a vain attempt to give it shape, though it seems he's stayed away from Carvers for the most part. His feet are bare. But it's his three eyes that demand attention. Two are heavy-lidded and Silver. An earthy, efficient shade. The third is Gold and implanted in a simple silver ring the man wears on the middle finger of his fat right hand.

We've interrupted his meeting.

Nearly thirty Coppers and Silvers pack the room. They're formed into two parties and sit across from one another at a giant's onyx table littered with coffee cups, wine carafes, and datapads. A blue holo document floats in the air between the two factions, obviously the object of their attention until the door shattered inward. Now they push back from the table, most too stunned yet to feel fear, or to even see us as the Howlers enter the room in ghostCloaks. But it isn't just Coppers and Silvers at the table.

"*Oh, shit,*" Victra sputters.

Among the professional Colors rise six Golden knights in full pulseArmor. And I know them all. On the left, a dark-faced older man wearing the pure black armor of the Death Knight, on either side of him are pudgy-faced Moira—a Fury, sister of Aja—and good old Cassius au Bellona. To the right are Kavax au Telemanus, Daxo au Telemanus, and the girl who left me on my knees in the old mining tunnels of Mars nearly one year ago.

Mustang.

17

||||||||||||||||||||||||

KILLING GOLDS

"Hold your fire!" I shout, pushing down Victra's weapon, but Sevro's barking orders, and Victra brings her weapon back up. We form a staggered line with our pulseFists and scorchers aimed at the Golds. We hold fire because we need Quicksilver alive, and I know Sevro's as stunned as I to see Mustang, Cassius, and the Telemanuses here.

"On the ground or we waste you!" Sevro screams, voice inhuman and magnified by his demonHelm. The Howlers join him, filling the air with a harpy's chorus of commands. My blood pumps cold. The alarm throbs around the roaring voices. Not knowing what to do, I point my pulseFist at the most dangerous Gold in the room, Cassius, knowing what must be going through Sevro's mind as he sees his father's killer in the flesh. My helmet syncs with the weapon, to illuminate weak points in his armor, but my eyes drink in Mustang as she sets down a cup of coffee, graceful as ever, and steps back from the table, the pulseFist implanted in the left gauntlet of her armor slowly beginning to blossom open.

My mind and heart war against each other. What the hell is she doing here? She's supposed to be in the Rim. Like her, the other Golds

aren't listening to us. They don't know who we are past our helmets.
No wolfcloaks today. They step back, eyes wary, judging the situation. Cassius's razor slithers on his right arm. Kavax slowly lifts himself from his chair along with Daxo. Quicksilver waves his hands
frantically.

"Stop!" he shouts, voice nearly lost in the chaos. "Do not fire! This
is a diplomatic meeting! Identify yourselves!" We've stumbled into the
middle of some negotiation, I realize. A surrender of Mustang's
forces? An alliance? Noticeably absent is the Jackal. Is Quicksilver
betraying him? He must be. So must the Sovereign. That's why this
place is so deserted. No servants, minimum security. Quicksilver
wanted only men he trusted at this meeting held so close under his
ally's nose.

My stomach lurches as I realize the rest of the room must think
we're Boneriders. Which means they think we're here to kill them,
and this is going to end only one way.

"*On the bloodydamn ground!*" Victra bellows.

"*What do we do?*" Pebble asks over the com. "*Reaper?*"

"*I claim the Bellona,*" Sevro says.

"Use stun weapons!" I say. "It's Mustang—"

"*Won't do shit against that armor,*" Sevro interrupts. "*If they lift
their weapons, kill the pricks. Full pulse charges. I'm not risking any
of our family.*"

"Sevro, listen to me. We need to talk to—" My words cut short
because he uses the master command built into his helmet to jam my
com output signal. I can hear them, but they can't hear me. I curse
futilely at him.

"*Bellona, stop moving!*" Clown shouts. "*I said stop.*"

Opposite Mustang, Cassius silently drifts through the Silvers,
using them as cover to close the gap between us. He's only ten meters
away. Getting closer. I sense Victra tensing beside me, hungry to be let
loose on one of the men who she blames for her mother's death, but
there's civilians between us and the Golds, and Quicksilver's a prize
we can't afford to lose.

My eyes judge the plump cheeks of the Silvers and Coppers. Not a
soul here is oppressed. Not a belly here has ever been hungry. These

are collaborators. Sevro would scalp them one by one if given a rusty knife and a few idle hours.

"Reaper . . ." Ragnar says quietly, looking to me for instruction.

"Take your hand away from the razor!" Victra shouts at Cassius. He stays quiet. Coming forward, certain as a glacier. Moira and the Death Knight follow after him. Kavax's helmet is slithering up to cover his head. Mustang's face is already covered. Her pulseFist active and pointed at the ground.

I know death well enough to hear it gather its breath.

I activate my external speakers. *"Kavax, Mustang, stop. It's me. It's—"*

"Stop moving, you piece of shit!" Victra snarls. Cassius smiles pleasantly and he lunges forward. Ragnar makes a weird twisting movement to my left, and one of the two razors he carries flies through the air and skewers the Death Knight through his forehead. The Silvers gape at the famous Olympic Knight teetering to the ground.

"KAVAX AU TELEMANUS," Kavax roars and rushes forward with Daxo. Mustang breaks sideways. Moira charges, lifting her pulseFist.

"Waste 'em," Sevro says with a snarl.

The room erupts. Air torn to shreds by superheated particles as the Howlers open fire at point-blank range into the crowded room. Marble turns to dust. Chairs melt into gnarled chunks of metal and kick across the floor. Meat and bone explode, filling the air with red mist, as Silvers and Coppers are caught in the crossfire. Sevro misses Cassius, who dives behind a pillar. Kavax is shot a dozen times, but he doesn't falter even as his shields overheat. He's going to smash into Sevro and Victra with his razor when Ragnar charges from the side and hits the smaller man so hard with his shoulder that Kavax is lifted clean off his feet. Daxo attacks Ragnar from behind, and three giants tumble to the side of the room, crushing two scrabbling Coppers half their size as they go. The Coppers scream on the ground, legs shattered.

Behind Kavax, Mustang takes two shots to the chest, but her pulse-Shield holds. She stumbles, fires back at us, hitting Pebble in her thigh. Pebble's lifted backward and flipped into the wall, leg shattered from the blast. She screams and clutches at it. Clown and Victra cover her, firing back at Mustang, dragging Pebble behind a pillar. Screwface and four other Howlers who guarded the door and kept Matteo outside now fire into the room from the hallway.

I stumble sideways, lost in the chaos, as the marble where I stood shatters. Silvers scramble under the table. Others kick away from their chairs, racing for the imagined safety of the columns on the fringes of the room. Hypersonic pulsefire rips between them, over their heads, through them. Buckling the columns. Quicksilver runs behind two Coppers, using them as human shields when shrapnel rips into them, and they all tumble down in a mess of limbs and blood.

Moira, the Fury, rushes Sevro to impale my friend from behind with her razor as he tries to move past Ragnar, who's fighting both Telemanuses, to get at Cassius. I fire my pulseFist point-blank into her side just before she reaches him. Her armor's pulseShield absorbs the first few rounds, rippling blue in a cocoon around her. She stumbles sideways, and if I did not continue to fire, she'd have nothing but a bruise in the morning. But my middle finger is heavy on the trigger of the weapon. She's an engineer of oppression, and one of the best minds of Gold. And she tried to kill Sevro. Bad play.

I fire till her shield buckles inward, till she falls to a knee, till she twitches and screams as the molecules of her skin and organs superheat. Boiling blood comes out her eyes and nose. Armor and flesh fuse together, and I feel the rage ride wild inside me, numbing me to fear, to sense, to compassion. This is the Reaper who laid Cassius low. Who slew Karnus. Who Gold cannot kill.

Moira's pulseFist fires wildly as the tendons of her fingers contract in the heat. Shooting into the ceiling on full automatic. Twitching sideways, whipping a stream of death across the room. Two Silvers running for cover explode. The glass of the viewport at the far end of the room, which looks out onto the space city, cracks perilously. Howlers scramble for cover till the pulseFist glows molten on Moira's left hand and the barrel overheats to melt inward with a corrupt fizzle. With that last gasp of rage, the wisest of the Sovereign's three Furies lies in a charred husk.

My only wish is that it could have been Aja.

I turn back to the room, feeling the cool hand of wrath guiding me, hungering for more blood. But all those that are left are my friends. Or once were. I shudder with hollowness as the rage leaves me as fast as it came. Replaced by panic as I watch my friends try to kill one another. The ordered lines have broken down into a hi-tech brawl. Feet sliding on glass. Shoulder blades slamming into walls. PulseFist battles between pillars. Hands and knees scrambling against the floor as pulseFists wail and blades clamor and hack.

And it's only now, only with this terrifying clarity, that I realize that there is only one common thread that binds them. It's not an idea. Not my wife's dream. Not trust or alliances or Color.

It's me.

And without me, this is what they will do. Without me, this is what Sevro has been doing. What an inevitable waste it seems. Death begets death begets death.

I have to stop it.

At the center of the room, Cassius stumbles after Victra through twisted chairs and shattered glass. Blood slicks the floor beneath them. Her damaged ghostCloak sparks on and off and she flashes between ghost and shadow like an undecided demon. Cassius cuts her again across the thigh and spins as Clown shoots at him, cutting Clown across the side of his head before bending back to dodge a shot from Pebble on the ground across the room. Victra rolls under the table to escape Cassius, slicing at his ankles. He jumps onto the table, firing his pulseFist into the onyx till it caves in the center, trapping her beneath. He's inches from killing her when Sevro shoots him from behind, the blast absorbed by Cassius's shield, but one that knocks him several meters to the side.

To the right, Ragnar, Daxo, and Kavax fight a duel of titans. Ragnar pins Kavax's arm to the wall with his razor, leaves the weapon, ducks, fires his pulseFist into Daxo at point-blank range. Daxo's shields absorb the blast, and his razor misses Rangar and takes out a chunk of the wall instead. Ragnar hits Daxo in his joints and is about to snap his neck when Kavax skewers him through the shoulder with a razor, screaming his family name. I rush to help my Stained friend, but as I do I feel someone to my left.

I turn just in time to see Mustang flying through the air at me, her helmet covering her face, her razor arching down to cut me in two. I bring my own razor up just in time. Blades slam together. Vibrations rattle down my arm. I'm slower than I remember, much of my muscle instinct lost to the darkness despite Mickey's lab and my training bouts with Victra. Plus Mustang's gotten faster.

I'm pressed back. I try to flow around Mustang, but she moves her razor like she's been at war for the last year. I try to slip to the side, like Lorn taught me, but there's no escape. She's smart, using the rubble, the pillars, to corner me. I'm being hemmed in, corralled by the flashing metal. My defense doesn't cave, but it erodes along the edges as I protect my core.

The blade parts an inch-deep gash through my left shoulder. Stings like a pitviper bite. I curse and she slices through more flesh. I'd shout at her to stop. Shout my name, something, if I had even half a second to breathe, but it's all I can do to keep my arms moving. I bend back just in time as she cuts a shallow gash through the neck of my scarab-Skin. Three quick cuts at the tendons of my right arm follow, just missing. Building a rhythm. My back's touching the wall. Cut. Cut. Stab. Fire opening up my skin. I'm going to die here. I call for help over my com, but they're still jammed by Sevro.

We've bitten off more than we can chew.

I scream in futility as Mustang's blade scrapes through three of my ribs. She spins the blade in her hand. Swings backhanded to cut my head off. I manage to deflect the razor into the wall with mine, pinning it above my head so her helmet is near my mask. I head-butt her. But her helmet's stronger than the composite duroplastic of my mask. She reels back her own head and slams it into mine, using my own tactic. A seam of pain splinters down my skull. I nearly black out. Vision rushing out, in. Still standing. Feel part of my mask crack off and slide off my face. Nose broken again. Seeing spots. The rest of the mask crumbles and I stare at the death-eyed horse helmet of Mustang as she prepares to end me.

Her razor arm draws back to deliver the killing stroke. And it stays there above her head. Trembling as she looks at my exposed face. Her helmet slithers away to reveal her own. Sweat-soaked hair clings to her forehead, darkening the golden luster. Beneath, her eyes are wild, and I wish I could say it's love or joy I see in them, but it's not. If anything, it's fear, maybe horror that draws the blood from her face as she stumbles back, gesturing speechlessly with her off-hand.

"Darrow . . . ?"

She looks over her shoulder to see the mayhem that still grips the room, our quiet moment a little bubble in the storm. Cassius flees, disappearing through a side door, leaving the corpse of the Death Knight and Moira behind. Our eyes meet before he disappears. Victra gives chase until Sevro reels her back in. The rest of the Howlers are turning toward Mustang. I take a step toward her, and stop when the tip of her razor pricks my collarbone.

"I saw you die."

She backs away toward the main door, boots sliding over the marble, crunching on bits of glass from the walls. "Kavax, Daxo!" she calls, a vein in her neck bulging from strain. "Pull back!"

The Telemanuses scramble to separate themselves from Ragnar, confused at who the masked man they are fighting is and why they're bleeding in so many places. They try to regroup on Mustang, both men rushing for her in a hasty retreat, but as they pass me to join her near the door, I know I can't just watch her go. So I whip my razor around Kavax's neck. He gags and reels against me, but I hold on. With the press of a button, I could retract my whip and sever his head. But I've no interest in killing the man. He falls only when Ragnar sweeps his leg and puts a knee into his chest. Slamming to the floor. Screwface and the others are on him, pinning him down.

"Don't kill him," I shout. Screwface knew Pax. He's met the Telemanuses, so he holds his blade and snaps at the newer Howlers to do the same. Daxo tries to rush to his father's aid, but Ragnar and I bar his way. His bright eyes stare in confusion at my face.

"Go, Virginia!" Kavax roars from the ground. "Flee!"

"I have the *Pax*. Orion is alive," Mustang says, eying the bloody Howlers who are at my back, coming for her and Daxo. "Don't kill him. Please." And then, with a sorrowful look to Kavax, she flees the room.

18

|||||||||||||||||||||||||

ABYSS

"What did she mean, Orion's alive?" I ask Kavax. He's as shell-shocked as I am, nervously eying the black-clad Howlers prowling through the room. We didn't lose one, but we're in shit shape. "Kavax!"

"What she said," he rumbles. "Exactly what she said. The *Pax* is safe."

"Darrow!" Sevro shouts as he reenters the room with Victra. They pursued Cassius through the blackened door on the far side of the room but return empty-handed and limping. "On me!" There's more I want to ask Kavax, but Victra's wounded. I rush to her as she leans against the shattered onyx table, hunched over a deep gash in her biceps. Her mask's off, face twisted and sweating as she injects herself with painkillers and blood coagulant to stem the flow from the wound. I see the hint of bone through the blood.

"Victra . . ."

"Shit," she says with a dark laugh. "Your boyfriend is faster than he used to be. Almost got him in the hall, but I think Aja taught him a little of your Willow Way."

"Looked like," I say. "You prime?"

"Don't worry about me, darling." She gives me a wink as Sevro calls my name again. He and Clown are bent over Moira's smoking remains. The terrorist lord is unfazed by the carnage around us.

"One of the Furies," Clown says. "Roasted."

"Good cooking, Reap," Sevro drawls. "Crispy on the edges, bloody down the middle. Just how I like. Aja's gonna be pissed—"

"You cut my coms," I interrupt angrily.

"You were acting a bitch. Confusing my men."

"Acting a bitch? The hell is wrong with you? I was using my head instead of just shooting everything. We could have done without murdering half the damn room."

His eyes are darker and crueler than those of the friend I remember. "This is war, boyo. Murder's the name of the game. Don't be sad we're good at it."

"That was Mustang!" I say, stepping close to him. "What if we killed her?" He shrugs. I poke his chest. "Did you know she would be here? Tell me the truth."

"Naw," he says slowly. "Didn't know. Now back up, boyo." He looks up at me impudently, like he wouldn't mind taking a swing. I don't back up.

"What was she doing here?"

"How the hell would I know?" He looks past me to Ragnar, who is pushing Kavax back toward the Howlers gathering in the center of the room. "Everyone prepare to squab out. We're gonna have to cut through an army to get out of this shit den. Evac point is ten floors up on the black side."

"Where's our prize?" Victra asks, eying the carnage. Bodies litter the ground. Silvers shivering in pain. Coppers crawling across the floor, dragging broken legs.

"Probably fried," I say.

"Prolly," Clown agrees, casting me a commiserating look as we move from Sevro to pick through the bodies. "It's a slaggin' mess."

"Did you know Mustang would be here?" I ask.

"Not at all. Seriously, boss." He glances back at Sevro. "What'd you mean he jammed your coms?"

"Stop jawin' and find the bloodydamn Silver," Sevro barks from the center of the room. "Somebody grab the Pink from the hall."

Clown finds Quicksilver at the opposite end of the room, farthest from the hallway door, to the right of the grand viewport that looks down onto Phobos. He's lying motionless, pinned under a pillar that broke from its place in the floor to fall sideways against the wall. The blood of others covers his turquoise tunic. Bits of glass jut from wounded knuckles. I feel his pulse. He's alive. So the mission wasn't a damn waste. But there's a contusion on his forehead from shrapnel. I call Ragnar and Victra, the two strongest of our party, to help pry the pillar off the man.

Ragnar wedges the razor he threw into the Death Knight's head under the pillar, using a rock as a fulcrum, and is about to heave upward with me when Victra calls for us to wait. "Look," she says. Where the pillar's top meets the wall, there's a faint blue glow along a seam that runs from the floor up the wall to form a rectangle in the wall. It's a hidden door. Quicksilver must have been rushing toward it when the pillar fell. Victra puts her ear against the door, and her eyes narrow.

"PulseTorches," she says. "Oh, ho." She laughs. "Silver's bodyguards are through there. Must have hid them in case things got tense. They're speaking *Nagal*." The language of the Obsidians. And they're cutting their way through the wall. We'd be dead if the pillar hadn't fallen and blocked the door.

Pure luck saved our hides. All three of us know it, and it deepens the anger I have with Sevro and calms a bit of the wildness in Victra's eyes. Suddenly she's seeing how reckless this was. We never should have rushed into this place without its blueprints. Sevro did what I would have done a year ago. Same result. The three of us share a common thought, glancing at the main door of the room. We don't have long.

Ragnar and Victra help me pry Quicksilver free. The unconscious man's legs drag behind him, broken, as Victra carries him back to the center of the room. There, Sevro is readying Clown and Pebble to push out from the room with our prisoners, Matteo and Kavax, who stares at me openmouthed. But Pebble can't even stand. We're all in shit shape.

"We've too many prisoners," I say. "We won't be able to move fast. And we don't have any EMPs this time." Not that they'd do anyone any good on a space station when all that separates us from space is inch-thin bulkheads and air recyclers.

"Then we trim the fat," Sevro says, stalking toward Kavax, who sits wounded and bound with his hands behind his back. He points his pulseFist into Kavax's face. "Nothin' personal, big man."

Sevro pulls the trigger. I shove him sideways. The pulse blast misses Kavax's head and slams into the ground near the slumped form of Matteo, nearly taking off the man's leg. Sevro wheels on me, pulseFist pointing at my head.

"Get that out of my face," I say down the barrel. Heat radiating into my eyes, causing them to sting so I have to look away.

"Who do you think that is," Sevro snarls. "Your friend? He's not your friend."

"We need him alive. He's a chip to barter. And Orion might be alive."

"Chip to barter?" Sevro snorts. "What about Moira? Had no problem frying her, but you spare him." Sevro squints at me, lowering his weapon. His lips curl back from his janky teeth. "Oh, it's for Mustang. Of course it is."

"He's Pax's father," I say.

"And Pax is dead. Why? 'Cause you let enemies live. This isn't the Institute, boyo. This is war." He jams a finger in my face. "And war is really bloodydamn simple. Kill the enemy when you can, however you can, as fast as you can. Or they kill you and yours."

Sevro turns from me, realizing now that the others are watching us with growing trepidation. "You're wrong about this," I say.

"We *can't* drag them with us."

"Halls are swarming, boss," Screwface says, returning from the main hall. "More than a hundred security personnel. We're slagged."

"We can cut through them if we go light," Sevro says.

"A hundred?" Clown says. "Boss . . ."

"Check your juice packs," Sevro says, squinting at his pulseFist.

No. I'll not let Sevro's shortsightedness ruin us.

"Slag that," I say. "Pebble, hail Holiday. Tell her evac is squabbed. Give her our coordinates. She's to park one kilometer beyond the glass, ass end our way." Pebble doesn't reach for her datapad. She glances at Sevro, torn between us, not knowing who to follow. "I'm back," I say. "Now do it."

"Do it, Pebble," Ragnar says.

Victra gives a small nod. Pebble grimaces at Sevro, "Sorry, Sevro." She nods to me and opens up her com to hail Holiday. The rest of the Howlers look to me, and it hurts knowing I've made them choose like this.

"Clown, grab Moira's datapad if it isn't fried and get the data from the console if you can. I want to know what contract they were negotiating," I say quickly, "Screwface, take Sleepy and cover the hall. Ragnar, Kavax is yours. He tries to flee, cut his feet off. Victra, you got any rappelling line left?" She checks her belt and nods. "Start tying us together. Everyone in the center of the room. Has to be tight." I turn to Sevro. "Lay charges at the door. Company's coming."

He says nothing. It's not anger behind his eyes. It's the secret seeds of self-doubt and fear coming to blossom, hate seeping into his eyes. I know the look. I've felt it on my own face too many times to count. I'm ripping away the only thing he's ever cared about. His Howlers. After all he's done, I make them choose me over him, when he doesn't trust I'm ready. It's an indictment of his leadership, a validation of the intense self-doubt I know he must feel in the wake of his father's passing.

It shouldn't have been that way. I said I'd follow and I didn't. That's on me. But this isn't the time for coddling. I tried words with him, tried using our friendship to make him see reason, but since I've been back I've seen him respond to things only with violence and force. So now I'll speak his bloodydamn language. I step forward. "Unless you want to die here, sack up and get moving."

His wrinkled little face hardens as he watches his Howlers run to do my bidding. "You get them killed, I'll never forgive you."

"Makes two of us. Now go."

He turns away, running toward the door to plant the remaining explosives from his belt. I remain looking around the broken room, finally seeing organization in the chaos as my friends work together. They'll all have deduced my plan by now. They know how manic it is. But the confidence with which they work breathes life into me. They put the trust in me that Sevro wouldn't. Still, I catch Ragnar glancing at the viewport three times now. All our suits are compromised. Not one of us will be able to stay pressurized in vacuum. I don't even have a mask. Whether we live or die is up to Holiday. I wish there was some way I could control the variables, but if the time in darkness taught me anything, it's that the world is larger than my grasp. Have to trust others. "Jammers on, everyone," I say, toggling my own on my belt. Don't want the cameras outside spotting anyone's exposed faces.

"Holiday is in position," Pebble says. I glance out the window to see the transport hovering a click beyond the window. Hardly larger than a pen tip at this distance.

"On my mark, we are going to fire at the center of the viewport," I tell my friends, making an effort to keep the fear from my voice. "Screwface! Sleepy! Get back here. Put your masks on the unconscious prisoners."

"Oh, goryhell," Victra mutters. "I was hoping you had a better plan than that."

"If you try to hold your breath, your lungs will explode. So exhale soon as the viewport shatters. Let yourself pass out. Have sweet dreams, and pray for Holiday to be as quick on the stick as Clown is in the bedroom."

They laugh and cluster tight, letting Victra wind her rappelling line through our munitions belts so we're together like grapes on a vine. Sevro's finishing laying explosives at the door, Sleepy and Screwface join us, waving at him to hurry.

"Attention," a voice booms from hidden speakers in the walls as Victra leans close to me to link me with Ragnar. *"This is Alec ti Yamato. Head of Security for Sun Industries. You are surrounded. Discard your weapons. Release your hostages. Or we will be forced to fire on you. You have five seconds to comply."*

There's no one in the room but us. The main doors are closed.

Sevro runs back to us from laying the charges. "Sevro, fastlike!" I shout. He's not halfway to us when he crumples to the ground like an empty can crushed by a boot. I'm slammed down to the floor by the same force. Knees buckling. Bones, lungs, throat all stomped down by massive gravity. My vision swims. Blood moving sluggishly to my head. I try to lift my arm. It weighs more than three hundred pounds. Security has increased the artificial gravity in the room, and only Ragnar's not on his belly. He's fallen to a knee, shoulders hunched and straining, like Atlas holding up the world.

"The hell is that . . ." Victra manages, on the floor looking past me to the door. It's opened, and through it comes not a Gray or an Obsidian or Gold. But a giant black egg the size of a small man, rolling sideways. It's smooth and glossy, and small white numbers mark its side. A robot. As illegal as EMPs. Augustus's great fear. Like reaching out of an oil spill, the metal morphs at the point of the egg to reveal a small canon, which aims at Sevro. I try to rise. Try to aim my pulse-Fist. But the gravity is too much. I can't even lift my arm to point the weapon. For all her strength, Victra can't either. Sevro's grunting on the floor, crawling away from the machine.

"The viewport!" I manage. "Ragnar. Fire at the viewport."

His pulseFist is at his side. Straining, he begins to lift it against the massive gravity. Arm shaking. Throat gargling that eerie war chant that sounds like a distant avalanche. The sound rises, an otherworldy bellow till his whole body convulses with effort and his arm draws level and the smallest of stars is born in his palm as the pulseFist gathers its trembling molten charge.

The entirety of my friend shudders and his fingers release the trigger. His arm wrenches back. The pulsefire leaps forward to scream into the center of the glass pane. The many stars ripple as the pane bends outward and cracks shoot down the window.

"*Kadir njar laga . . .*" Ragnar bellows.

And the glass shatters. Space drinks the air of the room. Everything slides. A Copper flips past us, screaming. She goes silent when she hits vacuum. Others who cowered during our brawl cling to the broken table in the center of the room. They wrap themselves around pillars. Fingers bleeding, nails cracking. Legs flailing. Grips giving out. Corpses flip end over end out into space as the abyss hungers for everything the building has. Sevro's ripped into the air away from the robot, lighter than our combined group. I reach for him and grab his short Mohawk till Victra wraps her legs around him and pulls him to her body.

I'm terrified as we slide toward the broken viewport. Hands shaking. Doubting my decision as I now stare it in the face. Sevro was right. We should have pushed into the building. Killed Kavax or used him as a shield. Anything but the cold. Anything but the Jackal's darkness from which I only just escaped.

It's just fear, I tell myself. It's just fear making me panic. And it's spread through my friends. I see the horror on their faces. How they look back at me and see that fear reflected in my own. I cannot be afraid. I've spent too long being afraid. Too long being diminished by loss. Too long being everything except what I need to be. And whether I am the Reaper, or whether it's just another mask, it's one I must wear, not just for them, but for myself.

"*Omnis vir lupus!*" I shout, kicking my head back to howl, exhaling all the air in my lungs. Beside me, Ragnar's eyes widen in wild ecstasy. He opens his massive mouth and bellows out a howl to make his ancestors hear him from their icy crypts. Then Pebble joins, and Clown, and even regal Victra. It's rage and fear leaving our bodies. Though space drags us across the floor to its embrace. Though death might come for us. I am home in this weird screaming mass of humanity. And as we pretend to be brave, we become so.

All except Sevro, who remains silent as we fly into space.

19

||||||||||||||||||||||||

PRESSURE

We rip through the broken viewport into vacuum at eighty kilometers an hour. Silence swallows our howling. A shock hits my body, like I've fallen into cold water. My body twitches. The oxygen expands in my blood, forcing my mouth to hiccup for air that isn't there. Lungs don't inflate. They're collapsed fibrous sacks. My body jerks, desperate for oxygen. But as the seconds tick by and I see the inhuman metal of Phobos's skyscrapers, and watch my friends linked together in the darkness, held together by hands and bits of wire, a stillness settles over me. The same stillness that came in the snows with Mustang, that came when the Howlers and I hunkered tight in the gulches of the Institute to roast goat meat and listen to Quinn tell her stories. I sink slowly into another memory. Not of Lykos, or Eo or Mustang. But of the cold Academy hangar bay where Victra, Tactus, Roque, and I first learned from a pale Blue professor what space does to a man's body.

"Ebulism, or the formation of bubbles in body fluids due to reduced ambient pressure, is the most severe component of vacuum exposure. Water in the tissues of your body will vaporize, causing gross swelling. . . ."

"My darling airhead, I'm well accustomed to gross swelling. Just ask your mother. And your father. And your sister." I hear Tactus say in the memory. And I remember Roque's laugh. How his cheeks blushed at the crudeness of the joke, which makes me wonder why he stood so close to Tactus. Why he cared so much about our bawdy friend's drug use and then wept by Tactus's bedside when he lay dead. The teacher continues. . . .

". . . and multiplicative increase in body volume in ten seconds, followed by circulatory failure . . ."

I feel sleepy even as pressure builds in my eyes, warping my vision and distending the tissue there. Pressure builds in my freezing fingers and aching, popped eardrums. My tongue is huge and cold, like an ice serpent slithering through my mouth into my belly as liquid evaporates. Skin stretches, inflating. My fingers are plantains. Gas in my stomach ballooning my gut. Darkness coming to claim me. I glimpse Sevro beside me. His face is freakish, swollen to twice its normal size. Legs still wrapped around him, Victra looks a monster. She's awake and staring at him with cartoonish, bloodshot eyes, hiccupping for oxygen like a fish out of water. Their hands tighten around each other's.

"Water and dissolved gas in the blood forms bubbles in your major veins, which travel throughout the circulatory system, obstructing blood flow and delivering unconsciousness in fifteen seconds. . . ."

My body fades. Seconds becoming an eternal twilight, everything slowed, everything so pointless and poignant as I see how ridiculous our human strength is in the end. Take us from our bubbles of life, and what are we? The metal towers around us look carved of ice. The lights and flashing HC screens like the scales of dragons frozen inside them.

Mars is over our heads, consuming and omnipotent. But in Phobos's fast rotation, we're already nearing a place on the planet where dawn comes and light carves a crescent into the darkness. Molten wounds still glow where the two nuclear bombs detonated. And I wonder, in my last moments, if the planet does not mind that we wound her surface or pillage her bounty, because she knows we silly warm things are not even a breath in her cosmic life. We have grown and spread, and will rage and die. And when all that remains of us is our steel monuments and plastic idols, her winds will whisper, her sands will shift, and she will spin on and on, forgetting about the bold, hairless apes who thought they deserved immortality.

I'm blind.

I wake on metal. Feel plastic against my face. Gasping around me. Bodies moving. The coldness of a shuttle engine rumbling under the deck. My body seizes and shivers. I suck down the oxygen. It feels like my head has caved in. The pain is everywhere and fading with each pulse of my heart. My fingers are their normal size. I rub them together, trying to orient myself. I'm shivering, but there's a thermal blanket on me, unsentimental hands rubbing me to promote circulation. To my left, I hear Pebble calling for Clown. We'll all be blind for several minutes as our optic nerves recalibrate. He answers her groggily and she nearly breaks down crying.

"Victra!" Sevro's slurring. "Wake up. Wake up." Gear rattles as he shakes her. "Wake up!" He slaps her face. She wakes with a gasp.

". . . the hell. Did you just hit me?"

"I thought . . ."

She slaps him back.

"Who is that?" I ask the hands that rub my shoulders through the blanket.

"Holiday, sir. We scooped you popsicles up four minutes ago."

"How long . . . How long were we out there?"

"'Bout two minutes, thirty seconds. It was a shitshow. We had to empty the cargo bay and have the pilot fly backward into you, then pressurize it on the fly. These carrots can't soldier, but they can damn well steer garbage ships. Still, if you hadn't been linked, most of you would be dead as lead. There's rubble and corpses floating around the sector now. HC crews crawling everywhere."

"Ragnar?" I ask fearfully, not having heard him yet.

"I am here, my friend. The Abyss will not claim us yet." He begins to laugh. **"Not just yet."**

20

||||||||||||||||||||||

DISSENT

We're in trouble, and Sevro knows it. Seizing command back from me as soon as we land in the dilapidated docking berth of a Sons of Ares safe house deep in industrial sector, he orders the still-unconscious Matteo and Quicksilver to the infirmary to be woken up, Kavax to a cell, and tells Rollo and the Sons to prepare for an assault. The Sons stare at us, dumbstruck. Our Obsidian disguises are obliterated. Particularly mine. The prosthetics on my face have fallen off in the battle. Contacts sucked off in the vacuum. Black hair dye thinned out from sweat. Still got my gloves, though. But these Sons don't look at a pack of Obsidians now. They're staring at a cadre of Golds, an Obsidian, a Gray, and at least one ghost.

"The Reaper . . . ," someone whispers.

"Keep your mouth shut," Clown snaps. "Not a word to anyone."

Whatever he says, soon the rumor will spread among them. The Reaper lives. Whatever the effect it'll have, it's not the right time. We may have avoided police pursuit, but such a high-profile kidnapping, not to mention the assassination of two high-level Peerless, will ensure that the full analytical weight of the Jackal's counterterrorism units is brought to bear on the evidence. Praetorian and Securitas antiterrorism tech squads will already be poring over the footage of the attack. They'll discover how we gained access to the facility, how we made our escape, and who our likely compatriots were. Every weapon, piece of equipment, ship used will be traced to its source. Society reprisals against lowColors throughout the station will be swift and brutal.

And when they analyze the visual evidence of our little vacuum escape, they'll see my face and Sevro's. Then Jackal himself will come, or he'll send Antonia or Lilath to hunt me down with their Boneriders.

The clock's ticking.

But that's supposing the authorities suspect that only Quicksilver was kidnapped. I don't know why Mustang and Cassius were meeting, but I have to assume the Jackal doesn't know about it. That's why I used our jammers. So the security cameras outside of Quicksilver's control wouldn't ID Kavax. If the Jackal saw him here, he'd know something was amiss with his alliance with the Sovereign and Quicksilver. And I want to keep that card in my pocket till I know how best to use it and can speak with Mustang.

But what will the Sovereign think when Cassius calls her to tell her Moira is dead? And what is Mustang's place here? There are too many questions. Too many things I don't know. But what haunts me as we run down metal halls, as my friends go to patch wounds and we pass armories where dozens of Reds and Browns and Oranges load weapons and buckle armor, is what she said.

"I have the *Pax*. Orion is alive."

With her, that could mean a dozen things, and the only one who will know is Kavax. I need to ask him, but Ragnar's already taken him down another hall to the Sons lockup and Sevro's stopped rattling off orders to others to address me. "Reap, they're gonna hit us, and hit us hard," he's saying. "You know Legion military procedures better than I do. Get to the datacenter, fastlike. Give me a timetable and their plan of attack. We can't stop them, but we can buy time."

"Time for what?" I ask.

"To blow the bombs and find a way out off this rock." He puts a hand on my arm, just as cognizant of those Sons watching as I am.

"Please. Get moving." He heads off down the hall with the rest of the Howlers, leaving me alone with Holiday. I turn to her.

"Holiday, you know Legion procedures. Get to the datacenter. Give the Sons the tactical support they need." She looks back down the hall to where Sevro has turned a corner. "You good with that?" I ask.

"Yes, sir. Where you going?"

I tighten my gloves. "To get answers."

"Virginia told us you were a Red after she left you. That is why we did not come to your Triumph," Kavax says up to me. He's bound to a steel pipe, legs splayed out on the floor. Still in his armor, red-gold beard dark in the low light. He cuts a menacing figure, but I'm surprised by the openness of his face. The lack of hatred. The clarity of excitement as his nostrils flare wide in recounting his tale to Ragnar and me. Sevro told the Sons that no one was to see Kavax. But apparently they don't think the rules much apply to the Reaper. Good on that. I don't yet have a plan, but I know Sevro's isn't working. I don't have time to navigate his feelings or struggle with him. The pieces are in motion, and I need information.

"She did not know yet what to do and so took our counsel as she did as a girl," Kavax continues. "We were on my ship, the *Reynard*, having roast mutton in ponzu sauce with Sophocles, though he did not like the sauce, when Agea Command called, saying the Sovereign's loyalist forces had attacked the Triumph in Agea. Virginia could not contact you or her father, and so feared a coup and sent Daxo and me from orbit with our knights.

"She stayed in orbit with the ships and finally contacted Roque when Daxo and I were already descending through atmosphere. Roque said the Sovereign had attacked the Triumph and wounded you and her father gravely. He urged her to come to one of his new ships, where he was taking you because the surface was no longer safe." I remember Roque talking on the shuttle as the Jackal leaned over me, not being able to hear him. We landed on a ship. The Sovereign was there. She never left Mars. She was hiding in Roque's fleet. Right under my nose. "But Virginia did not rush to your bedside." He grins jovially. "A fool in love would do so. But Virginia is clever. She saw through Roque's mendacity. She knew the Sovereign would not simply attack the Triumph. It would be a plan within a plan. So she sent word to Orion and House Arcos that a coup was under way. That Roque was a conspirator. So when the assassins struck, attempting to kill Orion and the loyal commanders on their bridge, they were ready. There were firefights on bridges. In staterooms. Orion was badly shot in the arm, but she survived and then Roque's ships opened fire on ours and the fleet fractured. . . ."

All this while Sevro and Ragnar were discovering that Fitchner was dead and the Sons of Ares base had been destroyed. And I lay paralyzed on the floor of Aja's shuttle as everything came apart. No. Not everything.

"She saved the crew's lives," I say.

"Yes," Kavax says. "Your crew is alive. The one you liberated with Sevro. Even many of your Legion, who we organized and managed to evacuate from Mars before the Jackal and Sovereign's forces took power."

"Where are my friends imprisoned?" I ask. "On Ganymede? Io?"

"Imprisoned?" Kavax squints at me, then bursts into laughter. "No, lad. No. Not a man or woman has left their station. The *Pax* is just as you left it. Orion commands, the rest follow."

"I don't understand. She's letting a Blue command?"

"Do you think Virginia would have let you live in that tunnel when you and Ragnar were on your knees if she did not believe in your new world?" I shake my head numbly, not knowing the answer. "She would have killed you on the spot if she thought you were her enemy. But when she sat before my hearth as a girl beside Pax and my children, what stories did I read them? Did I read them myths of the Greeks? Of strong men gaining glory for their own heads? No. I told them tales of Arthur, of the Nazarene, of Vishnu. Strong heroes who wished only to protect the weak."

And Mustang has. More than that. She's proven Eo right. And it wasn't because of me. It wasn't because of love. It was because it was the right thing to, and because mighty Kavax was more a father to her than her own ever was. I feel the tears in my eyes.

"**You were right, Darrow,**" Ragnar says. His hand falls on my shoulder. "**The tide rises.**"

"Then why are you here today, Kavax?"

"Because we are losing," he says. "The Moon Lords will not last two months. Virginia knows what is happening on Mars. The extermination. The savagery of her brother. The Sons are too weak to fight everywhere." His large eyes show the pain of a man watching his home burn. Mars is as much their heritage as it is mine. "The cost of war is too great for a certain defeat. So when Quicksilver proposed a peace, we listened."

"And what are the terms?" I ask.

"Virginia and all her allies would be pardoned by the Sovereign. She would become ArchGovernor of Mars and Adrius and his faction would be imprisoned for life. And certain reforms would be made."

"But the hierarchy would remain."

"Yes."

"**If this is true, we must speak with her,**" Ragnar says eagerly.

"It could be a trap," I say, watching Kavax, knowing the mind at work behind his bluff face. I want to trust him. I want to believe his sense of justice is equal to my love for him, but these are deep waters, and I know friends can lie just as well as enemies. If Mustang isn't on my side, then this would be the play to make. It would expose me, and there's no doubt in my mind that however she got on this station, she's got a nasty escort.

"One thing doesn't make sense, Kavax. If this is true, why didn't you make contact with Sevro?"

Kavax blinks up at me.

"We did. Months ago. Didn't he tell you?"

The Howlers are packing up by the time Ragnar and I rejoin them in the ready room. "It's all shit," Sevro's saying as Victra patches a gash on his back with resFlesh. Acrid smoke hisses up from the cauterizing wound. He throws down his datapad. It skitters into a corner, where Screwface collects it and brings it back to Sevro. "They've grounded everything, including utility flights."

"It's all right, boss, we'll find a way out," Clown says.

I entered the room quietly, nodding to Sevro that I'd like a word. He ignored me. His plan's a mess. We were due to stow ourselves away inside one of the empty helium haulers going back to Mars. We would have been gone before anyone even knew Quicksilver was kidnapped, and then detonated the bombs off-station. Now, like Sevro says, it's all shit.

"We obviously can't stay here," Victra says, putting the resFlesh applicator down. "We left enough DNA evidence for a hundred crime scenes back there. And our faces are everywhere. Adrius will send a whole legion for us when they find out we're here."

"Or blow Phobos out of the sky," Holiday mutters. She sits on a crate of medical supplies in the corner, studying maps with Clown on her datapad. Pebble watches them from her place on the table. Her leg's compressed with a gelCast, but the bone's not set. We'll need a Yellow and a full infirmary to fix what Mustang broke with a single shot. Pebble's lucky she was wearing scarabSkin. It minimized the burn damage. Still, she's in pain. Pupils large on a high dose of narcotics. It's let her inhibitions loose, and I note how obviously the pudgy-faced Gold is watching Clown lean across Holiday to point at the map.

"Helium-3 is Adrius's lifeblood," Victra says. "He won't risk this station."

"Sevro . . ." I say. "A moment."

"Busy right now." He turns to Rollo. "Is there any other way off this damn rock?"

The Red leans against the med room's gray wall next to a glossy paper cutout of a Pink model on one of Venus's white-sand beaches. "It's just cargo haulers down here," he says, silently noting how our Obsidian guises have been discarded. If it startles him how many of us are Gold, he doesn't let on. Probably knew from the start. His eyes linger on me the longest. "But they're all grounded. They got luxury liners and private yachts in the Needles, but you go up there, you folks are caught in a minute. Two, tops. There's facial-recognition cameras at every tram door. Retina scanners in the advertisement holos. And even if you got onto one of their ships, you gotta get past the naval pickets. Ain't like you can just teleport to safety."

"That'd be convenient," Clown mutters.

"We jack a shuttle and run the pickets," Sevro says. "Done it before."

"They'll shoot us down," I say tensely. It's pissing me off that he keeps ignoring my attempts to get him to the door.

"Didn't last time."

"Last time we had Lysander," I remind him.

"And now we got Quicksilver."

"The Jackal will sacrifice Quicksilver to kill us," I say. "Count on it."

"Not if we go straight vertical burn to the surface," Sevro says. "Sons have hidden tunnel entrances. We will fall from orbit and go straight underground."

"I will not do that," Ragnar says. **"It is foolhardy. And it abandons these noble men and women to slaughter."**

"I agree with Rags," Holiday says. She scoots away from Clown and continues looking at her datapad, monitoring police frequencies.

"Say you get off. What happens to us?" Rollo asks. "The Jackal finds out the Reaper and Ares were here and he'll tear this station apart piecemeal. Any Son left behind will be dead in a week. Did you think of that?" He makes a disgusted look. "I know who you are. We knew the second Ragnar walked into the hangar. But I didn't think Howlers ran. And I didn't think the Reaper took orders."

Sevro takes a step toward him. "You got another option, shitface? Or you just gonna run your mouth?"

"Yeah, I got one," Rollo says. "Stay. Help us take the station."

The Howlers laugh. "Take the station? With what army?" Clown asks.

"His," Rollo says, turning to me. "I don't rightly know how you're alive, Reaper. But . . . I was eating noodles by myself at midnight when the Sons leaked your Carving video onto the holoNet. Society cyber police shut down the site in two minutes. But once it was out . . . could find it on a million sites before I finished my bowl. They couldn't contain that. And then the Phobos servers crashed. You know why?"

"Securitas's cyber division pulled the plug," Victra says. "It's standard protocol."

He shakes his head. "Servers crashed because thirty million people were trying to access the holoNet at the same time in the middle of the night. Servers couldn't handle the traffic. Golds pulled the plug after that. So what I'm sayin' is if you march down to the Hive and tell the lowColors there you're alive, we can take this moon."

"Easy as that?" Victra asks skeptically.

"That's right. There's round about twenty-five million lowColors here crawling over one another, fighting for square meters, protein packages, Syndicate smack, whatever. Reaper shows his mug, all that goes to vapor. All that fighting. All that scrappin'. They *want* a leader, and if the Reaper of Mars decides to come back from the dead here . . . you won't have an army, you'll have a tide at your heels. You register? This will change the war."

He sends chills down my spine. But Victra's skeptical, and Sevro's quiet. Hurt.

"Do you know what a squad of Society Legionnaires can do to a mob of rabble?" Victra asks. "The weapons you've seen are geared to taking out men in armor. PulseFists. Razors. When they use coilguns or rattlers on mobs, a single man can fire a thousand rounds a minute. It sounds like paper tearing. Human body doesn't even know that sound is supposed to be frightening. They can superheat the water in your cellular structure with microwaves. And those are just Gray anti-mob squads. What if they unleash the Obsidian? What if Golds themselves come in their armor? What if they shut off your air? Your water?"

"What if we shut off theirs?" Rollo asks.

I frown. "Can you do that?"

"Give me a reason to." He looks at Victra, and by the bite in his voice, I know he knows exactly what her last name is. "They might be soldiers, *domina*. Might be able to put enough metal in my body that I bleed out. But before I was nine, I could strip down a gravBoot and piece it together in under four minutes. Now I'm thirty-eight and I can murder the lot of 'em ten ways till Sunday with a screwdriver and an electrical kit. And I'm sick and tired of not seeing my family. Of being stepped on and charged for oxygen, for water, for living." He leans forward, eyes glassy. "And there's twenty-five million of me on the other side of that door."

Victra rolls her eyes at the bravado. "You're a welder with delusions of grandeur."

Rollo steps forward and knocks a set of wrenches off a table. They clatter on the ground, startling Clown and Holiday, who look up from the datapad. Rollo stares up indignantly at Victra. She's easily a foot taller than him, but he doesn't break his gaze. "I'm an engineer. Not a welder."

"Enough!" Sevro snarls. "This isn't a bloodydamn debate. Quicksilver will get us off this rock. Or I'll start taking off his fingers. Then blow the bombs. . . ."

"Sevro . . ." Ragnar says.

"I am Ares!" Sevro snarls. "Not you." He shoves a finger up into Ragnar's chest and then points at me. "And not you. Finish packing the bloodydamn gear. Now."

He storms from the room, leaving us in awkward silence.

"**I will not abandon these men,**" Ragnar says. "**They have helped us. They are our people.**"

"Ares is cracked," Rollo says to the room. "Off his mind. You need—"

I wheel on the small man, picking him up with one hand and pinning him against the ceiling. "Don't you say a damn thing about him." Rollo apologizes, and I set him back on the ground. I make sure all the Howlers are listening. "Everyone stay put. I'll be right back."

I catch Sevro before he enters Quicksilver's cell in a gutted old garage that the Sons use to house generators now. Sevro and the guards turn when they hear me coming. "Don't trust me alone with him?" he sneers. "Nice."

"We need to talk."

"Sure. After he does." Sevro pushes open the door. Cursing, I follow. The room's a forlorn shade of rust. Machines older than some of the gear in Lykos. One rattles behind the thick Silver, coughing out the electricity that powers the lights bathing the man in a circle of light, and blinding him to anything beyond it. Quicksilver sits with his shoulders back in the metal chair in the center of the room. Arms bound behind his back. His turquoise robe is bloody and rumpled. Bulldog eyes patient and measuring. Wide forehead's covered in a thick sheen of sweat and grease.

"Who are you?" he hisses in irritation instead of fear. The door slams shut behind us. The man seems rather irritated with his predicament. Not disrespectful or angry, but professionally peeved at the meek measure of our hospitality and the inconvenience we've thrust upon him. He's not able to distinguish our faces due to the light blaring into his eyes. "Syndicate teethmen? Moon Lord dustmakers?" When we say nothing, he swallows. "Adrius, is that you?"

Chills creep down my spine. We say nothing. Only now, as he begins to suspect that we're the Jackal's men does Quicksilver seem truly afraid. If we had time, we could use that fear, but we need information fast.

"We need off this rock," Sevro says gruffly. "You're gonna make that happen, boyo. Or I pull off your fingers one by one."

"Boyo?" Quicksilver murmurs.

"I know you have an escape vessel, contingency—"

"Barca, is that you?" Sevro's caught off guard "It is you. Damn the stars, boy. You scared the shit out of me. I thought you were the gory-damn Jackal."

"You have ten seconds to give me something I can use, or I wear your rib cage as a corset," Sevro says, thrown by Quicksilver's familiarity. It's not his best threat.

Quicksilver shakes his head. "You need to listen to me, Mr. Barca, and listen well. This is all a misunderstanding. A vast misunderstanding. I know you may not believe it. I know you may think me mad. But you must hear me. I am on your side. I am one of you, Mr. Barca."

Sevro frowns. "One of us? What do you mean?"

"What do I mean?" Quicksilver laughs gruffly. "I mean exactly as I say, young man. I, Regulus ag Sun, chevalier of the Order of Coin, chief executive officer of Sun Industries, am also a founding member of the Sons of Ares."

21

||||||||||||||||||||||

QUICKSILVER

"A Son of Ares?" Sevro repeats, stepping into the light so Quicksilver can see his face. I stay back. It's a ludicrous claim.

"That's better. I thought I recognized your voice. More like your father's than you probably like. But yes, I'm a Son. The first Son, actually."

"Well, then slag me blind as a Pinkwhore," Sevro cries. "This *is* all just a misunderstanding!" He jumps forward and crouches beside Quicksilver to straighten the man's robe. "We'll get you cleaned up. Let you call your men. Sound good?"

"Yes, good, because you've managed to muck up something rather . . ."

Sevro hits the Silver right in his fleshly lips with a jab of his fist. It's an intimate, familiar bit of violence that makes me flinch. Quicksilver's head slams back against the chair. The man tries to move away, but Sevro pins him down easily. "Your tricks won't work here, fat little toad man."

"It's not a trick—"

Sevro hits him again. Quicksilver sputters, blood dribbling down his cracked lip. Tries to blink the pain away. Probably seeing spots. Sevro hits him a third time, casually, and I think it was for me, not the tycoon, because Sevro looks back into the darkness where I stand with impudent eyes. As if dangling moral bait in front of me so we can explode into conflict again. His moral creed has always been simple: protect your friends, to hell with everyone else.

Sevro pushes a knife into Quicksilver's mouth. "I know you think you're being clever, boyo," Sevro growls. "Saying you're a Son. Thinkin' you're so smooth. Thinkin' you can talk your way clear of us dumb brutes. But I've played this game with smarter kinds than you. And I've learned hard. Keen?" He pulls the knife sideways against Quicksilver's cheek, causing the man to move his head with the blade. Still, it splits the corner of his mouth just slightly.

"So whatever your garble, you ain't coming out on top of this, shit-brain. You're a rat. A collaborator. And it's time to reap what you've sown. So you're going to tell us how to get out of here. If you've got a ship hidden. If you can get us past the navy. Then you're going to tell us about the Jackal's plans, his equipment, his infrastructure; then you're going to give us the gear to equip our army." Quicksilver's eyes dart from the knife to Sevro's face.

"Use your brains, you little savage," Quicksilver snarls when Sevro takes the knife from his mouth. "Where do you think Fitchner got the money—"

"Don't say his name." Sevro points a finger to the man's face. "Don't you dare say his name."

"I knew your father. . . ."

"Then why'd he never mention you? Why does Dancer not know you? Because you're lying."

"Why *would* they know about me?" Quicksilver asks. "You never tie two boats together in a storm."

The words are a punch to the gut. Fitchner said the exact phrase when explaining why he didn't tell me about Titus. The Sons lost much of their technical ability when he died. What if there were two bodies to the Sons of Ares body? The lowColors, and the high? Kept apart in case one was compromised? It's what I would do. He promised me better allies if I went to Luna. Allies that would help make me Sovereign. This could be one of them. One who fled when Fitchner died. Who cut himself off from the contaminated body of the Sons.

"Why was Matteo in your bedroom?" I ask carefully.

Quicksilver stares into the darkness, wondering whose voice addresses him, yet now there's fear in his eyes, not just anger. "How . . . how did you know he was in my bedroom?"

"Answer the question," Sevro says, kicking him.

"Did you hurt him?" Quicksilver asks, enraged. *"Did you hurt him?"*

"Answer the question," Sevro repeats, slapping him.

Quicksilver trembles with anger. "He was in my room because he's my husband. You son of a bitch. He's one of us! If you hurt him . . ."

"How long has he been your husband?" I ask.

"Ten years."

"Where was he six years ago? When he worked with Dancer?"

"He was in Yorkton. He was the man who trained your friend, Sevro. He trained Darrow. The Carver made the body. Matteo sculpted the man."

"He's telling the truth." I step into the light so Quicksilver can see my face. He stares at me in shock.

"Darrow. You're alive. I . . . thought . . . it can't be."

I turn to Sevro. "He's a Son of Ares."

"Because he got a few facts right?" Sevro snarls. "You're actually serious."

"You're alive," Quicksilver murmurs to himself, trying to wrap his head around what is happening. *"How? He killed you."*

"He's telling the truth," I repeat.

"Truth?" Sevro moves his mouth like he's got a cockroach in it. "What does that even bloody mean? How could you possibly know that? You think you can get the truth outta some backroom-dealing shark like this. He's in bed with half the Peerless Scarred in the Society. He ain't just their tool. He's their friend. And he's playing you like the Jackal did. If he's a Son, why'd he abandon us? Why'd he not contact us when Pops died?"

"Because your ship was sinking," Quicksilver says, still staring at me in confusion. "Your cells were compromised. I had no way of knowing how deep the contamination went. I still don't know how the Jackal discovered you, Darrow. My only contact to the lowColor cells was Fitchner. Just like I was his contact for highColor cells. How could I reach out when I didn't know if it was Dancer himself who informed on you and made a power play to get rid of Fitchner?"

"Dancer would never do that," Sevro says with a sneer.

"How would I know that?" Quicksilver says in frustration. "I don't know the man." Sevro's shaking his head, overwhelmed by the absurdity. "I have videos. Conversations between myself and your father."

"I'm not letting you near a datapad," Sevro says.

"Test him," I say. "Make him prove it."

"I met your mother once, Sevro," Quicksilver offers quickly. "Her name was Bryn. She was a Red. If I wasn't a Son, how would I know that?"

"You could know that a dozen ways. Proves piss 'n shit," Sevro says.

"I have a test," I say. "If you are a Son, you'll know it. If you belong to the Jackal, you would have used it. Where is Tinos?"

Quicksilver smiles broadly. "Five hundred kilometers south of the Thermic Sea. Three kilometers beneath the old mining nexus Vengo Station. In an abandoned mining colony, the records of which were wiped from the internal servers of the Society by *my* hackers. The stalactites were carved hollow using Acharon-19 laser drills from my factories in spiral halls to maintain structural integrity. The Atalian hydrogenerator was built with plans designed by my engineers. Tinos might be the City of Ares, but I designed it. I paid for it. I built it."

Sevro sways there in stunned silence.

"Your father worked for me, Sevro," Quicksilver says. "First for the terraforming consortium on Triton, where he met your mother. Then in . . . less legitimate ways. Back then I was not what I am today. I needed a Gold. A hard-nosed Peerless Scarred, and all the legal protection that gives. One who owed me and was willing to play rough with my competitors. Off the books, you know."

"You're saying my father played mercenary. For you?"

"I'm saying he played assassin. I was growing. There was resistance in the marketplace to that growth. So the marketplace had to make room. You think all Silvers play it safe and legal?" He chuckles. "Some, maybe. But business in a crony-capitalist society is the craft of sharks. Stop swimming, the others will take your food and feed on your body. I gave your father money. He hired a team. Worked off-site. Did what I needed him to do. Until I discovered he was using my resources for a side project. *The Sons of Ares.*"

He makes a mockery of the words.

"But you didn't report him?" I ask skeptically.

"Golds treat sedition like cancer. I'd have been cut out too. So I was trapped. But he didn't want me trapped. He wanted a co-conspirator. Gradually he made his case. And here we are."

Sevro paces away, trying to make sense of it. "But . . . we've . . . been dying like flies. And you've been up here . . . humping your Pinks. Fraternizing with the enemy. If you were one of us . . ."

Quicksilver lifts his nose up, regaining what poise he lost during the beating. "Then I would have done what, Mr. Barca? Do tell. From your extensive experience in subterfuge?"

"You would have fought with us."

"With what? Hm?" He waits for an answer. None comes. Sevro's speechless. "I have a private security force of thirty thousand for myself and my companies. But they're spread from Mercury to Pluto. I don't own those men. They are Gray contractors. Only a fraction are owned Obsidians. I have the weapons, but I don't have the muscle to tussle with Peerless Scarred. Are you crazy? I use soft power. Not hard power. That was your father's purview. Even a minor house could wipe me out in direct conflict."

"You have the largest software company in the Solar System," Sevro says. "That means hackers. You have munitions plants. Military tech development. You could have spied for us on the Jackal. Given us weapons. You could have done a thousand things."

"May I be blunt?"

I grimace. "If ever there was a time . . ."

Quicksilver leans back to peer down his humped nose at Sevro.

"I've been a Son of Ares for more than twenty years. That requires patience. A long-eyed view. You've been one for less than a year. And look what's happened. You, Mr. Barca, are a bad investment."

"A bad . . . investment?"

It sounds ridiculous coming from a man chained to a metal chair with blood dribbling down his lips. But something in Quicksilver's eyes sells his point. This isn't a victim. It's a titan of a different plane. Master of his own domain. Equal, it seems, to Fitchner's own breed of genius. And more vast a character, more nuanced than I would have expected. But I reserve any affection for the man. He's survived by lying for twenty years. Everything is an act. Probably even this.

Who is the real man beneath this bulldog face?

What drives him? What does he want?

"I watched. I waited to see what you would do," he explains to Sevro. "To see if you were cut like your father. But then they executed Darrow"—he looks up at me, still confused on that note—"or pretended to, and you acted like a boy. You began a war you couldn't win, with insufficient infrastructure, materiel, systems of coordination, supply lines. You released propaganda in the form of Darrow's Carving to the worlds, to the mines, hoping for . . . what? A glorious rise of the proletariat?" He scoffs. "I thought you understood war.

"For all his faults, your father was a visionary. He promised me something better. And what has his son given us instead? Ethnic cleansing. Nuclear war. Beheadings. Pogroms. Whole cities shredded by fractious groups of Red rebels and Gold reprisals. Disunity. In other words, chaos. And chaos, Mr. Barca, is not what I invested in. It's bad for business, and what's bad for business is bad for Man."

Sevro swallows slowly, feeling the weight of the words.

"I did what I had to," he says, sounding so small. "What no one else would."

"Did you?" Quicksilver leans forward nastily. "Or did you do what you wanted to do? Because your *feelings* were hurt? Because you wanted to lash out?"

Sevro's eyes are glassy. His silence wounding me. I want to defend him, but he needs to hear this.

"You think I haven't been fighting, but I have," Quicksilver continues. "The Sovereign's opinion of the Jackal seems to have soured of late."

"Why?" I ask.

"I couldn't guess before, but now I'd bet anything it's because you escaped the Jackal's prisons. In any case, I saw an opportunity. I brought Virginia au Augustus and the Sovereign's representatives here to broker a peace that would give Virginia the ArchGovernorship of Mars and would remove the Jackal from power and put him in prison for life. It's not the end I wanted. But if what we're seeing on the Jackal's Mars is any indication, he is the single greatest threat to the worlds and our long-term goals."

"And yet you helped him consolidate power in the first place," I say.

Quicksilver sighs. "At the time, I thought him less of a threat than his father. I was wrong. And so were you. He needs to be removed."

The Jackal's been betrayed by two allies, then.

"But your plans for an alliance are slagged now."

"Indeed. But I don't mourn the opportunity lost. You're alive, Darrow, and that means this rebellion is alive. It means Fitchner's dream, your wife's dream, is not yet gone from this world."

"Why?" Sevro asks. "Why the bloodyhell would you want war? You're the richest man in the system. You're not an anarchist."

"No. I am not an anarchist, a communist, a fascist, a plutocrat, or even a demokrat, for that matter. My boys, don't believe what they tell you in school. Government is never the solution, but it is almost always the problem. I'm a capitalist. And I believe in effort and progress and the ingenuity of our species. The continuing evolution and advancement of our kind based on fair competition. Fact of the matter is, Gold does not want man to continue to evolve. Since the conquering, they have routinely stifled advancement to maintain their heaven. They've wrapped themselves in myth. Filled their grand oceans with monsters to hunt. Cultivated private Mirkwoods and Olympuses of their very own. They have suits of armor to make them flying gods. And they preserve that ridiculous fairy tale by keeping mankind frozen in time. Curbing invention, curiosity, social mobility. Change threatens that.

"Look where we are. In *space*. Above a planet we *shaped*. Yet we live in a Society modeled after the musings of Bronze Age pedophiles. Tossing around mythology like that bullshit wasn't made up around a campfire by an Attican farmer depressed that his life was nasty, brutish, and short.

"The Golds claim to the Obsidians that they are gods. They are not. Gods create. If the Golds are anything, they are vampire kings. Parasites drinking from our jugular. I want a Society free of this fascist pyramid. I want to unchain the free market of wealth and ideas. Why should men toil in the mines when we can build robots to toil for us? Why should we ever have stopped in this Solar System? We deserve more than what we've been given. But first, Gold must fall and the Sovereign and the Jackal must die. And I believe you are the sign I've been waiting for, Mr. Andromedus."

He nods at my gloved hands. "I paid for your Sigils. I paid for your bones, your eyes, your flesh. You are my friend's brainchild. My husband's student. The sum of the Sons of Ares. So my empire is at your disposal. My hackers. My security teams. My transports. My companies. All yours. With no reservations. No strings. No insurance policy." He looks at Sevro. "Gentlemen. In other words, I'm all in."

"Quite nice." Sevro applauds, mocking Quicksilver. "Darrow, he's just trying to buy you so he can escape."

"Maybe," I say. "But we can't blow the bombs anymore."

"Bombs?" Quicksilver asks. "What are you talking about?"

"We planted explosives in the refineries and the shipping docks," I say.

"That's your plan?" Quicksilver looks back and forth at us as if we're mad. "You can't do that. Do you have any idea what that would do?"

"An economic collapse," I say. "Symptoms including a devaluation of stock assets, a freeze of commercial bank lending, a run on local banks, eventual stagflation. And a breakdown of social order. Show us some respect when you talk to us. We're not dilettantes or boys. And it *was* our plan."

"Was?" Sevro asks, stepping back from me. "So now you're letting him dictate what we do."

"Things have changed, Sevro. We need to reassess. We've new assets."

My friend stares at me as if he doesn't recognize my face. "New assets? Him?"

"Not just him. Orion," I say. "You never told me Mustang contacted you."

"Because you would have let her manipulate you," he says without apology. "Like you did before. Like you're letting him now." He considers me, pointing a finger as he thinks he figures it out. "You're afraid. Aren't you? Afraid of pulling the trigger. Afraid of making a mistake. We finally have a chance to make Gold bleed and you wanna reassess. You wanna take time to look at our options." He pulls the detonator from his pocket. "This is war. We don't have time. We can take the bastard with us, but we can't miss this chance."

"Stop acting like a terrorist," I snarl. "We're better than that."

I stare down at him, furious in the moment. He should be my simplest, strongest friendship. But because of loss, everything is twisted between us. Even with him there's so many layers to the pain. So many levels of fear and recrimination and guilt for both of us. They once called Sevro my shadow. He's not any longer. And I think I've been bitter at him these last hours because they're proof of that. He's his own man with his own tides. Just as I think he's been bitter with me because I didn't come back as the Reaper. I came back a man he didn't recognize. And now that I'm trying to be the force he wanted, the force that's making decisions, he doubts me because he senses weakness and that's always made him afraid.

"Sevro, give me the detonator," I say coldly.

"Naw." He opens the detonator's priming shield, revealing the red thumb toggle inside the protective casing. If he presses down, one thousand kilograms of high-yield explosives will detonate across Phobos. It won't destroy the moon, but it'll demolish the moon's economic infrastructure. Helium will not flow for months. Years. And all the fears of Quicksilver will be realized. Society will suffer, but so will we.

"Sevro . . ."

"You got my father killed," he says. "You got Quinn and Pax and Weed and Harpy and Lea killed because you thought you were smarter than everyone else. Because you didn't kill the Jackal when you could. Because you didn't kill Cassius when you could. But unlike you, I don't flinch."

22

||||||||||||||||||||||||||||

THE WEIGHT
OF ARES

Sevro's thumb twitches for the detonation switch. But before he presses down, I activate a jamfield with the jammer on my belt, blocking the signal from leaving the room. "You son of a bitch," he snarls, rushing for the door to get beyond the field.

I reach for him. He spins under my hands. My jammer's not a strong one, so he doesn't need to get far away from me. He bowls into the hallway, I scramble after.

"Sevro, stop!" I say as I push into the hallway. He's already ten meters down the hall, running at full speed to get clear of my jamming field so his signal can go out. He's quicker than I am in these small hallways. He's going to escape. I pull my pulseFist out, aim it over his head, and fire it, but my aim is off and it nearly takes off his head. His Mohawk sizzles smoke. He stops dead in his tracks and wheels back on me, face feral.

"Sevro . . . I didn't mean . . ."

With a howl of rage he charges me. Caught off guard, I stumble back from the manic man. He closes in a flurry. I block his first punch, but an uppercut smashes into my jaw, slamming my teeth together. Rocking me back. My teeth close on a corner of my tongue. I taste blood and almost fall. If Mickey hadn't made bones proper, Sevro might've shattered my jaw. Instead, he curses, gripping his fist in pain.

I move with the uppercut and lash out with my left leg, kicking him so hard in the ribs that his whole body carries sideways into the wall, denting the metal bulkhead. I throw a straight jab with my right fist. He ducks under and my punch lands on duroSteel. Pain rattles up my arm. I grunt. He flies into me under the left elbow I swing at his head, ratcheting strikes into my stomach, aiming for my balls. I twist back, manage to grab one of his arms and swing him around as hard as I can. He slams face-first into the wall, spilling to the ground.

"Where is it?" I search his body for the detonator. "Sevro . . ."

He scissor-kicks my legs. Tangling them. Dropping me to the ground so we're grappling instead of trading punches. He's the better wrestler. And it's all I can do to keep him from choking me out from behind as his legs form a triangle, heels locked in front of my face, legs pressing in on both sides of my neck. I lift him off the ground, but I can't dislodge him. He's dangling upside down behind me, spine to my spine, heels still in my face, trying to elbow my balls through my legs from behind. I can't reach for him. I can't breathe. So I grab his calves on my neck and spin my body. He slams into the metal. Once. Twice. Then he finally lets go, scrambling off. I'm on him in a flash, throwing a tight series of kravat elbows into his face. He catches my chin with the crown of his head accidentally.

"Dumb . . . son of a bitch . . ." I mutter, stumbling back. He's gripping his own head in pain.

"Stupid lanky ass . . ."

He aims a kick at my midsection. I take the blow, catching the leg with my left arm, and exchange it for a haymaker right that crashes into his skull with all my weight behind it. He goes down hard, like I'm a hammer driving a nail into the floor. He tries to rise, but I push him down with a boot. He lies under it, heaving breaths. I'm dizzy and panting. Body hating me for what I'm doing to it.

"Are you done?" I ask him. He nods. I pull back my boot and extend a hand to help him up. He rolls to his back and reaches for it, then lurches up with his left boot heel straight into my groin. I fall and dry-heave beside him. Crippling nausea swells from my lower back into my balls and my stomach. Beside me, he's panting like a dog. At first I think he's laughing, but when I look up I'm shocked to see tears in his eyes. He lies on his back. Huge sobs make his rib cage shudder. He turns away, tries to hide from me to stop the tears from coming, but it makes it worse.

"Sevro . . ."

I sit up, feeling ripped apart by the sight of him. I don't hold him, but I put a hand on his head. And he surprises me by not flinching away, but instead crawling up to put his head on my knee. I put my other hand on his shoulder. In time the sobs slow and he blows the snot from his nose. But he doesn't move. It's like the moment after a lightning storm. The air kinetic and vibrating. After several minutes, he clears his throat and pushes himself up to sit with his legs folded under him in the center of the hall. His eyes are puffy, ashamed. He plays with his hands, the tattoos and Mohawk making him look like something pulled from a deranged children's book.

"You tell anyone I cried, I'll find a dead fish, put it in a sock, hide it in your room, and let it putrefy."

"Fair enough."

The detonator lies off to the side. Close enough so we can both reach for it. Neither of us do. "I hate this," he says weakly. "People like that." He glances up at me. "I don't want him to be a Son. I don't want to be like Quicksilver."

"You aren't."

He doesn't believe that. "At the Institute, I'd wake up in the morning. And I think I was still in my dreams. Then I'd feel the cold. And I'd slowly start remembering where I was, and there's dirt and blood under my nails. And all I want to do was go back to sleep. To be warm. But I knew I had to get up and face a world that didn't give a shit." He grimaces. "That's how I feel every morning now. I'm afraid all the time. I don't want to lose anyone. I don't want to let them down."

"You haven't," I say. "If anything, I let you down." He tries to interrupt me. "You were right. We both know it. It's my fault your father's dead. It's my fault that whole night happened."

"Was still a shit thing of me to say." He raps his knuckles on the ground. "I'm always saying shit things."

"I'm glad you said it."

"Why?"

"Because we've both forgotten we didn't get here on our own. You and I should be able to say anything to each other. That's how this works. It's how we work. We don't walk on eggshells. We talk to each other. Even if we say shit that's hard to hear." I see how alone he feels. How much weight he carried. It's how I felt when Cassius stabbed me and left me for dead at the Institute. He needs to share the weight. I don't know how else to tell him that. This stubbornness, this intransigence, looks insane from the outside, but inside he felt just as I did when Roque questioned me.

"Do you know why I helped you at the Institute when you and Cassius were gonna drown in that loch?" he asks. "It's cause of how they look at you. It wasn't like I thought you were a good primus. You were as smart as a bag of wet farts. But I saw them. Pebble. Clown. Quinn. . . . Roque." He almost trips over that last name. "I'd watch you at your fires in the gulches when Titus was in the castle. Saw you teach Lea how to cut a goat's throat even when she was afraid to do it. I wanted to do that too. To join."

"Why didn't you?"

He shrugs. "Was afraid you wouldn't want me."

"They look at you that way now," I say. "Don't you see that?"

He snorts. "Nah, they don't. The whole time, I tried to be you. Tried to be Pops. Didn't work. I could tell everyone just wished it was me that the Jackal captured. Not you."

"You know that's not true."

"It is," he says intensely, leaning forward. "You're better than I am. I saw you. When you looked down at Tinos. Saw your eyes. The love in them. The urge to protect those people. I tried feeling it. But every time I looked down at the refugees, I just hated them. For being weak. For hurting each other. For being stupid and not knowing what we've gone through to help them." He swallows and picks at the cuticles of his stubby fingers. "I know it's nasty, but it's what it is."

He seems so vulnerable here in this hall, the rage taken out of us from the fight. He's not looking for a lecture. Leadership has worn him down, alienated him from even his Howlers. Right now he's looking to feel like he's not like Quicksilver or the Jackal or any of the Golds we fight against. He's mistakenly assumed I'm something better than he is. And part of that is my fault.

"I hate them too," I say.

He shakes his head. "Don't . . ."

"I do. At least, I hate that they remind me of what I was, or could have been. Shit, I was a little idiot. You would have hated me. I was comfortable and arrogant and selfish on my knees. I liked being blind to everything because I was in love. And I thought for some reason that living for love was the most valiant thing in all the worlds. Even made Eo into something in my head that she wasn't. Romanticized her and the life we had—probably because I saw my father die for some cause. And I saw all he left behind, so I tried to cling to the life he abandoned."

I trace the lines on my palm.

"It makes me feel small to think I started doing all this for her. She was everything to me, but I was just a piece of her life. When the Jackal had me, that's all I could think about. That I wasn't enough. That our child wasn't enough. Part of me hates her for that. She didn't know all this would happen, wasn't even aware that the worlds had been terraformed. All she could have known was that she was making a point to the couple thousand people in Lykos. And was that worth dying for? Was that worth killing a child for?"

I gesture down the hall. "Now all these people think she was divine or something. A perfect martyr. But she was just a girl. And she was brave, but she was stupid and selfish and selfless and romantic; but she died before she could ever be more. Think how much she could have done with her life. Maybe we could have done this together." I laugh bitterly and lean my head against the wall. "I think the shittiest part about getting old is now we're smart enough to see the cracks in everything."

"We're twenty-three, dipshit."

"Well, I feel eighty."

"You look it." I flip him the crux, earning a smile. "Do you . . ." He almost doesn't finish the thought. "Do you think she watches you? From the Vale? Does your father?"

I'm about to say I don't know when I catch the intentness of his gaze. He's not asking about my family as much as he's asking about his own, maybe even Quinn, who he always loved but never had the courage to tell. With all his savagery it's hard to remember just how vulnerable he is. He's adrift. Alienated from Red and Gold. No home. No family. No view of a world after war. Right now I'd say anything to make him feel like he's loved.

"Yes. I believe she watches me," I say with more confidence than I feel. "And my father. And yours too."

"So they have beer in the Vale."

"Don't be sacrilegious," I say, kicking his foot. "Only whiskey. Streams of it as far as the eye can see."

His laughter stitches more of me together. Bit by bit, I feel like my friends are coming back to me. Or maybe I'm coming back to them. Suppose it's the same thing, really. I always told Victra to let people in. I could never take my own advice because I knew one day I'd have to betray them, that the foundation of our friendship was a lie. Now I'm with people who know who I am, and I'm afraid to let them in because I'm afraid of losing them, disappointing them. But it's this bond that Sevro and I share that makes us stronger than we were before. It's what we have that the Jackal doesn't.

"Do you know what happens after this?" I ask. "If we kill Octavia, the Jackal? If we somehow win?"

"No," Sevro says.

"That right there is a problem. I don't have the answer. I won't pretend to. But I won't let Augustus be right. I won't bring chaos into this world without at least a plan for something better. For that we need allies like Quicksilver. We need to stop playing terrorist. And we need a real army."

Sevro picks the detonator back up and breaks it in two. "What are your orders, Reap?"

23

||||||||||||||||||||||||

THE TIDE

Sevro and I stalk back into the ready room where the Howlers are packed and prepared to depart the station. Rollo and a dozen of his people watch us tensely from their side of the room. They know they're about to be abandoned. Quicksilver follows behind me, restraints left behind in his cell. He's agreed to our plan, with a few adjustments. "Well, look at this. . . ." Victra says, seeing our bruises and bloody knuckles. "You two finally talked." She looks to Ragnar. "See?"

"Shit's sorted," Sevro says.

"And the rich man?" Ragnar asks curiously. **"He wears no manacles."**

"That's because he's a Son of Ares, Rags," Sevro says. "Didn't you know?"

"Quicksilver's a Son?" Victra explodes into laughter. "And I'm secretly a Helldiver." She looks back and forth at our faces. "Wait . . . you're serious. Do you have proof?"

"I'm sorry to hear of your mother, Victra," Quicksilver says hoarsely. "But it is a pleasure to see you walking, truly. I've been with the Sons for over twenty years. I have hundreds of hours of conversations with Fitchner to prove it."

"He's a Son," Sevro says. "Can we move on?"

"Well, I'll be damned." Victra shakes her head. "Mother was right about you. Always said you had secrets. I thought it was something sexual. That you liked horses or something." Sevro shifts uncomfortably.

"So you find us a way off this rock, rich man?" Holiday asks Quicksilver.

"Not quite," he says. "Darrow . . ."

"We're not leaving," I announce. Rollo and his men stir in the corner. The Howlers exchange confused looks.

"Maybe you wanna tell us what's going on?" Screwface asks gruffly. "Let's start with who's in charge. Is it you?"

"Howler One," Sevro says, punching my shoulder.

"Howler Two," I say, patting his in turn.

"Prime?" Sevro asks. The Howlers nod in concert.

"First order of business, policy change," I say. "Who has pliers?" I look around until Holiday pulls hers from her bomb kit and tosses them to me. I open my mouth and stick the pliers to the back right molar where the achlys-9 suicide tooth was implanted. With a grunt I tear it out and set the tooth on the table. "I've been captured before. I will not be captured again. So this is worthless to me. I don't plan on dying, but if I do, I die with my friends. Not in a cell. Not on a podium. With you." I hand the pliers to Sevro. He jerks out his own back tooth. Spitting the blood on the table.

"I die with my friends."

Ragnar does not wait for the pliers. He pulls out his back tooth with his bare fingers, eyes wide with delight as he sets the huge bloody thing on the table. **I die with my friends.** One by one, they pass around the pliers, pulling out their teeth and tossing them down. Quicksilver watches all the while, staring at us like we're a pack of mad hooligans, no doubt wondering about what he's gotten himself into. But I need my men to lose this heavy mantle they wear. With that poison in their skulls, they felt the death sentences had already been read, and they were just waiting for the hangman to come knocking.

Slag that. Death'll have to earn its bounty. I want them to believe in this. In each other. In the idea that we might actually win and live.

For the first time, I do.

After I've detailed my instructions to my men and they depart to execute the orders, I return with Sevro to the Sons of Ares control room and ask for them to prepare a direct link. "To the Citadel in Agea, please." The Sons of Ares turn to look at me to see if they've misheard. "On the double, friends. We don't have all day."

I stand in front of the holo camera with Sevro. "Think they already know we're here?"

"Probably not quite yet," I reply.

"Think he's going to piss himself?"

"Let's hope. Remember, nothing about Mustang and Cassius being here. We're keeping that one in the pocket."

The direct holoLink goes through and the face of a wan young Copper administrator looks sleepily back at us. "Citadel General Com," she drones, "how may I direct your . . ." She blinks suddenly at our images on the display. Wipes sleep from her eyes. And loses all faculty of speech.

"I would like to speak with the ArchGovernor," I say.

"And . . . may I say who is . . . calling?"

"It's the bloodydamn Reaper of Mars," Sevro barks.

"One moment, please."

The Copper's face is replaced by the pyramid of the Society. Terribly predictable Vivaldi plays as we wait. Sevro taps his fingers on his leg and murmurs his little tune under his breath. *"If your heart beats like a drum, and your legs a little wet, it's because the Reaper's come to collect a little debt."*

Several minutes later, the Jackal's pale face appears before us. He wears a jacket with a high white collar, and his hair is parted on the side. He does not leer at us. If anything, he looks amused as he continues to eat his breakfast. "The Reaper *and* Ares," he says in a low drawl, mocking his own courtesy. He wipes his mouth on a napkin. "You departed so quickly last time I didn't have time to say farewell.

I must say, you're looking positively radiant, Darrow. Is Victra with you?"

"Adrius," I say flatly. "As you're no doubt aware, there has been an explosion at Sun Industries, and your silent partner, Quicksilver, has gone missing. I know it's a mess of jurisdiction, and the evidence won't be sorted for hours, maybe days. So I wanted to call and clarify the situation. We, the Sons of Ares, have kidnapped Quicksilver."

He sets his spoon down to sip from his white coffee cup.

"I see. To what end?"

"We will be holding him for ransom until you release all political prisoners illegally detained in your jails and all lowColors concentrated in internment camps. Additionally, you are to take responsibility for the murder of your father. Publicly."

"Is that all?" the Jackal asks, not displaying a flicker of emotion, though I know he's wondering how we discovered Quicksilver was his ally.

"You also have to personally kiss my pimply ass," Sevro says.

"Lovely." The Jackal looks off the screen to someone. "My agents tell me a flight moratorium was instituted ten minutes after the attack on Sun Industries and the vessel which fled the scene disappeared into the Hollows. Am I to assume then that you're still on Phobos?"

I pause as if caught off guard. "If you do not comply, Quicksilver's life is forfeit."

"Lamentably, I do not negotiate with terrorists. Especially ones who may be recording my conversation to broadcast it for political gain." The Jackal sips his coffee again. "I listened to your proposal, now listen to mine. Run. Now. While you can. But know, wherever you go, wherever you hide, you cannot protect your friends. I'm going to kill them all and put you back in the darkness with their severed heads for company. There is no way out, Darrow. This I promise you."

He kills the signal.

"Think he'll send the Boneriders before the legions?" Sevro asks.

"Let's hope. Time to get moving."

||||||||||||

The Hollows is a city of cages. Row upon row. Column upon column of rusty metal homes linked together in the null gravity as far as the eye can see here in the heart of Phobos. Each cage a life in miniature. Clothing floats on hooks. Little portable thermal press-grills sizzle with the foods of a hundred different regions of Mars. Paper pictures cling to iron cage walls by bits of tape, showing distant lakes, mountains, and families gathered together. Everything here is dull and gray. The metal of the cages. The limp clothing. Even the tired and wasted faces of the Oranges and Reds who are trapped here, thousands of kilometers from home. Sparks of color dance up from the datapads and holoVisor that glow through the city, bits of dream scattered on twisted scrap metal. Men and women sit penitent over their little displays, watching their little programs, forgetting where they are in favor of where they'd wish to be. Many have taped paper or blankets over the sides of their walls to give them some semblance of privacy from their neighbors. But it's the scent and the sound you cannot escape. The throaty unceasing rattle of cage doors slamming shut. Locks clicking. Men laughing and coughing. Generators humming. Public holoCans yapping and barking the dog language of distraction. All stirred and boiled together to make a thick soup of noise and shadowy light.

Rollo once lived in negative south end of the city. Now it is deep Syndicate territory. The Sons were chased out more than two months ago. I fly along the lines of plastic rope that weave through the cage canyons, passing dockworkers and tower laborers who climb back to their little cage homes. They jerk their heads toward the throaty thrum of my new gravBoots. It's an alien sound to them. One heard only over the holoVids or experiential virtual realities low world Greens hawk for fifty credits a minute. Most will never have seen a Peerless Scarred in the flesh. Much less one in full armor. I'm a terrifying spectacle.

It was seven hours ago that my lieutenants and I clustered together in the Sons of Ares ready room and I told them and Dancer back in Tinos my plan. Six hours since I learned of Kavax's escape from our detention cell—someone let him out. Five hours since Victra delivered

Quicksilver and Matteo back to their tower, where Quicksilver has spent the remainder of the night activating his own cells and contacts in the Blue Hives, making preparation for this moment. Four hours since Quicksilver joined his security teams with Sons of Ares and gave them access to his armories and his weapons depots, and we received word that two Augustus destroyers were inbound from the orbital docks. Three hours since Ragnar and Rollo took a thousand Sons of Ares to the garbage hangars on level 43C to prepare their skiffs. Two hours since one of Quicksilver's private yachts was prepped for launch. One hour since the Society destroyers deployed four troop transports to dock at the Skyresh Interplanetary Spaceport and the new coat of blood-red paint on my armor dried and I donned it to march to war.

All is ready.

Now I carve a wake of silence into the heart of the Hollows. My bone-white razor is on my arm. At my side flies Sevro, wearing the huge spiked helmet of Ares with pride. He brought it along, but the rest of his armor is borrowed from Quicksilver. It's cutting-edge tech. Better even than the suits we wore for Augustus. Holiday follows behind along with a hundred Sons of Ares.

The Sons are awkward on their gravBoots. Some carry razors. Others pulseFists. But, per my orders, not one wears a helmet as we fly. I wanted these lowColors of the stacks witnessing our treason, so that they feel emboldened by Reds and Oranges and Obsidians wearing the armor of the masters.

The faces are a blur. A hundred thousand peering from the homes in every direction. Pale and confused, most under the age of forty. Reds and Oranges brought here with false promises just like Rollo, with families down on Mars, just like Rollo.

Neighbors point in my direction. I see my name on their lips. Somewhere, the Syndicate watchmen will be dialing their superiors, relaying the news to the police or the Securitas antiterrorism apparatus that the Reaper lives and he is on Phobos.

I bait the beasts.

As I coast into the central hub of the city, I say a silent prayer, willing Eo to give me strength. There, like some pulsing electronic idol fenced in by metal bramble, a holographic display casts Society comedy programing one hundred meters long, fifty meters broad. It bathes the circle of cages around it in sickly neon light. Speakers laugh on cue. Blue light plays over my armor. Locks jingle as they're undone and cages are pushed open so their inhabitants can sit on the edge and dangle their legs off to watch me without looking through the cage bars.

Quicksilver's Greens focus their helmet cameras on me. The Sons array around, eyes smoldering out at the lowColors, my honor guard. Their red hair floating like a hundred angry torch flames. Holiday and Ares flank me to either side. Floating two hundred meters in the air. Surrounded by cages. Silence gripping the city except the laugh track of the comedy. It's sick and weird as it cackles out of the speakers. I nod to Quicksilver's Greens, and they cut the noise and somewhere in his tower, the hacker teams he's assembled hijack every broadcast on the moon and issue commands to secondary datahubs on Earth, Luna, the asteroid belt, Mercury, the moons of Jupiter, so my message will burn across the blackness of space, taking over the data web that links mankind. Quicksilver is proving his allegiance with this broadcast, using the network he helped the Jackal build. This is not like Eo's death. A viral video you have to dig for in the dark spaces of the holoNet. This is a grand roar across the Society, broadcasting on ten billion holos to eighteen billion people.

They gave these screens to us as chains. Today, we make them hammers.

Karnus au Bellona had his faults. But he was right when he said that all we have in this life is our shout into the wind. He shouted his own name, and I learned the folly in that. But before I begin the war that will claim me one way or another, I will make my shout. And it will be something far greater than my own name. Far greater than a roar of family pride. It is the dream I've carried and shepherded since I was sixteen.

Eo appears beneath me on the hologram, replacing the comedy.

A ghostly giant of the girl I knew. Her face is quiet and pale and angrier than in my dreams. Hair dull and stringy. Clothing drab and ragged. But her eyes burn out from her gray surroundings, bright as

the blood on her mangled back as she looks up from the metal whipping box. Her mouth barely seems to open. Just a sliver of space between her lips, but her song bleeds from her, voice thin and fragile as
a spring dream.

My son, my son
Remember the chains
When gold ruled with iron reins
We roared and roared
And twisted and screamed
For ours, a vale
Of better dreams

She echoes across the metal city louder than she echoed in that far-
off lost city of stone. Her light flickering across the pale faces watching from their cages. These Oranges and Reds who never knew her in
life, but hear her in death. They're silent and sad as she is walked to
the gallows. I hear my vain cries. See myself sagging against Gray
hands. Feel I'm there again. The hard-packed dirt on my knees as the
world falls out from under me. Augustus speaks with Pliny and Leto
as frayed hemp loops around Eo's neck. Hatred radiates from the
faces in the Stacks. I could no more stop Eo's death then than I can
stop it now. It's as if it always has been. My wife falls. I flinch, hearing
the rustling of her clothing. The creaking of the rope. And I look
down at the hologram, forcing myself to watch as the boy I was stumbles forward to wrap his hands with their Red Sigils around her kicking legs. I watch him kiss her ankle and pull her feet with all his feeble
strength. Her haemanthus falls, and I speak.

"I would have lived in peace. But my enemies brought me war. My
name is Darrow of Lykos. You know my story. It is but an echo of
your own. They came to my home and killed my wife, not for singing
a song but for daring to question their reign. For daring to have a
voice. For centuries millions beneath the soil of Mars have been fed
lies from cradle to grave. That lie has been revealed to them. Now
they've entered the world you know, and they suffer as you do.

"Man was born free, but from the ocean shores to the crater cities of Mercury to the ice waste of Pluto down to the mines of Mars, he is in chains. Chains made of duty, hunger, fear. Chains hammered to our necks by a race that we lifted up. A race that we empowered. Not to rule, not to reign, but to lead us from a world torn by war and greed. Instead, they have led us into darkness. They have used the systems of order and prosperity for their own gain. They expect your obedience, ignore your sacrifice, and hoard the prosperity that your hands create. To hold tight to their reign, they forbid our dreams. Saying a person is only as good as the Colors of their eyes, of their Sigils."

I remove my gloves and clench my right fist in the air as Eo did before she died. But unlike Eo, my hands bear no Sigils. Removed by Mickey when I was Carved in Tinos. I am the first soul in hundreds of years to walk without them. The silence in the Hollows gives way to sounds of shock, fear.

"But now I stand before you, a man unbound. I stand before you, my brothers and sisters, to ask you to join me. To throw yourselves on the machines of industry. To unite behind the Sons of Ares. Take back your cities, your prosperity. Dare to dream of better worlds than these. Slavery is not peace. Freedom is peace. And until we have that, it is our duty to make war. This is no license for savagery or genocide. If a man rapes, you kill him on the spot. If a man murders civilians, high or low, you kill him on the spot. This is war, but you are on the side of good and that carries a heavy burden. We rise not for hate, not for vengeance, but for justice. For your children. For their future.

"I speak now to Gold, to the Aureate who rule. I have walked your halls, broken your schools, eaten at your tables, and suffered your gallows. You tried to kill me. You could not. I know your power. I know your pride. And I have seen how you will fall. For seven hundred years, you have ruled over the dominion of man, and this is all you have given us. It is not enough.

"Today, I declare your rule to be at its end. Your cities are not your cities. Your vessels are not your vessels. Your planets are not your planets. They were built by us. And they belong to us, the common trust of man. Now we take them back. Never mind the darkness you spread, never mind the night you summon, we will rage against it. We will howl and fight till our last breath, not just in the mines of Mars, but on the shores of Venus, on the dunes of Io's sulfur seas, in the glacial valleys of Pluto. We will fight in the towers of Ganymede and the ghettos of Luna and the storm-stricken oceans of Europa. And if we fall, others will take our place, because we are the tide. And we are rising."

Then Sevro slams his fist against his chest. Once, twice, thumping it rhythmically. It is echoed by the two hundred Sons of Ares. Their fists pounding their chests. By the Howlers.

In the steel mesh of the cages men and women thump their fists into the walls till it sounds like the heartbeat rising through the bowels of this vampire moon; up through the Hives of Blues, where they sit drinking coffee and studying gravitational mathematics under the warm lights of their intellectual communes; through the Gray barracks in each precinct; among the Silvers at their trading desks; the Golds in their mansions and yachts.

Out through the black ink that separates our little bubbles of life before careening down into the halls of the Jackal's lonely hold on Attica, where he sits in his winter throne, surrounded by a sea of bent necks. There our sound rattles in his ears. There he hears my wife's heart beat on. And he cannot stop it as it goes down and down into the mines of Mars, playing on the screens as Reds beat on their tables and the Copper magistrates watch in swelling fear as the miners look hatefully up through the duroglass that keeps them imprisoned.

Her heart beats mutinously through the bustling oceanside promenades of the archipelagos of Venus as sailboats float proudly in the harbor and shopping bags hang in frightened hands and Golds look to their drivers, their gardeners, the men who power their cities. It beats through the tin-roofed mess halls of the wheat and soybean latfundia that cover the Great Plains of Earth, where Reds use machines to toil under the huge sun to feed mouths of people they will never meet, in places they will never be. It beats even along the spine of the empire, raging through the spiked city moon of Luna, passing by the Sovereign in her glass high refuge to thunder on down snaking electrical wires and drying clothing lines to the Lost City, where a Pink girl makes breakfast after a long night of thankless work. Where a Brown cook leans away from his stove to hear as grease spatters his apron, and a Gray watches from the window of his patrol skiff as a Violet girl smashes the front door of a Post Office and his datapad summons him back to the station for emergency riot protocols.

And it beats inside me, this terrible hope, as I know that the end has begun, and I am finally awake.

"Break the chains," I roar.

And my people roar back.

"Ragnar," I say into my com. "Bring it down."

The Greens cut to a different feed as the fists thump and the cages rattle. And we see a distant shot of the Society's military spire on Phobos. A goliath of a building with docks and vestibules for weapons. Efficient and ugly as a crab. From it, the Jackal maintains his grip on the moon. There, the Grays and Obsidians will be donning armor under pale lights, rushing through metal halls in tight lines, stocking ammunition belts, and kissing pictures of their loved ones so they can come down to the Hollows and make this heart stop beating. But they will never make it here.

Because, as fists pound even harder into cages, the lights of that military spire go black. All her power turned off by Rollo and his men with the access cards provided by Quicksilver.

We could have bombed the building, but I wanted a triumph of daring, of achievement, not destruction. We need heroes. Not another ash city.

And so, a small squadron of a dozen maintenance skiffs coasts into view. Flat, ugly fliers designed to port Reds and Oranges like Rollo to their construction work on towers. Craggy stingrays covered with barnacles. But it isn't barnacles that cling to them now. Another camera takes a closer angle, and we can see each skiff is covered with hundreds of men. Reds and Oranges in their clunky EVA suits, almost half the Sons of Ares on Phobos. Boots against the deck, harnesses latched into exterior buckles of the ship. They carry their welding gear and have Quicksilver's weapons patched onto their legs with magnetic tape.

Among them, two feet taller than the others, is their general, Ragnar Volarus, in armor freshly painted bone white, a red slingBlade painted on the chest and back.

As the skiffs near the Society military spire, they divide down the length of the building. Sons fire magnetic harpoons to tether the skiffs to the steel. And then they go with practiced ease along the lines, flying at implausible speeds as the little motors on their buckles pull them one by one along toward the building. It's like watching Reds in the mines. The grace and nimbleness even in the clunky suits dazzle.

More than a thousand welders pour onto the vast building like we did Quicksilver's spire, but they're not playing for stealth and they're better in null gravity than we were. Magnetic boots clutching metal girders, they skitter across the building, melting through the viewports and entering with extreme prejudice. Dozens are ripped to shreds as Grays inside fire railguns out the glass, but they fire back and pour inward. A ripWing patrol banks in along the outside of the building and rakes two of the skiffs with chain guns. Men turn to mist.

A Son fires a rocket at the ripWing. Fire blooms and vanishes and the ship cracks in half in a gout of purple flame.

The camera follows Ragnar as he breaches a window, enters a hall, and runs full-tilt into a trio of Gold knights, one who I recognize as the cousin of Priam, the man Sevro killed in the Passage and whose mother owns the deed to Phobos. Ragnar flows through the young knight without stopping. Swinging both his razors like scissors and ululating the war cry of his people, followed by a pack of heavily armed welders and laborers. I told him I wanted the spire. I didn't tell him how to take it. He walked off with Rollo, putting an arm around the man.

Now the worlds watch a slave become a hero.

"This moon belongs to you," Sevro says, roaring to the roiling cage city. "Rise and take it! Rise, men of Mars. Women of Mars, rise! You bloodydamn bastards! Rise!" Men and women are pulling themselves from their homes. Donning their boots and jackets. Pushing themselves toward us so that thousands clog the air avenues, crawling over the outside of the cages.

The tide has risen. And I feel a deep terror in wondering exactly what it will wash away. "Rape and murder of innocents is punishable by death. This is war, but you are on the side of good. Remember that, you little shitheads! Protect your brothers! Protect your sisters! All residents of sections 1a-4c, you are to take the armory in level 14. Residents of sections 5c-3f are to take the water-purification center on . . ."

Sevro seizes control of the battle and the Howlers and Sons disperse to organize the mob. It isn't an army but a battering ram. Many will die. And when they die, more will rise in their place. This is just one of the stack cities of Phobos. The Sons will supply them with weapons, but there won't be nearly enough to go around. Their sword is the press of flesh. Sevro will lead them, spend them, Victra in Quicksilver's spires will guide them, and the moon will fall to the rebellion.

But I will not be here to see it.

24

||||||||||||||||||||||||

HIC SUNT LEONES

Phobos is in uproar. Detonations shake the moon as Holiday and I run through the halls. Golds and Silvers evacuate the Needles in their flashing luxury yachts as kilometers beneath, the Hollows swarms with packs of lowColor mobs armed with welding torches, fusion cutters, pipes, black-market scorchers, and old-fashioned slug throwers. The mobs are overwhelming the tram systems and passages to gain access to the mid-sector and Needles while the Society military garrison, caught reeling from the attack on their headquarters, rushes to stop the upward migration. The Legions have training and organization on their side. We have numbers and surprise.

Not to mention fury.

No matter how many checkpoints the Grays blockade, how many trams the Grays destroy, the lowColors will seep through the cracks because they made this place, because they have allies among the mid-Colors, thanks to Quicksilver. They open derelict transportation tunnels, hijack cargo ships in the industrial sector, pack them full of men and women, and steer them for the luxury hangars in the Needles, or even toward the public Skyresh Interplanetary Spaceport, where cruise liners and passenger ships are being loaded with evacuees.

I'm remotely jacked into Quicksilver's security grid, watching high-Colors stampede over one another. Carrying luggage and valuables and children. Martian Navy ripWings and fast-moving fighters dart through the towers, shooting down the rebel ships rising from the Hollows toward the Needles. The debris from a destroyed lowColor skif crashes through the vaulted glass and steel ceiling of a Skyresh terminal, killing civilians, and shattering any illusion I might have had that this war would be sanitary.

Ducking away from a mob of lowColors, Holiday and I arrive outside a derelict hangar in the old freight garages, which haven't been used since before the time of Augustus. It's quiet here. Abandoned. The old pedestrian entrance is welded shut. Radiation signs warn potential scavengers away. But the doors open for us with a deep groan when a modern retinal scanner built into the metal registers my irises, as Quicksilver said it would.

The hangar is a vast rectangle skinned with dust and cobwebs. In the center of the hangar's deck sits a silver seventy-meter-long luxury yacht shaped like a sparrow in flight. It's a custom-built model out of the Venusian Shipyards, ostentatious, fast, and perfect for an obscenely wealthy war refugee. Quicksilver plucked it from his fleet to help us blend in with the migrating upper class. Its rear cargo plank is down, and inside the bird is filled to capacity with black crates stamped with the Sun Industries winged heel. Inside of which are several billion credits' worth of hi-tech weapons and equipment.

Holiday whistles. "Gotta love deep pockets. The fuel would cost my annual wages. Twice over."

We cross the hangar to meet Quicksilver's pilot. The trim young Blue waits at the bottom of the ramp. She has no eyebrows and her head is bald. Winding blue lines pulse beneath the skin where subdermal synaptic links connect her remotely to the ship. She snaps to attention, eyes wide. Clearly she had no idea who she was transporting until now. "Sir, I am Lieutenant Vesta. I'll be your pilot today. And I must say, it's an honor to have you on board."

There's three levels to the yacht, the upper and bottom for Gold use. The middle for cooks, servants, and crew. There's four staterooms, a sauna, and crème leather seats with dainty little chocolates and napkins sitting primly on armrests in the passenger cabin to the far back of the cockpit. I pocket one. And then a couple more.

As Holiday and Vesta prep the ship, I strip off my pulseArmor in the passenger cabin and unpack winter gear from one of the boxes. I dress in skintight nanofiber weave that's much like scarabSkin. But instead of black, it's mottled white and looks oily except for textured grips on the elbows, gloves, buttocks, and knees. It's crafted for polar temperatures and water immersion. It's also a hundred pounds lighter than our pulseArmor, is immune to digital component failures, and has the added benefit of not needing batteries. Much as I enjoy using four hundred million credits' worth of technology to make me a flying human tank, sometimes warm pants are more valuable. And we'll always have the pulseArmor if we need it in a pinch.

I'm struck by the silence in the cargo bay and the hangar as I finish lacing my boots. There's still fifteen minutes left on my datapad's timer, so I sit on the edge of the ramp, legs dangling off, to wait for Ragnar. I pull the chocolates from my pocket and slowly peel the foil off. Taking half a bite, I let the chocolate sit on my tongue, waiting for it to melt as I always do. And as always, I lose patience and chew it before the bottom half is melted through. Eo would make candy last for days, when we were lucky enough to have it.

I set my datapad on the ground and watch the helmet cameras of my friends as they wage my war for Phobos. Their chatter trembles out of the datapad's speakers, echoing in the vast metal chamber. Sevro's in his element, rushing through the central ventilation unit with hundreds of Sons loading themselves into the air ducts. I feel guilty for sitting here watching them, but we each have our parts to play.

The door we entered through opens with a groan and Ragnar and two of the Obsidian Howlers enter the room. Fresh from the battlefield, Ragnar's white armor is dented and stained. "Did you play gently with the fools, my goodman?" I call down from the ramp in my thickest highLingo. In reply, he tosses up to me a curule: a twisted gold scepter of power given to high-ranking military officers. This one is a tipped with a screaming banshee and a splash of crimson.

"The tower has fallen," Ragnar says. **"Rollo and the Sons finish my work. These are the stains of subGovernor Priscilla au Caan."**

"Well done, my friend," I say, taking the scepter in my hands. On it is carved the deeds of the Caan family, which owned the two moons of Mars and once followed Bellona to war. Among great warriors and statesmen, there's a young man I recognize standing by a horse.

"**What is wrong?**" Ragnar asks.

"Nothing," I say. "I knew her son is all. Priam. He seemed decent enough."

"**Decent is not enough,**" Ragnar says forlornly "**Not for their world.**"

With a grunt, I bend the curule against my knee and toss it back to him to show my agreement. "Give it to your sister. Time to go."

Glancing back at the hangar with a frown, he checks his datapad and files past me into the cargo hold. I try to wipe the blood from the curule off on my white suit's leg. It just smears over the oily fabric, giving me a red stripe on my thigh. I close the ramp behind me. Inside, I help Ragnar out of his pulseArmor and let him slip into the winter gear as I join Holiday and Vesta as they initiate preflight launch.

"Remember, we're refugees. Aim for the largest convoy heading out of here and stick to them." Vesta nods. It's an old hangar. So it has no pulseField. All that separates us from space are five-story-tall steel doors. They rumble as the motors begin to retract them into the ceiling and floor. "Stop!" I say. Vesta sees what caught my attention a second after I do and her hand flashes to the controls, stopping the doors before they part and open the hangar to vacuum.

"I'll be damned," Holiday says, peering out the cockpit to a small figure blocking our ship's path to space. "It's the lion."

Mustang stands in front of the ship illuminated by our headlights. Her hair washed white by the blinding light. She blinks as Holiday cuts the headlights from the cockpit and I make my way to her through the dim hangar. Her dancing eyes dissect me as I come. They dart from to my Sigil-barren hands to the scar I've kept on my face. What does she see?

Does she see my resolve? My fear?

In her I see so much. The girl I fell in love with in the snow is gone, replaced in the last fifteen months by a woman. A thin, intense leader of vast and enduring strength and alarming intellect. Eyes kinetic, ringed by circles of exhaustion and trapped in a face made pale from long days in sunless lands and metal halls. Everything she is dwells behind her eyes. She has her father's mind. Her mother's face. And a distant, foreboding sort of intelligence that can give you wings or crush you to the earth.

And just at her hip sits a ghostCloak with a cooling unit.

She has watched us since we arrived.

How did she get inside the hangar?

"'Lo, Reaper," she says playfully as I come to a halt.

"'Lo, Mustang." I search the rest of the hangar. "How did you find me?"

She frowns in confusion. "I thought you wanted me to come. Ragnar told Kavax where I could find you . . ." She trails off. "Oh. You didn't know."

"No." I look back up at the ship's mirror cockpit windows, where Ragnar must be watching me. The man's overstepped his bounds. Even as I arranged a war, he went behind my back and endangered my mission. Now I know exactly how Sevro felt.

"Where have you been?" she asks me.

"With your brother."

"Then the execution was a ruse meant to make us stop looking."

There's so much more to say, so many questions and accusations that could fly between us. But I didn't want to see her because I don't know where to begin. What to say. What to ask for. "I don't have time for small talk, Mustang. I know you came to Phobos to surrender to the Sovereign. Now why are you here talking to me?"

"Don't talk down to me," she says sharply. "I wasn't surrendering. I was making peace. You're not the only one with people to protect. My father ruled Mars for decades. Its people are as much a part of me as they are part of you."

"You left Mars at the mercy of your brother," I say.

"I left Mars to save it," she corrects. "You know everything is a compromise. And you know it's not Mars you're angry at me for leaving."

"I need you to stand aside, Mustang. This is not about us. And I don't have time to bicker. I'm leaving. So either you move or we open the door and fly through you."

"Fly through me?" she laughs. "You know I didn't have to come alone. I could have come with my bodyguards. I could have lain in wait to ambush you. Or reported you to the Sovereign to salvage the peace you ruined. But I didn't. Can you stop for a single moment to think why?" She takes a step forward. "You said to me in that tunnel that you want a better world. Can't you see that I listened? That I joined the Moon Lords because I believe in something better?"

"Yet you surrendered."

"Because I could not watch my brother's reign of terror continue. I want peace."

"This is not the time for peace," I say.

"Goryhell, you're thick. I know that. Why do you think I am here? Why do you think I've worked with Orion and kept your soldiers at their stations?"

I examine her. "I honestly don't know."

"I'm here because I want to believe in you, Darrow. I want to believe in what you said in that tunnel. I ran from you because I didn't want to accept that the only answer was the sword. But the world we live in has conspired to take everything I love away. My mother, my father, my brothers. I will not let it take the friends I have left. I will not let it take you."

"What are you saying?" I ask.

"I'm saying that I'm not letting you out of my sight. I'm coming with you."

It's my turn to laugh. "You don't even know where I'm going."

"You're wearing sealSkin. Ragnar's on board. You've declared open rebellion. Now you're leaving in the middle of the largest battle the Rising has ever seen. Really, Darrow. It doesn't take a genius to deduce that now you're using this ship to pretend to be a Gold refugee to escape and go to the Valkyrie Spires to beseech Ragnar's mother to provide an army."

Damn. I try not to let my surprise show.

This is why I did not want to involve Mustang. Inviting her into the game is adding another dimension I can't control. She could destroy my gambit with a single call to her brother, to the Sovereign, telling them where I am going. Everything relies on misdirection. On my enemies thinking I am on Phobos. She knows what I'm thinking. I can't let her leave this hangar.

"The Telemanuses know as well," she says, knowing my mind. "But I'm tired of having insurance plans against you. Tired of playing games. You and I have pushed each other away because of broken trust. Aren't you tired of that? Of the secrets between us? Of the guilt?"

"You know I am. I laid my secrets bare in the tunnels of Lykos."

"Then let this be our second chance. For you. For me. For both our people. I want what you want. And when you and I are aligned, when have we ever lost? Together we can build something, Darrow."

"You're suggesting an alliance . . ." I say quietly.

"Yes." Her eyes are afire. "The might of House Augustus and Telemanus and Arcos united with the Rising. With the Reaper. With Orion and all her ships. The Society would tremble."

"Millions will die in that war," I say. "You know that. The Peerless Scarred will fight to the last Gold. Can you stomach that? Can you watch that happen?"

"To build we must break," she says. "I was listening."

Still, I shake my head. There's too much to overcome between us, between our people. It would be a qualified victory, on her terms. "How could I ask my men to trust a Gold army? How could I trust you?"

"You can't. That is why I am coming with you. To prove I believe in your wife's dream. But you have to prove something to me. That you are worthy of *my* trust, in turn. I know you can break. I need to see that you can build. I need to see what you will build. If the blood we will shed is for something. Prove that, and you have my sword. Fail, and you and I will go our separate ways." She cocks her head at me. "So what do you say, Helldiver? Do you want to give it one more go?"

25

||||||||||||||||||||||||

EXODUS

I help unbuckle Mustang's pulseArmor in the cargo hold. "Cold gear is in here." I gesture to a large plastic box. "Boots in there."

"Quicksilver gave you the keys to his armory?" she asks, eying the winged heel on the boxes. "How many fingers did it cost him?"

"None," I say. "He's a Son of Ares."

"What now?"

I grin. Comforting knowing the world isn't an open book for her. The engines rumble and the ship rises underneath us. "Get dressed and join us in the cabin." I leave her behind to change in private. I was more gruff than I intended. But it felt strange smiling in her presence. I find Ragnar leaning back in his chair in the passenger cabin eating chocolates, white boots up on the adjacent armrest. "No offense, but what the hell are you doing?" Holiday asks me. She stands, arms crossed, between the cockpit and the passenger cabin. "Sir."

"Taking a risk," I say. "I know it might seem strange to you, Holiday. But I go back with her."

"She's the definition of the elite. Worse than Victra. Her father—"

"Killed my wife," I say. "So if I can stomach it, so can you." Holiday makes a whistling sound and heads back to the cabin, unhappy with our new ally.

"So the Mustang joined our quest," Ragnar says.

"She's getting dressed," I reply. "You had no right to let Kavax go. Much less tell him where we would be. What if they gave us up, Ragnar? What if they ambushed us? You would never have seen your home. If they find out we're there, they'll never let your people off the surface. They'll kill them all. Did you think of that?"

He eats another chocolate. "A man thinks he can fly, but he is afraid to jump. A poor friend pushes him from behind." He looks up at me. "A good friend jumps with."

"You've been reading *Stoneside,* haven't you?"

Ragnar nods. "Theodora gave it to me. Lorn au Arcos was a great man."

"He'd be glad you think so, but take everything with a grain of salt. The biographer took some liberties. Especially in his early life."

"Lorn would have told you that we need her. Now, in war. And after, in peace. If we do not bring her to our cause, then we will not win until every Gold is dead. That is not why I fight."

Ragnar rises to greet Mustang as she joins us. The last time they stood eye to eye, she had a gun pointed at his head. "Ragnar, you've been busy since I last saw you. Not a Gold alive doesn't know and fear your name. Thank you for releasing Kavax."

"Family is dear," Ragnar says. "But I warn you. We go to my lands. You are under my protection. If you play your tricks, if you play your games, that protection is forfeit. And even you will not survive long on the ice without me, daughter of the lion. Do you understand?"

Mustang bows her head respectfully. "I do. And I will repay your faith in me, Ragnar. I promise you that."

"Enough chatter. Time to buckle up," Holiday snaps from the cabin. Vesta's synced with the ship and pushing out of the hangar. We find our seats. There's twenty to choose from, but Mustang takes the one next to me in the left aisle. Her hand grazes my hip accidentally as she reaches for her seat harness.

Our ship departs the hangar, silently floating forward into the vacuum of the dim subcutaneous industrial world of Phobos. Pipes and loading docks and garbage bays as far as we can see. Closed off to the stars and the light of the sun. Few ships as lovely as ours have ever flown so far beneath the surface of Phobos. The word *LowSector* is rendered in white paint over an industrial transport hub where men pour into ships, and the ships trundle up out of this dim world toward the sector gates that the Sons have breached.

Our sleek yacht passes a motley fleet of slow-moving garbage haulers and freighters. Inside, men and women huddle quietly together in windowless, dirty steel cubes. Sweat drenches their backs. Their hands shake holding unfamiliar instruments: weapons. They pray they can be as brave as they've always imagined themselves to be. Then they'll land in some Gold hangar. The Sons will shout orders. The doors will open and they will meet war.

I pray silently for them, clenching my hands as I stare out the window. I feel Mustang watching me. Measuring the tides deep within.

Soon we leave the industrial Stacks behind, trading the dim recesses for the neon advertisements that bathe the space boulevards of the midSector. Manmade canyons of steel to either side. Trams. Elevators. Apartments. Every screen connected to the web has been slaved by Quicksilver's hackers, showing images of Sevro and the Sons overrunning security gates and checkpoints, painting scythes on walls.

And around us, the city of thirty million churns. Deep space commercial transports racing past little civilian taxis and skippers meant to go between the buildings here. Freighters soar from the Hollows up through the midSector toward the Needles. A flight of ripWings hunts through the streets above us. I hold my breath. With a flip of a trigger they could shred us. But they don't. They register our high-Color ship ID and hail us over the coms and offer an escort out of the warzone toward a current of yachts and skiffs that blaze quietly away from the moon.

"*Stirring speech,*" Victra purrs over the ship's com as I answer the call from Quicksilver's tower, her bored voice at odds with the warring world around us. "*Clown and Screwface just took Skyresh's main terminals. Rollo's men have seized the water cisterns for the midSector. Quicksilver's networks are broadcasting it all the way to Luna. Scythes popping up everywhere. There's riots in Agea, Corinth, every-*

where on Mars. And we're hearing the same from Earth and Luna. Municipal buildings are falling. Police stations burning. You've woken the rabble."

"They'll hit back soon."

"As you said, darling. We massacred the first responders the Jackal sent. Got a few Boneriders, just as we wanted. No Lilath or Thistle, though."

"Damn. Worth a shot."

"Martian Navy is on its way from Deimos. The Legions are coming, and we're making our final preparations."

"Good. Good. Victra, I need you to let Sevro know that we've added a member to our expedition. Mustang's joined us."

Silence from her. *"Am I on a private line?"*

Holiday tosses me a headset from the cockpit. I wrestle the headset on. "You are now. You don't agree."

The bitterness in her tone is acute. *"Here are my thoughts. You can't trust her. Look at her brother. Her father. Greed is in her blood. Of course she would ally with us. It fits her aims."* I watch Mustang as Victra speaks. *"She needs us because she's losing her war. But what happens when we give her what she needs? What happens when we're in her way? Will you be able to put her down? Will you be able to pull the trigger?"*

"Yes."

Victra's words linger as we pass Phobos's giant glass spires, cockpit skimming a dozen meters above the panes of the building. Inside roil little worlds of madness. The Rising has reached the Needles in this district of the city. LowColors push inexorably through the halls. Grays and Silvers barricading doors. Pinks standing in a bedroom over a bleeding old Gold and his wife, knives in hand. Three Silver children watching Ares on a wall-sized holo as their parents speak in the library. And at last, a Gold woman in a sky-blue cocktail dress, pearls about her neck, gold hair unbound to her waist. She stands near a window as Sons of Ares spread through the building, levels beneath her penthouse. Engulfed in her own drama, she raises a scorcher to her Golden head. Body stiff in imagined majesty. Her finger tightens around the trigger.

And we're past. Leaving her life and the chaos behind to join with the flow of yachts and pleasure craft that flee the battle for the safety of the planet. Most of the refugees call Mars home. Their ships, unlike ours, are not equipped for deep space. Now they scatter over the planet's atmosphere like burning seeds, most plunging straight for the spaceport of Corinth beneath us in the middle of the Thermic Sea. Others skimming over the atmosphere, disregarding designated transit lanes, racing past the Jackal's hastily erected blockade and the satellite level toward their homes in the opposite hemisphere. RipWings and wasps from the military frigates flash after them, trying to herd them back to the designated avenues. But entitlement and chaos are a poor mix. Mania grips these fleeing Golds.

"The *Dido*," Mustang says quietly to herself, eying a glass ship the shape of a sailboat to our starboard. "Drusilla au Ran's vessel. She taught me how to paint watercolors when I was little." But my attention is farther out, where ugly dark vessels without the flashing hulls or fanciful lines of the pleasure craft race toward Phobos. It's more than half the Martian defense fleet. Frigates, torchShips, destroyers. Even two dreadnaughts. I wonder if the Jackal is on one of those bridges. Likely not. It's probably Lilath who leads the detachment, or some other praetor newly appointed in his regime. Antonia has been dispatched to aid Roque on the Rim. Their ships will be packed with lifelong soldiers. Men and women as hard as we are. Many who fell in my Iron Rain. And they will cut through the mob I've summoned inside Phobos like paper. They'll be furious and confident: the more, the better.

"It's a trap, isn't it?" Mustang asks quietly. "You never meant to hold Phobos."

"Do you know how the Inuit tribes of Earth killed wolves?" I ask. She doesn't. "Slower and weaker than the wolves, they chiseled knives till they were razor sharp, coated them in blood and stuck them upright in the ice. Then the wolves would come up and lick the blood. And as the wolf licks faster and faster, he's so ravenous he doesn't realize until it's too late that the blood he's drinking is his own." I nod to the passing military vessels. "They hate that I was one of them. How many prime soldiers do you think those ships will launch at Phobos to take me, the great abomination for their own glory? Pride will again be the downfall of your Color."

"You're trying to get them on the station," she says, understanding. "Because you don't need Phobos."

"Like you said, I'm going to the Valkyrie Spires for an army. Orion and you might still have the remnants of my fleet. But we will need more ships than that. Sevro is waiting in the ventilation system of the hangars. When the assault forces land to take back the military spire and the Needles, they'll leave their shuttles behind in those hangars. Sevro will descend from his hiding place, hijack the shuttles, and return them home to their ships, packed with all the Sons we have left."

"And you honestly believe you can control the Obsidian?" she asks.

"Not me. Him." I nod to Ragnar. "They live in fear of their 'Gods' in the Board of Quality Control's Asgard Station. Golds in suits of armor playing at Odin and Freya. Same way that I lived in fear of the Grays in the Pot. As we were cowed by the Proctors. Ragnar's going to show them just how mortal their Gods really are."

"How?"

"**We will kill them,**" Ragnar says. "**I have sent friends ahead, months ago, to spread the truth. We will return to my mother and my sister as heroes, and I will tell them their gods are false with my own tongue. I will show them how to fly. I will give them weapons and this ship will carry them to Asgard and we will conquer it as Darrow conquered Olympus. Then we will free the other tribes and carry them away from this land on Quicksilver's ships.**"

"That's why you have a gorydamn armory back there," Mustang says.

"What do you think?" I ask her. "Possible?"

"Insane," she says, awed by the audacity of it. "Might be possible, though. Only *if* Ragnar can actually control them."

"**I will not control. I will lead.**" He says it with quiet certainty.

Mustang admires the man for a moment. "I believe you will."

I watch Ragnar as he looks back out the window. What passes behind those dark eyes? This is the first time I've felt like he's not telling me something. He already deceived me by releasing Kavax. What else does he plan?

We listen in tense silence to the radio waves crackle with yacht captains requesting docking clearance on the military frigates instead of continuing down to the planet. Connections are used. Bribes offered. Strings pulled. Men weep and beg. These civilians are discovering that their place in the world is smaller than they imagined. They do not matter. In war, men lose what makes them great. Their creativity. Their wisdom. Their joy. All that's left is their utility. War is not monstrous for making corpses of men so much as it is for making machines of them. And woe to those who have no use in war except to feed the machines.

The Peerless Scarred know this cold truth. And they have trained for centuries for this new age of war. Killing in the Passage. Struggling through the deprivation of the Institute so that they might have worth when war comes. Time for Pixies with deep pockets and expensive tastes to appreciate the realities of life: you do not matter unless you can kill.

The bill, as Lorn often said, comes at the end. Now the Pixies pay.

A Gold Praetor's voice cuts through the speakers of our ship, ordering the refugee ships to redirect toward authorized transit lanes and steer clear the navy warships or they will be fired upon. The Praetor cannot afford unauthorized vessels within one hundred kilometers of her ship. They could carry bombs. Could carry Sons of Ares. Two yachts ignore the warnings and are ripped apart as one of the cruisers fires railguns into their hulls. The Praetor repeats her order. This time it is obeyed. I look over at Mustang and wonder what she thinks of this. Of me. Wishing we could be somewhere quiet where a thousand things didn't pull at us. Where I ask about her instead of the war.

"Feels like the end of the world," she says.

"No." I shake my head. "It is the beginning of a new one. I have to believe that."

The planetscape below is blue and spackled white as we pretend to follow the designated coordinates along the western hemisphere at the equator. Tiny green islands ringed with tan beaches wink up at us from the indigo waters of the Thermic Sea. Beneath, ships jerk and burn as they hit atmosphere before us. Like phosphorous firecrackers Eo and I played with as children, kicking spasmodically and glowing orange, then blue, as heat friction builds along their shields. Our Blue veers us away, following a series of other ships who depart the general flow of traffic for their own homes.

Soon, Phobos is half a planet away. The continents pass beneath. One by one the other ships descend and we're left alone on our journey to the uncivilized pole, flying past several dozen Society satellites that monitor the southernmost continent. They too have been hacked into recycling information pulled from three years ago. We're invisible, for now. Not just to our enemies but to our friends. Mustang leans from her chair, peering up into the cockpit. "What is that?" She gestures to the sensor display. A single dot follows behind us.

"Another refugee ship from Phobos," the pilot answers. "Civilian vessel. No weapons." But it's closing fast. Trailing behind us by two hundred kilometers.

"If it's a civilian vessel, why did it just appear on our sensors?" Mustang asks.

"It could have sensor shielding. Dampeners," Holiday says warily.

The ship closes to forty kilometers. Something is wrong here. "Civilian vessels don't have that sort of acceleration," Mustang says.

"Dive," I say. "Get us through the atmosphere now. Holiday on the gun."

The Blue slips into defense protocols, increasing our speed, strengthening our rear shields. We hit atmosphere. My teeth rattle together. The ship's electronic voice suggests passengers find their seats. Holiday stumbles up, rushing past us to the tailgun. Then a warning siren trills as the ship behind us morphs on the radar display, sharp contours of hidden weapons blossoming from its formerly smooth hull. It follows us into atmosphere, and it fires.

Our pilot twists her thin hands in the gel controls. My stomach lurches. Hypersonic depleted uranium shells scar the canvas of clouds and icy terrain, superheating as they streak past. The ship jerks as we hit atmosphere ourselves. Our pilot continues to juke, twitching her fingers in the electric gel, face placid and lost in her dance with the pursuing craft. Her eyes distant from her body. A single droplet of sweat beading on her right temple and trickling down her jaw. Then a gray blur rips into the cockpit and she explodes in a shower of meat. Spattering the viewports and my face with blood. The uranium shell takes off the top half of her body, then rips through the floor. A second shell the size of a child's head screams through the ship between Mustang and me. Punching a hole in the floor and ceiling. Wind shrieks. Emergency masks fall into our laps. Warning sirens warble as pressure rushes from our ship, whipping our hair. I see the blackness of the ocean through the hole in the floor. Stars through the hole in the ceiling as our oxygen leaks out. The pursuing ship continues to fire into our dying ship. I huddle in terror with my hands over my head, teeth locked together, everything human in me screaming.

Laughter evil and inhuman rumbles so loud I think it's coming from the buffeting wind. But it comes from Ragnar, his head tilted back as he laughs to his gods. **"Odin knows we are coming to kill him. Even false Gods do not die easily!"** He throws himself from his seat and runs down the hall, laughing insanely, not listening as I shout for him to sit down. Shells whisper past him. **"I am coming, Odin! I am coming for you!"**

Mustang dons her emergency mask and pushes the release on her safety webbing before I can gather my thoughts. The ship bucks, slamming her into the ceiling and the floor hard enough to crack the skull of any but an Aureate. Blood spills over her forehead from a gash at her hairline and she clutches to the floor, waiting till the ship rolls again to angle herself so that she can use gravity to fall into the co-pilot chair. She lands awkwardly against the armrests but manages to drag herself into the seat and buckle in. More warning lights pulse on the blood-drenched console. I look back down the hall to see if Ragnar and Holiday are alive only to see a trio of shells savage the room behind us. My teeth clatter in my skull. Gut vibrating with the champagne flutes in the cabinet to my left. I can't do anything but hold on as Mustang tries to arrest our fall through orbit. The seat's gel webbing tightens against my rib cage. I feel the g-forces crushing me. Time seems to slow as the world beneath swells. We're through the clouds. On the sensor I see something small zip away from our ship and collide into the one trailing. Light flares behind us. Snow and mountains and ice floes dilate till they're all I can see through the broken cockpit window. Wind howls, shatteringly cold against my face. "Brace for impact," Mustang shouts over it. "In five . . ."

We plummet toward a sheaf of ice floating in the middle of the sea. On the horizon, a bloody ribbon of red ties the twilight sky to the ragged coastline of volcanic rock. A giant man stands atop the rock. Black and huge against the red light. I blink, wondering if my mind is playing tricks on me. If I'm seeing Fitchner before my death. The man's mouth is an open dark chasm into which no light escapes.

"Darrow, tuck in!" Mustang shouts. I lower my head between my knees, wrap my arms around it. "Three . . . two . . . one."

Our ship punches into the ice.

26

|||||||||||||||||||||||||

THE ICE

All is dark and cold as we sink into the sea. Water's rushed in through the mangled back of the ship and gurgles through the dozen gaping holes in the cockpit. We're already beneath the waves, the last air bubbling out into the darkness. The crash webbing synched tight around my body upon impact, expanding to protect my bones. But now it's killing me, dragging me down with the ship. The water is freezing needles against my face. SealSkin protects my body, though, so I cut through the webbing with my razor. Pressure building in my ears as I search frantically for Mustang.

She's alive and already working on escape. A light in her hand carves through the darkness of the flooded cockpit. Her razor's out. Cutting through her webbing like I did. I push myself through the flooded cabin toward her. The back of the ship is missing. Three levels of vessel torn off and floating elsewhere in the darkness with Ragnar and Holiday inside. My neck's locked up from whiplash. I suck at the oxygen from the mask that covers my nose and mouth.

Mustang and I communicate silently, using the signals of Gray lurcher squads. The human instinct is to flee the crash as fast as possible, but training reminds us to count our breaths. To think clinically.

There are supplies here we might need. Mustang searches in the cockpit for the standard emergency kit while I search for my equipment bag. It's missing, along with the rest of the gear in the cargo hold that we were bringing the Obsidians to seize Asgard. Mustang joins me, carrying a plastic emergency box the size of her torso, which she pulled from a cabinet behind the pilot's chair.

Taking a last breath, we leave the oxygen behind.

We swim to the edge of the torn hull, where the ship ends and the ocean begins. It is an abyss. Mustang turns off her light as I tie our belts together with a length of the crash webbing I took from my seat. Designed to keep the Obsidians trapped in their icy continent, the Carved creatures here are man-eaters. I've seen pictures of the things. Translucent and fanged. Eyes bulging. Skin pale, worming with blue veins. Light and heat attract them. To swim in open water with a flashlight would draw things from the deeper levels. Even Ragnar wouldn't dare.

Unable to see farther than a hand's breadth in front of us, we push away from the yacht's corpse in the black water. Fighting for every agonizing meter. I can't see Mustang beside me. We're sluggish in the cold water, limbs burning as they claw darkness; but my mind is locked and certain. We will not die in this ocean. We will not drown. I repeat it over and over, hating the water.

Mustang kicks my foot, disrupting our rhythm. I try to match it again. Where is the surface? There's no sun to greet us, to tell us we're near. It's wildly disorienting. Mustang kicks my leg again. Only this time I feel the ripple of the water beneath as something large and fast and cold swims in the depths below.

I slash down blindly with my razor, hitting nothing. Impossible to fight back the panic. I'm swinging at the darkness of the two kilometers of ocean that stretches beneath me and pumping my legs so desperately that I swim into the ice crust atop the water almost knocking myself out. I feel Mustang's hand on my back. Steadying me. The ice is dull gray skin that stretches above us. I stab my razor up into it. Hear Mustang doing the same beside me. It's too thick to push clear of. I grip her shoulder and draw a circle to signal my plan. I turn so my back is against hers. Together, nearly blind and out of oxygen, we cut a circle in the ice. I keep going until I feel the ice give slightly. It's too heavy to push up without traction. Too buoyant to pull down with just our arms. So I swim to the side so Mustang can savage the cylinder we've cut with her razor. Mincing the ice enough to push the emergency box through first. She follows and extends a hand to aid me. I slash blindly back down at the darkness and follow her up.

We collapse headfirst onto the rock-hard surface of the ice.

Wind rattles over our shaking bodies.

We're on the edge of an ice shelf between a savage coastline and the beginning of a cold, black sea. The sky throbs deep metallic blue, the South Pole locked in two months of twilight as it transitions to winter. The mountainous coastline dark and twisted, maybe three kilometers off, ice stretching all the way, punctured by icebergs. Wreckage burns on the coast's mountains. Wind rushes in off the open water ahead of a coming storm, whipping the waves into calamity so salt and spray hiss over the ice like sand buffeting through the desert.

Water geysers into the air fifty meters closer inland as someone fires a pulseFist from underneath the ice. Numb and frozen, we rush toward Holiday as she pulls herself free, Mustang trailing behind with the emergency box.

"Where is Ragnar?" I shout. Holiday looks up at me, face twisted and pale. Blood pools from her leg. A piece of shrapnel sticking through her thigh. Her sealSkin has kept her from the worst of the cold, but she didn't have time to don her suit's hood or gloves. She tightens a tourniquet around her leg, looking back into the hole.

"I don't know," she says.

"You don't know?" I rip free my razor and stumble for the hole. Holiday scrambles in front of me.

"Something is down there! Ragnar pulled it off of me."

"I'm going down," I say.

"What?" Holiday snaps. "It's pitch-black. You'll never find him."

"You don't know that."

"You'll die," she says.

"I won't let him go."

"Darrow, stop." She throws down the pulseFist and pulls Trigg's pistol from her leg holster and shoots it in front of my foot. "Stop."

"What are you doing?" I shout over the wind.

"I will shoot your leg out before I let you kill yourself. That's what you're doing if you go down there."

"You'd let him die."

"He's not my mission." Her eyes are hard. Unsentimental and clinical. So different from the way I fight. I know she'll pull the trigger to save my life. I'm about to lunge at her when Mustang flashes past to my left. Too fast for me to say anything or for Holiday to threaten her as she dives into the hole, a razor in her right hand, and in her left, a flare blazing bright.

27

||||||||||||||||||||||

BAY OF LAUGHTER

I rush to the hole. Water laps peaceably at the edge. The ice is too thick to see Mustang beneath the surface as she swims, but the flare glows gently through the meter of dirty ice, blue and wandering toward the land. I follow it. Holiday tries to drag herself after. I shout at her to stay and get the medkit for herself.

I follow Mustang's light. Razor skimming over the ice, tracing the light underneath for several minutes, till at last the light stops. It's not enough time for her to run out of breath, but it doesn't move for ten seconds. And then it begins to fade. Ice and water darkening as the light sinks into the sea. I have to get her out. I slam my razor into the ice, carving a chunk free. I roar as I jam my fingers into the cracks and lift it up, hurling it backward over my head to reveal water churning with pale bodies and blood. Mustang bursts to the surface, crying in pain. Ragnar's beside her, blue and still, pinned under her left arm as her right hacks at something pale in the water.

I stab my razor into the ice behind me and hold on to the hilt. Mustang reaches for my hand and I haul her out. Then we pull Ragnar out with a roar of effort. Mustang claws onto the ice, falling down with Ragnar. But she's not alone. A maggot white creature the size of a small man has latched itself to her back. It's shaped like a snail in full sprint, except its back is tough, hairy translucent flesh mottled with dozens of shrieking little mouths rimmed with needle teeth that gnaw into her back. It's eating her alive. A second creature the size of a large dog is stuck on Ragnar's back.

"Get it off!" Mustang snarls, slashing wildly with her razor. "Get it off of me!" The creature is stronger than it should be and crawls back toward the hole in the ice, trying to drag her back to its home. A gunshot echoes and the creature jerks as a slug from Holiday's bullet hits it square in the side. Black blood pulses out. The creature shrieks and slows enough for me to rush to Mustang and scalp the thing from her back with my razor. I kick it to the side, where it spasms as it dies. I cut Ragnar's beast in half, skinning it off his back, and hurl it to the side.

"There's more down there. And something bigger," Mustang says, struggling to her feet. Her face tightens as she sees Ragnar. I rush to him. He's not breathing.

"Watch the hole," I tell Mustang.

My massive friend looks so childish there on the ice. I start CPR. He's missing his left boot. The sock's halfway off. Foot jerks against the ice as I pump his chest. Holiday stumbles to us. Pupils huge from painkillers. Her leg's bound with resFlesh from the medkit. She collapses to the ice beside Ragnar. Tugs his sock back on his foot like it matters.

"Come back," I hear myself saying. Spit freezing against my lips. Eyelids crusty with tears I didn't even know I was shedding. "Come back. Your work isn't finished." The Howler tattoo is dark against his paling skin. The protection runes like tears on his white face. "Your people need you," I say. Holiday holds his hand. Both of hers not equal to the size of the massive six-fingered paw.

"Do you want them to win?" Holiday asks. "Wake up, Ragnar. Wake up."

He jerks beneath my hands. Chest twitching as his heart kicks. Water bubbles out of his mouth. Arms scrabbling at the ice in confusion as he coughs for air. He sucks it down. Huge chest heaving as he stares up at the sky. His scarred lips curl back into a mocking smile. **"Not yet, Allmother. Not yet."**

"We're fucked," Holiday says as we look over the meager supplies Mustang managed to scavenge from our vessel. We shake together in a ravine, finding momentary respite from the wind. It's not much. We huddle around the paltry heat of two thermal flares after having humped it across the ice shelf as eighty-kilometer winds shredded us with cold teeth. The storm darkens over the water behind us. Ragnar watches it with wary eyes as the rest of us sort through the supplies. There's a GPS transponder, several protein bars, two flashlights, dehydrated food, a thermal stove, and a thermal blanket large enough for one of us. We've wrapped it around Holiday, since her suit's the most compromised. There's also a flare gun, a resFlesh applicator, and a thumb-sized digital survival guide.

"She's right," Mustang says. "We have to get out of here or we're dead."

Our boxes of weapons are gone. Our armor and gravBoots and supplies sunken to the bottom of the sea. All that would have let the Obsidians destroy their Gods. All that would have let us contact our friends in orbit. The satellites are blind. No one is watching. No one except the men who shot us from the sky. The lone blessing is that they crashed as well. We saw their fire deeper in the mountains as we stumbled across the ice shelf. But if they survived, if they have gear, they will hunt us, and all we have to protect ourselves is four razors, a rifle, and a pulseFist with a drained charge. Our sealSkin is sliced and damaged. But dehydration will claim us long before the cold does. Black rock and ice span the horizon. Yet if we eat the ice, our core temperatures will lower and the cold will take us.

"We have to find real shelter." Mustang blows into her gloved hands, shivering. "Last I saw of the charts in the cockpit, we're two hundred kilometers from the spires."

"Might as well be a thousand," Holiday says gruffly. She chews her cracked bottom lip, still staring at the supplies as if they'll breed.

Ragnar watches us discuss wearily. He knows this land. He knows we can't survive here. And though he will not say it, he knows that he will watch us die one by one, and there will not be a thing he can do to stop it. Holiday will die first. Then Mustang. Her sealSkin is torn where the beast bit her and water leaked in. Then I will go, and he will survive. How arrogant must we have sounded, thinking we could descend and free the Obsidians in one night.

"Aren't nomads here?" Holiday asks Ragnar. "We always heard stories about marooned legionnaires. . . ."

"**They are not stories,**" Ragnar says. "**The clans seldom venture to the ice after autumn has fled. This is the season of the Eaters.**"

"You didn't mention them," I say.

"**I thought we would fly past their lands. I am sorry.**"

"What are Eaters?" Holiday asks. "My Antarctic anthropology ain't for shit."

"**Eaters of men,**" Ragnar says. "**Shamed castouts from the clans.**"

"Bloodyhell."

"Darrow, there must be a way to contact your men for extraction," Mustang says, determined to find a way out.

"There isn't. Asgard's jamming array makes this whole continent static. The only tech for a thousand kilometers is there. Unless the other ship has something."

"**Who are they?**" Ragnar asks.

"Don't know. Can't be the Jackal," I say. "If he knew who we were then he would have sent his fleet after us, not just one black-ops ship."

"It's Cassius," Mustang says. "I assume he came in a disguised ship, like I did. He's supposed to be on Luna. It was one of the positives of negotiating here. They get caught going behind my brother's back, it's as bad for them as for me. Worse."

"How'd he know which ship was ours?" I ask.

Mustang shrugs. "Must have sniffed out the diversion. Maybe he followed us from the Hollows. I don't know. He's not stupid. He did catch you in the Rain as well, going under the wall."

"Or someone told him," Holiday says, eying Mustang darkly.

"Why would I tell him when I'm on the gorydamn ship?" Mustang says.

"Well, let's hope it's Cassius," I say. "If it is, then they won't just hop on gravBoots and fly to Asgard for help, because then they'll have to explain to the Jackal why they were on Phobos to begin with. How'd it go down, anyway?" I ask. "It looked like a missile signature from the back of our ship. But we don't have missiles."

"The boxes did," Ragnar says. **"I fired a sarissa out the back of the cargo bay from a shoulder launcher."**

"You shot a missile at them while we were falling?" Mustang asks incredulously.

"Yes. And I attempted to gather gravBoots. I failed."

"I think you did just fine," Mustang says with a sudden laugh. It infects the rest of us, even Holiday. Ragnar doesn't understand the humor. My cheer fades quickly though as Holiday coughs and cinches her hood tighter.

I watch the black clouds over the sea. "How long till that storm hits, Ragnar?"

"Perhaps two hours. It moves with speed."

"It'll get to negative sixty," Mustang says. "We won't survive. Not with our gear like this." The wind howls through our ravine and the bleak mountainside around us.

"Then there's only one option," I say. "We sack up and push across the mountains, find the downed ship. If it is Cassius in there, he'll have at least a full squad of Thirteenth legion black ops with him."

"That's not a good thing," Mustang says warily. "Those Grays are better trained for winter combat than we are."

"Better than you," Holiday says, pulling back her sealSkin so Mustang can read the Thirteenth legion tattoo on her neck. "Not me."

"You're a dragoon?" Mustang asks, unable to hide the surprise.

"Was. Point is: PFR—Praetorian field regulations—mandate survival gear in long-range mission transport enough to last each squad a month in any conditions. They'll have water, food, heat, and gravBoots."

"What if they survived the crash?" Mustang says, eying Holiday's injured leg and our paltry weapons supply.

"Then they will not survive us," Ragnar says.

"And we're better off hitting them when they're still piecing themselves together," I say. "We go now, fast as we can, and we might get there before the storm lands. It's our only chance."

Ragnar and Holiday join me, the Obsidian gathering the gear as the Gray checks her rifle's ammunition. But Mustang's hesitant. There's something else she hasn't told us. "What is it?" I demand.

"It's Cassius," she says slowly. "I don't know for certain. What if he's not alone? What if Aja is with him?"

28

||||||||||||||||||||||||

FEAST

The storm falls as we climb along a rocky arm of the mountain. Soon we can see nothing beyond our party. Steel-gray snow gnaws into us. Blotting out the sky, the ice, the mountains inland. We duck our heads, squinting through the sealSkin balaclavas. Boots scrape the ice underfoot. Wind roars loud as a waterfall. I hunch against it, putting one boot after the other, connected with Mustang and Holiday by rope in the Obsidian way so we don't lose one another in the blizzard. Ragnar scouts ahead. How he finds his way is beyond me.

He returns now, loping over the rocks with ease. He signals for us to follow.

Easier said than done. Our world is small and furious. Mountains lurk in the white. Their hulking shoulders the only shelter from the wind. We scramble over bitter black rock that slices at our gloves while the wind tries to hurl us down gulches and bottomless crevasses. The exertion keeps us alive. Neither Holiday nor Mustang slow, and after more than an hour of dreadful travel, Ragnar guides us into a mountain pass and the storm breathes. Beneath us, impaled upon a ridgeline, is the ship that shot us from the sky.

I feel a pang of sympathy for her. Sharklike lines and flared starburst tail indicate she was once a long, sleek racing vessel of the famed Ganymede shipyards. Painted proud and bold in crimson and silver by loving hands. Now she's a cracked, blackened corpse impaled upside down on a stark ridgeline. Cassius, or whoever was inside, had a nasty time of it. The rear third of the ship sheaved off half a kilometer downhill from the main body. Both parts look deserted. Holiday scans the wreck with her rifle's scope. No sign of life or movement outside.

"Something seems off," Mustang says, crouched beside me. Her father's visage watches me from the razor on her arm.

"The wind is against us," Ragnar says. **"I smell nothing."** His black eyes scan the peaks of the mountains around us, going rock to rock, looking for danger.

"We can't risk getting pinned down by rifles," I say, feeling the wind pick up again behind us. "We need to close the distance fastlike. Holiday, you lay cover." Holiday digs a small trench in the snow and covers herself with the thermal blanket. We cover that with snow so only her rifle's peeking out. Then Ragnar slips down the slope to investigate the rear half of the ship as Mustang and I press for the main wreck.

Mustang and I slink low over rocks, covered by the renewed vigor of the storm, unable to see the ship till we're within fifteen meters. We close the rest of the distance on our bellies and find a jagged hole in the aft where the back half of the fuselage was shredded by Ragnar's missile. Part of me expected a camp of warColors and Golds preparing to hunt us down. Instead, the ship's an epileptic corpse, power flickering on and off. Inside, the ship is hollow and cavernous and almost too dark to see when the lights crackle off. Something drips in the darkness as we work our way toward the middle of the craft. I smell the blood before I see it. In the passenger compartment, nearly a dozen Grays lie dead, smashed into the floor above us by the rocks that speared the ship as it landed. Mustang kneels next to the body of a mangled Gray to examine his clothing.

"*Darrow.*" She pulls back his collar and points to a tattoo. The digital ink still moves even though the flesh is dead. Legio XIII. So it is Cassius's escort. I manipulate the toggle on my razor, moving my thumb in the shape of the new desired design. I press down. The razor slithers in my hand, abandoning its slingBlade look for a shorter, broader blade so I can stab more easily in the cramped environs.

There's no sign of any life as we move forward, let alone Cassius. Just the wind moaning through the bones of the vessel. A strange feeling of vertigo walking along the ceiling and looking up at the floor. Seats and belt buckles hanging down like intestines. The ship convulses back to life, illuminating a sea of broken datapads and dishes and gum packages underfoot. Sewage leaks from a crack in the metal wall. The ship dies again. Mustang taps my arm and points out a shattered bulkhead window to what looks like drag marks in the snow. Smeared blood black in the dim light. She signs to me. Bear? I nod. A razorback must have found the wreckage and begun feasting on the corpses of the diplomatic mission. I shudder, thinking of noble Cassius suffering that fate.

A grisly sucking sound makes its way to us from farther on in the ship. We press forward, feeling the dread of the scene before we enter the forward passenger cabin. The Institute taught us the sound of teeth on raw meat. But still, this is a horrifying sight, even for me. Golds hang upside down from the ceiling, imprisoned in their crash webbing, legs pinned by bent paneling. Beneath them hunch five nightmares. Their fur is grim and matted, once white but now clumped with dried blood and filth. They gnaw on the bodies of the dead. Their heads are those of massive bears. But the eyes that peer through the eye sockets of those heads are black and cold with intelligence. Standing not on four legs but two, the largest of the pack turns toward us. The ship lights throb back on. Pale muscled arms, slick with seal grease to ward off the cold, dark with blood from skinning the dead Golds, move from under the bear pelts.

The Obsidian is taller than I am. A crooked iron blade sewn into his hand. Human bones strung together with dried tendon as a breastplate. Hot breath billows from under the snout of the ursine skull he wears as a helmet. Slow and measured, the deep ululation of an evil war chant blossoms from between his blackened teeth. They've seen our eyes and one screams something unintelligible.

The ship wheezes and the lights go out.

The first cannibal vaults toward us through the cluttered hall, the rest behind him. Shadows in the darkness. My pale razor lashes forward and hews through his iron knife, through his breastplate and clavicle straight into his heart. I twist aside so he doesn't crash into me. His momentum takes him past me into Mustang, who sidesteps him and cuts his head clean off. His body spills to the ground past her, twitching.

An audible grunt, and a spear with a jagged iron end flies from one of the other cannibals. I duck under it and punch upward with my left hand, deflecting it into the ceiling, just over Mustang's head. Then the Obsidian behind slams into me as I rise. As large as I am. Stronger. More creature than man. Overwhelming me with the frenzy of a lost mind, he pins me to the wall and snaps at me with blackened, sharp-filed teeth. The lights of the ship flash illuminating the sores around his mouth. My arms are pinned to my sides. He bites at my nose. I turn my face just before he rips it off. Instead, his teeth sink into the meat at the base of my lower jaw. I scream in pain. Blood flows down my neck. He chomps down again, pulling at my face. Eating me alive as the lights go out. His right hand tries to work a knife through the sealSkin to slide it between my ribs and into my heart. The fabric holds.

Then the cannibal goes slack, twitching, and his body falls to the ground, spinal cord severed by Mustang from behind.

A black missile blurs past my face and slams into Mustang. Knocking her off her feet. The fletching of an arrow sticks from her left shoulder. She grunts, scrambling on the ground. I lunge away from her, toward the three remaining Obsidian. One's nocking another arrow, the second hefts a huge axe, the third holds a huge curved horn, which the cannibal brings through the bearhelm to its mouth.

Then a terrible howl comes from outside the ship.

The lights go out.

The darkness ripples with a fourth shape. Shadowy forms lashing at one another. Metal cutting flesh. And when the lights come back on, Ragnar stands holding the head of one Obsidian as he pulls his razor out of the chest of the second. The third, bow cut in half, pulls a knife, stabbing wildly at Ragnar. He hacks her arm off. Still she rolls away, mad, immune to pain. He stalks after her and rips off her helmet. Beneath is a young woman. Face painted white, nostrils slit open so she looks a snake. Ritual scars forming a series of bars under both eyes. She can't be more than eighteen. Her mouth slurs out something as she stares at the vastness of Ragnar, large even for her people. Then her wild eyes find the tattoos on his face.

"*Vjrnak,*" she rasps, not in terror, but fevered joy. "*Tnak ruhr. Ljarfor aesir!*" She closes her eyes and Ragnar cuts off her head.

"You prime?" I ask Mustang, rushing to her. She's already on her feet. The arrow sticks out from under her collarbone.

"What did she say?" Mustang asks past me. "Your Nagal is better than mine."

"I didn't understand the dialect." It was too guttural. Ragnar knows it.

"**Stained son. Kill me. I will rise Golden.**" Ragnar explains. "**They eat what they find.**" He nods to the Golds. "**But to eat the flesh of Gods is to rise immortal. More will come.**"

"Even in the storm?" I ask. "Can their griffins fly in this?"

His lips curl in disgust. "**The beasts do not ride griffin. But no. They will seek refuge.**"

"What about the other wreck?" Mustang asks, pressing on. "Supplies? Men?"

He shakes his head. "**Bodies. Ship munitions.**"

I send Ragnar to fetch Holiday from her post. Mustang and I stay with plans to search the ship for gear. But I remain standing motionless in the cannibals' charnel house even after Ragnar's slipped out into the snow. The Golds might have been enemies, but this horror makes life feel so cheap. There's a cruel irony to this place. It is terrifying and wicked, but it wouldn't exist unless Gold made it exist to create fear, to create that need for their iron rule. These poor bastards were eaten by their own pet monsters.

Mustang stands from examining one of the Obsidian, wincing from the arrow that's still imbedded in her shoulder. "Are you all right?" she asks, noting my silence. I gesture to the broken fingernails on one of the Golds.

"They weren't dead when they started skinning them. Just trapped."

She nods sadly and holds out her palm. Something she found on the Obsidian body. Six Institute class rings. Two Pluto Cyprus trees, a Minerva owl, a Jupiter lightning bolt, a Diana stag, and one which I pick from her palm, emblazoned with the Mars wolf head.

"We should look for him," she says.

I reach up to the ceiling to examine the Golds who hang upside down from their seats. Their eyes and tongues are gone, but I can see, mangled as they are, none are my old friend. We search the rest of the upside-down ship and find several small bedroom suites. In the dresser of one, Mustang finds an ornate leather box with several watches and a small pearl earring set in silver. "Cassius was here," she says.

"Are those his watches?"

"It's my earring."

I help Mustang remove the arrow from her shoulder in Cassius's suite, away from the gore. She makes no sound as I break off the tip, push her against the wall, and jerk the arrow out by its tail end. She curls in on herself, slumping down to her heels in pain. I sit on the edge of the mattress that's fallen from the ceiling and watch her hunch there. She doesn't like being touched when she's wounded.

"Finish up," she says, standing.

I use the resGun to make a shiny patch over the hole on the front and back, just under her collarbone. It stops the bleeding and will help repair the tissue, but she'll feel the wound and it'll slow her for days. I pull her sealSkin back up over her bare shoulder. She zips the front up for herself before patching the wound on my jaw as well. Her breath fills the air. She comes so close I can smell the dampness of the snow that's melted in her hair. She presses the resGun to my jaw and paints a thin layer of the microorganisms onto the wound. They scramble into the pores and tighten to make a fleshlike antibacterial coating. Her hand lingers on the back of my head, fingers wrapped in the strands of my hair, like she wants to say something but doesn't have the words. Nor does she find them by the time Holiday and Ragnar return. Hearing Holiday calling my name, I squeeze Mustang's good shoulder and leave her there.

Most of the ship's gear is gone. Several sets of optics missing from their cases. The armory missing entirely, scattered across the mountains as the ship came apart and the cargo hold ripped open. The rest has been torn through by Obsidians or broken in the crash. All I get is static from the transponder and com gear.

Ragnar discerns that Cassius and the rest of his party, some fifteen men, departed several hours before we reached the vessel. They stripped it bare of supplies. The Eaters likely descended as soon as it landed, otherwise Cassius wouldn't have left those Golds behind to be eaten. Supporting this idea, Mustang finds several Eater bodies nearer the cockpit, which means Cassius and his men were under attack as they left. Snow's almost covered the corpses. We stack the fresher bodies outside in the snow in case worse predators than Eaters come to visit.

After scavenging the ship for supplies, I have Mustang and Holiday seal us inside the galley. Fusing the two entrances shut with welding torches found in the ship's maintenance closet. The weapons and cold gear might have been stripped clean, but the ship's cistern is full, the water inside not yet frozen. And the galley's pantries are stocked with food.

It's passingly cozy in our shelter. The insulation traps our heat inside. The light from two amber emergency lamps bathes the room in soft orange. Holiday uses the intermittent power to cook a feast of pasta with marinara sauce and sausage over the galley's electric stoves as Ragnar and I plot a course to the Spires and Mustang sorts through the stacks of scavenged provisions, filling military packs she found in storage.

I burn my tongue as Holiday brings Ragnar and me heaping portions of pasta. I didn't realize how hungry I was. Ragnar nudges me and I follow his eyes to watch quietly as Holiday brings Mustang a bowl too and leaves her with a small nod. Mustang smiles to herself. The four of us sit eating in silence. Listening to our forks against the bowls. The wind shrieking outside. Rivets groaning. Steel gray snow piles against the small circular windows, but not before we see strange shapes moving through the white to drag off the corpses we set outside.

"What was it like growing up here?" Mustang asks Ragnar. She sits cross-legged with her back against the wall. I lay adjacent to her, a backpack between, on one of the mattresses Ragnar dragged inside the room to line its floor, on my third serving of pasta.

"It was home. I did not know anything else."

"But now that you do?"

He smiles gently. "It was a playground. The world beyond is vast, but so small. Men putting themselves in boxes. Sitting at desks. Riding in cars. Ships. Here, the world is small, but without end." He loses himself in stories. Slow to share at first, now it seems he revels in knowing that we listen. That we care. He tells us of swimming in the ice floes as a boy. How he was an awkward child. Too slow. Bones outracing the rest of him. When he was beaten by another boy, his mother took him to the sky for his first time on her griffin. Making him hold on to her from behind. Teaching him it is his arms that keep him from falling. His will. "She flew higher, and higher, till the air was thin and I could feel the cold in my bones. She was waiting for me to let go. To weaken. But she did not know that I tied my wrists together. That is as close to Allmother death as I have ever been."

His mother, Alia Volarus, the Snowsparrow, is a legend among her people for her reverence for the gods. A daughter to a wanderer, she became a warrior of the Spires and rose in prominence as she raided other clans. Such is her devotion to the gods that when she rose to power, she gave four of her own children to serve them. Keeping only one for herself, Sefi.

"She sounds like my father," Mustang says softly.

"Poor sods," Holiday mutters. "My ma would make me cookies and teach me how to strip down a hoverJack."

"And what about your father?" I ask.

"He was a bad sort." She shrugs. "But bad in a boring way. A different family in every port. Stereotypical Legionnaire. I got his eyes. Trigg got Ma's."

"I never knew my first father," Ragnar says, meaning his birth father. Obsidian women are polygamous. They might have seven children from seven fathers. Those men are then bound to protect the other children of her brood. **"He went to become a slave before I was born. My mother never speaks his name. I do not even know if he lives."**

"We can find out," Mustang says. "We'd have to search the Board of Quality Control's registry. Not easy, but we can find him. What happened to him. If you want to know."

He's stunned by the idea and nods slowly. **"Yes. I would like that."**

Holiday watches Mustang in a very different way than she did just hours before when we were leaving Phobos, and I'm struck by how natural this feels, our four worlds colliding together. "We all know your father." Holiday says. "But what is your ma like? She looks frigid, from what I've seen, just on the HC, you know?"

"That's my stepmother. She doesn't care for me. Just Adrius, actually. My real mother died when I was young. She was kind. Mischievous. And very sad."

"Why?" Holiday presses.

"Holiday . . ." I say. Her mother is a subject I've never pushed. She's held her back from me. A little locked box in her soul that she never shares. Except tonight, it seems.

"It's all right," she says. She pulls up her legs, hugging them, and continues. "When I was six, my mother was pregnant with a little girl. The doctor said there would be complications with the birth and recommended intervening medically. But my father said that if the child was not fit to survive birth, it did not deserve life. We can fly between the stars. Mold the planets, but father let my sister die in my mother's womb."

"The hell?" Holiday mutters. "Why not give her cell therapy? You got the money."

"Purity in the product," Mustang says.

"That's insane."

"That's my family. Mother was never the same. I'd hear her crying in the middle of the day. See her staring out the window. Then one night she went for a walk at Caragmore. The estate my father gave her as a wedding present. He was in Agea working. She never came home. They found her on the rocks beneath the sea cliffs. Father said she slipped. If he was alive now, he'd still say she slipped. I don't think he could have survived thinking anything else."

"I'm sorry," Holiday says.

"As am I."

"It's why I'm here, since that's what you were wondering," Mustang says. "My father was a titan. But he was wrong. He was cruel. And if I can be something else"—her eyes meet mine—"I will be."

29

||||||||||||||||||||||||

HUNTERS

By the time we wake, the storm has cleared. We bundle our-selves with insulation taken from the ship's walls and set out into the bleakness. Not a cloud mars the marbled blue-black sky. We head toward the sun, which stains the horizon a cooling shade of mol-ten iron. Autumn has few days left. We head for the Spires with plans of lighting fires as we go, in hopes of signaling the few Valkyrie scouts active in the area. But smoke will also bring the Eaters.

We scan the mountains as we pass, wary of the cannibal tribes and of the fact that somewhere ahead Cassius and maybe Aja trudge through the snow with a troop of special forces operators.

By midday we find evidence of their passing. Churned snow out-side a rocky alcove large enough for several dozen men. They camped there to wait out the storm. A cairn of stacked stones lies near the campsite. One of the stones has been carved with a razor and reads: *per aspera ad astra.*

"It's Cassius's handwriting," Mustang says.

Pulling off the rocks, we find the corpses of two Blues and a Silver. Their weaker bodies froze in the night. Even here, Cassius had the decency to bury them. We replace the rocks as Ragnar lopes ahead, following the tracks at a speed we can't match. We follow after. An hour later, manmade thunder rumbles in the distance, accompanied by the lonely shriek of distant pulseFists. Ragnar returns soon after, eyes shining with excitement.

"I followed the tracks," he says.

"And?" Mustang asks.

"It is Aja and Cassius with a troop of Grays and three Peerless."

"Aja is here?" I ask.

"Yes. They flee on foot through a mountain pass in the direction of Asgard. A tribe of Eaters harries them. Bodies litter the way. Dozens. They sprang an ambush and failed. More come."

"How much gear do they have?" Mustang asks.

"No gravBoots. ScarabSkin only. But they have packs. They left the pulseArmor behind just two kilometers north. Out of energy."

Holiday looks at the horizon and touches Trigg's pistol on her hip. "Can we catch them?"

"They carry many supplies. Water. Food. Injured men now too. Yes. We can overtake them."

"Why are we here?" Mustang interjects. "It's not to hunt Aja and Cassius down. The only thing that matters is getting Ragnar to the Spires."

"Aja killed my brother," Holiday says.

Mustang's taken aback. "Trigg? The one you mentioned? I didn't know. But still, we can't be pulled to the side by vengeance. We can't fight two dozen men."

"What if they reach Asgard before we reach the Spires?" Holiday asks. "Then we're cooked." Mustang's not convinced.

"Can you kill Aja?" I ask Ragnar.

"Yes."

"This is an opportunity," I say to Mustang. "When else will they be so exposed? Without their Legions? Without the pride of Gold protecting them? These are champions. Like Sevro says, 'When you have the chance to waste your enemy, you do it.' This is one time I'd agree with the mad bastard. If we can take them off the board, the Sovereign loses two Furies in one week. And Cassius is Octavia's link to Mars and the great families here. And if we expose her negotiations with you to him, we fracture that alliance. We sever Mars from the Society."

"An enemy divided . . ." Mustang says slowly. "I like it."

"**And we owe them a debt,**" Ragnar says. "**For Lorn, Quinn, Trigg. They came here to hunt us. Now we hunt them.**"

The trail is unmistakable. Corpses litter the snow. Dozens of Eaters. Bodies still smoking from pulsefire near a narrow mountain pass where the Obsidians sprang an ambush on the Golds. They did not understand the firepower the Golds could bring to bear. Huge craters pock the craggy slopes. Deeper imprints in the snow mark the passing of aurochs. Huge steerlike animals with shaggy coats that the Obsidian ride.

The pass widens into a thin alpine forest that skins an expanse of rolling hills. Gradually the craters decrease and we begin seeing discarded pulseFists and rifles and several Gray bodies with arrows or axes embedded in them. The Obsidian dead are closer to the Gold trail now and bear razor wounds. There's dozens with missing limbs, clean decapitations. Cassius's band is running out of ammunition and now Olympic Knights are doing the work up close. Yet the wind still crackles with gunfire kilometers ahead.

We pass moaning Obsidian Eaters who lie dying from bullet wounds, but it's only over a wounded Gray that Ragnar stops. The man's still alive, but barely. An iron axe is buried in his stomach. He wheezes up at an unfamiliar sky. Ragnar crouches over him. Recognition goes through the Gray's eyes as he sees the Stained's uncovered face.

"**Close your eyes,**" Ragnar says, pressing the man's empty rifle back in his hands. "**Think of home.**" The man closes his eyes. And with a twist, Ragnar breaks his neck and sets his head gently back on the snow. A shrill horn echoes across the mountain range. "**They call off the hunt,**" Ragnar says. "**Immortality is not worth the price today.**"

We pick up our pace. Kilometers to our right, Mounted Eaters on aurochs skirt the edges of the woods, heading for their high-mountain camps. They do not see us as we move through the pine taiga. Holiday watches the hunting party disappear behind a hill through the scope of her rifle. "They carried two Golds," she says. "Didn't recognize them. They weren't dead yet."

We all feel the chill.

It's an hour later that we spy our quarry beneath us in an uneven snowfield striped with crevasses. Two arms of forest hug the snowfield. Aja and Cassius chose an exposed route instead of continuing through the treacherous forest where they lost so many Grays. There's four left in the company. Three Golds and a Gray. They wear black scarabSkin, cloaked with pelts and extra layers they stripped from the dead cannibals. They move at a breakneck pace, the rest of their party massacred in the depths of the woods. We can't tell which is Aja or Cassius because of the masks and the similar shapes they make under the cloaks.

Initially, I wanted to lie in wait and ambush them to take the tactical initiative, but I remember how the optics were missing from their boxes and assume Aja and Cassius are both wearing them. With thermal vision, they'll see us hiding under snow. Might even see us if we hide inside the bellies of dead aurochs or seals. So instead, I have Ragnar lead me on the path he found to cut them off at a pass they must travel through and block their path to draw their eyes.

I'm panting beside Ragnar, coughing the cold out of aching lungs, when the party of four arrives on our chosen ground. They jog along the edge of a crevasse in improvised snowshoes, hunched against the weight of food and survival gear they drag behind them on little makeshift sleds. Textbook Legion survival skills, courtesy of the military schools of the Martian Fields. All four wear black optics visors with smoky glass lenses. It's eerie as they see us. No expressions on the optics or masked faces. So it feels like they expected us to be here waiting at the edge of the snowfield, blocking the pass out.

My eyes dart back and forth between them. Cassius is easy enough to distinguish by his height. But which of the four is Aja? I'm torn between two thick Golds, each shorter than Cassius. Then I see my old razormaster's weapon dangling from her belt.

"Aja!" I call, removing the sealSkin balaclava.

Cassius pulls off his mask. His hair is sweaty, face flushed. He alone carries a pulseFist, but I know its charge must be running low, based on the dispersion patterns of the dead cannibals behind them. His razor unfurls, as do the rest. They look like long red tongues, blood frozen on the blades.

"Darrow . . ." Cassius mutters, stunned by the sight of us. "I saw you sink . . ."

"I swim just as well as you. Remember?" I look past him. "Aja, you going to let Cassius do all the talking?"

Finally, she steps from the other to stand by the tall knight, removing from around her waist the rope that attaches her to her makeshift sled. She doffs her scarabSkin mask, revealing her dark face and bald head. Steam swirls. She scans the crevasses that thread their way through the snow, and the rocks and trees, the pen in the snowfield, wondering where my ambush will come from. She remembers Europa well enough, but she can't know who my crew was or how many survived.

"An abomination and a rabid dog," she purrs, eyes lingering on Ragnar before coming back to me. The scarabSkin she wears is unmarked. Can she really not have taken a single wound from the Obsidian? "I see your Carver has pieced you back together, ruster."

"Well enough to kill your sister," I say in reply, unable to keep the poison out of my voice. "Pity it wasn't you." She makes no reply. How many times have I seen her kill Quinn in memory? How many times have I seen her rob Lorn of his razor as he lay dead from the Jackal and Lilath's blades? I gesture to the weapon. "That doesn't belong to you."

"You were born to serve, not speak, abomination. Do not address me." She glances up to the sky where Phobos glitters on the eastern horizon. Red and white lights flicker around it. It's a space battle, which means Sevro has captured ships. But how many? Aja frowns and exchanges a worried look with Cassius.

"I have long awaited this moment, Aja."

"Ah, my father's favorite pet." Aja examines Ragnar. "Has the Stained convinced you he's tamed? I wonder if he told you how he liked to be rewarded after a fight in the Circada. After the applause faded and he cleaned the blood from his hands, Father would send him young Pinks to satisfy his animal lusts. How greedy he was with them. How frightened they were of him." Her voice is flat and bored of this ice, of this conversation, of us. All she wants is what we have to give her, and that is a challenge. After all the Obsidian bodies behind her, she still is not tired of blood. "Have you ever seen an Obsidian rut?" she continues. "You'd think twice about taking off their collars, ruster. They have appetites you can't imagine."

Ragnar steps forward, holding his razors in either hand. He unfastens the white fur he took from the Eaters and lets it fall behind him. It's strange being here surrounded by wind and snow. Stripped of our armies, our navies. The only thing protecting each of our lives: little coils of metal. The hugeness of the Antarctic laughs at our size and self-importance, thinking how easily it could snuff out the heat in our little chests. But our lives mean so much more than the frail bodies that carry them.

Ragnar's step forward is a sign to Mustang and Holiday in the trees.

Aim true, Holiday.

"**Your father bought me, Aja. Shamed me. Made me his devil. A thing. The child inside fled. The hope vanished. I was Ragnar no more.**" He touches his own chest. "**But I am Ragnar today, tomorrow, forever more. I am son of the Spires, brother of Sefi the Quiet, brother of Darrow of Lykos, and Sevro au Barca. I am the Shield of Tinos. I follow my heart. And when yours beats no more, foul Knight, I will pull it from your chest and feed it to the griffin of the . . .**"

Cassius scans the craggy rocks and stunted trees that cup the snowfield to his left. His eyes narrow when they fall upon a cluster of broken timber at the base of a rock formation. Then, without warning, he shoves Aja forward. She stumbles, and just behind her, where she stood, the head of their remaining Gray explodes. Blood splatters the snow as the crack of Holiday's rifle echoes from the mountains. More bullets tear into the snow around Cassius and Aja. The Fury moves behind the third Gold, using his body as cover. Two bullets slam into his scarabSkin, penetrating the strong polymer. Cassius rolls on his shoulder and uses much of the last juice from his pulseFist. The hillside erupts. Rocks glowing. Exploding. Snow vaporizing.

And under that noise is the sound of a bowstring releasing. Aja hears it too. She moves fast. Spinning as an arrow fired by Mustang from the woods careens toward her head. It misses by centimeters. Cassius fires on Mustang's position on the hill, shattering trees and superheating rocks.

Can't tell if she's hit. Can't spare the seconds to look because Ragnar and I use the distraction to charge, vision narrowing, slingBlade curving into form. Closing the distance over the snow. PulseFist glowing in his hand, Cassius turns just as I bear down on him. He fires the pulseFist. It's a weak charge that I dive beneath, hitting the ground and rolling up like a Lykos tumbler. He fires again. The pulseFist is dead, battery drained from firing on the hillside. Ragnar hurls one of his razors at Aja like a huge throwing knife. It flips end over end in the air. She doesn't move. It slams into her. She spins backward. For a moment I think he's killed her. But then she turns back to us, holding the razor by the hilt in her right hand.

She caught it.

A dark fear sweeps through me as all of Lorn's warnings about Aja come rushing back. "Never fight a river, and never fight Aja."

The four of us smash together, turning into a clumsy mash of cracking whips and clattering blades. Scrambling and twisting and bending. Our razors faster than our own eyes can track. Aja swipes diagonally at my legs as I go for hers; Ragnar and Cassius aim for each other's necks in quick no-look thrusts. Identical strategies, all. It's so awkward we all almost kill one another in the first half second. Yet each gambit misses by a hair.

We separate. Stumbling backward. Humorless smiles on our faces—a bizarre kinship as we remember we all speak the same martial language. All that hateful breed of human Dancer told me about before I was Carved, the ones Lorn lived among and despised all the while.

I shatter the weird peace first. Lashing forward in a tight series of thrusts at Cassius's right side, peeling him away from Aja so Ragnar can take her down singly. Behind Cassius, Mustang stirs from among the rubble. Rushing across the snow, huge Obsidian bow in hand. Still fifty meters away. I sweep my razor whip twice at Cassius's legs, retracting it into a blade as he swings diagonally at my head. The blow rattles my arm as I catch it halfway along the razor's curve. He's stronger than I am. Faster than he was the last time we fought. And he's practiced now against the curved blade. Training with Aja, no doubt. He forces me back. I stumble, fall, between his legs I see the Fury and the Stained tearing into each other. She stabs him through his left thigh.

Another arrow whispers through the air. It slams into Cassius's back. His scarabSkin holds. Off balance, he swings again in a tight set of eight moves. I throw myself backward just as the razor hisses through the air where my head had been. I sprawl on the snow, centimeters from the edge of a huge crevasse. Scrambling up as Cassius rushes me. I block another downward swing, teetering on the edge. I fall backward and push off the edge as hard as I can so I land and clear the other side, using my agility to avoid his onslaught. Behind him, Aja spins under Ragnar's blade, slicing at his hamstrings. She's peeling him apart.

Cassius pursues me, hurdling the crevasse and swinging down at me. I block the blade. It would have opened me from shoulder to opposite hip. I throw a rock at his face. Gain my feet. He slams his blade down again in a feint, pivots his wrist, and swings to carve off my knees. I stumble to the side, barely dodging. He converts his razor to a whip, cracks it at my legs, and rips them out from under me. I fall. He kicks me in the chest. Wind gushes out of me. He stands on my wrist, pinning my razor down, and is about to plunge his razor into my heart, his face a mask of determination.

"*Stop,*" Mustang shouts. She's twenty meters away, aiming her bow at Cassius. Hand quivering from the strain of the taut string. "I will put you down."

"No," he says. "You would . . ."

The bowstring snaps. He jerks his razor up to deflect the arrow. Misses, slower than Aja. The serrated iron tip punches through the front of his throat and out the back of his neck, the feather fletching scratching the underside of his dimpled chin. There's no spray of blood. Just a meaty, wet gurgle. He flops back. Hitting the ground hard. Gagging. Hacking hideously. His feet kick as he clutches the arrow. Hissing for breath, eyes inches from my own. Mustang rushes to me. I scramble to my feet, away from Cassius, and grab my razor from the snow, pointing it at his thrashing body.

"I'm prime," I say, tearing my eyes from my old friend as blood pools beneath him and he fights for his life. "Help Ragnar."

Over Cassius's body, we see the Stained and Aja whirling at each other on the edge of a crevasse. Blood paints the snow around them. All of it coming from Ragnar. But still he presses the woman knight back, a furious song cascading out of his throat. Beating her down. Overwhelming her with his two hundred and fifty kilograms of mass. Sparks flare from their blades. She caves before him now, unable to match the anger of the banished prince of the Spires. Heels skidding on the snow. Arm shuddering. Bending back away from Ragnar. Bending like a willow. His song roars louder. "No," I murmur. "Shoot her," I tell Mustang.

"They're too close. . . ."

"I don't care!"

She fires a shot. It rips inches past Aja's head. But it does not matter. Ragnar has already fallen into the trap the woman has laid for him, Mustang doesn't see it yet. She will. It's one of the many Lorn taught me. The one Ragnar could not have learned because he never had a razormaster. He only ever had his rage and years of fighting with solid weapons, not the whip. Mustang loads another arrow. And Ragnar swings down at Aja with a blacksmith's overhead strike, Aja raises her rigid blade to meet his. She activates the whip function. Her blade goes limp. Expecting to meet the resistance of solid polyenne fiber, Ragnar's whole weight carries down on empty air. He's athletic enough to slow the movement so his blade docsn't smash into the ground, and against a lesser opponent he would have recovered with ease. But Aja was the greatest student of Lorn au Arcos. She's already spinning to the side, contracting the whip back into a blade and using her momentum to hack sideways at Ragnar as she finishes her spin. The movement is simple. Laconic. Like one of the ballerinas Mustang and Roque would watch at Agea's opera house as I studied with Lorn, pivoting through a *fouetté*. If I didn't see the blood paint her blade and spray a delicate arc of red across the snow, I could be convinced that she missed.

Aja does not miss.

Ragnar tries to turn and face her, but his legs betray him. Crumpling underneath. His gaping wound a bloody smile against the white of his sealSkin. Aja cut into his lower back, through his spinal cord, and out the front of his stomach at the belly button. He flops down at the lip of a crevasse. Razor skipping across the ice. I howl in rage, in crushing disbelief, and charge Aja as Mustang fires her bow, running with me. Aja sidesteps Mustang's arrows and stabs Ragnar twice more in the stomach as he lies grasping his wound. His body jerks. The blade slides in and out. Aja sets her feet now, preparing for me, when her eyes go wide. She steps back, marveling at something in the sky above my head. Mustang fires twice in quick succession. Aja's head jerks. She twists away from us, spinning backward to the edge of the crevasse. Ice caves beneath her foot, crumbling off into the crevasse. Her arms windmill, but she can't regain her balance as her eyes meet mine and she pitches with the ice headfirst into the darkness.

30

||||||||||||||||||||||

THE QUIET

Aja is gone. The crevasse deep, sides narrowing away into dark-ness. I rush back to Ragnar as Mustang stares up at the hill-side and the clouds, bow at the ready. She only has three arrows left. "I don't see anything," she says.

"Reaper," Ragnar murmurs from the ground. His chest heaves. Panting heavily. Dark lifeblood pulses out of his open stomach. Aja could have finished him quickly with the two thrusts when he was on the ground. Instead, she stabbed his lower gut so he would suffer as he died. I push on the first wound, red to my elbows, but there's so much blood I don't even know what to do. A resGun can't fix what Aja has done. It can't even hold him together. The tears sting my eyes. Can hardly see. Steam billows from the wound. My frozen fingers tingling with warmth from the blood. Ragnar blanches at the blood, an em-barrassed look on his face as he whispers apologies.

"It could be the cannibals," Mustang says, regarding Aja's distrac-tion. "Can he move?"

"No," I say weakly. She glances down at him, more stoic than I am. "We can't stay here," she says.

I ignore her. I've watched too many friends die to let Ragnar go. I led him to fight Aja. I convinced him to come home. I will not let him slip away. I owe him that much. If it is the last thing I do, foolish or not, I will defend him. I will find some way to fix him, get him to a Yellow. Even if the cannibals come. Even if it costs me my life, I will not leave him. But thinking it doesn't make it true. Doesn't give me magical powers. Whatever plan I make, it seems the world is content to undo it.

"Reaper . . ." Ragnar manages again.

"Save your strength, my friend. It's going to take all of it to get you out of here."

"She was fast. So fast."

"She's gone now," I say, though I can't know for sure.

"I always dreamed of a good death." He shudders as he realizes again that he's dying. "This does not seem good."

His words fishhook a sob from my chest into my throat. "It's fine," I say thickly. "It'll be fine. Once we get you patched up. Mickey will fix you proper. We'll get you to the Spires. Call in an evac."

"Darrow . . ." Mustang says.

Ragnar blinks hard up at me, trying to focus his eyes. He reaches for the sky with a hand. "Sefi . . ."

"No. It's me, Ragnar. It's Darrow," I say.

"Darrow . . ." Mustang presses sharply.

"What?" I snap.

"Sefi . . ." Ragnar points. I follow his finger to the sky above. I see nothing. Just the faint clouds shifting in the wind that comes in from the sea. I hear only the sound of Cassius's hacking and the creak of Mustang's bow and Holiday limping toward us over the snow. Then I see why Aja fled as three thousand kilograms of winged predator pierces the clouds. Body that of a lion. Wings, front legs, and head that of an eagle. Feathers white. Beak hooked and black. Head the size of a grown Red. The griffin is huge, underside of its wings painted with the screaming faces of sky-blue demons. They stretch ten meters wide as the beast lands in the snow in front of me. The earth shakes. Its eyes are pale blue, glyphs and wards painted along its black beak in white. Upon its back sits a lean, terrible human, who blows mournfully on a white horn.

More horns echo from the clouds above and twelve more griffins slam down into the mountain pass, some clinging to the sharp rock walls above us, others pawing at the snow. The first griffin-rider, the one who blew the horn, is cloaked head to toe in filthy white fur and wears a bone helmet crested with a single spine of blue feathers, which trail down the back of the neck. Not a rider is under two meters tall.

"Sunborn," one of them calls in their sluggish dialect as she rushes to the side of their silent leader. The speaker strips her helmet to reveal a brutish face thick with scars and piercings before falling to her knee and touching her forehead with a gloved palm in a sign of respect. A blue handprint covers her face. "We saw the flame in the sky. . . ." Her voice falters when she sees my slingBlade.

The other riders strip their helms, dismounting in a rush as they see our hair and eyes. Not a rider among them is a man. The women's faces are painted with huge sky-blue handprints, a little eye drawn in the center of each. White hair flows in long braids down their backs. Black eyes peer from hooded lids. Iron and bone piercings bridge noses and hook lips and notch ears. Only the lead rider has yet to remove her helmet or kneel. She steps toward us, in a trance.

"Sister," Ragnar manages. "**My sister.**"

"Sefi?" Mustang repeats, eying the black human tongues on the prize-hook on the Obsidian's left hip. She wears no gloves. The backs of her hands are tattooed with glyphs.

"**Do you know me?**" Ragnar rasps. A tentative smile on quivering lips as the rider approaches. "**You must.**" The rider catalogues his scars from behind her mask. Eyes dark and wide. "**I know you,**" Ragnar continues. "**I would know you if the world were dark and we were withered and old.**" He shudders in pain. "**If the ice was melted and the wind quiet.**" She drifts forward, step by step. "**I taught you the forty-nine names of the ice . . . the thirty-four breaths of the wind.**" He smiles. "**Though you could only ever remember thirty-two.**"

She gives him nothing, but the other riders are already whispering his name, and looking at us as if by accompanying him and possessing a curved blade they've pieced together who I am. Ragnar continues, voice carrying the last of his strength.

"I carried you on my shoulders to watch five Breakings. And let you braid my hair with your ribbons. And played with the dolls you made from seal leather and threw balls of ice at old Proudfoot. I am your brother. And when the men of the Weeping Sun took me and a harvest of our kin to the Chained Lands, do you remember what I told you?"

Despite his wound, the man reeks of power. This is his land. This is his home. And he is as vast here as I was upon my clawDrill. The gravity of him draws Sefi closer. She collapses to her knees and strips away her bone helmet.

Sefi the Quiet, famed daughter of Alia Snowsparrow, is raw and majestic. Face severe. Angled like a crow's. Her eyes too small, too close together. Her lips thin, purple in the cold, and permanently pursed in thought. White hair shaved down the left side, braided and falling to the waist on the right. A wing tattoo encircled by astral runes is livid blue on the left side of her pale skull. But what makes her unique among the Obsidians, and the object of their admiration, is that her skin is without pocks or scars. The only ornament she wears is a single iron bar through her nose. And when she blinks down at Ragnar's wound, the blue eyes tattooed on the back of her eyelids pierce through me.

She extends a hand to her brother, not to touch him, but to feel the breath steam before his mouth and nose. It is not enough for Ragnar. He seizes her hand and presses it fiercely to his chest so she can feel his fading heartbeat. Tears of joy gather in his eyes. And when they spill from Sefi's down her cheeks to carve paths through her blue warpaint, his voice cracks. "I told you I would return."

Her eyes leave him to follow Aja's tracks into the crevasse. She clicks her tongue and four Valkyrie stake ropes into the snow and rappel down into the darkness to seek out Aja. The rest guard their warleader and watch the hills, elegant recurve bows at the ready. "We have to fly him to the Spires," I say in their language. "To your shaman."

Sefi does not look at me. "It is too late." Snow gathers on Ragnar's white beard. "Let me die here. On the ice. Under the wild sky."

"No," I mumble. "We can save you."

The world feels very distant and unimportant. His blood continues to leave him, but there is no more sadness in my friend. Sefi has chased it away.

"**It is no great thing to die,**" he says to me, though I know he doesn't mean it as deeply as he wants to. "**Not when one has lived.**" He smiles, trying to comfort me even now. But he wears the unjustness of his life and death upon his face. "**I owe that to you. But . . . there is much undone. Sefi.**" He swallows, his tongue heavy and dry. "**Did my men find you?**" Sefi nods, staying hunched over her brother, her white hair flying about her in the wind. He looks to me. "**Darrow, I know you think words will suffice,**" Ragnar says in Aureate lingo so Sefi cannot understand. "**They will not. Not with my mother.**" This was what he did not tell me. Why he was so quiet on the shuttle, why he carried dread upon his shoulders. He was coming home to kill his mother. And now he's giving me permission to do just that. I glance over to Mustang. She heard too, and wears her heartbreak on her face. As much for my shattered, fool's dream of a better world as for my dying friend. He shudders in pain and Sefi pulls a knife from her boot, unwilling to watch him suffer any longer. Ragnar shakes his head at her and nods to me. He wants me to do it. I shake my head as if I can wake up from this nightmare. Sefi stares at me fiercely, daring me to contradict her brother's last wishes.

"**I will die with my friends,**" Ragnar says.

I numbly let my razor slither into my hand and hold it over his chest. There's peace at last in Ragnar's wet eyes. It's all I can do to be strong for him.

"**I will give Eo your love. I will make a house for you in the Vale of your fathers. It will be beside my own. Join me there when you die.**" He grins. "**But I am no builder. So take your time. We will wait.**"

I nod like I still believe in the Vale. Like I still think it waits for me and for him. "Your people will be free," I say. "On my life, I promise this. And I will see you soon." He smiles as he stares up at the sky. Sefi frantically puts her axe in Ragnar's palm so that he can die as a warrior, a weapon in hand, and secure his place in the halls of Valhalla.

"No, Sefi," he says, dropping the axe and taking snow in his left hand, her hand with his right. "**Live for more.**" He nods to me.

The wind whips.

The snow falls.

Ragnar watches the sky, where the cold lights of Phobos glitter on as I silently slide the metal into his heart. Death comes like nightfall, and I cannot tell the moment when the light leaves him, when his heart no longer beats and his eyes no longer see. But I know he's gone. I feel it in the chill that settles over me. In the sound of the lonely, hungry wind, and the dread silence in the black eyes of Sefi the Quiet.

My friend, my protector, Ragnar Volarus has left this world.

31

||||||||||||||||||||||||

THE PALE QUEEN

I'm numb with grief. Unable to think of anything but how Sevro will react when he hears Ragnar has died. How my nieces and nephews will never braid another bow into the Friendly Giant's hair. Part of my soul has departed and will never return. He was my protector. He gave so many strength. Now, without him, I cling to the back of a Valkyrie as her griffin rises away from the bloody snow. Even as we soar through the clouds on great beating wings, even as I see the Valkyrie Spires for the first time, I feel no awe. Just numbness.

The spires are a twisting, vertiginous spine of mountain peaks so ludicrous in their abrupt rise from the arctic plains that only a maniacal Gold at the controls of a Lovelock engine with fifty years of tectonic manipulation and a solar system of resources could conspire to create them. Probably just to see if they could. Dozens of stone spires weave together like spiteful lovers. Mist shrouding them. Griffins making nests on their peaks, crows and eagles in the lower reaches. Upon a high rock wall, seven skeletons hang from chains. The ice is stained with blood and the droppings of animals. This is the home of the only race to ever threaten Gold. And we come stained in the blood of its banished prince.

Sefi and her riders searched the crevasse in which Aja fell; they found nothing but boot prints. No body. No blood. Nothing to abate the rage that burns inside Sefi. I think she would have remained over her brother's body for hours more, had they not heard drums beating in the distance. Eaters who had mustered greater strength and intended to challenge the Valkyrie for possession of the fallen gods.

Wrath stained her face as she stood over Cassius, her axe in hand. He is one of the first Golds she'll ever have seen without armor. Maybe the first aside from Mustang. And I think, stained with the blood of her brother, she would have killed him there on the snow. I know I would have let her, and so too would have Mustang. But she relented at the urging of her Valkyrie. Clicking her tongue to her riders, sheathing her axe and signaling them to mount. Now Cassius is tied to the saddle of a Valkyrie to my right. The arrow missed his jugular, but death might come for him even without a kiss from Sefi's axe.

We land in a high alcove cut into the highest reach of a corkscrew spire. Slaves from enemy Obsidian clans, eyes branded into blindness, receive our griffins. Their faces painted yellow for cowardice. Iron doors groan shut behind, sealing us off from the wind. The riders jump from their saddles before we land to help carry Ragnar away from us deeper into the rock city.

There's a commotion as several dozen armed warriors push their way into the griffin stable and confront Sefi. They gesture wildly at us. Their accents thicker than the Nagal I learned with Mickey's uploads and my studies at the Academy, but I understand enough to glean that the newer group of warriors is shouting that we should be in chains, and something about heretics. Sefi's women are shouting back, saying we are friends of Ragnar, and they point feverishly to the Gold of our hair. They don't know how to treat us, or Cassius, who several of the warriors pull away from us like dogs fighting for scrap meat. The arrow's still in his neck. Whites of his eyes huge. He reaches for me in terror as the Obsidians drag him across the floor. His hand grasps mine, holds for a moment, and then he's gone down a torch-lit hall, borne away by half a dozen giants. The rest cluster around us, huge iron weapons in hand, the stink of their furs thick and nauseating.

Quieting only when an old stout woman with a hand-shaped tattoo on her forehead pushes through their ranks to speak with Sefi. One of her mother's warchiefs. She gestures upward toward the ceiling with large hand motions.

"What is she saying?" Holiday asks.

"They're talking about Phobos. They see the lights from the battle. They think the Gods are fighting. These ones think we should be prisoners, not guests," Mustang says. "Let them take your weapons."

"Like hell." Holiday steps back with her rifle. I grab the barrel and push it down, handing them my razor. "This is bloody spectacular," she mutters. They shackle our arms and legs with great iron manacles, taking care not to touch our skin or hair, and jerk us toward a tunnel by the Spires guards, away from Sefi's Valkyrie. But as we go, I catch sight of Sefi watching after us, a strange, conflicted look on her white face.

After being dragged down several dozen dimly lit stairwells, we're shoved into a windowless cell of carved stone and stifling, smoky air. Seal oil smolders in iron braziers stinging our eyes. I trip on a raised flagstone and fall to the floor. There, I slam my chains against the stone. Feeling the anger. The helplessness. All the things happening so fast, whipping me around, so I can't tell which way's up. But I can think long enough to grasp the futility of my actions, my plans. Mustang and Holiday watch me in heavy silence. One day into my grand plan and Ragnar is already dead.

Mustang speaks more softly. "Are you all right?"

"What do you think?" I ask bitterly. She says nothing in reply, not the fragile sort of person to take offense and whimper out how she's just trying to help. She knows the pain of loss well enough. "We need to have a plan," I say mechanically, trying to force Ragnar out my mind.

"Ragnar was our plan," Holiday says. "He was the entire sodding plan."

"We can salvage it."

"And how the hell you expect to do that?" Holiday asks. "We don't have weapons anymore. And they don't exactly look tickled Pink to see us. They're probably going to eat us."

"These ones aren't cannibals," Mustang says.

"You're willing to bet your leg on that, missy?"

"Alia is the key," I say. "We can still convince her. It will be difficult without Ragnar, but that's the only way. Convince her that he died trying to bring their people the truth."

"Didn't you hear him? He said words wouldn't work."

"They still can."

"Darrow, give yourself a moment," Mustang says.

"A moment? My people are dying in orbit. Sevro is at war, and he's depending on us to bring him an army. We don't have the luxury of taking a bloodydamn moment."

"Darrow . . ." Mustang tries to interrupt. I keep going, methodically sorting through the options, how we must hunt down Aja, rejoin with the Sons. She puts a hand on my arm. "Darrow. Stop." I falter. Losing track of where I was, slipping away from the comfort of logic and falling straight into the emotion of it all. Ragnar's blood is under my nails. All he wanted was to come home to his people and lead them out of darkness like he saw me doing with mine. I robbed him of that choice by leading the attack on Aja. I don't cry. There isn't time for it, but I sit there with my head in my hands. Mustang touches my shoulder.

"He smiled in the end," she says softly. "Do you know why? Because he knew what he was doing was right. He was fighting for love. You've made a family of your friends. You always have. It made Ragnar a better man to know you. So you didn't get him killed. You helped him live. But you have to live now." She sits next to me. "I know you want to believe the best in people. But think how long it took for you to get through to Ragnar. To win over Tactus or me. What can you do in a day? A week? This place . . . it's not our world. They don't care about our rules or our morality. We will die here if we do not escape."

"You don't think Alia will listen."

"Why would she? Obsidians only value strength. And where is ours? Ragnar even thought he would have to kill his mother. She won't listen. Do you know the word for surrender in Nagal? *Rjoga*. The word for subjugation? *Rjoga*. What's the word for slavery? *Rjoga*. Without Ragnar to lead them, what do you think is going to happen if you release them on the Society? Alia Snowsparrow is a black-blooded tyrant. And the rest of the warchiefs are no better. She might even be expecting us. Even if we've hacked the Golds' monitoring systems, the Golds know she's his mother, then they could have told her to expect him. She could be reporting to them right now."

When I looked up at my father as a boy, I thought being a man was having control. Being the master and commander of your own destiny. How could any boy know that freedom is lost the moment you become a man. Things start to count. To press in. Constricting slowly, inevitably, creating a cage of inconveniences and duties and deadlines and failed plans and lost friends. I'm tired of people doubting. Of people choosing to believe they know what is possible because of what has happened before.

Holiday grunts. "Escaping won't be that easy."

"Step one," Mustang says as she slips free of her manacles. She used a little shard of bone to pick the lock.

"Where'd you learn that?" Holiday asks.

"You think the Institute was my first school?" she asks. "Your turn." She reaches for my manacles. "As I see it, we can rush them when they open the . . . what's wrong?"

I've pulled my hands back from her. "I'm not leaving."

"Darrow . . ."

"Ragnar was my friend. I told him I would help his people. I will not run to save myself. I will not let him die in vain. The only way out is through."

"The Obsidians . . ."

"Are needed," I say. "Without them, I can't fight Gold Legions. Not even with your help."

"All right," Mustang says, not belaboring the point. "Then how do you intend to change Alia's mind?"

"I think I'll need your help with that."

||||||||||

Hours later, we are guided to the center a cavernous throne room built for giants. It's lit by seal oil lamps that belch out black smoke along the walls. The iron doors slam shut behind us, and we're left alone before a throne, upon which sits the largest human being I've ever seen. She watches us from the far side of the room, more statue than woman. We approach awkwardly in our chains. Boots over the slick black floor till we come before Alia Snowsparrow, Queen of the Valkyrie.

Across her lap lies the body of her dead son.

Alia glares down at us. She is as colossal as Ragnar, but ancient and wicked, like the oldest tree of some primeval forest. The kind that drinks the soil and blocks the sun for lesser trees and watches them wither and yellow and die and does nothing but reach her branches higher and dig her roots deeper. The wind has armored her face in dead skin and calluses. Her hair is stringy and long, the color of dirty snow. She sits on a cushion of furs stacked inside the rib cage of the skeleton of what must have been the largest griffin ever Carved. The griffin's head screams silently down at us from above her. The wings spread against the stone wall, ten meters across. On her head is a crown of black glass. At her feet is her fabled warchest which is locked in times of peace by a great iron device. Her knotty hands are covered in blood.

This is the primal realm, and though I would know what to say to a queen who sits upon a throne, I have no bloodydamn clue what to say to a mother who sits with her own son dead in her lap and looks at me as though I am some worm that's just slithered up from the taiga.

It seems she doesn't much care that I've lost my tongue. Hers is sharp enough.

"There is a great heresy in our lands against the gods who rule the thousand stars of the Abyss." Her voice rumbles like that of an old crocodile. But it is not her language, it is ours. HighLingo Aureate. A sacred tongue, known by few in these lands, mostly the shaman who commune with the gods. Spies, in other words. Alia's fluency startles Mustang. But not me. I know how the low rise under the power of the mighty, and this merely confirms what I've long suspected. Slaggin' Gamma are not the only favored slaves of the worlds.

"A heresy told by wicked prophets with wicked aims. For a summer and a winter it has slithered through us. Poisoning my people and the people of the Dragon Spine and the Blooded Tents and the Rattling Caves. Poisoning them with lies that spit in the eye of our people." She leans down from her throne, blackheads huge on her nose. Wrinkles deep ravines around pitch eyes.

"Lies that say a Stained son will return and he will bring a man to guide us from this land. A morning star in the darkness. I have sought these heretics out to learn of their whispers, to see if the gods spoke through them. They did not. Evil spoke through them. And so I have hunted the heretics. Broken their bones with my own hands. Peeled their flesh and set them upon the rock of the spires to be eaten as carrion by the fowl of the ice." The seven bodies who dangled from the chains outside. Ragnar's friends.

"This I do for my people. Because I love my people. Because the children of my loins are few, and those of my heart many. For I knew the heresy to be a lie. Ragnar, blood of my blood, would never return. To return would mean the breaking of oaths to me, to his people, to the gods who watch over us from Asgard on high."

She looks down at her dead son.

"And then I woke into this nightmare." She closes her eyes. Breathes deep and opens them again. "Who are you to bring the corpse of my best born to my spire?"

"My name is Darrow of Lykos," I say. "This is Virginia au Augustus and Holiday ti Nakamura." Alia's eyes ignore Holiday and twitch over to Mustang. Even at nearly two meters, she seems a child in this huge room. "We came with Ragnar as a diplomatic mission on behalf of the Rising."

"The Rising." She dislikes the taste of the foreign word. "And who are you to my son?" She eyes my hair with more disdain than a mortal should have for a god. Something deeper is at play here. "Are you Ragnar's master?"

"I am his brother," I correct.

"His brother?" She mocks the idea.

"Your son swore an oath of servitude to me when I took him from a Gold. He offered me Stains and I offered him his freedom. Since then he has been my brother."

"He . . ." Her voice catches. "Died free?"

The way she says it intones that deeper understanding. One Mustang notes. "He did. His men, the ones you have hanging on the walls outside, would have told you that I lead a rebellion against the Golds who rule over you, who took Ragnar from you as they took your other children. And they would have told you, as well as all your people, that Ragnar was the greatest of my generals. He was a good man. He was—"

"I know my son," she interrupts. "I swam with him in the ice floes when he was a boy. Taught him the names of the snow, of the storms, and took him upon my griffin to show him the spine of the world. His hands clutched my hair and sang for joy as we rose through the clouds above. My son was without fear." She remembers that day very differently than Ragnar did. "I know my son. And I do not need a stranger to tell me of his spirit."

"Then you should ask yourself, Queen, what would make him return here." Mustang says. "What would make him send his men here, if he would come here himself if he knew it meant breaking his oath to you and your people?"

Alia does not speak as she examines Mustang with those hungry eyes.

"Brother." She mocks the word again, looking back to me. "I wonder, would you use brothers as you have used my son? Bringing him here. As if he is the key to unlocking the giants of the ice?" She looks around the hall so I see the deeds carved into the stone that stretches the height of fifteen men above us. I've never met an Obsidian artisan. They send us only their warriors. "As if you could use a mother's love against her. This is the way of men. I can smell your ambition. Your plans. I do not know the Abyss, oh, worldly warlord, but I know the ice. I know the serpents that slither in the hearts of men.

"I questioned the heretics myself. I know what you are. I know you descend from a lower creature than us. A Red. I have seen Reds. They are like children. Little elves who live in the bones of the world. But you stole the body of an Aesir, of a Sunborn. You call yourself a breaker of chains, but you are a maker of them. You wish to bind us to you. Using our strength to make you great. Like every man."

She leans over my dead friend to leer at me and I see what this woman respects, why Ragnar believed he would have to kill her and take her throne, and why Mustang wanted to flee. Strength. And where is mine, she wonders.

"You know many things of him," Mustang says. "But you know nothing of me, yet you insult me."

Alia frowns. It's clear she has no idea who Mustang is, and no wish to anger a true Gold, if, indeed, Mustang is one. Her confidence wavers only a fraction. "I have laid no claims against you, Sunborn."

"But you have. By suggesting he has evil wishes in store for your people, you too suggest that I collude with him. That I, his companion, am here with the same wicked intentions."

"Then what are your intentions? Why do you accompany this creature?"

"To see if he was worth following," Mustang says.

"And is he?"

"I don't know yet. What I do know is that millions will follow him. Do you know that number? Can you even comprehend it, Alia?"

"I know the number."

"You asked my intentions," Mustang says. "I will put it plainly. I am a warlord and Queen like you. My dominion is larger than you can comprehend. I have metal ships in the Abyss that carry more men than you have ever seen. That can crack the highest mountain in two. And I am here to tell you that I am not a god. Those men and women on Asgard are not gods. They are flesh and blood. Like you. Like me."

Alia rises slowly, bearing her huge son easily in her arms, and walks him to a stone altar and lays him upon it. She pours oil from a small urn onto a cloth and drapes it over Ragnar's face. Then she kisses the cloth. Looking down at him.

Mustang presses her. "This land cannot hold seed. It is ruled by wind and ice and barren rock. But you survive. Cannibals roam the hills. Enemy clans ache for your land. But you survive. You sell your sons, your daughters to your 'gods,' but you survive. Tell me, Alia. Why? Why live when all you live for is to serve. To watch your family wither away? I've watched mine go. Each stolen from me one by one. My world is broken. And so is yours. But if you join your arms with mine, with Darrow as Ragnar wanted . . . we can make a new world."

Alia turns back to us, beleaguered. Her steps are slow and measured as she comes before us. "Which would you fear more, Virginia au Augustus, a god? Or a mortal with the power of a god?" The question hangs between them, creating a rift words cannot mend. "A god cannot die. So a god has no fear. But mortal men . . ." She clucks her tongue behind her stained teeth. "How frightened they are that the darkness will come. How horribly they will fight to stay in the light."

Her corrupt voice chills my blood.

She knows.

Mustang and I realize it at the same terrible moment. Alia knows her gods are mortal. A new fear bubbles up from the deepest part of me. I'm a fool. We traveled all this distance to pull the wool from her eyes, but she's already seen the truth. Somehow. Some way. Did the Golds come to her because she is queen? Did she discover it herself? Before she sold Ragnar? After? It's no matter. She's already resigned herself to this world. To the lie.

"There's another path," I say desperately, knowing that Alia made her judgment against us before we ever entered the room. "Ragnar saw it. He saw a world where your people could leave the ice. Where they could make their own destiny. Join me and that world is possible. I will give you the means to take the power that will let you cross the stars like your ancestors, to walk unseen, to fly among the clouds on boots. You can live in the land of your choosing. Where the wind is warm as flesh and the land is green instead of white. All you need to do is fight with me like your son did."

"No, little man. You cannot fight the sky. You cannot fight the river or the sea or the mountains. And you cannot fight the Gods," Alia says. "So I will do my duty. I will protect my people. I will send you to Asgard in chains. I will let the Gods on high decide your fate. My people will live on. Sefi will inherit my throne. And I will bury my son in the ice from which he was born."

32

||||||||||||||||||||||

NO MAN'S LAND

The sky is the color of blood underneath a dead nail as we fly away from the Spires. This time, we are imprisoned, chained belly down to the back of fetid fur saddles like luggage. My eyes water as the wind of the lower troposphere slashes into them. The griffin beats its wings, muscled shoulders rippling, churning the air. We bank sideways and I see the riders tilting their masked faces up to the sky to see the faint light that is Phobos. Little flashes of white and yellow mar the darkening sky as ships overhead battle. I pray silently for Sevro's safety, for Victra's and the Howlers.

Words failed with Alia, as Mustang said they would. And now we are bound for Asgard, a gift for the gods to secure the future of her people. That is what she told Sefi. And her silent daughter took my chains and, with the help of Alia's personal guards, dragged me and Mustang and Holiday to the hangar where her Valkyrie waited.

Now, hours later, we pass over a land created by wrathful gods in their youth. Dramatic and brutal, the Antarctic was designed as punishment and a test for the ancestors of the Obsidians who dared rise against the Golds in the two-hundredth year of their reign. A place so savage less than sixty percent of Obsidians reach adulthood, per Board of Quality Control quotas.

That desperate struggle for life robs them of a chance for culture and societal progress, just as the nomadic tribes of the first Dark Ages were so robbed. Farmers make culture. Nomads make war.

Subtle signs of life freckle the bald waste. Roving herds of auroch. Fires on mountain ridges, glittering from the cracks in the great doors of Obsidian cities that are carved into the rock as they gather supplies and huddle behind their walls on the eve of the long dark of winter. We fly for hours. I fall in and out of sleep, body exhausted. Not having closed my eyes since we shared the pasta with Ragnar in our cozy hole in the belly of that dead ship. How has so much changed so quickly?

I wake to the bellow of a horn. *Ragnar is dead.* It's the first thought in my head.

I am no stranger waking to grief.

Another horn echoes as Sefi's riders close their gaps, drifting together into tight formation. We rise amidst a sea of ash-gray clouds. Sefi bent over the reins in front of me. Pushing her griffin hard toward a hulking darkness. We slip free of the clouds to find Asgard hanging in the twilight. It's a black mountain ripped from the ground by the gods and hung halfway between the Abyss and the ice world below. Seat of the Aesir. Where Olympus was a bright celebration of the senses, this is a brooding threat to a conquered race.

A set of stone stairs, precarious and seemingly unsupported, rises from the mountains tethering Asgard to the world below. The Way of Stains. The path all young Obsidian must take if they wish to gain the favor of the gods, to bring honor and bounty to their tribes by becoming the servants of Allmother Death. Bodies litter the Valley of the Fallen beneath. Frozen mounds of men and women in a land where carrion never rots and only the industry of crows can make proper skeletons. It is a lonely walk, and one we must make if the Obsidian are to approach the mountain.

This is what it takes to make an Obsidian afraid. I feel that fear now from Sefi. She has never walked this path. No Stained may stay among the people of the Spires or the other tribes. All are chosen by the Golds for service. Her mother never would have let her take the tests. She needed one daughter to remain as her heir.

Unlike Olympus, Asgard is surrounded by defensive measures. Electronic high-pitched frequency emitters that would make the griffins' eardrums bleed two clicks out. A high-charged pulse shield closer in that would hyper-oscillate the molecular structure of any man or creature by boiling the water in our skin and organs. Black magic to the Obsidian. But the sensors are dead today, compliments of Quicksilver and his hackers, and the cameras and drones that monitor our approach are blind to us, showing instead the footage recorded three years before, just as with the satellites. There is only one way to seek an audience with the gods, and that is along the Way of Stains through the Shadowmouth Temple.

We set down atop the forbidding mountain peak beneath Asgard where the Way of Stains is tethered to the earth. A black temple squats over the stairs like a possessive old crone. It's skin ravaged by time. Face crumbling to the wind.

I'm pulled off the saddle and fall to the ice, legs asleep after the long journey. The Valkyrie wait for me to rise with Mustang's help. "I think it's time," she says. I nod and let the Valkyrie push us after Sefi toward the black temple. Wind pours through the mouths of three hundred and thirty-three stone faces that scream out from the temple's front façade imprisoned beneath the black rock, wild eyes desperate for release. We enter under the black arch. Snow rolls across the floor.

"Sefi," I say. The woman turns slowly back to look at me. She's not cleaned her brother's blood from her hair. "May I speak to you? Alone?" The Valkyrie wait for their quiet leader to nod before pulling Mustang and Holiday back. Sefi walks farther into the temple. I follow as best I can in my chains to a small courtyard open to the sky. I shiver at the cold. Sefi watches me there in the weird violet light, waiting patiently for me to speak. It's the first time it's occurred to me that she's as curious of me as I am of her. And it also fills me with confidence. Those small dark eyes are inquisitive. They see the cracks in things. In men, in armor, in lies. Mustang was right about Alia. She would never listen. I suspected it before we entered her throne room, but I had to give it my best. And even if she had listened, Mustang would never trust Alia Snowsparrow to lead the Obsidian in our war. I would have gained an ally and lost another. But Sefi . . . Sefi is the last hope I have.

"Where do they go?" I ask her now. "Have you ever wondered? The men and women your clan gives to the gods? I don't think you believe what they tell you. That they are lifted up as warriors. That they are given untold riches in service of the immortals."

I wait for her to reply. Of course, she does not. If I can't sway her here, then we're as good as dead. But Mustang thinks, as do I, that we have a chance with her. More than we ever did with Alia, at least.

"If you believed in the gods, you would not have sworn yourself to silence when Ragnar ascended. Others cheered, but you wept. Because you know . . . don't you." I step closer to the woman. She's just above my own height. More muscular than Victra. Her pale face is nearly the same shade as her hair. "You feel the dark truth in your heart. All who leave the ice become slaves."

Her brow furrows. I try not to lose my momentum.

"Your brother was Stained, a Son of the Spires. He was a titan. And he ascended to serve the gods but was treated no better than a prized dog. They made him fight in pits, Sefi. They wagered on his life. Your brother, the one who taught you the names of the ice and wind, who was the greatest son of the Spires in his generation, was another man's property."

She looks up at the sky where the stars blink through the black-violet twilight. How many nights has she looked up and wondered what had become of her big brother? How many lies has she told herself so she can sleep at night? Now to know the horrors he suffered, it makes all those times she looked at the stars so much worse.

"Your mother was the one who sold him," I say, seizing the opportunity. "She sold your sisters, brothers, your father. Everyone who has ever left has gone to slavery. Like my people. You know what the prophets your brother sent said. I was a slave but I have risen against my masters. Your brother rose with me. Ragnar returned here to bring you with us. To bring your people out of bondage. And he died for it. For you. Do you trust him enough to believe his last words? Do you love him enough?"

She looks back to me, the whites of her eyes red with an anger that seems to have been long dormant. As if she's known of her mother's duplicity for years. I wonder what she's heard, listening for two and a half decades. I wonder even if her mother has told her the truth. Sefi is to be queen. Perhaps that is the right of passage. Passing down the knowledge of their true condition. Perhaps Sefi even listened to our audience with Alia. Something in the way she watches me makes me believe this.

"Sefi, if you deliver me to the Golds, their reign continues and your brother will have sacrificed himself for nothing. If the world is as you like it, then do nothing. But if it is broken, if it is unjust, take a chance. Let me show you the secrets your mother has kept from you. Let me show you how mortal your gods are. Let me help you honor your brother."

She stares at the snow as it drifts across the floor, lost in thought. Then, with a measured nod, she pulls an iron key from her riding cloak and steps toward me.

The stairs of the Way of Stains are frigid and gusty, and switch back devilishly into the sky through the clouds. But they are just stairs. We climb them without chains in the guise of Valkyrie—bone riding masks painted blue, riding cloaks, and boots too big for my feet. All loaned to us by three women who stayed behind to guard the griffin at the base of the temple. Sefi leads us, eight other Valkyrie coming behind. My legs shake from exertion by the time we reach the top and see the black glass complex of the Golds that crests the floating mountain. There are eight towers in all, each belonging to one of the gods. They surround the central building, a dark glass pyramid, like wheel spokes, connected by thin bridges twenty meters above the uneven snowy ground. Between us and the Gold complex is a second temple in the shape of a giant screaming face, this one as large as Castle Mars. In front of the temple lies a little square park, at the center of which stands a gnarled black tree. Flames smolder along its branches. White blossoms perch amidst the flames, untouched by the fire. The Valkyrie whisper to each other, fearing the magic at work.

Sefi carefully plucks a blossom from the tree. The flames scorch the edges of her leather gloves, but she comes away with a small white flower the shape of a teardrop. When touched it expands and darkens to the color of blood before wilting and turning to ash. I've never seen anything like it. Nor do I particularly give a piss about the showmanship. It's too cold for that. A bloody red footprint blossoms in the snow in front of us. Sefi and her Valkyrie stay deathly still, arms outstretched with fingers crooked in a gesture of defense against evil spirits.

"It's just blood hidden in the stone," Mustang says. "It's not real."

Still, the Valkyrie are overawed when more footprints begin to appear on the ground, leading us toward the god's mouth. They look to each other in fear. Even Sefi goes to her knees when we reach the stairs at the base of the temple's mouth. We mimic her, pressing our noses to the stone as the throat opens and out waddles a withered old man. Beard white. Eyes violet and milky with age.

"You are mad!" He howls. "Mad as crows to travel the stairs on the eve of winter!" His staff thumps each individual step in his descent. Voice squeezing the lines for all they're worth. "Bone and frozen blood is all that should remain. Have you come to request a trial of the Stains?"

"No," I rumble in my best Nagal. To take the trial of the Stains now would do nothing for us. We would only see the gods when we received the facial tattoos. And surviving a test of the Stained is something even Ragnar thought I was not prepared for. There's only one other way to bring the gods to me. Bait.

"No?" the Violet says, confused.

"We come to seek an audience with the gods."

At any moment, one of the Valkyrie could give us up. All it would take is a word. The tension works its way through my shoulders. Only thing that keeps me sane is knowing Mustang's on board enough with the plan to be bent on a knee beside me at the top of this damn mountain. That has to mean I'm not totally insane. At least I hope.

"So you *are* mad!" the Violet says, growing bored of us. "The gods come and go. To the abyss, to the sea down below. But they give no audience to mortal men. For what is time to creatures such as them. Only the Stained are worth their love. Only the Stained can bear the fever of their sight. Only the children of ice and darkest night."

Well this is bloodydamn annoying.

"A ship of iron and star has fallen from the Abyss," I say. "It came with a tail of fire. And struck among the peaks near the Valkyrie Spires. Burning across the sky like blood."

"A ship?" the Violet asks, now utterly interested, as we supposed he would be.

"One of iron and star," I say.

"How do you know it was no vision?" the Violet asks cleverly.

"We touched the iron with our own hands."

The Violet is silent, mind sprinting to and fro behind those manic eyes. I'm wagering he knows that their communications systems are down. That his masters will be eager to hear of a fallen ship. The last sight he might have seen was my speech before Quicksilver shut everything down. Now this lowly Violet, this eager actor banished to the wastes to perform a mummer's farce for barbaric simpletons has news his masters don't. He has a prize, and his eyes, when he realizes this, narrow greedily. Now is his time to seize initiative and gain favor in the eyes of the masters.

How sad, the dependability of greed to make men fools.

"Have you evidence?" he asks eagerly. "Any man may say he has seen a ship of the gods fall." Hesitating, fearful of the deception I work but disdainful of priests, Sefi produces my razor from her bag. It is wrapped in seal skin. She lays it on the ground in whip form. The Violet smiles, so very pleased. He tries to snatch it from the ground with a rag from his pocket, but Sefi pulls it back with the seal cloth.

"This is for the gods," I growl. "Not their whelps."

33

||||||||||||||||||||||||

GODS AND MEN

The priest ushers us through the temple's mouth, where we wait, kneeling on a black stone antechamber inside the mountain. The stone mouth grinds closed behind us. Flames dance in the center of the room, leaping up in a pillar of fire to the onyx ceiling.

Acolytes wander through the cavernous temple, chanting softly, draped with black sackcloth hoods.

"Children of the Ice," a divine voice finally whispers from the darkness. A synthesizer, like the ones in our demonHelms, layers the voice so it seems a dozen sewn together. The invisible Gold woman doesn't even bother to use an accent. Fluent as I in their language, but disdainful of the fact and of the people to which she speaks. "You come with news."

"I do, Sunborn."

"Tell us of the ship you saw," another voice says, this one a man. Less lofty, more playful. "You may look upon my face, little child." Remaining on our knees, we glance up furtively from the ground to see two armored Golds deactivating their ghostCloaks. They stand close to us in the dark room. The temple flames dance over their metallic god faces. The man wears a cloak. The woman likely didn't have time to don hers, so eager were they to attend us.

The woman plays Freya while the man is dressed as Loki. His metal visage like that of a wolf. Animals can smell fear. Men can't. But those who kill enough can feel the vibrations in that particular silence. I feel them now from Sefi. The gods are true, she's thinking. Ragnar was wrong. We were wrong. But she says nothing.

"It bled fire across the sky," I murmur, head down. "Making great roars and crashed upon the mountainside."

"You don't say," Loki murmurs. "And is it in one piece, or lots of little itty-bitty pieces, child?"

It is risky saying we saw a ship fall. But I knew no other ruse that would draw the Golds away from their holo screens in the middle of a rebellion, past their security systems and Gray garrison to meet me here. They're Peerless Scarred, trapped here on the frontier as their world shifts beyond these walls. Once, this post would have been considered glamorous, but now it's a form of banishment. I wonder about what crimes or failings brought these Peerless Scarred here to babysit the wastes.

"The bones of the ships litter the mountain, Sunborn," I explain, looking back at the ground so they do not insist I take away the riding mask that covers my face. The more groveling I do, the less curious I am. "Broken like a fishing boat laid upon mid-stern by a Breaker. Splinters of iron, splinters of men upon the snow."

I think that's a metaphor the Obsidians would use. It passes muster.

"Splinters of men?" Loki asks.

"Yes. Men. But with soft faces. Like seal skin in firelight." Too many metaphors. "But eyes like hot coals." I can't stop. How else did Ragnar speak? "Hair like the gold of your face." The Golds' metal masks remain impassive, communicating to one another over the coms in their helmets.

"Our priest claims you have a weapon of the gods," Freya says leadingly. Sefi produces the seal cloth once more, body tense, wondering when I will dispel the magic of the gods as I promised. Her hands tremble. Both Golds move closer, the slight ripple of pulseShields evident. I touch them and I fry. They have no fear. Not here on their mountain. Closer. Closer, you dumb bastards.

"Why did you not take this to the leader of your tribe?" Loki asks.

"Or to your shaman?" Freya adds suspiciously. "The Way of Stains is long and hard. To climb all this way just to bring this to us . . ."

"We are wanderers," Mustang says as Freya bends to look at the blade. "No tribe. No shaman."

"Are you, little one?" Loki asks above Sefi, voice hardening. "Then why are there blue tattoos of the Valkyrie on the ankles of that one?" His hand drifts to the razor on his hip.

"She was cast out from her tribe," I say. "For breaking an oath."

"Is it marked with a house Sigil?" Loki asks Freya. She reaches for the weapon's hilt in front of me when Mustang laughs bitterly, drawing her attention.

"On the handle, my goodlady," Mustang says in Aureate lingo, remaining on her knees as she strips off her mask and tosses it onto the ground. "You will find a Pegasus in flight. Sigil of the House Andromedus."

"Augustus?" Loki sputters, knowing Mustang's face.

I use their surprise and slip forward. By the time they turn back to me I've snatched the razor out from under Freya's hand and activated the toggle so it is the curved question-mark shape that has burned on hillsides, been cut into foreheads, and killed so many of their kind. The same they would have seen on the holoDisplays as I made my speech.

"Reaper . . ." Freya manages, pulling up her pulseFist. I hack her arm off at the shoulder, then her head at the jaw before hurling my razor straight into Loki's chest. The blade slows as it hits his pulse-Shield, frozen in midair for half a second as the shield resists. Finally the blade slips through. But it's slowed and the armor beneath holds. It embeds itself in the pulseArmor plate. Harmless. Until Mustang steps forward and swivel-kicks the hilt of the razor. The blade punches through the armor and impales Loki.

Both gods fall. Freya to her back. Loki to his knees.

"Mask off," Mustang barks as Loki's hands wrap around the blade sticking from his chest. She slaps his hands away from his datapad. "No coms." Holiday strips the razor from the man's hip as his pulseShield shorts. I take Freya's razor from her corpse. "Do it."

Sefi and her Valkyrie stare wide-eyed from their knees at the blood pooling beneath Freya. I remove Freya's helmet from her head to reveal the mangled face of a middle-aged Peerless Scarred woman with dark skin and almond-shaped eyes.

"Does this look like a god to you, Sefi?" I ask.

Mustang snorts a dark little laugh when Loki removes his mask. "Darrow. Look who it is. Proctor Mercury!" The pudgy, cherub-faced Peerless Scarred who endeavored to recruit me into his own house at the Institute before Fitchner stole me away. When last we saw each other five years ago, he tried to duel me in the halls as my Howlers stormed Olympus. I shot him in the chest with a pulseFist. He smiled all the while. He's not smiling now as he stares at the metal in his chest. I feel a pang of pity.

"Proctor Mercury," I say. "You have to be the least lucky Gold I've ever met. Two mountains lost to a Red."

"Reaper. You have to be shitting me." He shudders in pain and laughs at his own surprise. "But you're on Phobos."

"Negative, my goodman. That'd be my diminutive psychotic accomplice."

"Gorydammit. Gorydammit." He looks at the blade in his chest, grunting as he sits on his haunches and wheezes out breaths. "How . . . did we not see you . . ."

"Quicksilver hacked your system," I say.

"You're . . . here for . . ." His voice trails away as he looks at the Valkyrie rising to gather around the dead god. Sefi bends over Freya. The pale warrior traces her fingers over the woman's face as Holiday strips off her armor.

"For them," I say. "Bloodydamn right I am."

"Oh, goryhell. Augustus," our old proctor says turning to Mustang with a bitter laugh. "You can't do this . . . it's madness. They're monsters! You can't let them out! Do you know what will happen? Don't open Pandora's box."

"If they are monsters, we should ask ourselves who made them that way," Mustang says in the Obsidian tongue so Sefi can understand. "Now, what are the codes to Asgard's armory?"

He spits. "You'll have to ask nicer than that, traitor."

Mustang is deadly cold. "Treason is a matter of the date, Proctor. Must I ask again? Or must I begin trimming your ears?"

Beside Freya's body, Sefi dips her finger into the blood and tastes it.

"Just blood," I say, crouching beside her. "Not ichor. Not divine. Human."

I hold out Freya's razor for her to take. She flinches at the idea, but forces herself to wrap her fingers around the hilt, hand trembling, expecting to be struck by lightning or electrocuted like men are who touch pulseShields with bare hands. "This button here retracts the whip. This one controls the shape."

She cradles the weapon reverently and looks up at me, furious eyes asking which shape she should conjure. I nod to mine, trying to build kinship with her. And I do. If only in this martial way. Slowly her razor takes the shape of the slingBlade. The skin on my arm prickles as the Valkyrie laugh to one another. Vibrating with excitement, they pull their own axes and long knives and look at me and Mustang.

"There's five gods left," Mustang says. "How'd you ladies like to meet them?"

34

|||||||||||||||||||||||

GODKILLERS

W e drag the bodies of seven gods, two dead and five captured, behind us. I wear the armor of Odin. Sefi the armor of Tyr. Mustang the armor of Freya. All of which we pillaged from the armory on Asgard. Blood smears the stone of the hall. Feet slide and stumble as Sefi jerks one of the living Golds behind us by his hair. Her Valkyrie drag the rest.

We returned to the Spires on a shuttle stolen from Asgard, which we slipped through silently, using Loki's codes to access the armory and drape ourselves in the panoply of war before seeking the remaining gods out. Two we found in Asgard's mainframe leading a team of Greens attempting to purge Quicksilver's hackers from their system. Sefi with her new razor claimed the arm of one and beat the other unconscious, terrifying the Greens, two of which held up fists to me as silent acknowledgment of their sympathy for the Rising. With their help, we locked the others in a storage room as the two Green sympathizers connected me directly with Quicksilver's operations room.

We didn't reach Quicksilver himself, but Victra relayed news that Sevro's gamble worked. A little more than a third of the Martian defense fleet is under control of the Sons of Ares and Quicksilver's Blues. Thousands of the Society's best troops are trapped on Phobos, but the Jackal is hitting back hard, taking personal command of the remaining ships and recalling forces from the Kuiper Belt to reinforce his depleted fleet.

The rest of the Golds we located through the station's biometric sensor map in the lower levels. One practicing with her razor in the training rooms. She saw my face and dropped her blade in surrender. Reputation is a fine thing sometimes. The remaining two Golds we found in the monitoring bays, shifting back and forth between the cameras. They'd only just discovered that the footage was archival from three years before.

Now, all our Gold captives wear magnetic handcuffs and are tied together by long pieces of rope from Sefi's griffin, all gagged, all glancing around at the Spires like we've dragged them into the mouth of hell itself.

Obsidians of the Spires flock to us in the halls. Rushing from the deeper levels to see the strange sight. Most would only have seen their gods from a distance, as flashes of gold streaking over the spring snow at mach three. Now we come among them, our pulseShields distorting the air, our shuttle's pulse cannons melting open the huge iron doors which closed off the griffin hangar from the cold. The doors melt inward like the door on the *Pax* melted when Ragnar offered me Stains.

This is not how I intended to bring the Obsidians into my fold. I wanted to use words, to come humbly, in seal skin, not armor, putting myself at the mercy of the Obsidians to show Alia that I valued her people's worth. Valued their judgment, and was willing to put myself in peril for them. I wanted to do as I preached. But even Ragnar knew that was a fool's errand. And now I don't have time for intransigence or superstition. If Alia will not follow me to war, I'll drag her to it, kicking, screaming, like Lorn before her. For Obsidian to hear, I must speak in the only language they understand.

Might.

Sefi fires her pulseFist past my head at the doors leading to her mother's sanctuary. The ancient iron buckles. Bent and twisted hinges screaming. We flow past an army of prostrate giants who clutter the cavernous halls to either side. So much strength made frail by superstition. Once, when they were stronger, they tried to cross the seas. Built mighty knarrs to carry explorers across the oceans to seek out new lands. The Carved monsters the Golds sowed in the oceans destroyed each boat, or the Golds themselves melted them from the sea. The last boat sailed more than two hundred years ago.

We come upon Alia as she sits in council with her famed seven and seventy warchiefs. They turn to us now amidst large, smoking braziers. Huge warriors, with white hair to the waists, arms bare, iron buckles on waists, huge axes on backs. Black eyes and rings studded with precious metals glitter in the low light. But they're too stunned by the sight of the three-hundred-year-old iron doors suddenly glowing orange and melting away to speak or kneel. I draw up before them, still dragging the corpses of the Golds behind me. Mustang and Sefi hurl their captured Golds forward, kicking out their legs. They sprawl on the ground and stumble to their feet, attempting beyond all reason to maintain some dignity here surrounded by giant savages in the smoky room.

"Are these gods?" I roar through my helmet.

No one answers. Alia moves slowly through the parting warlords.

"Am I a god?" I snarl, this time removing my helmet. Mustang and Sefi remove theirs. Alia sees her daughter in the armor of her gods and she flinches back. Fear whispers over her lips. She stops near the five bound and gagged Golds as they finally find their feet. They stand over two meters tall. But, even bent and old as Alia is, she's a head taller than I. She stares down at the men and women who were once her gods before looking up at her last daughter. "Child, what have you done?"

Sefi says nothing. But the razor on her arm slithers, drawing the eyes of every Obsidian. One of their greatest daughters carries the weapon of the gods.

"Queen of the Valkyrie," I say as if we had never met. "My name is Darrow of Lykos. Blood brother of Ragnar Volarus. I am the warlord of the Rising, which rages against the false Golden gods. You have all seen the fires that rage around the moon. Those are caused by my army. Beyond this land in the abyss, a war rages between slaves and masters. I came here with the greatest son of the Spires to bring the truth to your people." I wave to the Golds, who stare at me with the hatred of an entire race. "They struck him down before he could tell you that you are slaves. The prophets he sent told it true. Your gods are false."

"Liar!" someone screams. A shaman with crooked knees and a bent spine. He babbles something else but Sefi cuts him off.

"Liar?" Mustang hisses. "I have stood upon Asgard. I have seen where your immortals sleep. Where your immortals rut and eat and shit." She twists the pulseFist in her hand. "This is not magic." She activates her gravBoots, floating in the air. The Obsidians stare at her in wonder. "This is not magic. This is a tool."

Alia sees what I have done. What I have shown her daughter and what I have now brought her people whether she wants it or not. We're the same cruel kind. I told myself I would be better than this. I failed that promise. But noble vanity can shine another day. This is war. And victory is the only nobility. I think that is what Mustang was looking for here with Obsidians. She was more afraid that I would allow my own idealism to let something loose that I could not control. But now she sees the compromise I'm willing to make. The strength I'm willing to exert. That's what she wants in an ally as much as she wants a builder. Someone wise enough to adapt.

And Alia? She sees how her people look at me. How they look at my blade, still stained with the blood of the gods, as though it were some holy relic. And she also knows I could have made her complicit in the Golds' crime. Could have accused her before her people. But instead I offer her a chance to pretend she is just learning this for the first time.

Lamentably, my friend's mother does not take the offer. She steps toward Sefi. "I carried you, birthed you, nursed you, and this is my reward? Treason? Blasphemy? You are no Valkyrie." She looks at her people. "These are lies. Free our gods from the usurpers. Kill blasphemers. Kill them all!"

But before the first warchief can even draw their blade, Sefi steps forward, lifts the razor I gave her, and decapitates her mother. Alia's head falls to the floor, eyes still open. The woman's huge body remains standing. Slowly it tips backward and thuds to the ground. Sefi stands over the fallen queen and spits on the corpse. Turning back to her people, she speaks for the first time in twenty-five years.

"She knew."

Her voice is deep and dangerous. Hardly rising above the level of a whisper. Yet it owns the room as surely as if she roared. Then tall Sefi turns away from the Golds, walks back through the gaggle of warchiefs to the griffin throne where her mother's fabled warchest has sat unopened for ten years. There, she bends and takes the lock in her hands and roars gutturally, like a beast, as she pulls at the rusted iron till her fingers bleed and the iron crumbles apart. She throws the old lock to the ground and rips open the chest, pulling free the old black scarabSkin her mother used to conquer the White Coast. Pulling free the red scale cloak of the dragon her mother slew in her youth. And hoisting high her great, black, double-headed axe of war called Throgmir. The rippling gleam of duroSteel catches in the light. She stalks back to the Golds, dragging the axe on the ground behind her.

She motions to Holiday, who removes the gags from the mouths of the Golds.

"Are you a god?" Sefi asks, her tone so different from her brother's. Direct and cold as a winter storm.

"You will burn, mortal," the man says. "If you do not release us, Aesir will come from the sky and rain fire upon your land. This you know. We will wipe your seed from the worlds. We will melt the ice. We are the mighty. We are the Peerless Scarred. And this millennium belongs to . . ."

Sefi slays him there with one giant swing, cleaving him nearly in twain. Blood sprays my face. I do not flinch. I knew what would happen if I brought them here. I also know there's no way I could keep them as prisoners. The Golds built this myth, but now it must die. Mustang moves closer to me, her sign that she accepts this. But her eyes are fixed on the Golds. She will remember this slaughter for the rest of her life. It is her duty and mine to make it mean something.

Part of me mourns the death of these Golds. Even as they die, they make these other taller mortals still seem so much lesser. They stand straight, proud. They do not quake in their last moment in this smoky room so far from their estates where they rode horses as children and learned the poetry of Keats and the wonder of Beethoven and Volmer. A middle-aged Gold woman looks back at Mustang. "You let them do this to us? I fought for your father. I met you when you were a girl. And I fell in his Rain," she glares at me and begins to recite with a loud clear voice the Aeschylus poem the Peerless Scarred use at times as a battle cry:

> Up and lead the dance of Fate!
> Lift the song that mortals hate . . .
> Tell what rights are ours on earth,
> Over all of human birth
> Swift of foot to avenge are we!
> He whose hands are clean and pure.
> Naught our wrath to dread hath he.

One by one they fall to Sefi's axe. Until only the woman is left, her head held high, her words ringing clear. She looks me in the eye, as sure of her right as I am of mine. "Sacrifice. Obedience. Prosperity." Sefi's axe sweeps through the air and the last god of Asgard flops to the stone floor. Over her body towers the blood-spattered Princess of the Valkyrie, terrible and ancient with her justice. She bends and removes the tongue of the female Gold with a crooked knife. Mustang shifts beside me in discomfort.

Sefi smiles, noticing Mustang's unease, and walks away from us to her dead mother. She takes the woman's crown and ascends the steps to the throne, bloody axe in one hand, glass crown in the other, and sits inside the rib cage of the griffin where she crowns herself.

"Children of the Spires, the Reaper has called us to join him in his war against false gods. Do the Valkyrie answer?"

In reply, her Valkyrie raise their blue-feathered axes high above their heads to drone out the Obsidian chant of death. Even the warchiefs of fallen Alia join. It seems the ocean itself crashes through the stone hallways of the Spires, and I feel the drums of war beating inside, chilling my blood.

"Then ride, Hjelda, Tharul, Veni, and Hroga. Ride Faldir and Wrona and Bolga to the tribes of the Blood Coast, to the Bleaking Moor, the Shattered Spine and the Witch Pass. Ride to kin and enemy alike and tell them Sefi speaks. Tell them Ragnar's prophets told true. Asgard has fallen. The gods are dead. The old oaths have been broken. And tell all who will hear: the Valkyrie ride to war."

As the world swirls around us and the ecstasy of war fills the air, Mustang and I look at one another with darkened eyes and wonder just what we have unleashed.

PART III

||||||||||||||||||||||||||||||||

GLORY

All that we have is that shout into the wind—
how we live. How we go. And how
we stand before we fall.

—Karnus au Bellona

35

|||||||||||||||||||||||||

THE LIGHT

For seven days after the death of Ragnar, I travel across the ice with Sefi, speaking to the male tribes of the Broken Spine, to the Blooded Braves of the North Coast, to women who wear the horns of rams and stand watch over the Witch Pass. Flying in grav-Boots beside the Valkyrie, we come bringing the news of the fall of Asgard.

It is . . . dramatic.

Sefi and a score of her Valkyrie have begun training with Holiday and me to learn to use the gravBoots and pulse weapons. They're clumsy at first. One flew into the side of a mountain at mach 2. But when thirty land with their headdresses kicking in the wind, the left of their faces painted with the blue handprint of Sefi the Quiet and the right with the slingBlade of the Reaper, folks tend to listen.

We take the lion's share of Obsidian leaders to the conquered mountain and let them walk the halls where their gods ate and slept, and show them the cold, preserved corpses of the slain Golds. In seeing their gods slain, most, even those who knew tacitly of their true condition as slaves, accepted our olive branch. Those who did not, who denounced us, were overcome by their own people. Two warchiefs hurled themselves from the mountain in shame. Another opened her veins with a dagger and bleeds out on the floor of the green houses.

And one, a particularly psychotic little woman, watched with great malevolence as we took her to the mountain's datahub where three Greens informed her of a planned coup against her rule, showing her video of the conspiracy. We loaned her a razor, a flight back home, and two days later she added twenty thousand warriors to my cause.

Sometimes I encounter Ragnar's legend. It has spread among the tribes. They call him the Speaker. The one who came with truth, who brought the prophets and sacrificed his life for his people. But with my friend's legend grows my own. My slingBlade's symbol burns across mountainsides to greet me and the Valkyrie when we fly to meet with new tribes. They call me the Morning Star. That star by which griffin-riders and travelers navigate the wastes in the dark months of winter. The last star that disappears when daylight returns in the spring.

It is my legend that begins to bind them. Not their sense of kinship with one another. These clans have warred for generations. But I have no sordid history here. Unlike Sefi or the other great Obsidian warlords, I am their untouched field of snow. Their blank slate on which they can project whatever disparate dreams they have. As Mustang says, I am something new, and in this old world steeped in legends, ancestors, and what came before, something new is something very special.

Yet despite our progress with gathering the clans, the difficulty we face is massive. Not only must we keep the fractious Obsidians from killing one another in honor duels, but many of the clans have accepted my invitation for relocation. Hundreds of thousands of them must be brought from their homes in the Antarctic to the tunnels of the Reds so they are beyond the reach of Gold bombardment, which will come when the Golds discover what has transpired here. All this while keeping the Jackal dumb and blind to our maneuvers. From Asgard, Mustang has led the counterintelligence efforts, with the help of Quicksilver's hackers to mask our presence and project reports consistent with those filed in previous weeks to the Board of Quality Control HQ in Agea.

With no way to move them without someone noticing, Mustang, a Gold aristocrat, has conceived the most audacious plan in the history of the Sons of Ares. One massive troop movement, utilizing thousands of shuttles and freighters from Quicksilver's mercantile fleet and the Sons of Ares navy to move the population of the pole in twelve hours. A thousand ships skimming over the Southern Sea, burning helium to set down on the ice before Obsidian cities and lower their ramps to the hundreds and thousands of giants swaddled in fur and iron who will fill their hulls with the old, the sick, the warriors, the children, and the fetid stink of animals. Then, under the cover of the Sons of Ares ships, the population will be dispersed underground and many of the warriors to our military ships in orbit. I do not think I know another person in the worlds who can organize it as fast as she does.

On the eighth day after the fall of Asgard, I depart with Sefi, Mustang, Holiday, and Cassius to join Sevro in overseeing the final preparations for the migration. The Valkyrie bring Ragnar with us on the flight, wrapping his frozen body in rough cloth and clutching him close in terror as our ship cruises just beneath the speed of sound five meters from the surface of the ocean. They watch in awe as we enter the tunnels of Mars through one of the many Sons' subterranean access points. This one an old mining colony in a southern mountain range. Sons lookouts in heavy winter jackets and balaclavas salute with their fists in the air as we pass into the tunnel.

Half a day of subterranean flying later, we arrive at Tinos. It is a hub of ship activity. Hundreds cluttering the stalactite docks, taxiing through the air. And it seems the whole city watches our shuttle as it passes through the traffic to land in its stalactite hangar, knowing it bears not just me and our new Obsidian allies, but the broken Shield of Tinos. Their weeping faces blur past. Already rumors swirl through the refugees. The Obsidians are coming. Not just to fight, but to live in Tinos. To eat their food. To share their already-crowded streets. Dancer says the place is a powder keg about to erupt. I can't say I disagree.

The disposition of the Sons of Ares is dour. They gather in silence as my ship's landing ramp unfurls. I go first down the ramp. Sevro waits beside Dancer and Mickey. He slams me into a hug. The beginnings of a goatee mark his stoic face. He holds his shoulders as square as he can, as if those bony things alone could hold up the hopes of the thousands of Sons of Ares who fill the docking bay to see the Shield of Tinos brought back to his adopted home.

"Where is he?" Sevro asks thickly.

I look back to my shuttle as Sefi and her Valkyrie carry Ragnar down the ramp. The Howlers are the first to greet them. Clown saying a respectful word to Sefi as Sevro steps past me to stand before the Valkyrie.

"Welcome to Tinos," he says to the Valkyrie in Nagal. "I am Sevro au Barca, blood brother to Ragnar Volarus. These are his other brothers and sisters." He motions to the Howlers, all of whom wear their wolfcloaks. Sevro produces Ragnar's bear cloak. "He wore this to battle. With your permission, I'd like him to wear it now."

"You were brother to Ragnar. You are brother to me," Sefi says. She clicks her tongue and her Valkyrie pass stewardship of her brother's body to Sevro. Mustang glances my way. Sefi's generosity strikes me as a promising sign. If she were a covetous creature, she would have kept his body in her lands and given him an Obsidian funeral pyre before burying his ashes in the ice. Instead, she told me she knows where his true home lies: with those who fought beside him, who helped him come back to his people.

Mustang moves closer beside me as the Howlers drape Ragnar's cloak over his body and carry him through the crowd. The Sons part for them. Hands reach to touch Ragnar. "Look," Mustang says, nodding to the thin black ribbons that the Sons have tied into their beards and hair. Her hand finds my smallest finger. A small squeeze sends me back to the woods where she saved me. Making me feel warm even as we watch Sevro leave the hangar with Ragnar's body. "Go." She nudges me his direction. "Dancer and I have a conference scheduled with Quicksilver and Victra."

"She needs a guard," I tell Dancer. "Sons you trust."

"I'll be fine," Mustang says, rolling her eyes. "I survived the Obsidians."

"She'll have the Pitvipers," Dancer says, examining Mustang without the kindness I'm used to seeing in his eyes. Ragnar's death has taken the spirit out of him today. He seems older as he waves Narol over and nods to the shuttle. "The Bellona on board?"

"Holiday's got him in the passenger cabin. His neck's still torn up so he'll need Virany to take a look at him. Be discreet about it. Give him a private room."

"Private? Place is crammed, Darrow. Captains don't even get private rooms."

"He's got intel. You want him shot before he can give it to us?" I ask.

"Is that why you kept him alive?" Dancer looks at Mustang skeptically, as if she's already compromising my decisions. Little does he know she'd have let Cassius die more readily than I ever would. Dancer sighs when I don't relent. "He'll be safe. On my word."

"Find me later," Mustang says as I depart.

I find Sevro slumped over Ragnar in Mickey's laboratory. It's a thing to hear of a friend's death, it's another to see the shadow of what they've left behind. I hated the sight of my father's old workgloves after he died. Mother was too practical to throw them away. Said we couldn't afford to. So I did it myself one day and she boxed my ears and made me bring them back.

The scent of death is growing stronger from Ragnar.

The cold preserved him in his native land, but Tinos has been suffering power outages and refrigeration units play second zither to the water purifiers and air reclamation systems in the city beneath. Soon Mickey will embalm him and make preparations for the burial Ragnar asked for.

I sit in silence for half an hour, waiting for Sevro to speak. I don't want to be here. Don't want to see Ragnar dead. Don't want to linger in the sadness. Yet I stay for Sevro.

My armpits stink. I'm tired. The scanty tray of food Dio brought me is untouched except the biscuit I chew numbly and think how ridiculous Ragnar looks on the table. He's too big for it, feet hanging off the edge.

Despite the smell, Ragnar is peaceful in death. Ribbons red as winter berries nestled in the white of his beard. Two razors rest in his hands, which are folded across his bare chest. The tattoos are darker in death, covering his arms, his chest and neck. The matching skull he gave me and Sevro seems so sad. Telling its story even though the man who wears it is dead. Everything is more vivid except the wound. It's innocuous and thin as a snake's smile along his side. The holes Aja made in his stomach seem so small. How could such little things take so large a soul from this world?

I wish he were here.

The people need him more than ever.

Sevro's eyes are glassy as his fingers glide over the tattoos on Ragnar's white face. "He wanted to go to Venus, you know," he murmurs, voice soft as a child's. Softer than I've ever heard it before. "I showed him one of the holoVids of a catamaran there. Second he put the goggles on I'd never seen anyone smile like that. Like he'd found heaven and realized he didn't have to die to go there. He'd sneak in and borrow my holo gear in the middle of the night till one day I just gave him the damn thing. Things are four hundred credits, max. Know what he did to repay me?" I don't. Sevro holds up his right hand to show me his skull tattoo. "He made me his brother." He gives Ragnar a slow, affectionate punch to the jaw. "But the big fat idiot had to run at Aja instead of away from her."

The Valkyrie still scour the wastes in vain for signs of the Olympic Knight. Her trail goes deeper into the crevasse before it is covered by the frozen black blood of some creature. I hope something found her and took her to its cave in the ice to finish her slowly. But I doubt it. A woman like that doesn't just fade. Whatever Aja's fate, if she's alive she'll find a way to contact the Sovereign or the Jackal.

"It was my fault," I say. "My shit plan to take Aja out."

"She killed Quinn. Helped kill my father," Sevro mutters. "Killed dozens of us when you were locked up. Wasn't your bad. You'd have lost me too if I were there. Even Rags couldn't have kept me from having a go at her." Sevro rolls his knuckles along the edge of the table, leaving little white creases in the skin. "Always trying to protect us."

"The Shield of Tinos," I say.

"The Shield of Tinos," he echoes, voice catching. "He loved the name."

"I know."

"I think he'd always thought himself a blade before he met us. We let him be what he wanted. A protector." He wipes his eyes and backs away from Ragnar. "Anyway. The little princeling is alive."

I nod. "We brought him on the shuttle."

"Pity. Two millimeters." He pinches his fingers together, illustrating how narrowly Mustang's arrow missed Cassius's jugular. After Sefi dispatched riders to the tribes, I took her and many of her warlords to Asgard aboard the shuttle to see the fortress there. I brought Cassius along as well and Asgard's Yellows saved his life. "Why are you keeping him alive, Darrow? If you think he's going to thank you for your generosity, you've got another thing coming."

"I couldn't just let him die."

"He killed my father."

"I know."

"Give me a reason."

"Maybe I think the world would be a better place with him in it," I say tentatively. "So many people have used him, lied to him, betrayed him. All that's defined him. It's not fair. I want him to have a chance to decide for himself what kind of person he wants to be."

"None of us get to be what we want to be," Sevro mutters. "Least not for long."

"Isn't that why we fight? Isn't that what you just said about Ragnar? He was made a blade but we gave him a chance to be a shield. Cassius deserves that same chance."

"Shithead." He rolls his eyes. "Just 'cause you're right doesn't mean you're right. Anyway, eagles are hated as much as the lions. Someone here's still going to try to pop him. And your girl too."

"She's got the Pitvipers with her. And she's not my girl."

"Whatever you say." He collapses into one of Mickey's stolen leather chairs and rubs a hand along his Mohawk's ridge. "Wish she'd taken the Telemanuses with her. If she had, you'd have slagged Aja hard." He closes his eyes and leans his head back. "Oh, hey," he remembers suddenly, "I got you some ships."

"I saw that. Thank you," I say.

"Finally." He snorts a laugh. "A sign we're making a difference. Twenty torchships, ten frigates, four destroyers, a dreadnought. You should have seen it, Reap. Martian Navy pumped Phobos full of Legionaries, emptied their ships and we just stole their assault shuttles, flew them back with the right codes, and landed them in their hangars. My squad didn't even fire a shot. Quicksilver's boys even hacked the PA systems in the navy ships. They all heard your speech. It was mutiny almost before we got on board, Reds, Oranges, Blues, even Grays. It won't work again, the PA system bit. Golds will learn to cut themselves off the network so we can't hack in, but it got 'em hard this week. When we unite with the *Pax* and Orion's other ships we'll have a real force to slag the Pixies."

It's moments like this that I know I'm not alone. Damn the world, so long as I have my mangy little guardian angel. If only I was so good at guarding him as he is at guarding me. Once again he's done all I could ask and more. As I marshaled the Obsidians, he ripped a gaping hole in the Jackal's defense fleet. Crippled a fourth of them. Forced the rest to retreat toward the outer moon of Deimos to regroup with the Jackal's reserves and await additional reinforcements from Ceres and the Can.

For a brief hour, he held naval supremacy over all of Mars's southern hemisphere. The Goblin King. Then he was forced to retreat to hunker close into Phobos, where his men eliminated the trapped loyalist marines by using Rollo's squads to cut off their air and vent them into space. I'm under no delusion. The Jackal won't let us have the moon. He might not care about its people, but he can't destroy the station's helium refineries. So another assault will come soon. It won't affect my war effort, but the Jackal will get tied down fighting the populace that we've woken. It'll drain his resources without trapping me. Worst possible situation for him.

"What are you thinking?" I ask Sevro.

His eyes are lost in the ceiling. "I'm wondering how long till it's us on the slab. And wondering why it's gotta be us on the line. You see vids and hear stories and you think of the regular people. The ones who got a chance at life on Ganymede or Earth or Luna. Can't help but be jealous."

"You don't think you've gotten a chance to live?" I ask.

"Not proper," he says.

"What's proper?" I ask.

He crosses his arms like he's a kid in a fort looking down at the real world and wondering why it can't be as magical as he is. "I dunno. Something far away from being a Peerless Scarred. Maybe a Pixie or even a happy midColor. I just want something to look at and say, that's safe, that's mine, and no one is going to try and take it. A house. Kids."

"Kids?" I ask.

"I don't know. I never thought of it till Pops died. Till they took you."

"Till Victra you mean . . . ," I say with a wink. "Nice goatee by the way."

"Shut up," he says.

"Have you two—" He cuts me off, changing the subject.

"But it'd be nice to just be Sevro. To have Pops. To have known my mother." He laughs at himself, harder than he should. "Sometimes I think about going back to the beginning and wondering what would have happened if Pops had known the Board was coming. If he'd escaped with my mother, with me."

I nod. "I always think about how life would have been like if Eo never died. The children I would have had. What I would have named them." I smile distantly. "I would have grown old. Watched Eo grow old. And I would have loved her more with each new scar, with each new year even as she learned to despise our small life. I would have said farewell to my mother, maybe my brother, sister. And if I was lucky, one day when Eo's hair turned gray, before it began to fall out and she began to cough, I would hear the shift of rocks over my head on the drill and that would be it. She would have sent me to the incinerators and sprinkled my ashes, then our children would have done the same. And the clans would say we were happy and good and raised bloodydamn fine children. And when those children died, our memory would fade, and when their children died, it would be swept away like the dust we become, down and away to the long tunnels. It would have been a small life," I say with a shrug, "but I would have liked it. And every day I ask myself if I was given the chance to go back, to be blind, to have all that back, would I?"

"And what's the answer?"

"All this time I thought this was for Eo. I drove straight on like an arrow because I had that one perfect idea in my head. She wanted this. I loved her. So I'll make her dream real. But that's bullshit. I was living half a bloodydamn life. Making an idol out a woman, making her a martyr, something instead of someone. Pretending she was perfect." I run my hand through my greasy hair. "She wouldn't have wanted that. And when I looked out at the Hollows, I just knew, I mean I guess I realized as I was talking that justice isn't about fixing the past, it's about fixing the future. We're not fighting for the dead. We're fighting for the living. And for those who aren't yet born. For a chance to have children. That's what has to come after this, otherwise what's the point?"

Sevro sits silently thinking over what I've said.

"You and I keep looking for light in the darkness, expecting it to appear. But it already has." I touch his shoulder. "We're it, boyo. Broken and cracked and stupid as we are, we're the light, and we're spreading."

36

||||||||||||||||||||||

SWILL

I run into Victra in the hall as I leave Sevro with Ragnar. It's late. Past midnight and she's only just arrived to help coordinate the final preparations between Quicksilver's security, the Sons, and our new navy, which I've given her command of until we're reunited with Orion. It's another decision that peeves Dancer. He's frightened I'm bestowing too much power on Golds who might have ulterior motives. Mustang's presence could be the straw that breaks the camel's back.

"How's he doing?" Victra asks regarding Sevro.

"Better," I say. "But he'll be glad to see you."

She smiles at that, despite herself, and I think she actually blushes. It's a new look for her. "Where are you going?" she asks.

"To make sure Mustang and Dancer haven't torn each other's heads off yet."

"Noble. But too late."

"What happened? Is everything prime?"

"That's relative, I suppose. Dancer's in the warroom ranting about Gold superiority complexes, arrogance, etc. Never heard him curse so much. I didn't stay long, and he didn't say much. You know he's not that sweet on me."

"And you're not that sweet on Mustang," I say.

"I've nothing against the girl. She reminds me of home. Especially considering the new allies you've brought us. I just think she's a duplicitous little filly. That's all. But it's the best horses that'll buck you right off. Don't you think?"

I laugh. "Not sure if that was innuendo or not."

"It was."

"Do you know where she is?"

Victra makes a sad little face. "Contrary to popular opinion, I don't know everything, darling." She moves past me to join Sevro, patting my head as she goes. "But I'd check the commissary on level three if I were you."

"Where are *you* going?" I ask.

She smiles mischievously. "Mind your own business."

I find Mustang in the commissary hunched over a metal bottle with Uncle Narol, Kavax, and Daxo. A dozen members of the Pitvipers lounge at the other tables, smoking burners and eavesdropping intently to Mustang, who sits with her boots up on the table, using Daxo as a backrest, as she tells a story about the Institute to the other two occupants of the table. I couldn't see them when I first entered, due to the bulk of the Telemanuses but my brother and mother sit listening to the tale.

". . . And so of course I shout for Pax."

"That's my son," Kavax reminds my mother.

". . . and he comes on over the hill leading a column of my housemembers. Darrow and Cassius feel the ground shaking and go screaming into the loch where they clung together for hours, shivering and turning blue."

"Blue!" Kavax says with a huge childish laugh that makes the Sons eavesdropping unable to keep their composure. Even if he's a Gold, it's difficult not to like Kavax au Telemanus. "Blue as blueberries, Sophocles. Isn't that right? Give him another, Deanna." My mother

rolls a jelly bean across the table to Sophocles, who waits eagerly beside the bottle to gobble it up.

"What's going on here?" I ask. Eying the bottle my brother's refill-
ing the Golds' mugs with.

"We're getting stories from the lass," Narol says gruffly through a
cloud of burner smoke. "Have a dram." Mustang wrinkles her nose
at the smoke.

"Such an awful habit, Narol," she says.

Kieran looks pointedly at our mother. "I've been telling both of
them that for years."

"Hello, Darrow," Daxo says, standing to clasp my arm. "Pleasure
to see you without a razor in your hand this time." He pokes me in the
shoulder with a longer finger.

"Daxo. Sorry about all that. I think I owe you a bit of a debt for
taking care of my people."

"Orion did most of the minding there," he says with a twinkle in
his eye. He returns gracefully to his seat. My brother's captivated by
the man and the angels tattooed on his head. And how could he not
be? Daxo's twice his weight, immaculate, and more well-mannered
than even a Rose like Matteo, who I hear is recovering well on one of
Quicksilver's ships, and is delighted to know I'm alive.

"What happened with Dancer?" I ask Mustang.

Her cheeks are flushed and she laughs at the question. "Well, I
don't think he very much likes me. But don't worry, he'll come
around."

"Are you drunk?" I ask with a laugh.

"A little. Catch up." She swivels her legs down and puts her feet on
the ground to clear a space on the bench beside her. "I was just getting
to the part where you wrestled Pax in the mud." My mother watches
me quietly, a little smile on her lips as she knows the panic that must
be going through me right now. Too shocked at seeing two halves of
my life collide without my supervision, I sit down uneasily and listen
to Mustang finish the story. With all that's transpired, I'd forgotten
the charm of this woman. Her easy, light nature. How she draws others in by making them feel important, by saying their names and letting them feel seen. She holds my uncle and brother in a spell, one

reinforced by the Telemanus' admiration for her. I try not to blush when my mother catches me admiring Mustang.

"But enough of the Institute," Mustang says after she's explained in detail how Pax and I dueled in front of her castle. "Deanna, you promised me a story about Darrow as a boy."

"How about the gas pocket one," Narol says. "If only Loran was here . . ."

"No not that one," Kieran says. "What about . . ."

"I have one," mother says, cutting off the men. She begins slow, words sluggish through the lisp. "When Darrow was small, maybe three or four, his father gave him an old watch his father had given him. This brass thing, with a wheel instead of digital numbers. Do you remember it?" I nod. "It was beautiful. Your favorite possession. And years later, after his father had died, Kieran here got sick with a cough. Meds were always in short ration in the mines. So you'd have to get them from Gamma or Gray, but each has a price. I didn't know how I was going to pay, and then Darrow comes home one day with the medicine, won't say how he got it. But several weeks later I saw one of the Grays checking the time with that old watch."

I look at my hands, but I feel Mustang's eyes on me.

"I think it's time for bed," mother says. Narol and Kieran protest until she clears her throat and stands. She kisses me on the head, lingering longer than she usually would. Then she touches Mustang's shoulder and limps from the room with my brother's help. Narol's men go with them.

"She's quite a woman," Kavax says. "And she loves you very much."

"I'm glad you met like this," I say to him, then to Mustang, "Especially you."

"How's that?" she asks.

"Without me trying to control it. Like last time."

"Yes, I would say that was quite the disaster," Daxo says.

"This feels right," I say.

"I agree. It does." Mustang smiles. "I wish I could introduce you to mine. You would have liked her better than my father."

I return the smile, wondering what this is between us. Dreading the idea of having to define it. There's an easiness that comes with being around her. But I'm afraid to ask her what she's thinking. Afraid to broach the subject for fear of shattering this little illusion of peace. Kavax awkwardly clears his throat, dissolving the moment.

"So the meeting with Dancer didn't go well?" I ask.

"I fear not," Daxo says. "The resentment he harbors runs deep. Theodora was more forthcoming, but Dancer was . . . intransigent. Militantly so."

"He's a cypher," Mustang clarifies, taking another drink and wincing at the quality of proof. "Hoarding information from us. Wouldn't share anything I didn't already know."

"I doubt you were very forthcoming yourself."

She grimaces. "No, but I'm used to making others compensate for me. He's smart. And that means it's going to be difficult to convince him that I want our alliance to work."

"So you do."

"Thanks to your family, yes," she says. "You want to build a world for them. For your mother, for Kieran's children. I understand that. When . . . I chose to negotiate with the Sovereign I was trying to do the same thing. Protecting those I love." The Telemanuses share a glance. Her finger traces dents in the table. "I couldn't see a world without war unless we capitulated." Her eyes find my Sigil-barren hands, searching the naked flesh there as if it held the secret to all our futures. Maybe it does. "But I can see one now."

"You really mean that?" I ask. "All of you?"

"Family is all that matters," Kavax says. "And you are family." Daxo sets an elegant hand on my shoulder. Even Sophocles seems to understand the gravity of the moment, resting his chin on my foot beneath the table. "Aren't you?"

"Yes." I nod gratefully "I am."

With a tight smile, Mustang pulls a piece of paper from her pocket and slides it to me. "That's Orion's com frequency. I don't know where they are. Probably in the belt. I gave them a simple directive: cause chaos. From what I've heard from Gold chatter, they're doing just that. We'll need her and her ships if we're going take down Octavia."

"Thank you," I say to them all. "I didn't think we'd ever have a second chance."

"Nor did we," Daxo replies. "Let me be blunt with you, Darrow: there is a matter of concern. It's your plan. Your design to use claw-Drills to allow the Obsidians to invade key cities around Mars . . . we think it is a mistake."

"Really?" I ask. "Why? We need to wrest the Jackal's centers of power away, gain traction with the populace."

"Father and I do not have the same faith in the Obsidians you seem to have," Daxo says carefully. "Your intentions will matter little if you let them loose on the populace of Mars."

"Barbarians," Kavax says. "They are barbarians."

"Ragnar's sister . . ."

"Is not Ragnar," Daxo replies. "She's a stranger. And after hearing what she did to the Gold prisoners . . . we can't in good conscience join our forces to a plan that would unleash the Obsidians on the cities of Mars. The Arcos women won't either."

"I see."

"And there's another reason we think the plan flawed," Mustang says. "It doesn't deal properly with my brother. Give my brother credit. He's smarter than you. Smarter than me." Even Kavax does not contest this. "Look what he's done. If he knows how to play the game, if he knows the variables, he'll sit in a corner for days running through the possible moves, countermoves, externalities, and outcomes. That's his idea of fun. Before Claudius's death and before we were sent to live in different homes, he'd stay inside, rain or shine, and piece together puzzles, create mazes on paper and beg me over and over again to try and find the center when I came back from riding with Father or fishing with Claudius and Pax. And when I did find the center, he would laugh and say what a clever sister he had. I never thought much of it until I saw him afterward one day alone in his room when he thought no one was watching. Shrieking and hitting himself in the face, punishing himself for losing to me.

"The next time he asked me to find the center of a maze I pretended I couldn't, but he wasn't fooled. It was like he knew I'd seen him in his room. Not the introverted, but pleasant frail boy everyone else saw. The real him." She gathers her breath, shrugging away the thought. "He made me finish the maze. And when I did, he smiled, said how clever I was, and walked off.

"The next time he drew a maze, I couldn't find the center. No matter how hard I tried." She shifts uncomfortably. "He just watched me try from the floor among his pencils. Like an old evil ghost inside a little porcelain doll. That's how I remember him. It's how I see him now when I think about him killing Father."

The Telemanuses listen with a foreboding silence, as afraid of the Jackal as I am.

"Darrow, he'll never forgive you for beating him at the Institute. For making him cut off his hand. He'll never forgive me for stripping him naked and delivering him to you. We are his obsession, just as much as Octavia is, as much as Father was. So if you think he's going to just forget how Sevro waltzed into his citadel with a clawDrill and stole you from under him, you're going to get a lot of people killed. Your plan to take the cities won't work. He'll see it coming a kilometer off. And even if he doesn't, if we take Mars, this war will last for years. We need to go for the jugular."

"And not just that," Daxo says, "we need assurances that you're not aiming to begin a dictatorship, or a full-demokracy in the case of victory."

"A dictatorship," I ask with a smirk. "You really think I want to rule?"

Daxo shrugs. "Someone must."

A woman clears her throat at the door. We wheel around to see Holiday standing there with her thumbs in her belt loops. "Sorry to interrupt, sir. But the Bellona is asking for you. It seems rather important."

37

||||||||||||||||||||||||||

THE LAST EAGLE

Cassius lies handcuffed to the rails of the reinforced medical gurney in the center of the Sons of Ares infirmary. The same place I watched my people die from the wounds they suffered to save me from his clutches. Bed after bed of injured rebels from Phobos and other operations on the Thermic fill the expanse. Ventilators whir and beep, men cough. But it's the weight of the eyes that I feel most. Hands reach for me as I pass through the rows of cots and pallets lying on the floor. Mouths whisper my name. They want to touch my arms, to feel a human without Sigils, without the mark of the masters. I let them as well as I can, but I haven't time to visit the fringes of the room.

I asked Dancer to give Cassius a private room. Instead, he's been set smack in the middle of the main infirmary among the amputees, adjacent to the huge plastic tent that covers the burn unit. There he can watch and be watched by the lowColors and feel the weight of this war the same way they do. I sense Dancer's hand at work here. Giving Cassius equitable treatment. No cruelty, no consideration, just the same as the rest. I feel like buying the old socialist a drink.

Several of Narol's boys, a Gray and two weathered ex-Helldivers, slump on metal chairs playing cards near Cassius's bedside. Heavy scorchers slung around their backs. They jump to their feet and salute as I approach.

"Heard he's been asking for me," I say.

"Most the night," the shorter of the Reds answers gruffly, eying Holiday behind me. "Wouldn't have bothered you . . . but he's a bloodydamn Olympic. So thought we should pass the word up the chain." He leans so close I can smell the menthol of the synth tobacco between his stained teeth. *"And the slagger says he's got information, sir."*

"Can he talk?"

"Yeah," the soldier grumbles. "Doesn't say much, but the bolt missed his box."

"I need to speak with him privately," I say.

"We got you covered, sir."

The doctor and the guards wheel Cassius's gurney to the far back of the room to the pharmacy, which they keep guarded under lock and key. Inside, among the rows of plastic medication boxes, Cassius and I are left alone. He watches me from his bed, a white bandage around his neck, the faintest pinprick of blood dilating between his Adam's apple and the jugular on the right side of his throat. "It's a miracle you're not dead," I say. He shrugs. There's no tubes in his arms or morphon bracelet. I frown. "They didn't give you painkillers?"

"Not punishment. They voted," he says very slowly, taking care not to rip the stitches on his neck. "Wasn't enough morphon to go around. Low supplies. As they tell, the patients voted last week to give the hard meds to the burn victims and amputees. I'd think it noble if they didn't moan all night from pain like lonely little puppies." He pauses. "I always wondered if mothers can hear their children weeping for them."

"Can yours?"

"I didn't weep. And I don't think my mother cares much for anything other than revenge. Whatever that means at this point."

"You said you had information?" I ask, to business because I don't know what else to say. I feel an ironclad kinship with this man. Sevro asked why I saved him, and I could aspire to notions of valor and honor. But the deepspine reason is I desperately want him to be a friend again. I crave his approval. Does that make me a fool? Disloyal? Is it the guilt speaking? Is it his magnetism? Or is it that vain part of me that just wants to be loved by the people I respect. And I do respect him. He has honor, a corrupted sort, but true honor nonetheless.

"Was it her or was it you?" he asks carefully.

"What do you mean?"

"Who kept the Obsidians from boiling out my eyes and taking my tongue? You or Virginia?"

"It was both of us."

"Liar. Didn't think she'd shoot, to tell the truth of it." He reaches up to feel his neck, but the manacles jerk his hands to a halt, startling him back into the room. "Don't suppose you could take these off? It's dreadful when you've got an itch."

"I think you'll live."

He chuckles as if saying he had to try. "So, is this where you act morally superior for saving me? For being more civilized than Gold?"

"Maybe I'm going to torture you for information," I say.

"Well, that's not exactly honorable."

"Neither is letting a man put me in a box for nine months after torturing me for three. Anyway, what the hell ever made you think I give a shit about being honorable?"

"True." He frowns, creasing his brow and looking startling, like something Michelangelo would have carved. "If you think the Sovereign will barter, you're wrong. She won't sacrifice a single thing to save me."

"Then why serve her?" I ask.

"Duty." He says the words, but I wonder how deeply he means them any longer.

In his eyes I glimpse the loneliness, the longing for a life that should have been, and the glimmer of the man he wants to be underneath the man he thinks he has to be.

"All the same," I say, "I think we've done enough evil to one another. I'm not going to torture you. Do you have information or are we just going to dance around it for another ten minutes?"

"Have you wondered yet why the Sovereign was suing for peace, Darrow? Surely it must have crossed your mind. She's not one to dilute punishment unless she must. Why would she show leniency to Virginia? To the Rim? Her fleets outnumber those of the Moon Lord rebels three to one. The Core is better supplied. Romulus can't match Roque. You know how good he is. So why would the Sovereign send us to negotiate? Why compromise?"

"I already know she wanted to replace the Jackal," I say. "And she can't very well have a full-scale rebellion on the Rim while trying to cuff his ears and fight the Sons of Ares. She's trying to limit her theaters of war so she can focus all her weight on one problem at a time. It's not a complicated strategy."

"But do you know why she wanted to remove him?"

"My escape, the camps, the disruptions in helium processing . . . I could list a hundred reasons why installing a psychopath as Arch-Governor could prove burdensome."

"All those are valid," he says, interrupting. "Convincing, even. And they are the reasons we provided Virginia."

I step back toward him, hearing the implication in his voice. "What didn't you tell her?" He hesitates, as if wondering even now if he should tell me. Eventually, he does.

"Earlier this year, our intelligence agents discovered discrepancies between the quarterly helium production logs reported to the Department of Energy and the Department of Mine Management and the yield reports from our agents in mining colonies themselves. We found at least one hundred and twenty-five instances where the Jackal falsely reported helium losses due to Sons of Ares disruption. Disruptions which didn't exist. He also claimed fourteen mines destroyed by Sons of Ares attacks. Attacks which never happened."

"So he's skimming off the top," I say with a shrug. "Hardly the first corrupt ArchGovernor in the worlds."

"But he's *not* reselling it on the market," Cassius says. "He's creating artificial shortages while he stockpiles."

"Stockpiles? How much so far?" I ask tensely.

"With the surplus inventory from the fourteen mines and the Martian Reserve? At this rate, in two years he'll have more than the Imperial Reserves on Luna and Venus and the War Reserve on Ceres combined."

"That could mean a hundred things," I say quietly, realizing just how much fuel that is. Three quarters of the most valuable substance in the worlds. All under the control of one man. "He's making a play for Sovereign. Buying Senators?"

"Forty so far," Cassius admits. "More than we thought he had. But there's another kink which he's involved them in." He tries to sit up straighter in his cot, but the manacles around his hands anchor him to a half-slouched pose. "I'm going to ask you a question, and I need you to tell me the truth." I'd laugh at the idea if I didn't see how serious he is. "Did the Sons of Ares rob a deep space asteroid warehouse in March, several days after your escape? About four months ago?"

"Be more specific," I say.

"A minor main belter in the Karin Cluster. Designation S-1988. Silicate-based junk asteroid. Nearly zero mining potential. Specific enough?"

I reviewed the entirety of Sevro's tactical operations when I was making my recovery with Mickey. There were several assaults on Legion military bases within the asteroid belts, but nothing remotely like what Cassius is talking about.

"No. There were no operations on S-1988 that I know of."

"*Gorydamn,*" he mutters under his breath. "Then we judged right."

"What was in the warehouse?" I ask. "Cassius . . ."

"Five hundred nuclear warheads," he says darkly.

The blood on his bandage has spread to the size of a gaping mouth.

"Five hundred," I echo, my own voice a distant, hollow thing. "What was their yield?"

"Thirty megatons each."

"World killers . . . Cassius, why would they even exist?"

"In case the Ash Lord ever had to repeat Rhea," Cassius says. "The depot lies between the Core and the Rim."

"Repeat Rhea . . . that's who you serve?" I ask. "A woman who stores enough nuclear warheads to destroy a planet, just in case."

He ignores my tone. "All evidence pointed to Ares, but the Sovereign thought it gave Sevro too much credit. She had Moira investigate it personally, and she was able to trace the tags of the hijacker's ship to a defunct shipping line formerly owned by Julii Industries. If the Sons truly didn't steal them, then the Jackal has the weapons. But we don't know what he's doing with them." I stand there, numb. Mind racing to piece together how the Jackal might utilize so many atomics. According to the Compact, the Martian military is only permitted twenty in its arsenal, for ship-to-ship warfare. All under five megatons.

"If this is true, why would you tell me?" I ask.

"Because Mars is my home too, Darrow. My family has been there as long as yours. My mother is still there in our home. Whatever the Jackal's long-term strategy is, the judgment of the Sovereign is that he will use the weapons here if his back is to the wall."

"You're afraid we might win," I realize.

"When it was Sevro's war, no. The Sons of Ares was doomed. But now? Look what's happening." He looks me up and down. "We've lost containment. Octavia doesn't know where I am. Whether or not Aja is alive. She has no eyes on this. The Jackal might know she tried to betray him to his sister. He's a wild dog. If you provoke him, he will bite." He lowers his voice. "You might be able to survive that, Darrow, but can Mars?"

38

||||||||||||||||||||||||||

THE BILL

"Five hundred nuclear warheads?" Sevro whispers. "*Holy bloodydamn shit*. Tell me you're joking. Go on."

Dancer sits quietly at the warroom table, kneading his temples.

"It's bullshit," Holiday grunts from the wall. "If he has them, he'd have used them."

"Let's leave the deductions to the individuals who have actually met the man, shall we?" Victra says. "Adrius doesn't function like a normal human."

"That's for damn sure," Sevro says.

"Still, it is a solid question," Dancer says, annoyed at the presence of so many Golds, particularly Mustang who stands beside me. "If he has them, why hasn't he used them?"

"Because that sort of escalation will hurt him almost as much as it hurts us," I say. "And if he uses them, the Sovereign will have every excuse to replace him."

"Or he doesn't have them," Quicksilver says dismissively. He floats before us, blue holoPixels shimmering over a display panel. "It's a ploy. Bellona knows what you care about, Darrow. He's plucking your heartstrings with notions of oblivion. It's bullshit. My techs would have seen major ripples if he was moving missiles. And I would have heard about plutonium enriching if the Sovereign had them built."

"Unless they're old missiles," I say. "Lots of relics lying about."

"And it's a big solar system," Mustang says evenly.

"I've got big ears," Quicksilver replies.

"Had," Victra says. "They're whittling them down as we speak."

The leaders of the rebellion sit in a semi-circle in front of a holo-projector which displays asteroid S-1988. It's a barren hunk of rock, part of the Karin sub-family of the Koronis Family of asteroids in the Main Belt between Mars and Jupiter. The Koronis asteroids are the base for heavy mining operations by an Earth-run energy consortium and home to several disreputable astral way stations for smugglers and pirates, most notably 208 Lacrimosa, where Sevro refueled on his journey from Pluto to Mars. The locals call the smuggler's cove Our Lady of Sorrows, where life is cheaper than a kilo of iced helium and a gram of demonDust, or so he says. He's unusually quiet about the place and his time there.

Gold warroom meetings are held in circles or rectangles because people facing one another are more likely to engage in intellectual conflict than people sitting side by side. Golds relish that. I'm trying a different tack, having my friends face the problem—the holoprojec-tor, so if they want to argue with one another, they have to crane their necks to do it.

"It's a shame we don't have the Sovereign's oracles," Mustang says. "Strap one on his wrist and see how forthcoming Cassius really is."

"Sorry we don't quite have the resources you're used to, *domina*," Dancer says.

"That's not what I meant."

"We could torture him," Sevro says. He's in the middle of the table cleaning his fingernails with a blade. Victra leans against the wall be-hind him, flinching in annoyance with each flake of nail that falls onto the table. Dancer is to Sevro's left. The meter-tall hologram of Quicksilver glows to his right, between us. Having declared Phobos a free city on behalf of the Rising, he functions as its Governor and now hunches over a small stack of thumb-sized heart oysters with a platinum octopus shucking knife, arranging the shells in five even mounds. If he's nervous about the Jackal's reprisals against his station, he doesn't look it. Sefi sweats underneath her tribal furs as she stalks along the perimeter of the table like a trapped animal, making Dancer shift in agitation.

"You want the truth?" Sevro asks. "Just give me seventeen minutes and a screwdriver."

"Should we really be having this talk with her here?" Victra asks of Mustang.

"She's on our side," I say.

"Are you sure?" Dancer asks.

"She was crucial to recruiting the Obsidians," I say. "She's connected us with Orion." I made contact with the woman after speaking with Cassius. She's burning hard with the *Pax* and a sizable remnant of my old fleet to meet me. Seems impossible I'd ever see the ornery Blue again, or that ship which was the first place to feel like home since Lykos. "Because of Mustang, we'll have a real navy. She preserved my command. She kept Orion at the helm. Would she have done that if she didn't have the same aims as us?"

"Which are?" Dancer asks.

"Defeating Lune and the Jackal," she says.

"That's just the surface of what we want," Dancer says.

"She's working with us," I stress.

"For now," Victra says. "She's a clever girl. Maybe she wants to use us to eliminate her enemies? Place herself in a position of power. Maybe she wants Mars. Maybe she wants more." Seems only yesterday my council of Golds was discussing whether or not Victra was worth trusting. Roque spoke up for her when no one else would. The irony is apparently lost on Victra. Or maybe she remembers Mustang's vocal distrust of her intentions a year ago and has decided to repay the old debt.

"I hate to agree with the Julii," Dancer says, "but she's right in this. Augustans are players. Not one's been born that hasn't been." Apparently Dancer wasn't impressed with Mustang's lack of transparency earlier. Mustang expected this. In fact, she asked to stay in her room, away from this so she wouldn't detract from my plan. But in order for this to work, in order for there to be some way to piece things together in the end, there must be cooperation.

They expect me to defend Mustang, which shows how little they know her.

"You are all being rather illogical," Mustang says. "I don't mean that as an insult, but simply as a statement of fact. If I meant you ill, I would have hailed the Sovereign or my brother and brought a tracking device on my ship. You know what lengths she would go to in order to find Tinos." My friends exchange troubled glances. "But I didn't. I know you will not trust me. But you trust Darrow and he trusts me, and since he knows me better than any of you do, I think he's in the best position to make the call. So stop whimpering like gorydamn children and let's be about the task, eh?"

"If you have a buzzsaw I could do it in around three minutes. . . ." Sevro says.

"Will you shut the hell up?" Dancer barks at him. It's the first time I've ever seen him lose his temper. "A man will lie through his teeth, say whatever you want to hear if you're pulling off his toenails. It doesn't work." He was tortured himself by the Jackal. Just like Evey and Harmony were.

Sevro crosses his arms. "Well, that's an unfair and massive generalization, Gramps."

"We don't torture," Dancer says. "That's final."

"Oh, yeah, right," Sevro says. "We're the good guys. Good guys never torture. And always win. But how many good guys get their heads put in boxes? How many get to watch their friends' spines cut in half?"

Dancer looks to me for help. "Darrow. . . ."

Quicksilver pops open an oyster. "Torture can be effective if done correctly with confirmable information in a narrow scope. Like any tool, it is not a panacea; it must be used properly. Personally, I don't really think we have the luxury of drawing moral lines in the sand. Not today. Let Barca have a go. Pulls some nails. Some eyes if need be."

"I agree," Theodora says, surprising the council.

"What about Matteo?" I ask Quicksilver. "Sevro shattered his face."

Quicksilver's knife slips on the new oyster, punching into the meat of his palm. He winces and sucks at the blood. "And if he hadn't have passed out he would have told you where I was. From my experience, pain is the best negotiator."

"I agree with them, Darrow," Mustang says. "We have to be certain he's telling the truth. Otherwise we're letting him dictate our strategy—which is classic counterintelligence on his part. It's what you would do." And it's what I tried to do till the torture started with the Jackal.

Victra, who has been silent on the issue till now, walks abruptly around the table into the holo projection so that black space and stars play across her skin. Jagged white-blond hair drifts in front of angry eyes as she pulls her gray shirt off. She's muscled and lithe beneath and wears a compression bra. A half dozen razor scars stretch three inches at a diagonal across her flat belly. There's more than a dozen on her sword arm. A few on her face, neck, clavicle.

"Some I'm proud of," she says of the scars. "Some I'm not." She turns to show us her lower back. It's a waxy melted swath of flesh where her sister left her mark in acid. She turns back to us, raising her chin in defiance. "I came here because I didn't have a choice. I stayed when I did. Don't make me regret that."

It's startling to see the vulnerability in her. I don't think Mustang would ever let her guard down in public like this. Sevro stares intensely at the tall woman as she tugs her shirt back on and turns back to the holo. She reaches for the asteroid with both hands to stretch the hologram. "Can we get better resolution?" she asks as if the matter is settled.

"The picture was taken by a Census Bureau drone," I say. "Nearly seventy years ago. We don't have access to the current Society military records."

"My men are on it," Quicksilver says. "But they're not optimistic. We're fighting a legion of Society counterattacks right now. Gory-damn maelstrom."

"This is when having your father around would come in handy," Sevro says to Mustang.

"He never mentioned anything like this to me," she replies.

"Mother did, once," Victra says thoughtfully. "Antonia and I. Something about nasty little goody bags that Imperators could collect on the fly if the Rim went off the tracks."

"That matches with what Cassius says."

She turns back to us. "Then I think Cassius is telling the truth."

"So do I," I say to the group. "And torturing him doesn't resolve anything. Cut off his fingers one by one, and what if he still says it's true? Do we keep cutting until he says it's not? Either way it's a gamble." I get a few reluctant nods and feel relief that at least one battle's won, if a little wary knowing how savage my friends can become.

"What did he suggest we do?" Dancer asks. "I'm sure he had a proposal."

"He wants me to have a holoconference with the Sovereign," I say. "Why?"

"To discuss an alliance against the Jackal. They give us intel, we kill him before he can detonate any bombs," I say. "That's his plan."

Sevro giggles. "Sorry. But that would be bloodydamn fun to watch." He pulls up his left hand and makes a talking motion with it. 'Hello, you old rusty bitch, you recall when I kidnaped your grandchild?'" He pulls up his right hand. "Why yes, my goodman. Just after I enslaved your entire race." He shakes his head. "No purpose in talking to that Pixie. Not until we're knocking on her doorstep with a fleet. You should send me and the Howlers after good old Jackal. Can't press a button without a head."

"The Valkyrie will attend this mission with the Howlers," Sefi says.

"No. The Jackal will invite a personal attack," I say, glancing at Mustang, who has already warned me off that course. "He knows us too well to be surprised by things we've done in the past. I'm not throwing lives away by playing into his understanding of our strengths."

"Do you have anyone inside his inner-circle, Regulus?" Dancer asks Quicksilver. Surprisingly, the two men seem to rather like one another.

"I did. Until your Grays broke Darrow out. Adrius had his chief of intelligence purge his inner circle. My men are all dead or imprisoned or scared shitless."

"What do you think, Augustus?" Dancer asks Mustang.

All eyes turn to her. She takes her time in replying.

"I think the reason you've managed to stay alive so long is because Golds are so consumed with the individual ego that they've forgotten how they conquered Earth. Each thinks they can rule. With Orion returning and Sevro's gains, your greatest strength now lies with your navy and an Obsidian army. Don't help the Sovereign. She is still the most dangerous enemy. You help her, she focuses on you. Sow more seeds of discord."

Dancer nods in agreement. "But are we sure the Jackal would actually use the nukes on the planet?"

"The only thing my brother ever wanted was my father's approval. He did not get it. So he killed my father. Now he wants Mars. What do you think he'll do if he doesn't get it?"

A menacing silence fills the room.

"I have a new plan," I say.

"I should bloodydamn hope so," Sevro mutters to Victra. "Do I get to hide inside anything?"

"I'm sure we can find something for you, darling," she says.

I nod my agreement.

He waves a hand. "Well, then let's hear it, Reaper."

"Hypothetically, assume we take half the cities of Mars," I say, standing and summoning a graphic from the table that shows a red tide flowing over the globe of Mars, claiming cities, pushing back the Golds. "Say we crush the Jackal's fleet in orbit when Orion joins us, even though we are outnumbered two to one. Say we shatter his armies. With the Valkyrie's help, we fracture the Obsidians away from the legions and have them join us, and we have a groundswell from the populace itself. The machines of industry grind to a complete halt on Mars. We've rebuffed the Society's countless reinforcements and we have insurrection in every street and we have cornered the Jackal after years of warfare. And it *will* take years. What happens then?"

"The machines of industry don't stop off of Mars," Victra says.

"They keep rolling. And they'll keep pumping men and materiel here."

"Or . . . ," I say.

"He uses the bombs," Dancer says.

"Which I also believe he'll use on the Obsidians and our army if we go ahead with operation Rising Tide," I say.

"We've been prepping the operation for months," Dancer protests. "With the Obsidians it might just work. You just want to scrap it?"

"Yes," I say. "This planet is why we fight. The strength of rebel armies throughout history is that they have less to protect. They can rove and move and are impossible to pin down. We have so much to lose here. So much to protect. This war won't be won in days or weeks. It will be a decade. Mars will bleed. And at the end, ask yourselves: What will we inherit? A corpse of what was once our home. We must fight this war, but I will not fight it here. I propose we leave Mars."

Quicksilver coughs. "Leave Mars?"

Sefi steps forward from the shadows of the stone room. "You said you would protect my people."

"Our strength is here, in the tunnels," Dancer continues. "In our population. That's where our responsibility lies, Darrow." He glances at Mustang, his suspicions clear. "Don't forget where you come from. Why you're doing this."

"I have not forgotten, Dancer."

"Are you so sure? This war is for Mars."

"It's for more than that," I say.

"For lowColors," he continues, voice gaining volume. "Win here and then spread across the Society. It's where the helium is. It is the heart of the Society, of Red. Win here, then spread. That's how Ares intended it."

"This war is for everyone," Mustang corrects.

"No," Dancer says territorially. "This is our war, Gold. I was fighting it when you were still learning how to enslave human beings at your . . ."

Sevro looks at me in annoyance as our friends descend into bickering. I give him a little nod and he pulls his razor and slams it into the table. It cuts halfway through and trembles there. "Reaper's trying to speak, you shitgobblers. Besides all this Colorism bores me." He looks around, terribly pleased with the silence. He nods to himself and waves a theatrical hand. "Reaper, please, continue. You were getting to the exciting part."

"Thank you, Sevro. I won't fall into the trap of the Jackal," I say. "The easiest way to lose any war is to let the enemy dictate the terms of engagement. We must do the thing the Jackal and the Sovereign least expect of us. Create our own paradigm so they're playing *our* game. Reacting to *our* decisions. We must be bold. Right now we've sparked a fire. Rebellions in almost all Society territories. We stay here, that means we are contained. I will not be contained."

I transfer the image on my datapad to the table so that the hologram of Jupiter floats in the air. Sixty-three tiny moons dot the periphery but the four great Jovian moons dominate its orbit. These four largest—Ganymede, Callisto, Io, and Europa—are referred to collectively as Ilium. Around those moons are two of the largest fleets in the Solar System, that of the Moon Lords, and that of the Sword Armada. Sevro looks so pleased he might faint.

I'm giving him the war he didn't even know he wanted.

"The civil war between Bellona and Augustus has exposed larger fault lines between the Core and the Outer Rim. Octavia's main fleet, the Sword Armada, is hundreds of millions of kilometers away from its nearest support. Excepting the Sceptre Armada around Luna it is the greatest weapon Octavia has. Octavia sent our good friend Roque au Fabii to bring the Moon Lords to heel. He has shattered every fleet that has been thrown against them, even with the help of Mustang, the Telemanuses, and the Arcoses, he has beaten the Rim down. On board these ships are more than two million men and women. More than ten thousand Obsidian. Two hundred thousand Grays. Three thousand of the greatest killers alive, Peerless Scarred. Praetors, Legates, knights, squad commanders. The greatest Golds of their Institutes. This fleet has been reinforced by Antonia au Severus-Julii. And it is the instrument of fear by which the Sovereign binds the planets to her will. It, like its commander, has never been defeated." I pause, allowing the words to sink in so they all know the gravity of my proposal.

"In forty days we're going to destroy the Sword Armada and rip the beating heart out of the Society war machine." I pull Sevro's razor out of the table and toss it back to him. "Now, I'll take your bloody-damn questions."

39

||||||||||||||||||||||||

THE HEART

Dancer finds me as I make final preparations to board the shuttle with Sevro and Mustang that will take us to the fleet in orbit. Tinos swarms with activity. Hundreds of shuttles and transports gathered by Dancer and his Sons of Ares leadership depart through the great tunnels to make their migration toward the South Pole, where they will still ferry the Obsidian young and old from their home to the safety of the mines, but the warriors will go to orbit to join my fleet. In twenty-four hours, they will move eight hundred thousand human beings in the greatest effort in Sons of Ares history. It makes me smile thinking how much happier Fitchner would be knowing the greatest endeavor of his legacy was to save lives instead of to take them.

After covering the evacuation with the fleet, I will burn hard for Jupiter. Dancer and Quicksilver will remain behind to continue what they started and hold the Jackal on Mars till the next evolution of the plan begins.

"It's haunting, isn't it," Dancer says, watching the sea of blue engine flares that flow past our stalactite up to the great tunnel in the ceiling of Tinos. Victra stands closely with Sevro at the edge of the open hangar, two dark silhouettes watching the hope of two peoples float away into the darkness. "The Red Armada goes to war," Dancer breathes. "Never thought I'd see the day."

"Fitchner should be here," I reply.

"Yes, he should," Dancer grimaces. "It's my greatest regret, I think. That he couldn't live to see his son wear his helm. And you become what he always knew you to be."

"And what's that?" I ask, watching a Red Howler jump twice with his gravBoots and rocket off the edge of the hangar to enter the open cargo hatch of a passing troop carrier.

"Someone who believes in the people," he says delicately.

I turn to face Dancer, glad that he's sought me out in my last moments here among my kin. I don't know if I'll ever return. And if I do, I fear he will see me as a different man. One who betrayed him, our people, Eo's dream. I've been here before. Saying goodbye on a landing pad. Harmony stood with him then, Mickey too as they said goodbye on that spire in Yorkton. How can I feel so melancholy for so terrible a past? Maybe that's just the nature of us, ever wishing for things that were and could be rather than things that are and will be.

It takes more to hope than to remember.

"Do you think the Moon Lords will really help us?" he asks.

"No. The trick will be making them think they're helping themselves. Then getting out before they turn on us."

"It's a risk, boy, but you like those, don't you?"

I shrug. "It's also the only chance we have."

Boots clomp on the metal deck behind me. Holiday moves past up the ramp carrying a bag of gear with several new Howlers. Life moves on, carrying me with it. It's been nearly seven years since Dancer and I met, yet it seems thirty on him. How many decades of war has he faced? How many friends has he said goodbye to that I've never known, that he's never even mentioned? People who he loved as much as I love Sevro and Ragnar. He had a family once, though he rarely speaks of them now.

We all had something once. We're each robbed and broken in our own way. That's why Fitchner formed this army. Not to piece us together, but to save himself from the abyss his wife's death opened in him. He needed a light. And he made it. Love was his shout into the wind. Same with my wife.

"Lorn once told me if he had been my father he would have raised me to be a good man. 'There's no peace for great men,' he said." I smile at the memory. "I should have asked him who he thinks makes the peace for all those good men."

"You *are* a good man," Dancer tells me.

My hands are scarred and brutal things. When I clench them their knuckles turn that familiar shade of white.

"Yeah?" I grin. "Then why do I want to do bad things?" He laughs at that, and I surprise him by pulling him into a hug. His good arm wraps around my hips. His head barely coming to my chest. "Sevro might've worn the helmet, but you're the heart here," I tell him. "You always have been. You're too humble to see it, but you're as great a man as Ares himself. And somehow, you're still good. Unlike that dirty rat bastard." I pull back and thump his chest. "And I love you. Just so you know."

"Oh, bloodydamn," he mutters, eyes tearing up. "I thought you were a killer. You gone soft on me, boy?"

"Never," I say, winking.

He pushes me off. "Go say goodbye to your mother before you go."

I leave him to shout at a group of Sons marines and work my way through the bustle, bumping fists with Pebble who Screwface pushes on a wheelchair toward a boarding ramp, tossing a salute to Sons of Ares I recognize, talking shit back to Uncle Narol who walks with a troop of Pitvipers. They're destined for a sabotage mission against the Jackal's deep space communication relays. My mother and Mustang stop talking abruptly when I arrive. Both look distraught.

"What's the matter?" I ask.

"Just saying goodbye," Mustang says.

My mother steps close to me. "Dio brought this from Lykos." She opens a little plastic box and shows me the dirt inside. My little mother smiles up at me. "You fly into night, and when all grows dark, remember who you are. Remember you are never alone. The hopes and dreams of our people go with you. Remember home." She pulls me down to kiss my forehead. "Remember you are loved." I hug her tight and pull back to see she has tears in her hard eyes.

"I'll be all right, Ma," I say.

"I know. I know you don't think you deserve to be happy," she says. "But you do, child. You deserve it more than anyone I know. So do what you need to do, then come home to me." She takes my hand and Mustang's. "Both of you come home. Then start living."

I leave her behind, confused and emotional. "What was that about?" I ask Mustang. Mustang looks at me as if I should know.

"She's afraid."

"Why?"

"She's your mother."

I walk up my shuttle's landing pad, with Sevro and Victra who join Mustang and I at the bottom. "Helldiver . . ." Dancer shouts before we reach the top. I turn back to find the gnarled man with his fist thrust in the air. And behind him the whole of the stalactite hangar watches me, hundreds of deckhands on mechanized loading trams, pilots, Blue and Red and Green, who stand at the ramps of their ships or on the ladders leading into their cockpits, helmets in hands, platoons of Grays and Reds and Obsidians standing side by side carrying combat gear and supplies—the scythe sewn onto shoulders, painted onto faces—as they board shuttles bound for my fleet. Men and women of Mars, all. Fighting for something larger than themselves. For our planet, for their people. I feel the weight of their love. I feel the hopes of all those people in bondage who watched as the Sons of Ares rose to take Phobos. We promised them something, and now we must deliver. One by one, my army raises their hands till a sea of fists clench as Eo's did when she held the haemanthus and fell before Augustus.

Chills run through me as Sevro and Victra and Mustang and even my mother raise their hands in union. "Break the chains," Dancer bellows. I raise my own scarred fist and step silently into the shuttle to join the Red Armada as it sails to war.

40

||||||||||||||||||||||

YELLOW SEA

The Yellow Sea of Io rolls in around my black boots. Great
dunes of sulfur-laced sand with razorback ridges of silicate
rock as far as the eye can see. In the steel blue sky, the marbled surface
of Jupiter undulates. One hundred and thirty times the diameter that
Luna appears from the surface of Earth, it seems the vast and evil
head of a marble god. War grips its sixty-seven moons. Cities hunker
under pulseShields. Blackened husks of men in starShells litter moons
while fighter squadrons duel and hunt troop and supply transports
among the faint ice rings of the gas giant.

It's quite a sight.

I stand upon the dune flanked by Sefi and five Valkyrie in black
pulseArmor waiting for the Moon Lord's shuttle. Our assault ship
sits behind us, engines idling. It's shaped like a hammerhead shark.
Dark gray. But the Valkyrie and Red dockworkers painted its head
together on our journey from Mars, giving the ship two bulging blue
eyes and a gaping mouth with ravenous bloodstained teeth. Up between the eyes, Holiday lies on her belly, sniper rifle scanning the rock
formations to the south.

"Anything?" I ask, voice crackling through the breathing mask.

"Nothin'," Sevro says over the com. He and Clown scout the little settlement two clicks away on gravBoots. I can't see them with the naked eye. I fidget with my slingBlade.

"They'll come," I say. "Mustang set the time and place."

Io is a strange moon. Innermost and smallest of the four great Galilean moons, she is a belt-notch larger than Luna. It was never her destiny to be fully changed by the Golds' terraforming machines. She's a hell Dante could be proud of. The driest object in the Sol System, rife with explosive volcanism and sulfur deposits and interior tidal heating. Her surface a canvas of yellow and orange plains broken by huge thrust faults from her shifting surface. Dramatic sheer cliffs rising from the sulfur dunes to scrape the sky.

Huge stains of concentric green freckle her equatorial regions. Finding crops and animals difficult to cultivate so far from the sun, the Society Engineering Corp covered millions of acres of Io's surface with pulseFields, imported dirt and water for three lifetimes on cosmosHaulers, thickened the planet's atmosphere to filter Jupiter's massive radiation, and used the planet's interior tidal heating to power great generators to grow foodstuffs for the entire Jupiter orbit and exportation to the Core and, more important, the Rim. She's a farm deck with the biggest breadbasket between Mars and Uranus with easy gravity and cheap land.

Guess who did all the labor.

Beyond the pulseFields is the Sulfur Sea stretching from pole to pole, interrupted only by volcanoes and lakes of magma.

I may not like Io. But I can respect the people of this land. Ionian men and women are not like humans of Earth or Luna or Mercury or Venus. They are harder, lither, eyes slightly larger to absorb the dimmed light six hundred million kilometers from the sun, skin pale, taller, and able to withstand higher doses of radiation. These people believe themselves most like the Iron Golds who conquered Earth and put man at peace for the first time in her history.

I shouldn't have worn black today. My gloves, my cloak, my jacket underneath. I thought we were going to the anti-Jupiter side of Io where sulfur dioxide snowfields crust the planet. But the Moon Lord's operation team demanded a new meeting point at the last moment, setting us on the edge of the Sulfur Sea. Temperature 120 Celsius.

Sefi walks up to stand beside me with her new optics scanning the yellow horizon. She and her Valkyrie have taken quickly to the gear of war, studying and training day and night with Holiday during our month and a half journey to Jupiter. Practicing ship-boarding and energy weapon tactics as well as Gray hand signals.

"How's the heat?" I ask.

"Strange," she says. Only her face can feel it. The rest benefits from the cooling systems in the armor. "Why would people live here?"

"We live everywhere we can."

"But Golds choose," she says. "Yes?"

"Yes."

"I would be wary men who choose such a home. The spirits here are cruel." Sand kicks up from the wind in the low gravity, floating down in wavering columns. It's Sefi who Mustang thinks I should be wary of. On our voyage to Jupiter, she has watched hundreds of hours of holofootage. Learning our history as a people. I keep track of her datapad's activity. But what concerns Mustang isn't that Sefi is fond of rain forest videos and experientials, but that she has spent countless hours watching holos of our wars, particularly the nuclear annihilation of Rhea. I wonder what she makes of it.

"Sound advice, Sefi," I reply. "Sound advice."

Sevro lands dramatically before us, spraying us with sand. His ghostCloak ripples away. "Bloodydamn shithole."

I dust off my face, annoyed. He was incorrigible the whole journey out here. Laughing, pulling pranks, and slipping off to Victra's room whenever he thought no one was looking. Ugly little man's in love. And for what it's worth, it seems to go both ways. "What do you think?" I ask.

"The whole place smells like farts."

"That your professional assessment?" Holiday asks over the com.

"Yup. There's a Waygar settlement over the ridge." His Howler wolf pelt kicks in the wind, jingling the little chains that connect it to his armor. "Buncha Red hunched goggle heads carting distillation gear."

"You've scanned the sand?" I ask.

"Ain't my first slag, boss. I don't like this face-to-face bullshit, but it looks clear." He glances at his datapad. "Thought Moonies were supposed to be punctual. Pricklicks are thirty minutes late."

"Probably cautious. Must think we've air support," I say.

"Yeah. Because we'd be bloodydamn shitbrains for not bringing some."

"*Roger that,*" Holiday says in agreement over the com.

"Why would I need air support when I've got you," I say, gesturing to Sevro's gravBoots. A plastic gray case sits on the ground behind him. Inside, a *sarrissa* missile launcher in foam padding. The same Ragnar used on Cassius's craft. If the need arises I've got myself a psychotic Goblin-sized fighter jet.

"Mustang said they'll be here," I say.

"*Mustang said they'll be here,*" Sevro mocks in childish voice. "They better. Fleet can't squat for long out there without being spotted."

My fleet waits with Orion in orbit since Mustang took her shuttle to Nessus, the capital of Io. Fifty torchShips and destroyers hunkered down, shields off, engines dark on the barren moon of Sinope as the larger fleets of the Golds swim through space closer in to the Galilean Moons. Any closer and the Gold sensors will pick us up. But as it hides, my fleet is vulnerable. With one pass a measly squadron of rip-Wings could destroy it.

"The Moonies will come," I say. But I'm not sure of it.

They're a cold, proud, insular people, these Jovian Golds. Roughly eight thousand Peerless Scarred call the Galilean Moons of Jupiter home. Their Institutes are all out here. And it is only Societal service or vacations for the wealthiest among them that takes them to the Core. Luna might be the ancestral home of their people, but it's alien to most of them. Metropolitan Ganymede is the center of their world.

The Sovereign knows the danger of having an independent Rim. She spoke to me of the difficulty of imposing her power across a billion kilometers of empire. Her true fear was never Augustus and Bellona destroying one another. It was the chance that the Rim would rebel and cut the Society in half. Sixty years ago, at the beginning of her reign, she had the Ash Lord nuke Saturn's moon, Rhea, when its ruler refused to accept her authority. That example held for sixty years.

But nine days after my Triumph, the children of the Moon Lords who were kept on Luna in the Sovereign's court as insurance toward their parents' political cooperation, escaped. They were assisted by Mustang's spies which she left behind in the Citadel. Two days after that, the heirs of the fallen ArchGovernor Revus au Raa, who was killed at my Triumph, stole or destroyed the entirety of the Societal Garrison Fleet in its dock at Calisto. They declared Io's independence and pressured the other more populous and powerful moons into joining them.

Soon after, the infamously charismatic Romulus au Raa was elected Sovereign of the Rim. Saturn and Uranus joined soon after that, and the Second Moon Rebellion began sixty years, two hundred and eleven days after the first.

The Moon Lords obviously expected the Sovereign would find herself mired on Mars for a decade, maybe longer. Add to that a certain lowColor insurrection in the Core and one can see why they assumed she would not be able to devote the resources needed to send a fleet of sufficient size six hundred million kilometers to quash their nascent rebellion. They were wrong.

"We've got inbound," Pebble says from her station at the shuttle's sensor boards. "Three ships. Two-ninety clicks out."

"Finally," Sevro mutters. "Here come the bloodydamn Moonies."

Three warships emerge from the heat mirage on the horizon. Two black *sarpedon*-class fighters painted with the four-headed white dragon of Raa clutching a Jovian thunderbolt in its talons escort a fat tan *priam*-class shuttle. The ship lands before us. Dust swirls and the ramp unfurls from the belly of the craft. Seven lithe forms, taller and lankier than I, walk down into the sand. Golds all. They wear kryll, organic breathing masks made by Carvers, over nose and mouths. Looks like the shed skin of a locust, legs stretching to either ear. Their tan combat gear is lighter than Core armor and complimented with brightly colored scarves. Long-barreled railguns with personalized ivory stocks are strapped to their backs. Razors hang from their hips. Orange optics cover their eyes. And on their feet are skippers. Lightweight boots that use condensed air instead of gravity to move their user. Skipping them over the ground like stones on a lake. Can't get much height, but you can move nearly sixty kilometers an hour. They're about a quarter the weight of my boots, have battery life for a year, and are dead cold on thermal vision.

These are assassins. Not knights. Holiday recognizes the different breed of danger.

"She's not with them," she says over her com. "Any Telemanuses?"

"No," I say. "Hold. I see her."

Mustang steps out of the craft, joining the much-taller Ionians. She's dressed like them, except without a rifle. Joined by another Ionian woman, this one with the forward hunching shoulders of a cheetah, Mustang joins us atop the dune. The rest of the Ionians stay near the ship. Not a threat, just an escort.

"Darrow," Mustang says. "Sorry we're late."

"Where's Romulus?" I ask.

"He's not coming."

"Bullshit," Sevro hisses. "I told you, Reap."

"Sevro, it's fine," Mustang says. "This is his sister, Vela."

The tall woman stares down her smashed-flat nose at us. Her skin is pale, body adapted for the low gravity. It's hard to see her face past the mask and goggles, but she seems in her early fifties. Her voice is one even note. "I send my brother's greetings, and welcome, Darrow of Mars. I am Legate Vela au Raa." Sefi slinks around us, examining the alien Gold and the strange gear she carries. I like the way people talk when Sefi circles. Seems a little more honest.

"Well met, *legatus*." I nod cordially. "Will you be speaking for your brother? I'd hoped to make my case in person."

The skin to the side of her goggles crinkles. "No one speaks for my brother. Not even I. He wishes for you to join him at his private home on the Wastes of Karrack."

"So you can lure us into a trap?" Sevro asks. "Better idea. How 'bout you tell your bitch of a brother to honor his bloodydamn agreement before I take that rifle and shove it so far up your farthole you look like a skinny Pixie shish kebab?"

"Sevro, stop," Mustang says. "Not here. Not these people."

Vela watches Sefi circle. Taking note of the razor on the huge Obsidian's hip.

"I could give a shit and piss who this is. She knows who we are. And she ain't got a little trickle goin' down her leg standing toe to toe with the bloodydamn Reaper of Mars, then she's got less brains than a wad of ass lint."

"He cannot come," Vela says.

"Understandable," I reply.

Sevro makes a grotesque motion.

"What is that?" Vela asks, nodding to Sefi.

"That is a queen," I say. "Sister to Ragnar Volarus."

Vela is wary of Sefi, as well she should be. Ragnar is a name known. "She cannot come either. But I was speaking in regards to that hunk of metal you flew here on. Is it meant to be a ship?" She snorts and turns up her nose. "Built on Venus, obviously."

"It's borrowed," I say. "But if you care to make an exchange . . ."

Vela surprises me with a laugh before becoming serious once more. "If you wish to present yourself to Moon Lords as a diplomatic party, then you must show respect for my brother. And trust the honor of his hospitality."

"I've seen enough men and women set aside honor when it's inconvenient," I say probingly.

"In the Core, perhaps. This is the Rim," Vela replies. "We remember the ancestors. We remember how Iron Golds should be. We do not murder guests like that bitch on Luna. Or like that Jackal on Mars."

"Yet," I say.

Vela shrugs. "It is a choice you must make, Reaper. You have sixty seconds to decide." Vela steps away as I confer with Mustang and Sevro. I motion Sefi over.

"Thoughts?"

"Romulus would rather die than kill a guest," Mustang says. "I know you don't have any reason to trust these people. But honor actually means something to them. It's not like the Bellona who just toss the word around. Out here a Gold's word means as much as his blood."

"Do you know where the residence is?" I ask.

She shakes her head. "If I did I'd take you there myself. They've got equipment inside to check for radiation and electronic trackers. They've studied you. We'll be on our own."

"Lovely." But this isn't about tactics. No short-term game here. My big play was coming out to the Rim knowing I had leverage the Sovereign doesn't. That leverage will keep my head on my shoulders better than anyone's honor. Yet I've been wrong before, so I double-check and listen now.

"Do the rules governing treatment of guests extend to Reds?" Sevro asks. "Or just Golds? That's what we need to know."

I glance back at Vela. "It's a fair point."

"If he kills you, he kills me," Mustang says. "I'm not leaving your side. And if he does that, my men turn against him. The Telemanuses turn against him. Even Lorn's daughters-in-law will turn against him. That's nearly a third of his navy. It's a bloodfeud he can't afford."

"Sefi, what do you think?"

She closes her eyes so her blue tattoos can see the spirits of this waste. "Go."

"Give us six hours, Sevro. If we're not back by then . . ."

"Wank off in the bushes?"

"Lay waste."

"Can do." He bumps my fist with his and winks. "Happy diplomacy, kids." He keeps his fist out for Mustang. "You too horsey. We're in this shit together, eh?"

She happily bumps his knuckles with her own. "Bloodydamn right."

41

||||||||||||||||||||||||||||

THE MOON LORD

The home of the most powerful man in the Galilean Moons is a simple, wandering place of little gardens and quiet nooks. Set in the shadow of a dormant volcano, it looks out over a yellow plain that stretches to the horizon where another volcano smolders and magma creeps westward. We set down in a small covered hangar in the side of a rock formation, one of only two ships. The other a sleek black racing craft Orion would die to fly next to a row of several dust-covered hover bikes. No one comes to service our vessel as we disembark and approach the home along a white stone walkway set into the sulfur chalk. It curves around to the side of the home. The entirety of the small property enclosed by a discreet pulseBubble.

Our escorts are at ease on the property. They file in ahead of us through the iron gate that leads to the grass courtyard into the home, removing their dust-caked skipper boots and setting them just inside the entryway beside a pair of black military boots. Mustang and I exchange a glance then remove our own. It takes me the longest to remove my bulky gravBoots. Each weighing nearly nine kilos and having three parallel latches around the boot that lock my legs in. It's oddly comforting to feel the grass between my toes. I'm conscious of the stink of my feet. Odd seeing the boots of a dozen enemies stacked by the door. Like I've walked in on something very private.

"Please wait here," Vela says to me. "Virginia, Romulus wishes to speak with you alone first."

"I'll scream if I'm in danger," I say with a grin when Mustang hesitates. She winks as she leaves to follow Vela, who noticed the subtlety of the exchange. I feel there's little the older woman misses, even less that she doesn't judge. I'm left alone in the garden with the song of a wind chime hanging from a tree above. The courtyard garden is an even rectangle. Maybe thirty paces wide. Ten deep from the front gate to the small white steps that lead into the home's front entrance. The white plaster walls are smooth and covered with thin creeping vines that wander into the home. Little orange flowers erupt from the vines and fill the air with a woodsy, burning scent.

The house rambles, rooms and gardens unfolding out from each other. There is no roof to the house. But there's little reason for one. The pulseBubble seals off the property from the weather outside. They make their own rain here. Little misters drip water from the morning's watering of the small citrus trees whose roots crack the bottom of the white stone fountain in the center of the garden. A little glance at a place like this was what led my wife to the gallows.

How strange a journey she'd think this was.

But also, in a way, how marvelous.

"You can eat a tangerine if you like," a small voice says behind me. "Father won't mind." I turn to find a child standing by another gate that leads off from the main courtyard to a path that winds around the left of the house. She might be eight years old. She holds a small shovel in her hands, and the knees of her pants are stained with dirt. Her hair is short-cropped and messy, her face pale, eyes a third again as large as any girl of Mars. You can see the tender length of her bones. Like a fresh-born colt. There's a wildness in her. I've not met many Gold children. Core Peerless families often guard them from the public eye for fear of assassination, keeping them in private estates or schools. I've heard the Rim is different. They do not kill children here. But everyone likes to pretend that they don't kill children.

"Hello," I say kindly. It's a fragile, awkward tone I haven't used since I saw my own nieces and nephews. I love children, but I feel so alien to them these days.

"You're the Martian, aren't you?" she asks, impressed.

"My name is Darrow," I reply with a nod. "What's yours?"

"I am Sera au Raa," she says proudly. "Were you really a Red? I heard my father speaking." She explains. "They think just because I don't have this"—she runs a finger along her cheek in an imaginary scar—"that I don't have ears." She nods up to the vine-covered walls and smiles mischievously. "Sometimes I climb."

"I still am a Red," I say. "It's not something I stopped being."

"Oh. You don't look like one."

She must not watch holos if she doesn't know who I am. "Maybe it's not about what I look like," I suggest. "Maybe it's about what I do."

Is that too clever a thing to say to a six-year-old? Hell if I know. She makes a disgusted face and I fear I've made a mistake.

"Have you met many Reds, Sera?"

She shakes her head. "I've only seen them in my studies. Father says it's not proper to mingle."

"Don't you have servants?"

She giggles before she realizes I'm serious. "Servants? But I haven't earned servants." She taps her face again. "Not yet." It darkens my mood to think of this girl running for her life through the woods of the Institute. Or will she be the one chasing?

"Nor will you ever earn them if you don't leave our guest alone, Seraphina" a low, husky voice says from the main entry to the house. Romulus au Raa leans against the doorframe of his home. He is a serene and violent man. My height, yet thinner with a twice broken nose. His right eye a third larger than mine set in a narrow, wrathful face. His left eyelid is crossed with a scar. A smooth globe of blue and black marble stares out at me in place of eyeball. His full lips are pinched, the top lip bearing three more scars. His dark gold hair is long and held in a ponytail. Except for the old wounds, his skin is perfect porcelain. But it's how he seems more than how he looks that makes the man. I feel his steady way. His easy confidence, as if he's always been at the door. Always known me. It's startling how much I like him from the moment he winks at his daughter. And also how much I want him to like me, despite the tyrant I know him to be.

"So what do you make of our Martian?" he asks his daughter.

"He is thick," Seraphina says. "Larger than you, father."

"But not as large as a Telemanus," I say.

She crosses her arms. "Well, nothing is as large as a Telemanus."

I laugh. "If only that were true. I knew a man who was nearly as large to me as I am to you."

"No," Seraphina says, eyes widening. "An Obsidian?"

I nod. "His name was Ragnar Volarus. He was Stained. A prince of an Obsidian tribe from the south pole of Mars. They call themselves the Valkyrie. And they are ruled by women who ride griffins." I look at Romulus. "His sister is with me."

"Who ride griffins?" The notion dazzles the girl. She's not yet gotten there in her studies. "Where is he now?"

"He died, and we fired him toward the sun as we came to visit your father."

"Oh. I'm sorry . . . ," she says with the blind kindness it seems only children still have. "Is that why you looked so sad?"

I flinch, not knowing it was so obvious. Romulus notices and spares me from answering. "Seraphina, your uncle was looking for you. The tomatoes won't plant themselves. Will they?" Seraphina dips her head and gives me a farewell wave before departing back down the path. I watch her disappear and belatedly realize that my child would be her age now.

"Did you arrange that?" I ask Romulus.

He steps into the garden. "Would you believe me if I said no?"

"I don't believe much from anyone these days."

"That'll keep you breathing, but not happy," he says seriously, voice having the clipped staccato delivery of a man raised in gladiatorial academies. There's no affectations here, no purring insults or games. It's a refreshing, if estranging, directness. "This was my father's refuge, and his father's before mine," Romulus says, gesturing for me to take a seat on one of the stone benches. "I thought it a fitting place to discuss the future of my family." He plucks a tangerine from the tree and sits on an opposite bench. "And yours."

"It seems a strange amount of effort to expend," I say.

"What do you mean?"

"The trees, the dirt, the grass, the water. None of it belongs here."

"And man was never meant to tame fire. That's the beauty of it," he says challengingly. "This moon is a hateful little horror. But through ingenuity, through will we made it ours."

"Or are we just passing through?" I ask.

He wags a finger at me. "You've never been credited for being wise."

"Not wise," I correct. "I've been humbled. And it's a sobering thing."

"The box was real?" Romulus asks. "We've heard rumors this last month."

"It was real."

"Indecorous," he says in contempt. "But it speaks to the quality of your enemy."

His daughter left little muddy footprints on the stone path. "She didn't know who I was." Romulus concentrates on peeling the tangerine in delicate little ribbons. He's pleased I noticed about his daughter.

"No child in my family watches holos before the age of twelve. We all have nature and nurture to shape us. She can watch other people's opinions when she has opinions of her own, and no sooner. We're not digital creatures. We're flesh and blood. Better she learns that before the world finds her."

"Is that why there are no servants here?"

"There are servants, but I don't need them seeing you today. And they aren't hers. What kind of parent would want their children to have servants?" he asks, disgusted by the idea. "The moment a child thinks it is entitled to anything, they think they deserve everything. Why do you think the Core is such a Babylon? Because it's never been told no.

"Look at the Institute you attended. Sexual slavery, murder, cannibalism of fellow Golds?" He shakes his head. "Barbaric. It's not what the Ancestors intended. But the Coreworlders are so desensitized to violence they've forgotten it's to have purpose. Violence is a tool. It is meant to shock. To change. Instead, they normalize and celebrate it. And create a culture of exploitation where they are so entitled to sex and power that when they are told no, they pull a sword and do as they like."

"Just as they've done to your people," I say.

"Just as they've done to my people," he repeats. "Just as we do to yours." He finishes peeling the tangerine, only now it feels more like a scalping. He tears the meat of it gruesomely in half and tosses one part to me. "I won't romanticize what I am. Or excuse the subjugation of your people. What we do to them is cruel, but it is necessary."

Mustang told me on our journey here that he uses a stone from the Roman Forum itself as a pillow. He is not a kind person. Not to his enemies at least, which I am, regardless of his hospitality.

"It's hard for me to speak to you as if you were not a tyrant," I say. "You sit here and think you are more civilized than Luna because you obey your creed of honor, because you show restraint." I gesture to the simple house. "But you're not more civilized," I say. "You're just more disciplined."

"Isn't that civilization? Order? Denying animal impulse for stability?" He eats his fruit in measured bites. I set mine on the stone.

"No, it's not. But I'm not here to debate philosophy or politics."

"Thank Jove. I doubt we'd agree upon much." He watches me carefully.

"I'm here to discuss what we both know best, war."

"Our ugly old friend." He glances once at the door to the house to make sure we're alone. "But before we move to that sphere, may I ask you a question of personal note?"

"If you must."

"You are aware my father and daughter died at your Triumph on Mars?"

"I am."

"In a way it's what began all this. Did you see it happen?"

"I did."

"Was it as they say?"

"I wouldn't presume to know who they are or what they say."

"They say that Antonia au Severus-Julii stepped on my daughter's skull till it caved in. My wife and I wish to know if it is true. It's what we were told by one of the few who managed to escape."

"Yes," I say. "It is true."

The tangerine drips in his fingers, forgotten. "Did she suffer?"

I hardly remember seeing the girl in the moment. But I've dreamed of the night a hundred times, enough to wish my memory was a weaker thing. The plain-faced girl wore a gray dress with a broach of the lightning dragon. She tried to run around the fountain. But Vixus slashed the back of her hamstrings as he walked past. She crawled and wept on the ground until Antonia finished her off. "She suffered. For several minutes."

"Did she weep?"

"Yes. But she did not beg."

Romulus watches out the iron gate as sulfur dust devils dance across the barren plain beneath his quiet home. I know his pain, the horrible crushing sadness of loving something gentle only to see it ripped apart by the hard world. His girl grew here, loved, protected, and then she went on an adventure and learned fear.

"Truth can be cruel," he says. "Yet it is the only thing of value. I thank you for it. And I have a truth of my own. One I do not think you will like . . ."

"You have another guest," I say. He's surprised. "There's boots at the door. Polished for a ship, not a planet. Makes the dust stick something awful. I'm not offended. I half expected it when you didn't meet me in the desert."

"You understand why I will not make a decision blindly or impetuously."

"I do."

"Two months ago, I did not agree with Virginia's plan to negotiate for peace. She left of her own accord with the backing of those frightened by our losses. I believe in war only insofar as it is an effective tool of policy. And I did not believe we stood in a position of strength to gain anything from our war without achieving at least one or two victories. Peace was subjugation by another word. My logic was sound, our arms were not. We never made the victories. Imperator Fabii is . . . effective. And the Core, as much as I despise their culture, produces very good killers with very good logistical supply and support. We are fighting uphill against a giant. Now, you are here. And I can achieve something with peace that I could not with war. So I must weigh my options."

He means he can leverage my presence into suing the Sovereign for better terms than she would have given if the war had continued. It's boldly self-interested. I knew it was a risk when I set this course, but I'd hoped he'd be hot-blooded after a year of war with the woman and would want to pay her back. Apparently Romulus au Raa's blood runs a special kind of cold.

"Who did the Sovereign send?" I ask.

He leans back in amusement. "Who do you think?"

42

||||||||||||||||||||||||

THE POET

Roque au Fabii sits at a stone table in an orchard along the side of the house, finishing a dessert of elderberry cheesecake and coffee. Smoke from a brooding dwarf volcano twirls up into the twilight horizon with the same indolence as the steam from his porcelain saucer. He turns from watching the smoke to see us enter. He's striking in his black and gold uniform—lean like a strand of golden summer wheat, with high cheekbones and warm eyes, but his face is distant and unyielding. By now he could drape a dozen battle glories across his chest. But his vanity is so deep that he thinks affectation a sign of boorish decadence. The pyramid of the Society, given flight with Imperator wings on either side, marks each shoulder; a gold skull with a crown burdens his breast, the Sigil of the Ash Lord's warrant. Roque sets the saucer down delicately, dabs his lips with the corner of his napkin, and rises to his bare feet.

"Darrow, it's been an age," he says with such mannered grace that I could almost convince myself that we were old friends reuniting after a long absence. But I will not let myself feel anything for this man. I cannot let him have forgiveness. Victra almost died because of him. Fitchner did. Lorn did. And how many more would have had I not let Sevro leave the party early to seek his father?

"Imperator Fabii," I reply evenly. But behind my distant welcome is an aching heart. There's not a hint of sorrow on his face, however. I want there to be. And knowing that, I know I still feel for the man. He is a soldier of his people. I'm a soldier of mine. He is not the evil of his story. He's the hero who unmasked the Reaper. Who smashed the Augustus-Telemanus fleet at the Battle of Deimos the night after my capture. He does not do these things for himself. He lives for something as noble as I. His people. His only sin is in loving them too much, as is his way.

Mustang watches me worriedly, knowing all I must feel. She asked me about him on the journey from Mars. I told her that he was nothing to me, but we both know that isn't true. She's with me now. Anchoring me among these predators. Without her I could face my enemies, but I would not hold on to so much of my self. I would be darker. More wrathful. I count my blessings that I have people like her to which I can tether my spirit. Otherwise I fear it would run away from me.

"I can't say it's a pleasure to see you again, Roque," she says, taking the attention away from me. "Though I am surprised the Sovereign didn't send a politico to treat with us."

"She did," Roque says. "And you returned Moira as a corpse. The Sovereign was deeply wounded by that. But she has faith in my arms and judgment. Just as I have faith in the hospitality of Romulus. Thank you for the meal, by the bye," he says to our host. "Our commissary is woefully militaristic, as you can imagine."

"The benefit of owning a breadbasket," Romulus says. "Siege is never a hungry affair." He gestures for us to take our seats. Mustang and I take the two facing Roque as Romulus sits at the head of the table. Two other chairs to the right and left of him are filled with the ArchGovernor of Titan and an old, crooked woman I don't know. She wears the wings of Imperator.

Roque watches me. "It does please me, Darrow, knowing you're finally participating in the war you began."

"Darrow isn't responsible for *this* war," Mustang says. "Your Sovereign is."

"For instilling order?" Roque asks. "For obeying the Compact?"

"Oh, that's fresh. I know her a bit better than you, poet. The crone is a nasty, covetous creature. Do you think it was Aja's idea to kill Quinn?" She waits for an answer. None comes. "It was Octavia's. She told her to do it through the com in her ear."

"Quinn died because of Darrow," Roque says. "No one else."

"The Jackal bragged to me that he killed Quinn," I say. "Did you know that?" Roque is unimpressed with my claim. "If he'd let her be, she would have lived. He killed her in the back of the ship while the rest of us fought for our lives."

"Liar."

I shake my head. "Sorry. But that guilt you feel in your skinny little gut. That's gonna stick around. Because it's the truth."

"You made me a mass murderer against my own people," Roque says. "My debt to my Sovereign and the Society for my part in the Bellona-Augustus War is not yet paid. Millions lost their lives in the Siege of Mars. Millions who need not have died if I had seen through the ruse and done my duty to my people." His voice quavers. I know the lost look in his eyes. I've seen it in my own in the mirror as I wake from a nightmare and stare at myself in the pale bathroom light of that same stateroom on Luna. All those millions cry to him in the darkness, asking him why?

He continues. "What I cannot understand, Virginia, is why you abandoned the talks on Phobos. Talks which would have healed the wounds that divide Gold and permit us to focus on our true enemy." He looks at me heavily. "This man wanted your father to die. He desires nothing but the destruction of our people. Pax died for his lie. Your father died because of his schemes. He's using your heart against you."

"Spare me." Mustang snorts contemptuously.

"I'm trying to . . ."

"Don't talk down to me, poet. You're the weeping sort here. Not me. This isn't about love. This is about what is right. That has nothing to do with emotion. It has to do with justice, which rests upon facts." The Moon Lords shift uncomfortably at the notion of justice. She jerks her head in their direction. "They know I believe in Rim independence. And they know I'm a Reformer. And they know I'm intelligent enough not to conflate the two or to confuse my emotions with my beliefs. Unlike you. So since your rhetorical plays here are going to fall on deaf ears, shall we spare ourselves the indignity of verbal jousting and make our propositions so we can end this war one way or another?"

Roque glowers at her.

Romulus smiles slightly. "Do you have anything to add, Darrow?"

"I believe Mustang covered it quite thoroughly."

"Very well," Romulus replies. "Then I shall say my peace and let you say yours. You are both my enemies. One has plagued me with worker's strikes. Anti-government propaganda. Insurrection. The other with war and siege. Yet here on the fringe of the darkness away from both your sources of power, you need me, and my ships, and my legions. You see the irony. My lone question is this. Who can give me more in return?" He looks first to Roque. "Imperator, please begin."

"Honorable lords, my Sovereign mourns this conflict between our people, as do I. It spawned from the seeds sown in previous disputes, but it can end now as Rim and Core remember that there is a greater, more pernicious evil than political squabbling and debate over taxes and representation. And that is the evil of demokracy. That noble lie that all men are created equal. You've seen it tear Mars apart. Adrius au Augustus has nobly fought the battle there on behalf of the Society."

"Nobly?" Romulus asks.

"Effectively. But still the contagion has spread. Now is our best chance to destroy it before it can claim a victory from which we may never be able to recover. Despite our differences, our ancestors all fell upon Earth in the Conquering. In remembrance of that, the Sovereign is willing to cease all hostilities. She requests the aid of your legions and armada in destroying the Red menace that seeks to destroy both Rim and Core.

"In return, after the war she will remove the Societal garrison from Jupiter, but not Saturn or Uranus." The ArchGovernor of Titan snorts contemptuously. "She will enter into talks in good faith regarding the reduction of taxes and Rim export tariffs. She will grant you the same licenses for Belt mining which Core companies currently hold. And she will accept your proposal for equal representation in the Senate."

"And the reformation of the Sovereign election process?" Romulus asks. "She was never meant to be an empress. She's an elected official."

"She will revise the election process after the new Senators have been appointed. Additionally, the Olympic Knights will be appointed by the vote of the ArchGovernors, not by order of the Sovereign, as you requested."

Mustang tilts her head back and laughs one hard note. "I'm sorry. Call me skeptical. But what you're saying, Roque, is that the Sovereign will say yes to everything Romulus might want until she's back in a position to say no." She blows air out of her nose comically. "Trust me, my friends, my family well knows the sting of the Sovereign's promises."

"And what of Antonia au Julii?" Romulus asks, noting Mustang's skepticism. "Will you deliver her to our justice for the murder of my daughter and father?"

"I will."

Romulus is pleased by the terms, and moved by Roque's comments about the Red menace. It doesn't help that his promises seem very plausible. Practical. Not promising too much or too little. All I can do to combat them is to embrace the fact that I offer them a fantasy, and a dangerous one at that. Romulus looks to me, waiting.

"Color notwithstanding, you and I have a common bond. The Sovereign is a politician, I am a man of the sword. I deal in angles and metal. Like you. That is my life blood. My entire purpose for being. Look how I rose in your ranks without being one of you. Look how I took Mars. The most successful Iron Rain in centuries." I lean forward. "Lords, I will give you the independence you deserve. Not half measured. Not transient. Permanent independence from Luna. No taxes. No twenty years of service to the Core for your Grays and Obsidians. No orders from the Babylon that the Core has become."

"A bold promise," Romulus says, showing the depth of his character by bearing the insult he must feel at a Red promising to deliver him his independence.

"An outlandish promise," Roque says. "Darrow is only who he is because of who is around him."

"Agreed," Mustang says cheerily.

"And I still have everyone around me, Roque. Who do you have?"

"No one," Mustang answers. "Just dear old Antonia, who has become my brother's quisling."

The words hit home with Roque and Romulus. I return to addressing the Moon Lords. "You have the greatest dockyard the worlds have ever seen. But you started your war too quickly. Without enough ships. Without enough fuel. Thinking the Sovereign would not be able to send a fleet here so quickly. You were wrong. But the Sovereign has made a mistake as well: all her remaining fleets are in the Core, defending moons and worlds against Orion. But Orion is not in the Core. She is with me. Her forces joined to the ships I stole from the Jackal to form the armada with which I will smash the Sword Armada from the sky."

"You don't have the ships for that," Roque says.

"You don't know what I have," I say. "And you don't know where I hide it."

"How many ships does he have?" Romulus asks Mustang.

"Enough."

"Roque would have you believe I am a wildfire. Do I look wild?" Not today, at least. "Romulus, you have no interest in the Core just as I have no interest in the Rim. This is not my home. We are not enemies. My war is not against your race, but against the rulers of my home. Help us shatter the Sword Armada, and you will have your independence. Two birds with one stone. Even if I do not defeat the Sovereign in the Core after we defeat the Poet here, even if I lose within the year, we will cause such damage that it will be a lifetime before Octavia can summon the ships, the money, the men, the commanders to cross the billion kilometers darkness again." The Moon Lords lean into my words. I may yet have them.

Roque scoffs. "Do you really think this self-styled liberator will abandon the lowColors in the Rim? In the Galilean Moons alone over a hundred and fifty million are 'enslaved.' "

"If I could free them, I would," I admit. "But I cannot. I recognize that and it breaks my heart, because they are my people. But every leader must sacrifice."

This receives nods from the Golds. Even if I am the enemy, they can respect my loyalty to my people, and also the pain I must feel. It is odd having such veneration in the eyes of my enemies. I am not used to it.

Roque also sees the nods. "I know this man better than any of you," he presses. "I know him like a brother. And he is a liar. He would say whatever it took to break the bonds that bind us together."

"Unlike the Sovereign, who never lies," I say lightly, drawing a few laughs.

"The Sovereign will honor her agreement," Roque insists.

"As she did with my father?" Mustang asks scathingly. "When she planned to kill him at the Gala last year? I was her lancer and she planned it right under my nose. And why? Because he did not agree with her politics. Imagine what she'd do to men who actually went to war with her."

"Hear, hear," the ArchGovernor of Titan says, rapping his knuckles on the table.

"And instead you would trust a terrorist and a turncoat?" Roque asks. "He has conspired to destroy our Society for six years. His entire existence is deception. How could you trust him now? How could you think a Red cares more for you than a Gold?" Roque shakes his head sadly. "We are *Aureate*, my brothers and sisters. We are the order that protects mankind. Before us was a race intent on destroying the only home it had ever known. But then we brought peace. Do not let Darrow manipulate you into bringing back the Dark Age that came before. They will purge all the wonders we have made to fill their bellies and sate their lusts. We have a chance to stop him here, now. We have a chance to unite once more, as we were always meant to. For our children. What world do you want them to inherit?"

Roque puts a hand over his heart.

"I am a Man of Mars. I have no love for the Core any more than you. The appetites of Luna have pillaged my planet long before I was born. That must change. And it will change. But not at the end of *his* sword. He would burn the house to fix a broken window. No, friends, that is not the way. To change for the better, we must look past the politics of the day and remember the spirit of our Golden Age. Aureate, united over all."

The longer this plays, the more likely Roque will convince them of their patriotism. Mustang and I both know it. Just as I knew I would have to sacrifice something in coming here. I'd hoped it would not be what I'm about to offer, but I know by the looks in the eyes of the Moon Lords that Roque's message has struck home. They fear an uprising. They fear me.

It's the great dread of the Sons of Ares, the great mistake Sevro made in releasing my Carving and taking the Sons to a true war. In the shadows we could let them kill each other. We were just an idea. But Roque has made them think the thought that unites all masters who have ever been: what if the slaves take my property for their own?

When my uncle gave me my slingBlade, he said it would save my life for the price of a limb. Every miner is told that so that he knows from the first day he steps in the mine, the sacrifice is worth it. I make one now for which I may never be forgiven

"I will give you the Sons of Ares," I say quietly. No one hears me through Roque's continued speech. Only Mustang. "I will give you the Sons of Ares," I repeat more loudly. Quiet falls over the table.

Romulus's chair creaks as he leans forward. "What do you mean?"

"I told you I have no interest in the Rim. Now I will prove it. There are over three hundred and fifty Sons of Ares cells throughout your territories," I say. "We are your dock strikes. We are the sanitation sabotage and the reason why Nessus's streets fill with shit. Even if you hand me over to the Sovereign today, the Sons will bleed you for a thousand years. But I will give you every single Son of Ares cell in the Rim, I will abandon the lowColors here and take my crusade to the Core, never coming through the asteroid belt as long as I live if you help me kill his bloodydamn fleet."

I stab a finger at Roque, who looks horrified.

"That is insanity," Roque says, noting the effect my words have had. "He's lying."

But I'm not lying. I've given orders for the Sons of Ares cells to evacuate across the Rim. Not many will make it out. Thousands will be captured, tortured, killed. Thus is war, and the peril of leadership.

"Lords, the Imperator is asking you to bow," I reply. "Aren't you tired of that? Of groveling to a throne six hundred million kilometers from your home?" They nod. "The Sovereign says I am a threat to you. But who has bombed your cities? Who has slain a million of your people? Who kept your children hostage on Luna? Slaughtered your father and daughter on Mars? Who burned an entire moon? Was it me? Was it my people? No. Your greatest enemy is the greed of the Core. The burners of Rhea."

"That was a different time," Roque protests.

"It was the same woman," I snarl and look to the Saturnian Gold to Romulus's left who pays rapt attention. "Who burned Rhea? The Sovereign has forgotten, because her throne sits with its back toward the Rim. But you see her glassy corpse every night in your skies."

"Rhea was a mistake," Roque says, falling into the pitfall that Mustang helped me prepare. "One that must never be repeated."

"Never repeated?" Mustang asks, springing the trap shut. She turns to Vela, who watches from the steps of the house with several other Ionian Golds. "Vela, my friend, may I please have my datapad?"

"Don't play her game," Roque says.

"My game?" Mustang asks coyly. "My game is facts, *Imperator*. Are those not welcome here or is rhetoric alone permissible? Personally, I trust no man who fears facts." She looks back to Vela, amused by her own barbs. "You can operate it for me, Vela. The password is L17L6363." She grins at my surprise.

Vela looks to her brother. "She might send a message to Barca."

"Deactivate my connection," Mustang says. Romulus nods to Vela. She deactivates it. "Look in datafolders, cache number 3, please." She does. At first the quiet Gold's eyes narrow, confused at what she's looking at. Then, as she reads, her lips curl back and the skin on her arms pucker with goose bumps. The rest of the small gathering watches her reaction with growing anxiety. "Illuminating, isn't it, Vela?"

"What is it?" Romulus demands. "Show us."

Vela glares hatefully at Roque, who is as confused as anyone, and walks the device to her brother. His face manages to remain impassive as he reads the data, fingers swiping through the files. I use Cassius's information against his master now, turning his gift into an arrow aimed at her heart. Mustang and I thought it would be better coming from her, however. Lending the lie to the credibility of her friendship with Romulus.

"Put it up," Romulus says, tossing the datapad to Vela.

"What is this?" Roque asks angrily. "Romulus . . ." His words falter as an image of Asteroid S-1988, part of the Karin sub-family of the Koronis family of asteroids in the Kuiper Belt between Mars and Jupiter, blossoms in the air. It rotates slowly over the table. The green stream of data beneath it spelling the Sovereign's doom. It's a series of falsified Society communiqués detailing the delivery of supplies to an asteroid without a base. The stream continues to roll, detailing high-level Society directives for "refueling" at the asteroid. Then it shows the footage of the ship I sent away from the main fleet to investigate the asteroid as the rest of us journeyed to Jupiter. Reds float through the dark warehouse. The small jets on their suits silent in the vacuum. But their Geiger meters, which are synced to their helms, crackle at the amount of radiation in the place. A far greater amount of radiation than is present in the legal five megaton warheads which are used in space combat.

Romulus stares at Roque. "If Rhea was not to be repeated, then why did your fleet empty a nuclear weapons depot before coming to our orbit?"

"We did not visit the depot," Roque says, still trying to process what he's seen and the implications of it. The evidence is compelling. All lies are better served with a hefty helping of the truth. "The Sons of Ares pillaged it months ago. The information is falsified." He's operating off of the wrong information. Which means the Sovereign has kept the Jackal's sedition tight to her chest. And now she pays for trusting so few. He's not prepared for this argument and it shows.

"So there *is* a depot," Romulus asks. Roque realizes how devastating the admission was. Romulus frowns and continues. "Imperator Fabii, why would there be a secret depot of nuclear weapons between here and Luna?"

"That's classified."

"Surely you jest."

"The Societal Navy is responsible for the security of . . ."

"If it was for security then wouldn't it be nearer a base?" Romulus asks. "This is near the edge of the asteroid belt on the path a fleet from Luna would use when Jupiter is in closest orbit to the sun. As if it was a cache meant to be acquired by an Imperator on the way to my home . . ."

"Romulus, I realize how this looks. . . ."

"Do you, young Fabii? Because it looks as if you were considering *annihilation* to be an option against people you call brother and sister."

"This information is clearly falsified. . . ."

"Except the existence of the depot . . ."

"Yes," Roque admits. "That exists."

"And the nuclear warheads. With that much radiation?"

"They're for security."

"But the rest of it is a lie?"

"Yes."

"So you didn't, in fact, come to my home with enough nuclear weapons to make our moons glass?"

"We did not," Roque says. "The only warheads we have aboard are for ship-to-ship combat. Five megaton yield, max. Romulus, on my honor . . ."

"The same honor you had when you betrayed your friend . . ." Romulus gestures to me. "When you betrayed honorable, Lorn. My ally, Augustus. My father, Revus. That honor by which you watched as my daughter's head was stomped in by a sociopathic matricide who takes orders from a sociopathic patricide?"

"Romulus . . ."

"No, Imperator Fabii. I do not believe you deserve the intimacy of using my given name any longer. You call Darrow a savage, a liar. But he came here wearing his heart on his sleeve. You came with the lies. Hiding behind manners and breeding . . ."

"ArchGovernor Raa, you must listen. There's explanation if you will just . . ."

"Enough," Romulus screams. Surging to his feet and slamming his large hand on the table. "Enough hypocrisy. Enough schemes. Enough lies you sniveling Core sycophant." He trembles finally with the rage. "If you were not my guest, I would hurl my glove at you and cut your manhood away in the Bleeding Place. Your lost generation has forgotten what it means to be Gold. You have forsaken your heritage. Suckling at the tit of power, and why? For what? Those wings on your shoulders? *Imperator*." He scoffs at the word. "You whelp. I pity a world where you decide if a man like Lorn au Arcos lives or dies. Did your parents never teach you?" They did not. Roque was raised by tutors, by books. "What is pride without honor? What is honor without truth? Honor is not what you say. It is not what you read." Romulus thumps his chest. "Honor is what you do."

"Then do not do this. . . ." Roque says.

"Your master did this," Romulus replies indifferently. "If she could not make us bow, she would make us burn. Again."

Mustang tries and fails to keep the smile from her face as Roque watches the Moon Lords slip through his fingers. A darkness enters his cultured voice. One which leaves my heart in tatters. To think that voice once defended me. Now he guards something far less loving. A Society that cares nothing for him.

I always wondered why Fitchner selected Roque for House Mars. Until his betrayal I had known him to be only the most gentle soul. But now the Imperator shows his wrath.

"ArchGovernor Raa, listen to me carefully," he says. "You are mistaken in believing we came here with intent to destroy you. We came to preserve the Society. Don't give in to Darrow's manipulation. You are better than that. Accept the Sovereign's terms, and we may have peace for another thousand years. *But* if you choose this path, if you renege on our armistice, there will be no quarter. Your fleet is ragged. Darrow's, wherever it hides, can be nothing more than a coalition of deserters in borrowed vessels.

"But we are the Sword Armada. We are the iron hand of the Legion and the fury of the Society. Our ships will darken the lights of your worlds. You know what I can do. You do not have a commander to match me. And when your ships burn, the knights of the Core will pour into your cities at the head flying columns and fill the air with ash enough to choke your children.

"If you betray your Color, the Compact, the Society—which is what this will be—Ilium will burn. I will acquaint you with ruin. I will hunt down every person you have ever known and I will exterminate their seed from the worlds. I will do so with a heavy heart. But I am a Man of Mars. A man of war. So know my wrath will be unending." He extends a thin hand. The wolf of House Mars' mouth is open in a silent, hungry howl. "Take my hand in kinship for the sake of your people and the sake of Gold. Or I will use it to build an age of peace upon the ashes of your house."

Romulus walks around the edge of the table so that he is facing Roque, the younger man's outstretched hand between them. Romulus draws his razor from where it is coiled on his hip. It rasps into rigid form. A blade etched with visions of Earth and of the Conquering. His family is as old as Mustang's, as old as Octavia's. He uses that blade to slice open his hand and suck the scarlet blood from the wound before drawing up and spitting it into Roque's face.

"This is a bloodfeud. If ever again we meet, you are mine or I am yours, Fabii. If ever again we draw breath in the same room, one breath shall cease." It is a formal, cold declaration that requires one thing of Roque. He nods. "Vela, see the Imperator to his shuttle. He has a fleet to prepare for battle."

"Romulus, you can't let him leave," Mustang says. "He's too dangerous."

"I agree," I say, but for another reason. I'd spare Roque from this battle. I do not want his blood on my hands. "Hold him prisoner until the battle is over, then release him unharmed."

"This is my home," Romulus says. "This is how we conduct ourselves. I promised him safe passage. He shall have it."

Roque dabs the blood and spit away with the same napkin he used for the cheesecake and follows Vela away from the table toward the steps that lead back into the home. He pauses there before turning back to face us. I cannot say if he speaks to me or the Golds gathered but when he recites his last words, I know they are for the ages:

> *"Brothers, sisters, till the last*
> *Woe that this has come to pass,*
> *By your grave, I shall weep*
> *For it was I who made you sleep."*

Roque bows minutely. "Thank you for the hospitality, ArchGovernor. I will see you shortly." As Roque leaves the assembly, Romulus instructs Vela to hold him until I am safely off Io.

"Hail my Imperators and Praetors," he tells one of his lancers. "I want them on holos in twenty minutes. We have a battle to plan. Darrow, if you would like to link in your Praetors . . ." But my mind is on Roque. I may never see him again. Never have a chance to say so many things which swarm my chest now. But so too do I know what letting him go could mean for my people.

"Go," Mustang says, reading my eyes. I rise abruptly, excusing myself and manage to catch Roque as he finishes tying his boots in the garden. Vela and several others are moving him toward the iron gate.

"Roque." He hesitates. Something in my voice causing him to turn and watch me approach. "When did I lose you?" I ask.

"When Quinn died," he says.

"You planned to kill me even when you thought I was a Gold?"

"Gold. Red. It doesn't matter. Your spirit is black. Quinn was good. Lea was good. And you used them. You are ruin, Darrow. You drain your friends of life, and leave them spent and wasted in your wake, convincing yourself each death is worth it. Each death brings you closer to justice. But history is littered with men like you. This Society is not without fault, but the hierarchy . . . this world, it is the best man can afford."

"And it's your right to decide that?"

"Yes. It is. But beat me in space, and it will be yours."

43

||||||||||||||||||||||||||

HERE AGAIN

Blood drips from Mustang's hand.

The voices of children drift through the air.

"My son, my daughter, now that you bleed, you shall know no fear." A young virgin girl with hair of white and feet bare on cold metal panels walks through the lines of kneeling giants carrying an iron dagger that drips with Aureate blood. "No defeat."

Gold armor etched with deeds of their ancestors. The boy's cloak innocent as snow. "Only victory." She slices the already-injured hand of Romulus au Raa, whose eyes are closed, his dragon armor white and smooth as ivory as his other hand holds his eldest son's hand. The boy is no older than seventeen, only just having won his year at the Ganymede Institute. His eyes are flashing and wild for the day. If only his intrepid young soul knew what waited on the other side of the hour. His older cousin kneels by his side, her hand on his knee. Her brother beside her. The family forming a chain across the bridge. "Your cowardice seeps from you." Behind the girl, more children walk through the fold, carrying the four standards of Gold—a scepter, a sword, and a scroll crowned with a laurel. "Your rage burns bright." She holds up the dripping dagger before Kavax au Telemanus and his youngest daughter Thraxa, a wild haired, freckle-faced, squat girl with her father's laugh and Pax's simple kindness. "Rise, children of Ilium, warriors of Gold, and take with you your Color's might."

Two hundred Gold Praetors and Legates rise. Mustang and Romulus at their head, flanked by the Telemanuses and House Arcos. Mustang lifts up her hand and smears the blood upon her own face. Two hundred killers join her, but I do not. I watch from the corner with Sefi as the combined officer corps of my Gold allies honors their Ancestors. Martian Reformers, Rim tyrants, old friends, old enemies clutter the bridge of Mustang's flagship, the two-hundred-year-old dreadnought *Dejah Thoris*.

"The battle today is to decide the fate of our Society. Whether we live under the rule of a tyrant or whether we carve our own destiny." Mustang catalogues the list of enemies for the day's hunt. "Roque au Fabii, Scipia au Falthe, Antonia au Severus-Julii, Cyriana au Tanus." Thistle. "These are wanted lives."

I've been here before, witnessing this benediction, and I can't help but feel I will be here again. It has lost none of its luster. None of the grandeur that so sheathes this remarkable people. They go to death not for the Vale, not for love, but for glory. We have never seen a race quite like them, nor will we again. After months surrounded by the Sons of Ares I see these Golds less as demons than falling angels. Precious, flaring so brilliantly across the sky before disappearing beyond the horizon.

But how many more days like this can they afford?

In the halls of our enemies, Roque will be reciting our names, and the names of my friends. He who kills the Reaper will have glory unending, bounty and renown. Young beasts with wide shoulders and angry eyes straight from the halls of the Core's schools will hunt me. Ready to make their name.

So too will the old Gray legionnaires hunt me. Those who see my rebellion as the great threat against mother Society. Against that union which they have loved and fought for their entire lives. And Obsidian will seek me, led by masters who promised them Pinks in exchange for my head. They will hunt my friends. They will say Sevro's name, and Mustang's, and Ragnar's because they do not yet know he is gone from us. They will hunt the Telemanuses and Victra, Orion, and my Howlers. But they cannot have them. Not today.

Today I take.

I stand looking down at my Gold allies. I am encased in militarized metal. Two point one meters tall, one hundred and sixty kilograms of death in a pulseArmor suit of blood-red. My slingblade is coiled around my right vambrace just above the wrist. A gravFist on my left hand. Built for collisions in corridors today, not speed. Sefi is just as monstrous as I in her brother's armor. Hate in her eyes seeing this host of enemies.

My allies needed to see her. To see me. To know beyond a shadow of a doubt that the Reaper is more alive than ever. Many of the Martians fell with me in the Rain. Some look at me with hate. Others with curiosity. And some—a very few—salute. But from most there's a contempt that will never be washed away. That's why I brought Sefi. Absent love, fear will do nicely in a pinch.

Upon hearing news that Roque's fleet has begun its journey from Europa, I make my farewell to Romulus and his coterie of Praetors who helped devise our battle plan. Romulus's handshake is firm. Respect between us, but no love. In the hangar, I say goodbye to Mustang and the Telemanuses. The floor vibrates as shuttles ferry the hundreds of Peerless back to their ships. "It seems like we're always saying farewell," I say to Kavax after he says his goodbyes to Mustang, lifting her up easy as he might a little doll and kissing her head.

"Farewell? It is not farewell," he rumbles with a toothy grin. "Win today and it becomes just a long hello. Much life left for the both of us, I think."

"I don't know how to thank you," I say.

"What for?" Kavax asks, confused, as per usual.

"The kindness . . ." I don't know how else to say it. "For watching over my friends when I'm not even one of you."

"One of us?" His ruddy face smirks. "A fool. You speak like a fool. My boy made you one of us." He looks across the hangar where Mustang speaks with one of Lorn's daughters-in-law near a transport. "She makes you one of us." It's all I can do to keep the tears from my eyes. "And if we damn all that, I say you're one of us. So one of us you are."

He lets Sophocles down from his shoulder perch to lope onto the floor. Circling, the fox jumps up onto my leg to dig something out of a joint in my armor. A jellybean. Thraxa puts a finger to her lips behind her father. The big man's eyes light up. "What fresh deliciousness is this, Sophocles? Oh, your favorite kind! Watermelon." The fox returns, jumping up onto his shoulder. "See! You have his benediction as well."

"Thank you, Sophocles," I say, reaching to scratch him behind the ears.

Kavax slams me into a hug before departing. "Take care, Reaper." He trundles up the ramp. "Fishing?" he booms down at me before he's gone ten meters.

"What?"

"Do Reds fish?"

"I never have."

"There is a river through my estate on Mars. We will go, you and I, when this is done and sit by the bank and toss our lines and I will teach you how to tell a pike from a trout."

"I'll bring the whiskey," I say.

He points a finger at me. "Yes! And we will be drunk together. Yes!" He disappears into the ship, throwing his arm around Thraxa and calling to his other daughters about a miracle he just witnessed. "I think he might be the luckiest of us," I say as Mustang comes up from behind me to watch the Telemanus ship depart.

"Is it ridiculous if I ask you to be careful?" she asks.

"I promise not to do anything rash," I reply with a wink. "I'll have the Valkyrie with me. I doubt anyone will want to tangle with us for long." She glances over my shoulder to where Sefi waits by my own shuttle, admiring the engines of other ships as they fly away. Mustang looks like she wants to say something, but is wrestling with how.

"You're not invincible." She touches the armor of my chest. "Some of us might want you around after all of this. After all, what's the point of all this if you go and die on me? You hear?"

"I hear."

"Do you?" She looks up at me. "I don't want to be left alone again. So come back." She raps her knuckles on my chest and turns to go to her ship.

"Mustang." I chase after her and grab her arm, pulling her back toward me. Before she can say anything, I kiss her there surrounded by metal and engine roar. Not some delicate kiss, but a hungry one, where I pull her head to mine and feel the woman beneath the weight of duty. Her body presses against me. And I feel the shudder of fear that this will be the last time. Our lips part and I sink into her, rocking there, smelling her hair and gasping at the tightness in my chest. "I'll see you soon."

44

||||||||||||||||||||||||||

THE LUCKY ONES

I pace my bridge like a caged wolf, his meal just beyond the bars. The kindness of me hidden again behind the Reaper's savage face. "Virga, are the Howlers in position?" I ask. Behind and below me, the skeleton crew of Blues chatter in their sterile pit. Faces illuminated by holoscreens. Subdermal implants pulsing as they sync with the ship. The captain, Pelus, a waifish gentleman who was a former lieutenant aboard the *Pax* when I first took the ship, awaits my orders.

"Yes, sir," Virga says from her station. "Forward elements of the enemy fleet will be within long-range guns in four minutes."

The arrogant might of Gold unfolds across the black of space. An unending sea of pale white splinters. I'd give anything to be able to reach out and shatter them. My own capital ships cluster in three groups around our powerful dreadnoughts above the north pole of Io. Mustang and Romulus marshal their forces around the south. And together, eight thousand kilometers apart, we watch Roque's fleet cross the void between Europa and Io to bring us battle.

"Enemy cruisers at ten thousand kilometers," a Blue intones.

There is no preamble for my fleet. No benediction or rite that we perform before battle like the Golds. For all our right, we seem so pale and simple compared with them. But there's a kinship here on my ship. One I saw in the engine rooms, in the gunnery stations, on the bridge. A dream that links us together and makes us brave.

"Give me Orion," I say without turning.

A holo of the overweight, ornery Blue ripples into life in front of me. She's half a hundred kilometers away in the heart of *Persephone's Howl,* one of my other four dreadnoughts, sitting in a command chair synced with every ship captain in my fleet save those of my strike force. Much of today relies upon her and the pirate fleet she's assembled in the months since last we saw one another. She's been raiding Core shipping lines. Drawing Blues to her cause. Enough to help the Sons staff the ships we stole from the Jackal with loyal men and women.

"*Big fleet,*" Orion says of our enemy, impressed. "*I knew I never should have answered your call. I was rather enjoying being a pirate.*"

"I can tell," I say. "Your stateroom's gaudy enough to a make a Silver blush." The *Pax* has been her home for the last year and a half. She took over my old quarters and filled it right up with the booty of her raids. Rugs from Venus. Paintings from private Gold collections. I found a Titian jammed behind a bookcase.

"*What can I say? I like pretty things.*"

"Well, pull this off today, and I'll find you a parrot for your shoulder. How about that?"

"*Ah! Pelus told you I was looking for one. Good man, Pelus.*" The waifish captain tilts his head genteelly behind me. "*Damn hard to find parrots when you can't dock planetside anywhere. We found a hawk, a dove, an owl. But no parrot. If you make it a red one I'll personally shoot a hole in Antonia au Severus-Julii's bridge.*"

"Red parrot it is," I say.

"*Good. Good. I suppose now I should go be about the battle.*" She laughs to herself and takes a tea from a valet on her bridge. "*Just want to say, thank you, Darrow. For believing in me. For giving me this. After today, Blue will have no master. Goodspeed, boy.*"

"Goodspeed, Admiral."

She vanishes. I glance back at the central sensor projection. The tactical readout floats before the windows as a to-scale globe of the Jupiter system. Four tiny inner moons orbit Jupiter more closely than the four huge Galilean Moons. My eyes focus on Thebe, the outermost of them and closest to Io. It's a small mass. Barely larger than Phobos. Long since mined for valuable minerals, and now the home of a military base that was blasted apart in the early days of the war.

"Sixty ticks till Howler coms go black," Virga intones from her station as Victra enters the bridge, wearing thick golden armor painted with a Red slingBlade on the chest and back.

"The hell are you doing here?" I ask.

"You're here," she replies innocently.

"You're supposed to be on the *Shout of Mykos*."

"This isn't the *Mykos*?" She bites her lip. "Well, I suppose I got lost. I'll just follow you around so that doesn't happen again. Prime?"

"Sevro sent you. Didn't he?"

"His heart's a black little thing. But it can break. I'm here to make sure it doesn't by keeping you nice and cozy. Oh, and I want to say hello to Roque."

"What about your sister?" I ask.

"Roque first. Then her." She elbows me. "I can be a team player too."

Grinning, I turn back to the pit. "Virga, give me a helmet patch to the Howlers."

"Aye, sir."

The com in my ear crackles. I activate my armor's helmet. The transparent heads up display shows me the tags on my crew, ranks, names, everything that's logged into the central ship register. I activate the com holo function and a semi-translucent collage of my friends' faces appear over the sight of my ship's bridge. *"'Sup boss?"* Sevro asks, his face is painted Red with warpaint but bathed in blue light from his mech's HUD display. *"Need a goodbye kiss or something?"*

"Just checking to make sure you're all tucked in."

"Your kin could've carved us a bigger nook," Sevro mutters. *"It's foot to face to fartbox in here."*

"*So you're saying Tactus would've liked it?*" Victra asks. She's patched into the panel so I hear her voice in link.

I laugh. "What didn't he like?"

"*Clothing, predominantly,*" Mustang replies from her own bridge. She wears her battle armor as well. Pure Gold with a red lion roaring on her chest.

"*And sobriety,*" Victra adds.

"*This moon smells like royal shit,*" Clown mumbles from his own starShell mech. "*Worse than a dead horse.*"

"*You're in a mech in vacuum,*" Holiday drawls. I hear the clang and shouts of the people behind her in the hangar bay of my ship. She wears a huge blue handprint on her face. Given to her by one of her Obsidians. "*It's likely not the moon.*"

"*Oh. Then it must be me,*" Clown says. He sniffs. "*Oh, ho. It's me.*"

"*I told you to shower,*" Pebble mutters.

"*Howler Rule 17. Only Pixies shower before battle,*" Sevro says. "*I like my soldiers savage, stinky, and sexy. I'm proud of you, Clown.*"

"*Thank you, sir.*"

"*Threka! Put your safety on,*" Holiday shouts. "*Now! Sorry. Bloodydamn Obsidians walking around with their fingers on the bloodydamn triggers. Shit is terrifying.*"

"Why do we laugh and speak like children?" Sefi booms over the com, so loud my eardrums rattle.

"*Bloodyshit in a handbasket,*" Sevro yelps. There's a chorus of curses at Sefi's volume.

"*Turn down your output volume!*" Clown snaps at the queen.

"I do not understand. . . ."

"*Your output . . .*"

"What is output . . . ?"

"*'The Quiet' is a bit of a misnomer, eh?*" Victra asks. Mustang snorts a laugh.

"*Sefi, bend down,*" Holiday barks. "*I can't reach. Bend down.*" Holiday's found Sefi in the hangar and helps her turn down her output volume. The Obsidian queen sleeps with her new pulseFist every night, but she's a bit behind on her understanding of telecommunication equipment.

"So, like the big girl asked, was there a reason for this little tête-à-tête?" Holiday says.

"Tradition, Holi," Sevro says, mimicking her twang. "Reap's a sentimental sap. He's probably going to give a speech."

"No speech," I say.

My odd little family whines and catcalls. "You're not going to admonish us to rage, rage against the dying of the light?" Sevro asks. But the joke feels strange, knowing it is what Roque would have said. My chest tightens again. I feel so much love for this band of misfits and oathbreakers. So much fear. I wish that I could protect them from this. Find some way to spare them the coming hell.

"Whatever happens, remember we're the lucky ones," I say. "We get to make a difference today. But you're my family. So be brave. Protect each other. And come home."

"You too boss," Sevro says.

"Break the chains," Mustang says.

"Break the chains," my friends echo.

Sevro's face becomes a snarl as he booms out: "Howlers go . . ."

"Ahhhwwwooooo." They howl like fools, cracking up. One by one, their images flicker away, and I'm left in the solitude of my helmet. I breathe and say a silent prayer to whoever is listening. Keep them safe.

I let the helmet slither back into the neck of my armor. My Blues watch me from their displays. A small coterie of Red and Gray marines stand by the door, waiting to escort me to the hangar. The strings of so many lives from so many worlds all intersecting here, at this moment around mine. How many will fray? How many will end this day? Victra smiles at me, and it seems I'm too lucky already for this day to end in joy. She should not be here. She should be across the void at the helm of an enemy battle cruiser. Yet she's here with us, seeking the redemption she thought she could never have.

"Once more unto the breach," she says.

"Once more," I reply. I address the crew. "How do you all feel?"

Awkward silence. They exchange nervous glances. Unsure of how to answer. Then a young Blue woman with a bald head bursts up from her console. "We're ready to kill some bloodydamn Golds . . . sir."

They laugh, tension broken.

"Anyone else?" Victra booms. They roar in reply. Marines as young as eighteen and as old as Lorn would be now slam their steel-heeled boots against the ground.

"Patch me through to the fleet," I command. "Broadcast on an open frequency to Quicksilver. Make sure the Golds can hear me so they know where to find me." Virga gives me a nod. I'm live.

"My friends, this is the Reaper." My voice echoes over the master com in all one hundred and twelve capital ships in my fleet, in the thousands of ripWings, in the leechCraft and the engine rooms and the medbays where doctors and newly appointed nurses walk through empty beds with crisp white sheets, waiting for the flood. Thirty-eight minutes from now Quicksilver and the Sons of Ares on Mars will hear it, and they'll boost the signal to the core. Whether we're alive at that time will depend on my dance with Roque.

"In mine, in space, in city and sky, we have lived our lives in fear. Fear of death. Fear of pain. Today, fear only that we fail. We cannot. We stand upon the edge of darkness holding the lone torch left to man. That torch will not go out. Not while I draw breath. Not while your hearts beat in your chests. Not while our ships yet have menace in them. Let others dream. Let others sing. We chosen few are the fire of our people." I beat my chest. "We are not Red, not Blue or Gold or Gray or Obsidian. We are humanity. We are the tide. And today we reclaim the lives that have been stolen from us. We build the future we were promised.

"Guard your hearts. Guard your friends. Follow me through this evil night, and I promise you morning waits on the other side. Until then, break the chains!" I pull my razor from my arm and let it take the shape of my slingBlade. "All ships, prepare for battle."

45

||||||||||||||||||||||||

THE BATTLE
OF ILIUM

R ed tribal drums played in the belly of one of my ships, *The
Evening Tide,* beat through the speakers in a martial rendi-
tion of the Forbidden Song. A steady undulation of defiance as we
roll toward the Sword Armada. I've never seen a fleet so large. Not
even when we stormed Mars. That was just two rival houses summoning allies. This is the conflict of peoples. And it is appropriately
massive.

Unfortunately, Roque and I studied under the same teachers. He
knows the battles of Alexander, of the Han armies, and Trafalgar.
He knows the greatest threat to an overwhelming power is miscom-
munication, chaos. So he does not overestimate the power of his force.
He subdivides into twenty smaller mobile divisions, giving relative
autonomy to each Praetor to create speed and flexibility. We face not
one huge hammer, but a swarm of razors.

"It's a nightmare," Victra murmurs.

I thought Roque would do this, but I still curse as I see it. In any
space engagement, you must decide if you're killing enemy ships or
capturing them. It seems he's intent on boarding. So we cannot slug it
out with them and hope for the best. Nor can we lure his fleet into my

trap from the first. They'll muscle through it and kill the Howlers. Everything depends on the one advantage we do have. And it's not our ships. It is not our hundred thousand Obsidians I have packed in leechCraft. It is the fact that Roque thinks he knows me, and so his entire strategy will be predicated on how I would behave.

So I decide to overshoot his estimation of my insanity and show him how little he really understands the psychology of Reds. Today I lead the *Pax* on a suicide mission into the heart of his fleet. But I don't begin the battle. Orion does, soaring forward ahead of me on *Persephone's Howl* with three quarters of my fleet. They cluster in spheres, the smallest corvettes still four hundred meters long. Most are half-kilometer-long torchShips, some destroyers, and the four huge dreadnoughts. Long-range missiles slither out from the Gold ships and from our own. Miniature computer-guided countermeasures are deployed. And then Roque's fleet flashes into motion and the black space between the two fleets erupts with flack, missiles, and long-range railgun munitions. Billions of credits' worth of munitions spent in seconds.

Orion shrinks the distance to Roque's fleet as Mustang and Romulus's ships hurtle toward the southern edge—per Io's pole—of Roque's formation, attempting to hit the only vulnerable place on a ship, the engines. But Roque's fleet is nimble and ten squadrons divide from the rest, orientating themselves so their bristling broadsides face the bows of the Moon Lord ships coming up from the planet's south pole and rake them with railgun fire. A hundred thousand guns go off simultaneously.

Metal shreds metal. Ships vomit oxygen and men.

But ships are made to take a beating. Huge hulks of metal subdivided into thousands of interlocking honeycombed compartments designed to isolate breaches and prevent ships from venting with one railgun shot. From these floating castles stream thousands of tiny one-man fighter craft. They swarm in small squadrons through the no-man's-land between our fleet and Roque's. Some packed with miniature nukes meant for killing capital ships. Helldivers and drillboys trained night and day in sims by the Sons of Ares fly with squadrons of synced Blues. They slash into the Society's war-hardened pilots led by ripWings striped with Gold.

Romulus's force peels away from Mustang's to link with Orion, while Mustang continues toward the heart of the enemy formation, preparing the way for my thrust.

We close to three hundred kilometers, and the mid-range rail guns open up. Huge barrages of twenty kilogram munitions hurtling through space at mach eight. Flak shields plume over the entire Gold formation. Closer to the ships, PulseShields throb iridescent blue as munitions crack into them and careen off into space.

My strike force lingers behind the main battle. Soon it will become a war of boarding parties. LeechCraft launching by the hundreds. Aggressive Praetors will empty their ships of their marines and Obsidians to claim enemy vessels, which they will then keep after the battle, per rules of naval law. Conservative Praetors will hoard their men till the last, keeping them to repel boarding parties and use their ships as their main weapon of war.

"Orion's given the signal," my captain says.

"Set course for the *Colossus*. Engines to ramming speed." My ship rumbles under my feet. "Pelus, the trigger's yours. Ignore torchShips. Destroyers or larger are the order of the day." The ship groans as we hurtle forward from the back of Orion's fleet. "Escorts keep tight. Match velocity."

We pass the artillery ships, then the four-kilometer-long *Persephone's Howl* as we emerge out the center of Orion's front with the enemy like a hidden spear, now driving into the fifty kilometers of no-man's-land, aiming for the heart of the enemy. Orion's ships fire chaff, creating a corridor to protect our mad approach. Roque will see what I intend now, and his capital ships drift back from mine, inviting me into the center of his huge formation as they rain fire down on my strike force.

Our shields flicker blue. Enemy munitions sneak through the chaff and punish us. We return fire. Raking a destroyer as we pass with a full broadside. It loses power. LeechCraft pour out of it to try and slip through our chaff tunnel, but our escorts shred the small craft. Still, we're hit by the guns of a dozen ships. Red glows around our shields. They fail in stages, local generators shorting out on our starboard side. Instantly, our hull is punctured in seven places. The honeycomb network of pressurized doors activates, shutting the compromised levels of my ship off from the rest. I lose a torchShip. Half a click off bow, a full barrage of rail-munitions rake her from stem to stern, fired by Antonia's dreadnaught the *Pandora*.

"Seems my sister is enjoying my ship," Victra says.

Bodies erupt out of the torchShip's bridge, but Antonia continues to fire on the much-smaller ship until the nuclear core of her engines implodes. Pulsing white twice before devouring the ship's back half. The shock wave pushes our craft sideways. Our EMP and pulse shielding holds, lights flickering just once. Something huge slams into the ten-meter-thick bulkhead beyond the bridge. The wall bends inward to my right. The shape of a railgun munition stretching the metal inward like an alien baby. Our gunners rip apart the 1.5-kilometer destroyer that fired on us, loosing eighty of our railguns directly into her bridge. Two hundred men gone. We're taking no prisoners at this stage. It's staggering the amount of violence the *Pax* can deal out. And staggering the amount we're taking. Antonia dissects another part of my strike force.

"*Hope of Tinos* is down," my Blue sensor officer says quietly. "*The Cry of Thebes* is going nuclear."

"Tell *Tinos* and *Thebes* helmsman to punch negative forty-five their midline and abandon ship," I snap. The ships obey and alter course to ram Antonia's flagship. She reverses her engines and my dying ships carry on harmlessly into space. One goes nuclear.

We're outmatched and outgunned here in the heart of the enemy formation. Trapped. No escape. A sphere forming around us. I only have four torchships left. Make that three.

"Multiple deck fires," an officer intones.

"Munitions detonations on deck seventeen."

"Engines one through six are down. Seven and eight are at forty percent capacity."

The *Pax* dies around me.

Roque's MoonBreaker looms ahead. Twice the length of my ship, three times the girth. A floating military dock city eight kilometers long. With a huge crescent bow, like a shark with an open mouth swimming sideways. She retreats from us at the same pace we advance. Making sure we cannot ram her as she punishes us with her superior weaponry. Roque thought I would pull a Karnus. Try to slam into their capital ship with my own. That's now impossible. Our engines are nearly done. Our hull compromised.

"All forward guns target their railguns and missile launchers on their top deck, carve us a shadow." I pull up a hologram of the ship and circle the area of fire with my fingers, directing the fire as Victra gives commands to the fighter groups which we've held on to till now. The ripWings scream out into space. The *Pax* rotates to present her main gunbanks to the *Colossus* to open a broadside.

It doesn't matter what we do at this stage. We're a wolf pinned to the ground by a bear and it's smashing our legs one by one, carving off our ears, our eyes, our teeth but keeping our belly nice and ready for a raking. My ship shudders around me. Blues rip out of sync, vomiting in the pits as the datanerves in the ships, to which they're linked, die one by one. My helmsman, Arnus, has a seizure as the engines are shredded.

"*The Dancer of Faran* is gone," Captain Pelus says. "No escape pods." It was a skeleton crew, but still forty die. Better than a thousand. Only two torchShips of my initial sixteen remain. They race around Antonia's *Pandora* behind us, but that ship is a black, hulking monster. She shreds the fastmovers till they're dead metal. And when escape pods launch from the quiet ships, she shoots them down. Victra watches the murder quietly. Adding it to Antonia's debt.

Roque is inviting us to launch our leechCraft, drawing the *Colossus* closer to my dead ship. A kilometer away now. I accept the invitation. "Launch all leechCraft at the surface of the MoonBreaker," I say. "Now. Fire the spitTubes."

Hundreds of empty suits fire out the spitTubes as they would in an Iron Rain. Two hundred leechCraft launch from the four hangars of my ship. Spewed out in a stream of ugly metal, each could carry fifty men to pump into the guts of the MoonBreaker. Controlled remotely by Blue pilots on board *Persephone's Howl,* they race fast as they can to cross the dangerous space between the two capital ships. And they're wiped away before they make it half the distance as Roque detonates a series of low-yield nuclear warheads.

He guessed my move.

And now my flight of ships is nothing but debris floating between the two vessels. Emergency sirens flash on the ceiling of my bridge. Our long-range sensors are down. Our guns smashed. Multiple deck breaches.

"Hold together," I murmur. "Hold together, *Pax*."

"We're receiving a transmission," Virga says.

Roque appears in the air before me. "Darrow." He sees Victra too. "Victra, it is done. Your ship is dead in the water. Tell your fleet to surrender and I will spare your lives." He thinks he can end this rebellion without putting us in the grave. The entitlement of it rankles me. But we both know he needs my body to show the worlds. If he destroys my ship and kills me, they'll never find me in the wreckage. I look at Victra. She spits on the ground in challenge. "What is your answer?" Roque demands.

I bend my fingers crudely. "Fuck you."

Roque looks off screen. "Legate Drusus, launch all leechCraft. Tell the Cloud Knight to bring me the Reaper. Dead or alive. Just make sure he's recognizable."

46

||||||||||||||||||||||

HELLDIVER

I look to the Blues at their station. Most were here when I took this ship. When I renamed her. They became pirates with Orion, rebels with me. "You all heard him," I say. "Well done. You did the *Pax* proud. Now say goodbye, get to your shuttle, and I'll see you soon. There's no shame in this." They salute and Captain Pelus opens the hatches in the bottom of the pit. The Blues begin their slide down the narrow shaft into the berth where there should be escape pods, but we replaced with heavily armored shuttles. My own escape pod is built into the side of the bridge. But Victra and I aren't escaping. Not today.

"Time to go, baby boy," Victra says. "Now."

I pat the doorframe of the bridge. "Thank you, *Pax*." I say to the ship. One more friend lost to the cause. I follow Victra and the marines in a sprint down the empty halls. Red lights pulse. Sirens wail. Small thumps reverberate through the hull as we go. Roque's leech-Craft will be swarming the *Pax* by now. Melting holes through her sides and pumping in boarding parties of Grays and Obsidians led by Gold knights. Instead of me, they'll find an abandoned ship. A molten circle throbs on the hallway wall beside a gravLift as we board. I watch the orange deepen till it is the color of the sun. The drums still beat through the speakers. *Thump. Thump. Thump.*

Victra leaves a mine behind as a present for the boarding party.

We hear it detonate ten levels above us as the gravLift deposits us on level negative three in the auxiliary hangar. Here my true assault force waits. Thirty heavy assault shuttles with their ramps down. Blues performing flight checks in the cockpits. Orange mechanics working furiously to prime engines, fill fuel tanks. Each ship is filled with a hundred Valkyrie in full smart armor. Reds and Grays accompany them in equal number for special weapons tasks. The Obsidians stomp their pulseAxes and razors as I run past, a thunderous chanting of my name. I find Holiday in the center of the hangar standing with Sefi and a coterie of Valkyrie who will be my personal squad. With them, praying in a small group, are the Helldivers I requested from Dancer. They're less than half the size of the Obsidians.

"Ship is breached," I say to Holiday. She jerks her head at a squad of Reds, who rush off to cover our back. "Distance is less than a click."

"No . . ." Holiday says with an elated laugh. "That close?"

"I know," I reply excitedly. "They want to get close so we can't shoot down their leechCraft."

"So now we give them a kiss," Victra says with a little purr for Holiday. "And some tongue."

Holiday bobs her cinderblock head up and down. "Then let's stop jawin'."

Sefi pulls a handful of dried mushrooms from a satchel. "God's bread?" she asks. "You will see dragons."

"War's scary enough, darling," Victra says. Then as an aside: "I one time tripped on that shit with Cassius for a week on the Thermic." She catches my look. "Well, it was before I met you. And have you ever seen him with his shirt off? Don't tell Sevro, by the way."

Holiday and I abstain from the mushrooms as well. Automatic weapons fire rattles from a hall just beyond the hangar. "The hour is here!" I boom to the three thousand Obsidian in the assault shuttles. "Sharpen your axes! Remember your training! *Hyrg la*, Ragnar!"

"*Hyrg la*, Ragnar!" they roar.

It means "Ragnar lives." The Queen of the Valkyrie salutes her razor to me and begins the Obsidian war chant. It spread through the black armored assault craft. A horrible dread sound, this time it is on my side. I've brought the Valkyrie to the heavens, and now I let them loose.

"Victra, you prime?" I ask, worried about Antonia being so near. Is my friend distracted by her sister?

"I'm gorydamn splendid, baby boy," the tall woman says. "Take care of that pretty little ass of yours." She slaps my butt before back-pedalling, blowing me an obnoxious kiss and jogging to her shuttle. "I'll be right behind." I'm left with the Helldivers. They're smoking burners, watching me with evil red eyes.

"First one through gets the bloodydamn laurel," I say. "Helmets on."

Little needs to be said to such men. They nod their heads and grin. We depart. I fly thirty meters upward on my gravBoots to land atop of one of the four clawDrills we confiscated from the platinum mining company in the inner asteroid belt. They stand in a row on the hangar deck, each fifty meters apart. Like grasping hands, the cockpit where elbow would be, the dozen drill bits on the deck where fingers would reach. Each is retrofitted by Rollo to have thrusters on the back and thick plates of armor extend down the sides. I slide into the cockpit, enlarged for my frame and armor, and slip my hands into the digital control prism.

"Fire them up," I say. A familiar thrum of energy goes through the drill, vibrating the glass around me. I grin like a madman. Perhaps I am one. But I knew I could not win this battle without altering the paradigm. And I knew Roque would never be driven into a trap or lured into an asteroid belt, for fear of exposing his larger force to ambushes. So I had only one recourse: hide my ambush in a flaw of character. He always preached for me to step back, to find peace. Of course he thought he knew how to beat me. But I'm not fighting as the man he knew today, as a Gold.

I'm a bloodydamn Helldiver with an army of giant, mildly psychotic women behind me and a fleet of state-of-the-art warships crewed by pissed-off pirates, engineers, techs, and former slaves. And he thinks he knows how to fight me? I laugh as the clawDrill shakes my seat. Filling me with a dormant, crazed sort of power. An enemy boarding party breaches the hangar from the same gravLift we took. They stare up at the huge claw drills and evaporate as Victra's shuttle fires a railgun at them from point-blank range.

"Remember the words of our Golden leader," I say to the Helldivers. "Sacrifice. Obedience. Prosperity. These are the better parts of humanity."

"*Bloodydamn slag,*" one says over the com. "*I'll show her the better part of my humanity.*"

"Drills hot," I order. They echo confirmation one by one. "Helmets up. Let's burn."

I flip the rotation toggle on my clawDrill clockwise. Beneath, the drill whirs. I plunge both hands forward in the control prism. Existence shakes. Teeth rattle. The metal deck sags under me. Molten metal peels back. I lurch ten meters down into the ship. Carving through the deck in five seconds. And the one after that. I sink again, falling through the floor of the hangar bay completely. Chewed metal around the cockpit. Then the next deck goes. Then the next. Heat builds along the drill as I slam through more of the ship, leaving the Valkyrie behind. Slow, the drill jams, slow and you die. And this speed is the pulse of my people. Momentum flowing into more momentum.

My clawDrill is building up a hell of a pace. Slamming through decks. Murdering metal with molten tungsten carbide teeth. I glimpse fractured sights of the other clawdrills ripping through the heart of the ship as we fall through the dimly lit barracks. Each drill glowing with heat and then slamming into the next deck. It is a glorious, horrible sight. Going through a mess hall. Through a water tank, then a hallway where a boarding party stumbles back from the debris and stares at the megalithic drills carving through the ship like the molten hands of some hilarious metal god.

"Don't slow," I roar, entire body convulsing in the seat. I'm out of control, going too fast, drill too hot. Then . . . nothing. I breach the belly of the *Pax*. Silence of space grips me. Weightless. I float like a spear through water toward the huge *Colossus*. LeechCraft bound for the *Pax* streak past me, one close enough I can see the captain's wide eyes inside the cockpit. Another flies straight into my superheated drill's mouth. Shredded in seconds. Men and debris cartwheel to the side. The other drills exit farther down the *Pax*'s belly, bursting into space, diving for the MoonBreaker. Around us, the battle rages. Blue explosions, huge fields of flak. Mustang's group racing along the edge of Roque's formations, exchanging punishing broadsides. Sevro still waits, hiding.

I can feel the confusion in the enemy gunners. I'm in the center of their leechCraft assault teams. They can't fire. Their computers won't even register the vessel classification. It'll look like a hunk of debris shaped like an arm from the elbow down. I doubt the bridge will even know what it is without seeing it with their naked eye.

"Blast engines," I say. The engines of the retrofitted clawDrill kick behind me and hurl me down at the black surface of the *Colossus*. Recognizing my threat, a ripWing sprays me with chain gun rounds. Thumb-sized bullets slam silently into the drill. The armor holds. Not so on the clawDrill beside mine. When a railgun round fired from a five-meter gun along the top-crest of the MoonBreaker punches through the cockpit, murdering the Helldiver in it, his ship shatters. One of his drillbits slams into my glass cockpit, cracking it. A dozen more rounds shred the leechCraft beside me. Roque might not know what the 30 meter projectiles coming from my ship are, but he's willing to kill his own men to stop their approach.

Gray metal blurs toward me. A railgun slug fired from the *Colossus* punches through three leechCraft in front of my ship before striking the bottom of my clawDrill, at the "wrist." It tears up the length of the drill, erupts up through the floor of my cockpit, between my legs, inches from my balls, scraping along my chest, almost taking my head off at the jaw. I jerk back and the slug slams into the metal support of the cockpit. Shattering the glass and bending the bar outward like a melting plastic straw. I gasp, knocked half unconscious by the kinetic energy transference.

White spots flash across my vision.

I shake myself. Trying to bring my senses back.

I've spun off course. This rig isn't meant for steering. About to slam into the MoonBreaker's deck. Instinct doesn't save me. My friends do. The clawDrill's engines are slaved to the bank of Blues back on Orion's ship. Someone reverses the thrusters at the last moment so I don't crash. I'm slammed back in my seat as the clawDrill slows and then lands gently onto the surface of the *Colossus*. I jerk in my seat, laughing in fear.

"Bloodydamn" I whoop to my distant saviors, whoever they are. "Thank you!"

But the clawDrill itself is all manual. Blues can't operate the digits any better than I can plot slingshots around a planet. My hands dance over the controls, flowing into my old mode of labor. I reactivate the drill, using my engines to push me down like a nail into the surface of the ship. Metal wheezes. Bolts rattle. And I begin to gnaw through the top layer of armor, which they said no leechCraft could penetrate.

Pressure hisses out around my drill. I ramp up the revolutions, my hands dancing through the controls, shifting the drill bits as they overheat, cycling through cooled units. Space disappears. I burrow into the warship. Carving not in a straight line, but a tunnel toward the front of the ship. One deck. Two decks. Chewing through halls and barracks and generators and gas lines. It's hideous and as savage a thing as I've ever done. I just pray I don't hit a munitions store. Men and women and debris fly out into space through the hole I've carved like autumn leaves sucked from the various deck levels I penetrate. Bulkheads will seal off the wound, but those caught between the bulkheads and the tunnel are good as dead.

Three hundred meters into the ship, my clawDrill breaks down. Drill bits spent and engine overheating. I reach down to pop my cockpit canopy to abandon the drill, but my hand slips on the lever. Blood coats it. I search my body frantically. But my armor isn't punctured. The blood isn't from me. It floats off the right cockpit wall, slick around the round railgun slug that pierced the three leechCraft to imbed itself in the support beam of my clawDrill. Bits of hair and a fragment of bone clump in the clotting blood.

I leave my clawDrill behind for the vacuum of the tunnel I carved. Air no longer gushing from the ship. It's calm now, the pressure already vented and the emergency bulkheads closed to quarantine the compromised hull. The gravity generator in this section of the ship must have been hit. My hair floats in my helmet.

I look up. At the end of the tunnel, where I penetrated the hull, is a little keyhole to the stars. A dead man drifts just beyond it, slowly spiraling. A shadow grips him as Antonia's flagship passes beyond, blocking the light reflected from Jupiter's surface. Like the man, I'm left in darkness. Alone in the belly of the *Colossus*. My com a flood of war-chatter. Victra is launching from our hangar. Orion and the Moon Lords are in flight, knocked off the poles of Io and bound for Jupiter. Mustang's flagship is now under assault by Roque's ship as Antonia leads the rest of his fleet after the retreating Telemanuses and Raas.

Still, Sevro waits.

Thirty meters above me, something moves out from one of the levels I carved through, peering into the twenty-meter-wide tunnel. My helmet identifies an active weapon. I fly upward, activating my pulse-Shield as I go only to find a young Gray staring at me through the plastic faceplate of an emergency oxygen mask. He floats, one arm holding a ragged length of metal wall. Blood coats him. Not his own. The body of one of his friends floats behind him. He's shaking. My drill must have gone through his entire platoon, and then space pulled their bodies out, leaving him alone here. The terror of me is reflected in his eyes. He raises his scorcher and I react without thinking. Putting my razor into the side of his heart, I make him a carcass. He dies wide-eyed and young and he floats there, upright till I put my foot on his chest so I can pull my blade out. We drift away from each other. Little droplets of blood dancing off my blade in the zero gravity.

Then the gravity generators reboot and my feet clomp to the floor. The blood splatters over them. His body flops to the ground. Light floods in behind me from the tunnel shaft. I pull myself away from the dead man and peer up into the tunnel to see a shuttle ripping in out of space. More follow. A whole cavalcade of assault craft led by Victra. RipWings chase them, but mounted guns on the back of the assault craft spray high-energy fist-sized rounds at them. Shredding the ripWings. More will come. Hundreds more. We must move fast. Speed and aggression our only advantage here.

Victra's transport slows dramatically in the tunnel beyond my level, just above the clawDrill. Valkyrie pour out to join me. More transports unload on levels above. Holiday and several Reds with battle armor move with the Obsidians, carrying breaching equipment across the airless room toward the bulkhead door that seals us off from the rest of the ship. They slam the thermal drill onto the metal. It begins glowing red. They deploy a pulseBubble over the metal hatch so that when we breach, we don't activate more bulkheads.

"Breach green in fifteen," Holiday says.

Victra stands to the side listening to enemy chatter. "Response teams inbound. More than two thousand mixed units." She's also patched to the strategic command on Orion's ship, so she can gather battle data from the huge sensor arrays on the flagship. Looks like Roque launched more than fifteen thousand men at us in his leech-Craft. Most will be in the *Pax* by now. Burrowed through to find me. Silly bastards. Roque gambled big, bet wrong. And I've just brought three thousand crazed Obsidian berserkers to a mostly empty warship.

The Poet is going to be pissed.

"Ten," Holiday says.

"Valkyrie, on me," I boom, lifting my hands in a triangle formation.

The hundred Obsidians step over the debris of the commissary and gather behind me, just as we trained them to do on the journey from Jupiter. Sefi's on my left hip, Victra's on my right and Holiday behind. The superheated metal door sags. The Reds and Grays back away. All along the tunnel on the ten levels I carved through, teams like this will be preparing to breach just like us. Two of the other clawDrills hit home. Two thousand Obsidians are breaching there as well. Grays, Reds, and a scattering of sympathizer Golds will lead them against the security forces who take trams and gravLifts to ferry themselves to the new battlefront inside the ship.

This is going to be a firestorm. Close quarters combat. Smoke. Screams. The worst of war.

"Full power to shields," I say in Nagal, facing the Valkyrie. They ripple iridescent as shields play over their armor. "Kill anything with a weapon. Harm nothing without one. Doesn't matter the Color. Remember our target. Clear me a path. *Hyrg la,* Ragnar!"

"*Hyrg la,* Ragnar!" they roar, beating their chests, embracing the madness of war. Most will have taken their beserker fungus in the shuttlecraft. They'll feel no pain. They move foot-to-foot, eager for the succor of battle. Victra vibrates next to me. I remember sitting with her in Mickey's lab as she told me how she loves the smell of battle. The old sweat in the gloves. The oil on the guns. The pulled muscles and shaking hands afterward. It's the honesty of it, I realize. That's what she loves. Battle never lies.

"Victra, stay at my side," I say. "Pair up for the Hydra if we encounter Golds."

"*Njar la tagag . . .*" Sefi says from behind me.

"*. . . syn tjr rjyka!*"

"There is no pain. Only joy," they chant, deep in the embrace of the god's bread. Sefi begins the war bellow. Her voice higher than Ragnar's. Her two wing-sisters join her. Then their wing-sisters, until dozens fill the com with their song, giving me a sense of grandeur as my mind tells my body to flee. This is why the Obsidians chant. Not to sow terror. But to feel brave, to feel kinship, instead of isolation and fear.

Sweat drips down my spine.

Fear is not real.

Holiday deactivates her safety.

"*Njar la tagag . . .*"

My razor goes rigid.

PulseWeapon shudders and whines, priming.

Body trembles. Mouth full of ashes. Wear the mask. Hide the man. Feel nothing. See everything. Move and kill. Move and kill. I am not a man. They are not men.

The chanting swells. . . . "*Syn tjr rjyka!*"

Fear is not real.

If you're watching, Eo, it's time to close your eyes.

The Reaper has come. And he's brought hell with him.

47

||||||||||||||||||||||

HELL

"Breach!" Holiday roars. The door falls open. I rush into the pulseField surrounding the breach point. Everything condenses. Sights, sounds, the movement of my own body. All a haze. Holiday's scatterFlash cackles through the two-meter opening in the bulkhead, frying any unshielded optic nerves on the other side. A secondary fusion grenade detonates. I jump through the hole into smoke, going right, Victra comes with. Sefi goes left. Enemy fire hits us immediately. My shield cackles with the sound of hail hitting a tin roof. The end of the hall a chaos of muzzle flashes and pulse fire. Superheated projectiles slice through the smoke.

I fire my pulseFist, arm jerking spasmodically. Ducking and moving so I don't block the entrance. Something slams into me. I stumble to the left wall, superheated particles screaming from my fist. My shield crackles with coilgun rounds that impact the energy barrier and fall, flattened to the ground at my feet. More Obsidian fill the hall behind me. They move so fast. It's a cacophony of sound. My tactical mind shoves the facts to the front. We're pinned down. Men die in the breach. Must move forward.

Something whizzes past my head. It detonates behind at the entrance. Limbs and armor slop onto the floor. The helmet mutes the massive noise, saving my eardrums. I stumble forward, trying to get out of the killzone. Another grenade lands among us. Detonating after an Obsidian dives upon it. More meat for the grinder. Must close the distance. Can't see anything in front of me. So much smoke. Fire.

To hell with this.

With a roar of frustration, I activate my gravBoots and rocket down the narrow hall eighty kilometers an hour toward our assailants, firing as I go. Flying a meter above the floor. Victra follows. It's a whole squad of twenty Grays led by a Gold legate in brilliant silver armor. I crash into the Gold. Razor outstretched, piercing his shield and spearing his brain. Crash to the ground. Arm pinned under me. The Gray response team separates from one another, keeping me at the center as I struggle to my feet. One shoots an ion-charge into my back. Blue lightning spasms over my shields, killing them. I stab one Gray through the neck with my razor. Two others fire into my chest. My armor dents with a dozen rounds. I stumble back. A heavy railgun with a boring round in the chamber levels at my head. I dip and dodge to the side, slipping on blood. Going down. The gun goes off and opens a hole the size of a man's head in the floor.

Then Victra smashes into the Grays. Bursting side to side with her gravBoots, an angry wrecking ball. Shattering bones between the walls and her heavily armored body. Then the Obsidians are among the Grays, hacking them to pieces with their pulseAxes. The Grays are screaming, falling back around the corner where they have fire support. A Gray's leg is slashed off by Sefi and he stumbles, firing his weapon into the wall. She rips his head clean off from behind.

This is horror.

The smoke. The twitching bodies and evaporation of blood as it boils out of charred wounds. A dying man's urine pools around my armor, hissing against the superheated barrel of my pulseFist as Victra helps me up.

"Thanks."

Her frightening bird helmet nods to me without expression.

As the rest of my platoon files through the breach, I move forward to the corner around which several of the Grays escaped. Another enemy response squad hastily sets up a heavy weapon mounted on a floating gravPod about thirty meters down near a gravLift entrance. When it fires, a quarter of the wall above me melts. I order Holiday take my place at the corner with Trigg's ambi-rifle.

"Four tins, one Gold," I say. "They've got a mounted QR-13. Slag 'em."

She adjusts her rifle's multi-use barrel. "Yessir."

At our breach point, six Valkyrie are down. A huge woman's helmet peels back into her armor. She vomits blood. Half her torso smokes, molten armor still melting her flesh. She tries to stand, laughing at the pain, high on god's bread. But this is a new type of war to these women with new injuries. Unable to support herself, the Obsidian slumps against a sister who calls to Sefi. The young Queen looks at the wounds and sees Victra shake her head. A quicker learner than the rest of them, Sefi knew well what this war would cost her people. But staring it in the face is something different altogether. She says something of home to the woman, something of the sky and the feathers at summer's twilight. I don't see the blade she slips into the base of the dying woman's skull until she pulls it back out.

A hologram of Mustang's face flashes in the corner of my screen. I open the link. *"Darrow, have you breached?"*

"We're in. Double for my teams. Pressing to bridge now. What's what?"

"You need to hurry. My ship's under heavy fire."

"We're in. You're supposed to bug out. Head to Thebe."

"Roque used EMPs." Her voice is tense. *"Our shielding kept us up, but half my fleet's engines are squabbed. We're sitting dead, punching it out with him. Soon as your clawDrill hit, the* Colossus *started shooting to kill. They're ripping us apart. We're outgunned, hard. Main batteries are already at half strength."* A sick feeling rises in my gut. Roque can see us on the cameras in his ship. He knows the strength of my boarding party. It's only a matter of time till I reach the bridge. Soon he'll make an announcement over the com for me to surrender or he'll kill her. *"Get to the gorydamn bridge and put him down. Register?"*

"Register." I turn to face my troops, "We gotta move," I say. "Victra, take squad command. I'm going digital. Sefi, range ahead."

"Holiday, anytime," Victra says eagerly, pacing back and forth in the hall. "The little lion needs our help. Come on! Come on!"

"Hold your tits," Holiday mutters, adjusting her rifle and toggling the corner-shot feature. The barrel joints rotate so it peeks around the wall and feeds the visual link directly into her bionic eye. Four quick bursts tear out of the gun. Thirty rounds each from the ammo magazine in the back of her armor. "Go."

Victra and I burst around the corner, eating up meters as a Gray tries to take his companion's place at the gun. I cut him down with my pulseFist and Victra exchanges a four move kravat set with the Gold, before skewering him with a thrust to the chest. I finish him with a stab to the throat. Holiday has her commandos haul the QR-13 with us, only able to keep pace with our long legs because of our heavy armor.

As we press for the bridge at a full-sprint, other elements of my invasion force make for vital ship functions with a new frantic speed. It's a lightning strike. Grays can't move with this speed because they rely on tactics, leapfrog maneuvers, corner-shots and sly tech. The Obsidian are straight battering rams. It's tempting to surge ahead, focus only on getting to the bridge. But I can't abandon my plan. My platoons need me to guide them using the battlemap on my HUD. Speaking to Red and Gray platoon leaders, I coordinate on the run as Victra leads us through the maze of metal halls and ambushes. As the platoons are pinned down, I use my com to maneuver other platoons through gravLifts and halls to flank entrenched security teams. It's an intricate dance. Not only are we racing against the destruction of Mustang's ship. But we're racing against the return of the leechCraft.

Roque knows this. And less than three minutes into our insertion, the ship goes into full lockdown protocol. All gravLifts and trams and bulkheads sealed off, creating a honeycomb of obstacles throughout the ship. We can only advance fifty meters at a time. It's a devilish system, pins down boarding forces as security teams with digital keys run about the ship at ease, flanking and creating deadly killboxes and cross-fires that can shred even a boarding party like mine. There's no way to combat it. This is the grind of war. No matter the tech or the tactics, it all comes down to terrifying moments crouching chalk-mouthed at a corner as a friend lays down cover fire and you try not to trip over the hi-tech gear that's wrapped around your body as you advance, head lowered, legs churning. It's not bravery, it's fear of shaming yourself in the eyes of your friends that keeps you moving.

As we melt our way through bulkhead after bulkhead, Sefi's Valkyrie feed the grinder. We're ambushed from every side. Some of the best warriors I've ever seen fall with smoking holes in the back of their helmets from Gray marksmen. They melt under pulseFist fire. They fall to a Gold knight flanked by seven Obsidian till Victra, Sefi, and I put them down with razors.

All this to reach the bridge. All this to reach a man who I could have reached out and touched the day before. If this is the cost of honor, give me a shameful murder. If I'd have stabbed Roque in the throat then, Valkyrie would not litter the ground now.

"Men and women of the Society Navy, this is the Reaper. Your ship has been boarded by the Sons of Ares . . ." I hear my voice over the ship's general com unit. One of my platoons has reached the communication mainframe in the back half of the ship. Every boarding party in my fleet has copies of the speech Mustang and I recorded together to upload to boarded enemy vessels. It exhorts lowColors to aid my units, to deactivate lockdown protocol if they can, to unlock doors manually if they cannot, and to storm the armories. Most of these men and women are veterans. It's unrealistic to expect the same sort of conversion as I had on the *Pax*'s crew, but every little bit helps.

The announcement works partially on the *Colossus*. It buys us precious time as we bypass several doors in seconds instead of the minutes it would take to melt through. Roque also turns off the artificial gravity, realizing by watching their tactics that my Obsidians don't have zero g experience.

Society Grays push their way through halls like seals under water, taking their revenge on my floating Obsidians, robbed of their closing speed, who've mauled so many of their friends. In the end, one of my teams reactivates the gravity. I have them decrease it to one-sixth

Earth standard so that my force is not encumbered by the heavy armor we wear. It's a blessing on our lungs and legs.

After cutting through a security team of Grays, we finally reach the bridge, battered and bloody. I crouch, panting and increase the oxygen circulation in my armor. Swimming in sweat, I activate a stim injection in my gear to keep me from feeling the gash in my biceps where a Gold's razor caught me. The needle bites into my thigh. Reports come from my other platoons that they've lost contact with the enemy, which means they're being consolidated by Roque, redirected, likely to us. Back to the bridge door, I stare across the circular, exposed antechamber to the bridge and remember how my instructor at the Academy demonstrated the geometric deadliness of the space for anyone besieging a starburst bridge design like this. Three halls from three directions lead to the circular room, including a gravLift in the center. It's indefensible, and Roque's marines are coming.

"Roque, darling," Victra calls up to the cameras in the ceiling as Holiday and her team set up the drill on the door. "How I have pined for you since the garden. Are you there?" She sighs. "I'll just assume you are. Listen, I understand. You think we must be wroth with you, what with the murder of my mother, the execution of our friends, the bullets in the spine, the poison, and a year of torture for dear Reaper and I, but that's not so. We just want to put you in a box. Maybe several. Would you like that? It's very poetic."

Holiday's remaining three commandos are attaching magnetic clamps to the door and mounting their thermal drill. She taps a few commands and the eye of the drill begins to spin.

Sefi returns from her scouting. Her helmet slithers back into her armor. "Many enemies come from tunnel." She points to the middle hall. "I killed their leader, but more Golds follow." She didn't just kill the leader. She brought his head back. But she's limping and her left arm bleeds.

"Oh, hell. That's Flagilus," Victra says, regarding the head. "He was in my school house. Very sweet fellow actually. Wonderful cook."

"How many are coming, Sefi?"

"Enough to give us a good death."

"Shit. Shit. Shit." Holiday punches the door behind me.

"It's too thick isn't it?" I ask.

"Yeah." She pulls her assault helmet off. Her Mohawk is mashed to the side. Tense face dripping with sweat. "Door's not VDY specs like the rest of the ship. It's Ganymede Industries. Custom. At least twice as thick."

"How long will it take to get through?" I repeat.

"At full burn? Fourteen minutes?" she guesses.

"Fourteen?" Victra repeats.

"Maybe more."

I turn, hissing the anger out. The women know as well as I that we don't have even five minutes. I hail Mustang's coms. No answer. Her ship must be dying. Bloodydamn. Stay alive. Just stay alive. Why did I ever let her out of my sight?

"We charge them," Victra's saying. "Straight down the middle hall. They'll run like foxes from hounds."

"Yes," Sefi says, finding a more kindred spirit in Victra than either might have thought prior to shedding blood together. "I will follow you, daughter of the sun. To glory."

"Piss on glory," Holiday says. "Let the drill do its work."

"And sit here to die like Pixies?" Victra asks.

Before I can say a word or do much of anything, there's a metallic wheeze behind me from the hydraulics in the wall as the door to the bridge opens.

48

||||||||||||||||||||||||

IMPERATOR

We surge onto the bridge, expecting an ambush. Instead, it's calm. Clean, lights dimmed, just as Roque prefers it. Beethoven streams out from hidden speakers. Everyone is still at their stations. Wan faces illuminated by pale light. Two Golds walk along the wide metal path that leads over the pits toward the front of the bridge where Roque stands orchestrating his battle before a thirty-meter-wide holographic projection. Ships dance among the sensors. Framed by fire, he cycles through images, issuing commands like a great conductor summoning the passion of an orchestra. His mind a beautiful, terrible weapon. He's destroying our fleet. Mustang's *Dejah Thoris* leaks flame from her oxygen stores as the *Colossus* and her three escort destroyers continue to hammer her with railguns. Men and debris float through space. This is just one part of the larger battle. The great host of his force, including Antonia, has pursued Romulus, Orion and the Telemanuses toward Jupiter.

To our left, twenty meters away, near the bridge's armory, a tactical squad of Obsidian and Grays secure their heavy weapons and listen intently to their Gold commanders, preparing to defend their bridge against me.

And just to our right, at the control panel by the now open door, unseen and unnoticed by anyone else on the bridge, trembles a small Pink in a white valet's uniform. The passcode display glows green under her hands. Her thin figure is frail against the backdrop of war. But the woman's face is set defiantly, her finger on the door's release button, her mouth spreading into the most delightful little smile as she shuts the door behind us.

All this in three seconds. The Gold infantry commander sees us.

Wolves, lovely as they are when they howl, kill best in silence. So I point to the left and the Obsidian surge toward the soldiers listening to the Gold. He shouts for them to turn, but Sefi is already on his men before they can lift their weapons. Dancing through them with her blades fluttering into faces and knees. Her Valkyrie smash into the rest. Only two guns go off by the time the Gold's body slides off the end of Sefi's razor and thumps to the floor.

Grays fire at us from the other side of the pit. Holiday and her commandos pick them off. My helmet slithers away. "Roque," I snarl as my men continue to kill.

He's turned now from his battle to see me. All the nobility in him, all the cold-blooded Imperator melting away, leaving him a stunned, startled man. Victra and I stalk across the bridge, Blues beneath us to every side, staring up at us in confusion and fear even as their ship is engaged in battle. Silently, Roque's two Praetorians come at us. Both wear black and purple armor adorned with the silver quarter moon of House Lune. We pair off on the metal bridge in the hydra. Victra taking the right, me the left. My Praetorian is shorter than I. Her helmet off, hair in a tight bun, ready to proclaim the grand laurels of her family. "My name is Felicia au . . ." I feint a whip at her face. She brings her blade up, and Victra goes diagonal and impales her at the belly button. I finish her off with a neat decapitation.

"Bye, Felicia." Victra spits, turning to the last Praetorian. "No substance these days. Are you of the same fiber?" The man drops his razor and goes to his knees, saying something about surrender. Victra's about to cut his head off anyway, when she glimpses me out of the corner of her eye. Grudgingly, she accepts his surrender, kicking him in the face and hands him over to our Obsidians who secure the bridge. "You like the clawDrills?" Victra asks, pacing to Roque's left. Hungry for the kill. "That's some poetic justice for you, you little backstabbing bitch."

The Blues still watch on, unsure of what to do. The boarding party that came for us now fills our place in the corridor outside the bridge. We left the drill, but it would take them ten minutes at least to breach the door.

The com on Roque's head buzzes with requests for orders. Squadrons he'd sent on attack runs now drift, over-exposed. Their commanders used to being guided by the invisible hand now fight blind to the overall battle. It's the flaw in Roque's strategy. The individual initiative now creates chaos, because the central intelligence has just gone silent.

"Roque, tell your fleet to stand down," I demand. I'm soaked with sweat. Hamstring pulled. Hand trembling with exhaustion. I take a heavy step forward. Boot clomping on the steel. "Do it."

He stares past me, at the Pink who let us onto the bridge. Voice thick with the betrayal of a lover instead of that of a master. "Amathea . . . even you?" The young woman is not shamed by his sadness. She pulls her shoulders back, anchoring herself to the spot. She removes the rose badge on her collar that marks her the property of the gens Fabii and drops it to the ground.

A tremor passes through my friend. "You romantic sop." Victra laughs. I close the distance between myself and Roque. Boots tracking blood over his gray steel deck. I point to the display behind him where Mustang's ship is dying. I can see the stars glittering through holes in her hull, but still the destroyers punish her. They're orientated off the bow of the *Pax*, thirty kilometers closer than her ship.

"Tell them to stop firing!" I say, pointing my razor at him. His own is on his hip. He knows how little it means to draw it against me. "Do it now."

"No."

"That's Mustang!" I say.

"She chose her fate."

"How many men did you send?" I ask coldly. "How many did you send to the *Pax* to bring me back here? Fifteen thousand? How many are on those destroyers?" I slide back the protective sheath over my datapad on my left forearm and summon the reactor diagnostics of the *Pax*. It pulses red. We've reversed the coolant flow to let the reactor overheat. A slight increase in the output demand and it goes thermal. "Tell them to cease fire or their lives are forfeit."

He lifts his gentle chin. "According to my conscience I can give no such order."

He knows what it means

"Then this is on both of us."

His head snaps toward his comBlue. "Cyrus, tell the destroyers to take evasive action."

"Too late," Victra says as I raise the output on the generator. It throbs an evil crimson on my datapad, washing us with its light. And on the hologram behind Roque, the *Pax* begins to release gouts of blue flame. Frantically responding to their Imperator, the destroyers halt their barrage on Mustang and try to jet away, but a bright light implodes in the center of the *Pax,* enveloping the metal decks and crumpling the hull as energy spasms outward. The shock wave hits the destroyers and, crumpling their hulls, smashes them into one another. The *Colossus* shudders around us and we're knocked through space as well, but her shielding holds. The *Dejah Thoris* drifts, lights dark. I can only pray that Mustang is alive. I bite the inside of my cheek to make me focus.

"Why didn't you just use our guns," Roque says, shaken by the loss of his men, of his destroyers, at being so outmaneuvered. "You could have crippled them. . . ."

"I'm saving these guns," I say.

"They won't save you." He turns back to me. "My fleet has yours in flight. They will decimate the remainder and return here and take the *Colossus* back. Then we'll see then how well you hold a bridge."

"Silly Poet. Haven't you wondered where Sevro is?" Victra asks. "Don't tell me you lost track of him in all this." She nods to the screen where his fleet pursues the routed forces of the Moon Lords and Orion toward Jupiter. "He's about to make his entry."

When the battle began, the outermost of the inner four moons of Jupiter, Thebe, was in far rotation. But as the battle dragged on, her orbit brought her closer, and closer, taking her across the path of my now-retreating navy, just under twenty thousand kilometers from Io. Led by Antonia's flagship, Roque's fleet pursued, as they should have, to complete the destruction of my forces. What they did not anticipate was that my ships had always planned to bring them to Thebe, the proverbial dead horse.

While I negotiated with Romulus, teams of Helldivers were melting caverns into the face of barren Thebe. Now, as Roque's battlecruisers and torchShips pass the moon, Sevro and six thousand soldiers in starShells pour out of the caverns. And out the other side of the moon pours two thousand leechCraft packed with fifty thousand Obsidians and forty thousand screaming Reds. Railguns spray. Flak deploys last minute. But my forces envelope the enemy, latching onto a their hulls like a cloud of Luna gutter mosquitos to burrow into their guts and claim the ships from the inside.

Yet even my victory carries betrayal. Romulus had Gold leechCraft of his own prepared to launch from the surface of the moon, so that he could capture ships as well to balance my gains. But I need the ships more than he. And my Reds collapsed the mouth of their tunnels at the same time Sevro launches. By the time he realizes the sabotage, my fleet will outnumber his.

"I could not lure you to an asteroid field, so I brought one to you," I say to Roque as we watch the battle unfold.

"Well played," Roque whispers. But we both know the plan works only because I have a hundred thousand Obsidian and he does not. At most, his entire fleet has ten thousand. Probably more like seven. Worse, how could he have known that I had so many when every other Sons of Ares attack has rested on the backs of Reds? Battles are won months before they are fought. I never had enough ships to beat him. But now my ships will continue to flee, continue to run away from his guns as my men carve his battlecruisers apart from the inside. Slowly his ships will become my ships and fire on the very vessels they're in formation with. You can't defend against that. He can vent the ships, but my men will have magnetic gear, breathing masks. He'll only kill his own.

"The day is lost," I say to the thin Imperator. "But you can still save lives. Tell your fleet to stand down."

He shakes his head.

"You're in a corner, Poet," Victra says. "There's no getting out. Time to do the right thing. I know it's been a while."

"And destroy what's left of my honor?" he asks quietly as a group of twenty men in starShells penetrate the rear hangar of a nearby destroyer. "I think not."

"Honor?" Victra sneers. "What honor do you think you have? We were your friends and you gave us up. Not just to be killed. But to be put in boxes. To be electrocuted. Burned. Tortured night and day for a year." Here in armor, it's hard to imagine the blond warrior to have ever been a victim. But in her eyes there's that special sadness that comes from seeing the void. From feeling cut away from the rest of humanity. Her voice is thick with emotion. "We were your friends."

"I swore an oath to protect the Society, Victra. The same oath you both swore the day we stood before our betters and took the scar upon our faces. To protect the civilization that brought order to man. Look upon what you've done instead." He eyes the Valkyrie behind us in disgust.

"You don't live in a bedtime story, whimpering little sod," she snaps. "You think any of them care about you? Antonia? The Jackal? The Sovereign?"

"No," he says quietly. "I have no such illusions. But it's not about them. It's not about me. Not every life is meant to be warm. Sometimes the cold is our duty. Even if it pulls us from those we love." He looks pityingly at her. "You'll never be what Darrow wants. You have to know that."

"You think I'm here for him?" she asks.

Roque frowns. "Then it's revenge?"

"No," she says angrily. "It's more than that."

"Who are you trying to fool?" Roque asks, jerking his head toward me. "Him or yourself?" The question catches Victra off guard.

"Roque, think of your men," I say. "How many more have to die?"

"If you care so much for life, tell yours to stop firing," Roque replies. "Tell them to fall in line and understand that life isn't free. It isn't without sacrifice. If all take what they want, how long will it be till there's nothing left?"

It breaks me to hear him say those words.

My friend has always had his own way of things. His own tides that come in and out. It is not in his nature to hate. Nor was it in mine. Our worlds made us what we are, and all this pain we suffer is to fix the folly of those who came before, who shaped the world in their image and left us the ruin of their feast. Ships detonate in his irises. Washing his pale face with furious light.

"All this . . . ," he whispers, feeling the end coming. "Was she so lovely?"

"Yes. She was like you," I say. "A dreamer." He's too young to look so old. Were it not for the lines on his face and the world between us, it would seem only yesterday that he crouched before me as I shivered on the floor of the Mars Castle after killing Julian and he told me that when you're thrown in the deep, there's only one choice. Keep swimming or drown. I should have loved him more. I would have done anything to keep him at my side and show him the love he deserves.

But life is the present and the future, not the past.

It's as if we look at each other from distant shores and the river between us widens and roars and darkens till our faces are pale shards of the moon in the deep night. More ideas of the boys we were than the men we are. I see the resolve forming in his face. The determination pulling him away from this life.

"You don't have to die."

"I have lost the invincible armada," he says, stepping back, his hand tightening on his razor. Behind him, the display shows Sevro's trap ruining the main body of his fleet. "How can I go on? How can I bear this shame?"

"I know shame. I watched my wife die," I say. "Then I killed myself. Let them hang me to end it all. To escape the pain. I've felt that guilt every day since. This is not the way out."

"My heart breaks for who you were," he says. "For that boy who watched his wife die. My heart broke in that garden. It breaks now knowing all you suffered. But the only solace was my duty, and now that has been robbed from me. All the remittance I've attempted to make . . . gone. I love the Society. I love my people." His voice softens. "Can't you see that?"

"I can."

"And you love yours." It's not judgment, not forgiveness that he gives me. It's just a smile. "I cannot watch mine fade. I cannot watch it all burn."

"It won't."

"It will. Our age is ending. I feel the days shortening. The brief light dimming upon the kingdom of man."

"Roque . . ."

"Let him do it," Victra says from behind me. "He chose his fate." I hate her for being so cold even now. How can she not see that beneath his deeds, he's a good man? He's still our friend, despite what he's done to us.

"I'm sorry for what happened, Victra. Remember me fondly."

"I won't."

He favors her with a sad smile as he strips the Imperator badge from his left shoulder and clutches it in his hand, drawing his strength from it. But then he tosses it to the ground. There's tears in his eyes as he strips away the other. "I do not deserve these. But I shall have glory by losing this day. More than you by vile conquest shall attain."

"Roque, just listen to me. This not the end. This is the beginning. We can repair what's broken. The worlds need Roque au Fabii." I hesitate. "I need you."

"There is no place for me in your world. We were brothers, but I would kill you, if only I had the power."

I'm in a dream. Unable to change the forces that move around me. To stop the sand from slipping through my fingers. I set this into motion but didn't have the heart or strength or cunning or whatever the hell I needed to stop it. No matter what I do or say, Roque was lost to me the moment he discovered what I am.

I step toward him, thinking I can take his razor from his hand without killing him, but he knows my intention and he holds up his off hand plaintively. As if to comfort me and beg me the mercy of letting him die as he lived. "Be still. Night hangs upon mine eyes." He looks to me, eyes full with tears.

"Keep swimming, my friend," I tell him.

With a gentle nod, he wraps his razor whip around his throat and stiffens his spine. "I am Roque au Fabii of the *gens* Fabii. My ancestors walked upon red Mars. They fell upon Old Earth. I have lost the day, but I have not lost myself. I will not be a prisoner." His eyes close. His hand trembles. "I am the star in the night sky. I am the blade in the twilight. I am the god, the glory." His breath shudders out. He is afraid. "I am the Gold."

And there, on the bridge of his invincible warship as his famous fleet falls to ruin behind him, the Poet of Deimos takes his own life. Somewhere the wind howls and the darkness whispers that I'm running out of friends, running out of light. The blood slithers away from his body toward my boots. A shard of my own reflection trapped in its red fingers.

49

|||||||||||||||||||||||

COLOSSUS

Victra is less shaken than I. She assumes command as I linger over Roque's corpse. His lifeless eyes stare at the ground. Blood thunders in my ears. Yet the war rages on. Victra's standing over the Blue operations pit, face drawn in determination.

"Does anyone contest that this ship now belongs to the Rising?" Not a sailor says a word. "Good. Follow orders and you'll keep your post. If you can't follow orders, stand up now and you'll be a prisoner of war. If you say you can follow orders but don't, we shoot you in the head. Choose." Seven Blues stand. Holiday escorts them out of the pit. "Welcome to the Rising," Victra says to the remainders. "The battle is far from won. Give me a direct link to *Persephone's Howl* and *Reynard*. Main screen."

"Belay that," I say. "Victra, make the call on your datapad. I don't want to broadcast the fact that we have taken this ship just yet."

Victra nods and punches her datapad several times. Orion and Daxo appear on the holo. The dark woman speaks first. *"Victra, where is Darrow?"*

"Here," Victra says quickly. "What's your status? Have you heard from Virginia?"

"A third of the enemy fleet is boarded. Virginia is aboard an escape pod, about to be picked up by the Echo of Ismenia. *Sevro's in the halls of their secondary flagship. Periodic reports. He's making headway. Telemanuses and Raa are pinching. . . ."*

"An even match," Daxo says. *"We'll need the* Colossus *to tilt the odds. My father and sisters have boarded the* Pandora. *They're striking for Antonia. . . ."*

Their conversation feels a world away.

Through my grief, I feel Sefi approach me. She kneels beside Roque. "This man was your friend," she says. I nod numbly. "He is not gone. He is here." She touches her own heart. "He is there." She points to the stars on the holo. I look over at her, surprised by the deep current she reveals to me. The respect she gives Roque now doesn't heal my wounds, but it makes them feel less hollow. "Let him see," she says, nodding to his eyes. The purest gold, they stare now at the ground. So I unscrew my gauntlet and close them with my bare fingers. Sefi smiles and I gain my feet beside her.

"Pandora is moving lateral to sector D-6," Orion says of Antonia's ship. On the display, the Severus-Julii ships are separating from the Sword Armada and firing at each other to try and skin away the leech-Craft which festoon them. She's shifting power to engines and away from shields and angling away from the engagement. *"Now D-7."*

"She's abandoning them," Victra says, dumbfounded. "The little shit is saving her own hide." The Society Praetors must not believe what they're seeing. Even if I brought the *Colossus* to bear on them, the fleets would be evenly matched. The battle would last another twelve hours and exhaust both our fleets. Now it crumbles apart.

Whether by cowardice or betrayal, I don't know, but Antonia just gave us the battle on a silver platter.

"She's left us a gap," Orion says. Her eyes go distant as she syncs with her ship captains and her own vessel, thrusting the huge capital ships into the region formerly occupied by Antonia, which brings them into the flank of the main enemy body.

"Do not let her escape!" Victra snarls.

But neither Daxo nor Orion can spare the ships to pursue Antonia. They're too busy taking advantage of her absence. "We can catch her," Victra says to herself. "Engines, prepare to give us sixty percent thrust, escalate by ten percent over five. Helmsman, set our course for the *Pandora*."

I make a quick assessment. Of our small battle at the rear of the warzone, we're the only ship still battle-ready. The rest are drifting rubble. But the *Colossus* has not yet made an action or a declaration that its bridge has been taken by the Rising. Which means we have an opportunity.

"Belay that," I snap.

"What?" Victra wheels on me. "Darrow, we have to catch her."

"There's something else that needs doing."

"She'll escape!"

"And we'll hunt her down."

"Not if she gets enough of a lead. We'll be tied here for hours. You promised me my sister."

"And I'll deliver. Think beyond yourself," I say. "Bridge shield down." I ignore the wrathful woman's glare and walk past Roque's body to peer into the blackness of space as the metal shielding beyond the glass viewports slides into the wall. In the far distance ships flicker and flash against the marble backdrop of Jupiter. Io is beneath us, and far to our left, the city moon of Ganymede glows, large as a plum.

"Holiday, recall all available infantry to protect the bridge and make safe the vessel. Sefi make sure no one gets through that door. Helmsman, set course for Ganymede. Do not make any Society ships aware the bridge is taken. Do I make myself clear? No broadcasts." The Blues follow my instructions.

"To Ganymede?" Victra asks, eying her sister's ship. "But Antonia, the battle . . ."

"The battle is won. Your sister made sure of that."

"Then what are we doing?"

Our ship's engines throb and we untangle ourselves from the wreckage of the *Pax* and Mustang's devastated strike group. "Winning the next war. Excuse me."

I wipe blood from my armored kneecap onto my face and let my helmet slither over my head. The HUD display expands. I wait. And then, as expected, a call from Romulus comes. I let it flash on the left hand side of my screen, altering my breathing so it seems I've been running. I accept the call. His face expands over the left eighth of my visor's vision. He's in a firefight, but my vision is as constricted as his. All I can see is his face in his helmet. *"Darrow. Where are you?"*

"In the halls," I say. I pant and crouch on a knee as if taking respite. "Pressing for the *Colossus*'s bridge."

"You're not in yet?"

"Roque initiated lockdown protocol. It's thick going," I say.

"Darrow, listen carefully. The Colossus *has altered trajectory and is headed for Ganymede."*

"The docks," I whisper intensely. "He's going for the docks. Can any ships intercept?"

"No! They're out of position. If Octavia can't win, she'll ruin us. Those docks are my people's future. You must take that bridge at all cost!"

"I will . . . but Romulus. He has nukes on board. What if it's not just the docks he's going for?"

Romulus pales. *"Stop him. Please. Your people are down there too."*

"I'll do my best."

"Thank you, Darrow. And good luck. First cohort, on me . . ."

The connection dies. I remove my helmet. My men stare at me. They haven't heard the conversation, but they know what I'm doing now. "You're going to destroy Romulus's dockyards around Ganymede," Victra says.

"Holy shit," Holiday mutters. "Holy shit."

"I'm not destroying anything," I reply. "I'm fighting my way through corridors. Trying to reach the bridge. Roque is ordering this move as his last act of violence before I claim his command." Victra's eyes light up, but even she has reservations.

"If Romulus finds out, if he even suspects, he'll fire on our forces and everything we've won today goes to ash."

"And who will tell him?" I ask. I look around the bridge. "Who will tell him?" I look to Holiday. "If anyone sends a signal out, shoot them in the head. Wipe the video memory from the whole ship."

If I ruin Ganymede's dockyards the Rim won't be able to threaten us for fifty years. Romulus is an ally today, but I know he will threaten the core if the Rising succeeds. If I must give Roque for this victory, if I must give the Sons on these moons, I will take something in return. I look down. Red bootprints follow my path. I didn't even realize I'd stepped in Roque's blood.

We carve our way free of the debris formed by Mustang's fleet and mine and break away from Jupiter toward Ganymede, leaving her behind. I feel the pulsing desperation as the Moon Lords send their fastest craft to intercept us. We shoot them down. All the pride and hope of Romulus's people are in the rivets and assembly lines and electric shops of that dull gray ring of metal. All their promises of power and future independence are at my mercy.

When I reach the sparkling gem that is Ganymede, I bring the *Colossus* parallel to the monument of industry they've built in orbit at her equator. The Valkyrie gather behind us at the viewport. Sefi staring in awe at the majesty and triumph of Gold will. Two hundred kilometers of docks. Hundreds of haulers and freighters. Birthplace of the greatest ships in the Sol System including the *Colossus* herself. Like any good monster of myth, the girl must eat her mother before being free to pursue her true destiny. That destiny is leading the assault on the Core.

"Men built this?" Sefi asks with quiet reverence. Many of her Valkyrie have fallen to a knee to watch in wonder.

"My people built it," I say. "Reds."

"It took two hundred fifty years . . . It's how old the first dock there is," Victra says, shoulder to shoulder with me. Hundreds of escape pods flower out from her metal carapace. They know why we're here. They're evacuating the senior administrators, the overseers. I'm under no delusion. I know who will die when we fire.

"There's still going to be thousands of Reds on there." Holiday says quietly to me. "Oranges, Blues . . . Grays."

"He knows that," Victra says.

Holiday doesn't leave my side. "You sure you want to do this, sir?"

"Want to?" I ask hollowly. "Since when has any of this been about what we want?" I turn to the helmsman, about to give the order when Victra puts a hand on my shoulder.

"Share the load, darling. This one's on me." Her Aureate voice rings clear and loud. "Helmsman, open fire with all port batteries. Launch tubes twenty-one through fifty at their center-line."

Together, we stand shoulder to shoulder and watch the warship lay ruin to the defenseless dock. Sefi stares out in profound awe. She has watched the holos of ship warfare, but her war until now, has been narrow halls and men and gunfire. This is the first time they see what a vessel of war can do. And for the first time, I see her frightened.

It's a crime that the marvel should die like this. No song. Nothing but silence and the unblinking gaze of the stars to herald the end of one of the great monuments of the Golden Age. And I hear in the back of my mind, that age old truth of darkness whispering to me.

Death begets death begets death . . .

The moment is sadder than I wanted. So I turn to Sefi as the dock continues to fall apart. The shattered bits drifting down to the moon, where they will fall into the sea or upon the cities of Ganymede.

"The ship must be renamed," I say, "I would like you to choose."

Her face is stained with white light.

"Tyr Morga," she says without hesitation.

"What's that mean?" Holiday asks.

I look back out the viewport as explosions ripple through the dock and her escape pods flare against the atmosphere of Ganymede. "It means Morning Star."

PART IV

||||||||||||||||||||||||||||||||||||

STARS

My son, my son

Remember the chains

When Gold ruled with iron reins

We roared and roared

And twisted and screamed

For ours, a vale

Of better dreams

—EO OF LYKOS

50

||||||||||||||||||||||||

THUNDER AND LIGHTNING

The Sword Armada is shattered. More than half destroyed. A quarter seized by my ships. The remainder fled with Antonia or in little ragged bands, rallying around the remaining Praetors to sprint for the Core. I sent Thraxa and her sisters in fast-moving corvettes out under Victra's command to reel Antonia in and recapture Kavax, who was captured by Antonia's forces while attempting to board the *Pandora*. I asked Sevro to go with Victra, thinking to keep the two of them together, but he went to her ship then returned a half hour before it departed, wrathful and quiet, refusing to discuss whatever it was that transpired.

For her part, Mustang is beside herself with worry for Kavax, though she makes a brave face. She'd lead the rescue mission herself if she weren't needed in the main fleet. We make repairs where we can to make the ships fit for travel. We scuttle the ships we can't save, and search the naval debris for survivors. A tentative alliance exists between the Rising and the Moon Lords, one that will not last long.

I've not slept since the battle two days ago. Neither, it seems, has Romulus. His eyes are dark with anger and exhaustion. He's lost an arm and a son on the day and more, so much more. Neither one of us could risk meeting in person. So all we have left between us is this holo conference.

"As promised, you have your independence," I say.

"And you have your ships," he replies. Marble columns stretch up behind him, carved with Ptolemaic effigies. He's on Ganymede, in the Hanging Palace. The heart of their civilization. "But they will not be enough to defeat the Core. The Ash Lord will be waiting for you."

"I hope so. I have plans for his master."

"Do you sail on Mars?"

"Perhaps."

He allows a thoughtful silence. "There's one thing I find curious about the battle. Of all the ships my men boarded, not one nuclear weapon over five megatons was found. Despite your claims. Despite your . . . evidence."

"My men found plenty enough," I lie. "Come aboard if you doubt me. It's hardly curious that they would store them on the *Colossus*. Roque would want to keep them under tight watch. We're only lucky that I managed to take bridge when I did. Docks can be rebuilt. Lives cannot."

"Did they ever have them?" Romulus asks.

"Would I risk the future of my people on a lie?" I smile without humor. "Your moons are safe. You define your own future now, Romulus. Do not look the gift horse in the mouth."

"Indeed," he says, though he sees through the lie now. Knows he was manipulated. But it is the lie he must sell to his own people if he wants peace. They cannot afford to go to war with me now, but their honor would demand it if they knew what I'd done. And if they went to war with me, I would likely win. I have more ships now. But they'd hurt me bad enough to ruin my real war against the Core. So Romulus swallows my lies. And I swallow the guilt of leaving hundreds of millions in slavery and personally signing the death warrants of thousands of Sons of Ares to Romulus's police. I gave them warning. But not all will escape. "I would like your fleet to depart before end of day," Romulus says.

"It will take three days to search the debris for our survivors," I say. "We will leave then."

"Very well. My ships will escort your fleet to the boundaries we agreed upon. When your flagship crosses into the asteroid belt, you may never return. If one ship under your command crosses that boundary, it will be war between us."

"I remember the terms."

"See that you do. Give my regards to the Core. I'll certainly give yours to the Sons of Ares you leave behind." He terminates the signal.

We depart three days after my conference with Romulus, making additional repairs as we travel. Welders and repairmen dot hulls like benevolent barnacles. Though we lost more than twenty-five capital ships during the battle, we've gained over seventy more. It is one of the greatest military victories in modern history, but victories are less romantic when you're cleaning your friends off the floor.

It's easy to be bold in the moment, because all you have is what you can process: see, smell, feel, taste. And that's a very small amount of what is. But afterward, when everything decompresses and uncoils bit by bit, and the horror of what you did and what happened to your friends hits you. It's overwhelming. That's the curse of this naval war. You fight, then spend months waiting, engaged only by the tedium of routine. Then you fight again.

I've not yet told my men where we sail. They don't ask me themselves, but their officers do. And again I give them the same answer.

"Where we must."

The core of my army is the Sons of Ares, and they are experienced in hardship. They organize dances and gatherings and force jubilation down war-weary throats. It seems to take. Men and women whistle in the halls as we distance ourselves from Jupiter. They sew unit badges onto uniforms and paint starShells in wild colors. There's a vibrancy here different from the cold precision of the Society Navy. Still they keep mostly to their Color, blending only when assigned to do so. It's not as harmonious as I thought it would be, but it's a start.

I feel disconnected from it all even as I smile and lead as best I know. I killed ten men in the corridors. Killed another thirteen thousand of my own when we destroyed the docks. Their faces don't haunt me. But that feeling of dread is hard to lose.

We have not yet been able to contact the Sons of Ares. Communications are blacked out across all channels. Which means Narol succeeded in destroying the relays as he promised. Gold and Red are just as blind now.

I give Roque the burial he would have wanted. Not in the soil of some foreign moon, but in the sun. His casket is made of metal. A torpedo with a hatch through which Mustang and I slip his body. The Howlers smuggled him from the overflowing morgue so we could say goodbye to him in secret. With so many of our own dead, it would not do to see me honor an enemy so deeply.

Few mourn the death of my friend. Roque, if he is remembered by his people, will forever be known as The Man Who Lost the Fleet. A modern Gaius Terentius Varro, the fool who let Hannibal encircle him at Cannae. Or Alfred Jones. The American general who went mad and lost his Imperium's dreaded mech division in the Conquering. To my people, he is just another Gold who thought himself immortal till the Reaper showed him otherwise.

It's a lonely thing carrying the body of someone dead and loved. Like a vase you know will never again hold flowers. I wish he believed as firmly in the afterlife as I once did, as Ragnar did. I'm not sure when I lost my faith. I don't think it's something that just happens. Maybe I've been worn down bit by bit, pretending to believe in the Vale because it's easier than the alternative. I wish Roque would have thought he was going to a better world. But he died believing only in Gold, and anything that believes only in itself cannot go happily into the night.

When it is my turn to say goodbye, I stare at his face and see nothing but memories. I think of him on the bed reading before the Gala, before I stabbed him with the sedative. I see him in his suit, pleading with me to come along with him and Mustang to the Opera in Agea, saying how much I'd delight in the plight of Orpheus. I see him laughing by the fire at her estate after the Battle of Mars. His arms around me as he sobbed after I came home to House Mars when we were hardly more than boys.

Now he is cold. Eyes ringed with circles. All the promise of youth fled. All the possibilities of family and children and joy and growing old and wise together are gone because of me. I'm reminded of Tactus now, and I feel tears coming.

My friends, the Howlers in particular, do not much like that I've let Cassius come to the funeral. But I could not stand the idea of sending Roque to the sun without the Bellona kissing him farewell. His legs are chained. Hands manacled behind his back with magnetic cuffs. I un-cuff them so he can say goodbye properly. Which he does. Leaning to kiss Roque farewell on the brow.

Sevro, pitiless even now, slams shut the metal lid after Cassius is done. Like Mustang, the little Gold came for me, in case I needed him. He has no love for the man, no heart for someone who betrayed me and Victra. Loyalty is everything to him. And, in his mind, Roque had none. So too with Mustang. Roque betrayed her as readily as he betrayed me. He cost her a father. And though she can understand Augustus was not the best of men, he was her father nonetheless.

My friends wait for me to say something. There's nothing I can say that will not anger them. So, as Mustang recommended, I spare them the indignity of having to listen to compliments about a man who signed their death warrants, and instead recite the most relevant lines of one of his old favorites.

Fear no more the heat o' the sun
Nor the furious winter's rages,
Thou thy worldly task hast done,
Home art gone, and ta'en thy wages;
Golden lads and girls all must
As chimney sweepers come to dust

"*Per aspera, ad astra,*" my Golden friends whisper, even Sevro. And with a press of a button, Roque disappears from our lives to begin his last journey to join Ragnar and generations of fallen warriors in the sun. I remain behind. The others leave. Mustang lingers with me, eyes following Cassius as he's escorted away.

"What are your plans for him?" she asks me when we're left alone.

"I don't know," I say, angry she would ask that now.

"Darrow, are you all right?"

"Fine. I just need to be alone right now."

"OK." She doesn't leave me. Instead, she steps closer. "It's not your fault."

"I said I want to be alone."

"It's not your fault." I look over at her, angry she won't leave, but when I see how gentle her eyes are, how open to me they are, I feel the tension in my ribs release. The tears come unbidden. Streaking down my cheeks. "It's not your fault," she says, pulling me close as I feel the first sob rattle my chest. She wraps her arms around my waist and puts her forehead into my chest. "It's not your fault."

Later that night my friends and I have supper together in the stateroom I've inherited from Roque. It's a quiet affair. Even Sevro doesn't have much to say. He's been quiet since Victra left, something gnawing in the back of his mind. The trauma of the past few days weighs heavy on all of us. But these few men and women know where we travel, and it's that knowledge that adds even more weight than the regular soldier carries.

Mustang wants to stay behind with me, but I don't want her to. I need time to think. So I quietly click the door shut behind her. I am alone. Not just at the table in my suite, but in my grief. My friends came to Roque's funeral for me, not him. Only Sefi was kind about his passing, because over the course of our journey to Jupiter she learned of Roque's prowess in battle and so respected him in a pure way the others can't. Still, of my friends, only I loved Roque as much as he deserved in the end.

The Imperator's stateroom still smells like Roque. I leaf through the old books on his shelves. A piece of blackened ship metal floats in a display case. Several other trophies hang on the wall. Gifts from the

Sovereign "For heroism at the Battle of Deimos" and from the Arch-Governor of Mars for "The Defense of Aureate Society." *Sophocles's Theban Plays* lies open on the bedside. I've not changed the page. I've not changed anything. As if by preserving the room I can keep him alive. A spirit in amber.

I lie down to sleep, but can only stare at the ceiling. So I rise and pour three fingers of scotch from one of his decanters and watch the holoTube in the lounge. The web is down thanks to the hacking war. Creates an eerie feeling being disconnected from the rest of humanity. So I search the old programs on the ship's computer, skimming through vids of space pirates, noble Golden knights, Obsidian bounty hunters and a troubled Violet musician on Venus, till I find a menu with recently played vids catalogued. The most recent dates to the night before the battle.

My heart thumps heavily in my chest as I sort through the vids. I look over my shoulder, like I'm going through someone else's journal. Some are Aegean renditions of Roque's favorite opera, *Tristan and Isolde,* but most are feeds from our time at the Institute. I sit there, my hand in the air, about to click on the feed. But instead I feel compelled to wait. I call Holiday on my com.

"You up?"

"Now I am."

"I need a favor."

"Don't you always."

Twenty minutes later, Cassius, chained hand and foot, shuffles in from the hall to join me. He's escorted by Holiday and three Sons. I excuse them. Nodding my thanks to Holiday. "I can take care of myself."

"Begging your pardon, sir, that's not exactly a fact."

"Holiday."

"We'll be right outside, sir."

"You can go to bed."

"Just shout if you need anything, sir."

"Ironclad discipline you have here," Cassius says awkwardly after she's left. He stands in my circular marble atrium, eying the sculptures. "Roque always did dress up a place. Unfortunately he's got the taste of a ninety-year-old orchestra first chair."

"Born three millennia late, wasn't he?" I reply.

"I rather think he would have hated the toga of Rome. Distressing fashion trend, really. They made an effort to bring it back in my father's day. Especially during drinking bouts and some of the breakfast clubs they had back then. I've seen the pictures." He shudders. "Dreadful stuff."

"One day they'll say it about our high collars," I say, touching mine.

He eyes the scotch in my hand. "This a social occasion?"

"Not exactly." I lead him into the lounge. He's slow and loud in the forty kilogram prisoner boots they've sealed his feet inside, but is still more at home in the room than I am. I pour him a scotch as he sits on the couch, still expecting some sort of trap. He raises his eyebrows at the glass.

"Really, Darrow? Poison isn't your style."

"It's a cache of Lagavulin. Lorn's gift to Roque after the Siege of Mars."

Cassius grunts. "I never was fond of irony. Whisky, on the other hand . . . we never had a quarrel we couldn't solve." He looks through the whisky. "Fine stuff."

"Reminds me of my father," I say, listening to the soft hum of the air vents above. "Not that the stuff he drank was good for anything more than cleaning gears and killing brain cells."

"How old were you when he died?" Cassius asks.

"About six, I reckon."

"Six." He tilts his glass thoughtfully. "My father wasn't a solitary drinker. But sometimes I'd find him on his favorite bench. Near this eerie path on the spine of the Mons. He'd have a whisky like this." Cassius chews the inside of his cheek. "Those were my favorite moments with him. No one else around. Just eagles coasting in the distance. He'd tell me what sort of trees were on the hillside. He loved trees. He'd ramble on about what grew where and why and what birds liked to roost there. Especially in winter. Something about how they looked in the cold. I never really listened to him. Wish I had."

He takes a drink. He'll find the spirit in the glass. The peat, the grapefruit on the tongue, the stone of Scotland. I can never taste anything but the smoke. "Is that Castle Mars?" Cassius asks, nodding to the hologram above Roque's console. "By Jove. It looks so small."

"Not even the size of the engines on a torchShip," I say.

"Boggles the mind, the exponential expectations of life."

I laugh. "I used to think Grays were tall."

"Well . . ." He smiles mischievously. "If your metric is Sevro . . ." He chuckles before growing serious. "I wanted to say thank you . . . for inviting me to the funeral. That was . . . surprisingly decent of you."

"You'd have done the same."

"Hmm." He's not sure of that. "This was Roque's console?"

"Yeah. I was going through his vids. He's rewatched most of these dozens of times. Not the strategies or the battles against other houses. But the quieter bits. You know."

"Have you watched them?" he asks.

"I wanted to wait for you."

He's struck by that, and suspicious of my hospitality.

So I press play and we fall back into the boys we were in the Institute. It's awkward at first, but soon the whisky dispels that and the laughs come easier, the silences stretch deeper. We watch the nights when our tribe cooked lamb in the northern gulch. When we scouted the highlands, listening to Quinn's stories by the campfire. "We kissed that night," Cassius says when Quinn finishes a story about her grandmother's fourth attempt to build a house in a mountain valley a hundred kilometers from civilization without an architect.

"She was climbing into her sleeping roll. I told her I heard a noise. We investigated. When she found out I was just throwing rocks into the dark to get her alone, she knew what I wanted. That smile." He laughs. "Those legs. The kind meant to be wrapped around someone, you know what I mean?" He laughs. "But the lady did protest. Put her hand in my face, shoved me away."

"Well, she wasn't an easy one," I say.

"No. But she did wake me up near morning to give me a kiss or two. On her terms, of course."

"And that is the first time throwing stones has ever worked on a woman."

"You'd be surprised."

There's moments I never knew existed. Roque and Cassius try to catch fish together only for Quinn to push Cassius in from behind. He takes a deep drink beside me now as his younger self splashes in the water and tries to pull Quinn in. We watch private moments where Roque fell in love with Lea, where they scouted the highlands in the dark. Their hands brushing innocently together as they stop for water. Fitchner surveying them from a copse of trees, taking notes on his datapad. We watch the first time they sleep snuggled under the same blankets in the gate's keep, and as Roque takes her off to the highlands to steal his first kiss only to hear boots on rocks and see Antonia and Vixus emerge from the mist, eyes glowing with optics.

They took Lea and when Roque fought, threw him off a cliff. He broke his arm and was swept down the river. By the time he returned, after three days of walking, I was supposedly dead by the Jackal's hand. Roque mourned for me and visited the cairn I built atop Lea only to find that wolves dug in and had stolen the body. He wept there by himself. Cassius grows somber witnessing this, reminding me of the distress on his face when he returned with Sevro to discover what had happened to Lea and Roque. And perhaps feeling guilty for ever allying himself with Antonia.

There's more videos, more little truths I discover. But the one viewed the most according to the holodeck was the time Cassius said he'd found two new brothers and offered us places as lancers to House Bellona. He looked so hopeful then. So happy to be alive. We all did, even I, despite what I felt inside. My betrayal feels all the more monstrous watching it from afar.

I refill Cassius's tumbler. He's quiet under the glow of the hologram. Roque's riding his dappled gray mare away from us, looking pensively down at his reins. "We killed him," he says after a moment. "It was our war."

"Was it?" I ask. "We didn't make this world. And we're not even fighting for ourselves. Neither was Roque. He was fighting for Octavia. For a Society that won't even notice his sacrifice. They'll play politics with his death. Blame him. He died for them and he'll just be a punch line." Cassius feels the disgust I intended. That's his greatest fear. That no one will care that he goes. This noble idea of honor, of a good death . . . that was for the old world. Not this one.

"How long do you think this goes on?" He asks pensively. "This war."

"Between us or everyone?"

"Us."

"Till one heart beats no more. Isn't that what you said?"

"You remembered." He grunts. "And everyone?"

"Until there are no Colors."

He laughs. "Well, good. You've aimed low."

I watch him tilt the liquor around in his glass. "If Augustus did not put me with Julian, what do you think would have happened?"

"Doesn't matter."

"Say it does."

"I don't know," he says sharply. He downs his whisky and pours himself another, surprisingly agile in in his cuffs. He considers the glass in irritation. "You and I aren't like Roque or Virginia. We're not nuanced creatures. All you have is thunder. All I have, lightning. Remember that dumb shit we used to say when we would paint our faces and ride about like idiots? It's the deepspine truth. We can only obey what we are. Without a storm, you and I? We're just men. But give us this. Give us conflict . . . how we rattle and roar." He mocks his own grandiloquence, a dark irony staining his smile.

"You really think that's true?" I ask. "That we're stuck being one thing or another."

"You don't?"

"Victra says that about herself." I shrug. "I'm betting a hell of a lot that she's not. That we're not." Cassius leans forward and pours me a drink this time. "You know, Lorn always talked about being trapped by himself, by the choice he made, till it felt like he wasn't living his own life. Like something was behind him beating him on, something to the sides winnowing his path. In the end, all his love, all his kindness, family, it didn't matter. He died as he lived."

Cassius sees more than just the doubt in my own theory. He knows I could talk about Mustang, or Sevro, or Victra changing. Being different, but he sees the undercurrent because in many ways his thread in life is the most like my own. "You think you're going to die," he says.

"As Lorn used to say, the bill comes at the end. And the end is on its way."

He watches me gently, his whisky forgotten, the intimacy deeper than I intended. I've touched a part of his own mind. Maybe he too has felt like he's marching toward his own burial. "I never thought about the weight on you," he says carefully. "All that time among us. Years. You couldn't talk to anyone, could you?"

"No. Too risky. Kind of a conversation killer. Hello, I'm a Red spy."

He doesn't laugh. "You still can't. And that's what kills you. You're among your own people and you feel a stranger."

"There it is," I say, raising a glass. I hesitate, wondering how much to confide in him. Then whisky talks for me. "It's hard to talk to anyone. Everyone is so fragile. Sevro with his father, with the weight of a people he hardly knows. Victra thinks she's wicked and keeps pretending like she just wants revenge. Like she's full of poison. They think I know the path here. That I've had a vision of the future because of my wife. But I don't feel her like I used to. And Mustang—" I stop awkwardly.

"Go on. What about her? Come on, man. You killed my brothers. I killed Fitchner. It's already awkward."

I grimace at the weirdness of this little moment.

"She's always watching me," I say. "Judging. Like she's keeping a tally of my worth. Whether I'm fit."

"For what?"

"For her? For this? I don't know. I felt like I proved myself on the ice, but it hasn't gone away." I shrug. "It's the same for you, isn't it? Serving at the Sovereign's pleasure when Aja killed Quinn. Your mother's . . . expectations. Sitting here with the man who took two brothers from you."

"You can have Karnus."

"He must have been a treat at home."

"He was actually fond of me as a child," Cassius says. "I know. Hard to believe, but he was my champion. Included me in sports. Took me on trips. Taught me about girls, in his way. He was not so kind to Julian, though."

"I have an older brother. His name's Kieran."

"Is he alive?"

"He's a mechanic with the Sons. Got four kids."

"Wait. You're an uncle?" Cassius says in surprise.

"Several times over. Kieran married Eo's sister."

"Did he? I was an uncle once. I was good at that." His eyes go distant, smile fading, and I know the suspicions that rest heavy on his soul. "I'm tired of this war, Darrow."

"So am I. And If I could bring Julian back to you, I would. But this war is for him, or men like him. The decent. It's for the quiet and gentle who know how the world should be, but can't shout louder than the bastards."

"Aren't you afraid you're going to break everything and not be able to put it back together?" he asks sincerely.

"Yes," I say, understanding myself better than I have for a long time. "That's why I have Mustang."

He stares at me for a long, odd moment before shaking his head and chuckling at himself or me. "I wish it was easier to hate you."

"There's a toast if I ever heard one." I raise my glass and he his, and we drink in silence. But before he parts with me that night, I give him a holocube to watch in his cell. I apologize in advance for its contents, but it's something he needs to see. The irony is not lost on him. He'll watch it later in his cell, and he will weep and feel lonelier still, but the truth is never easy.

51

|||||||||||||||||||||||||

PANDORA

Hours after Cassius has left me, I'm woken from a restless dream by Sevro. He calls my datapad with an urgent message. Victra has engaged Antonia in the Belt. She requests reinforcements, and Sevro's already got his gear and has Holiday mustering a strike team.

Mustang, the Howlers and I hitch a ride on the remaining Telemanus torchShip, the fastest left in the fleet. Sefi tried to come along, eager for more combat, but even after the victory at Io my fleet rides on a razor's edge. Her leadership is needed to keep the Obsidians in line. She's a peacemaker, and the punch line of Sevro's favorite new joke: what do you say when a seven-and-a-half-foot-tall woman walks into a room with a battle axe and tongues on a hook? Absolutely nothing.

Personally, I'm more worried that only a handful of strong personalities bind this alliance together. If I lose one, the whole thing might crumble.

We go full burn, straining the ships to reach Victra, but an hour before we arrive at her coordinates amidst a thicket of sensor-disrupting asteroids, we receive a brief encoded message that is patented Julii: *Bitch captured. Kavax free. Victory mine.*

We shuttle over from the lean Telemanus torchShip toward Victra's waiting fleet. Sevro picks nervously at his pant leg. Victra's won a great victory. She set out in pursuit with twenty strike craft. Now she possesses nearly fifty black ships—fast, nimble, expensive craft. Just the sort you'd expect of a trading family. None of the hulking behemoths the Augustuses and Bellona favor. All the black ships bear the weeping spear-pierced sun of the Julii family.

Victra waits for us on the deck of her mother's old flagship, the *Pandora*. She's splendid and proud in a black uniform with the Julii sun upon her right breast, a fiery orange line burning down the black pants, gold buttons sparkling. She's found her old earrings. Jade hangs from her ears. Her smile is broad and enigmatic.

"My goodmen, welcome aboard the *Pandora*."

Beside her stands Kavax, injured yet again, with a cast on his right arm and resFlesh coating the right side of his face. The daughters who raced ahead to find him flank him now and laugh as Kavax bellows a hello to Mustang. She tries to maintain propriety as she rushes to him and tosses her arms around his neck. She kisses him once on his bald head.

"Mustang," he says happily. He pushes her back and lowers his head. "Apologies. Deepest apologies. I cannot stop being captured."

"Just a damsel in distress," Sevro says.

"It seems the case," Kavax replies.

"Just promise me this is the last time, Kavax," Mustang says. He does. "And you're injured again!"

"A scratch! Just a scratch, my liege. Don't you know I've magic in my veins?"

"I have someone who has been dying to see you," Mustang says, looking back up the ramp. She whistles and inside the shuttle Pebble lets Sophocles go. Claws clatter behind me, then under me as he races through Sevro's legs, almost knocking my friend down, to jump onto Kavax's chest. Kavax kisses the fox with open mouth. Victra cringes.

"Thought you were in trouble," Sevro grunts up at her.

"I told you I had it under control," she says. "How far behind is the rest of the fleet, Darrow?"

"Two days."

Mustang looks around. "Where's Daxo?"

"Daxo is dealing with rats on the upper decks. Still some hardcore Peerless left. It's been a bitch digging them out," Victra says.

"There's barely any wreckage . . ." I say. "How did you do this?"

"How? I am the true heir of House Julii," Victra says proudly. "According to mother's will and according to birth. Antonia's ships—legally *my* ships—were run by stool pigeons, paid allies. They contacted me, thought the whole fleet was right behind my little harrying party. They *begged* me to spare them from the big bad Reaper . . ."

"And where are your sister's men now?" I ask.

"I executed three and destroyed their ships as an example to the rest. The disloyal Praetors which I could capture are rotting in cells. My loyalists and mother's friends have taken command."

"And will they follow us?" Sevro asks gruffly.

"They follow me," she says.

"That's not the same thing," I say.

"Obviously. They're *my* ships." She's one step closer to taking back her mother's empire. But the rest can only be done in peace. Still, it gives her an eerie independence. Just like Roque had when he gained ships after the Lion's Rain. It will test her loyalty, a fact Sevro does not seem entirely comfortable with. Mustang and I frown at one another.

"Property is a funny thing these days," Sevro says. "Tends to have opinions." Victra bristles at the challenge.

Mustang inserts herself. "I think Sevro means to say: now that you have your revenge, do you still intend to come with us to the Core?"

"I don't have my revenge," Victra says. "Antonia still breathes."

"And when she does not?" Mustang asks.

Victra shrugs. "I'm not good with commitment."

Sevro's mood sours even more.

Dozens of prisoners fill the ward's cells. Most Gold. Some Blue and Gray. All high ranking and loyal to Antonia. A canyon of enemies who glare out at me from the bars. I walk alone down the hall, enjoying the feeling of so many Golds knowing I'm their captor.

I find Antonia in the second to last cell. She sits against the bars of the cell that separates her from the adjacent one. Aside from a bruised cheek, she's as beautiful as ever. Mouth sensual, eyes smoldering behind thick eyelashes as she broods under the brig's pale lights. Her willowy legs are folded under her, black-nailed hands picking at a blister on her big toe.

"I thought I heard the Reaper swing," she says with a seductive little smile. Her eyes drift slowly up the length of me, eating every centimeter up. "You've been downing your protein, haven't you, darling? All big again. Don't fret. I'll always remember you as a weeping little worm."

"You're the only Boneriders left alive in the fleet," I say looking at the cell adjacent hers. "I want to know what the Jackal's planning. I want to know his troop positions, his supply routes, his garrison strengths. I want to know what information he has on the Sons of Ares. I want to know what his plans are with the Sovereign. Are they colluding? Is there tension? Is he making a move against her? I want to know how to beat him. And most of all, I want to know where the bloodydamn nuclear weapons are. If you give me this, you live. If you do not, you die. Am I clear?"

She didn't flinch at the mention of the weapons. Neither did the woman in the adjacent cell.

"Crystal clear," Antonia says. "I'm more than willing to cooperate."

"You're a survivor, Antonia. But I wasn't just talking to you." I slam my hand on the bars of the cell next to hers where a shorter, dark-faced Gold sits watching me with raw eyes. Her face is sharp, like her tongue used to be. Hair curly and more golden than last time I saw her—artificially lightened, same with her eyes. "I'm talking to you too, Thistle. Whichever of you gives us more information gets to live."

"Devilish ultimatum." Antonia applauds from the ground. "And you call yourself a Red. I think you were more at home with us than you are with them. Isn't that right?" She laughs. "It is isn't it?"

"You have an hour to think it over."

I walk away from them, letting them stew in it. "Darrow," Thistle calls after me. "Tell Sevro I'm sorry. Darrow, please!" I turn and walk back to her slowly.

"You dyed your hair," I say.

"Little Bronzie just wanted to fit in," Antonia purrs, stretching her long legs. She's more than a head and a half taller than Thistle. "Don't blame the runt, unrealistic expectations."

Thistle stares out at me, hands clutching the bars. "I'm sorry, Darrow. I didn't know it would go so far. I couldn't have . . ."

"Yes, you did. You're not an idiot. And don't be pathetic and claim to be one. I understand how you could do it to me," I say slowly. "But Sevro was supposed to be there. So were the Howlers." She looks at the ground, unable to meet my gaze. "How could you do that to him? To them?"

She has no answer. I touch her hair with my hand. "We liked you the way you were."

52

|||||||||||||||||||||||||

TEETH

I join Sevro, Mustang, and Victra in the brig's monitoring room. Two techs lean back in ergonomic chairs, several dozen holos floating around them at once. "They said anything yet?" I ask.

"Not yet," Victra answers. "But pot's stirred and I've cranked the heat."

Sevro's watching Thistle on the holoDisplay. "Did you want to talk with Thistle?" I ask.

"Who?" he asks, raising his eyebrows. "Never heard of her." I can tell he's wounded by seeing her again. Wounded even more because he tells himself to be hard, but this betrayal—by one of his own Howlers—cuts at his core. Still he plays it off. Not sure if it's for Victra, for me, or for himself. Probably all three.

After several minutes, Antonia and Thistle drip with sweat. Per my recommendation, we've made the cells forty degrees Celsius to amp up their irritability. Gravity is jacked up a fraction too. Just outside the realm of perception. So far, Thistle's done nothing but weep and Antonia has been touching the bruise on her cheek to see if any lasting damage has been done to her face. "You need to come up with a plan," Antonia says idly through the bars.

"What plan?" Thistle asks from the far corner of her own cell. "They're going to kill us even if we give them information."

"You weeping little cow. Pick your chin up. You're embarrassing your scar. You're House Mars, aren't you?"

"They know we're listening," Sevro says. "Least, Antonia does."

"Sometimes it doesn't matter," Mustang replies. "Highly intelligent prisoners often play games with their captors. It's the self-confidence that can make them even more vulnerable to psychological manipulation because they think they're still in control."

"You know this from your own extensive personal experience being tortured?" Victra asks. "Do tell me about that."

"Quiet," I say, turning up the holo's volume.

"I'm going to tell them everything," Thistle's saying to Antonia. "I don't give a shit about this anymore."

"Everything?" Antonia asks. "You don't know everything."

"I know enough."

"I know more," Antonia says.

"Who would ever trust you?" Thistle snaps. "Matricidal psychopath! If you even knew what people really thought about you . . ."

"Oh, darling, you can't really be so stupid." Antonia sighs sympathetically. "You are. So sad to watch."

"What do you mean?"

"Use your head, you little simpleton. Just try, please."

"Slag you, bitch."

"I'm sorry, Thistle," Antonia says, arching her back against the bars. "It's the heat."

"Or syphilitic madness," Thistle mutters, now pacing, arms wrapped around herself.

"How . . . base. It's in the upbringing really."

I consider pulling Thistle out, extracting the information she's willing to give. "Could be a ruse," Mustang says. "Something Antonia designed in case they were captured. Or maybe my brother's play. That'd be like him to sow misinformation. Especially if they just let themselves be captured."

"Let themselves be captured?" Victra asks. "There's over fifty dead

Golds in the morgues of this ship who would disagree with that statement."

"She's right," Sevro says. "Let it play. Might make Antonia open up more when we get her in a room."

Antonia closes her eyes, resting her head against the bars, knowing Thistle will ask what she meant by "use her head." And sure enough, Thistle does. "What did you mean when you said if I tell them everything, I'd have no more use?"

Antonia looks back at her through the bars. "Darling. You really haven't thought this through. I'm dead. You said it yourself. I can try to deny it, but . . . my sister makes me look like the village cat. I shot her in the spine and played acid drip with her back for almost a year. She's going to peel me like an onion."

"Darrow wouldn't let her do that."

"He's Red, we're just devils in crowns to him."

"He wouldn't *do* that."

"I know a Goblin that would."

"His name's Sevro."

"Is it?" Antonia couldn't care less. "Point's the same. I'm dead. You might have a chance. But they only need one of us alive for information. The question you have to ask yourself is if you tell them everything, will they still keep you alive? You need a strategy. Something to hold back. To barter incrementally."

Thistle approaches the bars that separate the women. "You're not fooling me." Her voice becomes brave. "But you know what, you *are* done. Darrow is going to win and maybe he should. And you know what? I'm going to help him." Thistle looks up at the camera in the corner of her cell, taking her eyes off Antonia. "I'll tell you what he's planning, Darrow. Let me make . . ."

"Get her out," Mustang says. "Get her out now."

"No . . ." Victra murmurs beside me, seeing what Mustang sees. Sevro and I look at the women in confusion, but Victra's already halfway to the door. "Open cell 31!" she shouts to the techs before disappearing through into the hall. Realizing what's happening, Sevro and I rush after her, knocking over a Green who's adjusting one of the holoscreens. Mustang follows. We break into the hallway and run to the brig security door. Victra's hammering on the door, shouting to be let in. The door buzzes and we fly in behind her, past the confused security guards who are gathering their gear, and into the cell block.

Prisoners are shouting. But even then I hear the wet *thwop, thwop, thwop* before we make it to Antonia's cell and see her hunched over Thistle. Her hands through the bars that separate their cells, drenched in blood. Fingers gripping Thistle's curly hair. The shattered remnants of the top of the Howler's skull bend around the bar as Antonia jerks Thistle's head toward her and against the bars between them one last time. Victra shoves open the magnetized cell door.

Antonia rises, grisly deed finished, bloody hands held in the air innocently as she bestows a little smirk upon her older sister. "Careful," she taunts. "Careful, Vicky. You need me. I'm the only one left with information to sell. Unless you want to stumble into the Jackal's maw you'll . . ."

Victra breaks Antonia's face. I can hear the brittle snap of bone from ten meters away. Antonia reels back, trying to escape. Victra pins her to the wall and beats her. Machinelike and eerily quiet. Elbow pumping back, driving from her legs, just as they teach us. Antonia's fingers claw at Victra's muscled arms, then go limp as the sound becomes wet and muddy. Victra doesn't stop. And I don't stop her, because I hate Antonia, and that dark little part of me wants her to feel the pain.

Sevro shoves past me and launches himself at Victra, pinning her right arm back and choking her with his left. He sweeps her legs and takes her backward to the floor, locking his legs around her waist, immobilizing her. Released from Victra's hold, Antonia flops sideways. Mustang lunges forward to keep her head from cracking on the sharp edge of the welded metal bed pallet. I kneel and reach through the bars to feel Thistle's pulse though I don't know why I bother. Her head is caved in. I stare at it. Wondering why I'm not horrified at the scene.

Some part of me has died. But when did it die? Why did I not notice?

Mustang is shouting for a Yellow. The guards picking up the call. I shake myself.

Sevro's letting go of Victra. She coughs from where he restrained her, shoving him away angrily. Mustang bends over Antonia, who's now snoring through her shattered nose. Face a ruin. Bits of teeth littering mashed lips. Except for her hair and Sigils, you can't even tell she's a Gold. Victra leaves the room without looking at her, pushing through the Gray guards so hard two of them fall down.

"Victra . . ." I call after her like there's something to say.

She turns back to me, eyes red, not with rage, but a fathomless sadness. Knuckles frayed open. "I used to braid her hair," she says forcefully. "I don't know why she's like this. Why I am." Half of one of her sister's broken teeth protrudes from the meat between her middle and ring knuckle. She pulls the tooth from her knuckles, and holds it up to the light like a child discovering sea glass on the beach before shivering in horror and letting it clatter to the steel deck. She looks past me to Sevro. "Told you."

Later that day, as the doctors tend to Antonia, the Sons go through Thistle's personal effects in her suite aboard the torchShip, the *Typhon*. Under a false bottom in a cabinet, they find the stinking, cured fur of a wolf. Sevro chokes up when Screwface brings it to him.

"Thistle cut her down," Clown says as the remaining original Howlers loiter around the room. Mustang gives them space, watching from the wall. Pebble, Screwface, and Sevro are with us. "When Antonia was crucified by the Jackal at the Institute, Thistle cut her down."

"I'd forgotten," I say from her desk.

Sevro snorts. "What a world."

"Remember when you had her fight Lea when Lea couldn't skin the sheep? Trying to make her tough," Pebble says with a little laugh. Sevro laughs too.

"Why are you laughing?" Clown asks. "You were still off eating mushrooms and howling at the moon back then."

"I was watching," Sevro says. "I was always watching."

"That's creepy, boss," Screwface says drolly. "What were you doing while you were watching?"

"Wanking in the bushes, obviously," I say.

Sevro grunts. "Only when everyone was asleep."

"Gross." Pebble wrinkles her nose and tucks the Howler cloak in her pack. "Howl on, little Thistle." The kindness in her eyes is almost too much to bear. There's no recrimination. No anger. Just the absence of a friend. Reminds me how much I love these people. Clown and Pebble leave hand in hand, Screwface taunting them all the while. I smile at the sight as Sevro and I linger behind. Mustang still hasn't moved from her place at the wall.

"What did Victra mean when she said 'told you'?" I ask.

Sevro glances at Mustang. "Ah it doesn't matter anymore." He acts like he's going to leave, but hesitates. "She called it off."

"It?" I ask.

"*Us.*"

"Oh."

"I'm sorry, Sevro," Mustang says. "She's going through a lot right now."

"Yeah." He leans against the wall. "Yeah. It's my fault, prolly. Told her . . ." He makes a face. "I told her I . . . *loved* her before the battle. Know what she said?"

"Thank you?" Mustang guesses.

He flinches. "Naw. She just said I was an idiot. Maybe she's right. Maybe I just read too much into it. Just got excited, you know." He looks at the ground, thinking. Mustang nods at me to say something.

"Sevro, you're a lot of things. You're smelly. You're small. Your tattoo taste is questionable. Your pornographic proclivities are . . . uh, eccentric. And you've got really weird toenails."

He swivels to look at me. "Weird?"

"They're really long, mate. Like . . . you should trim them."

"Nah. They're good for hanging on to things."

I squint at him, not sure if he's joking, and carry on as best I can. "I'm just saying, you're a lot of things, boyo. But you are not an idiot."

He makes no sign of having heard me. "She thinks she had poison in her veins. That's what she was talking about in the brig. Said she'd just ruin everything. So better just to cut it off."

"She's just scared," Mustang says. "Especially after what just happened."

"You mean what's happening . . ." He sits against the wall and leans his head back against it. "Startin' to feel like a prophecy. Death begets death begets death. . . ."

"We won at Jupiter . . . ," I say.

"We can win every battle and still lose the war," Sevro mutters. "The Jackal's got something up his sleeve and Octavia's only wounded. Scepter Armada is bigger than the Sword Armada, and they'll pull the fleets from Venus and Mercury. We'll be outnumbered three to one. People are gonna die. Probably most of the people we know."

Mustang smiles. "Unless we change the paradigm."

53

||||||||||||||||||||

SILENCE

After Mustang details the broad strokes of her plan to us and we finish laughing, analyzing and dissecting its flaws, she leaves us to ruminate on it and departs to rejoin the rest of the fleet with the Telemanuses. We stay behind with Victra and the Howlers to interrogate Antonia and oversee ship repair.

The beautiful Antonia is a thing of the past. The damage she suffered was superficially catastrophic. Left orbital bone pulverized. Nose flattened, crushed so brutally they had to pull it out of her nasal cavity with forceps. Mouth so swollen it makes a hissing sound as air goes between her shattered front teeth. Whiplash and severe concussion. The ship doctors thought she was in a ship crash until they found the imprint of House Jupiter's lightning crest in several places on her face.

"Marked by justice," I say. Sevro rolls his eyes. "What? I can be funny."

"Keep practicing."

When I question Antonia, her left eye is a swollen black mass. The right peers out at me in rage, but she cooperates. Perhaps now because she thinks threats against her carry a bit of merit, and that her sister is just waiting to finish the job.

According to her, the Jackal's last communiqué stated he was making preparations for our attack on Mars. He gathers his fleet around retaken Phobos and recalls Society ships from The Can and other naval depots. Similarly, there's an exodus of Gold, Silver, and Copper ships away from Mars to Luna or Venus, which have become refugee centers for disenfranchised patricians. Like London during the first French Revolution or New Zealand after the Third World War when the continents brimmed with radioactivity.

The problem with Antonia's information is that it's difficult to verify. Impossible really, with long range and intra-planetary communication essentially back to the stone age. For all we know the Jackal might have prepared contingency information for her to give us in case she was captured under duress. If she uses that information and we act on it, we could easily be falling into a trap. Thistle would have been crucial to our understanding of information. Antonia's murder of her was horrific, but tactically very efficient.

Holiday joins me on the bridge of the *Pandora* as I try to make that contact. I sit cross-legged on the forward observation post attempting to log in to Quicksilver's digital dataDrop again. It's late night shiptime. Lights dimmed. Skeleton crew of Blues manning the pit below guiding us back to the rendezvous with the main fleet. Shadowy asteroids rotate in the distance. Holiday plops down beside me.

"Fortify thyself," she says, handing me a tin coffee mug.

"That's nice of you," I say in surprise. "Can't sleep either?"

"Nah. Hate ships actually. Don't laugh."

"That's gotta be inconvenient for a Legionnaire."

"Tell me about it. Half of being a soldier is being able to sleep anywhere."

"And the other half?"

"Being able to shit anywhere, wait, and to accept stupid orders without going manic." She taps the deck. "It's the engine hum. Reminds me of wasps." She wiggles off her boots. "You mind?"

"Go on." I sip the coffee. "This is whiskey."

"You catch on quick." She winks at me boyishly.

She nods to the datapad in my hands. "Still nothin'?"

"Asteroids are bad enough, but Society is jamming everything they can."

"Well, Quicksilver gave them a run for it."

We sit quietly together. Hers isn't a naturally soothing presence, but it's the easy one of a woman raised in the agriculture backcountry where your reputation's only as good as your word and your hunting dog. We're not alike in many ways, but there's a chip on her shoulder I understand.

"Sorry about your friend," she says.

"Which one?"

"Both. You know the girl long?"

"Since school. She was a bit nasty. But loyal . . ."

"Till she wasn't," she says. I shrug in reply. "Julii is rattled."

"She talk to you?" I ask.

She laughs lightly. "Not a chance." She pops a laced burner into her mouth and lights up, I shake my head when she offers me a drag. The ship's air ducts hum. "Silence is a bitch, isn't it?" she says after a while. "But I guess you'd know that after the box."

I nod. "No one ever asks me about it," I say. "The box."

"No one asks me about Trigg."

"Do you want them to?"

"Nah."

"I never used to mind it," I say. "The silence."

"Well, you fill it with more things when you get older."

"Wasn't much to do in Lykos, 'cept sit around and watch the darkness in Lykos."

"Watch the darkness. That's so badass sounding." Smoke jets out of her nose. "We grew up near corn. Bit less dramatic. Shitloads of it far as you could see. I'd go stand in the middle of it at night sometimes and pretend it was an ocean. You can hear it whispering. It's not peaceful. Not like you'd think. It's malevolent. I always wanted to be somewhere else. Not like Trigg. He loved Goodhope. Wanted to enlist at the local precinct for policing duty or be a game warden. He'd be happy kicking it in the backwater till he was old, drinking with those idiots at Lou's, going hunting in early morning frost. I was the one who wanted out. Who wanted to *hear the ocean, see the stars*. Twenty years of service to the Legion. Cheap price."

She mocks herself, but it's curious to me that she's choosing to open up now. She found me here. At first I thought it was because she came to console me. But there's already whiskey on the squat woman's breath. She didn't want to be alone. And I'm the only one who knew Trigg even a little. I set my datapad down.

"I told him he didn't have to come with, but I knew I was draggin' him along. Told mom that I'd take care of him. Haven't even been able to tell her he's dead. Maybe she thinks we both are."

"Were you able to tell his fiancé?" I ask. "Ephraim, right?"

"You remembered."

"Of course. He was from Luna."

She watches me for a moment. "Yeah, Eph's a good one. Was with a private security firm in Imbrium City. Specialized in high-value property recovery—art, sculptures, jewels. A real pretty boy. They met at one of those themed bars when we were on leave from the Thirteenth. Venusian beach regalia. Eph didn't know about Trigg and me, that we were with the Sons and all. But I got a hold of him after we rescued you from Luna when I was out on a supply run. Used a web café. About week after I told him Trigg was gone, he sent a message saying he was going off-grid, joining the Sons on Luna. Haven't heard from him since."

"I'm sure he's all right," I say.

"Thanks. But we both know Luna's a cluster of shit right now." She shrugs. After a moment of picking the weightlifting calluses on her palms, she nudges me. "I want you to know, you're doing good. I know you didn't ask. And I'm just a grunt. But you are."

"Trigg would approve?"

"Yeah. And he'd piss his pants if he knew were we marching on—"

She's cut short as the holo above us beeps softly and one of the comBlue's calls up to me. I scramble to pick up my datapad. A single message is being broadcast across all frequencies into the belt. Our first contact with Mars since we went through the asteroid belt the first time. "Play it!" Holiday says. I do and a recording appears. It's a gray interrogation room. A man's covered in blood, shackled to a chair. The Jackal walks into frame to stand behind him.

"Is that . . ." Holiday whispers beside me.

"Yes," I say. The man is Uncle Narol.

The Jackal holds a pistol in his hand. *"Darrow. My Boneriders found this one sabotaging beacons in deep space. Really is tougher than he looks. Thought he might know your mind. But he tried to bite off his own tongue instead of talking to me. Irony for you."* He walks behind my uncle. *"I don't want a ransom. I don't want anything from you. I just want you to watch."* He lifts up the pistol. It's a slender gray slip of metal the size of my hand. The Blues in the pit gasp. Sevro rushes onto the bridge just as the Jackal points the gun at the back of my uncle's head. My uncle lifts his eyes to look into the camera.

"Sorry, Darrow. But I'll say hello to your father for—"

The Jackal pulls the trigger, and I feel another part of me slip away into the darkness as my uncle slumps in his chair. "Turn it off," I say numbly, the past flooding into me—Narol putting a frysuit helmet on my head as a boy, tussling with him at Laureltide, his sad eyes as we sat beneath the gallows after Eo's hanging, his laugh . . .

"Timestamp puts it at three weeks ago, sir," Virga, the comBlue says quietly. "We didn't receive it because of the interference."

"Did the rest of the fleet get this?" I ask quietly.

"I don't know, sir. Interference is marginal now. And it's on a pulse frequency. They've probably already seen it."

And I told Orion to keep all ships scanning in case we got lucky. It will leak.

"Oh, shit," Sevro mutters.

"What?" Holiday asks.

"We just set fire to our own fleet," I say mechanically. The fragile alliance between the highColors and low will shatter from this. My uncle was nearly as beloved as Ragnar. Narol is gone. Just like that. I feel helpless. I shudder inside. It's not real yet.

"What do we do?" Sevro asks. "Darrow?"

"Holiday, wake the Howlers," I say. "Helmsman, max thrust to rear engines. I want to be with the main fleet in four hours. Get me Mustang and Orion on the com. Telemanuses too."

Holiday snaps to attention. "Yes, sir."

Despite the interference, I reach Orion over the com and tell her to seal off all the ship bridges and to isolate control of the guns in case anyone decides to take a potshot at our Gold allies. It takes nearly thirty minutes for the Blues to connect me with Mustang. Sevro and Victra are with me now along with Daxo. The rest of his family is on their ships. The signal is weak. Interference causing static that wavers across Mustang's face. She's moving through a hall. Two Golds with her. *"Darrow, you've heard?"* she says, seeing the others behind me.

"Thirty minutes ago."

"I'm so sorry . . ."

"What's happening?"

"We received the communiqué. Some jackass tech pimped it to all the sensor chiefs," Mustang confirms. *"It's on the ship hubs throughout the fleet. Darrow . . . there's already movement against highColors on several of our ships. Three Golds on* Persephone *were killed fifteen minutes ago by Reds. And one of my lieutenants opened up on two Obsidian who tried to take her. They're dead."*

"Shit's hitting the fan," Sevro says.

"I'm evac-ing all my personnel back to our ships." There's gunshots in the background behind Mustang.

"Where are you?" I ask.

"On the Morning Star.*"*

"What the hell are you doing there? You have to get off."

"I still have men on here. There's seven Golds in the engine deck for logistical support. I'm not leaving them behind."

"Then I'm sending my father's guard," Daxo growls from his family's torchShips. *"They'll get you out."*

"That's stupid," Sevro says.

"No," Mustang snaps. *"You send Gold knights in here, and this turns into a bloodbath we don't recover from. Darrow, you have to get back here. That's the only thing that might stop this."*

"We're still hours out."

"*Well, do your best. There's one more thing . . . they've stormed the prison. I think they're going to execute Cassius.*"

Sevro and I exchange a look. "You need to find Sefi and stay with her," I say. "We'll be there soon."

"*Find Sefi? Darrow . . . she's leading them.*"

54

||||||||||||||||||||||||

THE GOBLIN AND
THE GOLD

My assault shuttle lands on the auxiliary deck of the *Morning Star* where Mustang was supposed to meet us. She's not there. Neither are the Golds she was rescuing. A coterie of Sons of Ares waits for us instead, led by Theodora. She carries no weapon and looks out of place surrounded by the armored men, but they defer to her. She tells me what's happened. My uncle's death sparked several small fights that escalated into shootings on both sides. Now several ships roil with conflict.

"Mustang has been taken by Sefi's men, along with Cassius and the rest of the highColor prisoners, Darrow," Theodora announces, assessing the rest of my lieutenants.

"Gorydamn savages," Victra mutters. "If they kill her this is done."

"They won't kill her," I say. "Sefi knows Mustang's on her side."

"Why would she do this?" Holiday asks.

"Justice," Victra says, drawing a look from Sevro.

"No," I say. "No I think it's something else altogether."

"Gorydamn marvelous." Victra nods back to space. "Looks like the Telemanuses are intent on slagging this all up." Another shuttle taxis into the hangar behind us. We gather as it lands. Storming down

the ramp before it even sets down, jumping to deck is the whole Telemanus clan. Daxo, Kavax, Thraxa, two other sisters I haven't met
land heavily behind them. Armed to the teeth, though Kavax's arm is
still in a sling. Behind them come thirty more of their House Golds.
It's a bloodydamn army.

"They're going to get us all killed," Holiday says. At my side, Sevro
blinks up at the disembarking war party.

"Death begets death begets death . . . ," he murmurs.

"Kavax, what the hell are you doing?" I ask as his family crosses
the hangar.

"Virginia needs our help," he booms, not breaking his pace until I
cut him off, blocking his way deeper into the ship. For a moment I
think he'll go through me. "We will not leave her to the mercy of savages."

"I told you to stay on your ship."

"Unfortunately we take orders from Virginia, not you," Daxo says.
"We know the ramifications of being here. But we will do what we
must to protect our family."

"Mustang even told you not to storm in here with knights."

"The situation has changed," Kavax rumbles.

"You want this to turn into a war? You want our fleet to shatter?
The fastest way you do that is marching in there with a show of Gold
force."

"We will not let her die," Kavax says.

"And what if they kill her because of you?" I ask. That's the only
thing that gives him pause. "What if they cut her throat when you
storm in there?" I step close so he can see the fear on my face too and
I can speak just loud enough for Daxo to hear as well. "Listen to me,
Kavax, the problem with that is that you leave the Obsidian only one
choice. Fight back. And you know they can. Let me handle this and
we'll get her back. Don't and we'll be standing over her casket tomorrow."

Kavax looks back to his lean son, always the moderating influence,
to see what he thinks. And to my relief Daxo nods. "Very well," Kavax
says. "But I will go with you, Reaper. Children, await my summons. If
I fall, come with all fury."

"Yes, father," they say.

Breathing a sigh of relief, I turn back to my men. "Where's Sevro?"

Sevro snuck away while we argued, to what purpose I don't know. We rush after him through the corridors, Victra behind us. Holiday leads, taking information from other Sons of Ares in through the optic implant in her eye. Her men have spotted the mob in the main hangar. They're holding a trial for Cassius for the murder of several dozen Sons of Ares, and, of course, Ares himself. No sign of Mustang. Where is she? She was supposed to stay out of sight. Meet us if she could. Did they catch her? Worse? When we reach the corridor that leads to the hangar, there's such a press of people we can barely get through, shoving Reds and Obsidians out of the way as I pass.

They're all shouting and pushing. Over their heads, near the center of the hangar, I see several dozen Obsidian and Reds astride the twenty-meter-high walkway that spans part of the hangar, high over the crowd. Sefi's at their center. Seven Golds hang dead from the walkway, suspended by rubber cable ligature, feet dangling five meters above the crowd, scalps hewn off. Aureate spines are tougher than average humans. Each of these men and women would have died horribly over several minutes from cerebral anorexia, watching the crowd beneath them curse and spit at them and hurl lugnuts and wrenches and bottles. Blood clots in a long ribbon cover their chins to their chests. Tongues removed by Sefi the Quiet. Cassius and several other prisoners await their own executions upon the walkway, kneeling beside their captors, bloody and beaten. Mustang is not with them, thank Jove. They've stripped Cassius to the waist and carved a bloody SlingBlade across his broad chest.

"Sefi!" I shout, but I can't be heard. Can't see Sevro anywhere. There's more than twenty-five thousand in a space meant for ten. Many are armed. Some wounded from the battle the week prior. All pressing into the hangar to watch the execution. The Obsidian stand titanic amidst the masses, like great boulders amidst a sea of lowColors. I never should have condensed most of the wounded and rescued crews into this hotbed of grief. The crowd has realized I'm here now and they part for me and begin to chant my name as if they think I've come to see justice done. The barbarity of it chills me. One of the men holding Cassius down is a Green tech who gave me coffee on Phobos. Most of the others I don't recognize.

One by one those Sons nearby recognize my presence. The quiet spreads around me.

"Sefi!" I snarl. "Sefi." At last she hears me. "What are you doing?"

"What you will not," she calls down in her own language, not in wrath, but acceptance that she performs an unsavory but necessary deed. Like a spirit of vengeance has drifted up from Hel. Her white hair hangs long behind her. Her knife is bloody from the tongues it has claimed. And to think I vouched for her. Let her name this ship. But just because a lion lets you pet it doesn't mean it's tame. Kavax is horrified by the scene. He's almost ready to call to his children, and would if Victra did not grip his arm and talk him down. There's fear in her eyes, too. Not just at the sight above, but at what could happen to her here. I shouldn't have brought the Golds with me.

There's moments in life where you're walking ahead so intent on your task that you forget to look down until you feel knee-deep in quicksand. I'm right there now. Surrounded by an unpredictable mob, looking up at a woman with the blood of Alia Snowsparrow running through her veins. My only defense a small circle of Sons of Ares and Golds. Holiday's pulling a scorcher. Victra's razor moves beneath her sleeve. I was too brash in storming in here. All this could go so wrong so quickly.

"Where is Mustang?" I call up to Sefi. "Did you kill her?"

"Kill her? No. The daughter of the Lion brought us from the Ice. But she stood in the way of justice, so she is in chains." Then she's safe.

"That's what this is?" I call up. "Justice? Is that what was given to Ragnar's friends who your mother hanged from the chains of the Spires?"

"This is the code of the Ice."

"You're not on the Ice, Sefi. You're on *my* ship."

"Is it yours?" This doesn't sit well with the lowColors among the crowd. "We paid for it in our blood."

"As did we all," I say. "What about the Ice was good? You left that place because you knew it was wrong. You knew your ways were shaped by your masters. You said you'd follow me. Are you a liar now?"

"Are you? You promised my people they would be safe," Sefi bellows down to me, pointing her axe, the weight of loss heavy upon her. "I have seen the works of these people. I have seen the war they make. The ships they sail. Words will not suffice. These Golds speak one language. And that is the language of blood. And so long as they live. So long as they speak, my people will not be safe. The power they have is too great."

"Do you think this is what Ragnar wanted?"

"Yes."

"Ragnar wanted you to be better than them. Than this. To be an example. But maybe the Golds are right. Maybe you are just killers. Savage dogs. Like they made you to be."

"We will never be anything more until they are gone," she says down to me, voice echoing around the hangar. "Why defend them?" She drags Cassius toward her. "Why weep over one who helped kill my brother?"

"Why do you think Ragnar gripped your hand instead of the sword when he died? He didn't want you to make your life about vengeance. It's a hollow end. He wanted more for you. He wanted a future."

"I have seen the heavens, I have seen the hells, and I know now that our future is war," Sefi says. "War until they fade in the night." She drags Cassius toward her and lifts her knife to carve out his tongue But before she does, a pulseFist fires and knocks the weapon from her hands and Ares, lord of this rebellion, slams down on the walkway wearing his spiked helmet of war. The Obsidians recoil from him as he straightens, dusts off his shoulders and lets the helmet slither back into his armor.

"What is he doing?" Victra asks me.

"You dumb shits," Sevro sneers. "You're touching my property." He stalks across the bridge toward Sefi. "Tsst. Get away." Several Valkyrie bar his way. He stands nose to chest with them. "Move, you albino sack of pubic hair."

The Obsidian moves only when Sefi tells her to. Sevro walks past the bound Golds tapping their heads playfully as he goes. "That one's mine," he says, pointing at Cassius. "Get your hands off him, lady." She doesn't move her knife. "He cut my father's head off and put it in a box. And unless you want me to do the same to you, you'll do me the courtesy of letting go my property."

Sefi backs away but does not sheath her knife. "It is your blood debt. His life belongs to you."

"Obviously." He shoos her away. "Stand up, you little Pixie," he barks at Cassius, kicking him with his boot and hauling him up by the cable around his neck. "Have some dignity. Stand up." Cassius rises to his feet, awkwardly. Hands behind his back. Face swollen from the beatings. The slingBlade livid on his chest. "Did you kill my father?" Sevro flicks him on his broad chest. "Did you kill my father?"

Cassius looks down at him. No measure of humor to the man, just pride, not the vain sort I've seen in him over the years. War and life have drained that vigorous spirit from him. This is the face, the bearing of a man who wants nothing more than to die with a little dignity. "Yes," he says loudly. "I did."

"Glad we cleared that up. He's a murderer," Sevro shouts to the crowd. "And what do we do to murderers?"

The crowd roars for Cassius's life. And Sevro, after making a show of cupping his ear, gives it to them. He shoves Cassius off the edge of the walkway. The Gold plummets till the cable around his neck snaps taut, arresting his fall. He gags. Feet kick. Face reddens. The crowd roars hungrily, chanting Ares's name.

Mobs are soulless things that feed on fear and momentum and prejudice. They do not know the spirit in Cassius, the nobility of a man who would have given his life for his family, but was cursed to live while they all died. They see a monster. A seven-foot-tall former god now mostly naked, humbled, strangling on his own hubris.

I see a man trying his best in a world that doesn't give a shit. It breaks my heart.

Yet I do not move, because I know I'm not witnessing the death of a friend as much as I'm seeing the rebirth of another. My company does not understand. Horror stains Kavax's face. Victra's too—even though she held little pity for Cassius all this time, I think she mourns the savagery she sees in Sevro. It's an ugly thing for any man to bear. Holiday pulls her weapon, eying the Reds nearby who point to Kavax. But they're missing the show.

I watch in awe of Sevro as he bounds up onto the railing, arms wide, embracing his army. Beneath, Cassius dangles and dies and the crowd beneath makes a game of seeing who can launch themselves high enough to pull his feet. None succeed.

"My name is Sevro au Barca," my friend cries out. "I am Ares!" He thumps his chest. "I have killed forty-four Golds. Fifteen Obsidian. One hundred and thirteen Grays with my razor." The crowd roars in approval, even the Obsidians. "Jove knows who else with ships, rail-guns, and pulseFists. With nukes, knives, sharp sticks . . ." He trails off dramatically.

They slam their feet.

He beats his chest again. "I am Ares! I am a murderer too!" He puts his hands on his hips. "And what do we do to murderers?"

This time no one answers.

He never expected them to. He grabs the cable from the neck of one of the kneeling Golds, wraps it around his own neck, and looking to Sefi with a demented little smile, winks and backflips off the railing.

The crowd screams, but Victra's stunned gasp is the loudest. Sevro's rope snaps taut. He kicks, choking beside Cassius. Feet scrambling. Silent and horrible. Face turning red, on its way to purple like Cassius's. They swing together, the Goblin and the Gold, suspended above the swirling crowd that's now stampeding trying to get up the ladder to the walkway to cut Sevro down, but in their madness they overload the ladder and it bends away from the wall. Victra's about to launch herself into the air on her gravBoots to save him. I hold her down. "Wait."

"He's dying!" she says frantically.

"That's the point."

It is not a boy who dangles on that line. It is not a brokenhearted orphan who needs me to pick him up. It's a man who has been through hell and now believes in the dream of his father, in the dream of my wife. It's a man I would die to protect even as he dies to save the soul of this rebellion.

Kavax is transfixed, watching Sefi who stares down at the curious scene. Her Obsidian are just as confused. They glance to her, searching for leadership. Ragnar believed in his sister. In her capacity to be better than the world that was given them, one in which there is no such thing as mercy, no such thing as forgiveness. Silently, she hefts her axe and swings it into Sevro's cable and then, reluctantly, Cassius's. Somewhere, Ragnar is smiling.

Both men tumble through the air to be caught by the swirling crowd beneath.

Kavax has not moved since Sevro jumped, watching Sefi with a profound look of confusion. Still with his hand on the com to call his children, but I lose him in the crowd. The Sons of Ares and Howlers have formed a tight circle around their leader, shoving others back. Sevro hacks for breath on all fours. I rush to him and kneel as Holiday helps Cassius, who wheezes on the ground to my left. Pebble drapes her Howler cloak over his body.

"Can you talk?" I ask Sevro. He nods, lips trembling from the pain, but his eyes are all fire. I give my arm and help him stand. I hold up a fist, demanding silence. Sons shout the others down till the twenty-five thousand breaths balance on the beating heart of my little friend. He looks out at them, startled by the love he sees, the reverence, the wet eyes.

"Darrow's wife . . ." Sevro croaks, larynx damaged. "His wife," he says more deeply. "And my father never met. But they shared a dream. One of a free world. Not built on corpses, but on hope. On the love that binds us, not the hate that divides. We have lost many. But we are not broken. We are not defeated. We fight on. But we do not fight for revenge for those who have died. We fight for each other. We fight for those who live. We fight for those who don't yet live.

"Cassius au Bellona killed my father. . . ." He stands over the man, swallowing before looking back up. "But I forgive him. Why? Because he was protecting the world he knew, because he was afraid."

Victra pushes her way to the front of the circle, watching Sevro who speaks now as if it was meant for her and her alone. "We are the new age. The new world. And if we're to show the way, then we better damn well make it a better one. I am Sevro au Barca. And I am no longer afraid."

55

||||||||||||||||||||||||||

THE IGNOBLE
HOUSE BARCA

"You're bloodydamn manic," I tell Sevro when we're alone in Virany's infirmary. Sevro's holding his neck laughing at himself. I kiss the top of his head. "Bloodydamn insane, you know that?"

"Yeah well I stole that one from your playbook; what does that say about you?"

"That he's insane as well," Mickey says from the corner. He's smoking his laced-burners. Purple smoke slithering from nostrils.

Sevro winces. "That slagging hurt. I can't even look sideways."

"You sprained your neck, damaged the cartilage, lacerations in your larynx," Dr. Virany says from behind her biometric scanner. She's a lithe, tan woman with that special small silence inside her reserved for people who have seen both sides of hardship.

"Just as I said when you came in. All these tools you use, Virany. Really where's the art in it?"

Virany rolls her eyes. "Another ten kilos on your body and you would have broken your neck, Sevro. Count yourself lucky."

"Good thing I took a shit before," he grumbles.

"Darrow's neck would have held up under the strain of fifty more kilos," Mickey brags idly. "The tensile rating of his cervical—"

"Really?" Virany says tiredly. "Can't you brag later Mickey?"

"Merely observing my own mastery," Mickey replies, giving me a little wink. He enjoys pushing the gentle Virany's buttons. Since he's employed her help in his project they've been spending most waking moments in his laboratory, much to Virany's chagrin.

"Ow!" Sevro yelps as she prods the back of his spine. "That's my body."

"Sorry."

"Pixie," I say.

"I almost broke my neck," Sevro complains.

"Been there, done that. At least you didn't have to get whipped."

"I'd rather have been whipped," he mutters, wincing as he tries to turn his neck. "Be better than this."

"Not being whipped by Pax," I reply.

"I saw the video, he wasn't swinging that hard."

"Have you ever been whipped? Did you see my back?"

"You see my bloodydamn eye at the Institute? Jackal had it plucked out with a knife, didn't see me whining."

"I had my whole bloodydamn body carved open," I say as the doors hiss open and Mustang enters. "Twice."

"Oh, it always comes back to the slagging Carving," Sevro mutters, wiggling his fingers in the air. "I'm so bloodydamn special, I had my bones peeled. My DNA spliced."

"Do they always do this?" Virany asks Mustang.

"Seems like," Mustang says. "Any chance I could bribe you to suture their mouths shut till they learn not to swear so much?"

Mickey perks up. "Well, it's interesting you ask . . ."

Sevro interrupts him. "How's the Gold holding up?" he asks Mustang. "You know?"

"Happy he still has a tongue," Mustang says. "They're suturing his chest in the infirmary. He has some internal bleeding from blunt trauma, but he'll live."

"You finally went to see him?" I ask.

"I did." She nods thoughtfully to herself. "He was . . . emotional. He wanted me to thank you, Sevro. He says he knows he didn't deserve it."

"Damn right he didn't," Sevro mutters.

"Sefi says the Obsidian will leave him be," I say.

"The Obsidian?" Mustang asks, my statement pulling her from her thoughts. "All of them."

I laugh suddenly. "I didn't even think about that."

"What's that?" Sevro asks.

"She spoke for the Obsidian now, not just the Valkyrie. Wasn't a slip of the tongue. Pan-tribalism wasn't in place before the riot," I say. "Must have used it to unite the other warchiefs under her direction."

"So . . . she pulled a coup?" Sevro asks.

I laugh. "Seems like."

"We'll see if it holds. Still . . . impressive," Mustang says. "They always told us never to let a good crisis go to waste."

Mickey shivers. "Obsidians playing politics . . ."

"So all that out there . . . was that strategy or was real?" Mustang asks Sevro.

"Dunno." Sevro shrugs. "I mean, gotta stop the cycle somewhere. Sucks, but dad's gone. No sense burning down the world to try and bring him back. You know? Cassius didn't kill dad because he hated him. They were both soldiers doing what soldiers do."

Mustang shakes her head, at a loss for words. So she sets a hand on his shoulder, and he knows how impressed she is. The compliment of silence is as deep a one as she can give, and Sevro favors her with a rare un-ironic smile. One that disappears when the door opens and Victra comes in. She's red-eyed and agitated.

"I need to talk to you," she says to Sevro.

"Get out," Sevro says when we don't move. "Everyone."

We wait outside the door as Victra and Sevro speak inside. "How long do you think it will take to make the voyage?" Mustang asks.

"Forty-nine days," I say, pulling Mickey back from the door where he cups his ear in an attempt to hear the happenings inside. "Key is keeping the Blues quiet."

"Forty-nine days is a long time for my brother to make plans."

Beyond our hull the worlds continue to turn. Reds are hunted. And though we've woken the spirit of the lowColors, and given this rebellion another victory, every day we spend crossing the distance to Core is another day that the Jackal can hunt our friends and the Sovereign can squelch the rebellions that plague her. My uncle's already gone. How many more will die before I return?

"This won't heal everything," Mustang says. "The Obsidians still killed seven prisoners. My people are wary of this war. The consequences. Particularly if Sefi now has united the tribes. That makes her dangerous."

"And more useful," I say.

"Until she disagrees with you again. This could go wrong at any moment."

She straightens as Mickey skitters back and the door to the infirmary opens. Sevro and Victra come out, both wearing smiles. "What are you two grinning about?" I ask.

"Just this." Sevro thrusts out a House Jupiter Institute ring. It's loose on his finger. I squint at it, not understanding right away. His own ring is missing and then I see it awkwardly jammed onto Victra's pinky. "She proposed," he says with delight.

"What?" I sputter.

Mustang's eyebrows shoot up. "Proposed . . . as in . . ."

"Yeah, boyo!" Sevro beams. "We're gettin' hitched."

Sevro and Victra marry seven nights later in a small ceremony in the auxiliary hangar of the *Morning Star*. When Victra asked me to give her away after they broke the news to us, I couldn't speak. I hugged her then as I hug her now before taking her arm and walking her through the small line of scrubbed and washed Howlers and towering Telemanuses. It's the cleanest I've ever seen Sevro, his unruly Mohawk combed to the side as he stands before Mickey. It is custom to have a

White give the benediction. But Victra laughed at the idea of tradition and asked Mickey.

The Violet's face glows now. Too much makeup on the day, but he's a ray of light all the same. From Carver to slaver to slave to wedding officiant, he's not had an easy road, but he's lovelier for it. He was delighted when Clown and Screwface asked him to join us for Sevro's bachelor night, and he howled along with us as we kidnapped Sevro from his room the night before and dragged him to the mess hall where the Howlers gathered to drink.

The animosity stemming from the riot has not abated entirely, but the wedding brings a sense of nostalgic normalcy. Surrounded by the insanity of war, it's a special hope given knowing life can go on. Though some Sons gripe about the marriage of the Red leader to a Gold, Victra's done enough to merit respect from the leaders within the Sons. And the bravery she showed in storming the *Morning Star* with Sefi and me around Ilium has bought her their respect. She shed blood for them, with them, so my fleet is quiet, at peace. At least for tonight.

I've never seen Sevro so happy. Nor so nervous as he was the hour before the ceremony when he combed his hair in my washroom. Not that you can do much with a Mohawk. "Is this insane? It seemed like a good idea yesterday," he asked, staring at himself in the mirror.

"And it's a good idea today too," I told him.

"You're not just saying that. Tell me the truth, man. I feel sick."

"Before I married Eo, I threw up."

"Bullshit."

"Got it all over my uncle's boots." A twinge of pain as I remember he's gone. "Wasn't that I was afraid of making the wrong decision. I was afraid she was. Afraid of not living up to her expectations . . . But my uncle told me that it's women who see us better than we see ourselves. That's why you love Victra. That's why you fight with her. And that's you why you deserve this."

Sevro squinted at me in the mirror. "Yeah, but your uncle was crazy. Everyone knows that."

"Even company then. We're all a little manic. Especially Victra. I mean she'd have to be to marry you?"

He grinned. "Bloodydamn right." And I rumpled his hair, hoping beyond all hope that they can have this little moment of happiness and maybe more after that. It's the best any of us can hope for, really. "Wish Pops was here, though."

"I think he's laughing his ass off somewhere that you have to stand on your tiptoes to kiss your bride," I said.

"Always was a prick."

Now Sevro shifts from foot to foot as I hand Victra over to him and he looks up into her eyes. I'm not even there. None of us are, not to them. The gentleness I see from the raging woman now is all it takes to know how much she loves him. It's not something she'd ever talk about. It's not her way. But the sharp edge she has for everything and everyone is dull tonight. Like she sees Sevro as a refuge, a place where she can be safe.

I rejoin Mustang as Mickey begins his flowery speech. It's not half so grandiloquent as I might have expected. The way Mustang nods along to the words, I know she must have helped him edit it down. Reading my mind, she leans over. "You should have heard the first draft. It was a spectacle." She sniffs me. "Are you drunk?" She looks back at the flushed Howlers and teetering Telemanuses. "Are they all drunk?"

"Shhh," I say and hand her a flask. "You're too sober."

Mickey is finishing the ceremony. ". . . a compact that can be broken only by death. I pronounce you Sevro and Victra Barca."

"Julii," Sevro corrects quickly. "Hers is the elder house."

Victra shakes her head down at him. "He said it right."

"But you're a Julii," he replies, confused.

"Yesterday I was. Today I'd rather be a Barca. Presuming you don't have problem with that and I don't have to become proportionally diminutive."

"It'd be lovely," Sevro says, cheeks glowing as Mickey continues and Sevro and Victra turn to face their friends. "Then I present you to your fellows and the worlds as Sevro and Victra of the Martian House Barca."

||||||||||||

The ceremony may have been small, but the celebration is anything but. Fleet-spanning, even. If my people know one thing it is how to survive hardship with celebration. Life's not just a matter of breathing, it's a matter of being. Word of Sevro's speech and his hanging spread through the ships, stitching the wounds back together.

But this day is the one that matters. The one that reaffirms the joy of life throughout my fleet. Dances are held on the smallest corvettes, on the destroyers and torchShips and the *Morning Star*. Flights of ripWings buzz bridges in celebratory formation. Swill and Society liquors flow among the milling crowds, which gather in hangars to sing and dance around weapons of war. Even Kavax, so stubborn in his fear of chaos and his prejudice against the Obsidians, dances with Mustang. Drunkenly hugging Sevro and Victra and clumsily attempting to forget the ballroom dreck of Gold dances and learn those of my people from a full-figured Red with a laughing face and a mechanic's grease under her nails. With them is Cyther, the awkward Orange who so impressed me a year a half ago in the garages of the *Pax*. He only just finished Mustang's special project this morning. Now he's drunk and turning his ungainly body around on the dance floor as Kavax roars approval.

Daxo shakes his head at his father's antics while sitting in reserve on the side, as always. I share a drink with him. "It's wine," I say.

"Thank Jove." He replies, delicately taking the glass. "Your people keep trying to give me some kind of engine solvent." He scans his datapad warily.

"I've got Holiday on security," I say. "This isn't a Gold party."

He laughs. "Thank Jove for that then as well." Finally he takes a sip from his wine. "Venusian Atolls," he says. "Very nice."

"Roque had good taste. Your father is a sight," I say, nodding to the dance floor where the big man sways along with two Reds.

"He's not the only one," Daxo replies shrewdly, following my eyes to Mustang who's now being spun about by Sevro. The woman's face is aglow with life, or maybe it's the alcohol. Hair sweaty and plastered on her forehead. "She loves you, you know," Daxo says. "She's just afraid of losing you, so she holds you far away." He smiles to himself. "Funny how we are, isn't it?"

"Daxo why aren't you dancing?" Victra says, striding up to him. "So proper all the time. Up! Up!" She hauls him up and pushes him onto the dance floor then collapses into his chair. "My feet. Raided Antonia's closet. Forgot she's got pigeon feet."

I laugh and Clown stumbles up to us, heavily drunk.

"Victra, Darrow. A question. Do you think Pebble is interested in that man?" he asks me, leaning against one of the tables as he chugs down another glass of wine. His teeth are already purple.

"The tall one?" Victra asks. Pebble's dancing with a Gray captain. "She seems to fancy him."

"He's terribly handsome," Clown says. "Good teeth too."

"I suppose you could always cut in," I say.

"Well, I wouldn't want to seem desperate."

"Jove forbid," Victra says.

"I think I'll cut in."

"I think it's a good idea," she says. "But you should bow first. To be polite."

"Oh. Then it's settled. I'll go right now." He pours another glass of wine. "After another drink."

I take the wine from him and push him on his way. Holiday appears in the doorframe to watch Clown's awkward interruption. He's bowing to Pebble and sweeping back his hand dramatically. "Oh, hell. He actually did it." Victra snorts champagne through her nose. "You should do the same with Mustang. Think she's trying to steal my husband away. *Husband*. That's a weird word."

"It's a weird world."

"Isn't it, though. *Wife*. Who'd have thought?"

I look her up and down. "On you, it seems to fit." I put my arm around her. "It seems to fit perfectly." She smiles radiantly.

"Sir," Holiday says, coming up to us.

"Holiday, come to have a drink?" I glance over at her, smile dying when I see the expression that marks her face. Something has happened. "What is it?"

She motions me away from Victra.

"It's the Jackal," she says quietly so as not to spoil the mood. "He's on the com for you. Direct link."

"What's the delay?" I ask.

"Six seconds."

On the dance floor, Sevro's spinning with Mustang clumsily, laughing because neither knows the dance the Reds around them perform. Her hair is dark from sweat on her temples, her eyes alight with the joy of the moment. None of them feel the sudden dread in me, in the world beyond. I don't want them to. Not tonight.

56

|||||||||||||||||||||||

IN TIME

He sits in a simple chair in the center of my circular training room wearing a coat of white with a gold lion to either side of his high collar. The stars above his glowing hologram are cold stains of light through the duroglass dome. This room was built to train for war and so it is here that I will grant my enemy an audience. I will not let him pervert this ship where Roque lived and where my friends celebrate by seeing or being anyplace else.

Even though he's millions of kilometers away, I can nearly smell the pencil-shaving scent of him. Hear the vast silence with which he fills rooms as I stand before his digital image. It's so lifelike if it did not glow I would think him here. The background behind him is blurred. He watches me enter the room. No smile on his face. No false pleasantness, but I can tell he's amused. His silver stylus spins in his one hand. The only sign of his agitation.

"Hello, Reaper. How are the festivities?" I try not to let my discomfort show. Of course he knows of the wedding. He has spies in our fleet. How close they are to me, I cannot tell. But I don't let the thought spread malignantly through me. If he could reach out and hurt us here, he already would have.

"What do you want?" I ask.

"You called me last time. I thought I should return the favor, particularly considering the message I sent of your uncle. Did you receive it?" I say nothing. "After all, when you arrive at Mars the cannons will speak for us. We may never see each other again. Strange, isn't that? Did you see Roque before he died?"

"I did."

"And did he weep for your forgiveness?"

"No."

The Jackal frowns. "I thought he would. It's easy to fool a romantic. To think he was right there when I took his girl. You went running by in the hall screaming Tactus's name, and he looked up in confusion. I pushed a sliver of Quinn's skull deeper into her brain with my scalpel. I thought about letting her live with brain damage. But the thought of her drooling everywhere made me sick. You think he still would have loved her if she drooled?"

There's a sound at the door, out of the camera's capture range. Mustang's followed me from the wedding. Taking in the scene, she watches quietly. I should turn off the holo. Leave this creature to himself, but I can't seem to part with him. The same curiosity that brought me here now anchors me to this spot.

"Roque wasn't perfect, but he cared about Gold. He cared about humanity. He had something he would die for. And that makes him a better man than most," I say.

"It's easy to forgive the dead," the Jackal replies. "I'd know." A tiny spasm of humanity moves across his lips. He may never say it, but the very tone of his voice tells me he is not without regret. I know he wanted his father's approval. But could it actually be that he misses the man? That he's forgiven his father in death and now mourns him?

He pulls a short gold baton up from his lap. With the press of a button, the baton extends to a scepter. One with the skull of a jackal overtop the pyramid of the Society. I had it commissioned for him more than a year ago. "I've not parted with your gift," he says. He traces the head of the jackal. "All my life I've been given lions. Nothing of my own. What does it say about me that my greatest enemy knows me better than any friend?"

"You the scepter, I the sword," I say, ignoring his question. "That was the plan." I gave it to him because I wanted him to feel loved. To feel like I was his friend. And I would have been, then. I would have helped him change like Mustang did. Like Cassius might. "Is it what you thought it would be?" I ask.

"What?"

"Your father's seat."

He frowns, considering which tack to take. "No," he says eventually. "No it is not what I expected."

"You want to be hated. Don't you?" I ask. "That's why you killed my uncle when you didn't need to. It gives you purpose. That's why you called me. To feel important. But I don't hate you."

"Liar."

"I don't."

"I killed Pax and your uncle and Lorn . . ."

"I pity you."

He recoils. "Pity?"

"ArchGovernor of all Mars, one of the most powerful men in all the worlds. With the might to do anything you like. And it's not enough. Nothing has ever been enough for you, nor will it be. Adrius, you're not trying to prove yourself to your father, to me, to Virginia, to the Sovereign. You're trying to matter to yourself. Because you're broken inside. Because you hate what you are. You wish you were born like Claudius. Like Virginia. You wish you were like me."

"Like you?" he asks with a sneer. "A filthy Red?"

"I'm no Red." I show him my hands, bare of Sigils. It disgusts him.

"Not even evolved enough to have a Color, Darrow? Just a *homo sapiens* playing in the realm of gods."

"Gods?" I shake my head. "You're no god. You're not even a Gold. You're just a man who thinks a title will make him great. Just a man who wants to be more than he actually is. But all you really want is love. Isn't that right?"

He snorts in derision. "Love is for the weak. The only thing you and I have in common is our hunger. You think that I cannot be satisfied. That I always yearn for more. But look in the mirror and you'll see the same man staring back at you. Tell your little Red friends what you like. But I know you lost yourself among us. You yearned to be Gold. I saw it in your eyes at the Institute. I saw that fever on Luna when I proposed that we should rule. I saw it when you rode that triumphal chariot up to the steps of the citadel. It's that hunger that makes us forever alone."

And there he strikes the core of me. That abyssal fear that the darkness made my reality. The fear of being alone. Of never finding love again. But then Mustang steps out to join me. "You're wrong, brother," she says.

The Jackal leans back at the sight of his sister.

"Darrow had a wife. A family he loved. He had just a little bit and he was happy. You had everything, and you were miserable. And you always will be because you covet." His foundation of calm begins to crumble. "That's why you killed Father and Quinn. Why you killed Pax. But this isn't a game, brother. This isn't one of your mazes. . . ."

"Do not call me brother, whore. You are no sister of mine. Opening your legs for a mongrel. For a beast of burden. Are the Obsidians next? I bet they are all queued up already. You are a disgrace to your Color and to our House."

I move angrily toward his holo, but Mustang puts a hand in the center of my chest and turns back to her brother. "You think you never had love, *brother*. But mother loved you."

"If she loved me why didn't she stay?" he asks sharply. "Why did she leave?"

"I don't know," Mustang says. "But I loved you too, and you threw that away. You were my twin. We were bound for life." There are tears in her eyes. "I defended you for years. Then I find out that it was you who had Claudius killed." She blinks through the tears, shaking her head as she finds her resolve. "I cannot forgive that. I cannot. You had love and you lost it, brother. That is your curse."

I step forward till I'm even with Mustang. "Adrius, we are coming for you. We will break your ships. We will storm Mars. We will burrow through the walls of your bunker. We will find you and we will bring you to justice. And when you hang from the gallows. When the door beneath you opens, when your feet do the Devil's Dance, then you will realize in that moment that this has all been for nothing, because there will be no one left to pull your feet."

The pale light of the holo vanishes as we close the connection, leaving us to the glass ceiling and stars beyond. "Are you all right?" I ask Mustang. She nods, wiping her eyes.

"Didn't expect to start crying like that. Sorry."

"To be fair, I think I cry more. But, forgiven."

She tries a smile. "Do you actually think we can do this, Darrow?"

Her eyes are red, the mascara she wore for the wedding stained by the tears. Her running nose is a ruddy pink, but I've never seen beauty as deep as hers is now. All the rawness of life flows through her. All the cracks and fears that make her who she is worn in her eyes. So imperfect and rough that I want to hold her and love her as long as I can. And for once, she lets me.

"We have to. You and I have a whole life ahead of us," I say, pulling her into me. It seems impossible a woman like this could ever want to be held by me, but she puts her head on my chest as I wrap my arms around her and I remember how perfectly we fit together as we hold each other and the stars and minutes pass distantly.

"We should return to the party," she eventually says to me.

"Why? I have everything I need right here." I look down at the crown of her golden head and see the darkness of her roots. I breathe in the full scent of her. If it ends tomorrow or in eighty years, I could breathe her the rest of my life. But I want more. I need more. I tilt her slender jaw up with my hand so that she's looking at me. I was going to say something important. Something memorable. But I've forgotten it in her eyes. That gulf that divided us is still there, filled with questions and recrimination and guilt, but that's only part of love, part of being human. Everything is cracked, everything is stained except the fragile moments that hang crystalline in time and make life worth living.

57

|||||||||||||||||||||||

LUNA

The Rubicon Beacons are a sphere of transponders, each as large as two Obsidian, floating in space one million kilometers beyond Earth's core, encircling the innermost domain of the Sovereign. For five hundred years, no foreign fleet has passed beyond their borders. Now, two months and three weeks after news of the destruction of the invincible Sword Armada reaches the Core, eight weeks after I proclaimed that we sailed on Mars, seventeen days after the Sovereign's declaration of martial law in all Society cities, the Red Armada approaches Luna, sailing past the Rubicon Beacons without firing a shot.

Telemanus torchShips race ahead at the vanguard to clear mines and scan for any traps left by Society forces. They're followed by Orion's Obsidian-filled heavy destroyers, painted with the all-seeing eyes of the ice spirits, then by the Julii fleet with Victra's weeping sun adorning the heavy dreadnought, the *Pandora*, the forces of the Reformers—the daughters-in-law of Lorn au Arcos come for justice and the gold and black ships bearing the lion of Augustus led by the battle-scarred *Dejah Thoris*. And finally my own vessels led by the greatest ship ever built and stolen, the indomitable white *Morning Star* painted with a seven-kilometer-long red scythe on her port and starboard sides. The holes we carved in her with our clawDrills are not mended all through the ship. But the armor has been replaced along the outer hull. The *Pax* died to give her to us. And what a prize she is. We ran out of paint on the bottom scythe, so it's a sloppy crescent moon, the symbol of House Lune. The men think it's a good omen. An accidental promise to Octavia au Lune that we have her marked.

War has come to the Core.

For three days they've known I was coming. We could not cover our entire approach from their sensors, but the chaos around the planet shows how unprepared they are for it. It is a civilization in turmoil. The Ash Lord has arrayed the Scepter Armada, the pride of the Core, around Luna in defensive formation. Caravans of trading vessels from the Rim clutter the Via Appia above the northern Lunar hemisphere, while backlogs of civilian vessels stagger their way back along the Via Flaminia, waiting to pass through inspection on the colossal Flaminius astroDock before their descent into Earth's atmosphere. But as we cross the Rubicon Beacons and encroach farther into Luna space, the vessels hurl themselves into a frenzy. Many bursting from their ordered queue to race for Venus, others trying to pass the Docks entirely and burn for Earth. They flare as silver and white Society fighters and fast-moving gun frigates shred engines and hulls. Dozens of vessels die to maintain order.

We're outnumbered, still vastly outgunned, but initiative is on our side, and so is the fear that all civilizations have of barbarian invaders.

The first dance of the Battle of Luna has begun.

"Attention unidentified fleet . . ." A brittle Copper voice echoes through an open frequency. *"This is Luna Defense Command: you are in possession of stolen property and in violation of Societal deep-space boundary regulations. Identify yourself and intentions with all haste."*

"Fire a long range missile at the Citadel," I say.

"That's a million kilometers away . . . ," the gunBlue says. "It'll be shot down."

"He bloodywell knows that," Sevro says. "Follow the order."

It took a campaign of counterintelligence not just in our transmissions to Sons cells throughout the Core, but among our ships and commanders to bring us here unnoticed. The Jackal will not be in position to help the Sovereign, nor will the *Classis Venetum,* the 4th Fleet of Venus. Or the *Classis Libertas,* the 5th Fleet of the inner Belt, which the Sovereign sent to Mars to aid the Jackal. At full burn all the ships will be three weeks away at current orbit. The lie worked. The spies in my ship leaked misinformation about our plans, just as I'd hoped.

That is the peril of a solar empire: all the power in all the worlds means nothing it if is in the wrong place.

Twenty minutes later, my missile is shot down by orbital defense platforms.

"New direct link incoming," the comBlue says behind me. "It's got Praetorian tags."

"Main holo," I say.

A Gold Praetorian with an aquiline face and gray at the temples of his short-cropped hair materializes in front of me. The image will appear on all bridges and holoscreens in the fleet. "Darrow of Lykos," he asks in an impeccably well bred Luna accent. "Are you in possession of *imperium* over this war fleet?"

"What need have I of your traditions?" I ask.

"Very well," the Gold says, maintaining propriety even now. "I am ArchLegate Lucius au Sejanus of the Praetorian Guard, First Cohort." I know of Sejanus. He's an eerie, efficient man. "I am come with a diplomatic envoy to your coordinates," he says dryly. "I request you stay further aggression and give my shuttle access to your flagship so we might relate the Sovereign and Senate's intentions in . . ."

"Denied," I say.

"I beg your pardon?"

"If any Society ship comes toward my fleet, they will be fired upon. If the Sovereign wishes to speak with me, then let her do it herself. Not through a lackey's mouth. Tell the hag we're here for war. Not words."

||||||||||||

My ship throbs with activity. Told only three days ago of our true destination, the men are filled with madcap excitement. There's something immortal to attacking Luna. Win or lose, we've forever stained the legacy of Gold. And in the minds of my men, and in the chatter we pick up over the coms from the Core planets and moons, there is real fear in the air. For the first time in centuries, Gold has shown weakness. Breaking the Sword Armada has spread the rebellion faster than my speeches ever could.

Soldiers salute as they pass me in the hall, making their way to their troop carriers and leechCraft. The squads are predominantly Red and defected Grays, but I see Green battletechs, Red machinists, and Obsidian scouts and heavy infantry in each capsule as well. I re-send the shuttle flight clearance order to the *Morning Star*'s flight controller with my authorization code. It's accepted and cleared. Most days I'd trust the order to stand on its own, but today I want to be sure, so I make my way to the bridge to confirm in person. The Red marine captain responsible for the security of the bridge shouts his men to attention when I enter. More than fifty armored soldiers salute me. The Blues in their pits continue in their operations. Orion's at the forward observation post where Roque once stood. Meaty hands clasped behind her back. Skin nearly as dark as her black uniform. She turns to me with those large pale eyes and that nasty white smile.

"Reaper, the fleet is nearly ready."

I greet her warmly and join her in looking out through the glass viewports "How does it look?"

"The Ash Lord is pulled up in defensive array. He seems to think we intend an Iron Rain before moving him off the moon. Sharp assumption. He has no reason to come to us. All the rest of the ships in Core will be headed here. When they get here we'll be the cockroach pinned between the ground and the hammer. He's assumed correctly we'll rush the engagement."

"The Ash Lord knows war," I say.

"That he does." She glances at her datapad. "What's this I hear about a flight clearance for a *sarpedon*-class shuttle from HB Delta?"

I knew she'd notice. And I don't want to explain myself to her now. Not everyone is as compassionate toward Cassius as I, even with Sevro sparing his life.

"I'm sending an emissary to meet with a group of Senators," I lie.

"We both know you're not," she says. "What's going on?"

I step closer so no one can overhear us. "If Cassius remains in the fleet while we go to war, someone will try to get past the guards and slit his throat. There's too much hate for the Bellona for him to stay here."

"Then hide him in another cell. Don't release him," she says. "He'll just go back to them. Rejoin the war."

"He won't."

She looks behind me to ensure we're not being overheard. "If the Obsidians find out . . ."

"This is exactly why I didn't tell anyone," I say. "I'm releasing him. You clear that shuttle. You let it go. I need you to promise me." Her lips make thin, hard line. "Promise me." She nods and looks back to Luna. As always, I feel she knows more than she lets on.

"I promise. But you be careful, boy. You still owe me a parrot, remember."

I meet Sevro in the hall outside the high security prisoner lockup. He's sitting atop the orange cargo crate and its floating gravRig drinking from a flask, left hand rested on the scorcher in his leg holster. The hall's quieter than it should be given its guests, but it's in the main hangars and gun stations and engines and armories where my ship pulses with activity. Not here on the prison deck. "What took you?" Sevro asks. He's in his black fatigues too, stretching uncomfortably against his new combat vest. His boots click together as his legs dangle.

"Orion was asking questions on the bridge about the flight clearance."

"Shit. She figure out we were letting the eagle fly?"

"She promised to let it go."

"She better. And she better keep her trap shut. If Sefi finds out . . ."

"I know," I say. "And so does Orion. She won't tell her."

"If you say so." Sevro wrinkles his face and downs the last of his flask as he glances down the hall. Mustang approaches.

"Guards are redeployed," she says. "Marine patrols are diverted from hall 13-c. Cassius is clear to the hangar."

"Good. You sure about this?" I ask, touching her hand. She nods.

"Not entirely, but that's life."

"Sevro? You still prime?"

Sevro hops down from the crate. "Obviously. I'm here, ain't I?"

Sevro helps me maneuver the gravRig through the brig's doors. The guard station is deserted. Food wrappers and tobacco dip cups all that remain of the Sons team who guarded the prisoners. Sevro follows me from the entrance down into the decagon room of duroglass cells, whistling the tune he made for Pliny.

"If your leg's a little wet . . . ," he sings as we stop before Cassius's cell. Antonia's cell is across from his. Her face swollen from her beating, she watches us hatefully without moving from her cell's cot. Sevro knocks on the duroglass separating us from Cassius.

"Wakey wakey, Sir Bellona."

Cassius wipes his eyes of sleep and sits up from his bed, taking in Sevro and I, but addressing Mustang. "What's going on?"

"We've arrived at Luna," I say.

"Not Mars?" Cassius asks in surprise. Antonia shifts in her cot behind us, just as startled by the news as Cassius appears to be.

"Not Mars."

"You're actually attacking Luna?" Cassius murmurs. "You're insane. You don't have the ships. How do you even plan to get past the shields?"

"Don't you worry about that, sweetheart," Sevro says. "We got our ways. But soon hot metal's gonna be sliding through this ship. And someone's likely gonna come in here and pop you in the head. Darrow here gets all sad thinkin' of that. And I don't like sad Darrow." Cassius just stares at us like we're mad. "He still doesn't get it."

"When you said you were done with this war, did you mean it?" I ask.

"I don't understand. . . ."

"It's pretty bloodydamn simple, Cassius," Mustang says. "Yes or no?"

"Yes," Cassius says from his cot. Antonia sits up to watch. "I am. How could I not be? It's taken everything from me. All for people who only care about themselves."

"Well?" I ask Sevro.

"Oh, please." Sevro snorts. "You think that's going to satisfy me?"

"What game are you playing at?" Cassius asks.

"Ain't no game, boyo. Darrow wants me to let you out." Cassius's eyes widen. "But I needa know you aren't gonna come try to kill us. You're all about honor and blood debts, so I need you to swear an oath so I can sleep soundly."

"I killed your father. . . ."

"You really should stop reminding me of that."

"If you stay here, we can't protect you," I say. "I believe the worlds still need Cassius au Bellona. But there's no place for you here. And there's no place for you with the Sovereign. If you give me your oath, on your honor that you will leave this war behind you, I'll give you your freedom."

Antonia bursts out laughing behind us. "This is hilarious. They're toying with you, Cassi. Just plucking you like a harp."

"Be quiet, you poisonous little brat," Mustang snaps.

Cassius eyes Mustang, judging our proposal. "You agreed to this?"

"It was my idea," she says. "None of this is your fault, Cassius. I was cruel to you, and I'm sorry for that. I know you wanted revenge on Darrow. On me . . ."

"Not on you, not ever on you."

Mustang flinches. ". . . but I know you've seen what revenge brings. I know you've seen what Octavia really is. What my brother really is. You're only guilty of trying to protect your family. You don't deserve to die here."

"You really want me to go?" he asks.

"I want you to live," she says. "And yes. I want you to go, and never come back."

"But . . . go where?" he asks.

"Anywhere but here."

Cassius swallows, searching himself. Not just seeking to understand what he owes honor or duty, but trying to imagine a world without her. I know the horrible loneliness he feels now even as we give him freedom. Life without love is the worst prison of all. But he licks his lips and nods to Mustang, not to me. "On my father, on Julian, I promise not to raise arms against any of you. If you let me go, I will leave. And I will never come back."

"You coward." Antonia punches the glass of her cell. "You gory-damn sniveling little whipped worm . . ."

I nudge Sevro. "Still your call."

He tugs the hairs of his little goatee. "Ah hell, you better be right about this, you pricklicks." Digging into his pocket he pulls out the a magnetic key card and Cassius's cell door unlocks with a heavy *thunk*.

"Then there's a shuttle waiting for you in the auxiliary hangar on this level," Mustang says evenly. "It's been cleared to fly. But you have to go now."

"That means *now,* shithead," Sevro says.

"They'll pop you in the back of the head!" Antonia is saying. "You traitor."

Cassius puts a tentative hand on the cell door, as if he's afraid he'll push and find it locked and we'll laugh at him and all the hope we've given him will be ripped away. But he has faith and, steeling his face, he pushes. The cell's door swings outward. Cassius walks out to join us. He holds out his hands to be cuffed.

"You're free, man," Sevro slurs, rapping the orange box heavily with his knuckles, "but you gotta get in the box so we can wheel you outta here without anyone seeing."

"Of course." He pauses and turns back to me to extend a hand. I take it, a strange feeling of kinship rising in me. "Goodbye, Darrow."

"Good luck, Cassius."

And for Mustang he pauses, wanting to reach out and wrap his arms around her, but she merely sticks out a hand, cold even now to him. He looks at her hand and shakes his head, not accepting her gesture. "We'll always have Luna," he says.

"Goodbye, Cassius."

"Goodbye."

He goes to the crate, which Sevro has opened and looks inside. Hesitating there, wanting to say something to Sevro, perhaps thank him one last time. "I don't know if your father was right. But he was brave." He extends a hand to Sevro as he did me. "I'm sorry that he's not here."

Sevro blinks hard at the hand, wanting to hate it. This does not come easy for him. He's never been a gentle soul. But he does his best and he takes the outstretched hand. They shake. But something feels wrong. Cassius won't let go. His face is cold, eyes unforgiving. His body rotates. So fast I can't stop him from jerking back on Sevro's hand, pulling my friend's smaller body forward toward him just as he swivels his hip, bringing Sevro to his right armpit like they're dancing, so he can strip Sevro's pistol from his leg holster. Sevro stumbles, fumbling for the weapon but it is already gone. Cassius shoves him off and stands behind him with the scorcher pressed to his spine. Sevro's eyes are huge, staring at me in fear. "Darrow . . ."

"Cassius no!" I shout.

"This is my duty."

"Cassius . . ." Mustang takes a step forward. Outstretched hand trembling. "He saved your life . . . Please."

"On your knees," Cassius says to us. "On your gorydamn knees." I feel myself teetering on the edge of a precipice, the darkness spreading out before me. Whispering to have me back. I can't reach for my razor. Cassius could easily shoot me down before I even pull it. Mustang goes to her knees and motions me to get down. Numbly, I follow her lead.

"Kill him!" Antonia's shouting. "Shoot the bastard!"

"Cassius, listen to me . . . ," I beg.

"I said on your knees," Cassius repeats to Sevro.

"My knees?" Sevro smiles wickedly. A mad gleam in his eye. "Stupid Gold. You forgot Howler rule number one. Never bow." He snatches up his razor from his right wrist, tries to spin around. But he's too slow. Cassius shoots him in the shoulder, jerking him sideways. The combat vest cracks. Blood sprays onto the metal wall. Sevro stumbles forward, eyes wild.

"For Gold," Cassius whispers and fires six more shots point-blank into Sevro's chest.

58

||||||||||||||||||||

FADING LIGHT

Blood erupts from Sevro's chest. Spraying my face. He stumbles. Drops his razor. Collapses to his knees, gasping in shock. I rush to him under the muzzle of Cassius's smoking weapon. Sevro's grasping at his chest, confused. Blood dribbles from his mouth. Bubbling out through his vest, staining my hands. He coughs it onto me. He's desperate to rise. To laugh it off. But nothing's working. His arms tremble. His breath ragged. Eyes huge, fear wild and deep and primal in him as Antonia cackles in delight from her cell.

"Don't die," I say frantically. "Don't die. Sevro." He shivers in my arms. "Sevro. Please. *Please*. Stay alive. Please. Sevro . . ." Without a final word, without a plea or a flicker of personality, he goes still, leaking red. Pulse fading away as tears stream down my face and Antonia howls in mockery.

I cry out in horror.

At the bleak evil I feel in the world.

Rocking there on the floor with my best friend.

Overwhelmed by this darkness and the hate and the helplessness.

Cassius stares pitilessly down at me.

"Reap what you sow," he says.

I rise with a horrible sob. He strikes me in the side of the head with the scorcher. I don't go down. I take the blow and pull my razor. But he hits me twice more and I fall. He takes my razor from me, holding it to Mustang's throat as she tries to rise. He points the gun at my forehead as I look up at him and is about to pull the trigger.

"The Sovereign will want him alive!" Mustang says.

"Yes." Cassius replies quietly, overcoming his anger. "Yes you're right. So she can peel him apart till you tell us your battle plans."

"Cassius, get me out of this damn cell," Antonia hisses.

Cassius moves Sevro's body over with his foot and pulls out the passcard to open her door. When Antonia exits her cell, she does so like a queen. Prisoner slippers making little tracks in Sevro's fresh blood. She knees Mustang in the face. Mustang goes down. My own vision wavers in and out. Nausea in my gut from a concussion. Warmth from Sevro's blood leaking through my shirt along the belly. Antonia sighs above me. "Ugh. The Goblin's still leaking everywhere."

"Guard them and get their datapads," Cassius orders. "We need a map."

"Where are you going?"

"Getting manacles." He tosses her the scorcher.

As he disappears around the corner, Antonia crouches over me, considering. She pushes the gun against my lips. "Open." She punches my testicles. "Open." Eyes rolling in pain, I open my mouth. She shoves the scorcher barrel inside. The alien metal presses against the back of my throat. Teeth scrape along the black steel. I gag. Feel bile coming up. She stares me hatefully in the eyes, crouched over my head, the barrel down my throat as my body convulses, only pulling it out as I vomit on the ground. "Worm."

She spits on me and takes our datapads and razors, tossing Sevro's to Cassius when he returns from the guard station. They fit me in a prisoner harness, a metallic muzzle-and-vest combination that interlocks the arms and pins them to my chest so that my fingers are touching the opposite shoulder, and dump me into the container we brought for him, forcing my knees to bend so I fit. I am unable to arrest my fall with my hands, and my head slams on the plastic at the bottom. Then they pile Sevro and Mustang in atop me like garbage and slam shut the crate. Sevro's blood drips down my face. My own leaks from the gash on the side of my head. Too dazed to weep or move.

"*Darrow . . .*" Mustang murmurs. "Are you all right?"

I don't answer her.

"You find a map?" I hear Cassius ask Antonia through the crate.

"And a jammer for cameras," she says. "I'll push. You range, if you can manage."

"I can manage. Let's go."

The jammer *pops* and the gravRig moves, taking us along with them. If Sevro and Mustang were not atop me, I could crouch and put my back into the lid, but their weight pins me down in the small container. It's hot. Smells like sweat. Hard to breathe. I'm helpless in here. Unable to stop them as they use the path I cleared for Cassius. Unable to stop them as they push us across the deserted hangar, up the ramp into the ship and begin preflight checks. "*Shuttle S-129, you are clear for departure, stand by for pulseShield deactivation,*" the flight officer says over the com from the distant bridge as the engines prime. "*You are go for launch.*"

Out from the belly of the war ship, my enemies smuggle me away from the comfort of my friends, the safety of my people, and the might of my army as it prepares for war. I hold my breath, expecting Orion's voice to come over the com. To ground the ship. For ripWings to shoot her engines out. None do. Somewhere, my mother will be making tea, wondering where I am, if I am safe. I pray she cannot feel this pain across the void, this fear that consumes me despite all my vaunted strength and foolish bluster. I'm afraid, despite what I know. Not just for myself, but for Mustang.

I hear Antonia and Cassius speaking beyond the crate. Cassius has broadcast an emergency signal from the craft. A few moments later, a cold voice crackles over the com.

"*Sarpedon shuttle, this is the LDC assault-runner Kronos; you have transmitted an Olympic distress signal. Please identify yourself.*"

"*Kronos,* this is the Morning Knight. Clearance code 7-8-7-Echo-

Alpha-9-1-2-2-7. I have escaped from imprisonment aboard the enemy's flagship and am requesting escort and docking clearance. Antonia au Severus-Julii is with me. We have valuable cargo. The enemy is in pursuit."

There's a pause.

"*Register, code accepted. Hold on the com. The next voice you hear will be the Protean Knight's.*" A moment later Aja's voice rumbles through the ship, filling me with dread. So she did survive the waste to find her way back home.

"*Cassius? You're alive.*"

"For now."

"*What is your cargo?*"

"The Reaper, Virginia, and the body of Ares," Antonia says excitedly.

"*The body . . . I want to see them.*"

Boots thud toward my container. The top opens and Cassius hauls Mustang out. Then he hauls me out and tosses me to the ground before the hologram. Small and dark in the holographic projector, Aja watches us with otherworldly calm. Antonia keeps Sevro's gun trained on my head as Cassius pulls up Sevro's head by his Mohawk to show his face.

"*Goryhell, Bellona.*" Aja says, excitement entering her voice. "*Goryhell. You've done it. The Sovereign will want to see you in the citadel.*"

"Before I do, I need you to assure me that no harm will come to Virginia."

"What are you talking about?" Antonia asks, wary how close Cassius stands near her with his razor. "She's a traitor."

"And she'll be imprisoned," Cassius says. "Not executed. Not tortured. I need your word, Aja. Or I turn this ship around. Darrow killed your sister. Do you want vengeance or not?"

"*You have my word,*" Aja says. "*No harm will befall her. I am sure Octavia will agree. We need her to settle things with the Rim. We're sending squadrons to intercept your pursuit. Re-direct to vector 41'13'25, circle the moon and await contact from the* Lion of Mars *for docking instructions. We can't clear your ship to land moonside. But ArchGovernor Augustus will be joining the Sovereign in the Citadel within the hour. I don't think he'll mind offering you a ride down."*

"The ArchGovernor is here?" Cassius asks, "I don't see his ships."

"Of course he's here," Aja replies. *"He knew Darrow was never going to Mars. His entire fleet is on the far side of Luna, waiting for them to attack my father's. This is his trap."*

59

||||||||||||||||||||||

THE LION OF MARS

Mustang and I are dragged down the cargo plank of the shuttle by Obsidians in black armor, each nearly as large as Ragnar and wearing the badge of the lion. I try to kick up at them, but they jam two-meter long ionPikes down into my stomach, electrocuting me. My muscles cramp. Electricity screaming through me. They toss me down to the deck, pulling me up by my hair so I'm on my knees staring down at the body of Sevro. Mercifully his eyes are shut. His mouth pink from smeared blood. Mustang tries to rise. A muffled thump as an Obsidian hits her in the stomach. Putting her back on her knees, gasping for breath. Cassius has been forced to his knees as well.

Antonia joins Lilath, who stands before us in black armor. A screaming gold skull on either shoulder and another in the center of the breastpiece. Down her sides are human rib-bones embedded in the armor. The first bonerider in all her barbaric finery. The Jackal's Sevro. Head shaved. Quiet eyes sunken in a small, pinched face that likes little of what it sees in the world. Behind her, tower ten young Peerless Scarred, heads shaved like hers for war. "Scan them," she orders.

"What the hell is this?" Cassius asks.

"Jackal's orders." Lilath watches carefully as the Golds scan me. Cassius suffers the indignity as Lilath continues. "Boss doesn't want tricks."

"I have the Sovereign's warrant," he says. "We're to take the Reaper and Virginia to the Citadel."

"Understood. We received the same orders. Bound there soon." She motions Cassius to stand as her men clear them. No bugs or devices or radiation tracking. Cassius dusts his knees off. I remain on mine as Lilath peers at Sevro, who one of the Obsidians has dragged down the ramp. She feels his pulse and smiles. "A fine kill, Bellona."

One Bonerider, a lofty, striking man with blazing eyes and a statue's cheekbones makes a little cooing noise. Tattooed fingers with painted nails tap his bottom lip. "How much for Barca's bones?" he asks.

"Not for sale," Cassius replies.

The man flashes an arrogant smile. "Everything's for sale, my goodman. Ten million credits for a rib."

"No."

"One hundred million. Come now, Bellona . . ."

"My title, *Legate Valii-Rath,* is Morning Knight. You may address me as sir or not at all. Ares's body is property of the state. It's not mine to sell. But if you ask me about it again, I will have more than words with you, sir."

"Will you have a rut?" Tactus's elder brother asks. "Is that what you mean?" I've never met the annoyingly aristocratic creature before, and I'm glad for it. Tactus seems the better of the bunch.

"You gorydamn savage," Mustang says through bloody teeth.

"Savage?" Tactus's brother asks. "Such a pretty mouth. That's not how you should use it." Cassius takes a step toward the man. The other Boneriders reach for their blades.

"Tharsus. Shut up." Lilath tilts her head, listening to a com in her ear as he returns to her side, lifting his nose. "Yes, my liege," she says into her com. "Barca is dead. I checked."

Antonia steps forward. "Is that Adrius? Let me speak with him."

She holds up a hand to the taller woman. "Antonia wants to speak with you." She pauses. "He says it can wait. Tharsus, Novas, uncuff the Reaper and spread his arms."

"What about Virginia?" Tharsus asks.

"Touch her, you die," Cassius says. "That's all you need to know." There's fear behind Cassius's eyes, even if he doesn't show it. He never would have brought her here if he could have helped it. Unlike the Sovereign's men, the Jackal is liable to do anything at anytime. Aja's guarantee of safety suddenly feels very frail. Why would the Sovereign send us here?

"No one will touch your prizes," Lilath says, voice that eerie one note. "Except the Reaper."

"I'm to deliver him . . ."

"We know. But my master requires compensation for past grievances. The Sovereign granted him permission while you were landing. Precautionary measures." She flashes her datapad. Cassius reads the order and goes a little pale, looking back at me. "Now may we proceed, or do you do care to fuss further?"

Cassius has no choice. He depresses the remote. The metal cuffs locking my hands to my chest open. Tharsus and Novas are there to grab my arms and haul them to the sides, wrapping their whip form razors around each wrist, pulling taut till my shoulders grind in their sockets.

"You're going to let them do this?" Mustang snarls at Cassius. "What happened to your honor? It is as false as the rest of you?" He's about to say something, but she spits at his feet.

Antonia smiles repugnantly, captivated by the sight of me in pain. Lilath takes my razor from Cassius and walks away toward the rip-Wings that escorted us into the hangar. There, she holds my sling-Blade up into one of the smoldering engines.

"Tell me, Reaper, did you piddle my baby brother. Is that why he was so besotted?" Tharsus asks as we wait. His perfumed locks fall over his eyes. He alone has not shaved his head. "Well, you're not the first to plow that field, if you catch my flow."

I stare straight ahead.

"Is he right or left handed?" Lilath calls over.

"Right," Cassius replies.

"Pollox, tourniquet," Lilath instructs.

I realize what they intend and my blood runs cold. It feels like it's happening to someone else. Even when the rubber tightens around my right forearm and the needle-pricks of sensation tingle through the tips of my fingers.

Then I hear my enemy.

The clicking of his black boots.

The delicate shift in everyone's mannerisms.

The fear.

The Boneriders part to watch their master enter out of the mouth of the main hall to the hangar bay, flanked by a dozen more towering Gold bodyguards with shaved heads. Each tall as Victra. Gold skulls laugh on their collars, on the handles of their razors. Bones rattle on their shoulders, finger joints taken from their enemies. Taken from Lorn, from Fitchner, from my Howlers. These are the killers of my time. Their arrogance drips from them. As they look at me, it isn't hate I see in their violent eyes, but a fundamental absence of empathy.

I told the Jackal I didn't hate him. That was a lie. It's all I feel watching him walk across the deck, the pistol he killed my uncle with hanging on a magnetic strip holster on his thigh. His armor gold. Roaring with Gold lions. Human ribs implanted along the sides of the torso, each carved with details I cannot make out. Hair combed and parted on the side. His silver stylus in his hand, twirling, twirling. Antonia takes a step toward him, but stops herself when she sees he's walking to Sevro and not to her.

"Good. The bones are intact." After he's examined Sevro's bloody body, he stands over his sister. "Hello, Virginia. Nothing to say?"

"What is there to say?" she asks through gritted teeth. "What words have I for a monster?"

"Hm." He takes her jaw between his forefingers, causing Cassius's hand to drift to his razor. Lilath and the Boneriders would cut him to pieces if he even drew it. "It is us against the world," the Jackal says softly. "Do you remember telling me that?"

"No."

"We were young. Mother had just died. I couldn't stop crying. And you said you'd never leave me. But then Claudius would invite you somewhere. And you'd forget all about me. And I'd stay home in a big old house and cry, because I knew even then I was alone." He taps her nose. "These next hours are going to test who you are as a person, sister. I'm excited to see what's beneath all the bluster."

He moves on to me, loosening my muzzle. Even on my knees my physicality dwarfs him. Fifty kilograms heavier. Still, his presence is like the sea: strange and vast and dark and full of hidden depths and power. His silence, his roar. I see his father in him now. He tricked me, guessing my play on Luna, and now I'm afraid all I've done is going to unravel.

"And here we are again," he says. I do not reply. "Do you recognize these?"

He runs his stylus down the ribs in his armor, coming closer so I can see the details. "My dear father thought a man's deeds make him. I rather think it's his enemies. Do you like it?" He steps even closer. One of the ribs shows a helmet with a spiked sunburst. Another rib shows a head in a box.

The Jackal is wearing Fitchner's rib cage.

Anger roars out of me and I try to bite his face, bellowing like a wounded animal, startling Mustang. I strain against the men holding me, trembling with rage as the Jackal watches me squirm. Cassius stares at the ground, avoiding Mustang's gaze. My voice croaks out of me, hardly my own. That deeper demon only the Jackal can summon from me. "I'm going to skin you," I say.

Bored of me, he rolls his eyes and snaps his fingers. "Put the muzzle back on." Tharsus binds my mouth. The Jackal opens his arms as if welcoming two long-lost friends to a party. "Cassius! Antonia!" he says. "Heroes of the hour. My dear . . . what happened?" He asks when he sees Antonia's face. They were lovers during my imprisonment. Sometimes I'd smell her on him as he came to visit me before the box. Or she'd drag a nail along his neck as she passed. He goes close to her now, taking her jaw in his hand, tilting her head to examine the damage done to her. "Did Darrow do this?"

"My sister," she corrects, disliking his examination. She mourned her face in our captivity more than she mourned her own mother's death. "The bitch will pay. And I'll have it fixed, don't worry." She pulls her head back from him.

"Stop," the Jackal says sharply. "Why fixed?"

"It's disgusting."

"Disgusting? My dear, scars are what you are. They tell your story."

"This is Victra's story, not mine."

"You're still beautiful." He pulls her down gently by her chin and kisses her lips delicately. He doesn't care for her. Like Mustang said, we're just sacks of meat to him. But while Antonia's as wicked a thing as I've ever met, she wants to be loved. To be valued. The Jackal knows how to use that.

"This was Barca's," Antonia says, handing the Jackal Sevro's pistol. The Jackal runs a thumb over the howling wolves engraved in the hilt.

"Fine work," he says. He strips his own gun from his magnetic holster and tosses it to a bodyguard before holstering Sevro's. Of course he takes my friend's pistol as a trophy.

His datapad flashes and he holds up a hand for silence. "Yes, Imperator?"

The grotesque Ash Lord appears in the air before the Jackal as a disembodied, gigantic head. Dark Gold eyes peer out from beneath twin thickets of eyebrows. His jowls hang over the high black collar of his uniform. *"Augustus, the enemy is under way. TorchShips in front."*

"They're coming for him," Cassius says.

"How many?" the Jackal asks.

"More than sixty. Half bearing the red fox."

"Do you wish me to spring the trap?"

"Not yet. I will assume command of your ships."

"You know the arrangement."

The Ash Lord's wide mouth makes a straight line. *"I do. You are to continue to join the Sovereign as planned. Escort the Morning Knight and his package to the Citadel. My daughter will take custody of him there. Go now, for Gold."*

"For Gold."

The head disappears.

The Jackal glances over to the Obsidians who pulled me down the cargo ramp. "Slaves, attend to Praetor Licenus on the bridge. You are no longer needed." The Obsidians leave without question. When they are gone, he eyes the thirty Boneriders. "The Morning Knight has given us an opportunity to win this war today. The Telemanuses will come for my sister. The Howlers and the Sons of Ares will come for the Reaper. They will not have them. It is upon our shoulders to deliver them to our Sovereign and her strategists in the Citadel."

He addresses Antonia and Cassius. "Set aside your little grievances. Today we are Gold. We can bicker when the Rising is ash. Most of you lived the darkness of the caves with me. You watched by my side as this . . . creature stole what was ours. They will take everything from us. Our homes. Our slaves. Our right to rule. Today we fight to keep what is ours. Today we fight against the dying of our Age."

They lean into his words, awaiting his orders hungrily. It's terrifying to see the cult he's built around himself. He's taken bits of me, of my speaking pattern, and transposed it onto his own behavior. He continues to evolve.

The Jackal turns from his men as Lilath brings back my slingBlade, red-hot from engine's heat, and hands it to him hilt first. "Lilath, you're to stay with the fleet."

"You're sure?"

"You're my insurance plan."

"Yes, my liege."

Antonia's not sure what they're talking about, and she doesn't like it one bit. The Jackal twirls my razor in his hand. And then looking between me and Mustang's he's struck by a thought. "How long were you imprisoned by Darrow, Cassius?"

"Four months."

"Four months. Then I believe you should do the honors." He flips the red-hot razor to Cassius, who smoothly catches it by its hilt. "Cut off Darrow's hand."

"The Sovereign wants him . . ."

"Alive, yes. And he will be. But she doesn't want him coming in to her bunker with his sword arm attached to his body, now does she?

We're to take all his weapons. Neuter the beast and let's be on our way. Unless . . . there's a problem?"

"No problem," Cassius says. Stepping forward, he lifts high the razor, metal throbbing with heat.

"Is this what you've become?" Mustang asks. Cassius suffers her gaze, shame on his face. "Look at me, Darrow," Mustang says. "Look at me."

I will myself to forget the blade. To watch her, taking strength from her. But as the superheated metal cleaves through the skin and bone of my right wrist, I forget her. I scream in pain, looking back where my hand was to see a stump lazily dripping blood through charred capillaries. Smoke from my burning flesh slithers into the air. And through the agony I can see the Jackal picking my hand up from the ground and holding it in the air. His newest trophy.

"*Hic sunt leones,*" he says.

"*Hic sunt leones,*" echo his men.

60

||||||||||||||||||||||||

DRAGON'S MAW

I think of my uncle as I cradle the charred stump of my right arm, shivering from pain. Is he with my father now? Does he sit with Eo by a woodfire listening to the birds? Do they watch me? Blood weeps through the blackened flesh at my wrist. The pain is blinding. Overtaking my entire body. I'm strapped beside Mustang into a seat in two parallel rows in the back of the military assault craft amidst thirty Boneriders. The overhead light pulses an alien green. The ship shudders from turbulence. Luna is in storm. Huge thunderheads swaddling the cities. Black towers penetrating the murky clouds. All along the rooftops, motes of light dance from the headlamps of Oranges and highReds, my own brethren, who slave under the military yoke, preparing weapons that will fell their Martian kin. Brighter flood lamps bathe military scenes. Black shapes trimmed with evil red beacons zip and float between towers as squadrons of ripWings patrol the sky and Golds in gravBoots jump between towers kilometers apart, checking on defenses, preparing for the storm above, saying last words to friends, to schoolmates, to lovers.

Passing the Elorian Opera House, I see a line of Golds perched on its highest crenellation, staring up at the sky, their glorious war helms spiked with horns so they look a troupe of gargoyles balanced there, silhouetted by lightning, waiting for hell to rain.

We drive toward the cauldron of clouds that swirls around the highest skyscrapers. Beneath the cloud layer, the interlocked skin of cityscape is quiet. Dark in anticipation of orbital bombardment, except for the veins of flame that bleed across the horizon from riots in Lost City. Flashing emergency vehicles dive toward the blazes. The city has gathered its breath for hours, for days, and, with exhalation bare moments away, her seams strain and her lungs stretch to bursting.

We taxi onto a circular landing pad atop the Sovereign's spire. There, Aja and a cohort of Praetorians meet us. The Boneriders unload with gravBoots before we land, covering the craft as it settles onto the pad. Cassius comes out, manhandling me along. He drags Sevro with his other hand like a deer carcass. Antonia shoves Mustang along. The weary winter rain of the city-moon drips down Aja's dark face. Steam rises from her collar and a brilliant white smile slashes the night.

"Morning Knight, welcome home. The Sovereign awaits."

A kilometer beneath the surface of the moon, the great gravLift known only in military myth as the Dragon Maw stops, hissing open to lead down a dimly lit concrete hall to another door emblazoned with the pyramid of the Society. There, blue light scans Aja's irises. The pyramid fractures in half, gears and huge pistons whirring. Technology here older than the Citadel above, ancient, from a time when Earth stood the only enemy Luna knew, and the great American railguns were the fear of all Luneborn. It's a testament to the architecture and the discipline of the Praetorians that the great bunker of the Sovereign has not had to change substantially for more than seven hundred years.

I wonder if Fitchner knew its inner workings. Doubtful. Seems a secret Aja would hoard. But I wonder if she even knows all the secrets of this place. Tunnels to the left and right of the narrow hall we pass through are long-ago collapsed, and I can't help but wonder who once walked through them, who collapsed them and why.

We pass heavily guarded rooms aglow with holo lights. Synced Blues and Greens lying back in tech beds, IVs hooked into their bodies as data streams through their brains via uplink nodes embedded in their skulls, eyes lost to some distant plane. It's the central nervous system of the Society. Octavia can wage a war from here even if the moon falls to ruin around her.

The Obsidians here wear black helmets with draconic shaped skulls and dark purple on their body armor. Gold letters spelling *cohors nihil* wind along the short-swords at their sides. Zero Legion. I've never heard of them, but I see what they guard: one last door of solid, unadorned metal, the deepest refuge of the Society. It dilates open with a groan and only then, a year and a half since I jumped out the back of her assault shuttle, do I see the silhouette of the Sovereign.

Her patrician voice echoes down the hall. ". . . Janus, who cares about civilian casualties? Does the sea ever run out of salt? If they manage an Iron Rain, you shoot them down, whatever the cost. The last thing we desire is for the Obsidian Horde to land here and link with the riots in Lost City. . . ."

The ruler of all I've ever fought against stands in a depressed circle at the center of a large gray and black room bathed in blue light from the Praetors and Ash Lord who surround her in holographic form. There's more than forty in a semicircle, the veterans of her wars. Pitiless creatures watching me enter the room with the dark, smug contentment of cathedral statues, as if they always knew it would come to this. As if they earned this end of mine and didn't luck into it just as they lucked into their birth.

They know what my capture means. They've been broadcasting it nonstop to my fleet. Trying to take our coms with hacking attacks to spread the word among my ships. Spreading it to Earth to quell the uprisings there, pimping the signal to the Core to forestall any more civil unrest. They'll do the same with my execution. The same with Sevro's dead body. And maybe Mustang, despite the deal Cassius thinks he's struck. Look what befalls those who rise against, they will say. Look how even these mighty beasts fall before Gold. Who else can stand against them? No one.

Their grip will tighten.

Their reign will strengthen.

If we lose today, a new generation of Gold will rise with vigor unseen since the fall of Earth. They will see the threat to their people and they will breed creatures like Aja and the Jackal by the thousands. They'll build new Institutes, expand their military, and throttle my people. That is the future that could be. The one Fitchner feared the most. The one I fear is coming as I watch the Jackal move past me into the room.

"His Obsidians are not trained in extraplanetary warfare," one of the Praetors is saying.

"You want to tell that to Fabii?" the Sovereign asks. "Or perhaps to his mother? She's with the other Senators who I had to corral in the Chamber before they could flee like little flies and take their ships with them."

"Politico cravens . . ." someone murmurs.

Aside from the glowing holographs, the room is occupied by a small host of martial Golds. More than I expected. Two Olympic Knights, ten Praetorians, and Lysander. Ten years of age now, he has grown nearly half a foot since last I saw him. He carries a datapad to take copious notes of his grandmother's conversation and smiles to Cassius as we enter, watching me with the wary interest you'd watch a tiger through duroglass. His crystal Gold eyes take in my bindings, Aja, and my missing hand. Mentally tapping the glass with a nail to see just how thick it is.

The two Olympic Knights greet Cassius quietly as we enter, so as not to disturb the Sovereign in her debriefing, though she's noted my presence with an emotionless glance. Both knights are heavily armored and ready to defend their Sovereign.

Above the Sovereign, a globular holo dominates the domed ceiling of the room, showing the moon in perfect detail. The Ash Lord's fleet is spread out like a screen to cover Luna's darkside, where the Citadel is, like a concave shield. The battle is well under way. But my forces have no way of knowing that the Jackal is just waiting to swing around their flank and hammer them against the Ash Lord's anvil. If only I could reach Orion, she might find some way to salvage this.

The Jackal quietly takes a seat to the side, patiently watching the Ash Lord give instructions to a sphere of torchShips.

"Cassius, you gorydamn hound," the Truth Knight says, voice a deep baritone. His eyes narrow and Asiatic. He's from Earth, and he's more compact than us Martians. "Is it really him?"

"Bones and heart. Took him from his flagship," Cassius says, kicking me to my knees and hauling back my head by my hair so they can better see my face. He tosses Sevro on the ground and they inspect the kill. The Joy Knight shakes his head. He's thinner than Cassius and twice again as aristocratic, from an old Venusian family. Met him once at a duel on Mars.

"Augustus too? Don't you just have all the luck. And Aja bagged the Obsidian. Fear and Love are going to get Victra and that White Witch. . . ."

"I'd kill to snag Victra," Truth says, walking around me. "That'd be a dance. Say, didn't you bed her, Cassius?"

"I never kiss and tell." Cassius nods to the battle. "How do we fare?"

"Better than Fabii. They're tenacious. Hard to pin down, keep trying to close so they can use their Obsidian, but the Ash Lord's keeping them at a distance. The ArchGovernor's fleet will be the hammer that wins this. They're already coming around their flank. See?" The knight looks longingly at the holo. Cassius notices.

"You could always join," Cassius says. "Order a shuttle."

"That would take hours," Truth replies. "We've four knights in engagement already. Someone has to protect Octavia. And my ships are being held in reserve protecting the dayside. If they make landfall, which is doubtful at this point, we'll need martial men on the ground. We'll have to wash his face."

"What?"

"Barca's face. It's too bloody. We'll make the broadcast soon, if we're not hacked again. Saboteurs were wrecking operations. More of Quicksilver's boys. All sorts of tech-head demokratic filth with delusions of grandeur. But we hit one of their dens last night with a lurcher squad."

"Best way to stop a hacker? Hot metal," Joy adds.

"The enemy is brave, I'll give them that," the Ash Lord is saying in the center of the room, his hologram twice again the width of his adjuncts'. *"Cutting off their escape but still they're standing toe-to-toe."* He's on a corvette in the back of his fleet, his signal being re-routed through dozens of other ships. The Ash Lord's fleet moves with beautiful precision, never allowing my ships within fifty kilometers.

Roque cared about casualties. Cared about not destroying the beautiful three-hundred-year-old ships I'd captured. The Ash Lord has no such restraint. He thuggishly smashes ships to oblivion. Damn their heritage, damn the lives, damn the expense, he's a destroyer. Here with his back to the wall he will win at all cost. It aches to see my fleet suffer.

"Report when you have further news," the Sovereign says. "I want Daxo au Telemanus alive, if possible. All others are expendable, including his father and the Julii."

"Yes, my liege." The old killer salutes and disappears. With a tired sigh, the Sovereign turns to look at her Morning Knight and extends her arms as if greeting a long-lost child. "Cassius." She embraces him after he bows, kissing his forehead with the same familiarity she once had for Mustang. "My heart broke when I heard what happened on the ice. I thought you were slain."

"Aja was right to think I was. But I'm sorry it took so long for me to return from the dead, my liege. I had unfinished business to attend."

"So I see," the Sovereign says, caring little for me. Focusing on Mustang instead. "I do believe you've won the war, Cassius. The both of you." She nods without a smile to the Jackal. "Your ships will make this a short battle."

"It is our pleasure to serve," the Jackal replies with a knowing smile.

"Yes," the Sovereign says in a strange, almost nostalgic way. Her fingers trace the scars on Cassius's broad neck. "Did they hang you?"

"Oh, they tried. It didn't quite take." He grins.

"You remind me of Lorn when he was young." I know she once said to Virginia that she reminded her of herself. The affection is more real than the Jackal has for his men, but she's still a collector. Still using love and loyalty as a shield to protect herself. The Sovereign gestures to me, wrinkling her nose at the metal muzzle around my face. "Do you know what he's planning? Anything that will compromise our endgame . . ."

"From what I glean he's planning an attack on the Citadel."

"Cassius, stop. . . ." Mustang snaps. "She doesn't care about you."

"And you do?" the Sovereign asks. "We know exactly what you care about, Virginia. And what you'll do to get it."

"By air or ground?" the Jackal asks. "The attack."

"Ground, I believe."

"Why didn't you mention this in space?"

"You were more concerned with chopping off Darrow's hand."

The Jackal ignores the barb. "How many clawDrills are there on Luna?"

"None working, not even in the abandoned mines," the Sovereign says. "We made sure of that."

"If he has a team coming, it'll be Volarus and Julii," the Jackal says. "They're his best weapons and helped him take the Moon-Breaker."

"Volarus is the Obsidian?" the Sovereign asks. "Yes?"

"Queen of the Obsidian," Mustang says. "You should meet her. You'd remind Sefi of her mother."

"Queen of the Obsidian . . . they are united?" the Sovereign asks Cassius warily. "Is that right? My politicos said pan-tribal leadership was impossible."

"And they were wrong," Cassius says.

Antonia seizes a moment to stand out in the Sovereign's eyes. "It's only the Obsidian in Darrow's fold, my liege. An alliance of the southern tribes."

The Sovereign ignores her. "I don't like it. We have hundreds of Obsidians in the citadel alone. . . ."

"They're loyal," Aja says.

"How do you know?" Cassius asks. "Are any from Mars?"

Octavia looks to Aja for confirmation. "Most," Aja admits. "Even Zero Legion. Martian Obsidians are the best."

"I want them out of the bunker," Octavia says. "Now."

One of the Praetorians moves to do her bidding.

"Is she as formidable as her brother?" Aja asks Cassius.

"Worse," Mustang says from her knees with a laugh. "Far worse and far brighter. She fights with a pack of warrior women. She has sworn a blood oath to find you, Aja. To drink your blood and use your skull as her chalice in Valhalla. Sefi is coming. And you cannot stop her."

Aja and Octavia exchange a wary look. "They would have to land first before making an assault on the citadel," Aja says. "It's impossible."

"How are they coming?" Cassius asks me. I shake my head and laugh at him behind my muzzle. Aja kicks the stump of my right hand. I almost black out as I curl around the wound in pain. "How are they coming?" Cassius asks. I don't reply. He motions to the Joy Knight. "Hold out his other arm." Joy grabs my left arm and pulls it out. "How are they coming?" he asks not me, but Mustang. "I will cut his other hand off if you do not tell me. Followed by his feet and nose and eyes. How is Volarus coming?"

"You're going to kill him anyway," Mustang sneers. "So fuck you."

"How slowly he dies is up to you," Cassius says.

"Who said they didn't already land?" Mustang asks.

"What?"

"They came in the grain ships from Earth, compliments of Quicksilver. Landed hours ago. And they're pressing for the Citadel now. Ten thousand strong. Didn't you know?"

"Ten thousand?" Lysander murmurs from his chair to the side of the holopit. His grandmother's Dawn Scepter lies on the table before him. A meter long length of gold and iron, it's tipped with the triangle of the Society and the withered heart of the Obsidian warlord who led the Dark Revolt nearly five hundred years ago. "The Legions are deployed to halt an invasion. The Obsidians will overrun our defenses before they can return."

"I will make ready the Praetorians and recall two legions," Aja says, striding for the door.

"No." Octavia stands motionless, thinking. "No, Aja, you stay with me." She turns to the Praetorian captain. "Legatus, go reinforce the surface. Take your platoon. There's no need for them here. I have my knights. Any ship approaching the Citadel should be fired upon. I don't care if it claims to carry the Ash Lord himself. Do you understand?"

"It will be done." Legatus and the remaining Praetorians rush out, leaving the room deserted save for Cassius, the three Olympic Knights, Antonia, the Jackal, the Sovereign, three Praetorian guards, and us prisoners. Aja presses her palm into a console near the door. The sanctum seals behind the Praetorians. A second, thicker door appears from the walls in a corkscrew, slowly locking us off from the world beyond.

"I'm sorry, Aja," Octavia says as the woman returns to her side. "I know you want to be with your men, but we already lost Moira. I couldn't risk losing you too."

"I know," Aja replies, but her disappointment is obvious. "The Praetorians will deal with the Horde. Shall we attend the other matter?"

Octavia glances over to the Jackal and he gives her the barest of nods. "Severus-Julii, come forward," Octavia says

Antonia does, surprised to have been singled out. A hopeful smile works its way onto her lips. No doubt she's to receive a commendation for her efforts today. She clasps both hands behind her back and waits before her Sovereign.

"Tell me, Praetor, you were conscripted to join the Sword Armada as it subjugated the Moon Lords in June of this year, were you not?"

Antonia frowns. "My liege, I do not understand. . . ."

"It's a fairly simply question. Answer it to the best of your abilities."

"I was. I led my family's ships and the Fifth and Sixth Legions."

"Under the pro tem command of Roque au Fabii?"

"Yes, my liege."

"Then tell me, how is it that you are still alive and your Imperator is not?"

"I only barely managed to escape the battle," Antonia says, seeing the danger in the line of questioning. Her voice modulates accordingly. "It was a . . . terrible calamity, my liege. With the Howlers hidden in Thebe, Roque . . . Imperator Fabii, fell into the trap twofold, through no fault of his own. Any would have done the same. I made an effort to rescue his command, to rally our ships. But Darrow had already reached his bridge. And torchShips were burning all around us. We did not know friend from foe. It's haunted my dreams, the sounds of the Obsidian Horde pouring through their ships. . . ."

"Liar." Mustang snorts her derision.

"And so you retreated."

"At grave cost, yes, my liege. I saved as many ships for the Society as I could. I saved my men, knowing they would be needed for the battle to come. It was all I could do."

"It was a noble thing, saving so many," the Sovereign says.

"Thank—"

"At least it would be if it were true."

"I beg your pardon?"

"I don't believe I have ever stuttered, girl. I do, however, believe you fled the battle, abandoning your post and your Imperator to the enemy."

"You are calling me a liar, my liege?"

"Obviously," Mustang says.

"I will not stand aspersions against my honor," Antonia snaps at Mustang, puffing up her chest. "It is beneath . . ."

"Oh, be still, child," the Sovereign says. "You're in deep waters here, with larger fish than you. You see, others escaped the battle, others who transmitted their battle analytics to us so we would know what happened. So we could assess the calamity and see how Antonia of the Severus-Julii disgraced her name and lost us the battle, abandoning her Praetor when he called for aid, fleeing for the belt to save her own hide, where she then lost her ships."

"Fabii lost the battle," she says vindictively. "Not I."

"Because his allies abandoned him," Aja purrs. "He might still have saved his command had you not thrown his formation to chaos."

"Fabii made mistakes," the Sovereign says. "But he was a noble creature and as loyal a servant to his Color. He was even honorable enough to take his own life, to accept that he had failed and to pay justly for it and ensure he would not be interrogated or bartered. His last act in destroying the rebel docks was the act of a hero. An Iron Gold. But you . . . you scurrilous craven, you fled like a little girl who pissed her Whiteday dress. You abandoned him to save yourself. Now you slander him in front of all. In front of his friend." She gestures protectively to Cassius. "Your men saw the reptile underneath, that is why they turned on you. Why you lost your ships to your better sister."

"I would see whoever lays these claims against me in the Bleeding Place," Antonia says, trembling with anger. "My honor will not be smeared by faceless, jealous creatures. It is sad that they would manufacture evidence to smear my good name. No doubt they have ulterior motives. Perhaps intentions against my company or my holdings or they seek to undermine Gold as a whole. Adrius, tell the Sovereign how ridiculous this all is."

But Adrius remains quiet. "Adrius?"

"I'd rather have the loyalty of a dog than that of a coward," he says. "Lilath was right. You are weak. And that is dangerous."

Antonia looks about like a drowning woman, feeling the water coming over her head, undertow pulling her down, nothing to grab onto, nothing to save her. Aja swells behind her like a dark wave as Octavia denounces her formally. "Antonia au Severus-Julii, matron of House Julii and Praetor First Class of the Fifth and Sixth Legions, by the power vested in me by the Compact of The Society, I find you guilty of treason and dereliction of duty in a time of war and hereby sentence you to death."

"You bitch," Antonia hisses at her, then to the Jackal, "You can't afford to kill me. Adrius . . . please." But she has no ships anymore. No face. Tears stream out of swollen eyes as she seeks some hope here, some way out. There is none, and when she meets my gaze, she knows what I am thinking. *Reap what you sow.* This is for Victra, and Lea, and Thistle, and all the others she would sacrifice so she could live. "Please . . . ," she whimpers.

But there is no mercy here.

Aja grasps Antonia's neck from behind. She shivers in horror, shrinking to her knees, not even attempting to fight as the huge woman slowly closes her hands and begins to strangle her to death. Antonia snorts, wriggles, and takes a full minute to die. When she has, Aja completes the execution by snapping her neck with a violent twist and tossing her atop Sevro's corpse.

"What an odious creature," the Sovereign says, turning from Antonia's body. "At least her mother had spine. Cassius, your shoes are filthy." Blood crusts the rubber soles of his prison slippers and spatters the green jumpsuit's legs. "There's a complex of sleeping quarters through there, a kitchen, showers. Clean yourself. My valet has been attempting to foist a meal on me for hours. I'll have him serve it here for you. You won't miss the battle. The Ash Lord has promised it will last another several hours, at the very least. Lysander, will you show him the way?"

"I won't leave your side, my liege," Cassius says very nobly. "Not till this is through and these monsters are put down." The Truth Knight rolls his eyes at the display.

"You're a good lad," she says before turning toward me. "Now it's time we dealt with the Red."

61

|||||||||||||||||||||||||

THE RED

Aja drags me to the Sovereign's feet at the center of the holopad. The cold sneer of command is etched deeply into the
tyrant's marble face. Her shoulders are weary though, pressed down
by the weight of empire and the shadowy mass of a hundred years of
sleepless nights. Her tightly bound hair is shot with deep rivers of
gray. Tendrils of blue worm through the corners of her eyes from re-
lapsed cellular rejuvenation therapy. She's had no peace from me.
Kneeling and bleeding though I am, it does my soul good to know I've
haunted her nights.

"Remove his muzzle," she tells Aja, who stands behind me, preparing to administer the Sovereign's justice. The Truth Knight and the
Joy Knight flank Octavia. Cassius stands over Mustang to the side in
his prisoner greens among the Praetorians while the Jackal watches
from his chair near Lysander, sipping a coffee brought by the valet. I
stretch my jaw as the muzzle comes off.

"Imagine a world without the arrogance of the young," Octavia
says to her Fury.

"Imagine a world without the greed of the old," I reply hoarsely.

Aja slams the side of my head with her fist. The world flashes black and I almost keel over.

"Why'd you take off his muzzle if you wanted him to be silent?" Mustang asks.

The Jackal laughs. "A fair point, Octavia!"

Octavia scowls at him. "Because we executed a puppet last time and the worlds know it. This is flesh and blood. The Red who rose. I want them to know it is he who falls. I want them to know that even their best is insignificant."

"Give him words and he'll just make another slogan," the Jackal warns.

"Octavia, do you really think my brother won't kill you?" Mustang asks. "He won't rest until you're dead. Until you're all dead. Till he takes your scepter and sits on your throne."

"Of course he wants my throne, who wouldn't?" the Sovereign says. "What is my charge, Lysander?"

"To defend your throne. To create a union where it is safer for subjects to follow than to fight. That is the role of Sovereign. Be loved by a few, be feared by the many, and always know thyself."

"Very good, Lysander," she says sadly.

"The purpose of a Sovereign isn't to rule. It's to lead," I say.

Not even hearing me, she turns to the Joy Knight, who is at the controls of the holodeck preparing her broadcast. "Is it ready?"

"Yes, my liege. Greens have restored the links. It'll go out live to the Core."

"Say your goodbyes to the Red . . . *Mustang*," Aja says, patting Mustang's head.

"Can't even do it yourself?" I ask the Jackal. "What a man you are."

He frowns. "I want to do it, Octavia," the Jackal says suddenly, rising from his seat and walking out to the holodeck.

"Olympic Knights carry out executive executions," Aja says. "It's not your place, ArchGovernor."

"I don't remember asking for your permission." Aja bares her teeth at the insult, but the Sovereign's hand on her shoulder restrains her tongue.

"Let him do it," the Sovereign says. Strange, the Sovereign's deference to the Jackal. It's out of character, but in keeping with the oddness I've felt between them on the day. Why would he be here, I wonder. Not Luna. That's obvious enough. But why would he come to a place where the Sovereign has absolute power over him? At any moment, she could kill him. He must have something over her, to buy himself immunity. What is his play here? I sense Mustang trying to divine the same answer as Aja moves away from me. The Joy Knight offers the Jackal a scorcher, but Adrius refuses. Instead, he picks Sevro's gun from his holster and twirls it around his index finger.

"He's no Gold," the Jackal explains. "He doesn't deserve a razor or a state death. He'll go like his uncle. In any matter, I very much would like to begin the transition as the hand of justice. Plus, offing Darrow with Sevro's gun is . . . more poetic, don't you think, Octavia?"

"Very well. Is there anything else you would like?" the Sovereign asks tiredly.

"No. You've been most accommodating." The Jackal takes Aja's place beside me as the Sovereign transforms before our eyes. The exhaustion burning away from her face as she adopts the serene, matronly visage I remember telling me: "Obedience. Sacrifice. Prosperity," time and time again from the HC in Lykos. Then, Octavia seemed a goddess so far beyond mortal ken that I would have given my life to please her, to make her proud of me. Now I'd give my life to end hers.

The Joy Knight nods to the Sovereign. A light glows softly above her, empowering the woman with the fury and warmth of the sun. It's just a spotlight. The lamp deepens its glow. The Jackal brushes an errant strand from his fastidiously parted hair and smiles fondly at me.

The broadcast begins.

"Men and Women of the Society," Octavia says. "This is your Sovereign. Since the dawn of man, our saga as a species has been one of tribal warfare. It has been one of trial, one of sacrifice, one of daring to defy nature's natural limits. Then, after years of toiling in the dirt, we rose to the stars. We bound ourselves in duty. We set aside our own wants, our own hungers to embrace the Hierarchy of Color, not to oppress the many for the glory of the few, as Ares and this . . . terrorist would have you believe, but to secure the immortality of the human race on principles of order and prosperity. It was an immortality that was assured before this man tried to steal it from us."

She points a long, elegant finger at me.

"This man, once a noble servant of you, of your families, should have been the brightest son of his Color. He was lifted up as a youth. Awarded merits of honor. But he chose vanity. To extend his own ego across the stars. To become a conqueror. He forgot his duty. He forgot the reason for order and has fallen into darkness, dragging the worlds with him.

"But we will not fall into that darkness. No. We will not bend to the forces of evil." She touches her heart. "We . . . *we* are the Society. We are Gold, Silver, Copper, Blue, White, Orange, Green, Violet, Yellow, Gray, Brown, Pink, Obsidian, and Red. The bonds that bind us together are stronger than the forces that pull us apart. For seven hundred years, Gold has shepherded humanity, brought light where there was dark, plenty where there was famine. Today we bring peace where there is war. But to have peace, we must destroy outright this murderer who has brought war to each and every one of our homes."

She turns to me with a callousness that reminds me of how she watched my duel with Cassius. How she would have let me die then sipped her wine and been about her dinner. I am a speck to her, even now. She's thinking past this moment. Past the time where my blood cools on the floor and they drag me off to be dissected.

"Darrow of Lykos, by the power entrusted in me by the Compact, I hereby find you guilty of conspiracy to incite acts of terror." I stare directly into the holoCam's optic lens, knowing how many countless souls watch me now. How many countless eyes will watch me long after I have gone. "I find you guilty of mass murder upon the citizens of Mars." I barely listen to her. My heart thunders in my chest. Rattling the fingers of my left hand. Pushing up into my throat. This is it. The end swarming toward me. "I find you guilty of murder." This moment, this fragment of time is my life in summary. It is my shout into the void. "And I find you guilty of treason against your Society. . . ."

But I want no shout.

Let that be for Roque. Let that be for the Golds. Give me something more. Something they cannot understand. Give me the rage of my people. The wrath of all people in bondage. As the Sovereign recites her sentence, as the Jackal waits to deliver it, as Mustang kneels on the ground, as Cassius watches me from among the Praetorians and Knights, waiting, and as Aja sees me look to the tall blond knight, she steps forward in trepidation because she knows something is wrong, I throw my head back and I howl.

I howl for my wife, for my father. For Ragnar and Quinn and Pax and Narol. For all the people I've lost. For all they would take.

I howl because I am a Helldiver of Lykos. I am the Reaper of Mars. And I have paid for access to this bunker with my flesh, all so I could come before Octavia, all so that I might either die with my friends or see our enemies brought to justice.

The Sovereign nods to the Jackal to execute the sentence. He presses the barrel to the back of my head and he squeezes the trigger. The gun kicks in his hand. Fire spits, scorching my scalp. Deafening sound ringing through my right ear. But I do not fall. No bullet carves through my head. Smoke swirls out of the barrel. And as the Jackal looks down at the gun, he knows.

"No . . ." He steps away from me, dropping the gun, trying to pull out his razor.

"Octavia . . ." Aja shouts, lunging forward.

But just then, in that beat of the heart, the Sovereign hears something behind the camera and turns to see a Praetorian guard with his head tilted, his pulseRifle thumping to the floor as a grisly red tongue protrudes from his mouth. Only it's not a tongue. It's Cassius's bloody razor that entered through the back of the Praetorian's skull and out between his teeth. It disappears back into the mouth. The three guards fall before the Sovereign can say a bloodydamn word. Cassius stands behind the slaughtered men, his head lowered, his razor red, his left hand holding the remote control to my restraints and Mustang's.

"Bellona?" is all the Sovereign can say before he presses the button. Mustang's steel vest unbuckles and falls to the ground. Mine follows suit. She dives for a dead Praetorian's pulseRifle. Unshackled, I rise, jerking my arms free and pulling the knife hidden inside the metal vest. I lunge toward the Sovereign. Faster than she can blink, I jam the blade through her black jacket into the softness of her lower belly. She gasps. Eyes huge. Inches from mine. I smell the coffee on her breath. Feel the flutter of her eyelashes as I stab her six more times in the gut and on the last, rip the metal up toward her sternum. Hot blood pours over my knuckles and chest as she spills open.

"Octavia!" Aja's charging me. Makes it halfway before Mustang, firing from her knees, shoots her in the armored side with the pulse-Rifle. The blast lifts Aja off her feet, slapping her across the room into the wooden conference table beside Sevro and Antonia's bodies, nearly crushing Lysander. Seeing their Sovereign stumbling backward, gut ripped open, the Truth Knight and the Joy Knight both wheel on Cassius, pulling their razors from their hips, their shields thrumming to life. Unarmored, wearing only his blood-spattered prison greens, Cassius flashes forward, skewering the surprised Truth Knight through his eye socket up through the roof of his skull.

The Jackal pulls my razor from his hip and slashes at me. I sidestep, coming at him. He swings again, screaming in rage, but I catch his arm and head butt him in the face before sweeping his legs and tackling him to the floor. I take my razor and stake his left arm to the floor so that he has no free hand. He screams. His spit spattering my face. Thrashing at me with his legs. I drop a knee into his forehead and leave him stunned and pinned to the floor.

"Darrow!" Cassius calls to me as he duels the Joy Knight. "Behind!"

Behind me, Aja's rising from the shattered remains of the table. Eyes wide with rage. I run from her to help Cassius and Mustang, knowing she'd kill me in seconds with my right hand gone. Blood darkens Cassius's green jumpsuit. His left leg has been slashed badly by the better-armored Joy Knight, who is using his weight and the pulsing aegis shield on his left arm to overwhelm Cassius. Mustang grabs two razors from the dead Praetorian and tosses one to me. I catch it on the run with my left hand. Toggle the hilt. Razor leaps to killing length. Cassius takes another slash to the leg and stumbles over a body, going down, blocking the second strike with the pulse-Fist, ruining the weapon. The Joy Knight's back is to me. He feels me coming, but it's too late. Silently, I jump through the air and swing a huge looping strike down at him from behind, left arm slowing as it meets the throbbing resistance of the pulseShield centimeters from the armor, then jerking as it cleaves into his sky-blue plate and through muscle and bone. Carrying from left shoulder to the right pelvis, parting his body at a diagonal. His body drips to the ground.

Silence in the room as the bodies hit the floor.

Mustang rushes to my side. She sweeps her golden mess of hair back, a fevered grin splitting her face. I help Cassius up from the ground.

"How was my acting?" he asks, wincing.

"Not quite as good as your swordwork," I say, looking at the bodies around him. He grins, more alive in battle than anywhere else. I feel a pang, knowing this is always how it should have been. Missing the days where we rode together in the highlands pretending we were lords of the earth. I grin back at him, wounded, bleeding, but almost whole for the first time I can remember.

"Will you two save the flirting for later," Mustang says.

Side by side with her, we turn together to face the deadliest human being in the Solar System. She's crouched over a terribly wounded Octavia, who has crawled to the edge of the holodeck and pants on her back, holding her stomach together with both hands. Octavia is pale and shivering. Tears stream down Aja's face and Lysander's, who has rushed into the pit to help his grandmother.

"Aja!" the Jackal screams from the floor. "Kill them! Open the door or kill them!" He's lost his mind. Thrashing about, trying to reach the whip toggle on the razor with his stump. It's three and a half feet above him and he just can't quite reach. "Open it!" he says through gnashing teeth.

But to open the door she must reach it. And to reach it, she must go through me and my friends then present her back to us while she enters the code. She's trapped in here till we're dead or she is.

"Aja, give us the Sovereign. Her justice is due," I say, knowing what Aja's reply to that will be, but minding the holodeck is still active. Still broadcasting as Gold blood wets the floor. Aja does not turn to look at us. Not yet. Her huge hands caress Octavia's face. She cradles the older woman like a mother holding her own child. "Stay alive," she tells her. "I will get you out of here. I promise. Just stay alive, Octavia."

Octavia nods weakly. Lysander touches Aja's arm. "Hurry. Please."

"Wear her down," Mustang whispers. "She's the one with the ticking clock."

"Don't let her pin you in a corner," I say. "Move laterally like we planned. Cassius, you can still take point?"

"Just try to keep up," he says.

Aja rises from her crouch to her full height, a brooding mass of muscle and armor, the greatest student of the greatest razormaster the Society has ever known. Face dark, unreadable. The deep blue Protean armor moving subtly with sea dragons. Shoulders nearly as broad as Ragnar's. I wish I could have brought Sefi here. A meter and a half of killing silver slithers out before Aja and she takes the winter stance of the Willow Way, sword raised like a torch off to the side, left foot forward, hips sunken, knees slightly bent. Mustang and I slide apart taking the right and left. Cassius, the best swordsman of us now, takes the middle. Aja's hungry eyes devour our weaknesses. The drag in Cassius's step, my missing right hand, Mustang's size, the arrangement of obstacles on the floor. And she attacks.

There are two strategies when fighting multiple opponents. The first is use them against one another. But Cassius and I have always been of one mind in battle, and Mustang is adaptable. So Aja chooses the second option: an all out attack on me before Cassius or Mustang can come to my aid. She deems me the weakest enemy. And she is right. Her whip cracks toward my face faster than I can bring my blade up. I flinch back, almost losing my eye. Throwing off my center of balance. She's on me, blade rigid, poking at me in a poetic frenzy of carefully constructed movements to bring my blade out of position across my body, so she can perform Lorn's maneuver called the Wing Scalp. Where she tries to lever her blade atop mine to touch the tip to my sword arm's shoulder and scrape down to the outside of my wrist to peel off the muscle and tendons along the way. I dance back, robbing her the leverage, navigating the corpses behind me as Cassius and Mustang close on Aja. Cassius is rushed in his approach, and he overextends, like I almost did.

But Aja doesn't use her razor. She activates her gravBoots in a quick burst and launches back at him, two hundred kilograms of armor and Peerless Scarred propelled by gravBoots crashes into flesh and bones. You can almost hear his skeleton creak. His body wraps around her, forehead smashing against her armored shoulder. He drips off her and she spikes him to the ground. Mustang rushes her flank to stop her from finishing Cassius off. But Aja was expecting the rush from Mustang and used Cassius to bait her. She slashes Mustang shallowly across the stomach, nearly opening her lower intestine.

I hurl my razor at Aja from behind. She somehow hears or feels it coming and bends sideways as it passes and sticks into the wall of the holodeck that separates it from the sitting room above. Aja's leg shoots out at Mustang, impacting her kneecap and jamming it backward. Can't tell if it dislocates, but Mustang stumbles back, razor outstretched and Aja turns back toward me, because I have no weapon.

"Shit shit shit shit shit," I hiss, scrambling toward the Praetorians to pick up one of their razors. I gain a pulseRifle and fire blindly behind me. Aja's pulseShield absorbs the munitions, throbbing crimson as she sprints at me and slashes the weapon from my hand. I escape again, rolling backward, taking a long burning gash on the back of my hamstrings, but gaining a razor as I jump out of the holodeck ring up to the sitting level several feet above. She picks up a pulseFist and shoots it at me. I dive down so she loses her shot. The steel ceiling above me bubbles and drips down. I roll to the side.

Razors keen on the deck bellow. I scramble back to the lip to get back in the fight. Aja's cutting us to ribbons and all fleeing does is allow her to turn back to Cassius and Mustang. She bears down on him, using his limp and the new wound in his shoulder against him. Mustang attacks from behind before he's cut down, but Aja bends when Mustang slashes, moving like she's studied the fight before it ever happened.

We're not going to put her down, I realize. This was our fear. Losing my hand was never part of the plan, either. One by one she's going to kill us.

I have a brief moment of hope when Mustang and Cassius finally pin Aja between them. I jump down to help the assault. The woman pivots and twirls like a willow caught among three tornadoes. She knows her armor will take our glancing blows but our skin can't take hers. She goes for shallow cuts, bleeding us out methodically, aiming for the tendons in our knees, arms, like Lorn taught us both. A sage digging the roots.

Her blade cuts deep into my forearm, lacerates my knuckles, taking off a corner of my pinky. I roar anger, but anger isn't enough. My instincts aren't enough. We're too spent, too overwhelmed by the monstrosity of her. Lorn trained her too well. Spinning, she delivers a two-handed thrust up into the right side of my rib cage. My world rocks. She lifts me up with a horrible bellow. My feet dangle half a meter above the deck. Cassius charges her and she flings me off the edge of her blade to parry his attack. I crash to the ground, my chest feeling like it is caving in on itself. Gasp for air, barely able to draw breath. Cassius and Mustang put themselves between Aja and me.

"Do not touch him," Mustang hisses.

The blade missed my organs, wedging itself between two of the reinforced ribs Mickey gave me, but I'm bleeding all over myself. Trying to stand, scrambling across the deck. The Jackal watches me from his place on the ground, exhausted from trying to free himself. He's grinning, despite the horror of bodies all around us, knowing Aja is going to kill me. The Sovereign's face distant and fading she watches too, propped up against the lip of the holodeck as it rises to the rest of the room, Lysander's hands holding her together. Aja looks at her in fear, knowing she has not long to live.

"How could you choose him over us?" Aja shouts in rage to Mustang and Cassius.

"Easily," Mustang replies.

Cassius pulls the syringe from the holster on his leg and tosses it across the room to me. "Do it before she kills us, man." I stumble to my feet as Aja tries furiously to get at me, but Cassius and Mustang have strength enough to batter her away. She roars in frustration. The three slipping on blood, my friends not long for this world standing toe-to-toe with her. I make it to the edge of the holodeck, opposite the Sovereign, and climb toward Sevro's body.

"You cannot run!" Aja shouts. "I will carve your eyes out. There's nowhere to run, you rusty coward!" But I am not running. I fall to my knees beside Sevro. The front of his chest is a chaos of laboratory blood and torn fabric from the entry wounds of Cassius's execution. I cut open his shirt with my razor. Six holes stare up at me from the combat vest Cyther made him, bits of Carved flesh looking so real. His face is quiet and peaceful. But peace isn't in his nature, and we haven't earned it yet. I pop open the syringe filled with Holiday's snakebite. Enough to wake the dead. Even those faking eternal sleep from Narol's wicked cocktail of haemanthus extract. I pull off his vest.

"Wakey, wakey, Goblin," I say as I lift high the syringe, praying the silent prayer than his heart doesn't fail, and plunge it straight into my best friend's chest. His eyes burst open.

"Fuuuuuuuuuck."

62

|||||||||||||||||||||||

OMNIS VIR LUPUS

Exploding upward out of the coma induced by the haemanthus oil in the flask he was drinking from before we freed Cassius, he flails past me, gaining his feet, looking around with manic, wild eyes, hands vibrating. Holding his heart, gasping in pain as I did when Trigg and Holiday brought me from my prison. The last thing he saw was my face in the brig, now to wake here, to be thrust into the battle, blood and bodies littering the floor. He stares at me with crazed, bloodshot eyes, pointing at my belly. "You're bleeding! Darrow! You're bleeding!"

"I know."

"Where is your hand? You're missing a fucking hand!"

"I know!"

"Bloodydamn." His eyes dart around, seeing the Jackal pinned and Octavia on the ground, Aja beating Cassius and Mustang back. "It worked! It fucking worked! We've got to help the Goldbrows, shithead. Get up! *Get up!*" He hauls me to my feet and shoves my razor back into my hand, rushing into the holopit, howling the hideous battle cry we made as children among the frozen pines. "I'm going to kill you, Aja! I'm going to kill you in your face!"

"It's Barca!" the Jackal screams from the ground. "Barca's alive!"

On the run, Sevro scoops up a pulseFist from a dead Praetorian and tramples over the Jackal's body, stomping on his face as he grabs the razor that pins the young ArchGovernor to the ground without stopping. He flies into Aja, firing with the pulseFist. Insane with the drugs and the victory he can smell.

The pulse blasts ripple over Aja's shield, spreading crimson around her silhouette, impairing her vision enough to finally let Cassius slip his razor through her guard. Still, she twists as it comes so it only takes her in the shoulder, but then Sevro is on her, stabbing her twice in the small of her back. She grunts in pain, backing away. I join the fray as Aja gains separation, stumbling back from us. But on the ground behind her, she leaves something few humans have seen: a thin ribbon of blood. It coats Sevro's razor. He wipes it from the tip of the blade and smears it between his fingers.

"Hahaha. Well look at that. You *do* bleed. Let's see how much more ya got in there." He hunches like an animal, stalking toward her as Mustang, Cassius, and I pin her between us, making a square around the greatest living Olympic Knight, like a wolfpack come upon a great panther of the forest. Shrinking before it as it charges, striking at its hindquarters, slashing its flanks. Bleeding it out. We're a prison of four. Sevro swishes his razor through the air, howling rabidly.

"Shut up!" Aja says, lashing out at him. But Sevro dances back and Cassius and I dart forward, stabbing at her. She parries Cassius's thrust at her neck and his two successive moves, but not in time to counter me. I feign a thrust at her abdomen and slash her shin instead, raking through the metal. Metal sparks and blood coats my blade. Mustang stabs her calf. I dart back as she wheels on me, making her overextend so Sevro can strike again. He does, furiously slashing the Achilles tendon on her right leg. She grunts and stumbles before lashing at him. He dances back.

"You're gonna die," he says with an evil little hiss. "You're gonna die."

"Shut up!"

"That one's for Quinn," he hisses as Cassius cuts through the tendons of her left knee. "This one's for Ragnar." I impale her right thigh with an underhanded thrust. "This one's for Mars." Mustang takes her arm off at the elbow. Aja looks down at the appendage on the ground, as if wondering if it belongs to her.

But she's given no respite. Sevro tosses aside his pulseFist, picks the Truth Knight's razor from the ground and jumps in the air to bring both his swords down into her chest, hanging there, a foot off the ground. Their faces inches from one another, noses nearly touching as Aja sinks to her knees, setting Sevro back on his feet.

"Omnis vir lupus."

He kisses her nose and jerks his razors out of her chest, letting them slither back into whips around his forearms. Arms outstretched, he backs away from the dying Protean Knight, greatest of her age as she pulses her last blood onto the cold floor. Still on her knees Aja's eyes drift hopelessly to the Sovereign, the woman who became mother to her sisters, who raised her, loved her as truly as any who rules the Solar System can love, and now dies along with her.

"I'm sorry . . . my liege." Aja wheezes wet breaths.

"Never be," Octavia manages from her place on the ground. "You burned bright, my Fury. Time itself . . . will remember you."

"Nah, prolly not," Sevro says pitilessly. "Nighty, night, Grimmus."

He lops off her head and kicks her in the chest. Her body teeters back and collapses to the floor, where he jumps atop it on all fours and howls. A deep moan escapes the Sovereign's mouth at the hideous sight. She shuts her eyes, leaking tears as we make our way to her and Lysander. Cassius and I limping together, his arm around my shoulders to take pressure off the leg he drags behind him. Mustang follows us. Sevro secures the Jackal by sitting on his chest and juggling a razor over his head.

Soaked in his grandmother's blood, Lysander grabs Octavia's razor from the ground and bars our way. "I won't let you kill her."

"Lysander . . . don't," Octavia says. "It's too late."

The boy's eyes are swollen with tears. The razor trembles in his hands. Cassius steps forward and extends a hand. "Drop the weapon, Lysander. I don't want to kill you." Mustang and I exchange a glance. One Octavia notices, and must make her soul shiver. Lysander knows he cannot fight us. His sense overcomes his grief and he drops the razor, stepping back to watch us hollowly.

Octavia's eyes are distant and dark, already halfway to that other world where even she does not reign. I thought there'd be spite in the end from her, or begging like Vixus or Antonia. But there's nothing weak in her even now. It's sadness and love lost that come in the end. She did not create the hierarchy, but she was its keeper in her time. And for that, she must be held accountable.

"Why?" Octavia asks Cassius, shaking from sorrow. "Why?"

"Because you lied," he says.

Wordlessly Cassius pulls the small holocube, a thumb-sized triangular prism, from his ammunition belt and sets it in her bloody hands. Images dance across its surfaces before floating into the air above the Sovereign's hands. The scene of Cassius's family dying plays, bathing her in blue light. Shadows move through a hall, becoming men in scarabSkin. They cut down his aunt in a hallway and the men move through and appear a moment later dragging children, which they kill with the razors and boots. More bodies are dragged and piled up, then lit on fire so there would be no survivors. More than forty children and non-scarred family members died that night. They thought they could heap the sin upon the shoulders of a fallen man. But it was the Jackal's work. He finished the war between the Bellona and the Augustuses, and the Sovereign's cooperation and silence was his price for my Triumph.

"You ask me why?" Cassius's voice is barely above a whisper. "It is because you are without honor. I swore an oath as an Olympic Knight to honor the Compact, to bring justice to the Society of Man. You swore the same, Octavia. But you forgot what that meant. Everyone has. That is why this world is broken. Maybe the next one can be better."

"This world is the best we can afford," Octavia whispers.

"Do you really believe that?" Mustang asks.

"With all my heart."

"Then I pity you," Mustang says.

And so does Cassius. "My heart was my brother. And I no longer believe in a world that says he was too weak to deserve life. He would have believed in this. In the hope for something new." Cassius looks over at me. "For Julian, I can believe that too."

Cassius hands me the two other holocubes from his pouch. The first is the murder of my friends at my Triumph. The second is for the Rim; when they see this recording, they will know I have a struck a blow for them. Politics never rests. I set the two holocubes in the Sovereign's hands to join the first. Rhea glows before her. A blue and white moon, gorgeous beside its brothers Iapetus and Titan as they orbit giant Saturn. Then over the moon's north pole, tiny slivers which you'd hardly notice flicker several innocent times, and mushrooms of fire bloom upon the surface of the blue and white planet.

As the nuclear fire blazes in the Sovereign's eyes, Mustang moves aside so I can crouch before the dying woman, speaking softly so she will know that justice, not vengeance, has found her in the end.

"My people have a legend of a being who stands astride the road leading to the world after. He will judge the wicked from the good. His name is the Reaper. I am not him. I'm just a man. But soon you will meet him. Soon he will judge you for all the sins you hold."

"Sins?" Octavia shakes her head, looking back to the three holos dancing in her hands, these drops in her ocean of sins. "These are sacrifices. What it takes to rule," she says, her hands closing around them. "I own them as I own my triumphs. You will see. You will be the same, Conqueror."

"No. I will not."

"In the absence of a sun, there can be only darkness." She shudders, cold now. I fight off the urge to put something over her. She knows what's being left behind. When she dies, the succession struggle will begin. It'll tear Gold apart. "Someone . . . someone must rule, or a thousand years from now, children will ask, 'Who broke the worlds? Who put the light out,' and their parents will say it was you." But I already know this. I knew this when I asked Sevro if he knew how this would end. I will not replace tyranny with chaos. There must be order, even if it is a compromise. But I don't tell her that. She swallows painfully, a struggle to even breathe. "Listen to me. You must stop him. You must . . . stop Adrius . . ."

Those are the last words of Octavia au Lune. And as they fade, the fire of Rhea cools in her eyes and life leaves a cold pupil surrounded by gold, staring into infinite dark. I close her eyes for her. Chilled by her passing, by her words, her fear.

The Sovereign of the Society, who has ruled for sixty years, is dead.

And I feel nothing but dread, because the Jackal has begun to laugh.

63

|||||||||||||||||||||||

SILENCE

His laughter rattles through the room. His face pale under the glow of the holo of the moon and the fleets pummeling one another in the darkness. Mustang has turned off the holodeck's broadcast and is already analyzing the Sovereign's data center as Cassius moves toward Lysander and I rise above Octavia's body. My body burns from wounds.

"What did she mean, stop him?" Cassius asks me.

"I don't know."

"Lysander?"

The boy's too traumatized by the horror around him to speak.

"Video went out to the ships and the planets," Mustang says. "People are seeing Octavia's death. Communiqué boards are flooding. They don't know who is in control. We have to move now before they marshal behind someone."

Cassius and I approach the Jackal. "What did you do?" Sevro's asking. He shakes the small man. "What was she talking about?"

"Get your dog off me," the Jackal says from under Sevro's knees. I pull Sevro back. He paces around the Jackal, still vibrating with adrenaline.

"What did you do?" I ask.

"There's no point in talking with him," Mustang says.

"No point? Why do you think the Sovereign let me in her presence," the Jackal asks from the ground. He comes up to a knee, holding his wounded hand to his chest. "Why she did not fear the gun on my hip, unless there was a greater threat keeping her in line?"

He looks up at me from under disheveled hair. His eyes calm despite the butchering we've done.

"I remember the feeling of being under the ground, Darrow," he says slowly. "The cold stone under my hands. My Pluto housemembers around me, hunched in the darkness. The steam on their breaths, looking to me. I remember how afraid I was of failing. Of how long I had prepared, how little my father thought of me. All my life weighed in those few moments. All of it slipping away. We'd run from our castle, fleeing Vulcan. They came so fast. They were going to enslave us. The last of our housemembers were still running through the tunnel by the time I rigged the mines to blow, but so were Vulcan. I could hear my father's voice. Hear him telling me how he was not surprised I failed so quickly. It was a week before we killed a girl and ate her legs to survive. She begged us not to. Begged us to choose someone else. But I learned then in that moment if no one sacrifices, then no one survives."

Cold fear wells in me, beginning in the deep hollow of my stomach and spreading upward. "Mustang . . ."

"They're here," she says, horrified.

"What's happening? What's here?" Sevro hisses.

"Darrow . . ." Cassius whispers.

"The nukes aren't on Mars," I say. "They're on Luna."

The Jackal's smile stretches. Slowly, he gains his feet and not one of us dares touch him. It all falls into place. The tension between him and the Sovereign. The subtle threats. His boldness in coming here into the Sovereign's place of power. His ability to mock Aja without consequence.

"Oh, shit. *Shit. Shit. Shit.*" Sevro pulls his Mohawk. "Shit."

"I never wanted to nuke Mars," the Jackal says. "I was born on

Mars. It is my birthright, the prize from which all things flow. Her helium is the blood of the empire. But this moon, this skeleton orb is, like Octavia, a treacherous old crone sucking at the marrow of the Society, crowing about what was instead of what can be. And Octavia let me ransom it. Just as you will, because you are weak and you did not learn what you should have at the Institute. To win, you must sacrifice."

"Mustang, can you find the bombs?" I ask. "Mustang!"

She's been struck dumb. "No. He would have masked the radiation signatures. Even if we could, we couldn't deactivate them. . . ." She reaches for the com to call our fleet.

"If you make the call, then I detonate a bomb every minute," the Jackal says, tapping his ear where a little com has been implanted. Lilath must be listening. She must have the trigger. That's what he meant. She's his insurance. "Would I really tell you my plan if you could do anything about it?" He straightens his hair and wipes blood from his armor. "The bombs were installed weeks ago. The Syndicate smuggled the devices across the moon for me. Enough to create nuclear winter. A second Rhea, if you will. When they were in place, I told Octavia what I had done and I told her my terms. She would carry on as Sovereign until the Rising was put down, which . . . has taken a surprising twist . . . obviously. And afterward, on the day of victory, she would convene the Senate, abdicate the Morning Throne and name me her successor. In return, I would not destroy Luna."

"That's why Octavia has the Senate rounded up," Mustang says in disgust. "So you could be Sovereign?"

"Yes."

I stand back from him, feeling the weight of the fight on my shoulders, the weakness in my body from the strain, the loss of blood, now this . . . this evil. This selfishness, it's overwhelming.

"You're bloodydamn mad," Sevro says.

"He's not," Mustang says. "I could forgive him if he were mad. Adrius, there are three billion people on this moon. You don't want to be that man."

"They don't care for me. So why should I care for them?" he asks. "This is all a game. And I have won."

"Where are the bombs?" Mustang asks, taking a threatening step toward him.

"Uh-uh," he says, scolding her. "Touch a hair on my head, Lilath detonates a bomb." Mustang's beside herself.

"These are people," she says. "You have the power to give three billion people their lives, Adrius. That is power beyond anything anyone should ever want. You have the chance to be better than Father. Better than Octavia . . ."

"You condescending little bitch," he says with a small laugh of disbelief. "You really think you can still manipulate me. This one is on you. Lilath, detonate the bomb on the southern Mare Serenitatis." We all look to the hologram of the moon above our heads, hoping beyond hope that somehow he's bluffing. That somehow the transmission won't go through. But a little red dot glows on the cool hologram, blossoming outward, a small almost insignificant little animation that envelops ten kilometers of city. Mustang rushes to the computer. "It's a nuclear event," she whispers. "There's more than five million people in that district."

"Were," the Jackal says.

"You freak . . ." Sevro shrieks, rushing the Jackal. Cassius gets in his path, knocking him back. "Get out of my way!"

"Sevro, calm down."

"Careful, Goblin! There's hundreds more," the Jackal says.

Sevro's overwhelmed, clutching his chest where his heart must be wrenching from the drugs. "Darrow, what do we do?"

"You obey," the Jackal says.

I force myself to ask: "What do you want?"

"What do I want?" He wraps a bit of cloth around his bleeding arm, using his teeth. "I want you to be what you always wanted, Darrow. I want you to be like your wife. A martyr. Kill yourself. Here. In front of my sister. In return, three billion souls live. Isn't that what you've always wanted? To be a hero? You die, and I will be crowned Sovereign. There will be peace."

"No," Mustang says.

"Lilath, detonate another bomb. Mare Anguis, this time."

Another red blossom erupts on the display. Nuclear fire ends the lives of millions. "Stop!" Mustang says. "Please. Adrius."

"You just killed six million people," Cassius says, not comprehending.

"They'll think it's us," Sevro sneers.

The Jackal agrees. "Each bomb looks like part of an invasion. This is your legacy, Darrow. Think of the children burning now. Think of their mothers screaming. How many you can save by simply pulling a trigger."

My friends look at me, but I'm in a distant place, listening to the moan of the wind through the tunnels of Lykos. Smelling the dew on the gears in the early morning. Knowing Eo will be waiting for me when I come home. Like she waits for me now at the end of the cobbled road, as Narol does, as Pax and Ragnar and Quinn and, I hope, Roque, Lorn, Tactus and the rest of them do. It would not be the end to die. It would be the beginning of something new. I have to believe that. But my death would leave the Jackal here in this world. It would leave him with power over those I love, over all I've fought for. I always thought I would die before the end. I trudged on knowing I was doomed. But my friends have breathed love into me, breathed my faith back into my bones. They've made me want to live. They've made me want to build. Mustang looks at me, her eyes glassy, and I know she wants me to choose life, but she will not choose for me.

"Darrow? What is your answer?"

"No." I punch him in the throat. He croaks. Unable to breathe. I knock him down and jump atop him, pinning his arms to the ground with my knees so his head is between my legs. I jam my hand into his mouth. His eyes go wild. Legs kicking. His teeth cut my knuckles, drawing blood.

The last time I pinned him down, I took the wrong weapon. What are hands to a creature like him? All his evil, all his lies, are spun with the tongue. So I grab it with my helldiver hand, pinning it between forefinger and thumb like the fleshy little baby pitviper it is. "This is always how the story would end, Adrius," I say down to him. "Not with your screams. Not with your rage. But with your silence."

And with a great pull, I rip out the tongue of the Jackal.

He screams beneath me. Blood bubbling from the mutilated stump at the back of his throat. Splashing over his lips. He thrashes. I shove off him and stand in dark rage, holding the bloody instrument of my enemy as he wails on the ground, feeling the hatred rolling through me and seeing the stunned eyes of my friends. I leave the com in his ear so Lilath can hear him wailing and I stalk to the holocontrols and hail Victra's ship. Her face appears, eyes widening at the sight of my face.

"*Darrow . . . you're alive . . .*" she manages. "*Sevro . . . The nukes . . .*"

"You need to destroy the *Lion of Mars*," I say. "Lilath is detonating the bombs on the surface. There's hundreds more hidden in the cities. Kill that ship!"

"*It's at the center of their formation,*" she protests. "*We'll destroy our fleet trying to get to it. It will take hours if we even manage.*"

"Can we jam their signal?" Mustang asks.

"*No.*"

"EMPs?" Sevro asks, coming up behind me. Victra's face brightens at the sight of him, before she shakes her head.

"*They have shielding,*" she says.

"Use the EMPs on the bombs to short-circuit their radio transmitters," I say. "Fire an Iron Rain and drop EMPs on the city till they're out."

"And plunge three billion people into the Middle Ages?" Cassius asks.

"*We'll be slaughtered,*" Victra says. "*We can't drop a Rain. We'll lose our army. And Gold will just keep the moon.*"

Another bomb detonates. This one nearer the southern pole. And then a fourth at the equator. We know the consequences to each one. "Lilath doesn't know exactly what's happened to Adrius," Cassius says quickly. "How loyal is she? Will she detonate all of them?"

"Not when he's still whimpering," I say. Least that's my hope.

"Excuse me," a small voice says. We turn to see Lysander standing behind us. We forgot about him in the mayhem. His eyes are shot red from tears. Sevro raises a pulseFist to shoot him. Cassius knocks it aside.

"Call my godfather," Lysander says bravely. "Call the Ash Lord. He will see reason."

"Oh, like hell . . ." Sevro says.

"We just killed the Sovereign and his daughter," I say. "The Ash Lord . . ."

"Destroyed Rhea," Lysander interrupts. "Yes. And it haunts him. Call him and he will help you. My grandmother would have wanted him to. Luna is our home."

"He's right," Mustang says, pushing me from the console. "Darrow, move." She's in that locked zone of concentration. Unable to relate her own thoughts as she starts opening direct com channels to the Gold Praetors in the fleet. The towering men and women appear around us like silvery ghosts, standing among the corpses they watched us make. Last to appear is the Ash Lord. His face stricken with rage. His daughter and master both dead by our hands.

"Bellona, Augustus," he growls, seeing Lysander among us. "Is it not enough . . ."

"Godfather, we have no time for recrimination," Lysander says.

"Lysander . . ."

"Please listen to them. Our world depends on it."

Mustang steps forward and raises her voice. "Praetors of the fleet, Ash Lord. The Sovereign is dead. The nuclear blasts you see destroying your home are not Red weapons. They come from your own arsenal which was stolen by my brother. His Praetor, Lilath, is overseeing the detonation of more than four hundred nuclear warheads from the bridge of *The Lion of Mars*. They will continue until Lilath is dead. My fellow Aureate, embrace change or embrace oblivion. The choice is yours."

"You are a traitor. . . ." one of the Praetors hisses.

Lysander walks off the holopad to the table where he sat earlier. He picks up his grandmother's scepter and returns as the Praetors are issuing threats to Mustang.

"She is no traitor," Lysander says, handing her the scepter. The blood of his grandmother staining his hands. "She is our conqueror."

64

||||||||||||||||||||||||

HAIL

The Lion of Mars dies an ignoble death, fired upon from all sides by loyalist and rebel alike. Watching Luna crackle with nuclear explosions did more to kill the bloodlust between the two navies than any peace or truce ever did. Few men truly like seeing beauty burn. But burn it does. Before the *Lion* is put to rest, more than twelve bombs detonate, carving new cities of fire and ash among those of steel and concrete. The moon is in turmoil.

As is the Gold Armada. With news of the Sovereign's death and the detonation of the bombs, the Society shudders beneath our feet. Wealthy Praetors are taking their personal ships and fracturing away, heading home to Venus, Mercury, or Mars. They do not stand together, because they do not know where to stand.

For sixty years Octavia has ruled. For most living, she is the only Sovereign they have ever known. Our civilization teeters on the brink. Electrical grids are down across the moon. Riots and panic spread as we prepare to leave the Sovereign's sanctum. There is an escape ship, but there is no escaping what we've done. We've carved the heart out of the Society. If we leave, what takes its place?

We knew we could never win Luna by force of arms. But that was never the goal. Just as it was not Ragnar's desire to fight until all Golds perished. He knew Mustang was the key. She always has been. That's why he risked our lives to let Kavax go. Now Mustang stands beneath the holo of the wounded moon, hearing the silent screams of the city as keenly as I. I step close to her.

"Are you ready?" I ask.

"What?" She shakes her head. "How could he do this?"

"I don't know," I say. "But we can fix it."

"How? This moon will be pandemonium," she says. "Tens of millions dead. The devastation . . ."

"And we can rebuild it, together."

The words flood her with hope, as if she's only just remembered where we are. What we've done. That we're together, alive. She blinks quickly and smiles at me. Then she looks at my arm, where my right hand used to be and touches my stomach where Aja stabbed me. "How are you still standing?"

"Because we're not yet done."

Battered and bloody, we join Cassius, Lysander, and Sevro before the door leading out of the Sovereign's inner sanctum as Cassius types in the Olympic code to open the doors. He pauses to sniff the air. "What's that smell?"

"Smells like a sewer," I say.

Sevro stares intensely at the razors he's taken from Aja, including the one belonging to Lorn. "I think it smells like victory."

"Did you shit your pants?" Cassius squints at him. "You did."

"Sevro . . ." Mustang says.

"It's an involuntary muscle reaction when you're fake executed and swallow massive amounts of haemanthus oil," Sevro snaps. "You think I would do that on purpose?"

Cassius and I look at each other.

I shrug. "Well, maybe."

"Yeah, actually."

He flips us the crux and makes a face, twisting his lips till it looks like he's going to explode. "What's happening?" I ask. "Are you . . . still . . ."

"No!" He throws his water bottle at me. "You stuck a needle full of adrenaline into my chest, asshole. I'm having a heart attack." He swats our hands as we try to help him. "I'm good. I'm good." He wheezes for a moment before straightening with a grimace.

"Are you sure you're prime?" Mustang asks.

"Left arm's numb. Probably need a Yellow."

We snort laughs. We look like walking corpses. Only thing keeping me up are the stim packs we found on the Praetorians. Cassius hobbles like an old man, but he's kept Lysander close to him, vetoing Sevro's offers to end the Lune bloodline here and now by drawing his razor. "The boy is under my protection," Cassius sneered. And now he walks with us as a sign of our legitimacy.

"I love you all," I say as the door begins to groan open. I adjust the unconscious Jackal, who I carry on my shoulder as a prize. "No matter what happens."

"Even Cassius?" Sevro asks.

"Especially me, today," Cassius says.

"Stay close," Mustang says to us, clutching the scepter tight.

The first great door parts. Mustang squeezes my hand. Sevro vibrates with fear. Then the second rumbles and dilates open to reveal a hall filled with Praetorians, their weapons drawn and pointed into the mouth of the bunker. Mustang steps forward bearing two symbols of power, one in each hand.

"Praetorians, you serve the Sovereign. The Sovereign is dead. A new star rises."

She continues walking toward them, refusing to break her step when she nears their line of bristling metal. I think a young Gold with furious eyes might pull the trigger. But his old captain puts a hand on the man's weapon, lowering it.

And they break for her. Parting and lowering their weapons one by one. They back away to let her pass. Their helmets slithering back into their armor. I've never seen a woman so glorious and powerful as she is now. She is the calm eye of the storm and we follow in her wake. Riding the Dragon Maw lift up in silence. More than four dozen of the Praetorians have come with us.

We find the Citadel in chaos. Servants ransacking rooms, guards leaving their posts in two and threes, worried for their families or their friends. The Obsidians we said were coming are still in orbit. Sefi is with the ships. We only created the ruse to draw men from the room. But it seems word has spread. The Sovereign is dead. The Obsidians are coming.

Amidst the chaos there is only one leader. And as we move through the Citadel's black marbled halls, past towering Gold statues and departments of state, soldiers gather behind us, their boots stamping over the marble halls to flock to Mustang, the one symbol of purpose and power left in the building. She lifts both her symbols of power high in the air, and those who first raise weapons against us see them and me and Cassius and the swelling mass of soldiers behind us and realize they're fighting the tide. They join us, or they run. Some take shots at us, or rush forward in small bands to halt our progress, but they're cut down before they get within ten meters of Mustang.

By the time we come before the great ivory-white doors to the Senate Chambers, behind which Senators have been sequestered inside by Praetorians, an army of hundreds is at our backs. And only a thin line of Praetorians bars our way to the Senate Chamber. Twenty in number.

An elegant Gold Knight steps forward, leader of the men guarding the chamber. He eyes the hundred behind us, seeing the purple adherents Mustang has gathered, the Obsidians, the Grays, me. And he makes a decision. He salutes Mustang sharply.

"My brother has thirty men in the Citadel," Mustang says. "The Boneriders. Find them and arrest them, Captain. If they resist, kill them."

"Yes, Lady Augustus." He snaps his fingers and departs with a fist of soldiers. The two Obsidians guarding the doors push them open for us and Mustang strides into the Senate Chamber.

The room is vast. A tiered funnel of white marble. At the bottom center is a podium from which the Sovereign presides over the ten levels of the chamber. We enter on the north side, causing a disruption. Hundreds of beady Politico eyes turn their entitled focus toward us. They will have watched the broadcast. Seen Octavia die. Seen the bombs wrecking their moon. And somewhere in the room, Roque's mother will stand up from her seat on her marble bench and crane her neck to watch our bloody band stomping down the white marble stairs to the bottom center of the great chamber, passing Senators to our right and left, bringing silence with us instead of shouts or protests. Lysander trails behind Cassius.

You can hear the rasping panicked breath of the Senate Majority Speaker as his Pink attendants help his withered form down from the podium where he was presiding over something of great importance. They were holding an election. Here, now, in the middle of chaos. And now they look like children who've been caught with their hands in the biscuit jar. Of course they would never suspect that the Praetorians guarding them would support rebels. Or that we could walk from the Sovereign's bunker unimpeded. But they've created a Society of fear. Where men and women must attach themselves to a rising star to survive. That's all this is. That simple human directive that allows for this coup to work. The old power is dead. See how they flock to the new.

Mustang takes the podium with the rest of us flanking her. I toss the Jackal to the ground so the Senate can see what has become of him. He's unconscious and pale from blood loss. Mustang looks at me. This is a moment she never wanted. But she accepts it as her burden just as I have accepted mine as Reaper. I see how it troubles her. How she will need me as I've needed her. But I could never stand where she stands or hold what she holds. Not without destroying everyone in this room. They would never accept it. If I am the bridge to the lowColors, she's the bridge to the high. Only together can we bind these people. Only together can we bring peace.

"Senators of the Society," Mustang proclaims, "I stand before you, Virginia au Augustus. Daughter of Nero au Augustus of the Lion House of Mars. You may know me. Sixty years ago Octavia au Lune stood before you with the head of a tyrant, her father, and laid her claim on the post of Sovereign to this Society."

Her keen eyes scour the room.

"I stand before you now with the head of a tyrant." She lifts her left hand to show the head of Octavia. One of the two objects which granted us passage here. Gold respects only one thing. And to change, they must be tamed by that one thing. "The Old Age has brought nuclear holocaust to the heart of the Society. Millions burned for Octavia's greed. Millions burn now for my brother's. We must save ourselves from ourselves before the inheritance of humanity is ash. Today I declare the beginning of a new age." She looks at me. "With new allies. New ways. I have the Rising at my back. A navy made of great Golden Houses which holds the Obsidian Horde in orbit. You have a choice before you." She tosses the head on the stone podium and raises her other hand. In it is the Dawn Scepter, bestowing upon the bearer the right to rule Society. "Bend. Or break."

A silence fills the chamber. So vast I feel it might swallow us all into itself and begin the war anew. No Gold will be the first to bend. I could make them. But better I bend for them. I fall to my knee before Mustang. Looking up into her eyes, I put my stump over my heart and feel myself swept away by the impossible joy of the moment. "Hail, Sovereign," I say. Then Cassius falls to his knee. And Sevro. Then Lysander au Lune and the Praetorians, and then one by one the Senators fall to their knees till all but fifty kneel and break the silence together, shouting with a single riotous voice: "Hail, Sovereign. Hail, Sovereign!"

A week after Mustang's ascension, I stand beside her to watch her brother hang. But for Valii-Rath and some ten men, the Jackal's Boneriders have been found and executed. Now their leader walks past me through the crowded Luna square. His hair is feathery and combed. His prisoner jumpsuit lime green. The lowColors around us watch in silence. A light dusting of snow falls from a thin skin of gray clouds. I'm nauseous from my radiation medication. But I came for her as she came for me to watch Roque buried. She's quiet and serene beside me. Face pale as the marble beneath our feet. The Telemanuses stand beside her, watching impassively as the Jackal climbs the stairs of the metal scaffold to where the White hangwoman waits.

The woman reads the sentence. Jeers are shouted from the crowd. A bottle shatters at the Jackal's feet. A stone splits his forehead. But he does not blink or buckle. He stands proud and vain as they loop the noose around his neck. I wish this would bring Pax back to us. That Quinn and Roque and Eo could live again, but this man has carved his mark in the world. The Jackal of Mars will never be forgotten.

The White moves for the lever, snow gathering on Adrius's hair. Mustang swallows. And the trapdoor opens. On Mars there's not much gravity, so you have to pull the feet to break the neck. They let the loved ones do it. On Luna there's even less. But no one comes forward from the crowd as the White extends the invitation. Not a soul lifts a finger as the Jackal's legs kick and his face purples. There's a stillness in me watching the sight. As if I'm a million kilometers away. I cannot feel for him. Not now. Not after all he's done. But I know Mustang does. I know this tears her apart. So I lightly squeeze her hand and guide her forward. She moves across the snow in a daze to grip her twin brother's feet. Looking up at him as if this were a dream. She whispers something and, lowering her head, she pulls down, showing him he was loved, even at the end.

65

||||||||||||||||||||||

THE VALE

In the weeks following the bombing of Luna and the ascension of Mustang, the world has changed. Millions lost their lives, but for the first time there is hope. In the aftermath of her speech to the Senate, dozens of Gold ships defected, joining the forces of Orion and Victra. The Ash Lord did his best to rally his navy, but with Luna burning, his fleet fracturing, and Mustang as Sovereign, it was all he could do to keep his own ships from falling into enemy hands. He retreated to Mercury with the core of his forces.

In his absence, Mustang has secured the cooperation of much of the military, particularly the Gray Legions and Obsidian slave-knights. She has used this political muscle to take the first steps to dismantling the Color Hierarchy and the Gold grip on military power. The Senate has been disbanded. The Board of Quality Control has been dissolved. Thousands face charges of crimes against humanity. Justice will not be so quick as it was with the Jackal, or so clean, but we will do the best we can.

I thought I might be able to rest after Octavia was dead, but we are not without enemies. Romulus and the Moon Lords remain on the

Rim. The Ash Lord aims to rally Mercury and Venus. Gold warlords have begun carving out claims. And Luna itself is a disaster. Overrun by riots and shortages of food and spreading radiation. She will survive, but I doubt she will ever look the same, no matter how much Quicksilver promises to rebuild the city to even greater heights.

My own body is in recovery. Mickey and Virany reattached my hand, which I retrieved from the Jackal's shuttle that set down on Luna. It will be months before I can write again, much less use a blade. Though I hope I have less cause for that in the coming days.

In my youth, I thought I would destroy the Society. Dismantle its customs. Shatter the chains and something new and beautiful would simply grow from the ashes. That's not how the world works. This compromised victory is the best mankind could hope for. Change will come slower than Dancer or the Sons want, but it will come without the price of anarchy.

So we hope.

Under the supervision of Holiday, Sefi has set off to Mars to begin the slow process of freeing the rest of her people, visiting the poles with medicine instead of weapons. I remember how dark her eyes seemed when she looked at one of the Jackal's nuclear craters in person. For now, she's embraced the legacy of her brother, and plans to settle on warmer land set aside for her people on Mars. Though she wishes to keep her people from the alien cities, I think she knows deep down that she will not be able to control them. The Obsidians will leave their prisons. They will grow curious, spread, and assimilate. Their world will never be the same. Nor will that of my people. Soon I will return to Mars to help Dancer lead the migration of Reds to the surface. Many will stay and continue the lives they know. But for others, there will be a chance for life under the sky.

I said farewell to Cassius the day before last as he departed Luna. Mustang wanted him to stay and help us shape a new, fairer system of justice. But he's had enough of politics. "You don't have to go," I told him as I stood with him on the landing pad.

"There's nothing for me here but memories," he said. "I've been living my life too long for others. I want to see what else is out there. You can't fault me for that."

"And the boy?" I asked, nodding to Lysander, who moved into the ship carrying a satchel of belongings. "Sevro thinks it's a mistake to let him live. What were his words? 'It's like leaving a pitviper egg under your seat. Sooner or later it's gonna hatch.'"

"And what do you think?"

"I think it's a different world. So we should act like it. He's got Lorn's blood in his veins as much as he's got Octavia's. Not that blood makes a difference anymore."

My tall friend smiled fondly at me. "He reminds me of Julian. He's a good soul, despite everything. I'll raise him right. Away from all this." He extended a hand, not to shake mine, but to give me the ring he took from my finger the night Lorn and Fitchner died. I closed his hand back around it.

"That belongs to Julian," I said.

He nodded softly. "Thank you . . . brother." And there, on a citadel landing platform in what was once the heart of Gold power, Cassius au Bellona and I shake hands and say farewell, almost six years to the day since we first met.

Weeks later, I watch the waves lap at the shore as a gull careens overhead. Whitecaps mark the dark water that lashes the northern beach's sea stacks. Mustang and I set our little two-person flier down on the east-northeast coast of the Pacific Rim, at the edge of a rain forest on a great peninsula. Moss grows on the rocks, on the trees. The air is crisp. Just cold enough to see your breath. It is my first time on Earth, but I feel like my spirit has come home. "Eo would have loved it here, wouldn't she?" Mustang asks me. She wears a black coat with the collar pulled up around her neck. Her new Praetorian bodyguards sit in the rocks a half kilometer off.

"Yes," I say. "She would have." A place like this is the beating heart of our songs. Not a warm beach or a tropical paradise. This wild land is full of mystery. It holds its secrets covetously behind arms of fog and veils of pine needles. Its pleasures, like its secrets, must be earned. It reminds me of my dreams of the Vale. The smoke from the fire we made of driftwood rises diagonally across the horizon.

"Do you think it will last?" Mustang asks me, watching the water from our place in the sand. "The peace."

"It would be the first time," I say.

She grimaces and leans into me, closing her eyes. "At least we have this."

I smile, reminded of Cassius as an eagle skims low over the water before rising up through the mist and disappearing in the trees that jut from the top of a sea stack. "Have I passed your test?"

"My test?" she asks.

"Ever since you blocked my ship from leaving Phobos, you've been testing me. I thought I passed on the ice, but it didn't stop there."

"You noticed," she says with a mischievous little grin. It fades and she brushes hair from her eyes. "I'm sorry that I couldn't just follow you. I needed to see if you could build. I needed to see if my people could live in your world."

"No, I understand that," I say. "But there's more to it. Something changed when you saw my mother. My brother. Something opened up in you."

She nods, eyes still on the water. "There's something I have to tell you." I look over at her. "You lied to me for nearly six years. Since the moment we met. In the Lykos tunnel you broke what we had. That trust. That feeling of closeness we built. Piecing that together takes time. I needed to see if we could find what we lost. I needed to see if I could trust you."

"You know you can."

"I do, now," she says. "But . . ."

I frown. "Mustang, you're shaking."

"Just let me finish. I didn't want to lie to you. But I didn't know how you would react. What you would do. I needed you to make the choice to be more than a killer not just for me, but for someone else too." She looks past me to the blue sky where a ship coasts lazily down. I hold my hand up against the autumn sun to watch it approach.

"Are we expecting company?" I ask warily.

"Of a sort." She stands. I join her. And she goes to her tiptoes to kiss me. It is a gentle, long kiss that makes me forget the sand under our boots, the smell of pine and salt in the breeze. Her nose is cold against mine. Her cheeks ruddy. All the sadness, all the hurt in the past making this moment all the sweeter. If pain is the weight of being, love is the purpose. "I want you to know that I love you. More than anything." She backs away from me, pulling me along. "Almost."

The ship skims over the evergreen forest and sets down on the beach. Its wings fold backward like a settling pigeon. Sand and salt spray kicked up by its engines. Mustang's fingers twine through mine as we trudge through the sand. The ramp unfurls. Sophocles sprints out onto the beach, running toward a group of seagulls. Behind him comes the voice of Kavax and the sweet sound of a child laughing. My feet falter. I look over at Mustang in confusion. She pulls me on, a nervous smile on her face. Kavax exits the ship with Dancer. Victra and Sevro come with, waving over to me before looking expectantly back up the ramp.

I used to think the life strands of my friends frayed around me, because mine was too strong. Now I realize that when we are wound together, we make something unbreakable. Something that lasts long after this life ends. My friends have filled the hollow carved in me by my wife's death. They've made me whole again. My mother joins them now on the ramp, walking with Kieran to set foot on Earth for the first time. She smiles like I did when she smells the salt. The wind kicks her gray hair. Her eyes are glassy and full of the joy my father always wanted for her. And in her arms she carries a laughing child with golden hair.

"Mustang?" I ask. My voice trembling. "Who is that?"

"Darrow . . ." Mustang smiles over at me. "That is our son. His name is Pax."

EPILOGUE

Pax was born nine months after the Lion's Rain, as I lay in the Jackal's stone table. Fearing that our enemies would seek the boy out if they knew of his existence, Mustang kept her pregnancy a secret on the *Dejah Thoris* until she was able to give birth. Then, leaving the child to be guarded by Kavax's wife in the asteroid belt, she returned to war.

That peace she intended to make with the Sovereign was not just for her and her people, but for her son. She wanted a world without war for him. I can't hate her for that. For keeping this secret from me. She was afraid. Not just that she could not trust me, but that I was not prepared to be the father my son deserves. That was her test, all this time. She almost told me in Tinos, but after conferring with my mother, she decided against it. Mother knew if I realized I had a son, I would not be able to do what needed to be done.

My people needed a sword, not a father.

But now, for the first time in my life, I can be both.

This war is not over. The sacrifices we made to take Luna will haunt our new world. I know that. But I am no longer alone in the dark. When I first stepped through the gates of the Institute, I wore

518 | PIERCE BROWN

the weight of the world on my shoulders. It crushed me. Broke me, but my friends have pieced me together. Now they each carry a part of Eo's dream. Together we can make a world fit for my son. For the generations to come.

I can be a builder, not just a destroyer. Eo and Fitchner saw that when I could not. They believed in me. So whether they wait for me in the Vale or not, I feel them in my heart, I hear their echo beating across the worlds. I see them in my son, and, when he is old enough, I will take him on my knee and his mother and I will tell him of the rage of Ares, the strength of Ragnar, the honor of Cassius, the love of Sevro, the loyalty of Victra, and the dream of Eo, the girl who inspired me to live for more.

ACKNOWLEDGMENTS

I was afraid to write *Morning Star.*

For months I delayed that first sentence. I sketched ship schematics, wrote songs for Reds and Golds, histories of the families and the planets and the moons that make up the savage little world I'd stumbled onto in my room above my parents' garage almost five years ago.

I wasn't afraid because I didn't know where I was going. I was afraid because I knew exactly how the story would end. I just didn't think I was skillful enough to take you there.

Sound familiar?

So I put myself in seclusion. I packed my bags, my hiking boots, and left my apartment in Los Angeles for my family's cabin on the wind-ripped coast of the Pacific Northwest.

I thought isolation would help the process, that somehow I would find my muse in the quiet and the fog of the coast. I could write sunup to sundown. I could walk among the evergreens. Channel the spirits of mythmakers past. It worked for *Red Rising.* It worked for *Golden Son.* But it didn't work for *Morning Star.*

In my isolation, I felt shuttered, trapped by Darrow, trapped by the thousand paths he could follow and the congestion in my own brain.

I wrote the initial chapters in that mental space. I suppose it helped their formation, giving Darrow a weird, sad mania behind his eyes. But I couldn't see beyond his rescue from Attica.

It wasn't until I returned from the cabin that the story began to find its voice and I began to understand that Darrow wasn't the focus anymore. It was the people around him. It was his family, his friends, his loves, the voices that swarm and hearts that beat in tune with his own.

How could I ever expect to write something like that in isolation? Without the coffee powwows with Tamara Fernandez (the wisest person I know without white hair), the early dawn breakfasts with Josh Crook where we conspire to take over the world, the Hollywood Bowl concerts with Madison Ainley, the hours of debate about Roman military warfare with Max Carver, the ice cream crusades with Jarrett Llewelyn, the Battlestar nerdouts with Callie Young, and the maniacal plotting with Dennis "the Menace" Stratton?

Friends are the pulse of life. Mine are wild and vast and full of dreams and absurdity. Without them, I'd be a shade, and this book would be hollow between the covers. Thank you to each and every one of them, named and unnamed, for sharing this wonderful life with me.

Every upstart needs a wise wizard to guide his path and show him the proverbial ropes. I count myself lucky to have a titan of my youth become a mentor in my twenties. Terry Brooks, thank you for all the words of encouragement and advice. You're the man.

Thank you to the Phillips Clan for always giving me a second home where I could dream aloud. And Joel in particular for sitting on that couch with me five years ago and wildly planning to make maps for a book that hadn't yet been written. You're a wonder and a brother in all but name. Thank you to my other brohirim: Aaron for making me write, and Nathan for always liking what I write, even when you shouldn't.

Thank you also to my agent, Hannah Bowman, who found *Red Rising* amidst the slush. Havis Dawson for guiding the novels into more than twenty-eight different languages. Tim Gerard Reynolds for giving me chills with his audiobook narration. My foreign publishers for their tireless efforts in trying to translate Bloodydamn or ripWing or anything Sevro says into Korean or Italian or whatever the local tongue.

Thank you to the peerless team at Del Rey for believing in *Red Rising* from the moment it first passed across your desks. I could not ask for a better House. Scott Shannon, Tricia Narwani, Keith Clayton, Joe Scalora, David Moench, you've got the hearts of Hufflepuffs and the courage of Gryffindors as far as I'm concerned.

Thank you to my family for always suspecting that my strangeness was a quality and not a liability. For making me explore forests and fields instead of the channels on the tube. My father for teaching me the grace of power unused, and mother for teaching me the joy of power used well. My sister for her tireless efforts on behalf of the Sons of Ares fan page, and for understanding me better than anyone else.

The most profound thanks must go to my editor, Mike "au Telemanus" Braff. If he didn't fully understand the extent of my neurosis before this book, he sure as hell does now. Few authors are as lucky as I am to have an editor like Mike. He's humble, patient, and diligent, even when I'm not. That this book was brought to you only a year after *Golden Son* is a miracle of his making. I doff my cap to you, my goodman.

And to each and every reader, thank you. Your passion and excitement have allowed me to live my life on my own terms, and for that I am ever grateful and humbled. Your creativity, humor, and support come through in every message, tweet, and comment. Getting to meet you and hear your stories at conventions and signings is one of the perks of being an author. Thank you, Howlers, for all that you do. Hopefully we'll have a chance to howl together soon.

Once I thought that writing this book would be impossible. It was a skyscraper, massive and complete and unbearably far off. It taunted me from the horizon. But do we ever look at such buildings and assume they sprung up overnight? No. We've seen the traffic congestion that attends them. The skeleton of beams and girders. The swarm of builders and the rattle of cranes . . .

Everything grand is made from a series of ugly little moments. Everything worthwhile by hours of self-doubt and days of drudgery. All the works by people you and I admire sit atop a foundation of failures.

So whatever your project, whatever your struggle, whatever your dream, keep toiling, because the world needs your skyscraper.

Per aspera, ad astra!

—*Pierce Brown*

ABOUT THE AUTHOR

PIERCE BROWN is the *New York Times* bestselling author of *Red Rising, Golden Son,* and *Morning Star.* While trying to make it as a writer, Brown worked as a manager of social media at a start-up tech company, toiled as a peon on the Disney lot at ABC Studios, did his time as an NBC page, and gave sleep deprivation a new meaning during his stint as an aide on a U.S. Senate campaign. He lives in Los Angeles, where he is at work on his next novel.

redrisingbook.com

@Pierce_Brown

Instagram: PierceBrownOfficial

To inquire about booking Pierce Brown for a speaking engagement, please contact the Penguin Random House Speakers Bureau at speakers@penguinrandomhouse.com.

ABOUT THE TYPE

This book was set in Sabon, a typeface designed by the well-known German typographer Jan Tschichold (1902–74). Sabon's design is based upon the original letter forms of sixteenth-century French type designer Claude Garamond and was created specifically to be used for three sources: foundry type for hand composition, Linotype, and Monotype. Tschichold named his typeface for the famous Frankfurt typefounder Jacques Sabon (c. 1520–80).